Sedition

By

Phil M. Williams

Printed in the United States of America.
First Printing, 2017.

Phil W Books.
www.PhilWBooks.com

ISBN: 978-1-943894-31-4

Cover design and interior formatting by Tugboat Design

Contents

A Note from Phil

Dear Reader,

If you're interested in receiving my novel *Against the Grain* for free, and/ or reading my other titles for free or .99 cents, go to the following link: http://www.PhilWBooks.com. You're probably thinking, *What's the catch?* There is no catch.

Sincerely,
Phil M. Williams

1: George and No Good Deed

George passed a Mobil station, glancing at the sign. *Diesel $2.32. That's not bad.* He drove down the four-lane highway to a strip mall. He took the turn wide, giving his tandem box trailer enough space. The woman in the opposite lane gripped her steering wheel with her eyes wide. *Relax. I'm not even close.* He parked in the back of the Giant grocery store lot. Thankfully there was space. His dually Ford pickup and fourteen-foot trailer took up two spots.

George cut the engine and picked up his phone from the cradle mounted on the dash. He sent a text.

George: I'm here. Back of the Giant parking lot.

A few minutes later came a reply.

Caden: running late be there in 15

George: OK

George stepped from the Ford and walked to the back of the trailer. He lowered the door that doubled as a ramp. *Last one.* He approached the black Ducati at the front of the trailer. Paperwork hung off the handlebars in a Ziploc bag. He undid the wheel locks, loosened the ratchet straps attached to the motorcycle, and removed them from the hooks built into the floor.

George walked the bike off the trailer and parked it next to his truck. Flecks of silver, embedded in the black paint, glistened in the sun. George stepped back, admiring the Italian craftsmanship. Cross-drilled rotors, Brembo brakes, and 1200 ccs from a liquid-cooled engine pumping out 150 horsepower. Or 30 more than a Honda Civic and 2,500 pounds lighter. *I hope Caden can handle this beast.*

He removed the rag from his pocket and gave the bike a once-over. He checked the time on his phone. *When they say fifteen, it usually means thirty.* George sat behind the wheel of his truck and returned his phone to the cradle. He turned the ignition to the left, activating the electrical. He tapped his phone, and a man spoke through the stereo speakers.

"This is Gary Cook of the *Alt News Podcast*, providing vital information in a changing world. It's Monday, May 7, 2018. It's a beautiful spring day, renewal all around me, but something's not quite right. Big changes are just over the horizon. It's important that we're alert and informed, so we can navigate whatever crisis comes our way. Today we have Jim Weaver, former dean of admissions at Albright College. He's here to talk to us about the college-loan bubble. Welcome, Jim."

"Thanks for having me on, Gary," Jim replied. "I'm a big fan of the show. What you do is invaluable."

"Thanks, Jim. I appreciate that. Could you tell the listeners a little about yourself?"

"I worked in college admissions for forty-two years, the last fifteen of those as the dean of admissions at Albright College in Reading, Pennsylvania. I'm retired now and, like your listeners, very concerned about my investments lasting until, well, … death." Jim chuckled.

Gary laughed. "You've been talking and writing about the college-loan bubble for a decade now. What evidence led you to believe that we, indeed, have a college-loan bubble?"

"If you look at college tuition plus room and board over the last thirty years, prices for private schools are up 247 percent. Public universities are up 362 percent. But, if you look at median household income growth over that same time, it's barely 20 percent. It's simple math really. The scary part is that we've let this go on for so long that there's no way to unwind this without a lot of pain."

"Wow, those are staggering numbers. Without the income to absorb these price increases, how have parents been able to send their kids to college?"

"With debt. Kids have taken out massive loans, all guaranteed by the US government."

"In 2011, we hit peak college enrollment, and it's been trending down ever since. Granted, it was a slow decline, but the past year has seen a collapse in college enrollments. What do you think is behind the change?"

"I think the kids finally figured out they've been sold a raw deal. We've told kids that, if they go to college and work hard, they'll get a degree, then a good job. That's simply untrue. Some professions require college degrees, like medicine or law, but, by and large, most degrees offered by colleges are worthless in this economy."

"Businesses don't care about your sociology degree," Gary said.

"Exactly," Jim replied.

"The kids not going to college, what are they doing?"

"Well, many of them are unemployed or underemployed and still living at home. Some bright ones are starting businesses or going to trade schools. There's a reason why the marriage rate in this country is collapsing along with the economy. No reason to marry if you can't support a family."

"The kids are wise to the rigged game."

"They are."

"Can you explain to the listeners how the debt, the decline of college enrollment, and the dreadful economy have converged to pop this bubble?"

"I'm not sure it's a dramatic pop, given the government backing for the loans, but, like I said earlier, it's just math. It was unsustainable twenty years ago, but we kept growing enrollments and raising prices. The students simply borrowed more money. Then, as the economy worsened, opportunities—especially for young people—have dried up. Now they can't pay their loans because they can't get jobs."

"And those loans can't be discharged in bankruptcy court," Gary said.

"We've sold our children into debt slavery," Jim said. "It sickens me."

"And colleges and universities are in bad shape financially as well."

"They are. They've spent like drunken sailors, competing for students, with massive facilities and sports complexes. Now, with the decline in enrollment, they're facing bankruptcy. Ten years from now, I think we have half the colleges and universities still in business."

"Plus, a lot of education's going virtual at a fraction of the cost. They don't need expensive infrastructure."

"This is true."

"Let's not forget the government's involvement in this," Gary said. "They distorted the market with free money. Now we have way-too-many colleges with way-too-many facilities and tons of college-educated kids with worthless degrees and mountains of debt."

"It's a terrible situation," Jim said.

"What do you think about Chairwoman Burnett's announcement last week?" Gary asked.

"I'm assuming you're talking about the purchase of the nonperforming student loans by the Fed?"

"To the tune of one hundred billion dollars a month."

"I saw that. It's not surprising. They'll try to reflate this bubble the same way they reflated the stock market, the bond market, and the housing market—with printed money."

"Do you think they'll be successful?" Gary asked.

"I suppose that depends on your definition of 'success,'" Jim replied. "I think they'll keep the zombie alive for a quite a few years, but, the longer they do, the more pain that'll ultimately be felt."

"I'm surprised bond yields are still as low as they are."

A Subaru STI with a throaty exhaust parked next to the motorcycle. George grabbed his phone, turned off the podcast, and stepped from his truck. A lanky twentysomething with a patchy beard fawned over the bike. As George approached, the guy looked up from the motorcycle.

"Are you George?"

"Yep." George extended his hand. They shook hands. "Nice to meet you, Caden."

"This is a nice bike," Caden said, a grin plastered on his face.

"It is."

A young woman stood by the Subaru, her arms crossed.

"Alyssa, come check this out," Caden said.

Alyssa frowned and trudged toward the bike, her arms still crossed. She was thin, with long legs and short-shorts. "This is a bad idea," she said.

"It gets way-better gas mileage than the Subaru."

She shook her head. "You know this isn't about gas mileage."

Caden grinned.

She placed her hands on her hips. "Just be careful, okay?"

"I need you to sign a couple things," George said, removing the paper-work from the handlebars. "Do you have your license?"

Caden showed his license and signed off on the condition of the bike. He retrieved his helmet from the Subaru and hopped on the Ducati.

"It has a lot of power," George said. "You've ridden before, right?"

"I got this," Caden replied.

The young man turned the key, and the motor roared to life. He squeezed the clutch with his left hand and tapped the gear into first with his foot. Caden smiled at Alyssa and shut the visor on his helmet. He cranked the throttle, let off the clutch, and he was gone. There was a little wobble at first, but he looked okay. Alyssa hopped in the car and drove after him.

George placed the carbon copies in the back pocket of his jeans and surveyed the shopping center. Three of the eight storefronts in the strip mall were vacant. He locked his truck and walked across the parking lot toward Starbucks. A campaign office was next door. The sign read Representative John Bradley.

George went into Starbucks to use the restroom and to purchase a coffee. He added creamer and stepped outside. As he started toward his truck, a young man with a shaved head and a long coat moved in the opposite direction. *A bit warm for a coat.* George craned his neck while the man hurried past with tunnel vision. George stopped and turned around, watching the man heading for the campaign office. The front of the office was all glass. Inside were rows of desks—no partitions—where people worked on laptops and phones.

When the man turned to open the glass door, George caught of glimpse of what was under his jacket. George dropped his coffee and ran toward the danger. Inside was a well-dressed man, standing with an equally well-dressed woman. The bald man entered the office, removed the AR-15 rifle from under his jacket, and leveled it at the well-dressed man. The office staff froze. Someone screamed.

George opened the door and barreled into the man's back, tackling him to the floor. The rifle fired. A single round echoed through the room. People flinched and ducked at the deafening pop. Office workers hid underneath their desks. George was on top of the man's back. The man let go of the rifle, and reached for his hip.

A man in a dark suit kicked the rifle out of their reach and pointed a handgun at George and the gunman. "Secret Service. Put up your hands," the dark-skinned agent said.

George rolled off the gunman who then rolled on his side and fired his handgun—three quick pops to the agent's chest. George lunged for the gunman, reaching for his right hand, as the agent collapsed to the floor. The gunman was a small person—sinewy but not very strong. George wrestled the handgun from the man's grasp and scurried to his feet. George pointed the Glock at the gunman.

"Don't move," George said, glancing at the AR-15 on the floor. It was out of the man's reach but dangerously close.

Office workers—mostly women, cowered behind and under desks. The well-dressed man was gone. The bald man pushed himself to one knee. Tattoos were visible on the backs of his hands. One hand read No Gods; the other, No Masters. He started to stand.

"Stay on your knees," George said, still pointing the Glock at the man.

The man knelt in front of George. He was in his early twenties maybe—fair skin.

"Put your hands up," George said.

The man glared at George and raised his hands over his head.

Sirens sounded in the distance.

"You fucked up," the gunman said. "You think you saved someone. You just killed millions."

The sirens were close—piercing. The lights whirled around the room. George's back was to the action outside.

"Put the gun down and turn around with your hands up," the guy on the bull horn said.

George's heart pounded in his chest. *They're gonna shoot me.* George slowly placed the handgun on the linoleum floor.

"Put your hands up and turn around," the guy with the bull horn repeated.

George raised his hands and slowly turned toward the parking lot. A handful of police cars and SUVs were parked in front of the building. Police officers pointed rifles at him over the hoods of their cars. More police vehicles raced toward the scene.

The gunman grabbed his rifle from the floor and the shooting resumed. Shots whizzed back and forth. George crumpled to the floor, his shoulder and leg burning. Pops behind him. Pops in front of him. George covered his head with his hands and curled into a ball. The shots ceased.

The door swung open. "Everybody down. Everybody down," several policemen said.

Then there was pressure on top of George. He couldn't breathe. His hands were wrenched behind his back.

"Stop resisting," a heavyset policeman said.

George grimaced. The handcuffs were cinched tight around his wrists. He was forced on his stomach. His jeans and T-shirt felt wet. He stared at the floor.

"Help," George said.

"Don't move," the heavyset policeman said.

"This shooter's dead," a police officer said.

"Cuff 'im anyway," another police officer said.

"We have an agent down. There's no pulse."

Someone gasped.

"This one's been shot," the heavyset policeman said. "There's a lot of blood."

"Let the paramedics deal with it."

"Help him," a woman said.

"Stay down, ma'am."

"Help him. He's not the one," she said, verging on hysteria. "He's bleeding. Do something."

"Calm down."

2: John and Everything's Political

John Bradley didn't hear the man at the door. He was focused on Donna, his chief of staff. She was the picture of professionalism. Her dark hair was in a tight bun, her makeup and skirt suit flawless. It was Donna that looked first, her expression changing from relaxed to wide-eyed in a microsecond. John turned and froze, looking down the barrel of a rifle. The gunman was pale, sweat beading on his shaved head. *I'm going to die.*

Someone tackled the gunman from behind. There was a pop. John flinched, instinctively ducking his head. Agent Barnes grabbed John and pushed him toward the back of the building, away from the wrestling men.

"Keep moving," Agent Barnes said.

They exited through the back door into a wide alleyway behind the strip mall. Dumpsters lined the fence. Agent Olson hurried toward them, his FN handgun drawn. Three more pops came from the office.

"Extraction," Barnes said.

Agent Olson hustled to the black SUV, scanning for threats. Barnes shoved John into the back seat of the Chevy Suburban. Barnes sat next to John and slammed the door. Agent Olson gunned the engine.

"Are you okay, sir?" Barnes asked. "Sir?"

John blinked and nodded. "I'm fine."

Agent Olson zipped through traffic.

Barnes talked into his cuff link that doubled as his microphone. "There was an assassination attempt. We're headed to the safe house. Legacy is secure and uninjured. We need an evac for Goldilocks and the three little bears." Barnes lowered his arm and pressed the earpiece tighter to his ear. He listened and put the cuff link near his lips again. "I believe Agent Stokes has the shooter under control, but I can't confirm." Barnes lowered his arm again.

"I need to call Linda," John said.

"Secret service will pick her up. They're en route," Barnes replied.

John's stomach churned. "My kids?"

"We're on it, sir. We have agents headed to the schools now. They'll meet us at the safe house."

"Donna, … my staff?"

"I believe Agent Stokes has it under control. The police have been notified."

John took a deep breath. "Thanks, Jake."

* * *

Gravel crunched under the tires of the Suburban. They passed fields of knee-high corn and cattle grazing in the pasture. The occasional farmhouse dotted the landscape, complete with run-down barns and silos. Three cars, marked Luray County Police, were parked in front of the last farmhouse on the road—a two-story stone colonial with a split-rail fence. There were no barns or silos, animals or fields of corn. This was a gentleman's farm.

A uniformed police officer stopped them at the wooden gate. Agent Olson showed his credentials, and the officer opened the gate and waved them through. Olson and Barnes escorted John into the farmhouse. John ducked his head on the way in. Agents Barnes and Olson were powerfully built men, but John was tall—an inch taller than Barnes and almost a foot taller than Olson.

Inside, the agents took John to a back office—no windows—with a brown leather couch and a cherrywood desk with a swivel chair. John sat at the desk. His cell phone rang again. He removed it from his suit jacket. It was the eleventh missed call.

"Can I answer it now?" John asked.

"Sorry, sir. Not yet," Agent Barnes replied.

John glanced at his phone—it was Donna calling—and silenced it. "What's the point of an encrypted phone then?"

"Sorry, sir. We need to figure out the situation before we give away any information."

"Let me know when you have."

"Yes, sir."

Barnes and Olson shut John in the office.

After the gun shots, the commotion, and the roar of the Suburban's V-8, the silence in the room was jarring. *Someone wanted to kill me.* John pictured the barrel of that rifle. He held up his hand in front of his face. It was shaky. He put his arm down and rubbed his hands together. *I think Stokes tackled him from behind. He'll receive a life-saving award. That'll be a photo op and a half. And the guy's black. That couldn't be more perfect. Especially running against Art.*

After a knock on the door, Linda spilled into the room, her angelic face streaked with tears. Agent Olson shut the door. John stood, and Linda rushed to him. She wrapped her arms around his waist, her face buried in his chest.

She sniffled. "I was so worried."

"I'm okay," John replied.

"I don't know what I'd do without you."

"I'm fine, really."

She looked up, her blue eyes glassy. "Someone tried to …"

"I know. Maybe I am a little shaken up. We should sit down."

"Agent Barnes said the kids are okay and should be here soon."

"That's good." John removed his suit jacket and placed it on the back of the swivel chair. He moved to the couch and sat down.

Linda curled up next to him. "What happened?" Linda asked. "Agent Barnes just said there was an assassination attempt and that you're unharmed."

John shook his head. "It all happened so fast. I was talking to Donna in the office, and this guy came in the front door and pointed a gun at me. One of those automatic rifles. This'll play great for my gun legislation."

Linda scowled. "Seriously, John?"

"There's always a silver lining."

She shook her head.

John continued. "Agent Stokes must have tackled him from behind. It was just in the nick of time, because the gun went off. It was the loudest thing I've ever heard. That's when Jake pushed me out the back door, and we came here."

"Was anyone hurt?"

"I don't know. I heard a few more shots, but we were already outside. I'm assuming Stokes had to shoot the guy."

"That's awful. What's this country coming to? It used to be that people were so patriotic. There's so much hate now."

"People *are* still patriotic. This is what domestic terrorism does. It makes people think these antigovernment radicals are more prevalent than they really are."

"Something needs to be done about these guns. It's crazy. Who the hell needs a machine gun?"

"We're working on it. We need to have enough buy-in from the public."

"How many shootings do we have to have before we have enough buy-in?"

"The latest poll we ran shows that most Americans support gun control legislation."

"But not a ban."

"No, but we may get an assault rifle ban."

High voices and other commotion came from the hall.

"The kids are here," Linda said with a smile, standing and opening the door.

John stood too.

A grinning little blond boy spilled into the room, wearing a miniature suit with the crest from his private school on the jacket.

John picked him up and gave him a hug.

"The agent was driving really fast," Bobby said. "It was *so* fun."

"It was?" John replied, setting his son on the couch.

Two girls, one teen and one preteen, entered the office. The older girl wore jeans; the younger one, her uniform—a plaid skirt and sweater. Olson closed the door.

"Why are we here?" asked Ellen, the older girl. She was a teen version of her mother. Beautiful silky blond hair, a perfect face, and an athletic build.

"Why don't you kids sit down," Linda said. "We have something to tell you."

The girls sat on either side of Bobby.

"Is it bad news?" Ellen asked.

"Everything's fine," John said.

Charlotte, the preteen, pursed her lips. She was short and chubby, with brown hair hanging past her shoulders.

"Someone tried to shoot me today," John said.

"What!" Ellen stood up. "Are you okay?"

"With a real gun?" Bobby asked.

"Oh my God," Charlotte said to herself.

"I'm fine," John said.

"Why?" Charlotte asked. "Why did they do that?"

"Because your father's a public figure," Linda replied. "Unfortunately, some people have a lot of hate in their heart, and they try to take that hate out on public figures."

"But that's why we have agents Barnes and Olson and Stokes and all the other secret service agents," John said.

Ellen sat down.

"Agent Stokes saved your father's life today," Linda said. "So, when you see him, make sure you thank him and give him a big hug."

"I like Agent Barnes the best," Bobby said.

"He saved me too," John said.

Ellen wrenched her hands. "Are people trying to hurt us? Is that why you took us out of school?"

"It was just a precaution, honey," John said.

"Nobody'll hurt any of you," Linda added.

A knock came at the door.

"Come in," John said.

Agent Barnes opened the door. "Sir, you may use your phone now."

"Thanks," John replied.

Bobby hopped off the couch and ran to Agent Barnes, hugging him around his thighs, his head against the agent's stomach. "Thank you for saving my dad."

Barnes blushed and smiled tightly. "You're welcome, buddy."

"I need to call Donna and check the news," John said to Linda.

Bobby let go of Barnes and returned to his mother.

"Is there a room with cable?" John asked Agent Barnes.

"Upstairs, sir, master bedroom," Barnes replied. "I can take you."

"Not necessary," John said.

John walked down the hallway to the stairs. More agents were in the living room; a few he'd never seen before.

A couple of agents greeted him with a nod. "Sir."

He climbed the wooden stairs to the second floor. The master bedroom was at the end of the hall. A king-size four-poster bed dominated the room, with its private bathroom to one side and an armoire against the wall. He opened the armoire and found a forty-eight-inch plasma. He grabbed the remote, flipped on the television, and turned the channel to WNN. A commercial was on. He called Donna.

"Jesus, John, I've been calling you," she said in lieu of a greeting. "Are you okay?"

"I'm fine," John replied. "Are you okay?"

"You don't sound too concerned."

"Of course I am. Are you hurt?"

"Not physically, apart from my eardrums."

"The shot *was* loud."

"Which one? The one you were there for, or the dozen that happened after you left?"

"I heard two or three more shots when Jake pushed me outside. I didn't know there were more than that."

"Agent Stokes is dead," Donna said.

"Shit." John paused for a moment. "What happened?"

"Some bystander saw the guy with the machine gun and tackled him—"

"I thought Stokes tackled him."

"No. They were on the ground, and Stokes came over and told them to put up their hands. The bystander rolled off the shooter, but the shooter had a handgun too. He shot Stokes. The bystander took the handgun from the shooter and held him at gunpoint. The police showed up a few minutes later. When the police told the bystander to drop his weapon, the shooter grabbed his rifle from the floor and started shooting again. The police shot back."

"Christ. Any injuries or, uh, … deaths, besides Stokes?"

"Just the shooter."

"Thank God. Anybody hurt?"

"The bystander was shot. Twice, I think. There was a lot of blood."

"Anyone on the staff?"

"A few bumps and bruises but nothing serious."

John exhaled. "That's a relief."

WNN returned from commercial break. *Breaking News* was scrawled across the bottom of the screen.

John turned up the volume. "Turn on WNN."

"I'm watching it," Donna replied.

They watched the news for eight minutes in silence. WNN cut to another commercial break.

"They know less than we do," John said.

"That's not surprising," Donna replied.

"There is a silver lining to all this, politically that is."

"I was thinking the same thing. Surviving an assassination attempt plays well with the public. It definitely helps bolster your credibility as a tough guy, which is always helpful for a nonveteran, antigun Democrat."

"I was actually hoping Stokes had saved my life. It would be a great story for black audiences. The bystander wasn't black, was he?"

"If only we were so lucky. You can still emphasize Stokes's heroism. You could talk about how an African-American man gave his life for you. The only color he saw was red, white, and blue."

John chuckled.

3: Katie, Baby Killer

Katie sat poolside in a chaise longue chair. She typed on her laptop, the hood of her sweatshirt over her head. A light breeze blew from the San Francisco Bay.

Crazy Davey123: Abortion is fucking awful. Don't want a kid, don't have sex. Fucking baby killer.

View all 474 replies

Jacob's Ladder: There's no justification for killing an unborn child. Katie, you said that a baby doesn't have the right to "survive off your body against your will." That is the most selfish, egotistical, sick statement I've ever heard. A fetus is a human being. Unsub. #BabyKiller

View all 332 replies

Katie: I doubt I'll convince you that a fetus isn't a life. But you should consider the following: A fetus is 100 percent dependent on its mother's body, unlike born human beings. Even if I concede that a fetus is a life, the "right to life" doesn't imply a right to use a woman's body. For example, people have the right to refuse to donate their organs, even if doing so would save the life of another.

CuddlyKitten77: If you can't be responsible, don't have sex.

View all 183 replies

Katie: It is your opinion that giving birth is the "responsible" choice.

What if the mother can't provide for the baby? In this situation, it's more responsible to have an abortion. This will prevent poverty and misery, not to mention the societal costs of increased criminality of unwanted children. Pro-choice is not about being pro-abortion. It's about the woman's right to have power over her own body.

"Why don't you get in?" Declan called out. "Babe?"

Katie looked up from her laptop. Declan sat in the hot tub adjacent the pool, with a pork pie fedora on his head. He leaned back. One arm was out of the water, resting on the sandstone pool deck, revealing a jungle of dark armpit hair and a wrist full of rubber bracelets.

"I'm trying to finish this," Katie said. "These crazy pro-lifers."

"I tried to tell you," he said. "You should stick to sex advice and making fun of Republicans."

"I'm trying to use my reach for something other than horny dudes and hit pieces."

"You getting in? Maybe you could use your reach for one horny dude." He grinned, his bushy beard concealing his dimples.

"Give me like twenty minutes."

"A slave to social media."

Katie scowled and went back to her laptop. An alert popped up on the lower corner of her screen. She clicked on it. "Holy shit."

"What?"

Katie watched the WNN breaking news report with a helicopter view of a strip mall and a storefront with a sign that read Representative John Bradley. The parking lot was littered with police cars and emergency vehicles.

"What is it?" Declan called out.

Katie was glued to the screen.

The newscaster Lisa Kelly said, "Earlier today an unidentified gunman entered the campaign office of Representative John Bradley of Virginia." WNN showed a close-up of the office with its shattered glass windows. "Eyewitness reports indicate that the gunman brandished an assault rifle and attempted to assassinate Congressman Bradley." They cut to pictures of AR-15s. "The Fairfax County Police Department reported that a secret service agent and the gunman were killed in the attack. No identities have been released." WNN cut to a square-jawed man with wavy hair cemented in place with product. "Our very own Chase Manning is on the ground."

Chase stood back from the police tape and vehicles but close enough to see the campaign office framed in the background. A middle-aged woman was next to him.

"Babe?" Declan said. He climbed out of the hot tub, grabbed a towel off the nearby chair, and dried himself.

"I'm here with Stacy Landry," Chase said into his microphone, "a volunteer for Representative Bradley's campaign and an eyewitness to the attack." The camera zoomed in on Chase and Stacy.

"This better be good," Declan said, with a towel around his waist. He put on his sweatshirt and walked toward Katie.

"Stacy, can you tell us what transpired here today?" Chase asked.

Declan peered over Katie's shoulder at the screen.

"I didn't notice the man at first," Stacy said, "but I heard someone scream, and I looked up from my computer, and there he was, pointing a gun at Congressman Bradley. He had one of those machine guns."

"What did the man look like?"

"He was white. He had a shaved head and a long jacket."

"What happened next?"

"A man came in from outside and tackled the man with the gun, and the gun went off."

"Was Congressman Bradley hit by the shot?"

"I don't know. I was under my desk after the gun went off. And a lot more shots were fired before it was over."

"Did you see if anyone was hurt?"

"The gunman and a secret service agent were shot and killed. And the guy who tried to help, he was shot."

"Thank you, Stacy, for your harrowing account." They cut to a close-up of Chase, Stacy now out of the picture. "Lisa, we still don't have an official comment from the secret service or Congressman Bradley's office."

They cut back to Lisa Kelly, a leggy blonde with heavy makeup. "Thank you, Chase," she replied. Lisa turned from Chase on the monitor to the camera. "We'll keep you updated as information becomes available."

"Holy shit," Katie said. "This is huge."

"Guy with a shaved head, assault rifle," Declan said. "You know what this is about."

Katie nodded. "I need to make a video."

She closed her laptop and hurried to the pool house. Declan ambled after.

The pool house was the same one-story, flat-roofed modern design as the main house. Katie set her laptop in the office—a small room with a glass desk—and went to her bedroom.

There her video camera was mounted atop a tripod and pointed at her king-size bed. She took off her sweatshirt and tossed it on the bed. Declan leaned against the doorway with a smirk. She removed her T-shirt, exposing her underarm hair and black bra. Katie reached behind her back and unclasped the bra, releasing her double Ds. Red marks were on her shoulders where the straps had dug into her pale skin. She rummaged through her dresser while Declan stared. Katie found *their* favorite pink T-shirt. She donned the shirt, sans brassiere.

Declan stepped closer, narrowing his eyes at her chest. "I can see why they like that one."

She frowned. "Turn on USN. What do the newscasters look like?"

"They do wear bras."

"They're not feminists."

She grabbed her camera and tripod, and hauled them to the office.

"Can you make sure I'm centered?" she asked, sitting in the chair behind the desk.

Declan turned on the camera and made a few adjustments. "You're good. You're not gonna prepare?"

Katie shook her head. "I want to record something quick to let my audience know I'm on top of the breaking news. I'll work on a video with in-depth analysis later tonight as they release more information."

"All right. You ready?"

Katie nodded.

Declan started recording. "You're on."

"Earlier today," Katie said, "there was an assassination attempt on Congressman John Bradley. Congressman Bradley is one of the good guys. He cares about racial equality and gender equality. He cares about helping the poor and the wealthy paying their fair share. He cares about women's rights and bringing the troops home. He's one of the few shining lights we have. He's someone who threatens the status quo and wants to bring power back to the people. This is why I believe an attempt was made on his life.

"The lamestream media hasn't identified the shooter yet, but an eyewitness described him as white, with a shaved head and a long coat. I'm not much of a gambling woman, but I bet he was an Anarchist. These antigovernment radicals are no different than the terrorists we've been fighting for almost twenty years now, and they are a much bigger threat than ISIS or Al Qaeda ever was.

"The Anarchist movement feeds on fear, fear of the government. This is why I believe they targeted Congressman Bradley. Because he represents the good in government. That doesn't help the Anarchist agenda, which needs you to be afraid, needs you to hate. They call us violent, but the Anarchists are the ones taking the law in their own hands. We only want to live in a society of rules and safety and fairness.

"I often cover government corruption on my channel. I know our government's not perfect, but that's why it's up to us to elect the right representatives to lead us. Congressman Bradley's one of the good guys. I'll record updates and in-depth analyses on the shooting as more information is released. Thanks, everyone. Stay tuned, and don't forget to subscribe."

Katie kissed her hand and blew it toward the camera.

4: Julie, My Match

Julie walked past the bar, her purse on her shoulder, a plastic bag in her grasp.

"Where you going so early?" Eric asked.

Julie stopped and turned to the bartender. Eric's dirty-blond hair was pulled back in a man bun. He sported the obligatory beard that was all the rage.

"Rodney sent me home. It's dead, in case you haven't noticed."

Eric turned and pointed at the television behind him. "Someone tried to kill some congressman." He faced Julie again. "It happened at the Giant shopping center not too far from here, so everyone's freaked out."

Julie watched the silent images on the screen and read the subtitles. *The Good Samaritan has been identified as George Smith Chapman, forty-one, a resident of Pennsylvania.*

An image popped up of a clean-shaven man with short dark hair, deep-set eyes, and a strong jaw.

"That's the dude who supposedly saved the congressman," Eric said. "A secret service agent was shot and killed."

Julie nodded and turned her attention to Eric, her shoulders slumped. "That's awful." She sighed. "Hopefully this blows over. Tips were terrible tonight."

"For me too." Eric narrowed his eyes at Julie. "You look like you could use some fun. I'm off in a couple hours. You wanna get a drink or something?"

"It's Monday night."

"I said, *or something.*"

She forced a smile. "I should get home but thanks." Julie started for the exit.

"Next time," he called out.

* * *

Julie drove through her neighborhood of mostly vinyl-sided townhomes. A few of the end units sprung for brick facing. For Sale signs were on every street and even a few foreclosures. Her parking lot was full and then some. She parked in her designated spot and turned off her headlights. She shuffled up the walk to her middle-unit townhome.

Inside, the lights and television were on in the family room. She exhaled, picked up the remote from the coffee table, and turned off the TV. She flipped off some of the lights and trudged to the kitchen. Julie set her purse, keys, and the plastic bag on the counter. The kitchen was cramped and filled with outdated appliances. A dining room was adjacent to the kitchen. She stepped to the stairs and looked upward. It was quiet.

"Max, come down here," she called out. "I brought dinner." She listened. Nothing. "Max, come down here." Still nothing.

Julie forced herself up the steps. She knocked on her son's bedroom door. There was no answer. She knocked harder. Still no answer. She opened the door and peeked inside. Max sat up on his bed, his pillow wedged between his back and the wall. He wore earbuds and focused on his iPad. The glow of the screen reflected off his wire-rim glasses.

"Hey, honey," Julie said.

He remained glued to the screen, his mouth half-open.

Julie moved closer to her son. "I brought some food."

He was unresponsive.

"Max," Julie said louder. "I know you hear me. Take those things out of your ears."

Max removed his earbuds. "What are you doing home so early?"

Julie mock-frowned. "Work was slow. Aren't you happy to see your mother?"

Max returned her frown.

Julie leaned over the bed and kissed Max on his chubby cheek.

As she stood up, he discreetly brushed the shoulder of his T-shirt against his cheek.

"I saw that," she said, grinning.

"I don't like lipstick."

"I'm not wearing any."

"What did you want?"

"I brought dinner. Are you hungry?"

"I had pizza."

"Oh."

"I was hungry. I didn't know you'd be home for dinner."

"That's okay, honey. What are you doing?"

He scowled. "Mom."

"What? I'm just interested."

He blew out a breath. "Reading."

"What are you reading? A comic?"

"They're graphic novels."

"Right. How was school today?

"Fine."

"Just fine?"

"Yeah, just fine."

"Anything interesting happen today?"

"No."

"Honey, I'm not trying to be a bother." Julie pursed her lips. "I guess I'll get out of your hair."

"Ellen Bradley got taken out of school because of the shooting."

"Are you talking about the shooting with the congressman?"

"Yeah, is there another one?"

"I hope not. Who's Ellen Bradley? Is she a friend?"

Max turned beet red. "No. She's the congressman's daughter."

"And she goes to your school?"

"Yeah, why?"

Julie lifted one shoulder. "I guess I'm just surprised she's not in private school."

"Her sister and brother go to a private school."

"You know a lot about this girl." Julie grinned. "Are you sure she's not a friend?"

Max blushed again. "Mom."

"Well, hopefully her dad's okay." Julie started for the door, stopped in the doorway, and turned around. "Max, honey, can you please not leave all those lights on downstairs? The electric bill's been expensive."

"Sorry."

Julie went back to the kitchen and heated up a plate of pecan-crusted chicken, garlic mashed potatoes, and green beans with onions. She sat down at the dining room table and scrolled through her Facebook feed as she ate.

Summer Caldwell has changed her profile picture. The new picture was of an attractive blonde in her forties, with a gray-haired man, flanked by two pretty teen girls wearing stretchy pants and blousy sweaters. The J.Crew family sat on a park bench, the Chesapeake Bay in the background.

An instant message popped up as she took a bite of chicken. *Speak of the devil.*

Summer: Have you signed up yet?

Julie: Do you ever stop?

Summer: No. You should know that.

Julie: I have not signed up.

Summer: Your dating market value is in decline.

Julie: That's just rude.

Summer: ☺ It's true. The pool of eligible bachelors willing to date someone your age with a child is getting smaller by the day.

Julie: Adding a ☺ doesn't make it less rude.

Summer: Or less true. I love you, sis. I'm just worried about you.

Julie: I'm fine. I have Max.

Summer: Not for long. In three years, he'll be off to college.

Julie: If I can afford it.

Summer: Don't be so fatalistic. A lot of government money is available for college. Especially with your income.

Julie: You mean, lack of income.

Summer: Well, we're going to pay a fortune for Abby and Heather.

Julie shook her head and stabbed at her green beans. *It must be rough.*

Summer: You still there?

Julie: I'm here.

Summer: Since I know you're so busy, I took the liberty of signing you up.

Julie: I don't want it. Seriously.

Summer: I already paid for a year and put all your info in. You might want to check it out to make sure it's correct. ☺

Julie: I think the ☺ actually makes it worse.

Summer: LOL. Love ya, sis. Username: Jules123 Password: Ineedtogetsome

Julie: ☹

Julie sighed and navigated to MyMatch.com. She smirked as she typed in the password. Her profile featured a three-year-old picture, but she hadn't really aged since then. *It is a good picture. Summer's fortieth birthday party, I think.* In the photo, Julie wore a knee-length skirt and a tight sweater, highlighting her athletic but feminine build. Her head was cocked a little, and her reddish-brown hair looked shiny. Her face was oval-shaped and symmetrical. She was smiling, with a glass of wine in her hand. *That might send the wrong message.*

She read through her profile.

Username: Jules123

Age: 37

Julie shook her head and edited the field.

Age: 40

Location: Fairfax, Virginia

Looking for: Male 30–50 for serious relationship

Height: 5'4"

Body Type: Athletic

I wonder if they have weight for men?

Hair: Auburn

Children: One teen boy

Personality: Sweet, easygoing, and happy

Julie deleted her personality traits. She thought for a moment, tapping her finger on her plump lower lip. She moved on.

Personality:

Relationship Status: Widow

Occupation:

Julie added the information.

Occupation: Waitress

Interests: Travel, theater, books, movies, music, nutrition, politics, psychology

She made several changes.

Interests: Books, movies, music, my son

Sports: Running, yoga, golf, tennis, sailing

Julie edited the field.

Sports: Running, yoga

Smoking: No

Under the statistics were a few closing paragraphs.

A Bit about Me:

I'm the type of woman who is just as comfortable at a sporting event as I am at a five-star restaurant. I'm sweet and fun, and beautiful from the inside out. For the right man, I'll be a great cook and a better friend. I love animals, but I don't have any of my own.

I'm looking for a serious relationship with the right man. It's important that he's kind, has a great sense of humor, and a professional career. No players and no games please.

Julie deleted those paragraphs. She stared at the blinking cursor for a few minutes. She logged out and went to bed.

* * *

Julie bounded down the steps in yoga pants, running shoes, and a long-sleeved running shirt that covered her butt. She filled up a glass of water in the kitchen. She stood at the counter, checking her email on her phone to find one entitled 282 Matches.

She sat down in the dining room with her water and her phone. She clicked the link to MyMatch.com. *Whoa.* She had fifty-three messages. She scanned through the first few. They were all pushing her age threshold: *forty-nine, forty-seven, fifty, forty-eight, forty-six.* She sighed. *The men always go younger.* She scrolled down and found someone forty. The subject of this man's message piqued her interest.

She clicked on it.

> From: Agent00777
> To: Jules123
> Subject: I think I know you. Go Vikings!
>
> Jules123,
>
> I could be wrong, but your picture bears a strong resemblance to a Julie Adams who I went to Woodbridge High School with. You still look great, by the way. You haven't changed a bit! Larry Nicholson here. You may not remember me. I was very skinny and not particularly popular. I was on the debate team. We won state my senior year, not that anyone cared. ☺
>
> I'm still thin, but at least I look normal now. Anyway, I always thought you were really nice and pretty in high school. I'd love to catch up sometime.
>
> Sincerely,
> Larry Nicholson (Class of '95)

She clicked on his profile. *Larry Nicholson. I don't remember him.* His profile picture was a headshot. He had short dark hair and a receding hairline that made his forehead look large. But it wasn't terrible. He wore hipster black-rim glasses and a polo. He was a little thin, but he did look normal. *At least he's healthy. And his message was sweet.* Julie scrolled through his profile.

Username: Agent00777

Age: 40

Location: Fairfax, Virginia

Looking for: Female 25–40 for serious relationship

Height: 5'11"

Body Type: Athletic

Hair: Brown

Children: None

Personality: Adventurous, outgoing

Relationship Status: Never married

Occupation: Government Agent (Really!)

Interests: Travel to exotic locales, books, politics, movies, music, candlelit dinners

Sports: Tennis, golf, running, weight training, sailing, racquetball, squash

Smoking: No

A Bit about Me …

I'm the quintessential nice guy. I open doors, and remember birthdays and anniversaries. I'm a great listener. I believe everyone wants to be heard. I believe in treating others the way I want to be treated.

I love adventure and the outdoors, whether it's overseas travel or just going for a hike. I would love to meet someone who I can be friends with first. I believe friendship is the unbreakable foundation of love.

It doesn't always pay to be the nice guy, but I know I'll eventually find the right nice girl. If you think we might be a good match, send me a message. I always respond.

Julie hovered her cursor over the Instant Message icon. She took a deep breath and clicked.

Jules123: I am Julie Adams, actually Julie Welch now. Thank you for the note. It was nice. How are you doing?

He responded a few seconds later.

Agent00777: Julie! It's great to hear from you.

The screen said he was still typing.

Agent00777: I'm doing well. Thanks for asking. I'm single. Obviously! I work for the IRS. I know. Nobody likes the IRS, but I investigate criminal enterprises. I put away bad guys, and I love it.

Jules123: That's great, Larry. It sounds like you're doing a lot of good in this world. I'm just a waitress.

Agent00777: I find it difficult to believe that you're *just* anything. Besides, people need to eat!

Jules123: ☺ That's sweet. I do have a son, Max. I suppose he's my big contribution to the world. He's a great kid.

Agent00777: See? I was right. You're a fantastic mom. The hardest job in the world.

Jules123: That's really nice of you to say.

Agent00777: How long have you been on MyMatch?

Jules123: Since last night. My sister signed me up. I wasn't happy about it.

Agent00777: Selfishly I'm glad she did.

Jules123: What about you? How long have you been on MyMatch?

Agent00777: About a year. I tried some of the other dating sites, but it was just a big meat market. Very superficial. At least here, people are looking for serious relationships.

Jules123: That's a relief. I wasn't sure what to expect.

Julie's phone chimed. She glanced at the number. It read Fairfax, Virginia. She sent the call to voice mail.

Agent00777: I know you just signed up and are probably interested in looking around, but I'd love to meet up for coffee or lunch. We're in the same city! It would be as friends of course. No pressure. You won't hurt my feelings if you're not interested.

Julie's stomach fluttered as she read the message. She thought about the proposal and typed a response.

Jules123: That sounds nice, Larry.

Agent00777: Great! I'll check my calendar and send you some dates and times. I look forward to it!

Jules123: Me too.

Julie's phone chimed. It was Fairfax, Virginia, again. She checked the time and sent the call to voice mail. *I need to get moving if I'm to make it to work on time.* Julie left her phone on the dining room table and stepped outside. It was a crisp and clear spring day. Her lawn was the shaggiest on the block. *Max needs to mow as soon as he gets home. I really don't want Dan to show up, complaining.*

Julie ran on the asphalt path that circled her neighborhood. She ran it twice and walked it twice. *Four miles. Not bad.* She stretched on her front stoop, her hair and shirt soaked with sweat. She stepped inside. Her phone was ringing.

She hustled to the kitchen, but the phone stopped ringing before she could pick it up. She checked the number. *Fairfax, Virginia.* She had five missed calls and four messages from that same number. Julie bit her lower lip. *Telemarketers aren't that persistent.*

She signed in to her voice mail and pressed One.

"Mrs. Welch, this is Principal Justine Taylor from Fairfax High School. I'm sorry to leave you this message instead of speaking to you directly, but I wanted you to know that Max had an accident today. He fell on the stairs, injuring his neck and hitting his head. He was taken to the Fairfax Hospital Emergency Room. The school nurse who examined him thinks he'll be fine, but we wanted to be cautious. You can never be too careful when dealing with a head trauma. Hopefully you'll get this message. In the meantime, I'll keep trying you. My direct line is 703-555-6533, extension 100."

5: George, Punching Bags

George lay in the hospital bed, hooked to an IV. His shoulder and leg were bandaged. An empty bed was next to him, and a television was affixed to the wall. He watched the news.

Lisa Kelly, the blonde newscaster, said, "We have Congressman John Bradley coming to us from an undisclosed location."

WNN cut to John. He stood in a windowless room, with an earpiece in his ear. He was fit, and his face looked younger than his silver hair.

"Thank you for connecting with us, Congressman," Lisa said. "Especially given the circumstances."

John was stoic. "You're welcome, Lisa. Thank you for having me."

"We've had unconfirmed reports that you were uninjured in the attack. Are those reports accurate?"

"They are. I was uninjured, but only because of the heroic actions of US Secret Service Agents Derrick Stokes, Jake Barnes, and Greg Olson. And of course the civilian bystander, George Chapman. I owe an enormous debt of gratitude to these men, especially Agent Stokes. As you know, Agent Derrick Stokes gave his life protecting me. He was a great man, and he will be sorely missed. My heart and prayers go out to his family."

"Such an amazing display of heroism." Lisa paused for a moment. "Can you walk us through the attack from your perspective?"

"I was talking to my chief of staff, and a man entered the front door. He removed an assault rifle from his jacket and pointed it at me. I remember thinking I was going to die. That's when Agent Barnes shielded me with his body, and George Chapman tackled the terrorist. I tried to help Mr. Chapman, but I was pushed out the back door. At that point, Agent Stokes had the

31

situation under control."

"But the terrorist managed to shoot Agent Stokes."

John exhaled. "Apparently the terrorist also had a handgun under his coat."

"We've had reports that both the assault rifle and the handgun had high-capacity magazines. Is that true?"

John nodded. "It is true."

"Do you think this attack could have been prevented with gun legislation?"

"As you know, Lisa, my gun control bill would have banned assault rifles and magazines capable of holding more than ten rounds of ammunition."

George turned off the television, set the remote on the bedside table, and picked up his phone. He checked his email. Nothing. *Good thing I didn't have any bikes on my trailer.*

George closed his email and scrolled through his favorite news wire. He clicked on a headline that grabbed his attention.

LEGAL SYSTEM OVERRUN WITH JURY TRIALS
By: Frank Redner
May 7, 2018

Ray Washington was arrested six months ago for felony possession of heroin with the intent to sell. He refused a plea bargain in favor of a jury trial. His court date is set for early 2020. Mr. Washington was asked why he refused the two-year prison sentence, which is ironically the same amount of time as his wait for a jury trial.

He said, "I'm not stupid. I can do the math. I see what's happening in this country. People are tired of being abused. I've been out on bail for six months, and, when I finally do go to trial, if I ever do, there's a good chance that one of the jurors might be an Anarchist. They think filling up the jails with druggies is a waste. All it takes is one Anarchist to win me my trial."

In 2016, 90 percent of criminal cases were never tried in court, defendants taking plea bargains instead. In the past two years, that number dropped to 88 percent in 2017, and 83 percent during the first quarter of 2018.

This may seem like a small percentage of cases request jury trials, but it is a volume increase of 70 percent in two years. The American legal system has been notoriously overburdened, with district attorneys arguing ten times as many cases as their private counterparts. But today the court system is bursting at the seams, with trial dates stretching out over two years into the future.

These extreme delays have angered defense attorneys and defendants. Civil liberties attorney Murray Feinstein said, "The state is overburdened, not because we have too many criminals but because we have too many laws. It is estimated that the average citizen commits three felonies a day. If the state wishes to criminalize and prosecute with such a wide net, they must maintain the defendants' constitutional right to a speedy trial. If they can't, they ought to decriminalize nonviolent offenses, such as drug possession."

In addition to lengthy judicial delays, anarchism has turned jury pools into potential minefields. One of the goals of many Anarchists is to dismantle the legal system by infiltrating juries and exercising jury nullification. Jury nullification occurs when a jury returns a verdict of "not guilty" despite its belief that the defendant is guilty of the crime. Anarchists believe that victimless crimes, such as drug use, should not be prosecuted. Some Anarchists believe that the state should not have the power to prosecute any crimes, even heinous ones, such as murder.

District attorneys are now forced to consume valuable resources and time they don't have researching potential jurors for connections to antigovernment ideologies. Many Anarchists are hiding in plain sight, registering as Republicans and Independents, not to support a political party but for the opportunity to be selected for a jury. This infiltration has resulted in a 110 percent rise in mistrials.

George looked up from his phone as a female nurse pushed a teenage boy into the hospital room, followed by a male nurse.

The chubby kid wore glasses, had a round face, and a bandage wrapped around his head. The nurses helped him into the bed next to George. The boy grunted as he moved.

"Are you okay?" the female nurse asked.

The male nurse exited the room.

"My neck hurts," the boy said.

"I know. It's gonna be sore for a few days." The nurse patted him on the hand.

An attractive woman in yoga pants burst into the room. She was breathless as she hurried to the boy's bedside. "Max, I am so sorry," she said. "I was out running, and I didn't have my phone. I just got the message from school. Are you all right?"

"I'm fine."

The nurse smiled at the woman. "You must be Max's mom?"

"I'm Julie Welch."

"It's nice to meet you, Mrs. Welch. I'm Amy. I'll be Max's nurse."

"Please call me Julie."

The nurse smiled again. "Of course."

"How's he doing?" Julie asked.

"He's gonna be just fine. He has a mild neck sprain and a concussion. We're putting him through our standard concussion protocol, which is, lots of rest and observation. We'd like to keep him overnight in case of seizures, but you should be able to take him home tomorrow."

"Thank you, Amy."

Nurse Amy turned to Max. "I'll be checking on you, but, if you need anything, my Call button is on your bedside table."

"Thank you," Max replied.

"Thank you," Julie echoed.

The nurse left the room.

"I'm so sorry, honey," Julie said. "I should've been here."

"It's not a big deal," Max replied.

"Principal Taylor said you fell on the stairs. What happened?"

"I fell on the stairs."

"But how?"

Max shrugged. "Tripped, I guess."

"Would you like me to get you something to eat or something to read?"

"Just my phone. It was in the pocket of my jeans. I don't know where they put my clothes."

* * *

"Visiting hours are about over," Julie said. "I should go home and get cleaned up. I didn't even shower after my run."

"That's gross, Mom," Max said, glancing up from his phone.

"I was worried about *you*, not my hygiene." Julie stood up with a smirk. "I'll be back at ten tomorrow morning to take you home." She bent over and kissed Max on the cheek. "Will you be okay by yourself?"

"I'll be fine."

"I love you, honey."

Max glanced at George, reading on his phone.

"Love you too, Mom," Max said quietly.

Julie left.

The lights were dim. Max watched the screen on his phone, his earbuds in. He alternately stared at George and stared at his phone.

"Excuse me, sir?" Max said, taking out his earbuds.

George looked at Max. "Yeah?"

"Are you George Chapman?"

"Yep." George placed his phone on his bedside table.

"The one on the news?"

"Afraid so. What's your name?"

"I'm Max ... Max Welch."

"Nice to meet you, Max."

"It's pretty cool, what you did."

"I was in the right place at the right time. Or the wrong place, depending on how you look at it."

"Did you see that they released the name of the terrorist?"

"I didn't."

"His name's Louis Allister. They said he was a veteran of Afghanistan and an Anarchist."

35

George didn't respond.

Max went back to his phone.

George closed his eyes.

"Do you wanna hear what he said on Facebook?" Max asked.

George opened his eyes. "Huh?"

"The terrorist wrote something messed-up on Facebook right before. You wanna hear it?"

"Okay."

"He wrote, 'No more will I be a hitman for bankers and war profiteers. This is a message to the ruling elite. We're coming for you. No rulers. No masters.' Sounds like a criminal mastermind out of a graphic novel. These Anarchists are pretty crazy, huh?"

"How do you figure?"

"This guy was in the military, then hates the United States so much that he tries to kill a congressman. I'd say that qualifies as crazy."

"If you're in the military and you're sent to war, it would stand to reason that you might see war up close and personal. And you might not agree with it."

"Do you agree with it?"

"I don't agree with violence."

"But you used violence to stop the terrorist," Max said.

George nodded. "You're right, but, to me, violence is justified if it's used in self-defense or to defend another."

Max was quiet for a moment. "Like standing up to a bully?"

"That's a good way of looking at it. So what are you in here for?"

"I fell and hit my head."

"That must've hurt."

* * *

Max tapped and scrolled on his phone as he polished off the last of his pancakes.

"How was your breakfast?" George asked.

Max scrolled through his phone. "Not bad actually."

"How's your head? You feeling better?"

Max didn't respond. George glanced from his breakfast to his roommate. Max stared into his phone, his face blank.

"You all right over there?" George asked.

Max's eyes were glassy. He stood from the hospital bed and snatched his bag from the nearby chair. Without a word, Max walked to the bathroom.

A few minutes later, Max emerged in baggy jeans and a long-sleeve T-shirt. He sat in the chair next to his bed.

"You taking off already?" George asked.

Max's face was blotchy. "Yeah."

"Well, I've enjoyed meeting you, Max."

Max looked away from George, toward the window.

"Anything you wanna talk about?" George asked.

"What?"

"Do you wanna talk about what was on your phone?"

"It's nothing." Max still looked away.

"When I was your age, I got picked on pretty bad. I had a face full of acne and barely two nickels to rub together. I remember being made fun of because I wore clothes that another kid's family had donated to Goodwill. The kid's initials were on the tag of my shirt. My dad was long gone, and my mother, ... well, she had some issues. The kids at school said a lot of stuff about my mother. I was too afraid to do anything about it. I was the school punching bag."

Max turned to George, his eyes red. "I'm not the school punching bag."

"I'm sorry. That's not what I meant. I'm just saying that I know school can be a cruel place. It's not unlike prison in a lot of ways."

"Yeah, well, it's a shitty place." Max hung his head. "And I can't get away from it."

"Sounds rough."

"Kids took pictures when I fell, and they posted these stupid memes on Instagram."

"You didn't fall, did you?"

Max lifted his head. "I did fall."

"But you had some help."

Max nodded.

George took a deep breath. "I'm sorry, Max. Two types of people are in this world. People who wanna be left alone, and people who won't leave you alone."

"What do you do with those people, the ones who won't leave you alone?"

"Seems to me you have three choices. Continue to take it, make them stop, or walk away."

"I can't stand it anymore, and I can't … I can't make it stop."

"Sometimes the only solution is to walk away."

"How am I supposed to do that? I have to go to school."

"Don't they have online school here?"

"My mom would never let me go virtual."

"Have you asked her?"

"No, but I know her. She talks about how she loved high school. She wouldn't understand."

"From what I saw yesterday, it looked like she really cared. I think it's worth a shot."

Max shrugged. "Maybe."

6: John and Leadership

Linda slept on her side, facing the wall. Rays of morning sunshine pierced the gaps in the curtains. John rolled toward her, toward her warmth. He lifted the cover and glanced at his wife. She wore black bikini underwear and a T-shirt. His pulse quickened as he gazed at the curve of her hips, her toned legs, and strawberry-hued skin. Her T-shirt had ridden up, exposing the small of her back.

John inched closer. He wrapped his arm around her and pressed his crotch against her backside. His semierect penis hardened as he moved. Linda opened her eyes, and her body went stiff. John moved his hand up her T-shirt and over her nipples.

"Honey," she said.

John tugged her underwear down to midthigh.

Linda rolled to her back and pulled up her underwear. "Honey, not now."

"Come on. I'm really stressed," John said.

"An agent is right outside our door, and this house is full of people," Linda replied in a hushed tone. "Someone needs to make breakfast."

John moved his hand under the silky fabric of her underwear. She slapped him across the face, and John removed his hand as if he'd been burned. Linda exited the bed.

John's face was flushed. "Jesus Christ, Linda. Was that necessary?"

"I said, *no.*"

"You said, *not now.* If I didn't push you, we'd never have sex."

"Keep your voice down."

"I don't know why I even bother. I was almost killed two days ago, and I can't even get a sympathy fuck."

39

Linda glared, her cheeks crimson. She started for the bathroom.

John popped out of bed and beat her to it. He stood between Linda and the bathroom door.

"Move," she said.

He stood with his arms crossed. "I'm not waiting around while you monopolize the bathroom. I have things to do that rank a bit higher in importance than fucking breakfast."

She pursed her lips, her eyes glassy. She opened her mouth and shut it.

"You're welcome to shower with me," he said with a smirk.

* * *

John buttoned his shirt and tucked it into his slacks. He picked up his phone from the dresser. There was a text.

Donna: Call me as soon as you get this. We have a situation.

The shower ran in the bathroom. He smiled to himself, knowing the hot water was waning. *I hope she enjoys the cold shower.*

John bounded down the stairs. He nodded to a couple of agents, not remembering their names. He shut the door to the office. A laptop was on the desk. He sat down in the swivel chair and powered on the computer. He pressed the Donna contact on his phone.

"We have a big problem," Donna said.

"That's a helluva way to greet someone first thing in the morning," John replied.

"Sorry."

"No, you're right to the point. I like that. Let me have it. Give me your best shot."

"There's video footage of the attack."

"Really?"

"Yes. Apparently Jeff Hutton recorded it with his phone."

"Who the hell's Jeff Hutton?"

"He's an intern, a college student. He just started."

"So, what's the problem?"

"The video shows an inconsistency between your account of what happened and what actually happened."

"Witnesses are notoriously unreliable. People will forgive a mistake."

Donna was quiet.

"You don't think so?"

"You said that you tried to help George Chapman but were taken away by the secret service."

"That's what happened."

"Not according to the video. The video doesn't show any indication that you made any effort to help Chapman. If anything, it shows you backing up before Jake pulled you away."

"I still don't see a problem. I was shot at. In my mind, I started to help Chapman. Everything happened so fast. I had a gun in my face, for Christ's sake."

"There are videos that show your interview in juxtaposition with the attack footage. The best one is set to music, and it replays what you said, like a refrain. It's quite catchy actually. It's trending on Twitter, and it already has over a million views on YouTube—"

"What's the damage?"

"It's tough to say, but it's not positive. It depicts you as the typical lying politician, which is exactly the opposite image we want to portray. People want someone different, and, to them, this is the same old bullshit."

"Jesus, Donna, I was almost killed. Doesn't that count for anything?"

"That's what the Democrats are saying, and this won't hurt your congressional reelection, but, to win the presidency, we need more than the Democrats."

"That's two and a half years away. You don't think it'll blow over?"

"I do, but the Republicans will dig it up and use it to portray you as a coward."

"I'm a coward?" John huffed. "Half these Republican fat fucks would've shit their pants."

"We need to address it before it gets out of control."

"There's nothing to address."

"The public disagrees."

John clenched his jaw. "Do you have something in mind?"

"I think we should set up an on-camera meeting with Chapman. To the public, Chapman's one of them right now. It would be good for you to show him some gratitude. I'm thinking something heartfelt. We'll draft a few different statements and poll them to find out which one plays best."

"I'm fine with that."

"I think we need to address the inconsistency in your story with a statement to the press."

"Is that necessary? Chapman'll be my best friend by the time I'm done with him."

"We can't leave any loose ends for the Republicans to exploit."

"I think it's a mistake to admit wrongdoing here."

"I agree," Donna replied. "I think we can craft a statement that touches on how stress can affect memory. We might get away with admonishing the press for focusing on a victim's faulty memory, instead of the heroism of the late Derrick Stokes."

"That might work."

"We'll poll it and find out before you stick your neck out there. How much longer will you be at the safe house?"

"Jake thinks today or tomorrow at the latest."

"That's good," Donna said. "I'd like for the meeting with Chapman to take place at the hospital. It's important that you see him before he's released. He's due for release tomorrow afternoon."

"I agree."

"We're already working on the statements. I'll send them to you as soon as I have them."

John was quiet for a beat. "Thanks, Donna."

"Are you okay?"

"I'm fine. What was the name of the intern who recorded the video?"

"Jeff Hutton."

"Get rid of him."

"That might not be—"

"I want him gone." John's cell phone buzzed. He glanced at the incoming call and groaned. "I have to go. It's the senator and his *wisdom*."

"Listen to him," Donna said, "but ultimately it's your career."

"Is it?" John clicked over to the incoming call. "Dad."

"I hope you plan on doing something about this ... this *discrepancy*," former Senator Bradley said.

John frowned. "I'm on it."

"Attempting to make yourself look stronger than you are makes you look weaker than you are. These days the public will forgive the veterans, billionaires, and celebrities, but not us academics. They see us as politicians, sitting in our ivory tower."

"It was a mistake. So forgive me if I wasn't thinking clearly while I was shot at."

"No, you weren't. The shot went into the floor. Your entire staff was shot at more than you. It would serve you better in the press to remember that. Play down your own danger and heroism, and emphasize the heroism of others. That's leadership."

7: Katie Likes JFK

Katie sat at her desk, watching the video of herself on the laptop screen. On-screen and offscreen, she wore a low-cut floral sundress—no bra of course. Her light brown hair draped down to her chest and curled at the ends. Thankfully her cleavage was uncovered.

"It's no surprise that USN picked up the video. Congressman Bradley is a major threat to the Republican establishment. We have to think about who stands to gain if Bradley's assassinated. Certainly the Republicans and of course the Anarchists. The shooter was a self-proclaimed Anarchist, but he was also a registered Republican. And now with the failed assassination attempt, they're attempting to assassinate the congressman's character."

Katie on the screen adjusted her black-frame glasses. "Congressman Bradley was almost killed, in a stressful, life-threatening situation that most of us will never experience. Memory is often unreliable in normal circumstances, but it is absolutely atrocious under stress. The man had a machine gun pointed in his face. In the congressman's mind, he thought he made an attempt to help George Chapman. He never said he *did* help Chapman, only that he made an attempt.

"We have to ask ourselves why the victim is blamed here. Are the producers of these videos blaming all the other people in the office who didn't help? Of course not because it's totally illogical. Our focus and blame should be on the shooter, the antigovernment Anarchist nutjob with Republican ties.

"There's a reason why they killed John and Robert Kennedy. The Kennedys represented real change in this country, the same way John Bradley does. John Bradley *will* be the Democratic candidate for president in 2020. I hope he survives long enough to be the change we want to see in this country."

She heard clapping—long, slow, loud claps. Katie looked up. It was Declan. He stood in a black T-shirt and his pork pie hat. His right arm was covered in Native American tattoos. He wasn't just another white guy; he was 1/32 Sioux.

"Nice speech," he said with a grin. "You have my vote."

Katie smiled. "Thanks."

"Are you about done?"

"Almost."

Declan sauntered behind the desk, behind Katie. He bent over and kissed her neck. He ran his hands inside her dress, over her breasts. She exhaled and tilted her head back, looking up at her boyfriend. He bent down and pressed his lips to hers.

"I think you're done now," Declan said.

Katie giggled. "Think so, huh?"

Declan nodded and moved around the desk to the camera. He ran a USB cable from the camera to the laptop. He pressed Record and checked the camera screen. Katie was centered nicely, her round face smiling back at him. Declan sashayed back around the desk. He swiveled Katie around in the chair, so she faced him. She looked up, with red cheeks and big blue eyes under her specs.

Declan kneeled in front of her, reached up her sundress, and slid her panties down her legs. He pulled her forward to the edge of the chair. Katie leaned back and draped her legs over Declan's shoulders. She gasped as he worked his tongue over her clitoris.

Katie was out of breath and flushed as Declan came up for air. He stood Katie up and pushed the chair aside. She turned toward the camera and bent over, placing her hands on the desk. He undid his belt, and pulled his skinny jeans and bikini briefs down to his knees.

Katie slid her arms from her dress, allowing her chest to dangle for the camera. He grunted and thrusted, watching Katie in real time, her face contorted on the laptop screen, and her breasts swaying back and forth. Declan moved faster, their skin smacking together. He gripped her hips tight and groaned as he climaxed.

Afterward Declan wiggled his hairy white ass back into his tight jeans. The camera was still rolling. Katie lifted her dress and put her arms back through the sleeves.

"I should get going," Declan said.

Katie turned around and pressed out her lower lip. "Already? You know I'm leaving in a few hours. I won't see you until Friday."

"Sorry, babe. I just stopped by to, uh—"

"Fuck your girlfriend?"

Declan laughed. "To wish you luck. But I can't stay. I'm interviewing that US Oil exec."

"Your dad's friend?"

"Yeah."

"Does he know it's a hit piece?"

Declan grinned. "What do you think?"

"Save the best questions for the end."

8: Julie and Friends

Julie glanced up at the clock as she hurried down the hall. Laughter came from the hospital room. *Is that Max?* She entered the doorway, her mouth open.

Max sat on a chair, next to a hospital bed with a man hooked up to IVs. They laughed as if they were the best of friends. *Did I miss something? He looks familiar.* The man had short dark hair, faint acne scarring on his cheeks, and eyes as black as coal.

"I'm so sorry I'm late," Julie said.

The laughter dissipated as Max turned from the man to his mother. "It's okay, Mom."

"You ready to go home?"

"This is George," Max said, glancing at the man in the hospital bed.

The dark-haired man raised his hand toward Julie.

"Hi, George," she said, then focused on Max. "You ready?"

"It's nice to meet you," George mumbled.

"Mom," Max said, "this is George Chapman from the news."

Julie did a double-take and narrowed her eyes. "Oh, … oh, I thought you looked familiar."

"It's nice to meet you," George said a little louder.

Julie forced a smile, then turned to Max. "We should get going."

Max stood. "It was cool talking to you, George."

George extended his hand. "Likewise, young man."

They shook hands.

Max grabbed his backpack and left the hospital room with his mother.

"How are you feeling?" Julie asked as the elevator door closed. "You look better."

Max shrugged. "I'm fine."

"That's good." Julie glanced at her son.

He stared at the floor numbers as they lit up on the elevator panel.

"I took time off work," she said. "The doctor thought it would be a good idea if I watched over you for a few days."

"You don't have to," he replied, still watching the floor numbers tick down. He stood a little straighter.

The elevator doors opened. "I wanted to," she replied.

They hiked through the lobby.

"I know we need the money, so you don't have to," Max said.

Julie grabbed her son's hand. "Your health's more important than money."

He stopped. "I'm fine, Mom. Really." He pulled back his hand.

They exited the building and continued through the parking lot in silence. Inside the car Julie put on oversize sunglasses before leaving. They edged along with the lunch hour traffic.

"So what were you two laughing about?" Julie asked, glancing at her son.

Max shrugged, his face buried in his cell phone screen. "I don't know. We talked about a lot of stuff."

"What kind of stuff?"

"Different stuff."

Julie pursed her lips. "Honey, would you please put that down? I'm trying to talk to you."

Max sighed and shoved his phone in the front pocket of his jeans. He looked out the passenger window.

"You two were laughing like you were the best of friends, which is weird, because you were in that hospital room for one day."

Max turned from the window. "Why is it weird? You're always telling me to make friends. I make a friend, and now I'm weird?" Max crossed his arms over his chest.

Julie exhaled. "I didn't say you were weird. I'm just concerned. When I suggested you try to make friends, I was thinking of someone your age."

"Nobody likes me."

"Oh, come on, honey. You're such a nice kid. That can't be true. You just need to open up."

"It is true," he said, glaring at his mother. "I don't have a single friend in that stupid school. And just because you were popular doesn't mean I can be.

You have no idea what it's like."

Julie pulled off the highway and parked in the back of a strip mall. She put the Honda in Park and turned her attention to her son.

Max hung his head. Julie placed her hand under Max's chin and tilted his face upward. His eyes were glassy.

"I'm sorry," Julie said. "I didn't know."

"I don't wanna go back to that school."

She placed her hand on top of his and squeezed. "Did that man say something to you?"

"He said a lot of things."

"Maybe we should take a few days to think about this before we make any rash decisions."

Max was quiet.

"It'll get better," Julie said. "I promise."

"You're not listening," Max said.

"I am listening. Talk to me."

"Forget it."

"Come on, honey. Please don't shut down. I'm trying to help you."

"No, you just want me to be okay because you can't deal with anymore disappointments."

Julie closed her eyes for a moment. "That's not fair. I'm doing the best I can."

Max looked down. "So am I."

"What would you like me to do?"

"I wanna finish school online."

"There's only six weeks left in the school year. I don't know if you can get into the virtual program at this point."

Max looked at his mother, his face blotchy. "I'm talking about next year. I'll finish this school year, but, after that, I'm done."

Julie bit her lower lip. "I'm just … I'm just worried about you being even more isolated at home by yourself."

"I eat lunch every day by myself in a packed lunchroom. I can't think of anything more isolating than that."

"If I consider this, you have to at least tell me what this George person said to you. All this feels like it's out of the blue."

"It's not out of the blue. George just told me the truth. He said that I deserve to be treated with respect, and, if I don't like the way someone's treating me, I can walk away."

"Honey, I don't think George has any special training with teens—"

"He was like me when he was in school, maybe worse. He knows what it's like."

"You don't think he's like one of those ..."

Max rolled his eyes. "One of those what, Mom?"

"You know, ... pedophiles."

Max blew out a breath. "He's not like that. Gimme a little credit. I'm not gonna be friends with some creeper."

"Are you friends with him?"

Max shrugged. "I don't know. He gave me his email and said I can contact him anytime. He's actually interested in what I have to say. He's a freaking hero, Mom, and he never said one word about that."

"I'm interested in what you have to say."

"You have to be."

Julie leaned over and hugged her son. After a moment, Max reciprocated. She released her son and said, "You're a good person, honey. One day people will see what I see."

Max nodded, his head down.

"I'm so sorry that you've been going through this. I love you."

Max looked at his mom. "I love you too, Mom."

Julie released the emergency brake, exited the mall parking lot, and drove home.

"Shit," Julie said, pulling into her parking space. "The grass."

A middle-aged man stood on the sidewalk with his arms crossed over his chest.

"I'll do it now," Max said.

"No. You need your rest."

"I can do it—"

"Go inside. I'll take care of it."

Julie took a deep breath and stepped from her Honda, her sunglasses still on. Max grabbed his backpack and shut the car door. Max ignored the greeting from the middle-aged man on the sidewalk and trudged toward the townhome.

"Good afternoon, Julie," the man said, staring at her overgrown lawn.

"Hi, Dan," she replied.

Dan Gordon wore khakis and a golf shirt tucked over his gut. He had a white mustache and a receding hairline.

"Grass grows pretty fast in the spring," he said.

"My son was in the hospital, but I'll get to it this weekend."

Dan turned to Julie, looking her up and down. "Has he been in the hospital for eighteen days?"

Julie raised her eyebrows. "Just the one night."

Dan nodded. "Huh. Lawn hasn't been cut for eighteen days."

"I'm sorry, Dan. I've been really busy at work."

"The lawn needs to be cut every week in the spring. When it gets real hot in the summer, you might be able to go every ten days. But you gotta monitor it."

"I'll put it on my phone calendar."

Dan sighed. "This is the third time in less than a year."

"I know. I'm sorry."

He stared at her chest.

Julie cringed at the possibility that her white T-shirt was wearing thin.

Dan lifted his gaze. "I'm not gonna fine you, but I can't keep givin' you special treatment."

Julie forced a smile. "Thanks, Dan."

He pushed his wire-rim glasses up his nose and grinned. "You're lucky I like you."

9: George and Violence Is Immoral

George sat in the chair next to the hospital bed, his bad leg straight, his good one bent. He wore jeans, no shirt. His T-shirt and shoulder sling were in his lap. He grunted, his shoulder grinding with pain as he wriggled into his shirt. With his T-shirt on, he struggled back into the shoulder sling.

A cane leaned against the chair. He used it to stand and limp to the window. It wasn't the cane of some dapper R&B star but of the rubber-and-metal geriatric variety. Outside, angry clouds peppered the parking lot with sheets of rain.

"Mr. Chapman?" a man asked.

George turned from the window. There he was, in the flesh—Congressman John Bradley with a power tie and a plastered smile.

"Yeah," George said.

John moved closer, a tightly wound woman at his side. She wore a skirt suit, with heels, panty hose, her blouse buttoned to her neck, and her hair pulled back in a tight bun. None of it looked comfortable.

"I'm Congressman Bradley, but I'm assuming you know that," he said.

"What can I do for you?" George replied.

"I would prefer to know what I can do for *you*."

George was quiet.

John's smile went flat. He looked George in the eyes. "Thank you for saving my life. I will never forget your selflessness and heroism. I am deeply indebted to you. Thank you." Congressman Bradley extended his hand.

They shook hands.

"You're welcome," George said.

"I know you don't have a ride from the hospital, so I've arranged for a couple of secret service agents to take you home."

"I appreciate that, but I need to pick up my truck and trailer from the plaza."

"We'll drive your truck home as well. Also I'd like to take you to lunch before you go."

"I'm sorry. I don't wanna do that."

John raised his eyebrows. "You don't want to go to lunch?"

"No, and I don't want your agents driving my truck or taking me home. I can manage on my own. Thank you for the offer though. Excuse me." George limped past the congressman and the woman toward the hall.

"Mr. Chapman?" Congressman Bradley said to George's back.

George peered into the hall, hoping for the orderly with his wheelchair. No orderly was found but there was a loitering camera crew and a couple secret service agents.

"Mr. Chapman," John said again.

George turned around, and Congressman Bradley and his henchwoman encroached on his personal space.

"Excuse me," George said, as he moved past them to the seat by the bed. George put his weight on his good leg as he eased into the chair.

"Let me give you a hand," John said, but it was too late.

"I'm fine," George said. "I'm leaving in a few minutes."

"Mr. Chapman, I'm the type of person who pays his debts. No doubt I owe you ... big time. I see that you're a proud man who's used to looking out for himself, but sometimes we all need a little help. Maybe not now or even ten years from now, but eventually we all need help. In the future, if you ever need anything, you can call me." John reached into the inside pocket of his jacket and removed a business card. He handed it to George. "My cell number's on the back."

George nodded. "Thank you."

"Call me anytime. I mean that."

George shoved the card in the front pocket of his jeans.

The woman approached. "Mr. Chapman, my name's Donna." She extended her hand to George.

They shook hands. "Nice to meet you," George said.

"I was hoping you might appear with Congressman Bradley on a news piece honoring your heroism."

"No thank you."

"This country's in crisis," John said. "You're a hero, Mr. Chapman. Americans identify with you. Your heroism and my gratitude is a perfect platform to bridge the gap between the people and our government. We can show that government really is for the people and by the people."

"Is that what you're selling?"

John put his hands on his hips. "I'm not selling anything. I'm just doing my part to keep this country together and give people hope."

"No thanks."

John clenched his jaw for a split second, then smirked. "This hasn't gone how I thought it would go. Is there any way I can convince you to change your mind?"

George shook his head. "I appreciate your gratitude but no."

"May I ask why?"

"Why I won't go on camera, or why I don't want your agents taking me and my truck to Pennsylvania?"

"Both."

"Who's paying for those agents and the vehicles and the fuel?"

"The federal government."

"No."

John chuckled. "No? I'm pretty sure I understand the budget items from my own office."

"People pay for it with taxation and inflation."

John's face turned down. "Is this about government largesse? Are you worried about wasting taxpayer funds?"

"No."

"That's good because your government also owes you a debt of gratitude."

"That may be, but I'm not gonna participate in an extortion racket to collect."

John raised his eyebrows. "Excuse me?"

"I think you heard me."

John shook his head. "You're an Anarchist."

George nodded, his jaw set tight.

Donna's eyes were wide, her mouth open.

John chuckled again. "Well, I didn't see that coming."

George glanced at the door, willing the orderly to appear.

"Let me ask you a question, off the record," John said.

"I didn't realize we were on the record," George replied.

"Did you know that the shooter was an Anarchist?"

"I do now but not then."

"If you could go back to that day, would you let him shoot me?"

Donna's eyes darted to John.

George scowled. "Unfortunately that young man didn't know what it means to be an Anarchist."

"Assault rifle, shaved head, an assassination attempt," John said. "Seems to me he knew exactly what it meant."

"Unfortunately neither do you."

A dark-skinned man with green scrubs walked into the room, pushing a wheelchair. "Mr. Chapman," he said, "are you ready to blow this joint?"

George smiled at the man. "Absolutely."

The orderly helped George into the chair and pushed him toward the door.

"Mr. Chapman," John said.

The orderly stopped.

"I meant what I said," John continued. "If you need anything, call me."

"I appreciate the sentiment, Congressman," George replied.

The orderly pushed George down the hall to the elevator.

"You got a ride home?" the orderly asked as he pressed the down arrow next to the elevator doors.

"I'm gonna get an Uber."

The elevator opened, and the man pushed George inside. "A lot of press is out front," the man said. "You want me to take you out back?"

"Please," George replied.

The man pushed B on the elevator panel. "I'll take you through the basement."

The orderly dropped off George in the back of the building at a covered walk with concrete benches.

"This okay?" the orderly asked.

"It's great, thanks."

With that, George was left alone, the rain pelting the roof of the covered walk, the grass, and asphalt around him. A few hospital personnel hustled past. George tapped on his Uber app and found a driver ten minutes away.

He booked the fare and shoved his phone back in the front pocket of his jeans.

A news van drove toward him. George looked around. He had no place to hide, not in his condition. The van stopped at the curb. A cameraman and a female reporter stepped from the van.

The camera was rolling and pointed at George.

The reporter, an attractive brunette with heavy makeup, stepped into George's personal space and said, "Hello, Mr. Chapman. I'm Corrinne Stevens from US News. How are you feeling?"

George was silent.

"Mr. Chapman, how are you feeling?"

George was still silent.

"How was your meeting with Congressman Bradley?"

George removed his phone from his pocket and checked the time. *Four minutes.* George frowned and shoved his phone back in his pocket.

"How does it feel to be a hero?" Corrinne asked.

George crossed his arms and looked straight ahead.

"Do you think the Anarchists are domestic terrorists?"

George closed his eyes for a moment. "Define terrorism," he said.

Corrinne raised her eyebrows. "Excuse me?"

"Define terrorism."

"It's, … umm, terrorizing people."

George glared at the camera. "It's the use of violence and intimidation in the pursuit of political aims. Governments throughout this world have killed 250 million of their own people in the past hundred years. Our government has killed over one million people in Iraq and another half-million in the so-called War on Terror from Afghanistan to Pakistan to Libya to Yemen and Syria. This doesn't include the millions who have been injured and maimed, and lost their homes and livelihoods. If you wanna talk about terrorists, let's start with the US government."

Corrinne's mouth was open. "Mr. Chapman, this is off topic. Do you care to comment on—"

"You can't tell the truth, can you?"

The reporter was dumbstruck.

"Of course you can't, because your government and corporate masters supply your network with a steady stream of propaganda that you gladly regurgitate to the American public because it's easy, it's profitable, and you don't have to worry about being sued."

A white Toyota Avalon pulled up behind the news van. George stood with the help of his cane. He limped toward the car.

"Why did you save Congressman Bradley?" Corrinne asked.

George turned toward the reporter. "Because violence is immoral."

10: John, Next Question

"That was a fucking disaster," Congressman John Bradley said. "Didn't you do any research on this guy?"

"We did," Donna replied, "but he doesn't have much of an Internet presence. No social media accounts. He has a profile as a shipper on Cycle Trader and eBay but no personal information beyond that. He does have an excellent online rating."

"I'm assuming he's not a registered voter."

"Actually he's registered as an Independent. We usually poll pretty well with Independents. That's why I thought this would work."

"Why would he register to vote? Aren't these Anarchists all about avoiding and subverting government?"

"They don't register to vote to actually vote. They do it to get on juries, so they can subvert the rule of law through jury nullification."

John shook his head. "Jesus, what is this country coming to? When I started in politics, I never would have dreamed that the most patriotic populace on the planet would change like this."

"Anarchists are a tiny minority. Less than 1 percent according to recent polls."

"Only 3 percent of Americans fought in the Revolutionary War against the British. Do you know what percentage of people actively supported that 3 percent?"

"I don't."

"Ten percent. Three percent willing to fight and with only 10 percent support. That's all they needed to overthrow the biggest empire the world had ever known back then."

Agent Olson drove John and Donna and Agent Barnes to the scene of the crime. They parked around back. Agents Barnes and Olson manned their posts. John and Donna stepped inside their campaign office. A half-dozen indispensable employees worked on laptops. The rest were given the week off. The floor was cleaned; the windows and glass door were repaired. If not for the bullet holes in the walls, the campaign headquarters appeared undisturbed, like nothing had happened.

"They did a nice job with the cleanup," John said.

"You sure you don't want them to fix the drywall?" Donna asked.

"We talked about this."

"The staff was traumatized. They may not come back, especially with the bullet holes to remind them of the attack."

"We need fighters for the presidential run. I'd rather they quit now than when we really need them. Besides, it'll look good as the backdrop for my statement tomorrow. We're in a war, Donna. I want the voters to know that I'm a fighter."

* * *

Dave the tech guy affixed a mike to John's lapel.

"Are you sure you don't need a teleprompter?" Donna asked.

John grinned. "You worry too much. It's all memorized." He tapped his head with his index finger. "Like a steel trap."

Donna smirked. "Make sure to call on Corrinne from USN to ask the first question. She'll ask about Chapman's comment. We need to deal with it head-on."

The press took their seats. John stepped up to the wooden podium in his campaign headquarters. Behind him was a wall with eight bullet holes. In front of him were lights, cameras, and an audience of newspersons arranged in neat rows.

"Thank you all for being here," John said. "First, I'd like to thank US Secret Service Agents Greg Olson, Jake Barnes, and Derrick Stokes for their heroism during the attack. Agent Stokes was killed while protecting me and, more important, while serving the United States of America." John paused, his hands gripping the edge of the podium. "I extend my heartfelt condolences to the Stokes family in this time of tragedy.

"Also I'd like to thank George Smith Chapman, the civilian bystander who tackled the shooter and thereafter sustained two gunshot wounds. If it weren't for him, I wouldn't be standing here today. I am deeply indebted to these four men.

"During the attack, I was afraid. I was afraid I'd never see my wife and children again." John looked down for a moment. "The fear and stress I felt affected my memory, my judgment, and my actions. This is not uncommon and something that victims of terrorism can attest to. I made a statement to the press shortly after the attack that I attempted to help Mr. Chapman. My statement reflected my memory. My statement and my memory of the event were faulty. I apologize for my error."

John stared into the cameras, unblinking. His upturned fist moved up and down with the cadence of his speech. "I hope, moving forward, we can concentrate on the heroism of the secret service agents and Mr. Chapman, not on the faulty memory of a terrorism victim. Furthermore, I was the least affected by this heinous act. I was fortunate enough to be escorted away from the violence after the first gunshot. My staff, on the other hand, withstood a barrage of at least fifteen bullets, eight of which created the holes in the wall behind me." John motioned to them. "It is only by the grace of God that nobody else was killed.

"A construction crew recently cleaned up our headquarters here. They fixed the windows shattered by bullets. They cleaned the glass shards and the blood from the floor. I asked that they leave the bullet holes in the drywall. It's a reminder to myself that I'm lucky to be alive. It's a reminder to myself to be grateful for the secret service agents assigned to me and for my staff who work tirelessly for me. It's a reminder to myself that every day I have on this earth is a gift, and I intend to make the most of it. It's a reminder to everyone here that we're in a war, not on the battlefield, but for the hearts and minds of everyday Americans. It's a war we intend to win. Thank you."

John took a deep breath. "I can take a few questions." A dozen hands reached for the ceiling. John pointed to an attractive brunette. "Corrinne."

She stood, wearing a skirt suit. "George Smith Chapman made a statement yesterday that the United States is a terrorist organization. Does this change your gratitude for his heroism or make you question his motives during the attack?"

"Mr. Chapman saved my life. I am grateful, as is my family. As far as his political ideology and opinions, I disagree, but we still have freedom of speech in this country, and that freedom applies to speech we don't agree with."

"Do you disavow his antigovernment statements?" Corrinne asked.

John frowned. "As I said, I disagree with his statements, but I will defend his right to free speech. Next question."

Hands from the audience went up again.

"Greg," John said, pointing to a dark-haired man.

Greg stood. "We've had reports that Jeff Hutton, the man who shot the video of the attack, has been fired from your campaign. Was he fired because you were embarrassed by the footage?"

"Considering Mr. Hutton was an unpaid volunteer, we have no obligation regarding his employment."

"Was he let go because of the footage he released?"

"No. Next question."

11: Katie and EROEI

Katie stood in a college classroom with seven hundred USC students crammed into the stadium seating. She wore a flowing black dress and a tiny microphone attached to her V-neck collar. Behind her, on the pulldown screen, was the title of her presentation: Social Media for Social Justice.

The audience hung on her every word. The guys in attendance were eager to impress their girlfriends with their progressiveness. And most of the gals were eager to assert their feminist power.

Katie said, "Everywhere you look, social and political movements are leveraging social media to reach more people and to improve their worldwide influence. BLM started as a Twitter hashtag, as well as *#RefugeesWelcome* and *#MarriageEquality*. The latter led to the legalization of same sex marriage in the United States and Ireland." Katie paced onstage, making eye contact with the audience, seeing head nods in agreement.

"Occupy Wall Street and the Arab Spring were effective in large part because of their use of social media to spread their messages of equality and fairness. After the Paris attacks in 2015, millions of Facebook users added the French flag to their profile picture.

"Of course social media cuts both ways. Humanity's at a crossroads today. Undoubtedly the social justice movements we've discussed have had incredible successes, but we've also seen a revival of other movements— movements fueled by hate and supercharged with social media."

The hopeful, engaged faces in the audience turned somber.

"The American Freedom Party is gaining support, and they may get a candidate on the ballot in a few states such as Idaho and Michigan. This political party is only interested in freedom for whites. The Aryan Nation has seen a resurgence in large part because of their exploitation of social media. The FBI classifies this group as a terrorist organization. Even the Ku Klux Klan is seeing an increase in membership. In 2016, their membership was estimated between five thousand and eight thousand. Today it is almost double that."

An audible gasp came from the crowd.

Katie paused, shaking her head. "If that's not scary enough, we have the American Nazi Party, an anti-Semitic, neo-Nazi organization based largely on the ideals of Adolf Hitler. Despite their principles of hate, this group has been successful in gaining members because of their claims of adherence to the American Constitution and the principles of the Founding Fathers of this country." Katie was silent for a moment, still pacing and making eye contact.

"We have a much bigger threat to our way of life than these white supremacist groups. The biggest threats to liberty and justice in this country are the Anarchists. The Anarchist movement is by far and away the most successful of these hate groups and by far and away the most successful at using social media. The fact that this group has no central authority and no rules governing it makes it more dangerous. In fact, describing it as a group is misleading. It's a loose amalgamation of individuals who believe government, in all its forms, should be destroyed."

Katie paused for effect, her jaw set tight. "These individuals are hiding in plain sight. Some have shaved heads and arms covered with tattoos, but many others look like you and me, have regular jobs, and families.

"Our government isn't perfect. For those of you who follow me online, you know I often rail against government corruption, but we can't give up on the institution that educates our children, feeds our poor, protects us, and cares for the old and sick. It's up to us to make it better. We have the power and the voice to influence and create policies that will give us the country we all deserve—a country that will serve as a shining example to others.

"Does anyone know how many people actually comment on a piece of media versus simply consuming it?"

"Very few," someone from the audience called out.

Katie nodded. "That's right. Nobody knows the exact number, but most people lurk in the background, consuming media but not making comments. The Anarchists on the other hand are fervent in their belief that they're right, and they're not afraid to voice their ideology. So it often seems like they're everywhere, when in fact, according to recent polls, they make up less than 1 percent of our population. However, a vocal and engaged 1 percent can do a lot of damage to this country. We're already very aware of what 1-percenters can do."

The audience laughed.

"So, when you're thumbing through your Facebook feed, and you see one of those taxation-is-extortion memes or the one with the cows ..."

The audience laughed again.

"Speak up. Defend this country and our way of life. Don't let them dominate your social media feed. We have to fight fire with fire. Thank you."

Katie took a bow, the applause washing over her.

After a beat, the audience stood and clapped louder.

She blushed and beamed.

A thin man with dark-rim glasses approached, walking onstage, holding a microphone.

Katie and the man shook hands as the applause dissipated.

"We'll have a question-and-answer period," the man said. "I hope everyone will stay. I imagine the discussion will be enlightening. Anyone who wants to ask Katie a question, please form a line behind the podium." The man gestured to the podium set up toward the bottom of the stadium seating.

A queue was already forming. A young woman with dark curly hair and a nose ring stepped up first to the podium. "Thank you, Katie," the woman said, "for all that you do to further the cause of feminism and social justice."

Katie smiled. "You're very welcome."

"President Reynolds and his administration have used drones in increasing amounts in countries like Yemen and Pakistan—countries we are not at war with. Our military has killed over a million people in Iraq—a war that started because of nonexistent weapons of mass destruction. Do you think the War on Terror has been an unlawful war?"

"That's a great question," Katie replied. "We've had a majority Republican congress, senate, and of course the presidency over the past six years. We have neoconservatives running our government and the military industrial complex making money hand over fist. My heart breaks for the people of the Middle East who've lost their homes, their jobs, and their loved ones. My heart breaks for our soldiers risking their lives for wealthy businessmen and corrupt politicians. Back to your question, I absolutely do believe it is a tragic and unlawful war."

The audience applauded. There were a few whistles.

Next a baby-faced man stepped up to the podium. He said, "You mentioned the meme, taxation is extortion. Do you believe taxation is extortion? If not, could you explain why?"

Katie nodded. "Taxation is not extortion. Taxation is necessary to even the scales, to give back to the less fortunate. Without taxation, we wouldn't have the funding necessary for government. Furthermore, taxation prevents bloodshed, because people will only take so much inequality. In my opinion, the problem with taxation is that there are too many loopholes for the wealthy."

The audience applauded.

The young man removed a scrap of paper from his pocket. "That doesn't explain why taxation isn't extortion." He read from the paper. "The definition of extortion is to obtain something, usually money, through force or threats. How many people would actually pay their taxes if they weren't forced to?"

"Taxation is perfectly legal and necessary for the polite society we all enjoy," Katie replied. "The government doesn't always use our tax dollars in the most efficient manner, but it is up to us to police the government, to vote for the right representatives."

"That still doesn't explain how it's not extortion."

"You can always leave. You can always move to Somalia or some other place where they don't have taxes. They also don't have clean water, sanitation, safety, and an educated populace."

Chuckles came from the audience.

"So, you're saying taxation is not extortion because the government provides us services, and it's legalized by law?"

Katie smirked. "That's an oversimplification, but that's part of it. There's also the social contract."

"What if I moved to a town in Italy, and the mafia provided protection services in exchange for 10 percent of my income? And the town voted that it was legal for the mafia to do this. Would it be extortion?"

Glares, scowls, and a few shouts of "Bullshit" came from the audience.

"I see what you're doing," Katie replied, "and this is exactly the type of esoteric, ridiculous argument that's perpetuated by the Anarchists. There's a huge difference between a criminal organization and a democratically elected republic."

"But the town voted."

"We should move on," the thin man said into his microphone. "Please step aside, sir."

* * *

Katie sat in a metal and pleather chair facing enormous windows. Outside, airplanes lifted off, landed, and hooked up to terminals. She sent a text.

> **Katie:** Hey, you. My flight is delayed, but I should be home by seven. R we still on for dinner?

Katie put her phone in her purse. She stepped to a refreshment kiosk, bought an iced coffee, and returned to her seat in the waiting area. When her phone buzzed, she fished it from her purse.

> **Declan:** Sorry, babe. Still working on the edit. Interview is FUCKED.

> **Katie:** ☹ I'm sorry, babe. Anything I can do to help?

> **Declan:** Don't think so.

> **Katie:** I'm just sitting here for the next two hours. Can I see it?

> **Declan:** In a minute. It's bad, just warning you.

> **Katie:** I'm sure you were wonderful.

Katie set her phone on her leg and watched the planes. A few minutes later, her phone buzzed.

> **Declan:** I sent the footage to your email.

> **Katie:** I'll look at it now. I love you.

Katie opened her email and clicked on the video from Declan. The video showed Declan and a white-haired man with a long face and arched eyebrows. The old man was identified on the screen as Carl Humphrey, CEO, Unico Oil & Gas. *I still can't believe he got Carl Humphrey. I suppose having a dad that's the CFO of Chevron helps.*

Declan started well, asking pertinent, but inoffensive questions. *Good, get him talking.*

Declan asked, "Do you think the oil and gas industry has hampered efforts by others to create a sustainable energy infrastructure based on solar and wind electricity?"

"No, I don't," Mr. Humphrey said. "We spend half-a-billion dollars a year researching alternative fuels. Everything from algae to ethanol to methanol to solar and battery technology."

Declan narrowed his eyes. "In 1949, your company was convicted of conspiracy to monopolize interstate commerce in the sale of buses, fuel, and supplies. Your coconspirators were Firestone Tire, Standard Oil of California, Phillips Petroleum, General Motors, and Mack Trucks. This conspiracy resulted in the dismantling of much of the electric transit infrastructure of our major cities."

Mr. Humphrey chuckled. "I know I look old, but I'm not that old. First, I was seven in 1949, so it wasn't my company then. Second, you ought to get your facts straight. These companies and mine were acquitted of conspiring to monopolize the transit industry, and the oil and gas industry didn't dismantle the electric lines. The transit industry did it themselves. They couldn't compete with oil. It was too damn cheap and too damn plentiful."

"There are photos—"

Mr. Humphrey waved his hand across his face. "I care about the facts, not some photos of piled-up streetcars. Electric streetcars were in decline long before 1949. In 1918, half of the streetcar lines were in bankruptcy."

"Do you think man's excessive use of oil and gas is sustainable in the long run?"

"Son, in the long run, we're all dead."

"From 1901 through 2017, ocean temperatures have risen at an average rate of 0.13°F per decade, with last year being the warmest on record. Do you think the burning of fossil fuels has contributed to this temperature rise?"

"I'm a petroleum engineer, not a climatologist."

"The oil and gas industry has been suppressing global warming reports for decades."

Mr. Humphrey frowned. "I can't speak for other companies, but why would we bother?"

"To ensure that we don't transition away from oil and gas."

He laughed. "Transition to what?"

"Solar, wind, biofuels, geothermal, tidal … hydroelectric."

"You have to look at the big picture. Oil and gas and coal provide about 80 percent of the world's energy needs. That includes electricity, transportation, shipping, home heating, the whole lot. We get about 10 percent from wood, biofuels, and waste, another 5 percent from nuclear. Hydroelectric another 1.5. Solar and wind and geothermal and these fancy renewables everyone's talking about only provide about 3 percent of the world's energy. It would be quite the undertaking to change that profile, and changing that profile would require quite a bit of our fossil fuel resources. Any idea how much rebar and concrete and steel go into a wind turbine?"

Declan pursed his lips. "No."

Mr. Humphrey leaned back in his chair and crossed his leg, his leather shoe on his knee. "In a 2.5-megawatt turbine, you need 630 yards of concrete and forty-five tons of steel for the rebar, and that's just for the base. You know how much oil you need to produce that amount of steel and concrete?"

Declan was silent.

"Six hundred and thirteen barrels. Since forty-two gallons of oil are in each barrel, that's roughly 25,000 gallons of oil just to make one base for one turbine. You still have to build the turbine. All the iron ore and minerals needed to complete the turbine don't get pulled from the ground with solar panels. Mineral resources are pulled out of the ground by massive diesel-powered machines. You know why?"

"Because guys like you have created a monopoly."

The old man shook his head. "I really do hope you produce this interview, because this is important. Fossil fuels, specifically oil, are incredibly dense sources of energy. This fuel can power the massive machines necessary to efficiently move and sort the earth to find the bits of minerals we need for modern society. That includes the minerals needed to produce wind turbines and solar panels."

Declan nodded. "If we use our fossil fuels to build an alternative energy infrastructure, we'll be much better off than burning it in our SUVs."

"Look, Declan. I agree with you. We should be conserving our fossil fuels and building an alternative energy infrastructure. Hell, I have more money than I need. My life's almost over, and I have children and grandchildren. I want them to have a nice standard of living in the future. The oil and gas industry is a dying industry, but, when we die, so do most of the comforts we all enjoy. Are you familiar with the term 'energy returned on energy invested'?"

"No."

"In 1930, the oil industry had a 100:1 ratio of energy returned on energy invested. In other words, they could use one barrel of oil to get one hundred back. Those extra ninety-nine barrels are what we used to power society and to pay people and to build our complex civilization. That make sense so far?"

"If your figures are correct."

Mr. Humphrey folded his hands in his lap. "Forty years later, the fields we drilled in 1970 were only at a 25:1 ratio of energy returned on energy invested. We had already exploited the cheap, easy stuff. By the '90s, we were drilling fields returning around 14:1. The stuff we're drilling today is maybe 3:1. It's barely worth doing anymore. You remember the BP disaster in 2010, with the *Deepwater Horizon*?"

"And BP got a slap on the wrist."

"Forget about the politics for a moment. They drilled what, at the time, was the deepest well ever drilled at 35,000 feet. That's almost seven miles deep. Think about that. It was an amazing feat of engineering. Now why would BP risk their capital and the men who worked that rig if they could drill a well on land or in shallow water?"

"I don't know."

Mr. Humphrey leaned forward. "They did it because the easy wells have already been drilled."

"All the more reason to transition to renewables."

The old man leaned back. "These other sources of energy have low energy returns. Ethanol is barely over 1:1. It would stop tomorrow without subsidies. People think they're helping farmers with ethanol, but they're killing poor people at the margins all over the world with higher corn prices. We still haven't made algae oil better than 1:1. Biodiesel's a little better at 2.5:1. Brazil has a good thing going with sugar cane at 8:1. Wind and solar do have a nice energy return at 20–30:1, but they produce electricity, not liquid fuels, and we haven't found an economic, long-lasting battery to make it work on a large scale. And we need fossil fuels to produce and maintain a solar and wind infrastructure."

"Why are you telling me this?"

"Because people need to know the truth. Government will never tackle this issue. It's too big, and talking about something this bleak is sure to kill any candidacy. I've been dealing with government officials for forty years, and I can tell you one thing for sure. They'll run this thing off the cliff, then find someone else to blame for the mess."

"What's the solution?"

Mr. Humphrey took a deep breath, his mouth downturned. "It's too late for solutions. It's like we're all on an airplane that's gonna crash. Some of us know it. Some of us are in denial, but most of us are just plain ignorant. Those of us in-the-know have a choice. We can put on our seat belts and get ready for impact, or we can party with the stewardesses."

Katie stared at the screen, dumbstruck. She blinked and tapped on her text messaging icon.

Katie: Declan, I just watched your interview. Call me. I want to talk to you about it.

She navigated to YouTube on her phone and responded to a few of the latest comments on her channel. She checked the most popular videos on YouTube. Her latest video was in the top ten for a few hours. Three of the top ten videos featured George Chapman. She'd seen these videos, but she didn't realize how popular they'd gotten. The raw footage of the attack remained well-viewed, as did the spoof video that featured Congressman Bradley saying that he helped Chapman and showing that he clearly did the opposite. The number one video was Chapman going off on some reporter and calling the US government a terrorist organization. She wasn't overly impressed by the video. *More ramblings by a pissed-off Anarchist. But people respond to something about him.*

Katie smiled wide and tapped the Declan contact on her phone.

"Babe, I really can't talk now," Declan said in lieu of a greeting. "I'm in the middle of research on solar."

"I thought the interview was really good. Shocking actually."

Declan exhaled. "The old man's a fucking nutcase."

"What he said isn't true?"

"I just found an MIT study that says it *is* possible to power the planet with solar."

"That's a relief. I figured he was being overly pessimistic."

"Big surprise, an oil exec talking out of his ass. And I can't use any of it. A big fucking waste of my time. Now I'm back to square one."

"I might have a solution for you."

"You have another oil exec who'll admit that they're ruining the environment?"

"What do you think about doing a documentary on this George Chapman guy?"

"Did you hear the crazy shit he said to that reporter?"

"Did you know that particular video is number one on YouTube?"

"Why are people so stupid?"

"We could show the public who this guy really is. We just have to ask the right questions. He'll reveal himself as a fool."

"He's definitely popular at the moment. We could make some money."

"The exposure would be huge for both of us."

12: Julie and Anarkooks

Julie spritzed hairspray to give her locks a bit more volume. Otherwise her hair was as flat as a pancake. She stood in front of the bathroom mirror, insecure about her appearance for the first time in a long time. She was still beautiful, but her age was showing on the margins—like those faint crow's feet around her eyes. She smiled, checking the lines between her mouth and nose. They were a little deeper. Her sister was right. She was running out of time.

She stepped from the bathroom, grabbed her purse off her dresser, and glanced at the clock. *Shit.* She hustled toward the stairs, stopping at Max's room on the way. She knocked.

"Come in," Max said.

She entered her son's bedroom. Max sat at his desk. He swiveled in his chair, away from his laptop. An email was on the screen.

"I'm going to meet Larry," Julie said. "How do I look?"

Max shrugged. "I don't know."

"You're no help." Julie glanced at his laptop screen. "Who are you emailing?"

"George."

"What are you two talking about?"

Max frowned. "Have you decided about me going virtual?"

"I'm really late. Can we talk about it later?"

"Fine."

Julie hurried downstairs, stepped outside, and shut the front door. The sun warmed her skin as she rushed to her car. Her lawn was mowed. Piles of clippings were strewn about the yard, and green mower tracks were left where she had turned the mower on the concrete sidewalk. Before she entered her car, she glanced across the street. Dan's blinds were parted; then they weren't.

She weaved in and out of traffic as she drove across town. Finally she parked at Panera Bread. The clock on her radio read 12:13. She shook her head. *He may have left.* She hustled inside the restaurant. It was crowded and noisy with plates clinking and people talking. She stood just inside and looked around. He walked toward her. He looked better in his profile picture, and he was shorter than advertised. He wasn't short though. *Why exaggerate?*

Larry approached with a grin on his face and good teeth. He was thin with small wrists, spindly fingers, small hands, a narrow neck.

"Julie," he said.

Julie forced a smile. "Larry."

He extended his hand.

"Sorry I'm late," Julie said, as she shook his hand.

"Don't worry about it. I just got here."

"You're a bad liar."

He chuckled. "I've been here for forty-five minutes."

Julie raised her eyebrows. *The time was twelve, right?*

"I was worried about being late," Larry said, "and I wanted to have time to get the lay of the land, so to speak."

"Well, I'm sorry I made you wait so long."

"Do you want to get in line?"

The couple took their place in the back of the line. They studied the menu and discussed what they wanted. Julie ordered a soup and salad, Larry a soup and sandwich.

"I got it," Larry said as the cashier looked at them expectantly.

"I have money," Julie, said, fumbling with her purse.

"Don't worry about it." Larry handed his credit card to the cashier.

Larry snagged the last available booth, near the bathroom. They sat down. He placed the receipt in front of him on the table, waiting for his name to be called.

"You look exactly the same," Larry said.

"That's nice of you to say, but I feel old. My sister said my dating market value is going down by the day."

Larry laughed. "Your dating market value?"

"Because I'm forty, and I have a son."

"Well, I guess we're in the same boat, because I'm forty too."

"Men become distinguished with age, but women become wrinkled old hags."

"Oh, come on. You look great, and I'm sure you'll look great when you're eighty."

"You're sweet."

Larry grinned. "So do you keep up with anyone from high school?"

"I have a few friends on Facebook, but we don't spend time together in real life."

"Me too. Apart from commenting on each other's pictures, we don't interact much. It's interesting how those people who seemed so important in high school can just disappear from your life."

"People definitely go their separate ways."

"You don't remember me, do you?" Larry asked.

Julie froze. "I, umm …"

"It's not a big deal. I was invisible in high school. Probably the worst four years of my life."

"That's awful. I'm sorry, Larry."

He shrugged. "Thankfully high school was a long time ago. You probably loved high school."

Julie frowned.

Larry held up his palms in surrender. "It's an observation, not an accusation. And I would rather you had a good experience than my miserable one. Believe me."

Julie's face softened. "I did enjoy it. My son hates it though. You two would probably get along."

"I'd love to meet him someday. What's he like?"

"He's different. Very smart. When he was in elementary school, they wanted him to skip a grade, but I decided against it, because socially he's always been a bit behind. He loves comics." She smiled. "Graphic novels. He gets mad when I call them comics. I think he wants to be a cartoonist. He makes the coolest cartoons on his computer."

Larry nodded. "I liked comics when I was a teenager. They were just comics then. For me, I liked seeing justice prevail and good triumph over evil. I guess that's why I put away criminals now."

"Larry, Larry," the person on the loudspeaker said.

"I think they called your name," Julie said.

Larry craned his neck toward the pickup counter. "I'll go check."

"Do you need some help?"

"I can handle it."

Larry returned with their food on a tray. They ate between bits of conversation.

"How's your sandwich?" Julie asked.

"Not great but edible," Larry replied. "Your salad?"

"It's good." Julie took a bite.

"You know, I had a huge crush on you in high school."

Julie almost choked on her walnut salad. She swallowed. "Really?"

Larry nodded. "Of course I didn't have the courage to even talk to you. And you had a pretty serious boyfriend, if I remember correctly. What was his name?"

Julie closed her eyes for a moment, her face rigid. "Justin."

"That's right, Justin, the football star." One side of his mouth turned up. "Whatever happened to him?"

Julie pursed her lips and set down her fork with a clang. "I married him, and he died."

Larry's eyes went wide. He spoke rapidly. "Oh, my God, I'm so sorry. I had no idea. I mean, I knew you were a widow from your profile, but I didn't know you married Justin."

"It's fine."

"No, it's not. I'm really sorry."

"It's okay." Julie picked up her fork and took another bite of her salad. She glanced at the analog clock on the wall.

"That's a bad sign."

Julie swallowed. "What's a bad sign?"

"You were checking the clock. I've ruined our date, haven't I?"

"I thought we were just meeting as friends?"

He blanched. "Of course. Sorry."

"You haven't ruined anything. I was thinking about Max. I have to work tonight, and I'm supposed to talk to him before I go. I was making sure I was okay on time. To be honest, I'm a bit anxious about it."

"Anything you want to talk about?"

"I can't imagine this is first-date material."

He grinned. "I thought we were just meeting as friends."

She smiled. "You got me."

"I think we've already talked about things we're not supposed to on a first date or meeting or whatever you want to call it. I am a good listener, if I do say so myself." He adjusted his black-rim glasses.

"Max fell on the stairs at school last week."

He leaned forward, his hands interlaced and his elbows resting on the table. "Is he okay?"

"He's fine, thank you. But he doesn't want to go to school anymore, or at least he doesn't want to go to the physical building anymore."

Larry furrowed his brow, lines erupting on his large forehead.

"He wants me to let him go to school online," Julie said. "He doesn't have many friends at school."

"Are you going to let him?"

Julie sighed. "It's more complicated than that. Do you know the guy who's been in the news, George Smith Chapman?"

"Yes, I hate that guy. What an asshole. Pardon my French."

"You might not want to tell Max that. I think Max idolizes him."

"I don't understand his popularity. I mean, he did do something patriotic, but then he disgraced everything this country stands for. Did you hear what he said?"

Julie nodded. "I saw the video. Max knows him personally, not just on those videos."

Larry raised his eyebrows.

"They were in the same hospital room, and now they're emailing back and forth. I guess they're friends."

"How old is your son?"

"He's fifteen."

"Now that's weird. I don't know what this Chapman guy wants with a fifteen-year-old kid. I'd be careful if I were you."

"That was my initial inclination. I asked Max if he thought George might be a pedophile." Julie whispered the word *pedophile*. "But Max seems certain that he's a good guy."

"They don't come out and tell you that they're pedophiles. They groom kids."

"I think Max feels connected to him because George shared how he had

had a rough time in school too." Julie sighed again. "Apparently George and Max talk about all sorts of things. Max hasn't given me any details, but now he wants to go virtual. Should I be worried?"

"I think you have cause for concern."

"You might be right."

"Maybe Max just needs to connect with someone who understands what he's going through—not that you don't understand, but you don't have that shared experience of having a tough time in school."

"I thought about that."

"If you ever want me to talk to him, just let me know."

"Oh, that's really nice of you to offer. That would definitely be beyond the call of duty for a first date."

Larry chuckled. "Well, not today. If you ever invited me over, and I met Max, I could casually talk about my time in school. Maybe it would give him someone to talk to other than that anarkook."

"Anarkook?"

He chuckled again. "It's what I like to call the Anarchists."

"I do think you two would hit it off."

"I'd love to take you out on a real date. Dinner next week?"

"I'd like that."

13: George Has Groundhog for Dinner

George sat at his kitchen table, eating scrambled eggs and checking his email on his laptop.

From: Katie@KatieTalk.com
To: GeorgeChapman2222@gmail.com
Subject: Interview

Mr. Chapman,

I hope you're healing well. My name is Katie Fitzgerald, and I run a blog, podcast, and YouTube channel that tackles a wide variety of political topics. I think you would make a fantastic guest on my show. My show is very popular, number fourteen among political shows on YouTube.

Your appearance would give your viewpoints a tremendous amount of exposure. You would reach a diverse and engaged audience. I would be happy to do the interview remotely via Skype. I would even be willing to travel to you if you prefer. I am that interested in meeting and interviewing you! I hope to hear from you soon.

Sincerely,
Katie Fitzgerald

George clicked Reply, typed *No thank you*, and clicked Send. He opened another email.

From: Maxxedout123@gmail.com
To: GeorgeChapman2222@gmail.com
Subject: Virtual

George,

I saw you on YouTube with that reporter. I have to say, it was pretty badass. It's the most popular video on YouTube. You should read the comments. People love what you said. I think I'm an Anarchist now. I know you said I need to make up my own mind, and I did. I did my own research, and it makes sense to me. Using violence to make people do things is wrong. It's really not that complicated. If you think about it, we learn anarchism in kindergarten, when we learn not to hit and take things from our classmates. This is ironic of course because kindergarten is paid for with violence. I think the problem comes not when we're taught the rules but when we're taught that the rules only apply to us.

I wanted to tell you that my mom and I are supposed to talk about me going to school online. I'm really hoping she goes for it, but I'm not sure she will. She just went on a date, which is superweird because she hasn't been on a date since my dad. I know she deserves to be happy, but it's still weird.

Before she left, she saw that I was emailing you, and she gave me a weird look and asked me what we're talking about. I think she's a little uncomfortable with us being friends. I think she's worried because usually you don't see kids who are friends with adults.

So, anyway, I asked her about the virtual school thing before she left, and she said she was late and would talk to me about it when she got back. Seems to me that she would have just said yes right there if that was what she was going to do. But she didn't, so that worries me. What should I do if she says no?

Max

George clicked Reply.

From: GeorgeChapman2222@gmail.com
To: Maxxedout123@gmail.com

Max,

It's nice to hear that you think of us as friends. I do as well. Friends are tough to come by, so I don't age discriminate. I understand your mother's concerns. She is welcome to contact me anytime if she feels uncomfortable. I certainly don't want to cause any problems.

I'm a little embarrassed by my outburst at the reporter. I haven't watched the video yet. I didn't think it would end up online, and I certainly didn't think it would be popular. It was stupid of me. I should have kept my mouth shut. It is nice that what I said is resonating with some.

I was impressed by your kindergarten analysis. I've never heard that before. It makes a lot of sense to me. You have a bright and logical mind. Anarchism may be the answer today, but never stop asking the questions, and always be open to new information. Truth is what we're after, wherever it takes us.

Regarding school, you're wrestling with a tough dilemma. I wonder if you've been completely honest with your mother about the gravity of your situation. If not, I think you should tell her the whole truth and nothing but the truth, as they say. I think, if she knew everything, she would be unlikely to say no. I know it's painful, but, as they also say, the truth will set you free.

Well, I should get going on my chores. I'm sure it'll take me twice as long in my condition. Good luck with your conversation. I'm pulling for you.

Your Friend,
George

He closed his laptop and stood from the rustic wooden table. George rinsed his plate and utensils at the sink and placed them on the drying rack. Sunlight pierced the south-facing windows. No windows were on the other walls of the one-story home. A rocket mass heater ran along the north wall. The heater featured a cob bench with a small metal opening on one end, and a tray filled with sticks. The other end had a flue that snaked up and out.

George wore canvas pants, a sweatshirt, a straw hat, and a handgun on his hip. His left arm was still in the sling, but he had some mobility. He slipped his headphones into his ears and tapped Play on his phone. Next to the front door was a wire basket and a .22 caliber rifle. He grabbed the wire basket and limped outside. To his right was a solar array on metal racking. In front of the earth-sheltered house was a meadow sloping downhill, edged with endless hardwood forests.

"This is Gary Cook of the *Alt News Podcast*, providing vital information in a changing world. It's Saturday, May 12, 2018. Today I have a very special guest. I'll be talking to Roger Glass, a geologist from Montana, about his export-consumption theory."

To the left and downhill twenty yards was another earth-sheltered structure, his greenhouse. Like his home, the roof here was covered with earth and meadow grasses and blended into the hill. George walked to the greenhouse. The south side was all glass. Near the greenhouse was a metal cage—a live trap. It was open, with melon rinds inside. A few hundred yards down the hill was a flat area with two buildings side by side: a small log cabin and a garage.

"Roger, welcome to the *Alt News Podcast*," Gary said.

"Thanks, Gary. I appreciate you having me on," Roger replied.

George hiked to the opposite side of the greenhouse to another trap, but this one was shut with a groundhog inside. As George approached the trap, the animal crashed headfirst into one side of the cage, then the other. Its nose was bloody.

"Could you explain your theory in laymen's terms?" Gary asked.

Roger said, "The world is producing and using around ninety-seven million barrels of oil per day. That includes natural gas liquids and heavy oils from oil sands. To put it another way, we're draining an Olympic-size swimming pool of oil every fifteen seconds."

George entered the greenhouse. It was humid and warm, the air sweet. Plants grew in raised beds, plumbed to a large fish tank. Lettuce, kale, radishes, peppers, eggplant, and basil grew in the six raised beds made out of cinder block and pond liner. Each planting space was twice the size of a coffin. Eight-foot-high trellises attached to the beds held melons and tomatoes and squash snaking in and out of the grids.

"That's a staggering amount of oil," Gary said.

"It is," Roger replied. "My theory is that, as world oil production peaks, the price of exported oil will increase, stimulating the economic growth and thereby the oil consumption in the oil-exporting countries. This will create a positive feedback loop with declining exports and higher prices."

"Do you have an example of your theory in action?" Gary asked.

"The United Kingdom and Indonesia track the theory very well," Roger replied. "These countries were net exporters. If you examine the seven years after the production peaks for the United Kingdom and Indonesia, you'll find that UK oil production decreased 7.8 percent per year, and their domestic consumption increased .2 percent per year. Exports fell a staggering 55.7 percent per year. Indonesia's numbers weren't quite as dramatic, but their exports declined on average 3.9 percent per year, and their consumption rose 4.1 percent per year. Their export decline was 28.9 percent per year."

George checked the pH of the five-hundred-gallon fish tank. The water was clear and populated by seventy tilapias about the size of his hand. He refilled the automatic fish feeder and then picked ripe produce, collected in his basket, doing everything with his right hand.

"Do you think we've reached the peak of world oil production?" Gary asked.

"I don't know," Roger replied. "The past few years we've been bumping along at ninety-six to ninety-seven million barrels of oil per day. I'm not sure we can produce anymore, especially with prices as low as they are."

George limped up the hill to his home. He put the produce in the refrigerator, grabbed a large bowl, the .22, and returned to the greenhouse. He set the bowl on the ground and stood behind the groundhog trap, waiting for the animal to settle down. He loaded a round in the chamber with the bolt action and pressed the button near the trigger, releasing the safety. His finger was straight and off the trigger as he moved the barrel into the cage. The groundhog was facing away when the round entered the back of his head. The animal spasmed and stood on its hind legs, before dropping to the floor of the cage.

George went into the greenhouse and grabbed a bucket and a plastic table with metal legs. He set up the table near the cage and pulled the hose next to his butcher station. The groundhog was still, a puddle of bright red blood near its head. He retrieved the animal and plopped it down on the table.

He took off his sling. George needed both hands to skin and gut the animal. Once the groundhog was butchered, he put the meat and fat into his bowl. The guts, skin, hair, head, and legs went into the bucket. He took his bowl of meat to the house and put it in the refrigerator. He returned to clean the table, and dump the gut bucket in the woods.

Gary said, "In 2006, you made a prediction of a future with four-hundred-dollar oil prices, which would equate to nine or ten dollars per gallon at the pump. Apart from the spike in 2008, we've had relatively stable oil prices. Today a barrel of oil trades for about fifty-four bucks a barrel."

Roger exhaled. "I never gave a time frame. Prices have been lower than I thought they'd be. We had more demand destruction in 2008 than I thought we would. The amount of shale oil coming out of the United States has been a surprise, but those wells start like gangbusters and deplete very rapidly, and many of those companies are losing money at fifty-dollar oil prices. I don't know if the economy can support four-hundred-dollar oil without imploding, but I still think an oil shock is likely."

"Are there any countries we should be watching today, in terms of declining oil exports?" Gary asked.

"Mexico may cease to export a single barrel of oil by 2020," Roger replied. "Mexico used to be the number two exporter to the United States."

"Are there any predictions you'd like to make for oil prices in the future?" Gary asked.

Roger laughed. "I think I'm done with predictions. I will say that we're dealing with a nonrenewable resource that's absolutely vital to everything we do, and we're using it at a staggering rate. It's gonna end in tears."

14: John Goes Fund-Raising

John Bradley stood on the flagstone patio, overlooking the Memorial Day celebration around the pool, on the lawn, and under the tent. Dark-skinned men and women in button-downs and bow ties served the elderly patrons. The party was crawling with secret service officers in suits and plainclothes.

"Isn't this grand?" Donna asked.

John turned, a bottle of beer in hand. She wore a blue and white floral sundress with an oversize hat.

"You look beautiful," he said.

She sidled up to him, resting her hands on the concrete railing, one hand briefly touching his. "You ready for this?"

"It's a party."

"Exactly. It's much easier to influence people when they're relaxed."

John was in a daze, wearing khakis and a blue blazer.

"You okay?" she asked.

He blinked. "I'm at that goddamn DCCC call center almost every day. You'd think I could take a day off from begging for money." The Democratic Congressional Campaign Committee raised money for the Democratic Party, often using politicians as telemarketers.

Donna was straight-faced. "Today isn't the day to take off. This is one year's worth of calls in one afternoon."

He downed the rest of his beer and set it on the railing. "If I had been born into a different family, I'd probably be a gym teacher and a lacrosse coach. I might even be a Republican."

She mock-gasped. "The hell you say."

John forced a smile. "Sorry, coming here ..."

"You want to talk about it?"

He shook his head and sighed. "Give me the rundown."

"You sure?"

"Yeah."

"Everyone needs to be acknowledged, but you should focus on four people. Walter Moody. General Gates—I'm assuming you remember not to call him Doug."

"I remember."

"And Carl Humphrey and Adam Doyle."

"I think you should distract them, maybe hike up your dress a bit but not too much. You don't want these old fuckers to have coronaries. While you're using your feminine wiles, I'll bump into them and steal their wallets. Instead of Bonnie and Clyde, it'll be Donna and John."

She shook her head, suppressing a grin.

"What?" He held up a palm. "It's more honest than what *we* do."

"Can you be serious for a minute?"

John made a somber face.

"This is important."

"All right." He bumped her hip with his. "You worry too much. With the exception of Doyle, I've known these guys forever."

"It was a friendlier, peripheral relationship through the senator and Will. This is different. This is business. Remember, Walter Moody is very serious, so no jokes, and call him Mr. Moody. He obviously doesn't like it when you call him Walter."

"Mr. Moody is moody and has a stick up his ass. Got it." John tapped his head with his index finger.

"He's concerned about the FDIC coping with the next banking crisis, so make sure he knows that you would support bailouts for national banks and takeovers for local and regional banks."

"Fuck the little guy. Got it."

She pursed her lips. "This is how it's done. Compromise."

"I know. Believe me. I know."

"And don't salute General Gates, like last year."

"Oh, come on. He was drunk. He thought it was funny."

"He wasn't that drunk. *You* were. The last thing we need is some paparazzi taking a picture of you saluting, like Gomer Pyle. Voters still worship the military, and they won't tolerate any perceived disrespect. And you can bet the Republicans would use it."

"No saluting the general, but I have to call him *General*. Got it. He wants to make sure I'll maintain defense spending, even though I'll be running as the peace president."

"Exactly," she replied.

"Carl Humphrey, CEO of Unico, likes me to call him Carl. He likes to talk about his wife, Barb, and his boys, Mark and Tom. He likes the Dallas Cowboys. He's concerned with the low cost of energy eating into his profits. I'll promise subsidies. That about right?"

"Good memory."

John taps his head again. "Like a steel trap."

Donna smiled.

"I don't know Adam Doyle very well," John said. "I think we've met a couple of times. He's a short guy, red hair."

"He's young, forty-five. Well, young for this crowd. He's the CEO of Armor Software."

"They were just awarded a contract with the DOD and Homeland Security."

Donna nodded. "They have software that's still in beta. According to our contact at the NSA, it'll revolutionize how we fight terrorism, specifically domestic terrorism."

"Plotting?" a white-haired man asked, approaching from behind.

"Will," John said, turning around. "How are you doing?"

Will held up his beer. He was tan, tall, and fit. "I'm happy not to be doing what you're doing."

John hugged his brother. They disengaged, and Will leaned forward, kissing Donna on the cheek.

"Donna," Will said, "you look great." He glanced at her hands. "I'm surprised you're not hitched yet."

"Still kissing frogs," Donna replied.

Will chuckled. "Well, you'll make some lucky guy very happy."

"That's the Bradley presidential charm."

"You know it's genuine because I'm not running for office. So, Donna, you think my coattails are strong enough to take my baby brother to the White House?"

"Let's not forget the senator's coattails," John said. "Did you actually make a decision without Dad's say-so?"

"Nobody makes it to the White House without help," Donna said.

"Maybe *she* should run," Will said with a smirk.

"She's too smart for that," John replied.

Will chuckled. "I'll second that."

"How are the boys?" John asked.

"Travis loves it at Nielson Bloomberg. Why wouldn't he? Making the kind of money he's making. Colleen's hoping he'll settle down soon. Chad, well, he's still at UVA for another year. He's taking after his uncle."

"I graduated in four years," John said.

"Barely."

"See this?" John asked Donna. "My big brother's still picking on me."

"Do I have to send you two to your rooms?" Donna asked.

"I'll take a spanking too," Will said, with a twinkle in his eye.

"How's Colleen?" John asked, reminding his brother of his wife.

Will winked at his brother. "She's doing great. She's with Linda and Mom inside."

"Time to hit the campaign trail. Watch out for this one." John lifted his chin to his brother. "He's been known to get handsy."

Will raised his hands in mock capitulation.

John walked down the steps of the patio, along the flagstone walkway toward the pool. He waved and beamed and said hello to partygoers along the way. He spotted Carl Humphrey at the bar. John stepped under the tent sheltering the white round tables and chairs, a dance floor, a string quartet, and the bar. Carl talked to the dark-skinned bartender, a scotch in hand. He looked sharp in his gray suit and Texas tie with his white hair combed straight back.

"Carl," John said, slapping the man on the back. "How 'bout them Cowboys?"

Carl turned to John straight-faced. "Considering its May, there's not much to say."

John held his smile, but his eyes were still.

Carl laughed. "I'm yanking your chain. You want a drink?"

John forced a chuckle. "You buying?"

Carl turned to the bartender. "My new friend Reggie has a nice single malt back there."

Reggie smiled, showing his bright white teeth.

"Reggie," Carl said, "could you please pour the congressman a healthy glass?"

The bartender poured the Scotch and set the glass on a coaster.

"Thank you, Reggie," John said, picking up the glass. John took a drink, the scotch burning his throat. "That's a helluva good scotch."

"Highland Park, twenty-five years old," Carl said. "You don't strike me as a scotch drinker."

"It's been a while," John said.

Carl nodded.

"How's Barb doing?"

Carl took a drink and swallowed. "She's fine."

"Mark and Tom?"

"You have a good memory, or someone on your staff does."

John raised his eyebrows.

"Let's cut the bullshit, John. I'm too damn old for it. You don't give a shit about my family any more than I give a shit about yours."

John smiled and held up his glass. "I'll toast to that."

Carl grinned, and they clinked glasses.

The old man took a drink. "I've lost a lot a money supporting Democrats. Why can't y'all win a goddamn election?"

"I've won my seat five times in a row, soon to be a sixth," John replied.

Carl waved his hand. "There's a majority Republican congress, and Art looks like the horse to back in 2020."

"The tide's turning, Carl. People are tired of the Republicans. They're looking for a change."

"You're the change candidate?"

"You said it."

"All right, I'll play along. Let's say I invest a truckload of cash behind your campaign. Let's say you win. How does that help me? Aren't you the alternative-energy candidate? Aren't you planning to tax the hell out of fossil fuels and give subsidies to a bunch of bankrupt solar manufacturers?"

"Look. I know where our energy comes from. Nothing will change that. I know that the oil and gas industry is struggling. I think subsidies are in order. I'll give subsidies to alternative energy to appease my base, but the oil and gas subsidies will be worth far more."

Carl shook his head. "We don't need subsidies. What we need is a fair commodities market, one that reflects the true supply-and-demand picture. As long as the Federal Reserve and their member banks can sell futures contracts for barrels of oil they don't have, with money they create out of thin air, they'll make the price whatever they want it to be."

"You want an inquiry into their commodities trading?"

Carl frowned. "I don't want an inquiry. We've had plenty of those, and it doesn't do a damn thing. I want it to stop."

"That's above my pay grade, even as president. I think you know that." John took a drink.

Carl also took a drink and set the glass on the bar. "These low prices'll end in shortages. Oil wells are shutting down. Nobody's drilling. They can only play the paper game for so long."

"You know how Americans are about high gas prices."

"We'll see how they do with no gas."

"Let's hope not."

Carl looked at Reggie. He was at the opposite end of the bar, giving the men their privacy. "Hey, Reggie, could you come over here for a moment?"

The bartender walked toward them with raised eyebrows.

"Are you a voter, Reggie?" Carl asked.

"Yes, sir," Reggie replied, his back straight.

"Are you a Republican or a Democrat?"

"I'm an Independent, sir. I vote for the best man for the job."

"Smart man." Carl grinned. "Hypothetically, in 2020, we have Representative Bradley here from Virginia." Carl nodded toward John. "And Secretary of State Arthur Coleman as the Republican candidate. I'm assuming you know who these men are?"

"I am familiar with Secretary Coleman. I shook his hand when I was in the army. I've seen Congressman Bradley on the news." Reggie looked down. "With the attack and all."

"Okay, great. You're a well-informed man, ready to do his civic duty. Do you vote for Mr. Bradley or Art Coleman?"

"I'm sorry, Congressman. I'd vote for Secretary Coleman."

"And that's where my money's going," Carl added.

John smiled at the bartender. "Thank you for your service, Reggie."

"You're welcome, sir."

"Secretary Coleman's former military, like you," John said.

"Yes, sir."

"And he's African American, like you."

"Yes, sir."

"Do you feel like he has more in common with you than I do, considering that I never served, and I'm white?"

"Yes. I don't mean any disrespect, sir."

"None taken, Reggie. What do you think is more important, the color of a man's skin or the actions of a man?"

"The actions."

"What's more important, whether a president has served in the military or his effectiveness as president?"

"His effectiveness."

"Did you know that thousands of veterans are dying because of delays and incompetence at the VA?"

Reggie nodded, his face rigid. "That doesn't surprise me. I can't stand my VA."

"Did you know that we have twenty-two veterans killing themselves every day?"

"No, sir, but that doesn't surprise me either."

"Art Coleman has been the Secretary of State for the last six years. He was a general in the army prior to that. Would you say that he has some culpability for these horrible tragedies?"

"Yes, sir. I would."

"My first order of business as president would be to clean up the VA system and to provide returning soldiers the care they deserve."

"I'd like to change my vote," Reggie said to Carl.

"Thank you, Reggie," John said.

Carl extended his hand to John. "We'll talk."

They shook hands.

John stepped away from the bar and surveyed the room. General Gates talked to a group of men with crew cuts. *Maybe later.* Walter Moody ate at a table by himself. John made a beeline for him.

"Mr. Moody, may I join you?" John asked.

The wrinkled man looked up. The skin around his mouth hung in a perpetual frown. His gray hair was short, receding, and slicked back. Moody pointed his steak knife at the chair next to him. "Have a seat, Congressman."

John sat, with one seat between them as a buffer.

Mr. Moody continued to eat as if John was invisible.

"How's the steak?" John asked.

Mr. Moody grunted the affirmative.

"Paul Volcker still looks good. I hope I look that good at ninety." Volcker was a former Federal Reserve chairman.

Mr. Moody nodded.

"He's a big man. Six-six maybe?"

Mr. Moody continued to eat.

"The housing market's starting to soften," John said. "Some of the major markets are down 10 percent over the past year."

Mr. Moody nodded.

"The default rates on college loans are rising."

The old man set down his fork and knife. He wiped his mouth with the napkin from his lap and narrowed his eyes at John. "As president, do you plan to be involved with monetary policy?"

"Nothing more than a mouthpiece when you need me."

"Do you think we ought to let this loan bubble burst on its own accord?"

"If you do that, it'll cause a ripple effect through the stock market, the debt markets, the housing market, and ultimately jobs and the economy. I think it would be an economic disaster."

He glared at John. "Good." Mr. Moody went back to his steak.

John stood up. "Nice talking to you, sir."

Moody's face softened. "It's about time for a Democratic president."

John spotted his other mark across the room. Adam Doyle was a short red-haired man with wire-rim glasses and some serious arm candy. His trophy wife had six inches on him, helped by model genes and heels. They nursed drinks; him a beer, her some fruity concoction. They spoke in hushed whispers. She didn't look happy.

"Adam," John said, grinning as he approached.

The ginger-haired man turned from his wife with raised eyebrows.

"Congressman John Bradley," John said.

Adam forced a smile. "It's good to see you again, Congressman."

"Please, call me John." John eyed the ex-model.

"This is my wife, Kim," Adam said, gesturing to the brunette.

John extended his hand.

She returned a limp-wristed handshake.

"It's a pleasure to meet you, Kim."

Her mouth turned up at John for a split second. "I'm going to the bathroom," she said. She strutted off, her head held high and her hips rocking as if she were on a catwalk.

"I hear Armor Software has some revolutionary products," John said.

"We're working on it," Adam replied.

"I'm a big proponent of using software instead of manpower, especially on the battlefield."

Adam nodded.

"You have to be bored."

"Excuse me?"

"You're a young successful guy with a beautiful wife. And here you are at what must feel like a retirement home."

Adam smiled. "I think Kim wants to leave."

John chuckled. "I could tell that from the other side of the room."

"That bad, huh?"

"I wouldn't worry about it. My wife's in the house with my mother. She's not interested in politics either."

"Neither am I."

"I told my chief of staff today that I should have been a gym teacher, so I know what you mean."

Adam laughed. "I should have designed video games."

"Instead you designed what I've been told is the software that will revolutionize how we fight terrorism. I have to say, I'm very impressed and intrigued."

"Well, it's classified and still in beta."

"I'm aware. I have contacts at the NSA."

Adam glanced around to make sure they were out of earshot of the other guests. "Between you and me, I did want to tell you something. During testing, we identified Louis Allister as a threat *before* the shooting."

John's eyes were wide. "How does the software identify a threat?"

"It's an algorithm, affected by many factors. Everything from demographics, social media, online purchases to banking and credit card data. We even track whether or not people cover their laptop camera."

"It would've been nice if they had picked him up beforehand."

"We didn't know for sure what he would do, and we certainly didn't know where and when. There are some legislative hurdles to picking up people before they've committed a crime."

John smirked. "As a lawmaker, I'm not sure I can get around that one."

"That's what we're working on."

John stepped a little closer, looking down on Adam. "Now I'm captivated."

Adam stifled a grin, like he had a secret that might land him a seat at the cool kids' table. "It collects data, from everyone, including crimes."

"What kind of crimes?"

"Anything we can track online. Purchases of drugs without a prescription, drug use pictures on Facebook, not paying sales tax, child pornography, even pictures of dead animals shot or trapped illegally. It even works state by state, where laws differ."

"That is impressive. You're banking on collecting evidence of criminality on the people who your software has identified as potential threats. What if they haven't committed a crime that your software can find?"

"With hundreds of thousands of regulations, thousands of federal criminal laws, plus state and local laws, the software almost always finds something. In our beta testing, 92 percent of people had offenses."

"Did Louis Allister have any offenses?"

"He was buying heart medication online, for what looked like his father."

"What if Allister was in the 8 percent?"

"Things can be done, but I'm really saying too much now."

John stepped back. "I understand. Keep up the great work."

They shook hands and exchanged business cards.

John said, "You ever need any help dealing with the vultures on Capitol Hill, let me know."

John stepped out of the tent, the sunshine warming his face and heating up his blue blazer. On the opposite side of the pool, the senator talked to General Gates. They were laughing. They shook hands and parted ways. John walked toward his dad. They met near the pool edge, the azure water sparkling in the sun.

"Dad," John said.

"John," the senator said, shaking his son's hand.

Former Senator William Bradley II was svelte and tall, with a full head of gray.

"How was Gates?" John asked, looking down a few inches on his dad.

The senator paused. "He's concerned about what an antiwar Democrat will do to the defense budget."

"We don't need his money," John said.

The senator glowered, his deep-set eyes like coal. "You're playing with the big boys now. You're not in a position to be choosy."

"What did you tell him?"

"The truth. The antiwar rhetoric is just that. Rhetoric."

15: Katie, Off the Record

Katie sat at her glass desk, reading George's reply on her laptop. "Shit," she said to herself.

She sent a text.

Katie: He said no, again.

Declan: Shit.

Katie: That's what I said.

Declan: Did you offer him money?

Katie: He said it's not about the money.

Declan: There are other Anarchists we could get.

Katie: Not one this popular. He stopped a terrorist attack on a congressman who might be our next president. We could go to his house. Corrinne Stevens put a camera in his face, and he eventually talked.

Declan: And he might put a gun in our face. Not out of the question for an Anarchist.

Katie: He won't shoot us. According to his background check, he doesn't have a criminal record.

Declan: What if he just says no?

Katie: "Off the record" interview.

Declan: That's on you. I'm not getting sued.

Katie: The guy's a trucker with a cabin he bought for 70K. He can't afford a lawyer. Besides, he'll say yes.

Declan: Flights to PA aren't cheap. I'm not sure I even have time for this.

Katie: Come on. I'll pay. It will be like a vacation.

Declan: To Pennsylvania?

Katie: Okay, maybe not a vacation but an adventure. You're between projects. What's a few days?

Declan: You sure on the address?

Katie: Pretty sure. Background checks are usually correct.

Declan: OK

Katie: ☺ I LOVE YOU. I'll check flights.

* * *

Declan drove the rental car, gravel crunching under the tires, and a hardwood forest encroaching the roadside. Katie peered out the window. Cabins and trailers were generously spaced and marked by rusted mailboxes.

"We're in the middle of nowhere," Declan said.

Katie glanced at the GPS. "It says we're off course."

"Maybe I missed a turn. We should turn around."

Katie spotted another mailbox. "It said ninety-eight on that mailbox. I think we're almost there."

A few miles farther, they found it. The metal mailbox was labeled 122. They turned onto the gravel driveway. There was a gentle slope uphill. It was a one-lane road, with briars, brush, and dense forest along the roadside. They came to a small clearing, a flat area with a garage and a log cabin.

Declan parked in front of the cabin.

They stepped from the vehicle. Declan twisted his upper body back and forth, working out the kinks. Katie reached into her pocket and turned on the hidden camera attached to her blouse. It was disguised as a button. The mike was attached to her bra and loosely covered.

"Did you turn it on?" Declan asked.

"I'm on," Katie replied.

Declan appraised the property. "You know you're in redneck country when the garage is bigger than the house."

Katie laughed.

They walked up the stone steps to the front door of the cabin. The windows were boarded up.

"It looks abandoned," Declan said.

Katie frowned and knocked on the door.

They waited. Katie knocked again, harder.

"I don't think anyone lives here," Declan said.

"Let's check the garage."

The garage was a two-car vinyl-sided box with rollup doors. Katie yanked on a garage door. It was locked. There were no windows. They checked the side door. It was locked.

Katie exhaled. "Well, shit."

Declan surveyed the area. The run-down cabin, the windowless garage. "I think we should get out of here."

Leaves rustled, and a twig snapped. The rustling continued. It was getting louder. Katie and Declan looked at each other, frozen.

George appeared from behind an ancient oak, a handgun holstered on his hip. "This is private property," he said.

Katie sucked in a breath, her hand on her chest. Declan stood behind her.

"Oh my God, you scared me," Katie said.

George was blank-faced. His clothes were worn and stained. *Is that blood?* He wore a straw hat that looked like it belonged in a rice patty.

"Mr. Chapman, I'm Katie Fitzgerald." She smiled. "You know? The one who's been emailing you like a crazy person?"

"I'm not doing the interview," George said. "I was clear."

Katie approached George. Declan hung back. "I don't know if you know this, but I live in San Francisco. My associate, Declan, and I have come a long way to see you." She motioned to Declan.

"Not my problem."

"Of course not. I was just hoping that you would do the interview when you saw me. I'm sincerely interested in what you have to say and so is the rest of America, as evidenced by the popularity of your video with Corrinne Stevens."

"It's not my video."

"The reason it's popular is because of you, not that dim-witted reporter. Please, Mr. Chapman. I would be eternally grateful."

He rubbed the dark stubble on his chin. "I'm sorry you came all this way, but I'm not doing the interview. Please leave."

"What about a conversation, off the record? No camera."

"Or audio?"

"No. I really am interested in what you have to say."

"I don't have anything to say."

"Then it'll be a very short off-the-record interview. Please, Mr. Chapman."

He huffed. "All right, come on."

George hiked toward the woods behind the cabin. Katie and Declan exchanged a glance and hurried after. George walked into the forest along an informal path. After a short walk, the trees opened up to a clearing, a meadow with long grasses and purple lupines. They followed George to a small house built into the hill. There was a solar array next to the home.

"Come in," George said, opening the front door.

Katie and Declan stepped inside, their eyes wide. They saw the entire house from the front door: a kitchen with a wooden table, a sitting area, and two rooms—a bathroom and a bedroom, their doors open.

"This is a really unique house," Katie said.

George grabbed a wooden chair from the sitting area and placed it next to the kitchen table. Now three chairs were around the table. "Have a seat," he said. "Would you two like something to drink?"

"No, thank you," Katie said.

"Declan?"

"I'm fine," Declan replied.

Declan and Katie sat down next to each other, and George sat across from them. He set his hat on the table and leaned back. His dark hair was short and matted.

"What would you guys like to talk about?" George asked.

"When Corrinne Stevens from USN questioned you, you seemed very angry with the US government. Are you angry with the US government?"

"Yes."

Katie and Declan glanced at each other.

"Care to elaborate?" she asked.

"No."

Katie scowled for a split second. "You said that governments around the world have killed 250 million people in the past hundred years. Do you have a source to back up that claim?"

"It's from a study done by the late professor R. J. Rummel at the University of Hawaii, and the figure's somewhere between 250 and 300 million to be exact."

"So, it's the wars you oppose?"

"I do oppose war, but that statistic doesn't include war deaths. These are democide deaths."

"Democide?"

"When people are killed by their own government."

"There have been despotic regimes such as Mao in China or Pol Pot in Cambodia. Surely you're not equating the United States with these regimes that murdered their citizens."

"That's a common argument made by government apologists. They take the most evil governments they can think of and compare it to their country. Then they say, 'See? We're not like that. We're so thankful for *our* government.' They're right. There are varying degrees of evil governments, but the apologists are still missing the big picture. All governments are evil because they *all* derive their power and wealth from coercion, intimidation, and violence."

Katie pursed her lips. "Do you realize that sounds insane?"

George responded as if she'd asked about the weather. "These ideas cause cognitive dissonance. If a person is taught to worship government through propagandistic schooling and rituals and media and culture, it makes sense to me that these ideas would seem insane. Most people will soothe their internal conflict with confirmation bias, by seeking out information that supports their previously held viewpoints."

"What you're saying isn't unique. This is Anarchist ideology, and not only is it insane but it's also dangerous and divisive."

"I don't care whose ideology it is. I care about whether or not it's true. And the truth is that all governments exist and continue because of violence, not because of voluntary support. Good ideas don't require violence for support."

"I've been a critic of the US government, but I also see the good it's doing here and around the world. Can you explain how it is that our government exists only through violence?"

"Where does the funding come from?" George asked.

"Taxes," Katie replied.

"And inflation. Of course, if we go down that rabbit hole, we'll be here all day talking about the history of central banking."

She rolled her eyes at Declan. "Okay."

"People don't have a choice about whether or not they pay their taxes or use their currency, which is debased. The government uses extortion backed up by violence to fund all their operations. What do you think would happen if taxes were optional?"

"People are inherently selfish. Taxes have to be an obligation, because otherwise we wouldn't have all the things that make our society a great place to live. We wouldn't have schools and roads and protection."

"So, to have schools and roads and protection, we create and give an institution the power to run a massive extortion and counterfeiting racket and to use our wealth to kill millions of innocent people overseas? I think we can find a way to provide those services peacefully."

"Like Somalia? They're an Anarchist society."

"Unfortunately, for the people there, that place was in bad shape with a centralized government, and it's still in bad shape. Are you familiar with a journal article entitled, *Better Off Stateless: Somalia Before and After Government Collapse*? It was written by Peter T. Leeson."

"No, I'm not." *How the hell am I supposed to know about some obscure journal article?*

"In the paper, Leeson compared eighteen welfare indicators of Somalians before and after the collapse of their government. He found that Somalians were notably better off now than with government. The other thing to keep in mind is that we've had many government failures worldwide. Governments don't have great track records. According to the 2017 Failed States Index, 21 percent of the world's countries have failing states. These are governments that are often predatory, dysfunctional, and on the brink of collapse. Also, according to the index, 56 percent of governments are in what they call a state of alert, meaning they are approaching failure. Essentially the majority of the world lives under a dysfunctional state." George paused.

"Maybe we should try something else."

"And you think that something else is anarchism?"

George shook his head. "I don't know, but I would like to have the freedom to decide for myself, and I would like others to have that same freedom."

"How would that work? We all have to agree."

"Look, I don't have all the answers, and people will never agree, but freedom means letting others say and do things you don't agree with."

"So people can just commit crimes then?"

"Anarchism is a society *without rulers*, not a society *without rules*. People smarter than me have ideas about dealing with crime without government. Medieval Ireland was an anarchic society that had a private legal system with mediators and professional jurors. I've heard of enforcement nonviolently through insurance contracts. Hell, even old-school shunning would be better than what we have today.

"We live in a country with the largest prison population in the world, a place where male rapes outnumber female because of our prison system, a place where one-third of us have a criminal record, not because we are immoral, but because, with so many laws, it becomes impossible for people to live without breaking them in some way. Have you read the book *Three Felonies a Day*?"

"I have, and I totally agree with the author's critique. I'm not sure if you've seen any of my work, but, if you have, you'll know that I'm very critical of our legal system. It's predatory, racist, and ineffective. I'm also very critical of government power, and I acknowledge that we need change, but, if I waved a magic wand and removed government, it would be a disaster."

"I agree. Big changes usually are. We don't have to remove government. We just have to remove the teeth of it. If support was voluntary, the power would truly be in the hands of the people. They could decide what to support and how much. Then our government would actually be held accountable, and people could decide for themselves if they wanted to participate."

Katie smirked. "That's great in theory, but it wouldn't work in the real world."

"You don't know that."

"Point to one successful anarchic society today."

"Are you two married?" George asked, glancing from Katie to Declan and back again.

"No," Katie said.

"But you're dating?" George asked.

"Yeah," Declan said.

"We are," Katie said.

George looked at Declan. "So, Declan, when you first met Katie, did you put a gun in her face and say, 'You better go out with me, or I'm putting you in a cage'?"

Declan scowled. "I know this argument."

"Then you know that the majority of our relationships are already anarchic and free. That's because voluntary associations work."

* * *

At the conclusion of the interview, they stood from the table and shook hands.

"You wanna help others," George said as he shook Katie's hand.

Katie nodded, her eyebrows arched.

George let go of her hand. "You're searching for answers."

"Excuse me?" she said.

"It's a good thing, the inquisitiveness, the desire to help others. Sometimes it helps to know the right questions to ask."

Katie put her hands on her hips. "And you'll tell me the right questions to ask?"

George shook his head. "No, but I have a book that might inspire quite a few questions." George walked past Katie and Declan to the bookcase in the sitting room. He pulled a thick book from the top shelf and stepped back to the kitchen. "It's *The Creature from Jekyll Island* by G. Edward Griffin." George handed the book to Katie. "You can keep it. I've already read it."

Katie took the heavy text in both hands. She smirked, shooting a glance at Declan. "Thanks."

George showed them back to their rental car. Katie gazed from the passenger window with the book in her lap, while Declan drove them away from George's house.

"You're quiet," Declan said.

Katie turned to Declan. Rubber bracelets dangled from his wrist, a wooden medallion around his neck. She remembered the story he had told her of the African medallion. She was impressed by his concern that the jewelry was ethically purchased from a Sudanese woman, not from some corporate sweatshop.

"I was just thinking," Katie said.

"You didn't let that guy get to you, did you?"

"No, ... no, of course not."

"That's good, because he was full of shit."

"Right." Katie pursed her lips. "He was different than I thought he'd be. He didn't know what questions I'd ask, but he seemed to have an answer for everything."

"Because he was talking out of his ass. We'll fact-check him and debunk him in the video. We'll expose him as the liar he is. It's fucking awesome that he kept talking about *truth*, because we can expose him as a hypocrite too."

16: Julie and Sport

Julie hovered over the stovetop, stirring spaghetti sauce. She heard footsteps coming down the stairs and into the kitchen.

"When are you gonna make a decision?" Max asked.

Julie exhaled and glanced over her shoulder at her son. "Honey, I don't have time to talk about this right now. Larry will be here any minute."

"This is bullshit."

Julie removed the sauce pan from the burner and turned to her son with a scowl. "Language."

"Well, it is. You've been putting this off for like a month."

"It hasn't been a month."

"Yes, it has. I remember because, when you went out on your first date with Larry, I sent George an email, saying that you said we'd talk about it when you got back. You wanna guess the date of that email?"

Julie held out her hands. "I have no idea."

"It was May 12." Max crossed his arms, his jaw taut. "It's June 9."

"You only have a couple weeks of school left. Why don't we talk about it when you get out? We'll both have a better perspective. And I don't think you should be discussing this with George."

"You don't want me to talk about it with George because you know you're wrong, and you're delaying the decision because you don't want me to go virtual."

Julie sighed. "Honey, I just want you to have some time and distance from school, so we can make a thoughtful decision, not an emotional one."

"*We*? You and I both know that you're the one making the decision."

"Honey."

"Why can't you decide now? I don't like this hanging over me, like the Sword of Damocles."

"The sword of what?"

"Damocles. It's a story about this guy who wanted to be king, so the king let him sit on the throne with a sword hanging over him connected to a single horse hair."

Julie smirked. "Where do you get this stuff?"

"Definitely not at school."

"I promise we'll make a decision after school lets out."

"Whatever."

The doorbell rang.

"Could you get the door?" Julie asked.

Max stomped to the front door.

Julie glanced at her reflection on the microwave oven. She brushed her auburn hair with her fingers. She checked her floral sundress for any sauce stains.

"Hey, sport," Larry said at the front door.

"My mom's in the kitchen," Max said.

Julie heard diverging footsteps, one set going upstairs, the other headed for the kitchen.

"There she is," Larry said.

Julie turned from the stove, as if his arrival were a surprise. "Larry."

He wore a short-sleeve, button-down shirt. It was tightly tucked into his khakis. He approached with a wide grin, a bouquet of roses in hand. "These are for you," he said.

"They're beautiful. Thank you." She took the roses. "I should put them in water." She searched her cabinets for a vase. "I thought I had a vase in here somewhere." Her cheeks reddened. She knew damn well she didn't have a vase. She couldn't remember the last time someone brought her flowers. "I guess this will have to do until I can find it." She put the flowers in a plastic water bottle and added water from the tap.

"It smells great," Larry said. "Is there anything I can do?"

"No, you just relax. Everything's pretty much ready. I made spaghetti but with spaghetti squash instead of pasta. It's very good and much better for you."

Larry nodded. "Sounds great. I hear gluten is pretty bad stuff. I can eat pretty much anything though."

"Oh, that reminds me." Julie slipped an oven mitt on her hand and opened the oven. She removed a tray of garlic bread. She set it on the stove-top and turned to Larry with a smile. "We have plenty of gluten too." Julie removed plates and glasses from the cabinets.

"Are you sure I can't do something?"

Julie turned to Larry and waved her hand across her face. "Just relax. I'll be right back."

She hurried from the kitchen to the bottom of the stairs. "Max, honey, would you please come down and set the table?" No response. "Max?"

A loud techno beat erupted from Max's room. She fast-walked back to the kitchen. "I'm sorry, Larry. I need to check on Max. Please sit down and make yourself at home."

"I'd really like to help."

"You can fill the water glasses, if you want, but please don't feel obligated."

"From the tap?"

Shit, I should have bought some bottled water or one of those Brita filters we would never remember to refill. "Yes."

Julie left her guest and climbed the steps in chunky heels, the techno beat getting louder with each step. She knocked on Max's door. No answer. She knocked harder. Nothing. She entered his room. Max was at his desk on his laptop, a cartoon under construction. She turned down the iPod plugged into a docking station, complete with speakers.

Max swiveled in his chair. "I was listening to that," he said.

"It's too loud, and it's time to eat."

Max stared at the carpet. "I don't like him."

Julie stepped closer to her son. She placed her hand under his chin and raised his gaze to meet hers. "We've only been on three dates, and we might just be friends. I don't know at this point. I know this is strange—"

"It's not strange. I don't like him."

Julie removed her hand from his chin. "You don't even know him."

"He called me *sport*. I know I don't like that."

"That's not a good reason not to like someone."

Max crossed his arms. "He's fake."

Julie squeezed her eyes shut for a moment. "Please don't do this to me. I'm trying. I'm *really* trying. I need you to try too."

"Whatever."

Julie took a deep breath, leaned into Max's personal space, and said, "If you can't be mature enough to come down, set the table, and be the nice young man that I brought you up to be, you're obviously not mature enough to go to school online."

Max's eyes widened. "Fine."

Max trudged down the steps after Julie. In the kitchen, three plates sat on the counter. Max yanked open a drawer, set silverware on the plates with a clang, and slammed the drawer shut. Larry watched the train wreck with his mouth open. Max blustered to the dining room, ignoring Larry.

"I put waters on the table," Larry said.

Julie smiled, her eyes still. "Thank you." She motioned with her eyes to the dining room and mouthed, *Sorry*.

"No big deal," Larry said.

Julie placed the garlic bread in a bowl and covered it with a cloth napkin. Max returned from the dining room, opened the refrigerator, and retrieved a can of Coke. He glared at Julie, daring her to forbid him the soda with dinner. Julie carried the food to the table, and Larry helped.

They sat at the dining room table for four. Larry and Julie sat close to each other at one corner. Max edged his seat as far away from the couple as possible. They passed the food around in silence, Max sending the spaghetti squash and the sauce around the table without putting any on his plate. He grabbed a stack of garlic bread and started eating.

"This looks great," Larry said, breaking the silence.

Max opened his soda. *Pfft.*

"Thanks, Larry," Julie said.

"So how's work been?" Larry asked, between bites.

Julie chewed, swallowed, and wiped her mouth with her napkin. "It's been good. Thanks for asking."

"What about you, Larry?"

Larry grinned. "I couldn't tell you before because it was confidential, but we arrested a big-time DC drug dealer for tax evasion. Did you know that that's how we got Al Capone? It was tax evasion."

"Wow, how exciting. Did you hear that, Max? Larry arrested a drug dealer. Sounds like one of your graphic novels, huh?"

"Not really," Max said with a mouthful of garlic bread.

"You know? I used to love comics—I mean, graphic novels," Larry said.

"I bet my parents still have them. I could find out. You'd be welcome to have them, if you want."

"That's really nice of you, Larry." Julie put her hand on top of his and squeezed. "Isn't that nice, Max?"

"Some of them are probably worth a lot of money," Larry added.

"No, thanks," Max said, not making eye contact.

"Well, if you change your mind, just let me know."

Max stood, grabbing his plate and Coke.

"Where are you going?" Julie asked.

"I'm finished," Max replied.

"Okay then."

Max set his plate in the sink. He walked past the dining room, holding his soda and two pieces of bread.

"No loud music," Julie called out as he stomped up the steps.

Julie frowned at Larry. "I'm really sorry about that. He's usually very well-behaved. I don't know what's going on with him lately."

"He's a teenager," Larry said. "That's enough."

"You probably want to run right about now."

Larry shook his head. "I'm not going anywhere."

Julie smiled.

They finished dinner and cleaned the dishes. Larry helped gratefully.

"Would you like to watch a movie?" Julie asked.

"Sure, but you pick the movie," Larry replied.

Julie and Larry browsed through the new releases on Netflix. They settled on a romantic comedy that Larry insisted was fine with him.

"Did you want popcorn or something to drink?" Julie asked. "I don't drink much, but I did buy a few beers."

"I'll have a beer if you will," Larry replied.

As the movie began, Julie sat close to him on the couch but not touching. Larry was on her right side. She sipped her beer with her left hand, keenly aware that her right hand was waiting to be held. Half an hour into the movie, her stomach fluttered as he placed his hand on top of hers. She turned her hand over, gripping his, her eyes on the screen. Halfway through the movie, Larry put his arm around her, and, shortly after that, she leaned against his chest. He smelled like cologne and aftershave. She felt his heart beating rapidly.

As the credits rolled, Julie sat up. "Did you want another beer?"

"I'll have one if you will," he replied.

Julie opened two more beers and handed one to Larry before sitting next to him on the couch. "What did you think of the movie?"

"It was okay."

"Not your cup of tea, huh?"

"Well—"

"You seem like a crime thriller guy."

"You have me pegged."

"Good triumphing over evil, right?"

He nodded. "Something like that."

They downed a couple more beers as they discussed old high school teachers.

Julie glanced at the clock on the cable box. "Wow, it's already eleven."

"Time flies when you're having fun," Larry replied.

"You're sweet, Larry Nicholson. How is it that you've never been married?"

Larry shrugged. "I don't know. I guess I haven't met the right girl." He grinned. "Present company excluded."

Julie giggled and stood from the couch. She sat back down, a little wobbly.

"Whoa," Larry said. "Are you okay?"

Julie continued to giggle. "I'm sorry. I get giggly when I'm buzzing."

"I thought *I* was a lightweight."

"I know. I haven't had any alcohol since New Year's. Are you feeling anything?"

"I'm okay. Not sure I'd pass a sobriety test, but I feel fine."

"I don't want you to get the wrong idea, but you can stay here tonight, if you want."

"That's not, um, … necessary. I'll be fine in an hour or so. I can sleep in my car if I have to."

"Sleep in your car? Don't be ridiculous." Julie stood up slowly and extended her hand. He took it and stood next to her. "Let's go up to bed. I'll stay on my side of the bed."

Larry glanced at the collection of beer bottles on the coffee table. "Maybe we should throw those out. I wouldn't want Max to get the wrong impression."

"Good idea."

They put the bottles in the recycle bin and tiptoed upstairs. A sliver of light shone under Max's door. Julie led Larry into the master bedroom with its queen-size bed topped with a floral comforter. Julie shut and locked the door.

"Do you mind if I use the restroom?" Larry asked, glancing at the master bath.

"Of course not," Julie said.

Larry shut the bathroom door. Julie hurried to the mirror over her dresser. She fluffed up her hair and smoothed out her dress. Larry didn't use the bath fan to drown out the sound of his urination. He flushed. She listened for the sound of the sink and breathed a sigh of relief when she heard it. He emerged from the bathroom, his shirt tucked in.

"I should go too," Julie said.

She flipped the fan on and peed. *I wonder if he thinks I'm not just peeing?* She flushed and cut the bath fan. *No, he'll know that's too fast.* She checked her hair and makeup. She fluffed her hair again and spritzed a bit of hair spray. She stepped into the bedroom. He stood, looking at the framed pictures on her dresser.

Shit.

Julie approached Larry. He stared at a photo of Justin, smiling, in his class A uniform, with his arm around Julie in her black evening gown.

Larry turned to Julie. "I didn't know he was in the military."

"That was from the army ball."

"Did he die in the war?"

Julie's face was taut.

"I'm sorry. If you don't want to talk about it, it's—"

"It's fine." Julie took a deep breath. "He died from complications from the war."

"I'm sorry. He made the ultimate sacrifice."

She had a lump in her throat. "He did."

"I wanted to join the marines, but ..." He adjusted his glasses. "Bad eyes. I was devastated. It was my dream."

"I'm sorry, Larry. But you're still serving the country."

Larry nodded. "You look beautiful."

Julie's face felt hot. "You're sweet." She put her hands on his hips and did what she'd wanted to do all night. She untucked his shirt. "Doesn't that feel more comfortable?" she asked.

Larry stepped closer and placed his hands on her lower back, pulling her against him. He pressed his lips to hers, soft at first. Julie's lips parted slightly, just enough to encourage more. Larry flipped like a switch. He jammed his tongue into her mouth and squeezed her ass. His hands moved over her body as if it were a race. He reached under her dress and plunged his hand between her legs.

Julie turned her head, unclamping his mouth from hers. She gasped. "Larry, Larry," she said. "Stop."

He was unresponsive, panting and grunting like a man possessed.

"Stop!"

Larry's eyes opened wide in recognition. He yanked his hand from her crotch and stepped back, breathless. "Sorry, … I'm sorry."

Julie was wide-eyed. "Maybe we should just go to sleep."

Larry's face was flushed. "I should go home. I doubt I'll sleep much in my condition."

"You can't drive yet."

He spoke rapidly. "I'll be fine. It's not your problem. I had a nice time, Julie. Thanks for dinner." He turned and opened the bedroom door.

"Larry, don't go. You can have the bed. I'll sleep on the couch."

"I'll find my way out."

"Larry."

He hurried down the stairs. Julie followed, but, like the superheroes he idolized, he was gone in a flash. Julie locked the dead bolt behind him and trudged back to her bedroom. She kicked off her shoes, unzipped her dress, and dropped it to the floor. She removed her lacy bra. It was the only one she had that wasn't from a discount store. She put on pajama pants and a T-shirt. She gazed at the picture of Justin and her on her dresser. She picked up the framed photograph, pulled back her comforter, and slipped into bed.

Julie pulled her knees to her chest, the picture close. She gazed at Justin, trying to find some indicator of what was to come. She had a lump in her throat. Tears filled her eyes and slipped down her face. Her body convulsed. She was sobbing now.

17: George and False Flags

George sat at his kitchen table, eating a lunch of grilled groundhog and mixed greens topped with grilled eggplant. His phone buzzed. It was a text.

Max: I loved the video you did with Katie.

George: What video?

Max: At your house. You talked about freedom and truth and how all governments are evil. Cool house by the way.

I'm so stupid.

George: I thought it was off the record. She got me.

Max: It backfired then.

George: I don't understand.

Max: Watch the video. **LINK**

George clicked the link. The title of the video was "Another Anarchist Hillbilly." The video was from Katie's point of view. She showed George's cabin and garage.

"You know you're in redneck country when the garage is bigger than the house," Declan said.

Declan and Katie looked around the cabin and garage. This was set to twangy music and sped up, so their motions appeared frantic.

"I felt like we were in *The Texas Chainsaw Massacre*," Katie said in voice-over.

The video slowed to normal speed.

"I think we should get out of here," Declan said.

Ominous music played. Leaves rustled. The camera panned to George, emerging from the woods, a handgun on his hip. A circle was drawn around the gun and another around the bloodstain on his T-shirt. The video cut to a close-up of Katie in a low-cut dress.

"I didn't know what he was going to do," Katie said, "but I couldn't take my eyes off that gun or the blood on his shirt. What kind of crazy person walks around his house with a gun? Does he think this is the Wild West? And where did the blood come from? Does he think he's some kind of weird cowboy? I mean, look at that hat. It's like something out of Huck Finn."

The video cut to George walking in the woods, the camera and Katie following behind. The video went back to Katie in her dress.

"I had no idea where he was taking us or why I was willing to go with him. Don't try this at home, boys and girls."

The video showed George taking them into his earth-sheltered home.

"He took us to this weird underground house," Katie said over the video. "He lives in a bunker, like he's waiting for a nuclear war."

The video cut to the interview. It periodically presented counterpoints to George's arguments, with additional snark added for emphasis. George's gift to Katie and his kindness at the conclusion of the interview were not included.

The video had over five million views and counting, with almost one hundred thousand dislikes and only ten thousand likes. His phone buzzed.

Max: Did you watch it?

George: I did. They invaded my privacy and made me look like a fool.

Max: You didn't look like a fool. You were awesome!

George: Well, people thought different. Lots of dislikes.

Max: Because they were mad at Katie. It's her channel. Read the comments.

George clicked on the video again and scrolled through the comments.

Rothbardian11: Typical propagandized liberal. Chapman serves up some truth, but Katie couldn't see truth if it bitch-slapped her across the face.

Bradley's Girl: I usually like Katie's videos, but I'm sorry she just seemed mean in this one.

Gary Player55: What a stupid whore.

Eric the Red: It's so fucked-up what they did. They trespassed and secretly recorded Chapman, who is obviously a private person. They probably thought he was too poor or too stupid to sue. Katie should be worried. That dude is smart.

Kelsie Donner: ☹ Unsub.

Gam Gam: I'd pay to see George Chapman debate President Reynolds.

Rick the Dick: Hahahahahahahahahahaha. You got served.

Luis Hiedler: Lib taken to school by an Anarchist. #fuckyeah

George's phone buzzed again.

Max: See what I mean?

George: Yes.

Max: I've never seen someone get burned like that on their own channel. You should make some comments.

George: I think I'll stay out of it. How's school going?

Max: Awful. So same as usual.

George: How many school days are left?

Max: Eight. Hopefully it'll be the last eight days I spend in that place. I don't know what I'll do if my mom doesn't let me go virtual.

George: If you tell her the whole truth, I think she'll see your perspective.

Max: I know. Maybe.

George: Other than school, how are you?

Max: I think Larry might be my mom's boyfriend now. He was over for dinner on Saturday.

George: How do you feel about that?

Max: It sucks.

George: Her having a boyfriend or the boyfriend?

Max: My dad has been gone eight years. A boyfriend I get, but Larry is a douchebag.

George: I'm sorry to hear that. Did he do something specific?

Max: No. I just think he's fake.

George: As hard as it is for you, I'm sure it's also very hard for her.

Max: Yeah. I gotta go.

George: Talk to you later.

George finished his lunch, cleaned his dishes, and limped outside. He wore muck boots over his canvas pants. The meadow was damp from last night's rain. The sun played peekaboo with the clouds. He slipped earbuds in his ears, tapped his phone a few times, and placed it in his pocket.

"This is Barry Krause from the *Extreme History Podcast*, and this is episode 317. Today I'll discuss a very effective propaganda technique utilized throughout history—the false flag attack. For those of you who don't know, a false flag attack is a covert operation designed to deceive in such a way that the operation appears as though it's being carried out by individuals, groups, or nations other than those who actually planned and executed the operation. It's an insidious form of terrorism and propaganda that not only instills fear in a population but is also often used to make people support the actual terrorist."

George hiked through the meadow, feeling the tips of the knee-high plants. He slipped through the briars and brambles at the forest edge. Under the dense tree canopy, the forest floor opened up, and hiking became easier.

"Many false flag attacks have been committed and confirmed by many governments," Barry said. "It's a common and very effective way for a government to exert control over their citizens. Joseph Stalin once said, 'The easiest way to gain control of a population is to carry out acts of terror. The public will clamor for such laws if their personal security is threatened.'

"Hermann Goering, a Nazi leader, explained the concept of a false flag quite succinctly. He said, 'Why of course the people don't want war. But, after all, it is the leaders of the country who determine the policy, and it is always a simple matter to drag the people along, whether it is a democracy or a fascist dictatorship or a parliament or a communist dictatorship. Voice or no voice, the people can always be brought to the bidding of the leaders. That is easy. All you have to do is to tell them that they are being attacked and denounce the pacifists for lack of patriotism and for exposing the country to danger. It works the same in any country.'

"Indeed, it does, Mr. Goering. Indeed, it does. Americans often cite 9/11 as the most obvious and controversial false flag. The Iraqis did not have weapons of mass destruction nor did they have any connection to the terrorists. I could go into detail here on engineering reports, but, even seventeen years later, still questions and speculations and misinformation exist. If I go down this rabbit hole, and I make a mistake, it will undermine the work we do here to provide the most accurate history we can. I'm going to avoid the pitfalls of 9/11.

"I'd like to analyze another American false flag attack, but I can verify this one and confidently source my information. This false flag is the Gulf of Tonkin incident or the public reason given for the Vietnam War. Much of the information I am about to provide is from the excellent book *Manufacturing Consent* by Noam Chomsky and Edward Herman.

"The incident began on July 30 and 31 of 1964 when Saigon naval vessels attacked North Vietnamese islands, eliciting a formal complaint from the North Vietnamese. On August 2, 1964, the US destroyer *Maddox* was conducting electronic espionage in the same general area, an area regarded by the North Vietnamese as their territorial waters. The *Maddox* was confronted by North Vietnamese patrol boats. Warning shots were fired, and the *Maddox* was hit by a single bullet. The *Maddox* and US aircraft destroyed or damaged the patrol boats. The *Maddox* and another destroyer, the *Turner Joy*, returned to the area the next day. On that same day and on August 4, Saigon naval vessels attacked North Vietnamese coastal facilities.

"US destroyers might've come under attack by North Vietnamese patrol boats on August 4, but Captain John Herrick of the *Maddox* wasn't sure and radioed that reports 'appear very doubtful' and that there were 'no actual sightings by *Maddox*'. Subsequent evidence indicates that no attack took place.

"On August 5, President Lyndon Johnson denounced the actions of the North Vietnamese as 'open aggression on the high seas,' and the US military retaliated by bombing North Vietnamese installations and destroying patrol boats.

"After testimony by then Defense Secretary Robert McNamara, in which he falsely claimed that the *Maddox* 'was operating in international waters, was carrying out a routine patrol of the type we carry out all over the world at all times,' Congress passed a resolution authorizing the president to 'take all necessary measures to repel any armed attack against the forces of the United States and to prevent further aggression.'

"The rest is history. The Gulf of Tonkin false flag led to the Vietnam War, a war that was genocidal, a war that reduced the Vietnamese population by 17 percent. To put the tragedy into perspective, 17 percent of the current US population is 56 million people."

George hiked toward the forest edge where rings of morel mushrooms could be found around a grove of elms. He removed his backpack and the paper bags inside. He filled his bags with the funky mushrooms that looked like pine cones. Despite the abundance of morels, he left far more than he took.

18: John's Nice View

John rolled off her, breathless. He was on his back, grinning. She rolled on to him, her leg draped over his and her head on his chest. Her crotch was warm on his thigh. He turned his head and kissed her on the lips. She smiled through the kiss.

Rays of sunshine brightened the white curtains. The thick comforter was bunched at the foot of the bed. A phone buzzed on the bedside table.

"Don't get it," she said.

"I won't," he replied.

Another phone buzzed on the opposite bedside table.

"Don't get it," he said.

"I won't," she replied.

After a beat, John wiggled out from under her, the afterglow fading.

She pushed out her bottom lip. "Not yet."

"You know my schedule." He slipped on his boxer briefs.

"Let's stay here forever."

"I wish." He put on his slacks. His chest was well-defined and covered in salt-and-pepper hair.

Donna groaned and scooted out of bed.

He stared at her subtle curves, the small of her back, her firm ass and legs.

She grabbed the bathrobe from the back of the chair and covered herself.

"Hey, I was enjoying the view."

She turned and mouthed a kiss his way. "Better to leave you wanting more."

John smirked and picked up his cell phone, checking the text. "Shit. It's Grace."

Donna picked up her cell phone from the bedside table. She checked the identical message from their head of public relations. "This guy won't go away," Donna said.

"Why do they keep covering him? Don't answer that. It was rhetorical."

John and Donna moved to the sitting area that overlooked the Jefferson Memorial and the Tidal Basin. They sat on the couch and watched the video of George Chapman being interviewed by Katie Fitzgerald. Two political pundits were debunking Chapman's theories and assertions, painting him as an extremist, while Corrinne Stevens moderated. They linked Chapman to John.

USN cut to a clip of John at a press conference.

On the video, John stood behind the podium in his campaign headquarters, with bullet holes over his shoulder. "Mr. Chapman saved my life. I am grateful, as is my family. As far as his political ideology and opinions, I disagree, but we still have freedom of speech in this country, and that freedom applies to speech we don't agree with."

USN cut to a screen split in thirds. Corrinne was on the left, her glasses unable to hide the beauty underneath. The man in the middle had a pudgy face, a full head of white hair, and wore round glasses. The man on the right had dark hair, small droopy eyes, and a downturned mouth—the human equivalent of a basset hound.

Corrinne said, "Alex, do you think Mr. Chapman's viewpoints are dangerous, and do you think Congressman Bradley is encouraging insurrection by not disavowing Chapman's words with more fervor?"

USN showed a close-up of the basset hound. Underneath the man, the caption read Alex Cooley, Political Strategist.

"I do think Mr. Chapman's viewpoints are dangerous," Alex replied. "I would go so far as to say, *treasonous*. At a time in this country when we're so divided, he's forging deeper fault lines. Having said that, Mr. Chapman is simply a rambling idiot whose fifteen minutes of fame are waning. As a veteran, I find Congressman Bradley's defense of his statements far more offensive."

"Ken, your counterpoint," Corrinne said.

They showed a close-up of the white-haired man. Underneath the man, his caption read RNC Chairman Ken Osborne.

"I found Chapman's statements to be distasteful and disrespectful," Ken said. "I'm not sure I'd go so far to say that Chapman's statements were treasonous, but legally he is stepping through a minefield. He could possibly be prosecuted under the Espionage and Trading with the Enemy Act which criminalizes antiwar speech and espionage. The Reynolds administration has used the Espionage Act to prosecute journalists who leaked classified government information. There's no reason to believe the president wouldn't also use the act to prosecute antiwar and antigovernment activists. If I were Representative Bradley, I'd distance myself from Chapman."

At the conclusion of the video, John tossed his phone on the coffee table and stood. "Corrinne's career is looking up."

Donna nodded. "She was in the right place at the right time."

"She has the right look for USN." John paced. "What are we going to do about this?"

"We're not doing anything until we poll it. This was on USN. We won't sway the Republicans either way. We have to keep the Democrats and at least half of the Independents. Based on Chapman's popularity, I would bet that your connection to him is positive. The Republicans are pandering to their patriotic viewers by calling him an idiot and a lunatic. From what I can tell, he's not crazy, and he's certainly not stupid."

"I agree with that. Chapman's problem is that he's too extreme."

"We'll be the moderate version."

"The change candidate, coming to DC to drain the swamp."

19: Katie and the Creature

Katie lay on her couch, her head propped up by a cushion, reading *The Creature from Jekyll Island*. She closed the text and set it on the coffee table. She had a sick feeling in the pit of her stomach. She shook her head. *This has to be bullshit.*

She picked up her cell phone, glanced at the time, and tapped her Contact for Declan.

"Hey," Declan said.

"It's already seven. Where are you?"

"Oh, shit. I lost track of time. I'm still working."

Katie clenched her jaw. "On what?"

"Research."

She exhaled. "*Now* you see the value of research?"

"I said I was sorry. What more do you want me to say?"

"What can you say? My channel's totally fucked. My reputation's totally fucked. But you said, you were sorry, so it's all better."

"I am sorry. I should have listened to you, okay? But I was worried that, if we didn't release it right away, his fifteen minutes of fame would've been over."

"Do you have any idea how many unsubs I've had?"

"You've also had five times as many subscribers."

"Yeah, the crazy Anarchists. Not exactly my audience. They just want to heckle me some more."

"At least you have an audience."

"Are you coming to dinner or not?"

"I can't—"

Katie ended the call. She hung her head, rubbing her temples. After a moment she stood, slipped on her flip-flops, and trudged outside onto the sandstone pool deck. The sun was low in the sky. She walked past the pool toward the glass-and-stone house. A modern design with a flat roof and a spectacular view of the San Francisco Bay. Katie opened the glass door and followed the smell of garlic to the kitchen. Susen worked over the Viking range, sautéing vegetables. Katie kissed her on the cheek. The old woman had jet-black hair and a squat stature that could be traced to her Mayan ancestors. A once-powerful civilization, many of the Mayan descendants were now enslaved in fields and kitchens.

"We just started, sweetheart," Katie's mom called out from the dining room.

"Coming," Katie called back.

"Hungry?" Susen asked.

Katie nodded, her face slack. "Smells good."

"What's wrong?" Susen removed the skillet from the stovetop.

Katie shrugged.

Susen added the steaming vegetables over a bed of quinoa. She squeezed Katie's hand. "Eat something. You'll feel better. You wanna talk after dinner, I'll be in my room."

Katie forced a smile. She carried her plate into the dining room. Her parents sat at the far end of a mahogany table that sat twelve. A chandelier the size of a fifties' jukebox hung over the table. Her place was set across from her mother and kitty-cornered from her father, who sat at the head of the table. Her parents ate steaks in addition to quinoa and sautéed vegetables. They drank water and red wine.

"It's 7:05," her dad said, glancing at Katie as she approached.

"The steaks were getting cold," her mom added.

Mary Fitzgerald was in her mid-fifties but could pass for a decade younger. She was an elegant woman in a conservative blue dress. She still had blond hair, but her hair stylist knew the truth. She wore tasteful but expensive jewelry.

Her dad chewed his steak, multitasking by cutting his meat as he did so.

"That's fine, Mom." Katie set down her plate and took her seat. "I was waiting on Declan. He's won't make it."

Mary pressed out her lower lip. "I'm so sorry to hear that."

"A man needs to keep his appointments," her dad said.

Katie frowned. "It's dinner, not a business meeting."

Peter Fitzgerald wore a blue blazer and a striped tie, his white hair parted to the side. He shook his head. "When I was courting your mother, if I said I'd be somewhere, you better believe I was there fifteen minutes early."

Mary beamed.

"It's not like that anymore," Katie said.

"I think you can do better," Peter said.

Katie cocked her head. "Dad."

"I won't say anymore."

They ate in relative silence. Katie set down her fork, her plate half-full.

"Dad, are you familiar with the book *The Creature from Jekyll Island*?" Katie asked.

He looked up from his plate, his eyebrows arched. "Written by G. Edward Griffin."

"You know it?"

"I read it many years ago."

"I just finished the part where he details the Mandrake Mechanism—"

Peter chuckled.

"What? Is it not true?"

"The 'Mandrake Mechanism' was named after a comic-book character from the 1940s, Mandrake the Magician. Do you know what his power was?"

Katie smirked. "I'm not well-versed in magicians from eighty years ago."

"He could create something out of nothing." Peter grinned, a gleam in his blue eyes. If it weren't for the wrinkles and age spots, you could almost see the mischievous young man underneath.

"Is it true? Is this how our money's created?"

The old man nodded. "Afraid so. Henry Ford once said, 'It is well-enough that people of the nation do not understand our banking and monetary system, for, if they did, I believe there would be a revolution before tomorrow morning.'"

Katie's eyes were wide. "Jesus Christ, Dad. So we've profited off this, this ... counterfeiting operation."

"It's more complicated than that," Peter said. "All this development you see around you wouldn't have been possible without a stable currency and a stable economic system."

"But it's not stable. According to the book, every thirty to forty years the system dies, and they make a new one."

"I suppose there is some truth to that."

"What do you mean there is *some* truth to that? Either it's true or not."

"Well, we had the gold standard from 1871 until World War I in 1914, then the gold exchange standard until 1944, the Bretton Woods system from '44 until 1971, and, since 1971, the entire world's been on the dollar standard. Admittedly the dollar standard is running on fumes."

Katie hung her head and rubbed her eyes with her thumb and index finger. "This is bad."

"You worry too much, sweetheart," Mary said. "We'll be fine."

Katie gaped at her dad. "Those crazy end-the-Fed people are right, aren't they?"

Peter chuckled. "It's easy to criticize. The system isn't perfect, but it's the one we have, and the one billions of people depend on."

Katie pushed away her plate, nauseated. "Everything we have is stolen."

"Katie," Mary said, scowling.

Peter pointed his steak knife at Katie. "I've worked since I was twelve-years old. I've never stolen so much as a stick of gum."

"USA Bank is part of the cartel," Katie said, standing from the table. "Excuse me." She walked away from her parents.

"Katie," Mary called out.

"Let her go," Peter said.

Katie walked past the kitchen and down a short hallway. She passed the laundry room and stopped at a door slightly ajar. She tapped on it.

"Come in," Susen said.

Susen sat in her rocking chair, wearing her reading glasses, reading a Spanish romance novel. Susen moved her bookmark and shut the book. Katie entered the room with a drawn face. She sat on the made bed across from the old woman.

"Are you okay?" Susen asked, removing her reading glasses.

Katie shrugged. "Do you remember the charity when I was in the seventh grade?"

Susen smiled. "You were always such a sweet girl."

"We went on that field trip to the strawberry farm, and the farmers worked so hard. I've never seen anyone work so fast in my entire life. I couldn't understand why I had so much and they had so little."

"You raised so much money. The farmers were grateful. I think I still have the article from the paper."

Katie shook her head. "It was only six thousand dollars. Not enough to even pay for one year of college for one of their children. The reporters just wanted to tell people what they wanted to hear."

"What do people wanna hear?"

"That we're good and kind and smart and special. But we're not." Katie hung her head, her eyes glassy. "I'm not." Tears slipped down her face.

Susen moved from the rocking chair to the bed and put her arm around Katie. Katie leaned against the old woman.

"Shh, shh. *Todo esta bien*," Susen whispered.

The old woman rocked Katie, like a baby.

After several minutes Katie sat up. Susen handed her the box of tissues from the bedside table. Katie dried her eyes and sopped up the mucus from her runny nose.

"I'm sorry," Katie said. "I'm too old to be crying to you like this."

Susen shook her head. "We're never too old to feel. You wanna tell me what this is about?"

"There's Declan, and my business is a disaster, and …" Katie chewed on her bottom lip.

"And what, *Katalina*?"

"I've been thinking things are one way, and I'm starting to think I'm wrong."

"*Nadie es perfecto.*"

Katie forced a smile. "Can we talk about something else?"

The old woman pursed her lips, her eyes beckoning Katie.

"Please," Katie said.

"*Esta bien.*"

"Are you looking forward to your summer trip?"

"Yes."

"Two more weeks. Your sons must be excited."

"I may not see Hector. He's in Mexico City, driving a cab. I worry about him. That air is very dirty."

"He's not farming anymore?"

Susen shook her head, frowning. "*El rio esta muy seco.* With no river, land's too dry to farm."

20: Julie and Question Authority

Julie slipped on her black pants and put on her polo. Her phone buzzed.

Larry: I'm sorry about what happened. I'm an idiot. I misread the signals, and I'm really sorry. You probably thought you'd never hear from me again. I'm also sorry it's taken over a week to apologize. I wanted to contact you, but I was afraid of rejection. I'm still afraid of rejection. If you don't text me back, I'll take that as a very big hint, and I won't bother you anymore. I really do like you … a lot. Hopefully you'll give me another chance.

Julie sat on her bed, staring at the screen. *I'm partly to blame. What the hell am I doing?*

Julie: I'm sorry too, and I like you too. Maybe we can take it slow?

Larry: Slow is fine with me! I just want to be in your life.

Julie: Would you like to come over for dinner on Friday?

Larry: I'd love to!

Julie: How about 7:00?

Larry: I'll see you then.

Julie: ☺

The doorbell rang. *Probably the UPS guy.* She stood and glanced at the clock on her dresser. *Still time for lunch before waiting on people eating lunch. Nothing worse than serving food on an empty stomach.* The doorbell rang again. She bounded down the steps in stocking feet.

Dan peered inside through the sidelight windows. Julie opened the door.

"I thought you were here," Dan said, holding a sealed envelope.

Julie exhaled. "What can I do for you, Dan?"

He held out the envelope. "This is for you."

Julie took the letter with her name on it. "What's this?" *I hope to God he's not inviting me somewhere.*

Dan pursed his lips. "Someone complained about your blinds in the living room. Remember when I warned you about this? I wanted to hand deliver the letter, so you didn't lose any days to comply, waiting for the mail."

Julie curled her lip in contempt and opened the letter. She skimmed it and glared at Dan. "Are you really going to fine me if I don't straighten my blinds?"

Dan held out his hands. "It's not up to me to decide. I have to enforce the rules. That's why I wanted to give this to you right away so you can fix it. I'd be happy to help, if you need a hand."

"I can handle it."

"Are you sure? Must be tough without a man around."

"I have to go, Dan. I'll fix it now."

"You have three days to—"

She shut the door. She walked over to her living room windows. Max had obviously tried to lower them to block the sun from the TV and had done it in a haphazard-Max sort of way. Julie fiddled with the strings, evening out the blinds. She lowered them all, so the windows were completely covered. She split one of the blinds and peered out the window. Dan stood on the sidewalk, staring at her. She stepped back from the window, a jolt of fear coursing through her veins. *What a creep.*

Julie's cell phone chimed. She fished it from her back pocket and checked the number. Her heart pounded as she answered.

"Hello, this is Julie Welch."

"Mrs. Welch, this is Principal Justine Taylor from Fairfax High School. I'm afraid we have a serious problem with Max. He's been removed from class and will not be allowed to return. You need to come to school and pick up your son, as he will not be allowed to ride the bus either."

"What? Why?"

"I need you to pick up your son, Mrs. Welch. We can go over the specifics when you arrive."

"I'll be there in ten minutes."

Julie called her boss to let him know she'd be late. She raced to the high school and parked in a visitor spot near the front entrance. She found the front office and entered, breathless. Two women sat behind an L-shaped wooden counter. Julie approached the older one.

"I'm Julie Welch. I'm here to pick up my son, Max."

The administrative assistant nodded, her face stern. "Have a seat," she said, motioning to the wooden chairs along the wall.

The assistant made a phone call from the desktop phone. She hung up and stepped out from behind the counter. "Principal Taylor will see you now."

She led Julie down a short hallway to the principal's office. Julie's legs felt weak, her stomach queasy. The assistant tapped on the door and opened it.

A tall dark-skinned woman stood from behind the desk. "Mrs. Welch, please come in," Principal Taylor said.

Max was slouched in one of the chairs in front of the desk. The assistant shut the door behind Julie as she approached the principal. Principal Taylor extended her hand across the desk. They shook hands.

"Please sit down," the principal said.

Julie sat in the seat next to Max. She tried to make eye contact with her son, but he stared at the floor.

"Max, would you like to tell your mother why you're in trouble?" Principal Taylor said.

Max looked up at his principal. "Not really."

Principal Taylor frowned at Max and turned her gaze to Julie. "Max created a cartoon parody of the school."

Julie's stomach relaxed. "He's in trouble for making a cartoon?"

"No." Principal Taylor pursed her lips. She wore a gray skirt suit, her hair pulled back in a tight bun. "He's in trouble for distributing the cartoon and inciting a food fight, a fist fight, and a walkout. Furthermore, his cartoon prominently featured a famous politician's daughter. This is extremely embarrassing for the school, especially after the recent tragedy her father suffered."

Julie's eyes were like saucers. "I don't understand."

Principal Taylor turned her laptop around and pushed it toward the edge of her desk. "Maybe you should watch it." She looked at Max. "Max, play the video for your mother."

Max blew out a breath. He stood and left clicked the video. He slouched back in his chair. Julie scooted to the edge of her seat, her eyes glued to the screen.

The cartoon started with a close-up of an animated version of Max, with one side of his mouth raised in contempt as he stood on the street corner. His likeness was remarkable. The character had the same wire-rim glasses, young round face, and straight hair combed forward. Cartoon Max was thinner than real life Max. A bus with bars on the windows pulled up beside Max. Fairfax County Public Prison System was written on the side of the bus. Cartoon Max put his hood over his head and stepped on the bus.

A dark boxy building loomed large in the distance. The bus stopped at the gray brick structure. There was a lightning strike in the distance, illuminating the sign in front, Fairfax Public Prison. The kids exited the bus and were met with cattle-prod-wielding teachers. The male teachers all wore khaki pants and blue polo shirts. The females wore khaki skirts and blue blouses. Some of the unruly kids were shocked with the cattle prods and forced inside.

Inside, cartoon Max was the only kid who walked alone. The other kids walked in packs. The kids in each gang dressed the same and had the same skin color. Max's skin was brighter and redder than the other white kids. As Max passed the gangs, they threatened him.

"We're gonna beat your bitch ass," said the gang of white kids.

"We're gonna fuck you up, white boy," said the gang of black kids.

"We're gonna kill you, faggot," said the gang of brown kids.

Cartoon Max opened his locker. His textbooks were stacked with the bindings visible. The titles were, *USA #1*, *The Military Saves the Day Again*, *All Wars Are Good Wars*, *Love It or Leave It*, *Be a Good Citizen or Else*. He opened *USA #1*. Stashed in the binding was a plastic shiv, carved to a point on one end and wrapped with athletic tape on the other. He glanced left and right and shoved it in the front pocket of his sweatshirt.

Max shut his locker. A few lockers away, a muscular teen boy with Justin Bieber hair leaned dangerously close to a busty brunette.

The boy said, "It'll be our little secret."

The girl said, "What about Ellen?"

"What she doesn't know won't hurt her."

"What about Colton?"

"He's a little bitch. What's he gonna do about it?" The boy stared at Max. "What the fuck are you lookin' at?"

Max went to class and sat in the back row. The female teacher made a list on the whiteboard. The list was titled Rules for Success.

1. Never question my authority or the authority of anyone in power.
2. Patriotism is the highest virtue.
3. The collective good is more important than the individual.
4. If you see something, say something.
5. To be good, we must follow **ALL** the rules.
6. The law = morality.
7. You are good if you follow the rules, bad if you don't.
8. It is your civic duty to exercise your right to vote.
9. The United States wages war to spread freedom and democracy.
10. Pay your taxes, shut the fuck up, and die.

After class, the cartoon showed Max pushing a tray along a steel lunch counter. Gray slop was heaped on his plate by a hair-netted old woman. Max pulled back his sleeve and extended his wrist to the cashier. The cashier scanned his barcode tattoo.

Max surveyed the lunchroom, balancing his tray of slop. Kids were segregated based on skin color. He sat by himself at an empty table. He stirred his slop, and little white grubs emerged. Max pushed away his tray.

A gang of white kids sat down at the opposite end of the table. He glanced at the kid with Justin Bieber hair. The kid was now with an attractive blonde.

"Oh, Ellen, you're the only one for me," the Justin Bieber–haired kid said. "I love you."

Ellen smiled. "I love you too, Tyler. You're the best boyfriend. I totally trust you."

Tyler glowered at Max. "What the fuck are you lookin' at, faggot?"

Max shrugged and placed his hand in his sweatshirt pouch pocket. Tyler stood up. He was tall and muscular. He grabbed Max by the collar of his sweatshirt, yanked him from his seat, and tossed him on the floor. Tyler bent over, put his hands around Max's neck, and squeezed. Max's face turned beet red. In the background, two female teachers were talking, oblivious to the fight.

Max reached into his pocket and removed the handmade shiv. He plunged it into Tyler's stomach. A close-up of Tyler's face showed how his eyes went wide with fright as he looked down at the shiv in his stomach.

Tyler let go of Max's neck, and he rolled out from under Tyler. Max gasped for air, and Tyler collapsed to the floor.

The female teachers glared at Max and pressed a big red button on the wall. The siren wailed, and all the kids lay face down on the linoleum, their hands extended. A couple of police officers stalked toward Max, who ran from the lunchroom, down a long hallway. At the end was a door with a window. Sunlight streamed through the window. The police officers chased Max as he sprinted for the door, the sunlight getting brighter with each step.

He reached the door and yanked on it. It didn't budge. The door was locked and chained. He turned around. The police officers approached, pointing Tasers.

"There's no way out," a police officer said.

They fired their Tasers, and Max fell to the ground, his body convulsing with electricity. The police officers dragged Max down the hall, away from the sunlight. They deposited him in an office that looked very much like the one Julie sat in, with bookshelves, a wooden desk, and a well-dressed black woman sitting behind it.

Cartoon Max slumped in the very same chair he sat in now. In the cartoon a placard on the desk read Warden Taylor.

"Max, Max, Max," Warden Taylor said. "What am I to do with you? You're a very poor student. You refuse to learn what we teach you. We have the correct answers. Don't you understand that we determine what is right and what is wrong? We have that power. And you?" She cackled. "You have nothing."

Max narrowed his eyes. "I can think for myself."

"We'll fix that." She picked up the phone on her desk and spoke into the receiver. "Give him the pills."

The door opened, and four teachers entered the room. They restrained Max as they force-fed him pills. Max thrashed and gasped, but he swallowed the pills.

The cartoon cut to Max walking in a herd of white kids, his skin no longer bright and tinged with red. It was the dull white of his gang.

The credits rolled, red lettering over a black screen:

Writer: Max Welch
Director: Max Welch

Voice-Over: Max Welch
Production: Max Welch
Animation: Max Welch

A quote appeared on-screen under the credits.

> They don't want a population of citizens capable of critical thinking. They don't want well-informed, well-educated people capable of critical thinking. They're not interested in that. That doesn't help them. That's against their interests.
> You know what they want? Obedient workers. People who are just smart enough to run the machines and do the paperwork, and just dumb enough to passively accept all these increasingly shitty jobs ...
> —George Carlin

The laptop screen went black. Julie scooted back in her chair, her face drawn. Principal Taylor shut the laptop. "Your son distributed this cartoon to a handful of students," Principal Taylor said, "who shared it with more students, who shared it with more students. Just before lunch, we had a fight in the hall between Tyler Lawson and Colton Blankenship, that was instigated by your son's cartoon. At lunch, we had a food fight inspired by the cafeteria scene. After lunch, we had over one hundred students leave school."

"I'm sure Max didn't intend for this to happen," Julie said. "He's normally very well-behaved. He was just being creative. I'm sure this was unintentional." Julie glanced at her son. He stared at the floor, his arms crossed. "Max?"

"Is that true, Max?" Principal Taylor asked.

Max raised his head, glaring at his principal. "The result was *exactly* what I wanted."

Julie gasped. "Max."

Principal Taylor sighed. "I'm suspending Max for the rest of the school year."

"Will this be on his permanent record? I'm hoping he can get a scholarship, because college is out of reach for—"

"Max will be required to disclose this suspension on his college applications. I'm sorry. Colleges *will* be aware."

Julie's eyes were glassy. "Please, Principal Taylor, please just give him another chance. He's a good kid. He lost his dad. Things have been hard. Deep down, he's a good kid. Please."

"Mrs. Welch, the cartoon showed your son stabbing another student. I sympathize, I do, but just about every discipline problem I handle has a sad backstory. I can't give your son special treatment, and I cannot in good conscience allow Max to be in this school."

"So, that's it?"

"I'm sorry, Mrs. Welch. There's nothing I can do. He is welcome to return next school year. He *will* have to meet regularly with one of our counselors."

"I'm not coming back to this shithole," Max said.

"Max," Julie said, glowering at her son. "Have you lost your mind?"

Max shook his head. "No, I've found it."

"I think it's best you take your son home before he digs himself a deeper hole," Principal Taylor said.

Julie led Max to the car, tears still in her eyes. Inside the car, her hands shook as she slipped the keys into the ignition. Max slouched into the passenger seat next to her. Julie placed her head in her hands and cried.

"Mom, it's gonna be okay," Max said.

Julie raised her head from her hands and turned to Max. She sniffled. "I don't understand why you would deliberately do this."

Max shrugged.

Julie wiped her eyes with the side of her index finger, smudging her mascara. "That's not good enough, young man. I demand to know why."

"Can we just go home?"

Julie shook her head. "Not until you talk to me. Really talk to me."

"You wouldn't understand."

"Does George have something to do with this?"

Max scowled. "This isn't his fault."

"All I know is that, since you met him, you're a completely different kid. You used to be so sweet."

"Where did that get me?"

"I don't know. I can't help you if you won't talk to me. Please honey, tell me."

"I walk around all day on edge because someone's gonna push me or smack me on the back of the head or give me a shoulder in the hallway—"

"We can tell Principal Taylor. It might change—"

"Can you just listen?"

"Sorry."

"The physical stuff isn't even the worst part. They laugh at me. They make fun of me. Even the girls. I can't take it anymore." His eyes were wet.

A few tears streaked down Julie's face. "When you fell, it wasn't an accident, was it?"

Max wiped his tears with the side of his fist, lifting his glasses from his nose in the process. He shook his head and pushed his glasses back into place.

"We're going back to Principal Taylor," Julie said. "She's going to get a piece of my mind."

"Mom, stop. I'm not doing that. It just makes it worse. And he never touched me anyway."

"Who never touched you?"

"That asshole Tyler."

"From the cartoon?"

Max nodded. "He's always messing with me. I was scared, and I backed away from him. I forgot that the stairs were behind me, and I fell."

"He can't do that. We'll get him expelled."

"Tyler will just say he didn't do anything, and they'll believe him, because everyone'll back him up. He's gonna get in trouble for the fight anyway."

"There has to be something I can do."

"It's over, Mom. Let me go virtual next year."

"What about college?"

"I don't wanna go to a regular college anyway. It's too expensive. And a degree doesn't even get you a job anyway."

"What do you want to do then?"

"Did you like my cartoon?"

Julie mock-frowned. "Is that a serious question?"

"Seriously. Forget about the fact that it got me into trouble. Did you think it was good?"

"It was very good." She smirked. "So good that it caused a riot."

He laughed. "I wanna be an animator. Technical schools are pretty cheap. Do you think I could do that?"

Julie put her hand on top of his. "Honey, you're very bright and very talented. You can do anything you put your mind to."

21: George and Consider the Source

George drove along US 15 South toward Virginia. Five motorcycles were in his box trailer. He drove in the right lane, passing cows grazing on pastures and thigh-high cornfields. He listened to a podcast through his truck stereo speakers.

"Welcome back to the *Abnormal Psych Podcast*. I'm your host, Everett Bush. Today we're revisiting the fascinating work of the late social psychologist Stanley Milgram. His most important work in my opinion was his experiment that measured obedience to authority figures.

"The experiment went like this. Individuals were brought into the lab and told that they were studying memory. Three people were involved in the experiment, the learner, the teacher, and the experimenter. The learner posed as another volunteer but was actually an actor. The learner was hooked up to an electroshock machine. The teacher, who was the only real volunteer and the subject of the experiment, was instructed by the experimenter to ask the learner a series of questions. When the learner answered incorrectly, the teacher was instructed by the experimenter to administer an electric shock. Prior to the experiment, the volunteer was given a shock to demonstrate the shock strength at the lowest level.

"The shocks increased in strength as the questioning and incorrect answers progressed. The actor in a separate booth could be heard wailing and crying out in pain each time the teacher administered a shock. After a certain number of voltage-level increases, the actor banged on the wall and complained about a heart condition. After several times banging on the wall and complaining about his heart, all responses by the learner stopped.

"Prior to conducting the experiment, Milgram polled forty psychiatrists from a medical school, and they believed that less than 1 percent of the subjects would administer the highest shock on the board.

"Throughout the experiment, the teachers showed signs of stress and tension, but two-thirds administered the final 450-volt shock. Milgram tested 636 subjects in eighteen different variation studies. In one variation, the uniformed experimenter was called away, and a nonuniformed participant took his place. Only 20 percent obeyed in this variation study. Milgram also found that 92.5 percent shocked to the maximum voltage when given an assistant to instruct, versus administering the shocks themselves."

George glanced at his fuel gauge. He took the next exit and followed signs for diesel.

"Milgram's experiment has been recreated around the world. Thomas Blass of the University of Maryland performed a meta-analysis of the experiment. He found that the percentage of subjects who inflicted fatal voltages averaged 61 percent in US studies and 66 percent in non-US studies.

"In *The Perils of Obedience*, Milgram wrote, 'Ordinary people, simply doing their jobs, and without any particular hostility on their part, can become agents in a terrible destructive process. Moreover, even when the destructive effects of their work become patently clear, and they are asked to carry out actions incompatible with fundamental standards of morality, relatively few people have the resources needed to resist authority.'

"Almost two-thirds of Americans administered a fatal shock, simply because someone in authority told them to do so. These people were not forced to deliver the shocks. They were not threatened. When I discuss Nazi Germany, people invariably think *they'd* be different. Milgram's experiment proves otherwise."

George parked next to a fuel pump with diesel at $2.55 a gallon. *Prices are up 10 percent in two months.* He cut the engine, stopped the podcast, and grabbed his phone from the cradle. He refueled and parked his truck in the back of the strip mall parking lot. In addition to the gas station, the mall had a grocery store, a Subway, and a couple of vacancies.

George locked his truck and hiked across the parking lot to the Subway. He ordered his food and paid. He sat in a lonely booth near the window, eating his sub and checking his email.

From: Katie@KatieTalk.com
To: GeorgeChapman2222@gmail.com
Subject: I'm sorry

Mr. Chapman,

I know you're probably mad at me. I took advantage of your kindness, and I'm very sorry. There's no excuse for what I did. If it's any consolation, in the video you were smart and patient, and I was mean and ignorant. Again I'm very sorry.

By the way, *The Creature from Jekyll Island* has been eye-opening to say the least. I'm not sure I want this information. I'm having trouble finding a perspective I can live with. I suppose it shouldn't be surprising that this isn't mainstream knowledge or taught in our schools.

My blog and YouTube channel have been undergoing quite a transition. I've lost a lot of subscribers, but I've gained many more. The new subscribers tend to be of the Anarchist/anti-government persuasion. I'm not sure if they showed up just to heckle me or if they think I'll have more George Chapman videos. Incidentally the video we did of you is the most watched video of the past week.

I would love to do more videos with you. I may not agree with everything you believe, but I'm coming around to some things. I do what I do because I care about people, and I think people will benefit from your message. Let me know. I will bend to your schedule.

Sincerely,
Katie Fitzgerald

George tapped reply.

From: GeorgeChapman2222@gmail.com
To: Katie@KatieTalk.com
Subject: Re: I'm sorry

Katie,

You lied to me. Honesty is something I greatly value. People are fallible, and I understand why you did what you did, but fame, vanity, and greed are not valid reasons to defraud someone. Having said that, I appreciate your contrition, and I see that you do care about others.

I don't have a message. I try to see the world as it is. I do that with logic and reason and, most important, by learning from others who are a heck of a lot smarter than me.

I'd like to help you out, but I don't think I'm the right messenger. Others are vocal and would be happy to appear in your videos.

Good Luck,
George Chapman

George tapped Send. He opened another email.

From: MarleneCooke@wnn.com
To: GeorgeChapman2222@gmail.com
Subject: Debate Appearance

Mr. Chapman,

My name is Marlene Cooke. I am a producer for the WNN television program *Crosstalk*. In July, we will be debating policies for the prevention of domestic terrorism. Given your political views and personal experience as a victim of domestic terrorism, I think you'd make a fabulous guest.

Our multiguest debate format allows for more alternative viewpoints than most news programs. This would be a terrific opportunity and platform for your message.

I know your time is extremely valuable. I am authorized to offer compensation for your appearance. Please let me know if you are interested.

Sincerely,
Marlene Cooke
Producer, *Crosstalk*

George tapped Reply. He thumb-typed, *No thank you*, and tapped Send. George gathered his trash and deposited it in the nearby bin. His phone buzzed as he returned to the table. He sat down and checked the text.

Max: You want the good news or the bad news?

George: The good news.

Max: My mom is letting me go virtual.

George: That's great. Good for you.

Max: I also got suspended.

George: Really? Why?

Max: It was awesome. I did this video. Watch this **LINK**.

George watched the video on his phone.

George: I'm impressed. The story, the production value. VERY well done. You're talented. There's no doubt about that. I'm assuming that your school obtained the video?

Max: I released it to some kids who I knew would spread it around. The principal got mad because it caused a fist fight, a food fight, and a walkout. Also because the Ellen character is Ellen Bradley, Congressman Bradley's daughter.

George: And the Tyler character?

Max: Her boyfriend.

George: And?

Max: He's a bully.

George: Sounds like you killed two birds with one stone.

Max: Huh?

George: I'm proud of you for standing up for yourself. It took a lot of courage. Hopefully you're not in too much trouble.

Max: My mom is fine. I told her the truth, like you said I should.

George: I read this book by Professor Randy Pausch, who was dying. He wanted to give one final lecture before he died. At the end, he said, "If I could only give three words of advice they would be, 'Tell the truth.' If I got three more words, they would be, 'All the time.'"

Max: Thanks, George.

George: You're welcome, Max. And here I was bracing myself for bad news.

Max: That wasn't the bad news. I think it's crap by the way. <u>**Link**</u>

George tapped the link. A white-haired man stood on the stoop of a sprawling stucco rambler. He was tanned, muscular, and wore a tank top and shorts.

A young woman shoved a microphone in his face. "Mr. Chapman, would you like to comment on your son's recent statements that the US government is a terrorist organization?"

He frowned, his forehead erupting in wrinkles. "It's Colonel Chapman."

"Colonel Chapman, do you agree with your son's statement that the US government is a terrorist organization?"

"Of course not."

"Your son described the US government as a massive extortion and counterfeiting racket. Do you support his statements?"

"I do not."

"Your son blamed the US military for killing millions of innocent people overseas. Do you support his statements?"

Colonel Chapman crossed his beefy arms. His weathered face reflected his sixty-five years on Earth, but his physique was of a much younger man. "Look, lady, his statements are idiotic. What on earth would possess you to think I would support 'em?"

"Do you feel responsible for your son's anti-American views?"

"You need to get your facts straight. First of all, my son is Captain Robert Chapman. I haven't seen George since he was little. If it wasn't for you people, I wouldn't know him from a hole in the ground."

"Why did you abandon your son?"

He glowered at the reporter. "If you're lookin' for a culprit, I suggest you look into his mother. Now get the hell off my stoop." He retreated into the house, slamming the door behind him.

The video cut to a USN news desk and a well-coiffed anchorman alongside a mugshot of a straggly haired waif of a woman.

The anchorman said, "George Chapman's mother was Vicki Banks, who died of a heroin overdose in the year 2000. She had two felony drug convictions and served two years in a state penitentiary. A source close to the Banks family told us that George Chapman moved out of his childhood home as a sixteen-year-old and failed to graduate high school. He was described as awkward and a loner."

22: John and Absence Makes the Heart Grow Colder

John blasted Guns N' Roses on his car stereo as he drove through the posh neighborhood of enormous houses with checkerboard-striped lawns. He waved at the secret service detail parked out front. His house was a classic redbrick colonial with black shutters. He parked in the garage and shut the door behind him with a press of the remote.

He entered the house from the garage, the smell of honey-glazed salmon wafting in the air. Linda readied four plates at the center island. Her eyes flicked to John, then back to the plates.

"I didn't make you a plate," Linda said, not looking at him. "You're never home for dinner."

John glanced at the extra piece of fish still in the pan. "That's okay. I'll fix mine." He moved toward her, like a hunter hoping not to frighten his prey.

She froze, her body rigid as he kissed her on the cheek.

John took his briefcase and keys to his office. He took off his suit jacket, placed it on the back of the desk chair, and returned to the kitchen. He grabbed a plate from the cupboard and served himself the last piece of salmon and a heap of peas and mashed potatoes.

"Dinner's ready," Linda called out from the bottom of the stairs.

"Coming," Bobby called back.

"Can you get your sisters?"

"I'll get 'em."

"Want me to get the drinks?" John asked.

Linda turned from the stairs, barely glancing at John. "I got it." She bristled past him for the cupboard. She removed four glasses and carried two to the refrigerator. She filled them with filtered water from the refrigerator door.

John grabbed the other two glasses, queueing behind Linda. "I'm sorry I haven't been home lately."

She shrugged. "It's not a problem for me." She took the water to the center island.

John filled his glasses. The kids bounded down the steps.

"Dad," Bobby said. He ran across the hardwood and hugged John.

"Hey, buddy," John said, grinning, holding out the waters, trying not to spill them. "How was school today?"

Bobby let go. He wore a T-shirt with an angry T. rex and *Bobosaurus* scrawled underneath. "It was good. Did you know that a *Micropachycephalo-saurus* has the longest dinosaur name?"

John smirked. "A what?"

The girls entered the kitchen with sullen faces.

Bobby enunciated. "*Micro-pachy-cephalo-saurus*. It means, small thick-headed lizard. Mrs. Jordan said it wasn't relevant. I think it's only 'cause she couldn't say it. Did you know that a male T. rex had a twelve-foot-long penis?"

John laughed.

Linda turned to her son. "What did I tell you about saying things for shock value?"

Bobby frowned. "To not do it. I didn't tell Mrs. Jordan about the T. rex penis, but I wanted to."

Linda sighed. "Progress." She looked at her daughters. "Grab your plates, girls. It's getting cold."

The Bradley family sat at the wooden dining table, a chandelier overhead. The girls picked at their food; John and Bobby devoured theirs.

"I don't like fish skin," Bobby said.

"You don't have to eat it," Linda replied.

Bobby pushed out his lips and hung a piece of fish skin, like a scaly mustache.

John chuckled.

"Don't play with your food," Linda said.

Charlotte twisted her chubby face. "Gross." She pushed away her half-eaten plate.

John set down his fork. "I was thinking that, after dinner, we could all watch a movie and make ice cream sundaes."

"Yes." Bobby thrust his fist into the air.

"May I be excused?" Charlotte asked.

"You're not hungry?" Linda asked.

Charlotte glared at her brother. "No."

"Okay. Take your plate to the kitchen."

"What about the movie?" John asked Charlotte.

"I have homework," Charlotte replied and left the dining room.

"Ellen? You want to pick the movie?" John asked.

Ellen pushed peas around her plate. "I have homework too."

"Yes, I get to pick," Bobby said.

"It's a school night," Linda said. "Not tonight."

"Aww, Mom."

John exhaled. "Your mother's right. We'll do it this weekend."

"No, we won't," Bobby said.

"Sure we will," John said.

"No, we won't. It'll be just like the other times."

"I'm sorry, buddy. My job's very demanding. I promise I'll do my best to be home this weekend. How's that sound?"

Bobby narrowed his eyes at his dad and went back to his food, now crushing his peas instead of eating them. "Whatever," he said under his breath.

"How's school, Ellen?" John asked.

"Fine," she said, not looking up. Her long blond hair hung mere inches from her food. Her eyes flicked to Linda. "May I be excused?"

"You may," Linda replied.

Ellen started to stand.

"Not yet," John said.

Ellen sat back down.

"Something's obviously bothering you," John said.

"So?" Ellen said.

"So, I'd like to know what it is. Maybe I can help."

"I don't wanna go to Fairfax anymore."

"Why?"

She shrugged.

"Ellen."

"What, Dad? You wanna help me? Let me go to Saint Stevens." She glanced at her mother. "May I be excused now?"

Linda nodded. Ellen took her plate to the kitchen and trudged upstairs.

"I'm done too," Bobby announced. "Can I watch TV?"

"May I," Linda said.

"*May I* watch TV?"

"You may."

Bobby took his plate to the kitchen and headed off for the family room.

"What's wrong with Ellen?" John asked Linda.

"There was an incident at school," Linda replied.

John furrowed his brow. "What do you mean, an *incident*?"

"One of her classmates made a cartoon that depicted Ellen and her boyfriend, Tyler. In the cartoon, Tyler was stabbed to death."

John's eyes widened. "Who made this cartoon?"

"Max Welch. He's in Ellen's grade. Ellen said the boy is always staring at her, but she doesn't know him."

"Is he dangerous?"

"I don't know, but Ellen's beside herself. The cartoon also showed Tyler seeing another girl. I guess it was true because it caused a fight between Tyler and the other girl's boyfriend. Ellen broke up with Tyler. She feels humiliated by the whole thing."

"She shouldn't feel humiliated. She didn't do anything wrong."

"Well, she does." Linda glared at John. "It makes perfect sense that she feels humiliated, because that's what it feels like when someone you love betrays you."

"She's fifteen. She doesn't know what love is."

"If you say so."

"I hope this kid was expelled."

"Principal Taylor told me that he was suspended for the rest of the school year."

John scowled. "That's barely a punishment. How many school days are left?"

"Not very many."

"So he'll be back next year?"

"Yes."

"I'll take care of it."

23: Katie and Hypocrisy

Katie sat in a booth, eating a salad topped with shitake mushrooms. Across from her were two attractive blond women. They also had salads but seemed more interested in the fried onions they shared.

"You two are coming to Todd's company barbecue, aren't you?" Penny asked. "It's on the twenty-third."

Penny wore a sleeveless red dress that buttoned in the front. She had straight blond hair parted down the middle and a symmetrical face. Todd certainly had his trophy.

"I have to check my schedule," Katie replied.

"I have my sister's wedding, remember?" Lindsey said. She was dressed in all white, with bright red lipstick.

Penny pushed out her lower lip. "Oh, come on. It'll be dreadful without you two."

"I'd much rather go to your hubby's barbecue. Believe me," Lindsey said. "My sister's wedding's in Missouri. Did I tell you what her redneck fiancé posted on Facebook?"

Katie didn't respond.

"I can only imagine," Penny said.

"It was some stupid meme," Lindsey said. "It said, 'Liberal Democrats' at the top, and underneath it said something like, 'Let's take a working man's income and give it to someone who refuses to work.'"

Penny shook her head, frowning. "That's just like Todd's best friend, Wade. Total Republican. I mean, they've had the White House for the last two terms, and what have they done but create more war, more poverty, and more global warming?"

"They've also had congress," Katie added.

"Exactly, they've had congress too," Penny said.

Lindsey said, "My sister's fiancé also posted a meme that had a picture of some old guy, and it said something like, 'Global warming? In my day, we called it summer.'"

"When did we become a nation of idiots and assholes?" Penny asked.

"I don't know, but I'll be at a wedding with over one hundred of them. There's no way I'm getting through it sober."

Katie sighed, her face turned down.

"What?" Lindsey asked.

Katie shrugged. "I didn't say anything."

"You just sighed like you didn't agree, and you've been cranky this whole lunch."

"Forget it."

"She's right," Penny said. "I'm not trying to be mean, but you have been acting bitchy. What's going on with you?"

"You two complain about global warming and these idiots, but what are you actually doing about it?"

Lindsey crossed her arms over her chest. "I post things to bring awareness on my Facebook page. I have two thousand friends."

"That's not doing anything. That's talking about it."

Penny scowled at Katie. "What are *you* doing about it?"

"Nothing. I'm no better. I live in a huge inefficient house, just like you two. I buy a bunch of shit I don't need. We're part of the problem, not the solution."

"Jesus, Katie, you don't have to be so dramatic," Lindsey said. "Is this about Declan?"

Katie shook her head. "No. I'm just tired of the hypocrisy. Who's to say we would have been better off with the Democrats? Maybe we would, but maybe things would be just as fucked-up as they are now. Maybe we're not asking the right questions."

"Now you sound like the Anarchist I just unfriended," Lindsey said. "You sound so nihilistic. It's not becoming."

Katie stood from the table, riffling through her purse.

"Where are you going?" Penny asked.

Katie slapped a twenty on the table. "I don't know." She walked away.

* * *

Katie sat on her couch with her laptop warming her legs.

From: Katie@KatieTalk.com
To: GeorgeChapman2222@gmail.com
Subject: I don't know why I'm contacting you

George,

You told me to call you George once, and this doesn't feel like a Mr. Chapman sort of email. I want you to know that, since we met, my life has been flipped upside down and shaken. I don't blame you. Well, I suppose I do, but I know it's not your fault. You're simply the messenger. The problem is, the message sucks. If I could go back in time and not know about the contents of *The Creature from Jekyll Island*, I might choose to be ignorant.

My father is the CEO of USA Bank. My family and I have profited off the counterfeiting operation. My whole life I thought I was a good person. All I ever wanted to do was help. I'm not helpful. I'm vapid and materialistic and arrogant. I'm just another leech on the productive efforts of people.
I feel lost. I don't know who I am, and I don't know what to do.

Sincerely,
Katie Fitzgerald

Katie clicked Send and set her laptop on the coffee table. She grabbed the blanket off the couch, pulled it around her, and drifted off to sleep. A couple hours later, her eyes fluttered and then opened. She reached for her laptop and set it on the couch next to her. She revived it and checked her email.

From: GeorgeChapman2222@gmail.com
To: Katie@KatieTalk.com
Subject: Re: I don't know why I'm contacting you

Katie,

I'm sorry that you're having a tough time. It is painful to learn something unpleasant, especially something that makes you question your worldview. This happened to me as a child, when my father left. I didn't know it then, but I went through Elisabeth Kübler-Ross's five stages of grief.

You probably know this, but the stages are denial, anger, bargaining, depression, and acceptance. The good news is, it sounds like you've moved through the first three stages rather quickly. It sounds like you're stuck on what I think is the hardest part, depression.

You're a strong person, Katie. I'm confident that you'll reach acceptance, and you'll be healthier and happier in the long run.

As far as your family's wealth and how it was created, that's not your fault. People are kept in the dark by the media, education, government propaganda, and even friends and family. Now that you've been exposed to the light, what are you going to do? My guess would be that you'd do exactly what you want to do—help people. You'll just do it more effectively.

Good Luck,
George

24: Julie and Kill Him with Kindness

Julie left the restaurant, the afternoon sun warming her face. She wore her uniform—black pants and a white polo. Her phone chimed in her purse as she walked across the parking lot. Standing next to her car, she retrieved her phone. She checked the number, frowned, and answered.

"Hello, this is Julie Welch." Julie opened her car door and sat in the driver's seat.

"Mrs. Welch, this is Principal Taylor. Max's suspension has been upgraded to a possible expulsion. A hearing is set in two weeks. I was calling to let you know."

Julie's heart pounded. "I don't understand. You said he was suspended. Now he's expelled? What does this mean?"

"Nothing's been decided yet. The hearing in two weeks is to decide."

"What happens if Max is expelled?" Julie gripped the phone in one hand, her other balled into a fist.

"He won't be able to return to Fairfax High School, but there are alternative—"

"He's not coming back. He's going to attend cyberschool."

"Not if he's expelled. He won't be permitted to attend any activities sanctioned by this school. That includes school dances, extracurricular activities, and cyberschool."

Julie's face felt hot. "What's he supposed to do then?"

"Alternative schools have online programs."

"Did you know that Max was being bullied?"

"There were no reports—"

"He was being bullied. Every single day my son was being abused in *your*

151

school, and you throw him away like trash."

Principal Taylor spoke in a firm voice. "There's no need for—"

"Why the change? It doesn't make any sense."

"It's not a change. The initial punishment was to ensure the safety of the students and the faculty. The hearing for expulsion is standard procedure for an offense that involves death threats against another student."

Julie clenched her jaw. "This isn't right. Someone got to you, didn't they?"

"Mrs. Welch, this isn't Hollywood. My top priority is safety—"

"For who? Obviously not for Max."

"I can't help a student if I don't know about the problem."

"But you can throw him away when he causes trouble? Max made a cartoon. He didn't hurt anyone."

"Quite a few students were hurt by your son's cartoon."

"What about freedom of speech? Doesn't Max have freedom of speech?"

"In school, he doesn't."

"My son will *not* return to your school, so you can take your hearing and shove it up your ass." Julie ended the call with a shaky finger.

She drove to the grocery store and shopped in a daze, her thoughts dominated by Max's future or lack thereof. Afterward Julie drove home.

Cool air chilled her skin as she entered her townhome. Julie heaved grocery bags on the kitchen counter. She checked the thermostat, shook her head, and moved the setting from 65 to 72 degrees.

Julie stomped upstairs to Max's room and knocked.

"Come in," Max said.

Julie opened the door and stepped inside.

Max turned away from his laptop. A cartoon was on-screen of a crowd, a man behind a podium, and a banner that read George 2020.

"Don't touch the thermostat. The electric bills are very expensive." Julie narrowed her eyes at Max. "Do you understand me?"

Max blanched. "It gets hot upstairs."

"Then take your laptop downstairs."

"What about sleeping?"

"Sleep downstairs too if you have to."

"Is it really that much money?"

"In case you haven't noticed, we're not rich. Don't touch the thermostat."

He scowled. "Fine."

Julie pursed her lips. "I'm sorry for getting angry."

"Whatever."

Julie took a deep breath. "Principal Taylor called me. They're having a hearing to determine whether or not to expel you."

Max shrugged. "So what? I'm not going back there anyway."

"If you're expelled, you can't go there for cyberschool either."

"There's a bunch of cyberschools. Screw them."

Julie smirked. "Well, start looking for one."

Max smiled.

"Dinner's at seven." Julie turned for the door.

"Can I invite a friend to dinner?"

Julie turned to her son, her eyebrows raised. "On one condition."

"What?"

"Be nice to Larry tonight."

Max smacked his tongue off the roof of his mouth. "Does he have to come over?"

"Well, no, but I want him to. Be nice, okay?"

"Fine."

"Who's the friend? Someone you met at school?"

"No, I mostly talk to him online, but he's really nice."

Julie knitted her brow. "You have met him in person, haven't you?"

"I'm not stupid."

Julie put her hands on her hips. "You didn't answer my question."

"Yes, I've met him in person."

* * *

"I was hoping to get here earlier," Larry said, as he followed Julie into the kitchen. "It took me forever to get out of there because of a demonstration outside the IRS building."

"A demonstration?" Julie asked, opening the refrigerator.

"A bunch of protestors," Larry said.

"What were they protesting?" Julie scanned the inside of the fridge.

"Taxes."

"In June?" Julie placed a bag of lettuce on the counter and a pepper on the cutting board.

"Yes, I can't imagine what it'll be like next April. A bunch of them had signs that read Taxation Is Theft. Everyone hates taxes, but it's the price we pay to live in the greatest country in the world." Larry glanced around the kitchen. "So what can I do to help?"

"You can prepare the salad," Julie said, opening the fridge again. She snagged a red onion and a carrot, then set them on the counter. "Or you can just keep me company."

She turned around and looked at Larry. He wore khaki shorts, a tucked-in polo, and bright white sneakers. His legs were skinny, hairy, and almost as white as his shoes.

"Thank you for inviting me over," Larry said, moving closer and stepping into her personal space.

"You're welcome. It's nothing fancy."

"I know you want to take it slow, which I'm totally okay with but"—he sucked in his lower lip—"is it okay if I kiss you?"

She nodded, and he pressed his lips to hers. The kiss was soft and tender, almost chaste. Larry stepped back.

She smiled.

"I really like you, Julie. I want you to know that."

Her face felt hot. "I like you too, Larry."

He grinned. "I'll do the salad."

"Great. I'll work on the chicken."

Julie opened the cupboard and removed a glass baking dish.

"Do these need to be washed?" Larry asked.

"They do."

Larry brushed against her backside on his way to the sink, a pepper and carrot in hand.

"I hope you don't mind, but Max is bringing a friend to dinner," Julie said.

Larry shook the excess water from the veggies and returned to the cutting board. "That's probably a good thing."

"Why's that?"

Larry grabbed a knife from the block. He stared at the large kitchen knife. "I know he's not especially fond of me."

"That's not true," Julie said.

Larry cut into the pepper. "I'm pretty good at reading people."

"I'm sorry. It's not you. He's going through a tough time right now."

Larry shook his head. "It's totally understandable given the circumstances.

I have a plan." He turned to Julie, holding up the knife.

Her eyes widened.

"I'm going to kill him with kindness."

25: George and Guess Who's Coming to Dinner

"Take 495 North for seven miles," the GPS said, in a female voice. George drove in the right lane, the traffic heavy. A podcast played through his stereo speakers.

"This is Gary Cook of the *Alt News Podcast*, providing vital information in a changing world. It's Friday, June 15, 2018. Robert Frost once said, 'A bank is a place where they lend you an umbrella in fair weather and ask for it back when it begins to rain.'

"Today I will examine banking. To fully understand banking and the Federal Reserve System, we must understand the wizard behind the curtain. We must understand fractional reserve banking and how money is created in our economy. Pay attention because this impacts everyone.

"Let's say you move to a new town, where a new bank's opened. You deposit $1,000 into the bank. You, as the depositor, now have a $1,000 asset, your bank account, and the bank has a $1,000 liability, your same bank account. A federal rule permits banks to lend 90 percent of their deposits to people who wish to borrow money. In reality banks often loan closer to 100 percent, but, in the spirit of simplicity, let's stick to the rule.

"Banks make a profit by charging a higher interest to borrowers than they pay in interest to depositors. Currently savings accounts yield less than 1 percent, while a car loan would probably be 5 percent or so, depending on your credit rating. Banks profit from the difference or the spread.

"Our fictional bank is quick to lend 90 percent of your $1,000 to your new neighbors. Your neighbor borrows $900 and buys a butchered hog from a farmer. The farmer then deposits the $900 into the bank. Another neighbor borrows 90 percent of the $900, which is $810. The neighbor buys groceries, and the grocer deposits the money in the bank, and like magic 90 percent of the $810 is available for loan. The next neighbor can borrow $729. And on and on it goes. This is fractional reserve banking, and this is how banks can and do turn $1,000 into $10,000.

"You might be wondering what would happen if all the depositors came into the bank and withdrew their deposits. There is only $1,000 on reserve, so most of the depositors would not receive their money. This is called a bank run, and it's happened many times throughout history.

"My explanation still has two problems. If everyone repays their loans all at once, all the cash money in the system is extinguished, … but what about the interest on the loans, and where the heck did the original $1,000 come from?

"For that answer, we need to take a look at the Federal Reserve. When the US government wishes to spend more money than it has, which is a common occurrence, the US Treasury Department will print Treasury bills, bonds, and notes, which are the same thing with different maturities and interest rates. For example, if you purchased a one-year bond with a face value of $100 and an interest rate of 2 percent, in one year, at the maturity date, the US Treasury will pay you $100 plus $2 in interest. These bonds, bills, and notes are sold in scheduled auctions. They are mostly purchased by banks, other large financial institutions, and the central banks of other countries.

"In the auction example, we still don't have any *new* money. New money is created when the Federal Reserve buys a Treasury bond, bill, or note from a bank. When the Federal Reserve makes this purchase, it pays for the bond with money created out of *thin air*.

"I know it sounds crazy, but here's a quote from a Federal Reserve article. 'When you or I write a check, there must be sufficient funds in our account to cover the check, but, when the Federal Reserve writes a check, there is no bank deposit on which the check is drawn. When the Federal Reserve writes a check, it is creating money.'"

"Take Exit 236 West toward Fairfax," Miss GPS said.

George exited the beltway.

"Take 236 West for two miles," Miss GPS said.

Gary Cook continued. "G. Edward Griffin in *The Creature from Jekyll Island* wrote, 'The bottom line is that congress and the banking cartel—the Federal Reserve—have entered into a partnership in which the cartel has the privilege of collecting interest on money which it creates out of nothing, a perpetual override on every American dollar that exists in the world. Congress, on the other hand, has access to unlimited funding without having to tell the voters their taxes are being raised through the process of inflation.'

"The Federal Reserve doesn't simply buy Treasury bonds. Since 2009, the Fed has purchased over four-trillion-dollars' worth of mortgage-backed securities. These purchases have made the Federal Reserve the single largest owner of real estate in the United States. Their recent scheme to purchase nonperforming college loans is reminiscent of the 2008–2009 housing crisis. They claim that they're purchasing these loans to save the economy, but, the truth is, they're purchasing the loans to increase the power, control, and wealth of the Federal Reserve System and their member banks. College loans are the only type of debt that can't be discharged in a bankruptcy. Our kids are being sold into debt slavery to the Federal Reserve with counterfeit money.

"The ability to create money out of thin air and lend at interest is the power to control governments and economies and to profit off just about every person on this planet. There's a reason why they shroud the counterfeiting sleight-of-hand in complexity. There's a reason why something this important isn't taught in government schools and isn't common knowledge.

"Turn right onto Colonial Commons Drive," Miss GPS said.

George took the turn wide, watching his box trailer in the side mirror.

Gary Cook continued, "Former Bank of England President Sir Josiah Stamp said, 'Bankers own the earth. Take it away from them but leave them the power to create money and control credit, and, with a flick of a pen, they will create enough to buy it back.'"

"You have arrived at your destination," Miss GPS said.

George turned off the GPS and the podcast. He drove around the block, looking for a place to park his truck and trailer. He found a stretch of road where a few work trucks were parked. He pulled along the curb and cut the engine. The sun was dropping in the distance, but it was still bright.

George glanced down at his stained T-shirt and then at his suitcase on the passenger seat. He leaned over and unzipped it. He changed T-shirts, retrieved a long-sleeve button-down shirt, and took a swig of mouthwash. Still swishing the mouthwash around, he opened the cooler in the extended cab and retrieved a cloth bag filled with produce. George stepped from the truck and locked the vehicle with his key fob. The air was thick and sticky with humidity. He spat the mouthwash on the grass and hiked the quarter mile to his destination.

George stood in front of the townhome. He set the bag of produce on the ground, put on the dress shirt, buttoned it, and picked up the bag. He rang the doorbell.

Max opened the door with a toothy grin. "Come on in."

George stepped inside, wiping his boots on the mat. "Should I take off my boots?"

Max shrugged. "I don't think so."

George wiped his boots again and followed Max into the living room with its greenish-brown sectional, recliner, and forty-eight-inch DLP.

"Do you wanna sit down?" Max asked.

"Sure," George said, taking a seat at the end of the couch.

"Is your friend—" Julie said as she rounded the corner. Her mouth hung open at the sight of George.

He stood from the couch and approached Julie. She wore fitted jeans and a blousy top.

She forced a smile. "George."

He extended his hand. "Mrs. Welch. Thank you for inviting me to dinner."

Julie's eyes flicked to Max, then back to George. "You're welcome." They shook hands. "Please call me Julie."

George nodded. He held up the cloth bag. "This is for you."

Her eyebrows arched as she took the bag. She looked inside at the tomatoes, eggplant, and peppers. "What beautiful produce."

"I just picked it a couple days ago, so it should be pretty fresh."

"At the store?"

"It's from my garden."

Julie's face brightened. "Oh, that's really thoughtful. Do you need the bag back?"

"No."

"Thank you, and please have a seat." Julie motioned to the sectional. "Dinner will be ready shortly."

George moved back to the couch.

"May I speak to you in the kitchen?" Julie asked Max.

Max frowned.

"Excuse us for a moment," Julie said to George, taking the produce with her.

George heard hushed voices in the kitchen.

"You said you were bringing a friend," Julie said.

"He is my friend," Max said in a normal voice.

"Shh, he'll hear you."

"Fine with me."

"Is everything okay?" a man asked.

"I'll be in the living room with my *friend*," Max said.

"Max brought George Chapman to dinner," Julie said in the kitchen.

"Sorry about that," Max said to George, returning to the couch.

"Are you sure it's okay that I'm here?" George asked.

"It's fine."

"Your mother didn't know I was coming to dinner."

Max whispered, "She said I could invite a friend."

George frowned. "I should go. I don't wanna cause any problems."

"You can't go now. She'll feel guilty for running you off."

George shook his head, his frown receding. "I'll stay for dinner, but I should go shortly afterward. I don't wanna overstay my welcome."

Julie poked her head into the living room. "Dinner's ready, you two."

George followed Max to the dining room.

"The famous George Chapman," the smiling skinny man said. "Or maybe it's infamous. I'm Larry Nicholson, Julie's boyfriend."

Max scowled; Julie blushed.

George extended his hand. "George."

"It's nice to meet you," Larry said as they shook.

"Waters are on the table," Julie said, "but we also have beer and wine."

"I'll have a beer," Max said.

"No, you won't," Julie replied with a smirk.

"I'll grab myself a beer," Larry said. "George, you want one?"

"No, thank you," George replied.

They took seats around the square table for four, everyone in close proximity. They passed around the baked chicken, salad, and green beans.

"It smells really good," George said, placing a chicken breast on his plate with the serving fork.

Julie smiled briefly. George stared at Julie for a second, then took the green beans from Max. George waited for everyone to start eating before he picked up his silverware. They ate in silence.

"So what do you do, George?" Larry asked, breaking the silence.

George glanced up from his plate, chewing. He swallowed. "I deliver motorcycles."

"You mean, like a truck driver?"

"I drive a truck but not an 18-wheeler. It's just a pickup truck with a covered trailer."

"Is there much money in delivering motorcycles?"

"Enough to live on."

"How does it feel to be an Internet celebrity?" Larry restrained a grin.

George's jaw tensed, then relaxed. "The attention's mostly online, so it doesn't change my day-to-day activities." George looked at Julie. "This is really good. Thank you." He took a bite of chicken.

"You're welcome," she replied.

"Yeah, Mom, this is good," Max echoed.

"Yes, thank you for such a wonderful meal," Larry said, jumping on the bandwagon.

"Are you away from home a lot?" Julie asked George.

George nodded. "About half the time I'm on the road. The other half, I'm at home."

"All that driving must get boring," Larry said.

"I keep my mind occupied with audiobooks and podcasts."

"Is that where those ideas came from?"

George narrowed his eyes at Larry. "What ideas?"

"The ones in your videos and on the news."

"We really shouldn't get into politics," Julie said to Larry.

"I get a lot of information from audiobooks and podcasts," George said.

"So those ideas aren't really yours?" Larry said.

"Larry," Julie said.

Max glared at Larry.

"I'm just curious," Larry said. "I'm not trying to be rude."

"Just about everything you can think of has already been thought of,"

George said. "The trick is figuring out what's true and what's not."

"Is that what it is? Truth?"

"As far as I know. I am open to information that might change my mind." George went back to his food.

"Uh-huh."

"The video George did with Katie Fitzgerald has over one hundred million views," Max said.

"Wow, that's a lot," Julie said.

"Do people recognize you?" Larry asked.

George chewed and swallowed. "Like I said, 'the attention's mostly online.'" He looked at Julie. "How do you like it here in Fairfax?"

"It's expensive, but the tips are good where I work, and my mother, my sister, and her family are close by."

George nodded. "That's nice that you have family around."

"It is. Of course we don't see each other as much as we should. Everyone's always so busy."

"Is your father nearby?"

Her face went still. "He died of a heart attack a couple of years ago."

That was a dumb question. "I'm very sorry," George said.

Julie shook her head. "It's fine."

Larry put his hand on top of hers.

"What about you?" Julie asked, changing the subject. "I don't even know where you live."

"I live in central Pennsylvania, in the mountains," George said. "The closest town is Shamokin, about fifteen miles away."

"George has a supercool house," Max said. "It's partly underground. He can heat it with a few sticks."

"Your house is a bunker, isn't it?" Larry asked. "Are you afraid of a nuclear war?"

Max furrowed his brow. "His house isn't a bunker. It's earth-sheltered. Why would it have all that glass on the south side if it were a bunker? That stupid USN lady said that."

"Max," Julie said, giving her son a look.

"Larry works at the IRS," Max said to George, the corners of Max's mouth quivering upward.

Larry sat a little straighter, his thin chest puffed up. "I help put away tax evaders. Many times they've committed far worse crimes. I actually had protestors in front of my office today."

George took a bite of green beans.

"What were they protesting?" Max asked.

"Taxes," Larry said. "They held Taxation Is Theft signs. You agree with that, don't you, George?"

"Larry, politics," Julie said, imploring him with her eyes.

George swallowed. "I don't see how it's not."

"I have a Libertarian friend who tries to make this argument, but the sixteenth amendment allows for taxation."

"Slavery was abolished with the thirteenth amendment in 1865."

"I don't see what that has to do with taxation."

"Slavery was immoral in 1864 when it was legal, the same as it was immoral in 1865 when it was illegal. The rules don't change what is. Taking something from someone without their permission is theft. I suppose technically taxation is extortion, but I'm splitting hairs. Some argue that it's free-range slavery."

Larry adjusted his glasses, one side of his mouth raised in contempt. "By living in the United States and benefitting from the government, you're agreeing to the implicit social contract to follow the rules of the land. If you don't like it, you can move to another country."

"Why should I leave? I'm not the one running a counterfeiting and extortion racket."

Larry rolled his eyes toward Julie. "Come on, George. You don't really believe that, do you? There aren't any cameras around."

George turned to Max. "You got any big plans for the summer?"

"I have a big animation project."

"Yeah? What's it about?"

Max grinned. "It's a surprise, but I'll show you when it's done."

"I look forward to it."

"Max is a talented animator," Julie said.

"And storyteller and producer," George added, glancing at Max.

Max beamed.

"How do you expect the government to fund itself without taxes?" Larry asked, changing the subject.

"Larry," Julie said, her head cocked.

"I don't," George replied.

"Then there's no law and order, no protection, no help for the poor, no roads, no EPA, no schools, and a million other things we all depend upon to live. Do you ever stop to think about that?"

"Yeah, I do."

"Then you know how idiotic it is to endorse Anarchist ideology. You know, you've probably influenced millions of young people to hate their government."

George let out a tired breath. "I doubt very many people care what I have to say."

"You influenced Max to create a video that got him suspended."

"Larry, stop," Julie said.

Max glowered at Larry. "You don't know what you're talking about."

"I care about Max," Larry said, his eyes flicking to Max, then settling on George. "He may not go to college because of you. You may have ruined his life."

"Larry." Julie's eyes bulged.

"Just because your life is empty and small, doesn't mean you have to ruin the lives of others. I'm so sick of people like you criticizing this country. You should thank your lucky stars that you live in the United States. You don't even have a high school diploma, for Pete's sake, and yet you have a house and a truck and a job."

"That's enough!" Julie said.

Larry showed his palms. "That's all I was going to say."

George stood, glaring at Larry. "Max has his whole life in front of him. He'll be successful with or without college." George turned to Max. "I'm sorry for talking about you like you're not here." He looked at Julie. "I'm sorry for, … well, I apologize for my rude behavior. I should be going. Thank you for your hospitality."

26: John, Drain the Swamp

John sat at a glass table opposite an attractive newswoman. The WNN logo was in the background; the camera ran in the foreground.

Lisa Kelly's dyed blond hair and professional makeup knocked a decade off the fortysomething correspondent. "Here at WNN, we've had an increase in reports of vandalism, tax evasion, and domestic terrorism. This lawlessness has been attributed to the growing Anarchist movement in this country, and George Smith Chapman is at the epicenter of this movement. Do you think it's possible Chapman's involvement in your rescue from an Anarchist assassination attempt was choreographed to increase the popularity of Chapman and, by extension, antigovernment Anarchists?"

"I suppose anything's possible, Lisa," Congressman John Bradley said. "However, given that Chapman was shot twice, I don't think so. I think Chapman was an innocent bystander who did something heroic, and I'm grateful for that."

"Chapman's an Anarchist, and the Anarchists would like to see the abolishment of government and people like you, Congressman. You've taken some criticism for not disavowing Chapman's antigovernment rhetoric. Do you still believe Chapman should be free to engage in antigovernment speech?"

"To set the record straight, I disavow Mr. Chapman's antigovernment rhetoric. I've devoted my life to public service. This country was built on the ideals of freedom and democracy, and, as much as I disagree with Chapman's beliefs, I still defend his right to freedom of speech."

Lisa's long legs were crossed. "Even if his speech has resulted in an increase in domestic terrorism?"

"There's no concrete proof of that assertion. Causation does not equal correlation. The Anarchist movement has been successful because our government has failed the citizens of the United States. People are angry, and they're looking for change. We do need major reform in government. The Republicans have had complete control of congress and the presidency for the past six years, and what do we have to show for it? We have more war, more poverty, and the biggest wealth gap we've ever seen. We all know that anarchism and chaos aren't the answer. That's like throwing the baby out with the bath water. But we do need real change. We need to drain the DC swamp and get rid of the snakes."

Lisa smiled, her teeth bright white. "Congressman Bradley, are you planning to bring change to Washington with a run at the White House in 2020?"

John sported a crooked grin. "I still have to win my congressional seat in November."

"Your last three campaigns have been landslide victories. I think your congressional seat is safe." Lisa smiled again. "A recent poll had you as the front-runner for president."

"That's very flattering." John paused. "If I do decide to run, I'll be sure to let you know."

27: Katie's Confirmation Bias

Katie sat in front of the pool on a chaise longue, an umbrella positioned overhead to protect her fair skin. The whiz of the gardener's Weed eater played in the background. She typed on her laptop.

From: Katie@KatieTalk.com
To: GeorgeChapman2222@gmail.com
Subject: Pretty Please!

George,

You said, with my newfound knowledge, I will help people more effectively. So, my newfound knowledge is telling me to work with you and to not stop pestering you until you give in. I KNOW we can be a great team. I KNOW we can do something great together. I KNOW you might say no. I also KNOW that I won't give up.

Will you please, please, please—with whipped cream, sprinkles, and three cherries on top—appear in a series of videos? I would like for you to debate some well-known Republican and Democrat bloggers.

I've been studying anarchism and the Anarchist movement. It's very fractured. You have anarcho-capitalists, anarcho-communists, anarcho-syndicalists, anarcho-naturism, anarcho-feminism, anarcho-pacifism, and I'm sure many others. From what I've been reading online, these Anarchist groups seem to hate each other, as if they're fighting for members. Not only that, they often sound insane.

In contrast, when we talked, your ideas made sense to me. Do you consider yourself an Anarchist? I assume you do, but I don't think I ever asked. If so, which sect? I think the Anarchist movement is in desperate need of a logical, levelheaded spokesperson. That should be you. I have the platform, and you have you.

Just say yes, and I'll do all the work. You just have to show up to your computer and do the debates. I'll make it as easy for you as possible.

Sincerely,
Katie Fitzgerald

Katie clicked Send. She replied to a few comments on her YouTube channel. She opened Facebook and scrolled through her feed. Katie's friend Penny had posted a meme that pictured President Henry Reynolds, his mouth open in midsentence. The meme read *Did you know that one out of three Reynolds supporters are just as stupid as the other two?* Katie clicked Like. Katie continued to scroll through her feed, found some videos with cute animals, recipes for healthy meals, pictures of beautiful families in beautiful places, but mostly her feed was riddled with pro-Democrat and anti-Republican videos, links, opinions, and memes. She clicked Like on almost everything.

She read another meme posted by Penny. This one pictured an obese woman eating chocolate-covered ice cream on a stick. The meme read VOTE REPUBLICAN. IT'S EASIER THAN THINKING. She hovered the cursor over the thumbs-up icon. She thought about what George had said to her about confirmation bias.

These ideas cause cognitive dissonance. Most people will sooth their internal conflict with confirmation bias by seeking out information that supports their previously held viewpoints.

It hit her like a two-by-four to the cranium. She moved her cursor away from the thumbs-up icon. She scrolled through her feed counting the pro-Democrat posts against other ideologies.

Katie exhaled, shaking her head. *Shit, I'm biased.* She closed Facebook and opened her email to find a response from George.

From: GeorgeChapman2222@gmail.com
To: Katie@KatieTalk.com
Subject: Re: Pretty Please!

Katie,

I think your assessment of anarchism and the warring factions is correct. There are a lot of divisions, disagreements, and insanity. I do consider myself an Anarchist. I believe the initiation of force is immoral. Therefore, the institution of government in its current form is also immoral. Voluntary associations are the way by which we conduct the majority of our lives, and this voluntary association is how I would like all the associations in my life to be. Maybe a more correct term for me would be a voluntarist.

I don't know enough about all the Anarchist sects to tell you where I agree and where I disagree. I try to live my life by the law of reciprocity—or the Golden Rule, if you're religious. *Do unto others as you would have done to you* works pretty well for me.

I appreciate your persistence and your interest in anarchy, but, as I said before, I don't think I'm the right messenger. I think you can do better. Also the news media has already exposed information about my parents that I would have rather been kept private. I don't want to be in the spotlight. I'm sorry.

Good Luck,
George Chapman

28: Julie and Slowing Down

Larry merged his Corvette onto the highway. "I really do think you're a fantastic mother," he said.

Julie turned toward Larry from the passenger seat. "Oh, I don't know."

Larry glanced at Julie through his dark-rim glasses. "You are. Trust me. I know Max thinks he and I are so different, but I was a lot like him as a kid. He appreciates you. He's just going through a rough patch. I know he's mad at me for what I said to George on Friday, but it's because I care."

"I appreciate that, Larry, but in the future—"

"I know. You're right. I need to keep my big mouth shut. Like I said, 'It won't happen again.'"

"Thanks. It's hard enough for Max to see me dating. It's probably best you don't act too parental with him."

"You're right."

Julie stared out the passenger window. She counted three foreclosure notices and many more For Sale signs as they drove through her neighborhood.

"Did you enjoy your dinner?" Larry asked, as he parked in a visitor's space. The engine idled.

Julie turned from the window. "It was very good, thank you. I think those margaritas went straight to my head."

Larry smiled. "I had a good time."

"Me too."

"I am really sorry about Friday."

"It's okay."

Larry exhaled and looked down at his steering wheel. "I guess I should get going. Those margaritas went straight to my head too, but I should be fine to drive."

"You can stay, if you want. You should probably leave in the morning before Max gets up, but that won't be until ten at the earliest."

"Are you sure? I don't want to push you."

Julie pursed her lips. "I'm sure."

Larry cut the engine.

They went inside and crept upstairs. At the opposite end of the hall, a swath of light emanated from the bottom of Max's door. They entered Julie's bedroom. She locked the door behind them.

Julie kicked off her wedged heels, giving Larry an obvious height advantage. He approached, putting his hands around her lower back. They kissed, soft, their tongues lightly touching. He tasted like the Andes Chocolate Mints they'd had after dinner. His hands slid down to the hem of her skirt, and he pulled it upward, exposing her black bikini underwear. Still kissing, he tugged her underwear down to midthigh. She helped, sliding them down her legs.

She gasped as he brushed his fingers over her clitoris. He removed his hand from her crotch and undid his belt and khaki shorts. His shorts fell to his ankles. Larry's pace accelerated as if he were suddenly in a race. He was breathless and panting as he yanked his white briefs down to his thighs, releasing his erection.

"Larry, wait," Julie said.

Larry pushed her against the dresser and pressed his pelvis forward. His penis wasn't inside her but between her thighs.

"Larry, stop." She squirmed, but he had her pinned against the dresser.

He was a man possessed, grunting, and rubbing his penis against her thighs.

"Larry, stop!"

He groaned, his penis spasming. She felt the warm fluid on her thighs. He shuddered, and his breathing slowed. He stepped back, his penis semi-flaccid. She pulled down her skirt, covering her naked lower body. His face was flushed, his eyes averted as he pulled up his pants and underwear. Larry cleared his throat. "I'm sorry. I think we, uh, drank too much."

"Did you not hear me?"

"Did you say something?"

"I told you to stop."

Larry's eyes were wide, his eyebrows arched. "You did? I didn't hear anything. Are you sure? Oh, my God, I would never …"

"I'm pretty sure."

"Are you certain?"

"Fairly certain."

Larry held up his hands in defense. He was talking fast. "I didn't hear anything. I was planning just to go home. I would never want to make you feel uncomfortable. You know that."

Julie felt nauseated. "It's late. I'm not feeling too well. We should just go to bed."

Larry frowned. "It's the alcohol. Would you like me to get you some medicine? Pepto or something?"

"No, I'm fine. Do you mind if I use the bathroom first?"

"Of course not."

Julie grabbed her pajamas, went to the bathroom, and locked the door behind her. She set her pajamas on the edge of the sink and removed her skirt. Her inner thighs were sticky. She took a shower. Afterward she dried herself and put on her pajama pants and T-shirt. She washed her face and brushed her teeth. She leaned on the sink and stared into the mirror. Sans makeup, in the bright lights, her wrinkles were on full display. *Is this the best I can hope for? Is this my market value?* She hung her head. *I don't know what the hell I'm doing.*

Julie entered her bedroom. Larry was in bed, breathing heavy. His clothes were in a neat pile on the floor. She tiptoed to the opposite side of the bed, and lifted the covers. Larry wore only his tight white underwear. His body was pale, freckled, and thin. She slipped into bed, her body tight to the edge. Eventually she drifted off to sleep.

* * *

Julie's eyes fluttered. His lips were on her cheek. He came into focus. He was grinning, his glasses on, his hair brushed and parted to the side. His forehead was massive in comparison to his weak chin. If his eyes were as big as his glasses, he'd pass for an alien.

"Good morning, sleepyhead," Larry said.

He was naked except for his briefs.

"What time is it?" Julie asked.

"It's still early. A little after seven," Larry replied.

Larry pressed his lips to hers. He tasted like toothpaste.

Julie pulled away. "Sorry," she said, covering her mouth with her hand. "I haven't brushed my teeth."

"Your mouth's fine. I brushed my teeth because my morning breath is hit or miss. Don't worry. I didn't use your toothbrush. I found a new one under the sink. Mine's the purple one."

"How long have you been up?" Julie asked.

"A couple of hours. I'm a morning person."

"I see that."

He kissed her again and rolled on top of her, straddling her, most of his weight on his hands. "I was hoping we could, … you know? I feel like I owe you after last night."

Julie's eyes widened. "Oh, no, that's not necessary—"

"It is." Larry smiled. "You know? I've been told I'm a very good lover." He leaned back on his knees, his briefs now tented, and tugged on Julie's pajama pants.

"Larry, don't." Julie wiggled out from under him and stood.

Larry sat on his haunches like a puppy, his smile fading with his erection.

"We're moving too fast again. Can we slow things down a bit?" Julie asked.

"Yeah, sure. Whatever you want."

"I'm sorry. It's been a long time since I've been in a relationship."

"I really like you, Julie. I thought the feeling was mutual." Larry hung his head.

"I'm just confused. I need some time, okay?"

29: George and Soil to Dirt

George drove past corn and soybean farms with massive metal sprinkler systems on wheels. It was a race between the water and the evaporative power of the summer sun. A podcast played through his speakers.

"This is Gary Cook of the *Alt News Podcast*, providing vital information in a changing world. It's Sunday, June 24, 2018. On the *Alt News Podcast*, we discuss a wide variety of important topics, and today is no different. In fact, today's guest and I will be discussing one of the most important elements to the survival of all living things—soil. Today we have soil scientist Dr. Hope Traylor from The Soil Institute. Welcome, Dr. Traylor."

"Thank you, Gary. I'm happy to be here," Dr. Traylor said.

"I've been reading your latest book, *Soil to Dirt*, and I must say that the information is well-researched, interesting, but also sobering and even a bit terrifying."

"My intention isn't to scare, but the data does that on its own."

"That's for sure," Gary said. "Could you tell us a little about your book and hit us with some of that scary data?"

"Sure. First let me clarify the difference between soil and dirt. Soil is alive with billions of microscopic bacteria, fungi, protozoa, and *nematodes*. Soil will also likely contain earthworms, arthropods, and other crawling insects."

"My skin's starting to crawl."

She chuckled. "Dirt on the other hand is lifeless and dependent on synthetic fertilizers and chemicals. Modern farming practices essentially strip-mine rich soils, causing water pollution and soil erosion. The soil erosion is so bad that topsoil blowing off our farms and down our waterways is the biggest export by weight in the United States. Furthermore, the soil erosion sends the chemicals we apply to our land into our drinking water and our oceans."

"Would you say modern farming's unsustainable?"

"Yes. We're seeing massive dead zones in the ocean downriver from farming areas. Our food is much less nutritious. For example, a head of broccoli in 1950 contained on average 12.9 milligrams of calcium per gram of dry weight. A head of broccoli today has only 4.2 milligrams of calcium per gram of dry weight. Yet this isn't just about broccoli and calcium. It pretty much runs the gamut of macro and micronutrients for all our foods produced by modern farming and is a direct result of growing our food in lifeless soil. Fourteen percent of the world's population is undernourished now. I see that number going much higher in the future."

George paused the podcast and parked in the back of the parking lot, his truck and trailer taking up two spaces. He cut the engine and stepped from his truck. The heat of the sun warmed his face. He stretched his arms, twisted his torso, and hiked across the parking lot to the shiny, metal-clad diner.

Inside were a half-dozen truckers scattered throughout. George was greeted by a chubby middle-aged waitress.

"Just you, sugar?" she asked.

"It's just me," George replied.

"Well, come on then." She motioned for George to follow. "I'll give you the best seat in the house."

She sat George in a booth by the window. "This all right?" she asked.

"It's perfect." George sat down. "Thank you."

"My name's Beth, and I'll be takin' care of you. What would you like to drink?"

"Water, please."

"Comin' right up." She winked, turned on her sneakers, and marched toward the counter.

George removed his vibrating phone from the front pocket of his jeans to find a new text.

> **Max:** Thanks for coming over on Friday. Sorry it was a disaster. Larry is a dick. Thank you for what you said. I know you may not want to, but I hope you will come over again. You are my only friend at this point, if you don't count my mom, which I don't because parents have to like you. By the way, my mom asked for your email. She said it was nothing bad. I gave it to her. I hope that's OK.

Beth returned to the table with a large glass of ice water and a plastic-covered menu.

"Here's your water," she said, setting the glass on the table, "and here's a menu. Our lunch special is Greek meat loaf. It's real good."

"I'll have the meat loaf," George said, returning the menu to Beth.

She grinned. "A man who knows what he wants. Comin' right up."

Beth left, and George went back to his phone.

George: Max, my friend list is pretty short too. It's not the quantity of friends that matters but the quality. You are someone of high quality. In regard to Friday, I'm sorry I lost my cool. I let Larry get under my skin, and I apologize for that. I'd be happy to come back and visit, provided it's okay with your mom. When I was young, my mother had some boyfriends. I know it's hard to take. I don't know Larry well enough to make a definitive judgment, but, from what you've told me about your mother, she's a kind, compassionate woman. I'm sure she'd appreciate it if you tried to keep the peace. And no problem on giving your mom my email.

Your friend, George

George tapped Send and checked his email.

Another one from Katie. He exhaled, tapped Reply, and thumb-typed. *Katie, I'm on the road. I won't be back until Wednesday. I'll think about it then, but I'm still leaning toward no.* He tapped Send. The next email had to be from Max's mother.

From: Jules8910@hotmail.com
To: GeorgeChapman2222@gmail.com
Subject: Thank you and Sorry

Mr. Chapman,

Max gave me your email. I hope it's okay that I contact you.

My son idolizes you. Max is smart, but he's also awkward, and he doesn't have many friends. He considers you his friend. I'm not trying to put undue pressure on you, but I thought you should know that.

To be honest, I was concerned about Max befriending an older male, but I do think you've had a positive influence on him. The expulsion wasn't good (I don't blame you), but he's more confident, even happier. He's still a moody teenager, but he's been better lately. So thank you for that.

Also I wanted to apologize for Larry's behavior on Friday. He's very patriotic, so I think your views threaten him. I think you handled the situation with class. I appreciate that, and I appreciate how you stood up for my son. Max said that you often travel through Virginia. You are welcome to visit Max whenever you're in town.

This will sound strange, but I was wondering if you've had any luck with online dating? You look about my age, and Max said you weren't married, so I was wondering if you are on any dating sites? I'm not hitting on you, I swear. Max goes on and on about how you have an answer for everything. I guess I was wondering if you've cracked the code to successful online dating? I've been out of the dating game for quite a while, and everything seems different and weird. Maybe my sister's right—my dating market value is low because I'm a forty-year-old mom. I guess I have to lower my standards.

Thank you again,
Julie

George tapped Reply.

Beth approached. "Here's your salad, sugar," she said, setting the iceberg lettuce and tomato salad in front of him.

George looked up from his phone. "Thank you."

"Meat loaf will be out shortly." Beth's ample hips rocked back and forth on the way back to the kitchen.

George dug into his salad and went back to his email.

Phil M. Williams

From: GeorgeChapman2222@gmail.com
To: Jules8910@hotmail.com
Subject: Re: Thank you and Sorry

Julie,

There's no need to thank me. I enjoy Max's company. He's very bright, insightful, and funny. I'm happy he's doing better. Structured schools tend to suck the life out of creative types like Max.

I will do my best to be a friend to Max. I know what it's like to feel ostracized.

As far as my confrontation with Larry, please don't worry about it. I feel bad that I reacted emotionally, but I'm certainly not angry with anyone. It's water under the bridge as far as I'm concerned.

Online dating is something I tried, but I didn't meet anyone. I live in a remote part of the country, and the pool of single people nearby is pretty small. I went on three first dates but never a second date, if that's any indication of my success. It must have been my ugly mug.

I didn't like the superficiality of the process. People measuring people by income and height and profile pictures airbrushed or from younger days. The tallest men with the most money—or at least the ones who say they have the most money—seem to do well. I'm average height with a below-average income. Not exactly Mr. Right but I'm okay with that.

I think when choosing a partner in life, virtue should be the quality we seek. Is the individual a good person, and do they make you a better person? I think that's a standard worth maintaining. I don't know anything about dating market values, but, based on what I've seen and what Max has told me, you're a kind, compassionate person, and that value can't be measured in dollars and inches because it's priceless. Sorry for sounding like a MasterCard commercial.

Sincerely,
George Chapman

30: John's for Sale

John entered the narrow hallway, a dozen doors on either side of the corridor. Some were open; some were closed. He trudged to the end of the hallway where a counter held two warming coffeepots with a bulletin board on the wall. Tacked to the bulletin board were a few sheets of paper with a list of names and dollar figures. He was still at the top of the list with $37 million raised for the party. He poured coffee, creamer, and sugar into a disposable cup.

John took his coffee to the nearest open office. He shut the door behind him. The office was tiny, six by six maybe. John could stand in the middle of the room and touch the walls on either side of him with his long wingspan. A desk, a chair, a computer, a telephone, and a headset were provided, along with a laminated flow chart on the wall and a duplicate taped to the desktop. The walls were eggshell white with black scuff marks on the lower portion and the baseboards.

John exhaled and took his seat. He turned on the computer, logged in, and put on the headset. A list of names appeared. He took a sip of coffee and clicked on the first one.

Name: Dr. Nathan Mitchell (Make sure to address him as Dr.)

Gender: Male

Age: 62

Wife: Jacqueline Mitchell (Goes by Jackie)

Children: Emily, Sam

Address: 8400 Roseland Estates

Fairfax Station, Virginia 22039

Occupation: Dean of Admissions, George Mason University

Political Concerns: Maintaining government-backed student loans and grants. Tell him that you will increase funding for Perkins Loans and Pell Grants.

Home Phone

Work Phone

Cell Phone

Email

John preferred to contact their cell, but the DCCC didn't have that number. John clicked on the work phone link.

The phone rang in his headset.

"Admissions office, this is Debbie."

John glanced at the script attached to the desk, but he knew it by heart. "Hi, Debbie, this is Congressman Bradley. I'm calling for Dr. Nathan Mitchell. I'd like to invite him to the annual DCCC dinner in Washington with Congresswoman Nancy Pelosi, Senator Elizabeth Warren, and many other leaders of the Democratic Party."

"Oh," Debbie said. "I'm usually not supposed to bug him, but I bet he'd like to talk to you, Congressman. Let me see if he's available."

"Thank you so much, Debbie."

John memorized Nathan's stats while he waited.

The line clicked. "This is Dr. Mitchell."

"Good morning, Dr. Mitchell. This is Congressman John Bradley." John paused.

"Good morning, Congressman. What can I do for you?"

"I'm calling to invite you to the annual DCCC dinner in Washington with Nancy Pelosi, Senator Elizabeth Warren, and many other leaders of the Democratic Party, myself included. This is a unique opportunity to come together with party leaders in support of the Democratic Congressional

Campaign Committee. Do you have a moment to hear more about the dinner?"

"Yes."

"Thank you. The event begins on Friday, September 21, with an intimate dinner with the house Democratic leadership and members of congress. The next day follows with a morning panel discussion with top political strategists and members of congress, followed by a luncheon and photo opportunity with the members of congress in the afternoon. The evening will consist of a reception and dinner with an address from our Democratic leadership. Would you join me in Washington, DC, September 21 and 22 by purchasing a table for yourself and three guests for $33,400? This amount allows the DCCC to fund an entire polling budget for a congressional district." John paused to let the donor speak, as the script suggested.

"That's quite a large sum of money, don't you think?" Dr. Mitchell said. "I'm an educator not a billionaire."

"The education of our young people and the resolution of the college loan crisis is a top priority of the Democratic Party. Increased funding for Pell Grants and Perkins Loans are something we support, unlike the Republicans. I'm concerned that, if we don't win the house in 2018, the Republicans are likely to gut public education at the worst possible time."

Dr. Mitchell sighed. "That's my fear as well. New enrollments are plummeting. We need to stem the tide and make it more attractive for young people to attend a university."

"Many of my fellow members of congress would love to talk to you about possible policy solutions."

"I suppose I do have a bird's eye view."

"With a table, you could bring the whole family."

"How many seats did you say were in a table?"

"Four."

"That would be enough for my wife and me and our two children. I suppose it would be an experience."

"And an opportunity."

"Yes, I suppose it *would* be an opportunity."

Hook. Line. And sinker.

* * *

Donna followed John into his office, shutting the door behind them. John's congressional office was furnished with a mahogany desk, a sitting area with leather chairs and a couch, and a large window overlooking sunny DC.

John took off his suit jacket and draped it over the chair in the sitting area. He removed his tie and placed it on top of his jacket.

"How was the DCCC?" Donna asked.

John frowned. "It's like a call center in Mumbai." He shook his head. "I'm not a congressman. I'm a glorified telemarketer. How are the numbers from the campaign office?"

"Pretty good. A little over 70K today."

John sighed. "I did more than that in three hours."

"That's why you'll be the next president."

There was a knock at the door. Donna opened it.

"Come in, Grace," she said.

A tiny middle-aged woman with cat-eye glasses and a skirt suit entered the office.

"Good afternoon, Grace," John said, unbuttoning his cuffs.

"Hi, John," she said, narrowing her eyes at the congressman. "You look tired. Are you getting enough rest?"

"I'll sleep when I'm dead."

Grace scowled at John. "That won't be too long from now if you keep it up."

"She has a point," Donna said.

"All right, you two," John said, sitting on the couch. "Let's get down to business."

Grace and Donna sat in the leather chairs opposite John. Grace had a pen and notepad at the ready, Donna a tablet.

"From a PR perspective," Grace said, "I think we should announce at your victory party in November. People will be optimistic, and there'll be plenty of exposure."

"I agree," Donna said.

"Playing devil's advocate," John said, "won't people question my commitment to this office? I'll be announcing my candidacy for president immediately after I'm elected to another term in congress. Why not wait until 2019, after the New Year?"

"We've polled it," Donna said. "People don't think like that. They'll be more excited *because* you're running for president. It's like discovering The Beatles before they hit it big. Besides, unless someone tries to kill you again, you won't have another opportunity with more press."

John nodded. "Let's plan for the November announcement then."

Grace said, "I'd like to run a social media campaign immediately after the announcement for brand awareness. Facebook, Twitter, and Instagram. Something to appeal to the younger voters."

"I agree," Donna said. "We need to concentrate on younger voters." Donna turned to Grace. "I'd also like to target Independents with the social media campaign."

Grace nodded. "We can do that. The targeting on Facebook and Twitter is very precise. I can also run a parameter in the targeting that excludes anyone who likes anything Republican."

"That's good," Donna said. "Republicans won't jump ship anyway. No sense wasting ad dollars on them. We should probably exclude Libertarians as well but include Green Party people."

Grace scribbled on her notepad. She looked up. "I'd like to run a campaign in August for the midterm election, starting small and increasing the ad spending as we go into November."

"The Republicans aren't running a serious candidate," John said.

"Ideally we spend a minimal amount for the congressional campaign," Donna said. "We'll need a war chest for the 2020 run."

"I just need the advertising budgets," Grace said.

"I should have those by next week," Donna said.

Grace stood. "Is there anything else?"

"I think we're done," John said. "Donna?"

"That's it," Donna said. "I'll have those budgets by next week."

"Thank you, Grace," John said.

"Get some rest," Grace replied and exited the office.

"You want to slip out and meet at the Mandarin?" John asked Donna. "We could order room service for dinner."

"Did you forget about your phone appointments?" Donna replied.

John groaned. "Is that today?"

"You have Carl Humphrey at four and Walter Moody at six. Carl wants to talk about the possibility of new refinery regulations."

"I'm assuming he's against it?"

"Actually he's for them."

"What's the catch?"

"He, or more accurately his lawyers, want to write the policy."

"He's looking for a leg up on his competitors."

"Exactly." Donna paused for a beat. "Moody will want to know where you stand on bringing back Glass Steagall."

John smirked. "To the public I love it. To Moody, don't worry. We won't let it pass."

Donna smiled. "Right again." She glanced at the clock on her tablet. "It's almost four. Carl doesn't like to be kept waiting. His information's on your calendar." She stood.

"We could still meet later."

"We'll see." Donna left the office.

John checked the calendar on his phone and called Carl Humphrey, CEO, Unico Oil & Gas.

"John, how are you?" Carl said.

"I'm well. I'd ask you how you're doing, but I wouldn't want you to think I actually care."

Carl laughed. "No bullshit out of a Democrat. Now that's gotta be a first."

John chuckled. "There's a first time for everything."

"I set up this appointment with Donna because I have some legislation that I'd like for you to sponsor."

"Can you give me the specifics in laymen's terms?"

"Basically it makes it more difficult to build a new refinery in the United States. I figure you can support a bill that shows your constituents that you're against big oil."

"This would be good for companies that have existing refineries with no intention of building new ones."

Carl chuckled. "You don't miss a trick, John. Oil and gas is a dying industry. We don't need new refineries for domestic supply. With crude so damn cheap, the bulk of Unico's profits are from refining. If new refineries come on line, it'll cut into my main source of profit."

"And what do I get in return?"

"You'll be in my good graces."

"Do you know what the average return on investment is for a congressman?"

"I reckon you're gonna tell me."

"For every dollar invested, business gets $220 back. If I'm gonna sponsor your bill, I need a serious financial commitment from you."

"I'll tell you what. You sponsor the bill, and I'll let you invoice me two hundred grand worth of speaking engagements. If the legislation passes, you can bank on ten times that amount for your presidential run."

"The contributions can't come from Unico," John said.

"Don't worry. This isn't my first rodeo. I can send the money through a few of our more environmentally friendly subsidiary businesses." Carl chuckled again. "I wouldn't wanna dirty your good name with oil."

"Send it over."

"Nice doin' business with you, Congressman." Carl hung up.

John smiled wide and leaned back on the couch. His office door opened. Donna hurried to the sitting area, her heels clicking on the floor.

"There was another attack," Donna said, her eyes wide. She picked up the remote from the coffee table and turned on the flat screen attached to the wall.

The bottom of the screen read *Breaking News: Suicide Bombing at the Federal Reserve.* Footage showed extensive damage. The massive building had a hole the size of a pickup truck where the front doors used to be. Windows were shattered. The marble facade and the front steps were charred. The scene crawled with Capitol Police, Federal Reserve Police, and DC Metropolitan Police officers.

Lisa Kelly from WNN spoke over the images. "At just after 4:00 p.m. today, a suicide bomber detonated himself near the entrance to the Federal Reserve. We do not have any information on casualties yet or on the identity of the terrorist, but we will provide that information as it becomes available."

31: Katie and Anarchy Versus Democracy

Katie parked her rental car in front of the abandoned cabin and George's garage. She grabbed her laptop bag and stepped from the sedan. It was warm—mid-eighties—and quiet. Beams of sunlight pierced the tree canopy. She surveyed the area. *No sign of George.*

She hiked past the old cabin to the forest path. She found the clearing and the meadow. It was like a Monet—red and yellow flowers dotting the landscape. Butterflies danced from flower to flower. George was next to his earth-sheltered home, hanging laundry. The clothesline was shaped like an umbrella. He looked her way, and she waved. He wore canvas pants and a faded T-shirt. Katie advanced, passing the ground-mounted solar array and attached antenna. George pinned a pair of pants as Katie approached.

"You're probably surprised to see me," Katie said.

He frowned. "I'm not."

"I wasn't kidding about not taking no for an answer."

"I see that."

"Will you do the interviews then?"

George exhaled. "We need to talk terms."

"Oh, okay. I just thought we'd do the interviews, keep it casual and fun."

George narrowed his eyes. "You planning on monetizing these videos with advertising?"

"Well, yes, but it's my channel. It's the cost of doing business."

"How much does it cost to run your channel?" George asked.

"It depends. Ten to fifteen thousand a year, depending on how much travel I do, and how many times I need a cameraman."

"Best case scenario, how much are you hoping to earn from these videos?"

"I have an established platform so …"

"How much?"

Katie bit the bottom corner of her lip. "Maybe a thousand dollars in ad revenue per video."

George pinned a T-shirt to the clothesline. "And how many videos did you wanna do?"

"I was hoping to do one a week."

"For how long?"

"I don't know. For as long as it's popular."

"How long do you think it'll be popular?"

"A year?" Katie winced.

George let out a low whistle. "So, about fifty-two thousand dollars minus ten or so for expenses."

"I know that might seem like a lot of money, especially around here, but in San Francisco, it's nothing. I still live with my parents."

George nodded. "I'll do your videos on one condition." He pinned another T-shirt to the clothesline. "If you make more than $100,000 profit on my videos in one year, I would like half of the additional profit to be donated to the Permaculture Research Institute in Australia and the other half to a charity of your choice."

"The Permaculture Research Institute?"

"I like what they're doing with regenerative agriculture and sustainable housing."

"I doubt we'll make that much money."

"You never know."

"Is that it?" Katie asked.

"That's it."

She smiled. "Deal. We don't need a contract, do we?"

"No, but if you go back on your word again, I'm done. Do you understand?"

"Yes." Katie held out her hand, and they shook.

Katie helped George hang the rest of his laundry.

"No dryer?" she asked as she picked up a damp T-shirt from the basket.

"Dryers use too much electricity," George said. "The sun does just fine."

"Did you hear about the terrorist attack on the Federal Reserve?"

"I saw that."

"Two Federal Reserve Police officers died."

George nodded as he hung a pair of pants.

"The bomber was an Anarchist," Katie said.

"Not a good one or a smart one."

"Why do you say that?"

"Anarchism is a nonviolent movement. The state is violent and coercive, but anarchism is about voluntary associations. Second, the state has a monopoly on violence. They're very good at violence. Even if anarchism was a violent movement, it's stupid to try to beat the state at their own game." George picked up the empty wicker basket. "Would you like something to drink?"

"Please," Katie replied.

George led Katie into his home. He filled a glass from the tap and handed it to her.

"Where's your partner in crime?" George asked, sitting at the kitchen table.

Katie sat across from him. "Declan's working on his documentary. He kind of bailed on this project."

"I'm sorry to hear that."

"Oh, it's not like that. We're fine."

George nodded. "What's involved with these interviews?"

"Basically I have a starter question. It'll be a question that, given your ideology, you'll be on one side of, and the other person will be on the opposite side. I'd like to do a series of debates with popular Democrat and Republican bloggers, YouTubers, and I'd even like to try to get some actual politicians."

"And I can do this here? I don't have to go anywhere?"

"How's your Internet? I saw you have an antenna."

George nodded. "I'm close to a Verizon tower. I have their wireless Internet for laptops. The antenna's a signal booster."

"Can you play video without any buffering?"

"Yeah."

"Then it should be fine."

"When's the first interview?"

Katie grinned. "In a few hours."

* * *

Katie installed the necessary software on George's computer. She gave him a microphone. Katie sat at the kitchen table in front of her laptop and microphone. George was set up in his room at his desk. The conference call screen was split in thirds. George on the right, Katie in the middle, and Vance Riddle on the left.

"Thank you for being here, Vance," Katie said.

"You're welcome, Katie," he replied.

Vance Riddle had a manicured beard, close-cropped brown hair, and beady eyes. His large nose was slightly sunburned.

"I'll do the intro, and I'll post the debate topic on the bottom of the screen," Katie said. "Once the debate topic goes up, we can begin. It's the same topic we discussed. Vance, would you like to go first?"

"I would," Vance replied.

"Are you okay with that, George?"

"Fine with me," George replied.

"Here we go." Katie pressed Record and smiled at the camera on her laptop. "Hi, everyone. This is Katie Fitzgerald of Katie Talk. Today I'm kicking off a series of debates with George Smith Chapman, entitled 'Anarchy Versus Democracy.' Mr. Chapman has graciously agreed to appear in a series of debates with notable political bloggers, YouTubers, and politicians from the left and the right. In this installment of 'Anarchy Versus Democracy,' we have the irreverent and very popular Democrat vlogger Vance Riddle. You can read, watch, and follow Vance at the links below. Welcome, Vance."

"Thank you for having me, Katie," he replied.

"And of course we have the most famous Anarchist in America, the controversial George Smith Chapman. Welcome, George."

George was blank-faced. "Hello, Katie."

"Our topic today is, 'Does government make us safe?' Vance?"

"It's funny, you know?" Vance said. "These Anarchists wanna abolish the government, but, when something bad happens, who do they call? They call the police for protection, just like everyone else. I'll even concede that our government isn't perfect, that there are instances of government abuse. But, when government abuse occurs, another branch of government fixes the problem. This is why we have the checks and balances of the executive, legislative, and judicial branches.

"A lot of evil people are out there. Without the government to protect us, it would simply be a situation of might makes right. We'd have a bunch of warring tribes, killing each other and taking what they want. We need the rule of law to protect our rights. Without government, there's no protection whatsoever." Vance smiled.

"George, your counterpoint," Katie said.

George began, "Mr. Riddle said, 'When something bad happens, Anarchists call government for protection, just like everyone else.' He's correct, but the problem with this argument is that the government has a monopoly on law and police. Our options are limited by the violence of the state.

"I'm not afraid of my fellow citizen. I have the power to defend myself against a criminal. I do not have the power to defend myself against the state. We all know ignorance of the law is no defense, yet no single lawyer is familiar with all the approximately four thousand federal criminal laws and three hundred thousand regulations that carry criminal penalties, plus the untold state and local laws, codes, and ordinances. Civil liberties attorney Harvey Silverglate found that the average American commits three felonies a day. This excessive government regulation makes us less safe because nearly every person runs the risk of being chewed up and spat out by the state.

"Excessive laws and regulations give tremendous power to law enforcement to selectively enforce. Nearly one in three Americans has an arrest record. One out of thirty-one Americans are under corrections custody through parole, probation, and incarceration. The United States has the largest prison population in the world. Approximately 60 percent of inmates in federal prison are incarcerated for nonviolent crimes, where they are often assaulted and raped. This is the reason why more males are raped in this country than females.

"Meanwhile, hundreds of thousands of rape kits remain untested, and law enforcement has no specific duty to protect the public. *Warren v. The District of Columbia* established that law enforcement has no specific duty to protect the public—"

"I'm gonna stop you for a moment," Vance said. "I've given you far more time than I had. First of all, I'm well aware of the abuses of our justice system. I report on the abuse of minorities on my channel on an almost daily basis. I don't agree that we're still arresting people for smoking a plant in many states. The problems George outlined should be addressed. That I agree with, but you don't throw away the very apparatus we need to do that. This is why we need to get involved and make things better. This is our government. We get what we vote for. It's *we the people*. It's up to us to have an ethical government. It's a choice."

"Let's say I had a Coke and a Pepsi," George said, "and I asked, 'Would you like to have one of my sodas?' Would that be a choice?"

"Yes."

"What if I said, 'Would you like to buy one of my sodas?' Still a choice?"

"Yes. I know what you're getting at."

"What if I said, 'You *must* buy one of my sodas, and you can choose which one to buy, but, if your neighbors choose the soda you didn't choose, you'll have to buy the majority soda.' Is that a choice?"

Vance curled his lip in contempt. "These sophomoric arguments get us nowhere. These Anarchists think they have these clever analogies. They're not. They're simplistic, childish arguments that have no business among serious political thought. Without government, what's to stop a foreign power from taking over and enslaving the nation? I think we could do with a much smaller military, but we do need protection from foreign powers."

George said, "Governments often attack governments because of some aggression perpetrated by one or both governments. Economic sanctions, bombings, past wars, and secret coups would not occur to fan the flames of war in a free society, because they could not tax or print money to fund wars and other acts of aggression.

"Another incentive to invade a government-controlled territory is because there are tax bases and clear centers of power to be conquered. In a free society, there's no tax base and no centers of power. From the perspective of the invading government, what's the gain? With no tax base or government buildings to occupy and a population that views government power as illegitimate, they can't just waltz in and propagandize the people to pay taxes and accept their new master."

"I call bullshit on that," Vance said. "Governments go to war for resources all the time. Who's to stop another country from stealing oil fields from these supposedly free people?" Vance threw up air quotes when he said "free."

"In a free society," George said, "the inhabitants understand that they're responsible for their own protection. They will have already either hired private security, armed themselves, or both. With many local private security firms in a free society, well-armed and effective protection forces could band together. Imagine the nightmare for a foreign power invading a peaceful country where each citizen has a personal means of protection. The invasion might be successful, but the occupation would be a disaster. Think Afghanistan times a hundred. I doubt they would get the oil out without spending far more money than they're making to protect pipelines, massive oil fields, and tanker trucks, all of which are combustible."

Vance crossed his arms.

"In addition to the logistic and strategic nightmare," George continued, "it would be a public relations disaster. As the invader, how do you justify your aggression against a peaceful society? Sure, you'd lie and propagandize, but you can't fool everyone. I believe in the inherent goodness of human beings. There'd be an outcry of support for the peaceful society and condemnation for the invader. There'd be protests within the invading country, as I doubt the people would be too enthused about having their hard-earned money used to invade a peaceful country. Who knows? Military support might be offered by an enemy of the invader or a trading partner of the peaceful society."

"What about the private invader from within?" Vance said. "Who's to stop my rich asshole neighbor from creating his own army and taking whatever he wants? This is why the Anarchist argument is utopian bullshit."

"The neighbor still has to contend with an armed populace and many armed private security companies. In addition he'd have the problem of funding his invasion. Government wars are paid for with debt, taxation, and inflation. A private person would have to fund his invasion out of his own pocket. He can't tax anyone. He can't inflate the currency, and he might not even secure financing."

"Banks finance wars all the time," Vance said.

"They do, but they do it because there is a tax base, and the profitable monopoly of the central bank is protected by the government. But for the average private person in a free society, a bank would not be protected by the government and would have to exist on the profitability of their loans. The bank would say, 'Your invasion plan is not profitable. We cannot loan you the money because we don't think we'll be paid back. Not only that, if our customers found out we financed something so despicable, we'd be run out of business.'

"A private person would be forced to finance a war entirely from his own pocket, and he would have to hire soldiers for exorbitantly high wages, because most people would rather work a job than attack a bunch of people who did nothing to them. You also have to remember that he doesn't have the massive propaganda machine that attracts young men to work for low wages despite terrible conditions and the possibility of injury and death—"

"When has there ever been a successful Anarchist society?" Vance asked.

"May I finish?"

Vance raised his hands. "Katie, he's had enough time."

"I'll give you the final word," Katie said. "Let him finish."

George continued, "On the opposite side, those defending themselves from his invasion would have the moral high ground, and that moral high ground would attract those who want to protect the oppressed. They would attract hired soldiers who would work for much less to be a part of the cause. People are much more likely to fight for a just cause. There's a reason propaganda is so important to war."

"Wow, talk about propaganda," Vance said, "you've been spouting quite a bit of Anarchist propaganda. Again, when has there ever been a successful Anarchist society?"

"Medieval Ireland for one thousand years or about four times longer than the United States has been in existence."

Vance rolled his eyes. "Government can be a very powerful force for democracy and justice for all, and it can also be a force for tyranny. George described some of the tyranny, but none of the democracy and justice. The freedoms we all enjoy in this country are because government granted us those rights. Make no mistake, the only reason we aren't slaves to greedy capitalists is because of our government. There's no doubt that we need reform, but these silly abolishment ideas are the ramblings of single men who are still living in their mother's basements."

32: Julie and Judgment When Aroused

Julie sat at the linen-covered table across from Larry. The candlelight danced in Larry's glasses like mini-infernos.

Julie surveyed the restaurant. Every table was occupied in the cozy dining area. The diners were mostly couples. The older ones talked to the waitstaff about the food. The younger ones stared at their phones more than each other.

The blond waitress took their plates. "Would you like dessert?" she asked.

"Nothing for me," Julie replied.

"I'd like a cappuccino," Larry said.

The waitress nodded. "Yes, sir." She left the table.

"As I was saying," Larry said, "this Anarchist who detonated himself in front of the Federal Reserve is emblematic of the movement. They're a bunch of violent thugs, seeking power by exploiting the powerless. Actually they're a bunch of losers who blame the government for all their problems."

Julie pursed her lips.

"The past few weeks I've thought about the bombing every day at work, wondering if the IRS is their next target. Something needs to be done, don't you think?"

Julie lifted one bare shoulder. "I don't know. Whatever the government does in response will create more violence."

Larry frowned. "Please tell me that you're not serious. This is how the terrorists win. This is how they become emboldened to do it again—bigger. We need to start rounding them up for hate speech. That'll put an end to it. The sooner we start, the less collateral damage there'll be. If we wait too long, we could end up in a civil war."

Julie exhaled, glancing over Larry's shoulder.

"You're not paying attention," he said.

"Sorry. I need to go to the restroom." Julie grabbed her purse and stood from the table. Her napkin fell from her lap to the floor. She picked it up, placed it on the table, and stepped to the bathroom.

She locked the door behind her. The bathroom contained a mirror over the sink and a single toilet. She peed, flushed, and pulled up her underwear. She washed her hands and stared into the mirror. Her blue eyes were empty. She straightened the spaghetti straps of her little black dress. A piece of metal was visible over her chest from the safety pin used to cinch up her dress and cover her cleavage. As she exited the bathroom, her phone buzzed. She opened her tiny black purse and extracted her phone. An email from George. She sat on the wooden chair just outside the bathroom.

From: GeorgeChapman2222@gmail.com
To: Jules8910@hotmail.com
Subject: In the Neighborhood

Julie,

How are you? I hope you're well.

I'm in sunny Florida. It's not near as fun as it sounds. Earlier today it was 102 degrees with near 100 percent humidity. With the sun going down, it's a "chilly" 88. I'm very thankful for the air-conditioning in my truck. Did you know that when car manufacturers first started offering air-conditioning, it was a huge status symbol, so much so that people without AC drove around on hot days with their windows up? I think people would be happier if they didn't worry about the opinions of others.

I'm really off track now. The reason for this email is: I'll be in northern Virginia next Friday, July 6. Max asked me to stop by for a visit. I told him that I'd love to drop by, but I wanted to clear it with you first. I won't stay long, and please don't feel obligated to feed me. I'll show up on a full stomach. However, if this isn't a good time, we can do it another time.

Thanks,
George

Julie tapped Reply and typed with her thumbs.

From: Jules8910@hotmail.com
To: GeorgeChapman2222@gmail.com
Subject: Re: In the Neighborhood

George,

You're welcome to come by next Friday. What time do you think you'll be here? Please do come on an empty stomach. I'll be cooking dinner anyway. One extra place is no work at all.

You asked how I am, and I know nobody wants an honest answer, but I'm still struggling with dating. Maybe I don't know how to be in a relationship anymore. Do you ever feel like that? How are you doing by the way?

Julie

Julie pressed Send and shoved her phone in her purse. She returned to the table and slid into her seat.

"You were gone for a long time," Larry said.

"I was fixing my hair," Julie replied.

"Looks the same to me."

Their waitress placed a cappuccino in front of Larry.

"Maybe you can settle a dispute," Larry said to the waitress.

She forced a smile.

"Are you familiar with the Anarchist bombing from two weeks ago?" he asked.

Her eyes flicked to Julie, then to Larry. "Yes."

"Well, my girlfriend thinks that we shouldn't do anything about the Anarchist movement, whereas I think that people who are speaking out against the government should be arrested for hate speech. What do you think?"

"You don't need to answer," Julie said.

"Can I get you anything else?" the waitress asked.

"An answer to my question," Larry said, with a smirk.

The waitress held her head high. "I don't think people should be arrested for what they say."

"Even if what they say leads to the death of innocent people?" Larry said.

"Could we have the check, please?" Julie asked.

The waitress set the leather booklet on the table and marched away. Julie glanced at the check and removed a fistful of cash from her purse.

Larry grabbed the check. "Put that away," he said. "I'll put it on my credit card."

"You really don't have to pay all the time," Julie said. "At least take the cash for my half of the meal."

"You know I won't take your money."

Julie shoved the cash back into her purse. "Thank you for dinner, Larry."

"It was my pleasure."

Larry studied the check. He inserted his credit card into the placeholder and set the booklet on the edge of the table. The waitress took his credit card and bill without making eye contact. She returned a few minutes later and placed the booklet on the table.

"Thank you," she said, her eyes still. And she was gone.

"She was a bit rude," Larry said. He grabbed his credit card, filled in the tip amount, signed the receipt, and closed the booklet. "You ready to go?"

Julie nodded.

Outside in the humid night air, Julie stopped, her hands free. "I'll meet you in the car," she said. "I left my purse in the restaurant."

Julie returned to the table. Thankfully her purse was still there. The booklet with the bill still sat on the edge of the table. She opened it. The meal charge was $132.35. The tip line was crossed off with a single stroke of the pen. The total after the tip was $132.35. Julie left thirty dollars in cash.

She was quiet on the ride home. Larry jabbered on about some case at work. He parked his Corvette in the visitor spot across from Julie's townhome.

"You okay?" Larry asked. "You've been really quiet tonight."

"I'm just tired," Julie replied.

"Me too."

"Maybe we should call it a night."

Larry yawned. "I agree. I'm beat."

Julie shut her eyes for a moment. *Go home.*

Larry followed Julie inside and they trudged upstairs. Larry shut the bedroom door behind them and pressed the lock on the handle.

Julie set her purse on the dresser and slipped off her heels. Larry wrapped his arms around her waist from behind and kissed the nape of her neck. Julie wiggled from his grasp and turned around. "Not now, Larry. I'm tired."

"Come on," he said. "I've been patient."

"I'm going to bed." Julie stepped toward the bed, her folded pajamas in a neat pile on the comforter. Larry hovered behind her, his breath labored against the back of her neck, his body mere inches from hers. As she reached for her pajamas, he pushed against her, his hands on her back, forcing her to bend over the bed. Julie struggled, but Larry's weight and hands kept her in place. He lifted her dress and rubbed his crotch against her backside. He was aroused.

"Larry, no."

He used one hand to undo his belt and unzip.

With less pressure on her back, Julie managed to turn over and sit up.

He stood, wild eyed, his fly open, his penis pointing to the ceiling. Larry pushed her back down.

She was now faceup, her legs hanging off the bed.

He tried to force her legs open with his knees.

Julie smacked him across the face. "Get the fuck off me!" Julie said.

Larry stepped back, his eyes shrinking.

Julie stood and kneed him in the groin.

He dropped like a sack of potatoes. He lay on the carpet, groaning. "Why'd you do that?" he asked.

"Get out of my house," she said.

After a moment, he struggled to his feet, buckled his belt, and zipped up. He wore no underwear for the occasion. Larry held up his hands in surrender. "I'm sorry. I don't know what came over me."

Julie opened the bedroom door. "Get out, and don't call me again."

Max stood at the opposite end of the hallway. "What's going on?" he asked.

"Nothing," Julie said. "Go back to bed."

Larry hurried downstairs and outside.

"Are you okay, Mom?" Max asked.

"I'm fine. I'm just tired."

Max went into his room. Julie shut her door, leaned against it, and slid to the carpet. She pulled her knees to her chest and sobbed. A few minutes later, Julie stood, sniffling and shaky. She changed into her pajamas and retrieved her phone from her purse. She climbed into bed, swiped the screen, and found a new email.

From: GeorgeChapman2222@gmail.com
To: Jules8910@hotmail.com
Subject: Re: Re: In the Neighborhood

Julie,

Thank you for the invite. I look forward to seeing you and Max then. I'm not certain on the time yet, but I'm thinking between 4:00 and 6:00 p.m. I'll give you a more exact time on that day. I wish I could be more precise. You never know with traffic around the beltway.

I appreciate your honesty, and I'm sorry you're having a tough time. I understand how you feel. I'm not sure I've ever known how to be in a relationship. If you ever want to talk, I'm here.

George

Julie tapped Reply.

From: Jules8910@hotmail.com
To: GeorgeChapman2222@gmail.com
Subject: Re: Re: Re: In the Neighborhood

George,

I think Larry just tried to rape me.

She deleted the email and started again.

From: Jules8910@hotmail.com
To: GeorgeChapman2222@gmail.com
Subject: Re: Re: Re: In the Neighborhood

George,

Do you ever feel like you're destined to be alone? Do you ever feel like the stars are aligned against you?

I think I would like to talk sometime. 703-555-9802.

Julie

She took a deep breath and tapped Send. She pulled her knees into the fetal position and closed her eyes. The phone chimed; her eyes opened. The screen read *Pennsylvania 717-555-4212 calling.* Her heart pounded. She swiped right.

"Hello," she said.

"Julie, it's George. I'm sorry for calling you so late. I thought maybe you needed someone to talk to."

"I'm fine, really." She had a lump in her throat. "I didn't mean for you to call right away."

"Oh, it's just, uh … It's just your email seemed sad. I know I don't know you very well, but I wanted to see if you were okay."

"I'm okay."

"Good. I'm sorry to bother you. I should go."

"It's not too late for you, is it?" She clutched the phone as if it were a lifeline.

"No, it's not." He paused for a moment. "I do feel like I'm destined to be alone."

"What?"

"Your question from your email. I've felt like I was destined to be alone ever since I was a kid. It gets easier."

"What gets easier?"

"Being alone."

"When?"

There was another pause. "I'm sorry. That was stupid. I don't know if it'll get easier for you."

"Larry attacked me tonight."

"Are you okay? Did he hurt you?"

She choked out a laugh. "I'm fine. He's the one you should be asking. I kneed him pretty hard."

"Where is he now?"

"He's gone."

"So you're not in any danger?"

"No."

"Did you call the police?"

"I just want to forget about it. With my luck, I'd get arrested for assault."

"I'm very sorry that you went through that."

Julie was silent. Fresh tears filled her eyes.

"Julie? Are you still there?"

"I'm here."

"Good."

"I should've known better. This isn't the first time. I mean, the other times weren't like this, but he was overly aggressive a couple times before, but ... I don't know. I thought he was a nice guy." She exhaled. "I'm freaking clueless."

"You're not. This kind of thing is a lot more common than most people think. I read this book six years ago, called *Predictably Irrational*. It's by this psychology and behavioral economics professor from Duke named Dan Ariely. Anyway, one of the studies he detailed in his book had to do with the judgments and decision-making of men when they're aroused versus when they aren't."

"Do I even want to know how they did this test?"

"The men got themselves into an aroused state and answered survey questions. Then they compared the results from when they took the survey not aroused. One of the questions was, 'Would you keep trying to have sex after your date says no?' When the men were normal, 20 percent said they would. When they were aroused, 45 percent said they would, a 125 percent increase."

"That's awful."

"It is."

"Do you have that book in front of you?"

"No, why?"

"Where did you get those statistics?"

"I remembered them."

"The exact statistics from a book you read six years ago?"

"I have a pretty good memory."

"I'll say. I can reread the same novel every couple of years because I forget the plot."

"A good memory isn't always a good thing."

"Thank you for calling, George."

"You're welcome."

"Will you stay on the phone with me until I fall asleep?" Julie asked.

"Yes."

33: George and the Friend Zone

George sat in his truck, parked along the curb, just outside Julie's neighborhood. His phone buzzed.

Max: Something is up. No more Larry. My mom changed clothes like three times already tonight. She's acting nervous, and she keeps asking questions about you. Is there something between you two?

George: We're friends.

Max: When did that happen?

George: We email sometimes, and we've talked on the phone a couple times.

Max: Hmm. She didn't tell me about that. Do you think she's pretty? Don't lie.

George: Yes, but don't worry. There's nothing between us.

Max: If you like her, you should at least try to hold her hand tonight. Otherwise, you could get friend-zoned.

George laughed.

George: I'm here in the neighborhood. Does your mom need more time to get ready?

Max: She's ready.

George: See you in a few minutes.

George exited his truck with two cloth bags full of produce. He hiked along the sidewalk to Julie's townhome. He took a deep breath and rang the doorbell.

Julie appeared wearing a knee-length sundress and a perfect smile. "Hi," she said.

George matched her smile in spirit if not beauty. "You look nice."

She blushed. "So do you. Come in." She motioned him inside.

George wiped his boots on the mat and followed. He wore jeans and an untucked button-down shirt with the sleeves rolled up.

"I brought you some produce." He held out the bags, his arms taut.

"That's really sweet of you," Julie replied.

Julie led George into the kitchen. He set the bags on the counter. The kitchen smelled like baked fish and dill.

Julie peered inside the bags. "Wow, the produce looks beautiful. I hope we're not taking all your food."

"There's so much in the summer, much more than I can eat. You're doing me a favor."

"I know you were coming this way but ..." She looked at George, her blue eyes dilated. "Thank you for coming."

George returned her gaze. "Thank you for inviting me." Her auburn hair was shoulder length and brushed to the side. Her face was radiant, with high cheekbones, and perfectly proportioned features.

"Hey, George," Max said, appearing in the kitchen.

George turned and grinned. "Hey, Max. It's good to see you." George offered his hand, and they shook.

"What are we having?" Max asked.

"Baked tilapia with dill and sweet potatoes and salad," Julie replied. "And I have something special for dessert."

"Sounds great," George said.

"George eats tilapia all the time," Max said. "He just harvested like seventy of them from his aquaponics farm."

Julie's mouth flatlined. "Oh, sorry, George. I didn't know—"

"I love tilapia with dill," George said.

George and Max set the table and filled glasses with water. Julie removed the fish from the oven. They readied their plates in the kitchen and sat down to eat in the dining room.

George and Julie stole glances at each other.

Max talked about an animated video he was working on. "I think I'm already good enough to get paid," Max said. "It would be pretty badass to get paid for doing something I'd do for free."

"I think you *are* good enough," George said. "And that's the best type of job. It never feels like you're at work."

After dinner and peach cobbler for dessert, all three of them cleared the table. Julie washed dishes, and, despite her protests, George loaded the dishwasher.

Max stretched his arms over his head and yawned. "I'm pretty tired. I'm gonna go to bed."

"It's only eight o'clock," Julie said, glancing at the clock on the oven.

"It was good to see you," Max said to George, shaking his hand. Max discreetly mouthed, *Friend zone.* "Good night, kids."

"Good night, honey," Julie replied with a smirk.

Max left the kitchen and went upstairs.

Julie hung her dishcloth on the drying rack. "He's something else."

George smiled. "You'll have to turn this thing on," he said. "I don't have a dishwasher."

Julie grabbed the detergent from under the sink, squeezed some gel into the receptacle, and turned on the machine.

"Thank you for dinner," George said. "I had a good time."

"You're welcome. Would you like some tea or coffee?"

"No, thank you." George shoved his hands in his pockets.

"Beer? Water?"

"No, thank you."

Julie wrung her hands, out of code words for "spend more time together."

"You don't have to entertain me. I can leave."

Julie's mouth turned downward. "Do you want to leave?"

"No, but I don't wanna overstay my welcome."

"Will you sit with me for a little bit before you go?"

"Of course."

They settled in the family room on the couch, a few feet of space between them, the television black.

"How's work?" George asked.

"Remember when you told Max that the best job to have is one you'd do for free?"

George nodded.

Julie huffed. "Well, I wouldn't do my job without the pay, that's for sure."

"What *would* you do without the pay?"

She lifted one shoulder. "I have no idea. What about you?"

"I'm not sure either. I think my life's been more about survival than self-actualization."

"You're different," Julie said.

George looked at the coffee table.

Julie covered his hand with hers. "It's not a bad thing."

George forced a smile. He turned his hand over and squeezed. Her hand was small and soft. George chuckled to himself.

"What?" she replied, not unkind.

"Max said that I should hold your hand tonight, otherwise you might relegate me to the friend zone."

Julie giggled. "That kid."

"He is funny … and smart."

Her laughter dissipated. She sighed.

"Did I say something wrong?" George asked.

"No, I just can't figure out why he doesn't have any friends."

"Max is a good friend and a good person. His time will come. It's good that you got him out of that school. It's not a place for the empathetic."

Julie was quiet.

"You okay over there?" George asked.

"I'm fine." Her face was somber.

"You sure?"

"Can I be honest with you?" Julie asked.

"I hope so," George replied.

"I wonder about you too."

"What about me?"

"I like you, George. You seem kind and down-to-earth."

"Seem?"

"I was burned by a guy who I thought was nice literally a week ago. And then I went to you for comfort. I could have gone to my sister or my mother, but I chose to confide in a man I barely know."

George removed his hand from hers. "Why *didn't* you go to your sister or your mother?"

She balled her hand into a fist. "I don't know."

"You don't have to tell me, but I think you do know."

She scowled. "Fine. My sister thinks she's better than me. And you know what? She's right. She has the perfect family, the perfect husband, the perfect house, and my life's a perfect mess. When I confide in her, she's a little too happy, like my pain makes her grateful for what she has."

"I'm sorry," George said.

"I love my mother, but she refuses to talk about anything real. It's all surface stuff with her. If I talk about anything unpleasant, she gives me a canned response, like, 'It'll get better,' then she quickly changes the subject." Julie huffed.

"I don't even talk to anyone in my family, much less confide in them."

Julie rubbed her temples for a moment. "Clearly something is wrong with me. Larry had some serious red flags, and I didn't see them, or I ignored them." She shook her head. "And now I feel like I'm ignoring them again. You're a man without any attachments whatsoever. That's not normal."

George pinched the bridge of his nose. "You're right, it's not normal. I'm forty-one with no family, no friends, no wife, no ex-wife, no kids. There's five bright red flags for you." George stood. "Maybe it's best to stop this before we venture out of the friend zone. Thank you for dinner. I should go."

Julie rose from the couch and put her hand on his forearm. "Please don't. I'm sorry."

"Me too." George walked out the front door.

"George, wait," Julie called out in his wake.

Outside, it was approaching dusk. It was warm and humid. He hurried to his truck. George climbed into the cab and shut the door. He leaned his head on the steering wheel. He thought about his red flags, how they reinforced each other in a vicious cycle.

He heard tapping on his window. George sat up and turned.

Julie stood there, her blue eyes glassy. "May I talk to you?" she asked, her voice muffled by the glass.

George opened the door and slid across the bench seat, giving her space to join him. Julie climbed into the cab and shut the door.

"I was rude," Julie said. "You've been nothing but nice to me and my son. I'm sorry–"

"No, you're right to be concerned. I'm not by myself because I'm a well-adjusted great guy."

"Then why?"

George stared through the windshield. "You don't wanna hear this."

"I do."

George turned to Julie. "You wanna hear how my dad left when I was six, and the only thing I remember about him are the beatings? You really wanna hear that?"

"Yes. I'd like to be here for you, like you were for me."

George shut his eyes for a moment and hung his head.

Julie scooted across the bench seat toward George. She placed her hand on his. "That must've been incredibly hard," Julie said.

George raised his gaze, staring at the fiery orange orb hanging low in the sky. "When I was a kid, I used to climb to the top of this mountain by my house and watch the sunset."

"Sounds beautiful."

"It was. I found this old tent in the woods. I used to sleep out there until it was too cold."

"How old were you?"

"Eight."

"Your mother didn't mind you being out in the woods all by yourself at that age?"

George took a deep breath. "She was high or sick and her boyfriends, … well, my mother fell for the abusive type. I spent as little time as possible at home. When I was sixteen, I gotta job working as a laborer for a landscape company half an hour away from my hometown, so I dropped out of school and rented a basement from an old couple near my job.

"I never spoke to my mother again. She died of an overdose when I was twenty-three, but I didn't find out until a few years after. I was making a little money at the time, and I wanted to help her. Maybe get her into a treatment facility. I guess I had finally forgiven her. Her old boyfriend told me that she had died. That was that."

"I'm so sorry, George. I didn't—"

"I need some air." George opened the passenger door and stepped outside. He bent over and put his hands on his knees, sucking in the humid air.

Julie appeared and placed her hand on his back.

He stood upright, drawing in a deep inhale.

"Are you okay?" she asked.

"Yeah."

She stepped into his personal space and hugged him tight. After a moment, George reciprocated. Her body felt warm and forgiving. He pulled back, their arms still intertwined. She tilted her head up, and he pressed his lips to hers.

34: John and the Art of the Deal

John sat by himself in a secluded booth. The lighting was dim, and the restaurant was mostly empty—too late for lunch and too early for dinner. A short red-haired man with wire-rim glasses entered the restaurant with his head on a swivel. John raised his arm.

"Adam," John said.

Adam turned toward John's voice and stepped to the booth. Adam slid into the seat opposite John.

"Thank you for meeting me," John said.

"I don't have a lot of time," Adam replied.

A young waitress, wearing khaki pants and a white shirt, approached. "What can I get you two?"

"Nothing for me," Adam said.

"They have great burgers here," John said.

"I'll have a coffee."

"Cheeseburger, fries, and a Coke," John said with a wink to the waitress.

She blushed and took their orders to the kitchen.

John turned his attention from the waitress's ass to Adam. "I heard the NSA is moving up the time table for implementation of Armor Software. The Federal Reserve attack must have you guys scrambling."

"I can't talk about that," Adam said, stone-faced.

"Was the suicide bomber on your list?"

Adam nodded.

"Your software will revolutionize how we fight the War on Terror."

"We're hoping."

"Don't be so modest."

The waitress approached with a coffee and a Coke. "Here you are," she said.

"Thank you," John said.

She blushed again. "You're welcome. Food will be ready in a few minutes."

Once the waitress was out of earshot, John said to Adam, "You just moved to DC from California, right?"

"It's been a year."

"California to DC. The private sector to the public sector. Must've been quite the culture shock."

"I'm not following."

John leaned forward, his elbows on the table and his hands clasped. "Business is done differently in the public sector. It's not about profit and loss. It's about power. Plenty of good contractors are out on their asses, not because they weren't doing a good job but because they couldn't navigate the DC swamp."

Adam furrowed his freckled brow. "Is that a threat?"

John showed his hands, with a big grin. "Come on, Adam. I don't make threats. I make deals." John put his elbows back on the table. "Here's the deal. I'm a loyal guy, and I have a good memory."

Adam clenched his jaw. "What do you want from me?"

"This isn't a zero-sum game. That's the art of the deal. We both come out ahead. Otherwise what's the point?"

Adam nodded.

"I'd like to count on you for information from time to time, and you can count on me for support for your company."

"We already have the support of congress," Adam said.

"Very few of them know exactly what your company does. I could speak out against the tyrannical *1984* style software that's being used to spy on the free people of the United States. That would play very well for my presidential run. People just don't trust the government anymore." John grinned. "And for good reason, don't you think?"

"If you become president, and that's a big if, you'll be begging for Armor Software. Like you said, we'll revolutionize how we fight the War on Terror. And, if you lose, nobody will give a shit what you say."

"Are you sure you haven't been in DC longer than a year?" John chuckled.

Adam remained blank-faced.

"There's more than one way to skin a cat. It would be a shame if we found something incriminating in your past. Or how about Kim? She was a model, right? I bet we can find her coke dealer."

Adam narrowed his eyes at John.

"You need a clean record for the kind of security clearance you have. If you put the company in jeopardy, I'm sure your board of directors and shareholders would be happy to give you a nice severance package."

"There's nothing in my past," Adam said.

"Yet." John smiled for a beat to let that sink in. "If that doesn't work, there's always nationalization. I doubt the free-market Republicans would give a shit, not when it's a matter of national security."

Adam exhaled; his shoulders slumped. "What do you want?"

"Just information. From time to time, I'll ask you for some information, and, in return, you'll have my undying devotion and support. Like I said, I'm a loyal guy with a good memory."

35: Katie and Declan

Katie sat on her couch, watching Declan's documentary—a hodgepodge of historical footage and interviews with fat-cat CEOs, socialists, and critics of capitalism. Periodically Declan paused the film to explain an important detail or behind-the-scenes fact.

After the credits rolled, Declan stopped the video, closed his laptop, and turned to Katie. "What did you think?" he asked, like a dog, desperate for approval.

Katie raised one shoulder. "It was good."

Declan scowled. "What does that mean?"

"What do you mean?"

"You shrugged when you said, 'It was good.'"

"No, I didn't."

"Yes, you did."

Katie sighed. "Whatever you say."

"See? That's what I'm talking about." Declan crossed his tattooed arms over his chest. "This is important, and you're like, '*Whatever.*'"

"I think it'll be great for your audience."

"But not yours?"

"My audience isn't the same as it used to be."

"So what? Anarchists hate capitalism. This should be right up their alley."

"That depends on which sect you're talking about. Anarcho-communists hate capitalism, but the anarcho-capitalists don't. If I recommend your documentary, I'll have millions of ancaps blasting it for inaccuracies on monopolies and corporations."

"What inaccuracies?"

"You talked about the Standard Oil monopoly, but the ancaps will say that Standard Oil had already lost market share from 90 percent to 60 percent when they were broken up by the government. And one of the reasons they had such a market share to begin with was because Rockefeller bribed governments."

"You can't be serious."

"I am serious. I've been studying Anarchist philosophy. They'll also say that corporations are corrupt because the owners of the corporations have their personal wealth protected by the corporate veil. Therefore, the company can act unethically, and the owners don't have to worry about being held personally liable."

"No shit. I talked about how corporate personhood is wrong."

"They'll say that corporations only exist because of the force and violence of government. They'll say that, without the corporate veil to hide behind, businesses would act more ethically, because the owners would be held personally liable for the actions of the business."

"Fucking ancaps are so stupid. Who the hell's supposed to enforce this liability?" Declan showed his palms. "The courts are government institutions."

"The ancaps endorse nonviolent solutions. Some talk about insurance companies and private courts. Others think the market will come up with the most elegant and effective solution."

Declan stood from the couch. "Listen to yourself, Katie. You sound like one of them."

Katie stayed seated. "Maybe I am one of them."

"Please tell me that you're joking," Declan replied.

Katie remained quiet.

"Why won't you give me a plug?"

"I told you. My audience is not the right audience for you."

His nostrils flared. "I'm your boyfriend. Jesus, you're so fucking selfish. Maybe if I could show my tits, I'd have a popular channel on YouTube."

Katie rose from the couch, her body shaking. "Fuck you."

"The truth hurts, doesn't it?" Declan stroked his beard.

"Get out," Katie said, pointing to the door.

Declan grabbed his laptop from the coffee table. "I'm done." He walked out, leaving the door open.

Katie shut the door behind Declan and returned to the couch. She curled up on the couch in the fetal position. *I'm done with him.* Tears slid across her face. Her phone buzzed on the glass coffee table, signaling a text. A few minutes later, her phone chimed. She ignored the phone. The chime stopped, followed by a beep for a new voice mail. Her phone chimed again. Katie spewed out a breath and sat up. She wiped her face with the sleeve of her T-shirt. She picked up her phone, surprised that it wasn't Declan. She swiped right.

"Hi, Penny," Katie said.

"It's alive. I thought you dropped off the face of the earth." Penny had an edge to her voice.

"Sorry."

"*Sorry* doesn't even begin to cut it. You act like a crazy person at lunch, and then you go all MIA for the past three weeks. You don't return my texts, my phone calls."

"I'm going through some stuff."

"I'm supposed to be your friend. You can't talk to me?"

"Declan and I broke up. At least I think we did."

Penny's voice softened. "Are you okay?"

"It's for the best."

"You didn't answer my question. Are you okay?"

Katie sniffled. "I will be."

"I met someone last night who would be perfect for you."

Katie frowned. "Declan and I broke up, like, fifteen minutes ago."

"He's very sweet, very successful, and very single."

"I don't think—"

"He can be your rebound guy."

36: Julie and a Great Memory

The timer was down to one minute. Julie and George stood in the kitchen, waiting on the lasagna in the oven.

"Thank you for stopping by again," Julie said.

"Thank you for your hospitality," George replied, staring at her.

"Why are you looking at me that way?" Julie asked, holding his gaze.

"I like looking at you."

Julie's face felt hot.

Max entered the kitchen. He narrowed his eyes at George and Julie. "What are you guys doing?"

They turned to Max.

"Just talking," Julie said.

"Just talking," George echoed.

Max laughed. "More like making google eyes at each other."

Julie grinned. "That's googly eyes, honey."

"Don't stop on my account," Max said, glancing in the oven window. "Smells good. I love lasagna."

The timer beeped.

"Let's eat," Julie said.

They readied their plates in the kitchen and sat down to eat in the dining room. Toward the end of the meal, Max talked about George's latest video.

"That Alex Cooley guy's a total dick," Max said.

Julie frowned. "Max, language."

Max shrugged. "What? He is. You should watch the video. He tried to argue that the military keeps us safe by taking the fight to the terrorists, so they don't come here. George blasted him with the statistics on the civilians

217

we've killed and how it's creating more terrorism and making us less safe." Max looked at George. "What was that stat about how much more global terrorism we've had since 9/11?"

"Terrorism fatalities have increased 500 percent since 9/11," George replied. "Per an article in *The Guardian* from 2014. I suspect it's even higher now. An organization called the Institute for Peace was indexing and publishing global terrorism fatalities. They're no longer operating. I don't know for sure, but I think they were shut down for distributing *inconvenient* statistics."

"By who?" Julie asked.

"I don't know. Neoconservatives, the military industrial complex, central bankers? A lot of groups benefit from war."

Julie nodded. "Where do you learn all this stuff?"

"I read a lot. On the road, I listen to podcasts. I like history and psychology and science. I'm no expert though."

"You do have a really good memory."

Max laughed. "That's an understatement. I'm telling you, Mom. You need to watch his debates. He knows all these crazy statistics. When the person he's debating tells him that he's making something up, George cites his source. Not just where it came from, but the exact date if it's from the newspaper or the exact page if it's from a book." Max looked at George. "That statistic from *The Guardian* about the 500 percent increase in terrorism, what was the exact date of the article?"

"November 18, 2014," George replied.

Max grinned at Julie. "Told ya."

"That's incredible," Julie said. "How many of these debates have you done?"

"We do one a week," George replied. "We've done three so far. Katie wants to continue for as long as I'm willing and people are interested."

"People are definitely interested," Max said. "All three of his videos have over one million views already."

"That's wonderful," Julie said.

"I have an idea." Max popped out of his seat. "I'll be right back." Max ran upstairs.

Julie gazed at George, smiling. His black hair was short, naturally a little spikey. He was clean-shaven with small dark eyes that were sharp as lasers.

George looked up from his food. "Do I have something on my face?"

"No. ... I was just thinking that—"

"I found it," Max called out as he bounded down the stairs. He set a box of Trivial Pursuit cards on the table and sat down. "I wanna ask George some questions."

Julie's eyes flicked to George, then to Max. "George may not want to answer questions."

"Just a few," Max said to George.

"It's okay," George said. "There'll probably be things I don't know."

"I bet not." Max retrieved a card from the box. "What New York island does the Statue of Liberty stand on?"

"Originally the island was Bedloe Island. The name was changed to Liberty Island in 1956."

"See?" Max said to Julie. "What's the common name for sodium chloride?" Max frowned and answered his own question. "That's too easy. Salt." Max narrowed his eyes at George. "I have a better question. When did people first start making salt ... and where ... and how did they do it?"

George said, "Historians don't know for certain, but the earliest evidence of salt processing is about eight thousand years ago. People around the area that's Romania today were boiling spring water to extract the salts. There's also a similar area in China from about the same time period."

Julie's eyes were wide. "This is amazing. Do you have a photographic memory?"

"I'm no expert, but, as far as I know, the photographic memory is a myth. There is the eidetic memory. With an eidetic memory, a person can recall images and auditory information in great detail, but the memories fade quickly. Apparently 2 to 10 percent of children have this memory, but they lose it as they get older. This is why kids are so good at learning foreign languages. This type of memory is very rare in adults, but there are adults with great memories. I think I'm just a person with a good memory."

"That's for sure," Julie said.

Max read from another card. "Yerevan is one of the oldest continuously habited cities. It is the capital of what country? And how old is the city? That's my bonus question."

"Yerevan is the capital of Armenia," George replied. "It was established in 782 BC by King Argishti."

"Why don't you go on *Jeopardy*?" Max asked. "You'd make a fortune. You wouldn't have to deliver motorcycles ever again."

"I have stage fright."

"I don't understand."

"I get nervous in front of an audience."

"Really? But you just answered those questions in front of me and my mom. And you do the videos."

"A couple of people is okay. When I do the videos, I'm just having a conversation with whoever I'm debating and Katie. With an audience of people, it's different."

"Maybe you could get some help. Like therapy or something."

"Let's not pry," Julie said to Max.

"It's okay," George said. "I tried therapy, and it did help. When I was younger, I doubt I could have done the videos. I think I would've froze. I'm not sure I would've come here either. I don't need to be in front of large groups of people, so it's not a problem."

"But you could be rich," Max said.

"Max," Julie said with raised eyebrows.

"I'm just saying."

George hung his head.

"I'm sorry, George," Max said.

George looked at Max. "Don't be sorry. You're absolutely right. I have some limitations."

"I don't think you do."

George forced a smile. "I appreciate that."

"George said he'll be in Virginia next weekend," Julie said, changing the subject. "I was thinking about having a cookout. What do you two think?"

"I'll bring some more produce," George said.

"Are you coming by to see me or my mom now?" Max asked with a straight face.

There was a moment of silence.

Julie's mouth hung open.

George cleared his throat. "I'd like to visit with you both if that's okay."

Max laughed. "I'm just messing with you guys."

George chuckled.

Julie smirked at her son. "Why don't you help clear the table?"

They cleared the table and set the dishes in the sink.

Julie looked through the kitchen window. "There's still a little daylight left," she said. "How about a walk?"

"That sounds good," George replied.

Julie turned to Max. "You want to come for a walk with us?"

"I'm not a dog," Max replied.

George and Julie stepped outside. Dan was across the street, staring at them. Julie ignored Dan as they walked past.

"That guy was staring at us," George said when they were safely out of earshot. "Do you know him?"

"That's Dan," Julie said. "He's the HOA president and a first-class creep. I've had a few infractions for my grass being too long."

"I didn't know you were such a badass."

Julie grinned. "I am kind of a badass. Not only do I mow when I damn well please but, when Max's principal scheduled a hearing to expel him, I told her to shove her hearing up her ass."

George laughed and made Julie reenact the conversation with Max's principal.

They walked on the asphalt path that encircled Julie's neighborhood. The path bordered a small swath of woods on one side, endless townhomes on the other. The summer heat dissipated as the sun dropped low on the horizon. Halfway around the circle, George held Julie's hand.

"You really do have an amazing memory," Julie said.

"Thanks."

"I don't want you to think this is a judgment, but why didn't you finish school? You must've been an excellent student."

George was quiet for so long that Julie wasn't sure if he would answer her question.

"I told you a little about my family," he said.

She nodded.

"I went to school with dirty clothes, poor hygiene, and low self-esteem. I was a small kid too. A late bloomer. I think that was partly because I wasn't eating well. As you can imagine, the other kids harassed me."

Julie squeezed his hand.

"My second-grade teacher was right out of school. Bright-eyed and bushy-tailed. I think she knew I was being picked on, and she wanted to help. I was a good student, so when she recognized the kids who got the best grades on tests and quizzes, I started to get a lot of attention. She made a huge fuss over me. I think she thought, if the other kids knew I was smart, they'd like me. It ended up being another thing for the kids to harass me about. So I missed a few questions on purpose, just to get out of the spotlight.

"When I was in high school, I was a C student on purpose. I skipped school a lot. I spent a lot of time in the woods. I liked the peace and quiet. I learned to forage and hunt and trap from some books in the library. I wasn't doing it for sport. I was hungry. I was still the doormat of my class. My face was in bad shape. That didn't help my popularity. You can still see the acne scaring." George let go of Julie's hand and pointed at his cheek.

"It's not noticeable," Julie said. "I think you're very handsome."

George blushed and took her hand again. "Now I know you're just being nice."

37: George, *the* Anarchist

George drove Julie's Honda through the upscale neighborhood. Julie was in the passenger seat, Max in the back on his smart phone. Lawns were bright green in the middle of a heat wave. Jeeps and sports cars graced the driveways, no doubt the vehicles of the cool kids. The German sedans and SUVs were tucked away in three- and four-car garages. The mansions were oriented toward the road with no concern for the power of the sun and no need to harness passive solar energy. These suburbanites had multiple air conditioners, multiple gas furnaces, and multiple bank accounts more powerful than the seasons.

"Thank you for coming," Julie said.

George glanced from the road to Julie. "Thank you for inviting me."

Julie wore a knee-length sundress that showed off her runner's legs. Her auburn hair was parted on the side and hung to her shoulders. She brushed an errant strand from the corner of her eye.

"Are you okay?" George asked. "You look nervous."

"I'm fine," she replied with too much conviction.

"She's nervous about you meeting everyone," Max said, his eyes still locked on his phone.

"Is that true?" George asked.

"That's not entirely true," Julie replied.

"Aunt Summer can be a big B sometimes, and Uncle Jason can be a big D," Max said.

Julie turned and scowled at her son. "Your aunt is a very nice person, and your uncle is all bark and no bite."

Max laughed. "And Grandma always agrees with everything they say."

Julie turned back to George. "My sister's certainly not a big B. Jason can be opinionated, but his heart's in the right place." Julie paused, then winced as she said, "Can you avoid talking about politics?"

Max laughed again. "This is gonna be awesome."

"Not helping," Julie said.

"What?" Max said.

"You know what."

"George should be able to say whatever he wants."

"It's fine. I'll stay away from politics," George said.

"It's just they're pretty serious Republicans," Julie said to George. "Jason's a partner in some law firm in DC. He knows a lot of government people, even a few congressmen and senators."

"It's a birthday party, not a debate. It'll be fine."

Julie pointed out the stone mansion, but it was hard to miss. A long line of shiny vehicles hugged the curb, pointing the way. They parked at the end of the line and hiked to the house. Max carried the gift and George a cloth bag filled with produce. Julie opened the door without knocking and entered the marble-floored foyer with George and Max behind her. A spiral staircase stood before them and a hand-painted mural of a vineyard was on one wall.

"Summer?" Julie called out.

"In the kitchen," Summer replied.

They walked through the dining room on the way to the kitchen. A cluster of teen girls sat at the dining room table, looking at their phones. A striking blond was at the center of the clique.

"Happy birthday, Heather," Julie said to the blond.

The teen looked up from her phone. "Thanks, Aunt Julie," she said without enthusiasm. She went back to her device.

"This is my friend, George."

"Hi, Heather," Max said.

The birthday girl didn't respond. She was lost in her own world, a world in which she was the center.

The kitchen was filled with massive stainless-steel appliances and a center island counter covered in catered Mexican food. An older woman stood, hovering over a cake, writing with icing. Summer set a jug of sangria on the center island. She was a tall, lithe, blonde—pretty, but slightly less so than Julie. She smiled wide and tottered over on her wedged heels. Her shorts were short, and her legs were long and athletic.

"Hey, sis," Summer said.

Julie smiled, and they hugged.

The older woman set down the icing dispenser and joined the group. She had white hair to her shoulders. She looked to be in her late fifties but had to be pushing seventy.

"Hi, Grandma," Max said, hugging the old woman.

"Hello, honey," Grandma said to Max.

"Hi, Mom," Julie said, hugging her mother.

Summer kissed Max on the cheek with a big smack of her glossed lips. She pulled back, her hands now perched on Max's shoulders. "Let me look at you," she said. Summer pinched Max's chubby cheek. "Still such a cutie-pie."

Max turned beet red, aware of the nubile girls in close proximity. "Where do I put this?" Max asked, holding up the gift.

Summer let go of his cheek. "Everything's out back on the patio. Lots of cute girls." She winked at her nephew.

Max started for the patio, still beet red.

"Food's getting cold. Why don't you make yourself a plate first?" Summer said.

"I'll come back," Max replied as he walked away.

"Don't embarrass him," Julie said to Summer.

Summer smirked. "Embarrassing kids is the only fun I get to have."

"He's sensitive."

"He's fine."

"He could use some toughening up," Grandma said.

"George, this is my mom, Helen," Julie said, motioning to Grandma.

"It's really nice to meet you," George said.

Helen shook his hand, her eyes narrowed. "It's nice to meet you as well."

Summer turned her attention to George. She looked him up and down, from his short dark hair to his deep-set eyes to his clean-shaven face to his best gray T-shirt, jeans, and finally his boots. Her eyes moved back to his face as if she'd made a definitive judgment with a single scan of her eyes.

"And this is Summer," Julie said, motioning to her sister.

George and Summer shook hands. "I've heard a lot about you. Some of it good," he said, with a smile.

Summer burst into laughter, no doubt fueled by the sangria. "I need to keep my eye on you," she said, pointing at George.

George held up the cloth bag. "I brought you some produce from my garden."

"Oh, thank you," Summer said, taking the bag. She peered inside at the tomatoes, peppers, and eggplant. "Should I refrigerate these?"

"You don't have to," George said, "but they'll last longer in the fridge."

"You're the fella on the news, making everybody so mad," Helen said.

"Mom, you need to stop watching US News," Julie said.

"Then how am I supposed to know what's going on?"

"It's propaganda, not news."

"President Reynolds said we need to be careful of Internet news, because that's fake news."

Summer had the Sub-Zero open, searching for space, but the massive fridge was packed to the gills with food that would eventually be thrown away. She shut the fridge and set the cloth bag on the center island. "I'll find space later," Summer said.

"So how's everything at the house?" Julie asked Helen, changing the subject.

Helen frowned. "The yard man won't take the clippings. He puts it in my trash can, but my trash man comes in the morning, so the grass stinks up my trash for a week. I think he should take the clippings with him. I tried to tell him, but he doesn't even speak English. How do you live in the United States and not know how to speak English? It should be a law."

"Did you call the company?" Julie asked.

"I did. They wanted to charge me five more dollars. Isn't that ridiculous? I told them that was highway robbery."

"He could recycle the clippings back into the yard," George suggested.

Helen scrunched up her face as if she'd tasted something bitter. "It makes an awful mess. Clippings everywhere."

Summer called out toward the clique of girls sitting at the dining room table. "Heather, did you say hello to your aunt and George?"

"Yeah," Heather called back, annoyed.

"Heather's being a brat," Summer said to Julie in a hushed tone.

"Why?" Julie asked, matching her tone.

"She's mad because she thinks she's not getting a car."

"I thought you—"

"It's a surprise." Summer winked. "Why don't you two make your plates? Everyone's on the patio."

George and Julie readied their plates.

Summer said to Helen, "We're going to the patio. Are you coming, Mom?"

"It's too hot," Helen replied. "I'll be out a little later, when it cools off."

Summer led George and Julie downstairs. The walkout basement featured a full bar, pool table, foosball table, movie theater, and a gym. They stepped outside on the patio.

Teen girls and boys stood, talking in groups, drinking bottled specialty beverages—the coolest thing short of alcohol. Max was on the periphery of a group of boys. Nine adults sat around the rectangular table, talking, drinking beer and sangria. The massive patio was concrete and flagstone with built-in stone benches and five-figures' worth of wicker furniture. A banner hung over the back doors which read Happy Sweet Sixteen, Heather.

Summer set the sangria on the table. She introduced George to her husband, Jason, and their friends—a few neighbors and two of Jason's coworkers and their wives. Jason sat at the head of the table with a bottle of beer. He had short salt-and-pepper hair. He was barrel-chested and soft around the middle. Summer sat at the opposite end of the table from Jason and beckoned Julie to sit next to her. This left George at the only remaining seat, kitty-cornered from Jason.

"Have a seat," Jason said.

George set down his plate. "Where are the drinks?"

"Sangria's on the table for the women." He smirked. "We also have beer and scotch inside at the bar." Jason stood as if to get George a drink. Jason wore khaki shorts, a polo, and sandals—the apparent uniform for the adult men at the party.

"Water would be great, but I can get it," George replied.

Jason eased back into his seat.

"Bottled water's in the cooler," Summer said, pointing to the cooler at the end of the patio near the gift table and a trash can.

George stepped to the cooler and looked inside—bottled water and a wide variety of overpriced specialty fruit drinks that claimed ingredients from exotic locales. George shut the cooler and peered into the trash can. It was filled with empty and half-empty plastic bottles. He grabbed an empty water bottle from the trash and scanned the back of the house. He stepped to the outdoor faucet and filled up the bottle.

"Is the bottled water gone already?" Jason called out from the table.

George turned around with the full bottle of tap water. "No, there's quite a bit left." George approached the table, all eyes on him.

Jason grinned, nearly cracking up with laughter. "Then why are you filling up a used bottle from the spigot?"

George shrugged and sat in his seat next to Jason. "I don't wanna contribute to the plastic." George bit into a steak fajita.

Jason laughed and half the table joined in. George continued to eat, unfettered.

"I agree," one of the wives said. "The kids leave the bottles everywhere, and they don't even finish them. It's such a waste. The oceans are filled with plastic, you know?"

"Teri's our resident environmentalist," Jason said, motioning to the tiny tan woman. "She drives a Tesla but lives in a mansion like the rest of us."

"Jason." Summer shot her husband a look from across the table. "If we all did our part like Teri, the world would be a better place."

Jason held up his hands. "You're right." He looked at George. "So are you an environmentalist?"

"I'm not sure what you mean by that," George replied.

"One of those save-the-polar-bear types with hemp clothing and over-priced composters that they don't use."

"I use my overpriced composter," Teri said with a smile.

Jason said, "Don't worry, Saint Teri, protector of Gaia. I wasn't talking about you. I just think, in general, the environmental movement is long on fashion and short on substance."

"George lives in an off-grid house that he built himself," Julie said, "and he hunts and grows a lot of his own food."

"I had a lot of help with the house," George said. "I was more like the general contractor."

"I would love to live in an off-the-grid house," Teri said.

"What do you hunt?" Jason asked.

"Deer and turkey," George said. "I trap rabbits and groundhogs."

"You eat them?" one of the wives asked.

"Yeah. There wouldn't be much point in killing them if I didn't."

"Groundhog?"

"It's actually not bad, and they're easy to trap, so it's not much work at all."

"That's gross," Summer said, her nose scrunched.

Jason's cell phone chimed. He reached into the pocket of his shorts and glanced at the screen. "I think it's the guy," he said, looking across the table at Summer. He connected the call. "Hello." Jason listened. "Fifteen minutes?" He listened again. "Great. See you then." Jason disconnected the call. "He'll be here in fifteen minutes," Jason said to Summer, then turned to George. "We bought Heather a car. She doesn't know it yet. It's being delivered on a flatbed."

The adult guests finished their food and congregated on the driveway, Heather still inside, sulking and oblivious. The flatbed wrecker parked in the street with a shiny new Volkswagen Beetle. The rumor filtered through the young people as the car was driven off the tilted flatbed.

By the time Heather ran outside, the wrecker was gone, and all that was left was her birthday surprise. She jumped up and down, high-pitched screaming, her friends joining in the celebration, no doubt recognizing the peripheral benefits of rides and adventures to come. After well-deserved hugs and kisses given to Jason and Summer, the birthday girl zoomed out of the neighborhood with two male suitors and two of her closest friends. The rest of the teens were disappointed at their second-rate status in Heather's life smacking them upside the head. Despite the dis, they stayed, waiting for her return. Besides, there was still the promise of cake.

Heather returned from her joyride and blew out her candles. The teens and the men had cake. The adult women avoided it like it was poison. Julie was the only exception. The women were fitter than most of the men. Outside of the teen boys, George was the only man without a first-world paunch. The men had their trophies, and the women had their resources. Biology is often crass when coupled with civilization.

After cake, the teens cleared out, leaving paper plates and half-empty glass and plastic bottles behind. The adults returned to the table on the patio and to the alcohol. George ended up next to Jason again, not on purpose.

"We weren't going to buy her a car, but, with the way the stock market's been"—Jason smiled like the cat that ate the canary—"let's just say, we've done well."

"It's been quite a run over the last decade," one of the men said.

"I remember in 2008 when everyone thought the world was ending," another man said.

"It turned out to be the opportunity of a lifetime," Jason said. "I wouldn't be surprised to see the Dow at 40,000 in the next couple of years. What do you think about the stock market, George?"

"I don't invest in the stock market," George replied.

"You don't even have an opinion? From what I've seen on the news, you have a lot of opinions."

"Don't be pushy, Jason," Julie said.

"I'm not being pushy. I'm just asking a question."

George took a sip of water. "I think the stock market's overvalued because the valuations are based on future growth that's unrealistic because of debts growing faster than natural resource and energy extraction, the limits of which we're starting to encounter."

"Whoa." Jason smiled wide and slapped the table. "That was a mouthful. So you're a Malthusian?"

"What's a Malthusian?" one of the men asked.

"A follower of Thomas Malthus," Jason said. "He was an economist from the early 1800s who thought population growth would outstrip agriculture and a bunch of people would die, sending us back to a subsistence lifestyle. He was proved laughably incorrect with the agricultural revolution."

"He didn't know we'd use diesel-powered machines and petrochemicals to feed ourselves," George said. "Without oil, the planet would have a tough time supporting seven billion people. Our use of energy tracks population growth very well. If we were to have less energy, we'd likely have less people."

Jason chuckled. "Please tell me that you're not one of those peak-oil believers. I had one in my office. He was so freaked out in 2008 when gas was over $4 a gallon. Yet here we are, ten years later, with gas barely over $2."

"Peak oil's just an observation of how oil fields produce during their life span. The world uses an Olympic swimming pool worth of oil every fifteen seconds. It's only a matter of time before we're forced to live on less."

"That's astounding," Teri said. "A swimming pool every fifteen seconds?"

George nodded toward her. "It is."

"We've been hearing this crap since the seventies," Jason said. "Jimmy Carter tried to sell us this shit. It's funny, you know? Democrats bitch about

President Reynolds, but Democrats and Republicans have been enjoying low gas prices and fat 401(k)s."

"That's true," one of the men said.

"What do you think about President Reynolds?" Jason asked George.

"You don't have to answer," Julie said, glaring at Jason.

"I think he's an asshole," Teri said.

"We know what you think," Jason said to Teri. "She's in love with John Bradley, which is interesting, because he'd be dead if not for George here." Jason looked at George with a straight face. "Do you ever wish you had let Congressman Bradley die?"

"Are you serious?" Julie said, scowling at Jason.

"It *is* a good question," Summer said. "These Anarchist terrorists want to kill government officials. They say so themselves."

"George is *not* a terrorist!" Julie said.

"It's okay," George said to Julie.

"It's not fair to put George on the spot for your drunken amusement," Julie said.

Jason frowned. "Come on, Julie. Everyone here knows George is an Anarchist. Hell, he's *the* Anarchist. It's the elephant in the room that we're all tiptoeing around. He wants to destroy the US government. I, for one, would like to know why."

"I'd prefer not to discuss politics," George said. "If you wanna know why I believe what I believe, watch my videos. I'm very transparent."

"That's a cop-out," Jason said. "He's afraid that he'll be proven wrong. Intellectually embarrassed in front of his new girlfriend."

"That's enough, Jason," Julie said.

"Jason does have a point," Summer said. "I've watched some of George's videos, and he literally wants no government. Who would take care of the poor and the old? What about the military and the police? Who's going to keep us safe? As a mother, a Mad Max world wouldn't work for me."

George took a deep breath. He looked from Jason to Summer then back again. "I oppose the state because everything the state has, has been stolen. Everything the state will ever have, will be stolen. If the state were a good idea, they wouldn't have to force us to support it with violence and coercion." George stood from the table.

"That makes no sense," Jason said. "We the people are the government.

We can't steal from ourselves. And we're not forced to support the government. That's ridiculous."

"Why do you pay your taxes?"

Jason was dumbfounded for few seconds. "Every country has taxes."

George shrugged and looked at Summer. "May I use your restroom?"

"Sure. We have seven. I'm sure you'll find one."

As George left the table, Julie stood and met him at the back door. She grabbed his hand. "I'm sorry," she mouthed.

"He's fine. He's a big boy," Jason called out.

"It's okay," George said, squeezing her hand. He let go and entered the house.

George used the restroom but didn't return to the patio. He walked upstairs. Helen, Julie's mother, dozed on a recliner in the living room. George opened the front door and stepped outside. It was still warm, the orange sun low on the horizon.

Max sat on the front steps, playing a game on his phone. His cheeks were flushed, his brow dotted with perspiration. His oversize T-shirt and baggy jeans concealed his shape. He glanced back at George. "Hey," Max said.

"How are you doing?" George asked.

Max shrugged. "These rich kids are stuck-up."

George sat down on the steps a few feet away from him. "Wealth is a blessing and a curse."

Max still played his game. "I'd take that curse any day."

"If you're given everything, if your life is too easy, you don't develop any grit or determination. You run the risk of becoming an entitled a-hole."

"They're already entitled assholes." Max turned off his game and shoved his phone in the pocket of his jeans. "I heard Uncle Jason talking shit."

George laughed. "He certainly voiced his opinions. Your grandmother seems nice."

Max lifted a shoulder. "She poked my stomach and told me I need to exercise."

George's jaw tensed. "That's not right."

"She's always comparing me to Heather. Of course she's perfect and I'm …" Max hung his head.

"You're the most talented teenager I've ever met."

Max looked at George.

"You remember what I told you about my life when I was your age?"

Max nodded.

"If I could go back in time and tell myself one thing, I would tell myself not to care what people think about me."

Max nodded again.

The front door opened, and Julie stepped onto the stone stoop. "Hey, guys," she said.

George and Max turned their heads toward Julie.

"You ready to go home?" she asked.

"Yes," they said in unison.

38: John and the Homefront

John was in his home office, the door closed, his cell phone to his ear.

"You want me to leave Linda?" John asked, his voice hushed.

"I won't ask you to do that, but I need something real," Donna replied through the phone.

"It'll happen whether we're together or not. Linda and I are like roommates at this point—roommates who barely tolerate each other."

"If you're divorced, you can forget about the presidency. You won't even be nominated."

"I'd get divorced after the election."

"We still couldn't be together."

John sat at his desk. He ran his hand over his face. "Why not?"

Donna huffed. "Think about it, John. The press would have a field day with me. My career, my life, would be over. I'd never work in this town again. I'd be a pariah worse than Monica Lewinsky."

"Fuck 'em. I'd be a pariah with you, and we'd be together—really together. I care more about you than I do about my career *or* my legacy."

"You shouldn't." Donna was quiet for a moment. "I should go."

"I'll make a reservation at the Mandarin on Monday." John waited for a reply. "Donna, are you still there?"

"I'm here." She sighed. "I'll see you on Monday."

"Good night." John disconnected the call and set his phone on the desktop. He leaned back in his chair, his hands behind his head. He thought about what it would be like to be unencumbered by a wife and children and a political career where he was beholden to so many.

The doorbell brought John back to reality. He glanced at the time on his phone. It was after nine. *It's a little late for visitors.* John left his home office for the front door. He passed Bobby watching a war movie on the way. Linda had already answered the door and was in the foyer talking to Ellen's boyfriend. Tyler was obviously attracted to Linda, evident by his proximity to her, his saucerlike eyes, flushed face, and smiley mouth. He was still too young and inexperienced to know how to hide it. *What a fucking douchebag.*

Linda would never do anything, but she was enjoying the attention. Tyler was tall and wiry—probably had nice abs under his T-shirt. He had that Justin Bieber hair that all the girls liked.

"Congressman Bradley," Tyler said with a big grin as John approached.

John narrowed his eyes. "It's a bit late, don't you think?"

"Ellen and I are going to see *Fifty Shades Freed*. It starts at ten."

"Like hell you are." John crossed his arms over his chest. "You're not taking my daughter to some X-rated movie."

"John, it's not an X-rated movie," Linda said.

Tyler's shit-eating grin was gone, replaced by a dumbfounded gape. "It's, uh, rated R. It's not that bad." Tyler paused, recovering. He spoke quicker now, as if he expected to be cut off at any second. "I didn't even wanna see that. Ellen likes the books. I think it's totally stupid. Some billionaire who's like in his twenties and wants to, like, feed Africa or some crap, and he's all buff and has a big ..." Tyler cleared his throat.

John glared at Tyler.

"Like I said, the movie's stupid, but Ellen, you know, she, uh, likes the books."

Ellen bounded down the spiral staircase, with long legs and short shorts, her silky blond hair halfway down her back.

Tyler stared, his mouth open. "You ready to go?" Tyler asked as Ellen strutted toward them.

She smiled, her teeth white and straight. "Yes."

Tyler put his hand on the door handle.

"Hold on a second," John said. "I expect you home by midnight."

Ellen scowled. "Dad, the movie starts at ten, and they have previews, and the movie's at least two hours. Then we have to drive home. It'll probably be closer to one."

"I expect you to come home directly from the movie, no stopping off anywhere for any reason." John glowered at Tyler. "Straight back here after the movie."

"Yes, sir. We'll come right back," Tyler said, his back ramrod straight.

"Have fun, you two," Linda called out as they exited.

"Not too much fun," John added.

John followed Linda into the kitchen. Machine gun fire emanated from Bobby's movie in the family room.

"I thought they broke up," John said.

"They're back together now," Linda replied.

"I don't like him."

Linda laughed and grabbed a glass from the cupboard. "He reminds me of you."

"He's only interested in sex," John said, his voice low, aware of Bobby in the next room.

Linda laughed again, this time verging on hysterics. She sighed.

John was straight-faced. "I don't see what's so funny."

"Do you want to be the pot or the kettle?"

"I was *not* like that."

"If you say so."

"Do you think she's having sex?" John asked in a low volume.

Linda filled her glass with water from the fridge door. She took a sip and pursed her lips.

"Do you think she's having sex?" John asked again.

"I'm not sure."

"If she gets pregnant, she'll be like Bristol Palin. Her life will never be the same. It might cost me the presidency."

Linda smirked. "There it is. We all have to conform to your standards for your career. You forced Ellen to go to public school for your career, which is where she met Tyler to begin with. We all have to dress a certain way, look a certain way, talk a certain way. We're people, not ornaments."

"These aren't my standards. I didn't make the rules. And, for the record, I didn't force Ellen to do anything. I asked her."

"And you knew she'd do anything for you."

John took a deep breath. "Aren't you worried she'll get pregnant?"

"She's on the pill."

John widened his eyes. "What? When did you make that decision?"

"A couple of months ago."

"Jesus, she's already having sex?"

"I don't know if she is. Last I heard, she was thinking about it. But don't worry. There won't be any evidence of her impropriety for the tabloids to dissect."

John shook his head. "Why didn't you talk to me before getting her birth control?"

"I make a lot of decisions without you." She narrowed her eyes. "You're never here."

"That's bullshit, Linda. You could've talked to me."

"No, what's bullshit is you expecting to be involved in decisions when you're never here. And, even when you are here, you're in your office working." Linda went upstairs.

John walked to the family room. Bobby lay on the couch, mesmerized by the Iraqi battlefield on the screen. He wore pajamas decorated with little dinosaurs. John sat on the nearby recliner. "Hey, buddy," John said.

"Hey, Dad," Bobby replied, still glued to the screen.

An Iraqi woman tried to throw a grenade at a platoon of American marines. She was shot by a sniper in the nick of time.

"Should you be watching this?"

Bobby grabbed the remote and paused the movie. "It's *American Sniper*. Did you know he killed the most people ever?"

"He did what he had to do to protect Americans, but it would've been better if he'd never been there and never had to kill anyone."

"I'm gonna be a marine and go to war. I'll be a hero, and, after that, I'm gonna be in the secret service, like Agent Barnes, and I'll be a hero again."

John rubbed the back of his neck. "You don't have to go to war to be a hero."

"I know, but that's the best way."

39: Katie, Fun and Flirty

Katie stood in front of her bathroom mirror. She wore a shirt dress that hung to her knees and clung to her curves. Her light-brown hair was in loose waves. Penny had told her to wear something "fun and flirty." *This is as fun and flirty as I get.* She also told her to shave and wear a bra. Apparently this guy was pretty straight-laced.

Six months ago, Katie would've told Penny that she shaved for no man, and she wore a bra when she wanted to, not for sexist conventions. But here she was with shaved legs and armpits, and wearing a bra.

Her phone buzzed. It was a text.

Declan: I really need to talk to you.

Katie shook her head and thumb-typed a Reply.

Katie: No. I told you that it's over. Stop texting me.

"*Katalina?*" Susen called out from the living room. "You have company."

"Coming," Katie called back.

Katie's phone chimed. It read, *Declan calling.* She sent the call to voice mail and checked the time on her phone. *Two o'clock. He's right on time.* She exited the bathroom, headed for the living room.

Zach stood behind Susen, his hands in the pockets of his khaki pants. Susen smiled, turned on her sneakers, and left her with this man she'd never met. He grinned as she approached. Zach was wiry and short, about the same height as Katie. *I bet he weighs less than me.*

"Katie?" he asked.

"Hi, Zach," she replied.

He extended his hand. They shook.

His hands were small and soft.

"It's really nice to meet you," he said.

Katie smiled. "You too."

He was cute in a nerdy sort of way. He looked young, even though she knew he was thirty-five—ten years older than her. He reminded her of Patrick Dempsey without all the hairiness.

"Are you ready?" he asked.

Zach walked with her outside and opened the passenger door of his car for Katie. His Nissan Altima sedan was relatively new but not flashy. They drove through San Francisco to Castro Street. Zach found a parking space a few blocks away from the restaurant. He parallel parked along the street, the nose of his car pointed downhill.

He fed the meter, and they hiked uphill toward the restaurant. It was warm but breezy. Victorian-style buildings and townhomes lined the wide sidewalk. Small trees were landlocked by concrete. Electric wires hung over the road, hookups for the trackless electric buses that climbed the hills of San Francisco better than anything that ran on diesel.

They walked past shops, boutiques, Philz Coffee, a realtor, Wells Fargo bank, and a Human Rights Campaign Center. Zach held the door open to Anchor Oyster Bar.

The seafood place was cozy with a handful of people on stools along the counter and the tables half-full. The hostess sat them by the window.

"Have you ever been here?" Zach asked.

"No," Katie replied.

"The clam chowder's unbelievable. Oysters too, if you like them."

Katie nodded. "I do."

The waitress appeared. Katie ordered the oysters; Zach ordered the clam chowder. The waitress took their orders to the kitchen.

"Why did you want to go out with me?" Katie asked.

He chuckled. "You're direct."

"Is that a problem?"

He flashed his palms. "No problem here. I like direct. I saw a picture of you and Penny together. I asked Penny who you were, and I told her that I thought you were pretty and that I'd like to meet you." A grin tugged at the corners of his mouth.

"What else? You're leaving out something."

"I may have watched all your videos."

She smirked. "I'm not sure how I feel about that."

"Flattered. You should feel flattered. It's interesting how your political position has changed over the past year."

"Let me guess. You're a Democrat?"

"Politics already? Isn't that a little dangerous?"

"You started it. Besides, I thought we were being direct."

"I'm not a fan of the Republicans or the Democrats."

Katie raised her eyebrows. "Libertarian?"

"I guess you can put me in that box."

"Wow, a Libertarian in San Francisco. You're like a Big Foot sighting."

Zach laughed. "What about you? From what I can tell from your videos, you were a Democrat, and now you're an Anarchist?"

"I'm *leaning* toward anarchism. I'm not sure if I'm there yet."

He nodded.

"Penny told me that you're a software developer."

"I work for Armor Software," Zach said.

"I've heard of it," Katie replied. "What do you guys do?"

"We do database software. Mostly for government agencies."

"How did you get into that?"

"My roommate at Stanford was Adam Doyle. He's the CEO."

40: Julie and Rose River Falls

Julie sat in the passenger seat of her Honda, leafing through a worn paperback entitled *Waterfall Hikes of the Shenandoah Mountains*. George drove them along Skyline Drive in the Shenandoah Mountains of Virginia. The road was windy and steep, a short stone wall the only barrier between the road and oblivion. The road cut through a forest with leaves in every shade of green possible.

"Have you hiked them all?" Julie asked.

"Yes," George replied. "A few I've hiked many times. I drive through here every couple of months. I usually stop and stretch my legs with a hike. I found that little book in a shop in Luray at least ten years ago."

"Which one do you want to do?"

"It's up to you. Every one of those hikes is worth the walk."

Julie went back to the book. "The trailhead for Dark Hollow Falls is coming up at Mile Marker 51. It says we can see Dark Hollow Falls and Rose River Falls. It's six miles round trip."

"Rose River Falls is probably my favorite."

They passed Mile Marker 36.

"It's in fifteen miles," Julie said. "Let's do it." Her phone buzzed. She glanced at the text.

Verizon: As of August 8, 2018, you've used 50 percent of your data.

She placed her phone inside the center console. "I need to stop checking my phone every time it buzzes. If it wasn't for Max, I'd turn it off. At work last night, I saw so many couples on their phones. They're at a nice restaurant, and they're fiddling with their phones instead of talking to each other."

"Smart phones and social media are literally rewiring people's brains," George said, glancing from the road to Julie and back. "I listened to this psychologist talk about it. He did this really interesting study, and he found that the average college student unlocks their phone sixty times a day, and they use it a little less than four minutes each time. So they're interrupted sixty times, and they spend about 240 minutes on their phones. Think about what that does to concentration and deep thought."

"If I was interrupted sixty times a day, I wouldn't get anything done, much less think deeply."

"And with social media, people are constantly scrolling through their feeds, getting quick doses of information, which gives them dopamine hits and encourages more scrolling. Again people are thinking about the information from a very shallow perspective. Then you have the Likes, which assures that people only see the information they want to see. This creates an online echo chamber of confirmation bias and herd behavior."

"Confirmation bias is when people look for information to enhance what they already believe, right?"

George nodded. "Exactly."

"Do you think smart phones and social media make people more susceptible to propaganda?"

"I do. I also think it's undermining relationships. People have hundreds if not thousands of fake friends and very few real friends. Of course Katie's been collecting a ton of fake friends for me, so I shouldn't talk."

"What about the Internet?" Julie asked.

"I think the Internet's a double-edged sword. We don't live in a world like George Orwell's *1984* where information is restricted. We live in a world more like Aldous Huxley's *Brave New World*. People are docile, distracted by entertainment, and overloaded with information. It requires deep thought and concentration to wade through the propaganda to find the truth."

"But that deep thought and concentration is in short supply."

"It is."

"By design?" Julie asked.

"I don't know. Maybe. What do you think?"

"It wouldn't surprise me."

George parked near Mile Marker 51. They stepped out of the Honda and grabbed their packs. It was hot and humid, not a cloud in the sky. Julie surveyed the parking lot. Only one other car was there.

"Not too many people today," Julie said.

"This hike can get crowded on the weekend, but it's nice and quiet during the week," George said.

They walked from the parking area to the trailhead.

Julie led the way, following the blue blazes painted on the trees. It was noticeably cooler under the tree canopy but still muggy. Julie stopped, touching a massive tree next to the trail. "What kind of tree is this?"

"An oak," George replied.

As they continued on the trail, George pointed out the different trees—mostly mixed hardwoods: oaks, chestnuts, maples, ash, and birch. Mountain laurels and serviceberry grew in the understory.

As they neared the falls, Julie heard the cascading water. They were alongside the creek now—a branch of the Rose River. The banks of the creek were lush with fauna. They passed a man with his black lab.

"It's beautiful down there," he said.

They reached Dark Hollow Falls rather quickly. It was only a mile from the parking lot and mostly downhill. The falls were wide, multitiered, the rocks covered in moss. They hiked to the bottom, where a thigh-high pool of water gathered. Julie and George stood on rocks, gazing up at the seventy-foot-high cascading waterfall.

"Wow. So gorgeous," Julie said.

George nodded, staring at *her*.

They sat on a rock, enjoying the view, and sharing some trail mix before moving on. They hiked a couple more miles, the trail a slight decline, the Rose River alongside them. As they approached the Rose River Falls, the sound of falling water was louder. The Rose River Falls had two tiers. The top tier was a gentle cascade to a shallow pool. From here was a nice view over the cliff edge to the second tier—a steep cascade with multiple waterfalls, walled by stone on three sides, ending in a round pool.

"Look at that," Julie said with her hands on her hips. "It's beautiful." She smiled at George. "Can we get down there?"

"Yeah, just be careful with the wet rocks," George replied.

They picked their way down the steep embankment, holding on to trees, George always there to offer his hand. At the base of the falls, the whoosh of water reverberated off the stone walls and made normal conversation impossible. The waterfalls fell forty-feet, the river broken in three parts by the rock formation, to be reunited in the pool.

Julie stepped to the edge, bent over, and put her hands in the water. She said, "It's cool."

George showed his palms. "I can't hear you."

She stood and moved into his personal space. She spoke, her lips inches from his. "The water's cool."

He nodded.

"Thank you for taking me here," she said, slipping her arms around his waist.

George pulled her close. "You're welcome."

They leaned toward each other, their lips meeting in the middle.

After a moment, they separated, and Julie said, "Do you want to get in?"

George glanced down at his canvas pants. "I'm not dressed for it."

Julie had a crooked grin. "You could take them off."

George laughed.

"What? Only one car was in the lot, and that guy was going the opposite way." Julie removed her T-shirt, revealing her black sports bra.

"It's still early. People could've come later than us."

"Maybe." Julie untied her boots and slipped off her shoes and socks. She slid her shorts down her legs.

Before he could protest, she waded into the water in her black underwear and sports bra. Julie turned around in the waist-deep pool and beckoned him with a wave of her arm. "Come on," she said, although she was sure he couldn't hear her.

George removed his T-shirt. He had a nice build—not weight-lifter bulky but muscular, like someone who eats right and works hard. George stripped to his gray boxer briefs and waded into the water.

Julie stood under the waterfall, mist and river water dousing her. She was laughing. George moved under the water with her. Julie wrapped her arms around him. They were laughing together now, embraced, the power of the Rose River crashing over them.

41: George and Universal Morality

George drove through the Blue Ridge Mountains on a cloudless day. A podcast played on his stereo.

"Welcome to the *Abnormal Psych Podcast*. I'm your host, Everett Bush. It's Friday, November 2, 2018. Today we're revisiting the fascinating work of the late psychologist Lawrence Kohlberg, who studied the moral development of human beings. Kohlberg's theory says that moral reasoning, which is the basis for ethical behavior, has six identifiable stages. As a person rises on the scale, at each stage the person is better equipped for navigating moral dilemmas. The six stages of moral development are grouped into three levels—preconventional morality, conventional morality, and postconventional morality. Two stages are at each level.

"Level one or preconventional morality consists of mostly children nine years old or younger. At this level, we don't have our own personal code of morality. Our moral code is shaped by the adults around us and the consequences of breaking or following the rules. In stage one, we are good to avoid being punished. If someone is punished, we believe they must have done wrong. In stage two, we recognize not just one right view is given by the authorities. Different people have different viewpoints.

"Level two or conventional morality includes most adolescents and adults. At this level, we internalize the moral standards of our adult role models, but we do not question. Our morality is based on the cultural norms of the group we belong to. In stage three we are good to garner approval of others. In stage four, we become aware of the rules and laws of society. We follow the rules in order to obey the law and to avoid guilt."

George gazed at the endless fieldstone wall built on the roadside. Miles upon miles of beautifully stacked and mortared stone. *I wonder how many labor hours that took?*

Everett Bush still lectured through the speakers. "Level three or postconventional morality includes only 10 to 15 percent of people. According to Kohlberg, this level requires abstract thinking that many are incapable of. At this level, we choose our own principles, and our moral reasoning is based on justice and the rights of the individual. In stage five we understand that rules and laws might exist for the greater good, but, at times, they will work contrary to the interests of certain individuals. In stage six we have developed our own set of moral guidelines which may or may not fit the law. Yet the principles are universal. They apply to everyone. At this final stage we are prepared to defend human rights, justice, and equality, even if it means going against society and paying the consequences of disapproval and even imprisonment. Kohlberg thought that very few people ever reached stage six."

George passed a Lookout sign. He pulled off the parkway and parked in the empty lot. He cut the engine, grabbed his phone from the cradle, and stepped from his truck. He stretched his legs walking to the lookout. George stood on the fieldstone wall and gazed at the Blue Ridge Mountains, the tops covered in conifers. The midslopes were covered in the red and yellow foliage of ash and buckeye trees. The oaks and hickories in the valley had yellowish-green leaves. He sat on the wall for a while, the sun on his face. He thought about Julie.

His phone buzzed in his pocket, waking him from his trance. He retrieved it and swiped right.

Katie: We are #1. That's right. We have the most-watched political channel on YouTube for October. From the bottom of my heart, thank you! ☺

George: Congratulations, Katie!

Katie: It was all you. By the way, your friend Max sent me something awesome! It's supposed to be a surprise, so I won't tell you what it is. I will say that that kid is talented.

George: Max is very smart and creative.

Katie: I'd like to renegotiate our deal. I've already sent a small fortune to the Permaculture Research Institute. This Geoff Lawton guy was so grateful. He invited us to Australia so he could thank us in person. I was hoping we can raise the 100K profit cap. If we keep this up, we could have a million-dollar channel. I could cut you in for 10 percent.

George: That's great news! You're helping people. That's exactly what you said you wanted to do. I'm not interested in a cut.

George's phone buzzed.

Max: I made something for you. Click the **link.**

George clicked the link. The video was entitled "George 2020." George pressed play. The video buffered several times because of the spotty cell service in the mountains. It was a mashup of highlights from the debates he had been doing. Max had done a fantastic job picking out the best clips and arranging them in an order that told the story of the Anarchist philosophy of morality and nonviolence. He also skewered Republicans and Democrats with their own words, illuminating their hypocrisies.

George: Great job! Katie was very impressed as well. I'm assuming the *George 2020* was tongue-in-cheek.

Max: What is tongue-in-cheek? The video is trending on Twitter.

George: Tongue-in-cheek is like a joke.

Max: It is a joke. Do you think Katie might give me a job?

George: You should ask her. It's worth a shot. How's school going?

Max: Virtual is the best. I get my work done in like 3–4 hours and with no D-bags to deal with. They posted my first-quarter grades yesterday. I got all As.

George: That's great to hear. Congratulations!

Max: Thanks, but I don't care about the grades. I care about the learning, and I don't accept anything they say without additional research.

George: You're a wise man, Max.

Max: My mom wants me to ask you if you'll still be here next Friday.

George: I'm still on schedule.

Max: She just asked me a bunch of other stuff. I told her that I feel like a middle-school girl, passing notes. I said, *She can call you herself.*

George: Hah!

George swiped right on the first chime and pressed his phone to his ear. "Hey," George said.

"Hey, yourself," Julie replied. "Where are you?"

"Blue Ridge Mountains on the North Carolina–Virginia border. It's beautiful. I wish you were here."

"Me too."

"Are you working tonight?"

"Yes, I traded shifts. I'm working all weekend so next weekend I can spend it with you."

"I can't wait."

"How many bikes are in your trailer?"

"I have five to be delivered in the next couple days."

"Please drive carefully. I kind of like having you around."

"Kind of?"

Julie giggled. "I wouldn't want you to get too cocky."

"Too late."

"Will you call me when you get to the hotel?"

"I will." George paused. "I was thinking about you today. I like this quote by George Harrison of The Beatles. He said, 'There's no past, and there's no future. All there is ever is the now.' He's right. The past is over, and the future isn't guaranteed. That's why right now is so important."

"What are you saying?"

"I, uh, … I thought about waiting until I get back, but I want you to know now, because time is this unknown quantity for everyone. You just never know."

"You're worrying me. Are you okay?"

"I'm fine. I'm better than fine." George cleared his throat. "These past four months with you have been the happiest of my life. I wanted to tell you that, and I wanted to tell you that I love you."

Her voice caught. "I love you too."

42: John 2020

John stood behind the podium on a stage that covered center court at the EagleBank Arena—home of the George Mason University Patriots. The crowd was electric and ten thousand strong. They cheered and waved Bradley 2018, Bradley 2020, and Drain the Swamp signs. He was flanked by his wife, Linda, and the kids, Ellen, Charlotte, and Bobby. The girls wore conservative dresses; Bobby, a blue suit, with an American flag pin, just like his dad.

Donna was in the background with Grace. Television cameras were in the foreground. Agents Olson and Barnes scanned the audience for threats. A handful of other agents worked the crowd. They didn't expect any trouble. Everyone had been through the metal detectors.

John waited for the crowd to quiet. He smiled and waved periodically, starting another round of exaltation. He was happy to wait.

"We did it," John said into the microphone and shook his fist.

More applause sounded throughout the arena.

Finally they quieted. "Thank you," John said. "This is very humbling. I really appreciate your support as Americans but, more important, as people."

More cheers came.

"I'd like to acknowledge my family." He motioned to his wife. "My wonderful wife, Linda." Then his children. "The best kids a father could hope for, Ellen and Charlotte and my little man, Bobby."

The crowd was on their feet now, applauding.

"Of course I'd like to thank everyone who helped on the campaign. We had hundreds of volunteers, and I have the hardest-working staff in politics. Donna and Grace, thank you for keeping me pointed at the goal." John turned around and winked at the two ladies. "I wouldn't be standing here today if it weren't for the brave secret service officers who protect me and my family. My friend Agent Derrick Stokes died so I can be here today. It's a debt I can never repay. But I'll honor his death by being the best husband, father, and public servant that I can be."

Even more cheers erupted.

John smiled, letting the adulation wash over him. "Now I know many of you are here to celebrate my congressional victory, but I'm not naive. This is a rather large crowd for an incumbent reelection to congress, and I've heard a lot of talk about the 2020 presidential race. I've been surprised and flattered by the outpouring of support I've had for a 2020 presidential run. I think we're all tired of Republican warfare and crony capitalism. It's about time we drained the swamp."

The crowd applauded.

"The answer to the question many of you came to hear is, yes. Right here, right now, I'm announcing my candidacy for president of the United States of America in the 2020 election."

Pandemonium ensued. Applause and whistles reverberated through the arena.

New George 2020 signs were hoisted. The zeros in 2020 each contained a bloodred Anarchist A. They were everywhere.

John's smile evaporated.

The crowd booed. It was hard to tell if the boos were directed at the George Chapman supporters or if they were booing John Bradley. Fairfax County Police officers and secret service agents grabbed the George supporters, but there were too many of them. The cops barely made a dent. In fact, they made it worse by drawing more attention to the protestors.

John and his family were escorted offstage by Agents Olson and Barnes and taken to the home locker room, its wooden lockers housing basketball jerseys hanging in each one. The carpet was green and trimmed with yellow. Away from the media, John's family left his side to be replaced by Donna. She wore a skirt suit, her hair pulled back in a tight bun.

"What the fuck was that?" John asked Donna in a hushed voice.

"I don't know. We certainly didn't anticipate—"

"Jesus Christ, Donna, your job is to anticipate these things."

She scowled. "Nobody could've predicted this. *Nobody.* I do have a solution though."

John ran his hand over his face. "This is a fucking nightmare."

"Do you want to stand here and cry, or do you want to fix it?"

"I'm not crying." John smirked. "Well, maybe a little."

Donna shook her head. "George Chapman is popular because his brand is managed by Katie Fitzgerald."

"Who the hell is Katie Fitzgerald?"

"She has the number one political channel on YouTube. I did some research on some of her older videos. Guess who she compared to JFK?"

John grinned. "Yours truly?"

"Bingo. And I think she would work for us."

"Doing what?"

"Whatever we want."

43: Katie's Past and Future Collide

Katie sat behind her glass desk, looking at her laptop. *Holy shit. The most popular hashtag on Twitter is #George2020.* She navigated to YouTube. Several popular videos showed the protest at Congressman Bradley's victory party. *I need to interview George and get his reaction. Bradley must be pissed.* Her phone buzzed. She picked it up and checked the text.

> **Max:** Katie, the video I sent you made a lot of money in ad revenue. I think I have proven my worth, and I'd like to work for you. I want a 50/50 split on the ad revenue for videos I do by myself. I will edit and mix for you for 25 percent.

> **Katie:** 40/60 on videos you do and 15 percent on editing and mixing. Also, you need to get your videos approved by me before you make them. I will send them back to you if there are quality issues.

Katie set her phone back on her desk. Almost immediately it buzzed again. She grabbed her cell.

> **Max:** Deal.

> **Katie:** I'll send you a contract. Welcome to the number one political channel on YouTube.

* * *

Katie fastened a wooden necklace around her neck. She gave herself a once-over in her mirror. She looked pretty in a simple cotton dress and a cardigan. Her curvy body always looked better in dresses. Her phone buzzed.

> **Zach:** I'm here. Susen let me in. I'm waiting on the pool deck. No rush.

Katie smiled and grabbed her purse. She exited the pool house and saw Zach on the opposite side of the pool, staring out over the San Francisco Bay. The sun was low on the horizon, breezy, but warm for November—mid-sixties. Katie sidled up to him, slipping her arm around his waist.

Zach turned to her with a smile that reached his eyes. "You look beautiful," he said.

"You don't look half bad yourself," she replied. That was the truth. His dark hair was cutely disheveled, and his jeans and untucked button-down fit him nicely.

"It's a great view."

"I love it here."

"Why don't we eat here tonight? I'll call for carry out. We can light candles. It'll be dark by the time we get the food. We can watch a movie afterward."

Katie smiled. "I'd like that."

"Did you still want Italian?"

Katie nodded. "Unless you want something else."

"Italian's fine with me."

Zach and Katie checked the menu on his phone. After deciding, Zach called the restaurant and ordered.

"It'll be forty-five minutes," Zach said.

They relaxed on the pool deck, talking and enjoying the weather. Half an hour later, they drove to the restaurant.

Paradiso Restaurant and Bar was a hole in the wall. A place with great food for the locals that hadn't been spoiled by the San Francisco guide books. Zach opened the door to the restaurant for Katie. They walked past the bar to the carry-out window.

"I'm here to pick up an order for Zach," he said to the old woman.

"It'll be just a few minutes," she replied.

Katie surveyed the bar and seating area with only five square tables and another five booths along the wall. The bar had a dozen stools, half of which were taken by a group of hipsters. They reminded her of Declan's friends. *Shit.* That's because they *were* Declan's friends. And there was Declan, a beer in hand, glaring her way.

Katie whispered in Zach's ear. "My ex-boyfriend Declan is at the bar over there."

Zach looked over to Declan and his entourage. "Which one?"

"Don't stare."

Declan slid off his bar stool and ambled toward them. He was dressed like a wannabe revolutionary—tight black jeans, a tight black T-shirt, and black bracelets.

"Hey, Katie," Declan said.

"Declan, how are you?" Katie asked.

Declan shrugged. "Who's your friend?"

Katie froze.

"I'm Zach," he said, holding out his hand.

Declan looked down on Zach with one side of his mouth raised in contempt.

Zach dropped his hand after Declan made no effort to shake.

"You're like a different person," Declan said, staring at Katie as if Zach were invisible. "Is that a fucking cardigan?"

"Don't be a dick," Katie said.

"Oh, I'm a dick? You're the one who threw me away like trash, and then you wouldn't even talk to me. And now you look like a 1950s' housewife with this little corporate man-boy."

"You're drunk," Katie said. "Why don't you go back to your friends?"

Declan glowered at Katie. "You're a fucking sellout."

"Hey," Zach said.

Declan wobbled back to his friends.

Katie put her hand on Zach's forearm. "Don't worry about it."

They suffered through a couple minutes of Declan staring. Finally their food was ready. Zach positioned himself between Katie and the bar as they walked toward the exit. Declan slid off his bar stool and gave Zach a little shoulder as they stepped past. Zach took the impact in stride and didn't react.

In the parking lot, Declan appeared with two of his buddies, Royce and Oliver.

Katie and Zach stood next to Zach's Nissan.

"Were you going out with this little man-boy behind my back?" Declan asked.

"Are you serious, Declan? We broke up four months ago. You need to move on," Katie said.

"Let's go back inside," Royce said.

"You should listen to Royce," Katie said.

Declan raised his bearded chin to Zach. "Hey, man-boy, walk away so Katie and I can talk."

"Would you like to talk to him in private?" Zach asked Katie.

Her arms were crossed over her chest. "Absolutely not."

"No can do, bracelets," Zach said to Declan. "Why don't you go back inside?"

Declan stepped closer, looking down on Zach. "I'll do whatever the fuck I want." Declan turned his attention back to Katie. "I can't believe you're with this square. Look at him. Fucking corporate shill."

"Are you done?" Katie asked.

"No, I wanna talk to you alone."

"Dude, calm down," Oliver said.

"You're done," Zach said.

Declan puffed up his chest. "Walk away, man-boy."

Zach didn't move.

"I said, 'Walk away'!" Declan shoved Zach.

Zach stumbled back against his car, dropping the bag with their food on the asphalt.

"Don't touch him," Katie said.

Zach recovered and threw an upper cut to Declan's stomach. Declan collapsed to the asphalt and wheezed, the wind knocked out of him.

Zach stood over Declan. "Deep breaths, bracelets."

Declan's buddies bent over their fallen comrade.

"Is he okay?" Katie asked.

"He's fine. It's just his wind," Zach said.

"We'll take care of him," Royce said.

Declan still wheezed but less so.

Katie squatted next to Declan. "I broke up with you because you're a hypocrite. You're masquerading as some sort of revolutionary man of the people, but it's bullshit. You don't care about anybody but yourself."

44: Julie and Casualties of War

The teakettle whistled. Julie and George stood from the couch. They wore sweats, their relationship already favoring comfort over superficiality.

Julie placed her hand on his forearm. "I'll get it. You sit."

She walked to the kitchen and removed the kettle from the burner. As she readied two cups of herbal tea, her phone buzzed on the counter. It was a text from Larry. Her heart pounded as she opened the text. It was a picture of Larry kissing a beautiful woman on a white sandy beach. He was reddish-tan and shirtless; she was blonde and bikini-clad. They looked happy. Julie deleted the text and blocked his number. *Why would he send me this?*

Julie carried the teas to the family room and placed them on the coffee table. She sat next to George, her face blank.

"You okay?" George asked.

"I just got a text from Larry," Julie replied.

George raised his eyebrows. "What did it say?"

"Nothing. Just a picture of him kissing a woman on a beach. Why would he send me that?"

"Was the woman attractive?"

"Yes, very."

George rubbed the stubble on his chin. "I think it's a big FU. He's saying this attractive woman likes me, so I must be valuable, and you're missing out."

She huffed. "He's such a creep."

"He may have hired the woman for the picture."

"Well, I blocked his number." She blew on her tea. "Do you think I have anything to worry about?"

"Is this the first time he's contacted you since you broke up?"

"Yes. Don't you think it's weird that he's contacting me now, after all this time? It's been over four months." Julie sipped her tea.

"Yeah, I do, but he probably rationalized everything that he did. He probably believes *he's* the wronged party, maybe even that you broke his heart. People can obsess over rejection for a long time, especially men."

Julie shook her head, scowling. "If he thinks that I wronged him, he's truly insane."

"Will you let me know if he contacts you again?"

"Can we talk about something else? He makes my skin crawl."

George nodded. "I was thinking how it would be nice to have a garden here. I could install it for you." He sipped his tea.

"Sounds good," Julie said, "but it also sounds like work."

"I'll do the hard part of prepping the garden, and I'll tend it when I come to visit. You just have to do some harvesting and weeding while I'm away."

"When would you put the garden in?"

"Not until spring. I'll bring you some seed catalogues to look over."

Max descended the stairs, his laptop under his arm like a book.

"Hi, honey. Want some tea?" Julie asked, cradling her cup.

"No, thanks," Max said as he approached. "I need to show George something." Max opened his laptop on the coffee table.

George and Julie leaned forward.

"Check it out." Max pointed at the screen with a wide grin. "*George2020* is the most popular hashtag on Twitter."

George forced a smile. "That's great, Max. You started that."

"We should really do it."

"Do what?" George asked.

"Run for president."

George's mouth turned down. He placed his teacup on the coffee table.

"I know what you're gonna say," Max said. "You could never win. But I disagree. You had like a thousand people at John Bradley's victory party. People already want you to be president, and you're not even trying. Imagine if we tried."

"I appreciate your optimism, Max, but I don't think it's possible to even get on all the ballots, much less win. And, even if it was possible, it's not something I wanna do."

"Why not?"

George grinned. "Well, for one, who's gonna deliver all these motorcycles?"

Max crossed his arms. "Seriously, why not?"

George's smile receded. "Because everything that the government does is funded and backed by violence."

"You could do some really good things."

"Even if I'm doing good things, and I think some politicians really do wanna do good things, I'm still using the violence of the state to make people do what I want. It's not ethical."

"People are tired of being lied to. They want someone who tells the truth."

"The crowd's fickle. They don't know what they want."

Max closed his laptop. "I still think we should do it."

* * *

They were covered by the comforter, their bodies intertwined, their breathing heavy. Julie laid her head on George's bare chest, and he wrapped his arms around her. They relaxed, coming down from their endorphin release. He pressed his lips to her forehead.

Julie smiled. "I wish we could stay like this forever."

"Me too."

"What time do you have to go tomorrow?"

"I should probably be on the road by eight."

"How did I get so lucky?" she asked.

"Did you win the lottery?"

She tilted her head up, her eyes on his. "You know what I mean."

"I think it's the other way around."

Julie kissed him on the cheek. She rolled to her back and propped her head with a pillow. "I thought all the good ones were married."

"Maybe I'm one of the bad ones."

Julie frowned. "Seriously, you had to have at least been close."

George nodded. "Once."

Julie waited for George to elaborate, but he was silent. "Spill it, Chapman."

George laughed. "It's not that interesting." He paused for a beat. "I was engaged. We had been dating for a couple years. I hid my money at my house because I don't trust the banks. I showed her where it was, in case something happened to me. It turned out she was less trustworthy than a central banker.

She stole everything and left. I never saw her again."

Julie's face fell. "That's awful."

George nodded. "I haven't had the best of luck with people."

She grabbed his hand and squeezed. "I don't know how anyone could ever be mean to you."

He leaned over and kissed her. "You mind if we change the subject?"

"Do you think you could be president? I mean, if you had a billion dollars, a staff, and all the things you need to run a campaign?"

"I seriously doubt it."

"Let's pretend that you're the president. What would you do?"

"I'd dissolve the Federal Reserve, legalize competing currencies, and abolish taxation. The currency and taxation empowers the government to enslave us and to make war. Granted, in reality, I'd never complete any of those tasks. Congress wouldn't support any of those things. I doubt American citizens would either. I'm not sure Americans are ready for real freedom."

"You really think Americans wouldn't support that?"

"Almost every person on this planet's been propagandized since birth to believe that their government's necessary and virtuous. It's embedded in our culture, our education, even in our friends and family. You remember that football player from a few years ago, the one who kneeled during the national anthem?"

"Yes."

"People literally lost their minds over that. Why should anyone be forced to stand for a piece of cloth that symbolizes the institution that enslaves us?"

"I think people were upset because he did it in front of soldiers."

"So what?"

Julie pursed her full lips. "I know they might be misled, but the soldiers do mean to protect us."

"These wars make us less safe, not to mention the civilian casualties overseas."

Julie scowled and inched away from George.

"I'm surprised you'd say that," George continued. "You know the statistics on the increase in terrorism since 9/11."

"I just don't think we should blame the soldiers. They deserve our respect."

George shook his head. "No, they deserve our disrespect. It's our respect that encourages more young men to join the military. Maybe if we didn't respect mass murder in this society, young men wouldn't wanna participate in it."

Julie slipped out of bed and snatched her pajamas and underwear from the floor. She dressed quickly. George exited the same side of the bed and also dressed.

"It's the politicians who people should be angry with," Julie said. "It's not the soldiers' fault."

George pulled up his sweatpants. "I don't dispute that the politicians are culpable, far more culpable than the soldiers. But it's the regular person who becomes the trigger man. Stanley Milgram determined that 60 percent of Americans will electrocute someone to death simply because someone in authority tells them to do so." He slipped his T-shirt over his head. "This narrow-minded allegiance is deadly, and, if we support soldiers afflicted with this hysteria, we're part of the problem. It's like telling the addict, 'Great job smoking that crack today.'"

Julie was red-faced. "So my husband was just a narrow-minded trigger man—a murderer?"

George showed his palms. "Maybe we shouldn't talk about this."

"No, we should. Answer my question." She crossed her arms over her chest.

"It's complicated." He put on his hooded sweatshirt.

"Somehow I think you can explain it."

George frowned. "If a military aggresses upon another country or especially civilians, the casualties in my opinion are murders. The problem is the propaganda always justifies the aggressive action."

"You sound like a politician. Answer the question." Julie's eyes were glassy. "Are soldiers murderers?"

"Some of them are. Some of them act as an accessory to murder. The medical personnel aren't, but their salaries *are* derived from extortion."

Julie hung her head, her voice barely audible. "They just do what they're told."

"That's the problem," George said softly. "Even a child hears, 'Would you jump off a cliff if your friends did it or told you to do it?' People are ultimately responsible for what they do."

"Would you like to know what Justin did?"

George was silent.

"He was a drone pilot. So, in your eyes, he was definitely a murderer."

George didn't respond.

"Who the hell are you to judge anyway?" Julie asked. "You were never in the military."

"Do I have to become a serial killer to know that it's wrong to murder?"

Julie blew out a breath. "You don't have any idea what it's like to be a soldier."

"That's true, but twenty-two veterans kill themselves every day for some reason—"

"Fuck you." Tears slipped down Julie's face. "They're not just numbers. They're people. Justin wasn't just a number." Julie crumpled to the floor, her head in her hands, her body racked with sobs.

George knelt beside her. "I'm sorry. You said he died in a car accident." He placed his hand on the middle of her back.

She stiffened. "Get out."

He removed his hand and stood. He trudged to the dresser, zipped up his duffel bag, and left without a word.

Julie thought of that long-ago day. Justin had said he wasn't feeling well. That wasn't uncommon. Julie and Max had gone to her parents' house for the afternoon. She was happy he wasn't coming. Justin had been so withdrawn since he got out of the army. He wouldn't or couldn't work. He refused to go to therapy. He was like another child—a grown, dependent, damaged child. Julie did everything without any help.

The first thing she had noticed upon returning home was the envelope taped to the door. *Julie* was scrawled across the front in Justin's handwriting. He wrote that he was sorry. To not let Max in the basement. That he loved her and Max, but he didn't deserve to live.

The images scrolled through her mind like a twisted slideshow. The plastic sheet Justin had laid on the floor. His body contorted and twisted. The blood and brain matter. The handgun. The holes in his head.

"Through and through," the detective had said when he thought Julie wasn't listening.

45: George and the Petrodollar

George drove north on US 15 through southern Pennsylvania. The traffic was light. The moon cast dim light on the mostly leafless trees and fallow fields that bordered the highway. He replayed his argument with Julie over and over in his mind. *I should have known. She was so vague with the car accident story.* He tapped on his phone and played a podcast. He needed a distraction.

"This is Barry Krause of the *Extreme History Podcast*, and this is episode 342. It's Sunday, November 11, 2018, and today I'll be examining the petrodollar. The petrodollar isn't something you'll find in your high school history book, but it's been critical to American wealth since 1974. To really understand the petrodollar, we have to go back to the Bretton Woods agreement.

"In 1944, global financiers and politicians met in Bretton Woods, New Hampshire. The International Monetary Fund and the World Bank were established during this meeting with the goal of stabilizing exchange rates of national currencies, and facilitating international trade. At the time, national currencies were valued according to the gold exchange standard. This is different than the gold standard, where currencies are backed by gold. The gold exchange standard valued a currency based on how much gold they could buy on the open market. This was simply supply and demand. The bankers and politicians hated it because they couldn't manipulate it.

"With the Bretton Woods agreement, they eliminated the gold exchange standard and replaced it with the dollar standard. The world would now peg their currencies to the dollar, and the United States would peg their currency to gold at thirty-five dollars an ounce. At the time, the US government had two-thirds of the world's gold, yet it was illegal for US citizens to own gold.

"During the fifties and sixties, the US government ran large trade deficits to pay for the Korean War, the Great Society Programs, and the Vietnam War. Dollars became very abundant in comparison to gold. Predictably foreign governments holding US dollars exchanged them for gold, and the massive American gold hoard diminished rapidly.

"John Butler wrote in *The Golden Revolution*, 'By July 1971, the US gold reserves had fallen sharply to under $10 billion, and, at the rate things were going, would be exhausted in weeks. Treasury Secretary John Connally was tasked with organizing an emergency weekend meeting of Nixon's various economic and domestic policy advisers. At 2:30 p.m. on August 13, they gathered, in secret, at Camp David to decide how to respond to the incipient run on the dollar.'

"'Nixon's solution, pressed by the banking community, was to abandon the gold dollar standard. In his speech, the president informed Americans that he had directed Connally to suspend temporarily the convertibility of the dollar into gold or other reserve assets. He promised this would defend the dollar against the speculators.'

"'Temporarily', to Nixon and the bankers pulling the strings, meant 'forever'. The US government could now fund outlandish budgets without restraint, and the bankers would be there to siphon off the profits. There was only one problem. What if people lost faith in the value of the dollar and paper money? If that happened, there would be bank runs and a rush to dump worthless dollars for real tangible assets. The bankers and the US government wanted inflation, just not so much that people lost confidence in the money itself. In fact, the stated goal of the Federal Reserve is 2 percent inflation. It sounds so small and so benign, but 2 percent inflation results in a 50 percent devaluation of the dollar in thirty-six years. Put another way, every thirty-six years they've stolen half of every dollar in existence. That is in *addition* to taxation.

"Without gold backing, what would provide demand and, therefore, value to those infinite dollars being spread domestically and abroad? Enter the petrodollar.

"In 1974, a series of talks took place between then Treasury Secretary William Simon, former President Richard Nixon, former Secretary of State Henry Kissinger, and then Saudi King Faisal. The purpose of the meetings was to convince King Faisal to sell Saudi Arabia's massive stockpile of oil only in US dollars and then to consider recirculating his dollar profits into US treasury securities. In return, the United States government offered military protection for Saudi Arabia's oil fields, weapons for their own military, and, perhaps most important, protection from Israel.

"The Saudi royal family accepted the deal. With the Saudis on board, the other oil-producing nations wanted in. A year later, all the oil-producing nations of OPEC had agreed to price their oil in dollars and to hold their surplus oil proceeds in US government debt securities in exchange for US military protection and weapons.

"Nixon, Kissinger, and Simon had replaced the demand for dollars from the failed Bretton Woods arrangement with the petrodollar system. The artificial demand for dollars soared due to the increasing demand for oil around the world. The petrodollar system has brought tremendous wealth to the United States. It is a system that must be maintained at all costs.

"The petrodollar system has been challenged from time to time. Saddam Hussein was once a critic of the US dollar. He referred to it as the 'currency of the enemy' and in 2000 began selling Iraqi oil in euros. We all know what happened next.

"Former Libyan leader Muammar al-Gaddafi also made the mistake of defying the petrodollar and the central bankers, by proposing a gold-backed dinar to be used in Africa. His plan was to stop selling oil in US dollars— only accepting payment in the gold dinar. Libya had close to 150 tons of gold and similar amounts of silver. Ultimately Gaddafi was killed and sodomized by a bayonet. Libyan oil is still sold in dollars today.

"Bashar al-Assad and Syria dropped the dollar for the euro in 2006. The Syrians paid the price with a civil war and US bombings in 2017.

"Iran's been poking the bear for the past two decades. They created the Iranian Oil Bourse in 2005 and stopped accepting US dollars in 2007. Also in 2007, President Mahmoud Ahmadinejad tried to persuade OPEC members to move away from the dollar, which he called a 'worthless piece of paper.' Iran has been sanctioned by the United States and the European Union. Economic hardship in Iran has been the result. In October 2012, their currency, the rial, collapsed in value.

"Just this past Friday, Iran announced that they entered into an agreement with Iraq to sell Iraqi oil on the Iranian Oil Bourse, outside of the US dollar of course. The mainstream news buried the story, but make no mistake, this is a devastating blow to the United States. The US has spent a fortune in Iraq over the past three decades. This has been done, not to steal oil, like many critics say, but to maintain the status of the petrodollar. Iraq has come full circle with their intention to sell oil outside of the US dollar. It stands to reason that Iraq and Iran believe the United States is too weak to do anything about it.

"Make sure to join me next week as I delve deeper into Iranian history. I'll tackle the nationalization of Iranian oil by Prime Minister Mossadegh, much to the chagrin of the company we now know as British Petroleum. This led to a CIA- and MI6-backed coup to install the shah of Iran. I'll cover that and much more. Until next time, this is Barry Krause of the *Extreme History Podcast*.

George turned on the radio and listened to music. He cracked his window to keep from falling asleep. Gravel crunched under his tires as he drove on the narrow road that led to his home.

He parked in front of his boarded-up cabin. The clock on his radio read 2:24 a.m. He exited his truck, his legs stiff. He unlocked his garage, opened the roll-up doors, and flicked on the overhead lights.

George's phone buzzed. He ignored it and backed his trailer into the garage. He unhooked the trailer from his truck and then backed his pickup into the garage. He shut the roll-up doors.

His phone buzzed again. He fished his phone from his pocket and swiped right. He leaned against his truck.

> **Julie:** I can't sleep. I feel really bad about what I said to you. I'm sorry. It hurts to believe Justin died for nothing. I hope you can forgive me. I love you.

> **Julie:** If you're still awake, please let me know you're okay. I'd be devastated if something happened to you because I made you leave in the middle of the night. I have this sick feeling in the pit of my stomach that you fell asleep while driving.

> **George:** I'm home, and don't worry. I'm in one piece. I understand why you were upset. It's a terrible situation. It must have been unbelievably hard. It still must be. If you want to talk, I'm here. I love you, and I'll call you in the morning. Try to get some sleep.

46: John and United We Stand

John and Donna sat on the couch in John's congressional office.

"I think we should keep our options open," Donna said.

"He's arguably the most successful campaign strategist alive," John said.

"He's also pushing seventy."

"This guy's a winner."

"He lost his last important campaign—your brother's reelection."

John frowned.

"Does he know anything about running a campaign in the digital age?" Donna asked.

"You can ask him."

"I plan to," Donna replied.

"By the way, did you take care of your accounts?"

"I'm in cash, short-term treasuries, and gold."

"Good. The last time I had a warning this severe was in 2007. We've had a decade-long bull run fueled by the printing press, the VIX is at all-time lows, interest rates have nowhere to go but up, and the public is all-in."

"Hopefully the downturn lasts through the election," Donna said. "It would be nice for Art and the Republicans to have a little egg on their faces."

The phone rang on John's desktop. He rose from the couch, walked to his desk, and picked up the phone. John listened for a moment. "Send him in."

Donna stood from the couch. She looked the part of the professional woman with her skirt suit, heels, and hair pulled back.

The door opened, and a young blonde ushered the white-haired man inside.

"Frank," John said with a wide grin.

"It's good to see you, John," Frank replied as they shook hands.

Donna sidled up to the men.

"This is Donna Hayes, my chief of staff and right-hand woman," John said to Frank.

"It's nice to see you again, Frank," Donna said with a nod to the man. They shook hands.

John raised his eyebrows to Donna.

"We met at the Memorial Day party," Donna said.

Frank had tiny wire-rim glasses too small for his big block-shaped head. He looked like an elderly Fred Flintstone in a three-piece-suit.

"Would you like something to drink?" John asked.

"No, thank you," Frank replied. "I had too much coffee this morning."

"Why don't we sit?" John said, motioning to the sitting area.

Frank sat in a chair, John and Donna on the couch opposite.

"I appreciate you taking the time to meet with me," Frank said. "You two must be busier than a one-armed paper-hanger."

John laughed. "It's been hectic."

"Well, it's just the beginning."

"What made you decide to come out of retirement?" Donna asked.

"She's down to business. I like that," Frank said to John, then looked at Donna. "I don't golf. I don't fish. I don't like cruises, and I don't like eating dinner at four in the afternoon. I'm a campaign strategist, not a retiree."

"A lot has changed in six years."

"You wanna know if this old dog can still hunt?"

"No," Donna replied. "I want to know if you're prepared to run a campaign in the digital age."

Frank smiled. "You don't mince words. That's for sure."

"We are planning to hire an expert in social media marketing," John said.

Donna narrowed her eyes at John.

"Look," Frank said. "I'm not gonna blow smoke up your ass. It's gonna be an uphill battle. Art'll be a formidable opponent. You can count on that. He's black, so he's bound to redirect some black Democrat votes his way. He's a decorated soldier and general, so he'll have the military, the bootlickers, the warmongers, and everyone afraid of their own shadow, which is a big group these days. He'll have a lock on most of the Republican vote. He might lose a few racists, but even the white supremacists hate liberal Democrats more than black people. To top it all off, he comes from a working-class background. You better believe they'll paint you as a spoiled silver-spoon blue blood that can't relate to the average Joe."

"Sounds bleak," John said.

"That's why you need me."

"I don't mean to be rude, but I'll be blunt," Donna said. "You lost with an incumbent president. How do you expect to win under these circumstances?"

"Will and I are great friends, so I don't think he'll deny or be offended by the facts. If you ask him, he'll tell you that his heart wasn't in it. He took Hank too lightly. Will didn't listen to me." Frank leaned forward in his chair, looking directly at John. "I think your brother was relieved when he lost. Will was finished with politics long before politics was finished with him. This is an entirely different scenario. With your charisma and my plan, we'll win." Frank leaned back, waiting for the inevitable.

There was a moment of silence.

"I'll bite," Donna said. "I'd like to hear your plan."

Frank grinned. "I thought you'd never ask. We can forget about the Republican votes, so no point in playing the man in the middle. We need to keep as many of the Democrat votes as possible. We need a healthy chunk of the Independent vote, and we need the new voters—the young people."

"Tell us something we don't know," Donna said.

Frank said, "This George Chapman character could destroy our campaign, or he could be the key to victory. It depends on how we frame our message. I've done some independent polling, and, if Chapman were on the ballot, he'd have 9 percent of the popular vote."

Donna's mouth hung open. "That can't be right. People who identify as Anarchists are less than 2 percent of the population."

"This is true, but somewhere around 8 percent of voters will vote for the candidate who they think is the best person, regardless of party. And 69 percent of voters think politicians aren't trustworthy. Chapman has 9 percent of the popular vote, because people think he's honest, and they like him as a person."

"People hate him," Donna said.

"And we've picked up quite a few residual haters from our association with him," John added.

"He is polarizing," Frank said. "But that'll happen with an extreme position."

"Do you think he'll run? His *George2020* hashtag is everywhere."

"I doubt it, but we can still ride his popularity. Do you have a whiteboard or a pad of paper? I'd like to illustrate my point."

"I think so," Donna said, standing. She left the room.

John and Frank shot the shit until Donna returned with a young receptionist carrying a whiteboard. The blonde set up the whiteboard next to Frank.

"Thank you, Madison," Donna said.

Madison shut the door behind her.

Frank stood and removed a notepad from the inside pocket of his suit jacket. He scribbled numbers on the board, occasionally glancing at his notepad.

202,000,000 Registered voters
126,000,000 Registered voters who actually vote
76,000,000 Potential voters sitting at home (38 percent do not vote)

12 percent Not Political (minus 88 percent don't vote) = 3 million voters
4 percent Libertarian (minus 24 percent don't vote) = 6 million voters
1 percent Green Party (minus 23 percent don't vote) = 1.5 million voters
34 percent Independent (minus 46 percent don't vote) = 37 million voters
26 percent Republican (minus 20 percent don't vote) = 42 million voters
23 percent Democrat (minus 22 percent don't vote) = 36 million voters

Art– 42 R, 3 D, 14 I = 59 million votes
John– 33 D, 23 I = 56 million votes
Libertarian & Green Party Candidates = 7.5 million votes

Not Political Voters= 3 million votes up for grabs and many more sitting on the couch. (Need to mobilize this group to vote.)

Electoral College Blue States:
West Coast, CO, and NM = 94
East Coast = 101
Northern Midwest = 56
TOTAL 251 electoral votes

NEED 270 out of 538 to win

Frank turned from the board.

Donna raised one side of her mouth in contempt. "Now we know exactly how we'll lose."

John frowned.

"I also know how we'll win," Frank said. "Twelve percent of registered voters identify as not political. This amounts to 24 million people. Eighty-eight percent of these people don't vote. If we can get a sizable amount of these 88 percent couch-sitters to vote, we have a chance to win the popular vote, which will help us where it counts—the electors."

"Not an easy task," John said.

"Anyone wanna guess what percentage of the *not political* category indicated that they'd vote for Chapman?"

"Twenty-five percent?" Donna asked.

"Fifty-nine percent," Frank replied.

John let out a low whistle.

"The second thing we have to do," Frank said, "is we have to win Pennsylvania."

"The twenty electoral votes in Pennsylvania put us over 270," John said.

"Anyone wanna guess who's from Pennsylvania?" Frank grinned.

"Chapman," John said.

"All roads lead to Chapman."

"This is about convincing the Chapman fans to vote for me."

"Bingo," Frank said. "You're already tied to Chapman with the shooting. You're antiwar, like Chapman. You're the antiestablishment candidate, right?

That appeals to Chapman supporters. The key is gonna be connecting with the Chapman supporters without going too far and losing your base. Your message has to be all about peace abroad and peace at home. People are tired of the endless wars. This'll play well against the Republicans, and we take a supposed weakness, your lack of military service, and turn it into a strength. You prefer diplomacy over war."

"Sounds pretty damn good," John said. "And we might have an ace in the hole."

Frank raised his eyebrows.

"Apparently the young woman who handles Chapman's social media was a fan of mine."

"Katie Fitzgerald?" Frank asked.

"You don't miss a trick," Donna said.

"Like I said, retirement wasn't for me."

"We don't know if she's still a fan," John said, "but, at one point, she was a hard-core Democrat. Something tells me that we can convince her to come over to the winning team."

"We need to figure out how we want to use her," Donna said.

"And Chapman," Frank said. "Maybe we can get him to tone down his message and endorse us in exchange for a cabinet position. You'd be surprised how quickly principles are thrown out the window when real power is on the table."

"We definitely need Chapman to tone down his message," John said.

"At the very least," Donna said, "I'd like to see Chapman's videos before they're posted. We could front-run them with a similar but more rational message."

"I'd give Fitzgerald a call before she's co-opted by the Libertarians," Frank said.

"I'm on it," Donna said.

"And one more thing. *Drain the Swamp* can't be the slogan for our campaign. It's fine to say it on occasion, but it's too negative for the peace candidate that's gonna bring us together. I was thinking, *United We Stand*."

John nodded and glanced at Donna. "That's good."

"I agree," Donna said.

"When can you start?" John asked.

Frank smiled wide. "I already have."

47: Katie and the Compromise

Katie sat at her desk checking her email on her laptop. One particular email caught her attention. She opened it.

From: DonnaHayes@JohnBradley.house.gov
To: Katie@KatieTalk.com
Subject: Opportunity

Katie Fitzgerald,

Congressman Bradley and I are impressed with your digital marketing skills. I'd like to discuss an opportunity with you. It's sensitive in nature, so I've attached a digital nondisclosure agreement. Please look it over, sign if you're interested in talking, and provide a contact number.

Sincerely,
Donna Hayes
Chief of Staff for Congressman John Bradley

Katie opened the nondisclosure agreement. It was pretty standard. She provided her digital signature and sent it to Donna, along with her cell phone number. Katie's phone buzzed on the glass desktop. She picked it up and swiped right.

Zach: I'm about to board the plane to DC. I'll miss you. I was thinking we could go away for the weekend when I get back.

Katie smiled and texted a response.

Katie: I'm missing you already. A weekend vacation sounds perfect.

Katie returned to her laptop. She finished her email and checked the latest YouTube comments. She no longer responded to them as there were too many, and they were mostly sophomoric, crude, or insane.

Her phone chimed. *Restricted Number.* Katie swiped right.

"Hi, this is Katie."

"Hello, this is Donna Hayes, Chief of Staff for Congressman Bradley. Thank you for taking my call."

"You're welcome."

"Like I said in my email, Congressman Bradley and I are impressed with your skills as a digital marketer. We'd like to collaborate with you."

"I appreciate the compliment. I'm not sure how we'd collaborate, but I'd love to book Congressman Bradley for a debate with George Chapman. Given their history—"

"That wouldn't work for the congressman."

"I know my platform isn't exactly Democrat-friendly anymore, but all of our guests are treated fairly."

"Congressman Bradley doesn't want to debate Mr. Chapman. Like I said, he'd like to cooperate with Mr. Chapman."

"Politically they're not in agreement," Katie said. "Not even close."

"We think the agreements outweigh the differences. For example, the congressman is staunchly antiwar, antigovernment corruption, and pro-reform. Of course Mr. Chapman is an advocate for a stateless society, but we won't get there overnight. Supporting Congressman Bradley is a rational stepping stone to a more egalitarian and peaceful society. We agree with Mr. Chapman's sentiments. We just feel that our society's not ready for that yet. Experts agree that a stateless society would result in tremendous suffering. That point is moot, however, because a stateless society won't occur in our lifetime, possibly ever."

"What are you asking for?"

"We'd like an endorsement from Mr. Chapman, and we'd also like for Chapman to tone down his message, to make it more palatable for the general public and more in line with our message."

"Why not ask him directly?"

"We don't think he'll agree."

Katie exhaled. "Well, you're right."

"That's why I contacted you."

"I don't have any control over what George supports or says. I'm simply the conduit."

"Maybe you can influence him. There would be a cabinet position for Mr. Chapman, if he complies. We're also looking for a head of social media for the presidential run. This position would continue as the White House Press Secretary. If you can secure the endorsement, the position is yours."

"I have the most popular political channel on YouTube channel. Why would I work for you?"

"Correction, you have George Chapman. He won't be there forever. But this is the opportunity of a lifetime. This is real politics, not some YouTube channel talking about hypothetical societies that'll never happen."

Katie pursed her lips. "What if I can't convince George to endorse Congressman Bradley or to tone down his message?"

"I understand it's a tall order. If that's not possible, we'd at least like to see new videos one week before their release. This will help us to stay on top of the message and to craft appropriate responses to the media."

Katie shook her head. "Let's cut the shit, Donna. You're going to front-run the videos. You'll craft a similar but less extreme message and glean some juice from our video when it comes out. People will invariably search for similar themes, and your message will be there, feeding off our scraps. What I can't figure out is why you'd want to be more connected to George. I thought Congressman Bradley wanted to distance himself from George?"

"Like I said, Congressman Bradley's message isn't so different from Mr. Chapman's."

"Why would I do this? I'm assuming the job offer's off the table."

"The head of social media position would be off the table, but Congressman Bradley would be quite appreciative, and we would still consider you for a position in the future."

Katie shook her head. "I need something tangible. I won't do anything for some hypothetical job and the congressman's supposed appreciation. You must think I'm an idiot."

Donna sighed. "I assure you that's not the case. I might be able to convince the congressman to offer a monthly consulting fee."

"Let me know when you have an amount."

"I'm emailing you a list of the political positions we would like for Mr. Chapman to alter. The email is coming from an anonymous account, so you won't recognize the address. The subject is List. The nondisclosure agreement is in effect for the incoming email. I'll get back to you on the consulting fee. I hope we can work together." Donna disconnected the call.

Katie set down her phone and checked her laptop for a new email. Nothing. She refreshed her email. *There it is.*

From: LovesLacrosse112233@gmail.com
To: Katie@KatieTalk.com
Subject: List

- Cannot say that the US government is immoral. It is acceptable to criticize governments unfriendly to the United States.
- Cannot say that taxation is theft.
- It is acceptable to criticize the corruption of politicians, but he cannot criticize Congressman Bradley.
- It is acceptable to say that the current government is corrupt and how it is up to citizens and good politicians like Congressman Bradley to change it.
- It is acceptable to be antiwar, but under no circumstances can he criticize the troops or the military.
- It is acceptable to criticize the drug war, but he cannot criticize police officers.
- It is acceptable to be in favor of better police training, but he cannot blame police officers for accidental or controversial shootings.
- It is acceptable to criticize a tax code that favors the wealthy, but he cannot support no taxation or a flat tax.
- He must be supportive of clean energy and a believer in anthropogenic global warming.
- He must be a supporter of a woman's right to choose.

- It is acceptable to be an advocate for gun rights, but he must also be an advocate for increased gun legislation. Specifically limits on magazine capacities, assault rifle bans, and more thorough background checks.
- He cannot support domestic terrorism or terrorism abroad.
- He cannot support anarchism. He can say that anarchism would be nice in theory, but he must say that it cannot work in practice.

This list is not exhaustive. When in doubt, mirror Congressman Bradley's position.

Katie scowled at the screen. *George'll never agree to that.*

48: Julie's Drowning

Julie sat across from her boss, Rodney.

"I'm sorry, Julie," he said. "I don't have a Saturday shift available."

"I really need the money," Julie replied.

Rodney adjusted his wire-rim glasses. He was a big man with a keg-size gut. "I'll put you on the list for a Saturday shift. It may take a while for one to open up. I have seven people ahead of you. I do have a Monday lunch shift. I know that's the worst shift."

Julie stood from the wooden chair. "Thanks, Rodney. I'll take it." Julie put on her coat and trudged from the back office toward the bar.

Busboys and servers were readying tables for the lunch crowd. The bartender, Eric, stared up at the flat screen behind the bar. Julie stopped at the bar and watched the television. President Henry "Hank" Reynolds spoke behind a podium. Hank Reynolds had blue eyes, blond hair mixed with gray, a square jaw, and was built like a linebacker.

The US News logo was in the lower left corner. The headline *Breaking News: Stock Market Crash, Trading Halted* was scrawled across the bottom of the screen. The lower right corner of the screen had down arrows and red numbers. *DJIA: 18,500. Down 9.8 percent. S&P 500: 1998. Down 10.4 percent. Nasdaq: 5233. Down 10.8 percent.*

"Our financial markets are under attack today by foreign speculators—many from China and Russia and Iran," President Reynolds said. "This isn't the first time our markets have been attacked by those who wish to do us harm, and it won't be the last. We've always recovered from these attacks, only to be stronger on the other side.

"In a globalized world, we aren't the only ones suffering today. Despite the current turmoil, the United States is still the safest place in the world to invest. I'm looking at it as a buying opportunity. The strongest companies in the strongest economy in the world are on sale today." USN cut to the news desk.

Eric muted the television, set the remote behind the bar, and turned his attention to Julie. Eric smirked. "Good thing I don't have any money to lose."

"Me neither," Julie replied.

"How did it go with Rodney?"

"No Saturday shifts are available right now. I did pick up Monday lunch."

"That sucks. Mondays are the worst."

"Hopefully a Saturday will open up."

Eric grinned and stroked his manicured beard. "We could always go out on Saturday. Make lemons out of lemonade."

"You mean, lemonade out of lemons."

He chuckled. "Yeah, right. Come on. It'll be fun."

"I have a boyfriend."

Eric clutched his heart. "You really know how to hurt a guy."

Julie cocked her head. "Wouldn't you rather go out with someone your own age?"

"You're not that much older than me. What are you, like, thirty?"

Julie laughed. "You're sweet. Try forty."

"We're only twelve years apart."

"See you tomorrow, Eric."

Julie left the restaurant and drove her old Honda toward home. The muffler was louder than usual. *A hole maybe? Not like I can afford to fix it.* She turned up the radio to drown out the exhaust noise.

On Public News Radio, a man said, "The Fed will backstop this crash, just like it's done every time we've had a downdraft over the past decade."

Julie flipped through the stations, settling on some peppy music—anything to take her mind off her finances. She drove through her neighborhood. Most of her neighbors had Bradford pear trees with brown leaves still clinging for dear life. Her neighbors complained about the cheap softwood tree that split too easily and grew too fast and too big for a townhome. For Sale signs and foreclosure notices appeared on every street. She parked in her spot, still singing along with the radio. She cut the engine and stepped from her car, humming the pop tune. She hiked up her front walkway, paused at her front door, and fished her keys from her purse.

"We need to talk," a man said.

Julie jumped and dropped her keys on the concrete stoop. She turned around.

Dan stood blank-faced. He wore jeans pulled up too high and a Redskins sweatshirt. He moved closer.

Julie bent down and picked up her keys. "I can't talk right now," Julie said, shoving her key in the lock. "I'm really busy."

"I've noticed," Dan said.

Julie turned back to Dan. His chin disappeared in his hanging neck skin. "Noticed what?" she asked.

"You got that George Chapman fella comin' around quite a bit. I'd be careful. We gotta lot of patriotic people in this neighborhood."

Julie clenched her fists. "It's none of your business who I invite to my home. I don't appreciate you watching me."

His mouth turned down. "Don't flatter yourself, missy. I'm not goin' outta my way. I was in law enforcement for thirty years. I notice *everything*. I've seen you two walkin' around the neighborhood. But I didn't come here to talk about who you're sleepin' with."

"Then *what*, Dan?"

He huffed a breath from his nose like a bull. "I've been nothin' but nice to you. All I get is attitude in return. I came here to talk to you about your HOA dues and the fines you got rackin' up. I know times are tough, so I'm tryin' to help you. Do you wanna lose your house?"

"I took another shift at work."

"With your dues and late fees, you owe almost five hundred dollars."

Julie pinched the bridge of her nose. "I'm working on it."

"I have the power to waive those late fees," Dan said, a grin tugging on the corners of his mouth. "Hell, I could waive the dues too."

Julie breathed a sigh of relief. "You'd do that for me?"

He narrowed his beady eyes at Julie. "Depends."

"Depends on what?"

"Depends on your attitude." He pursed his lips.

"I'll put a check in the mail today." She turned to the door, unlocked it, and pushed inside.

"You can bring it over to me," Dan said over her shoulder.

Julie shut the door and leaned back against it. She hung her head and massaged her temples. An electronic beat emanated from Max's room—not overly loud. She trudged to the kitchen and opened a drawer. She removed her checkbook and a stack of bills. She paid the smaller bills: car insurance, power, water, cell phones, cable, Internet, and minimums due on the credit cards.

Julie called the cable company and canceled the service. She had $643.21 left in her account, and her interest-only mortgage payment was $1,080, with another $480 in HOA dues and fees. She removed her phone from her purse and tapped her Summer contact.

"I haven't heard from you in a while," Summer said, in lieu of a greeting.

"I know. I'm sorry," Julie replied. "I've been busy."

"Busy being in love." Her sister had an edge to her voice. "How is the infamous George Chapman?"

"He's good. He's at home. He'll be back in town in a couple of weeks." Julie paused for a beat. "I was wondering if I could borrow a little money?"

"You can't be serious. We lost a small fortune in the stock market today. We're not in a position to be giving away money."

"I'll pay you back. You're not giving me anything. It's just a loan. I hate to even ask, but I have to pay my mortgage."

"You haven't paid us back from the last time."

"I know. I'm sorry. I'll pay that back too."

Summer exhaled. "Maybe you should ask George. He must be doing well. He's all over the Internet."

"He doesn't get paid for that."

"I don't know what to tell you. We all have to stand on our own two feet."

"You're right. I'm sorry." Julie ended the call.

She held her phone in her hand, thinking about George and his fiancée who stole everything he had. She thought about Max. *Absolutely not. He just started with Katie last week, and whatever he does earn, that's for his life.* She tapped another contact on her phone. *Calling Mom.*

"Hello," Helen said.

"Hi, Mom," Julie said.

"Hi, honey."

"I don't want to beat around the bush. I'm in a bit of a jam." Julie paused. "Could I borrow a thousand dollars to pay my mortgage? I'll pay you back. I promise."

Helen blew out a breath.

"Mom, are you still there?"

"I'm here. It's not a good time. My retirement portfolio took quite a tumble. I have an appointment with my financial advisor. I'm going to give him a piece of my mind."

"I *will* pay you back. I picked up another shift at work."

Helen sighed. "Julie, you're a forty-year-old woman. It's no longer my responsibility to take care of you. You should be taking care of me at this point."

"I know. I'm sorry. I wouldn't ask, but ... I don't know what else to do." Julie wiped the corners of her eyes.

"I'll put a check in the mail."

"Thank you, Mom."

"This is the last time. Don't ask me again."

49: George Says, "It's a Rigged Game."

George sat at his kitchen table, eating breakfast, his laptop open in front of him. He watched the latest video, and the editing work of Katie and Max. The title of the video was "The Stock Market Is Still Overvalued."

In the video, George was shown from the chest up. He said, "Historically speaking the stock market has been a solid place to park your money over the past hundred years. If you go back to January 1918, the S&P 500 was 7.21. A hundred years later, we're around 2000." The screen displayed a chart showing the S&P 500 over time. "That looks great, right? Over a hundred years, it's about a 5.8 percent compound rate of return plus a 4.3 percent average dividend yield, for a total return of 10.1 percent. Adjusted for inflation, the real rate of return would be 7.1 percent. Theoretically, if you invested a thousand dollars in the S&P 500 a hundred years ago, today it would be worth about a million bucks.

The video cut back to George. "A few problems exist with this scenario repeating itself in the future. Stock prices are largely determined by projected earnings and earnings growth. Even after the 12 percent price cut of last week, stocks are still largely overvalued in my opinion." The video cut to pictures of harried and despondent traders. "The price-to-earnings ratio of the S&P 500 is still a frothy 23.7." A chart on the screen showed historical PE ratios and an average around 16.6. "To put this in perspective, if you were to invest in a company with a 23.7 price-to-earnings ratio, it would take you 23.7 years for that company to repay your investment *if* that company maintained the same earnings *and* they distributed all of their profits in the form of a dividend. Of course they don't. Currently the dividend ratio payout for the S&P 500 is 38 percent, so it would take closer to sixty years to repay your investment with dividends." The video showed a chart of historical dividend ratio payouts. Payouts were 90 percent in the 1930s.

George in the video continued. "You're probably thinking that the company could grow earnings and make your investment much more profitable. You're right. The company *could* grow earnings, and historically that's been true." The video cut to a graph that presented historical earnings growth. "The flip side is the company could contract and become less profitable. The million-dollar question is whether companies are likely to grow in the future or to contract?

"To answer that question, we have to look at what drives revenues and profits. What do all these companies need to operate?" Video footage of an automobile assembly line appeared. "They all require natural resources to operate. Metal and energy and rubber and a million other things in the case of a carmaker." A video footage clip showed a massive excavator moving earth into a dump truck the size of a house. "And, if they are to grow, they'll need exponentially increasing amounts of those natural resources." The video cut to a deepwater drilling ship.

"If you overlay a graph of worldwide energy use over earnings growth, you'll find that they track in lockstep." The video presented graphs of earnings growth and energy use. When the graphs were overlaid, it reflected almost perfect synchronicity. "Underneath all the complexity and technology in our society, we depend on the natural world. The question then becomes, can we extract these natural resources in ever-increasing quantities to continue the exponential growth of the past 150 years of industrialization?

"The answer to this question is all around us. It's in the degraded topsoil of our farms." Footage followed of massive combines motoring through endless waves of grain. "The declining amount of new oil field discoveries." A graph appeared, showing a peak in oil field discoveries in 1964 and a decline since that time. "The decrease in concentrated ore bodies." A clip of video footage revealed a massive open pit mine in Utah, one kilometer deep. "The pollution of our fresh water and air and oceans." The video cut to a world map of the hundreds of ocean dead zones, most clustering along the coastlines. "And the decline in diversity of our plant and animal species."

The video now showed George. "In addition to the constraints on growth from the natural world, we also have to contend with the graft of Wall Street, central banks, and governments. The stated inflation goal of the Federal

Reserve is 3 percent. For many years, it was 2 percent." Clips of video footage projected the shiny-headed Ben Bernanke announcing the 2 percent goal, then footage of the middle-aged Chairwoman Paula Burnett in her pearls and pantsuit announcing the 3 percent goal.

The video cut back to George. "Three percent doesn't sound so bad, right? Well, the devil's in the details. I'll give an example to illustrate the effect of inflation on investments."

George spoke over an image of a whiteboard. A digital marker was used to illustrate his point. "Let's say you invested $100,000 in ABC, Incorporated, in 2018, and you held the stock for a decade. In that decade, your investment appreciated in value to $150,000. In 2028, you sold the stock for a 50 percent return, with a $50,000 capital gain. That's great, right? Like I said, 'The devil's in the details.'

"We have to factor in inflation. Three percent inflation for ten years would mean that your original $100,000 can no longer buy $100,000 worth of stuff. In fact, you would need $134,391 in 2028 to buy the same $100,000 worth of stuff in 2018. So you have a real return on investment of $15,609 after factoring in inflation. It gets worse. You have to pay a 15 percent capital gains tax on the full $50,000 appreciation. This is why the government loves inflation. That's another $7,500 out of your profit. You end up with a measly $8,109 in exchange for risking $100,000 of your hard-earned money and tying it up for ten years."

The whiteboard read:

2018 Initial investment in ABC, Inc. = $100,000
2028 Investment value of ABC, Inc. = $150,000
Return on Investment = $50,000
3 percent compounded inflation over ten years on $100,000
= $134,391
Real Return on Investment = $50,000 - $34,391 = $15,609
Capital Gains Tax = $50,000 x .15 = $7,500
Real Return after Taxes = $8,109 (Less than 1 percent yearly compounded return over the decade)

The video cut to George. "The stock market is a rigged game for the common man. For example, in the past ten years, JPMorgan's in-house trading group has had four days of losses." The video presented daily trading revenues and totals for JPMorgan. "Four days in *ten years*. This isn't trading. Trading involves risk. This is a rigged casino, with the board tilted in favor of the big banks. JPMorgan averages $80 million per weekday in trading revenues or about $20 billion per year."

The video showed George again. "Every trade entails a buyer and a seller. If JPMorgan's the winner, who's the loser? We are. The common man. It's the 'dumb money' that isn't privy to insider information, high-frequency algos, thin-air money, pump-and-dump schemes, front-running, quote-stuffing, stop-running, and collusion.

"In general, the common man's not equipped financially to handle the ups and downs of the stock market." The video showed historical data on the Dow Jones Industrial Average, with red lines on the various troughs and green lines on the peaks. "This makes us easy prey for their trap. Let's imagine that you're a regular guy with a decent job in the 1920s." Here's a cartoon of a guy working on a Studebaker automobile assembly line.

"You work hard. You raise your family, and you even have a little left over to save." The cartoon guy shoved cash under his mattress. "In the 1920s people were making money in the stock market, so you start investing your money. In September of 1929, you're ecstatic. The Dow Jones just hit a high of 381.17. You're caught up in the euphoria, and you invest all of your money. The market proceeds to crash for the next three years from 381 down to 41.22. At this point you've been laid off, and you had to liquidate your stocks at the bottom to pay for things like food and your mortgage." The cartoon guy waits in a breadline with his empty pockets turned inside out.

The video cuts back to George. "Meanwhile the wealthy and connected sold at the top, so they had the cash to swoop in and buy all these companies for pennies on the dollar. This is one way wealth is transferred from the common man to the wealthy and connected. A more recent example of this phenomena is the crash of 2008, where the Dow Jones hit a low of 6547 in March of 2009." The video showed a chart of the DJIA from 2008 to the present. "Many regular people were forced to liquidate 401(k)s and investments to survive job losses. Meanwhile the wealthy and connected bought at the bottom, and they rode the market all the way to Dow 20,000 in January 2017."

The video showed George again. "In my opinion, we'll have a very sharp deflation in the stock market and housing, with high unemployment and more foreclosures. At the bottom, the connected will buy everything at fire-sale prices. Then the Federal Reserve—in concert with the US Treasury—will flood the world with currency, causing a spike in prices. The connected people will take that quickly inflating currency and spend it on tangible things of value, like land, natural resources, water, oil, gold, silver, rare earth minerals, art, you name it. The common man will be so fearful at this point that he'll hold tight to the rapidly depreciating currency.

"This could be the largest wealth transfer in the history of the world as people, and, more important, as governments and banks transition from paper and abstract financial instruments to tangible real wealth. We are at the beginning of the deflation. I suspect the rats are jumping ship now."

The video ended with a cartoon of politicians and bankers jumping off a sinking ship into the water. George in real life laughed at Max's handiwork. George recognized President Reynolds and Fed Chairwoman Burnett among the rats.

George stopped the video. It already had millions of views. George picked up his cell phone and tapped his Katie contact.

"What did you think?" she asked, bubbling with excitement.

"You guys did a great job with the graphics and the editing," George replied.

"It's the top trending video on Twitter."

"That's great, Katie. I'm glad you hired Max."

"So am I." She paused for a beat. "On another subject, I'd like to reach a more mainstream audience. I think we can influence many more people if you toned down the message a bit."

"What do you mean by 'tone down the message'?"

"This video wasn't too bad, but the last video you did—where you argued that the US government was immoral— that offended a lot of people."

"I find tax slavery offensive. I also find mass murder offensive."

Katie exhaled. "That's what I'm talking about. I understand why you say things like that, but most people aren't ready to hear that yet."

"I agree. They're not ready. Most people will never be ready. But I won't pervert the truth to win popularity. The second this becomes a popularity contest is the second I'm done."

50: John and Iran

John, Donna, and Frank sat in the sitting area of John's congressional office, glued to the flat screen on the wall.

Lisa Kelly sat behind the WNN news desk with a somber expression. The headline at the bottom of the screen read *Breaking News: Attack on Iran.*

Lisa said, "At midnight, Iranian time, on April 8, 2019, a coalition of US and Israeli military forces attacked Iranian nuclear, military, and infrastructure targets. Two months prior, US and Israeli intelligence uncovered evidence that Iran was less than one year away from completion of a nuclear weapon capable of reaching Israel. We have live footage of Tehran, courtesy of Al Jazeera."

WNN cut to the city. The high-rises were lit by fire and moonlight. Dark mountaintops loomed in the background.

John pressed Mute on the television. "Nothing we don't already know."

"Art's press conference is in about fifteen minutes," Frank said.

"While we wait," Donna said, "I'd like to talk to you two about hiring Katie Fitzgerald to head up our social media."

"She's had no influence over Chapman's message," John said.

"That may be, but she has helped *our* message," Donna replied. "Five months ago, 3 percent of the people who liked our Facebook page also liked George Chapman's page or one of the other pages affiliated with his name. Since we've been front-running his videos and refining our message to be a more balanced and sane version of his, that number has climbed to 16 percent–"

"That's because we've been targeting his audience with marketing."

"Yes, but we've used Katie's insider information to craft the perfect messages at the perfect time. And, more important, we've increased our social media exposure—as far as video views and page views—by 73 percent."

Frank's eyes bulged under his specs. "That's incredible."

John nodded. "Great work, Donna."

"The majority of the kudos goes to Katie Fitzgerald. Her social media consulting and, of course, the insider information has been invaluable. I know she wasn't able to influence Chapman to change his message, but his message is still relegated to the mostly antigovernment, while our message is resonating with the antiwar and those who are fed up with the current administration. I think Katie can help us spread our message to the young voters, and I think she'd be an excellent addition to the staff. Grace is over-whelmed, and I don't think she's equipped for the job. She'd be more effective if she concentrated on public relations and traditional marketing."

"Why not just keep Katie where she is?" Frank asked. "If it ain't broke, don't fix it."

"I think her days with Chapman are numbered," Donna said. "The Internet is figuring out that we're connected. A couple of videos claim Chapman's a paid shill for us. There hasn't been much traction yet, but Chapman's bound to figure it out."

"She may not be interested in jumping ship," Frank said. "She must be making a fortune with her YouTube channel."

Donna shook her head. "She's not making a fortune. She has some sort of weird agreement with Chapman. Apparently the majority of the ad reve-nue from his videos goes to charity. And, like I said before, I think her days with Chapman are numbered. Without him, her channel won't be nearly as popular."

"What do you think, Frank?" John asked.

"I'd hire her before someone else does," Frank replied.

"We're in agreement then," Donna said.

* * *

They watched the flat screen on the wall. Secretary of State Arthur "Art" Coleman stood behind a dark wooden podium with a cluster of micro-phones attached. The Great Seal of the United States was emblazoned on the front of the podium. Behind him were blue curtains.

Art had light-brown skin, close-cropped white hair, and wire-rim glasses atop his nose. He was tall and fit for a man in his sixties.

Art said, "As part of a US-Israeli coalition, we attacked Iran at midnight on April 8. The first phase of the attack involved American and Israeli fighter jets and drones. Targets included Iranian air defense systems, ballistic missile bases, launch facilities, and air bases. We destroyed their missile bases, ensuring that Riyadh and Kuwait City are safe from retaliation. We're cautiously optimistic that the Iranian air defense systems have been destroyed.

"The second wave targeted military bases, roads, bridges, refineries, power plants, and, most important, nuclear sites. We do have confirmation that the nuclear sites have been destroyed with no US or Israeli casualties. I attribute this to the exemplary planning and execution of the men and women of our armed forces."

Art surveyed the audience. "I'll take questions now." Hands were raised. He pointed to a dark-haired young woman. "Dana?"

Dana stood. "Secretary Coleman, you mentioned that you were cautiously optimistic about the destruction of Iran's air defense systems. Are some missile sites still operable?"

"It's been confirmed that Iran's missile sites have been destroyed, but they do have Russian-made S-400 missile systems. These systems are mobile, so we aren't certain that we've destroyed them all. Like I said, we're cautiously optimistic." Art paused for a moment. "Next question." Art pointed to a middle-aged man. "Andrew?"

Andrew stood. "The nuclear sites were reportedly hardened structures. Were bunker-busting bombs used?"

"Yes, the GBU-57 Massive Ordnance Penetrator was used to ensure destruction of the underground facilities. Next question." Art pointed to a young brunette. "Brenda?"

Brenda stood. "Will ground troops be deployed?"

"We're hoping for a diplomatic solution, but we are ready and prepared to deploy ground troops if necessary."

At the conclusion of the press conference, John again muted the television with a frown. "No casualties." He shook his head. "The Republicans will have people flying American flags on their cars, chanting, 'We're number one.'"

"We'll be fine," Frank said. "This is good for us. These wars might start optimistic and clean, but they always end up pessimistic and messy. First of all, even if everything goes off without a hitch, gas prices will go higher. Hell, the Strait of Hormuz is tighter than a bull's butt in fly time. It wouldn't take much to block it, shutting off 20 percent of the world's oil. You can already bank on another dollar added to gas prices, but, if the strait's shut, all bets are off."

"Stock market is down 3 percent today," Donna added. "That's 47 percent since last November. I don't care how patriotic people are, no way will the Republicans survive the crash. People are upset. They've seen their retirements go up in smoke in five months."

"We better not count that chicken until it hatches," Frank said. "You can bet the Fed will goose the markets with funny money prior to the election. Everyone loves a comeback."

"Even if Iran isn't a disaster prior to the election," John said, "we can still hammer Art on the mess they created in Syria and Libya."

"I agree," Donna replied.

"I think you should make a strong statement against the war," Frank said to John.

"It's too soon," John said. "People will say that I don't support the troops."

"It'll be unpopular with the right, but, when this blows up in their faces, and it will, you'll be there to say, 'I told you so.'"

"It's a gamble," Donna said, "but I agree with Frank."

51: Katie and Sand

"Iran hasn't attacked anyone in over two hundred years," John said on his live TV broadcast as Katie stood in her living room, glued to the screen. Congressman John Bradley spoke from a wooden podium, an American flag and a House of Representatives flag behind him.

"This is more warmongering by the Republican neocons, and I won't stand idly by while people are being killed. Remember what they said when we attacked Iraq? Remember that? Weapons of mass destruction and yellow cake. All of it a lie. A lie to increase their power and control over you and the rest of the world. This nation is supposed to be about freedom. We're supposed to set the example for peace and prosperity." John shook his head, his hands gripping the podium, and his jaw clenched. "This isn't it." He marched off camera.

Our next president.

Katie turned off the television and stepped outside onto the pool deck. She moved to the edge and gazed down at the San Francisco Bay. The sea sparkled in the sunlight. Tiny boats dotted the water. The breeze increased, and she zipped up her sweatshirt. Katie walked inside the main house. The kitchen smelled like caramelized onions.

Susen was at the stovetop, preparing lunch, her long black hair flowing down her back. Susen turned toward Katie with a toothy grin. "You hungry?"

"Starved." Katie smiled and sidled up to Susen. She kissed the old woman on the cheek.

"Why don't you go sit in the dining room with your father while I finish up?" Susen said.

Katie walked into the dining room; her dad was reading a newspaper.

The headline on the back page read "Gas Prices Spike."

"What are you doing home?" Katie asked.

Peter Fitzgerald folded the paper and set it on the table. "I'm playing hooky."

Katie cocked her head and sat kitty-cornered from her father. "No, really. Why are you home? And where's Mom?"

"She's at a charity luncheon, and I needed a day off."

"I don't think I've ever seen you miss a day of work."

"Well, there are more important things than work." He gazed at Katie for a moment. "Don't let your job define you. That's a mistake I made long ago."

Katie raised her eyebrows. "What's going on, Dad? Are you sick?"

Peter chuckled. "I'm fine. Times are certainly changing, but I'm fine. How are you doing? Still fighting the system?"

"I know you don't agree with my political viewpoints—"

"I don't disagree, but it's hard for me to be against the system that I've benefitted from. Upton Sinclair said—"

"'It is difficult to get a man to understand something when his salary depends on his not understanding it.'"

"Exactly."

"But you do understand the system."

Susen entered the dining room with two steaming plates of vegetables over quinoa, one with grilled chicken, the other without. She set the plates in front of Katie and Peter.

"Smells great," Peter said.

"Thank you," Katie said.

"I'll be right back with some water," Susen said. A moment later, she returned with waters.

Katie and Peter ate. They engaged in some small talk about what he planned to do with his day off. Apparently, absolutely nothing.

"Why don't we go to the Presidio?" Katie asked.

* * *

Katie and her father strolled on the sandy path adjacent to the beach. Beyond the beach was the San Francisco Bay and the Golden Gate Bridge. Joggers and dog-walkers passed them on the trail. It was a breezy and bright April day. Katie was comfortable in her sweatshirt. Peter wore a light jacket.

"How's Zach doing?" Peter asked.

"He's good," Katie replied. "I really do like him."

"The other night your mother said, 'He could be the one.'" Peter glanced at his daughter, then back to the path.

Katie's face felt hot. "He might be."

"Well, I like him."

Katie smiled to herself, thinking of the past five months with Zach.

"Of course Declan could make just about anyone look good."

Katie punched her dad in the arm, not hard. "Dad."

Peter grinned, his blue eyes sparkling in the sun. "I'm glad you gave him his walking papers. What a phony."

"Okay, enough ex-boyfriend commentary. I think you should be on the hot seat."

Peter glanced at a park bench. "Speaking of seat, I need a break."

They sat on the bench, overlooking the path and the bay.

Peter groaned as he sat.

"Why are you really home today?" Katie asked, sitting next to Peter.

"I've decided to retire."

Katie turned to her dad. "Really? When?"

"Not yet but in the next year or so."

"I didn't think you'd ever retire."

"I think it's time. I've been working since I was twelve. I'm not sure I ever had the chance to figure out what I really wanted to do with my life."

"I thought you loved your job?"

Peter took a deep breath. "I'm at the pinnacle of my profession, and what I do doesn't ..." Peter shook his head. "When it's all said and done, the good you do in the world is what matters."

"Does this have anything to do with the stock market? I know things are bad."

"We knew this was coming. We don't have total control of the markets, but we do have a lot of control. By 'we,' I mean, 'the Treasury, the Fed, foreign central banks, and member banks,' like mine. The Fed influences interest rates and the money supply. Member banks do the Fed's bidding by buying US Treasuries so the US government can finance insane budgets. Hell, the Fed's purchased five-trillion-dollars' worth of treasuries directly. If it wasn't for the banks, there'd be no market for government debt. Then we buy stocks to prop up the market, or we sell to shake lose the weak hands. We've been selling during the crash, and—when we hit rock bottom, and all the weak hands have sold—we'll buy back everything again at a nice discount and ride the wave up. Rinse and repeat." Peter stared at the beach. "It's all built on sand. The economy ... our lives. Sand."

"What are you saying?"

"We have a debt-based monetary system. Therefore, more borrowing must occur every year in order for it to function. The problem is, anything that must increase by some measure each year is, by definition, an exponential system, and every exponential system eventually fails."

"Is USA Bank failing?"

"The money itself is failing."

"Like the dollar?"

Peter nodded. "All fiat currencies. It's all interconnected. The stock market, the bond market, currencies. They're all predicated on exponential growth in economic activity. Real economic growth has been elusive for quite some time. We've made up for it with fake growth. Massive amounts of government and consumer debt, 0 percent interest rates, digital money printing, and abstract derivatives. People have been mostly compliant, happy to rack up debts and accept that the digits in their computer represent real wealth. When I was a young man, people threw parties when they paid off their homes. Now they have interest-only loans and rent furniture." Peter gazed at the Golden Gate Bridge. "The tide's turning. People are losing faith."

"What happens when people lose faith?"

Peter turned to Katie. "A big reset and a new system brought to you by the same people who controlled the old system."

They walked back to the car, and Peter drove them home. Their conversation was subdued. Katie was flustered by what her dad had told her but didn't want to show it.

At home, in the garage, Katie leaned over and kissed her dad on the cheek. "You should play hooky more often," she said.

He smiled. "I enjoyed our time together."

"Well, I guess I should get back to fighting the system, while we still have one to fight."

Katie hopped out of the Mercedes and entered the house through the garage. She returned to the pool house. Her phone chimed as she entered the door.

"Hi, Donna," Katie said.

"Hello, Katie," Donna replied. "Did you see Congressman Bradley's statement about Iran?"

"I did. I was impressed."

"We're not so different after all." Donna paused for a beat. "Listen. I called because I would like to offer you a full-time position as our head of social media. It comes with a generous salary and benefits, and the press secretary position is at the end of the rainbow if we win the presidency."

"What about George?"

"There's still a cabinet position for him, if he'll endorse the congressman."

"He won't do it."

"You might be surprised what people will do. You don't need to make a decision today. Take the weekend to think it over. Get back to me on Monday. I'll email you the formal offer and the employment agreement."

"Thank you, Donna," Katie said, without enthusiasm.

"I know you're conflicted, but this is a good thing, Katie. We're in a position to make a real difference in the world."

"Thank you. I'll get back to you on Monday."

Katie moved to her desk and opened her laptop. She made a list.

Pros of Taking Job
Steady salary
A real job with health care!
Prestige
Chance to make a difference
Work in congress, and maybe the White House
I can move out of my parents' house
George will leave the channel anyway when he finds out what I've done.

Cons of Taking Job
Will no longer be helping the charities
George will hate me
Max will hate me
Audience will say I'm a sellout
Maybe I am a sellout

Katie shut her laptop and picked up her cell phone. She tapped her Zach contact.

"Hi, sweetie," he said.

"You must be by yourself," Katie replied.

Zach laughed. "How'd you know that?"

"Because, when you're around work people, you're very formal. You called me Katherine last week."

"I don't want people to be annoyed. Nothing is more annoying than a couple in love."

Katie giggled. "Hey, I called you because I wanted to run something by you. Do you have a minute?"

"I'm all ears."

"I got a job offer to be the head of social media for Congressman Bradley. And, if he wins the election, I'd be the White House press secretary."

Zach didn't respond.

"What do you think?" Katie asked.

"What about George and the Anarchist movement?"

"Did you see Congressman Bradley's statement about Iran?"

"I saw it."

"Then you see how antiwar he really is. He has a real chance of winning the presidency in 2020, especially with the stock market crash. People are tired of war. I'd like to be part of bringing peace to the world."

"You think the government brings peace?"

"An antiwar president could bring peace."

"Seems like you've already made up your mind."

"You sound disappointed. You're in DC half the time anyway. It wouldn't change much for us. We'd just see each other in a different city."

"Is this really what you want?"

"Yes."

"Then it doesn't matter what I think."

Katie scowled. "What the hell does that mean?"

Zach exhaled. "It means you'll do what you want regardless of what I say."

"I don't make that much money. Not for how much I work. I have no benefits, and I'm entirely dependent on George. What happens when he walks?"

"I get it."

"No, you don't. You have a good job. You have benefits, a house of your own—"

"It's fine. I get it. We'll see each other in DC."

"I should go. I need to call George."

"I'll call you later," Zach said.

"Okay."

Katie ended the call and tapped her George contact.

"Hey, Katie," George said.

In the background, Max said, "Can I talk to her after you? I need to tell her about the hacking."

"I need to talk to you for a minute," Katie replied.

"Sure. Max needs to talk to you too."

"Can you go somewhere private?"

"Okay, hold on. Max and I are fixing Julie's toilets. They all run constantly." George's voice was muffled as he said to Max, "Can you finish up?"

"Don't forget. I need to talk to her," Max said in the background.

"I won't forget," George replied.

Katie heard his footsteps followed by the shutting of a door.

"I'm outside. Go ahead."

Katie said, "Did Max say something about hacking?"

"Yeah, he thinks that someone's getting our videos before they're released. Some guy did a video called, 'George Chapman's a Shill for Congressman Bradley.' The guy claims that Bradley and I staged the terrorist attack together."

"So what? He's just an idiot then."

"That part is idiotic, but the guy does have some evidence that's pretty compelling. He matched up our videos with press conferences and videos released by Bradley, and it appears that we cover very similar topics."

"I don't think it's a big deal that we cover similar topics."

"The problem is, Bradley's information comes out right before ours, so it looks like we're working together. The shill video does have a hundred thousand views. I think we should look into it. Maybe they're hacking our network."

Katie took a deep breath. "They're not hacking our network." She paused for a beat. "I gave them the videos."

"Why would you do that?"

"I got a job offer from Congressman Bradley to be their head of social media."

George blew out a breath. "This is really disappointing."

"I'm sorry, George."

"I'm assuming the only reason you're telling me this is because you plan on taking the job."

"They're impressed with what I've done with our social media."

"I imagine they are," George said. "You're the best."

Katie bit her bottom lip. "I really am sorry."

"I guess we're done."

"We don't have to be. They offered you a cabinet position if he wins the presidency, which is looking more and more likely. You'd just have to endorse him."

"I'm not interested. What about Max?"

"I won't have any more work for Max. He made that cartoon that portrayed Congressman Bradley's daughter and her boyfriend. I don't think Bradley would want Max working on his campaign."

"Max could continue with our channel. He's done a fantastic job over the past five months."

"He has, and I've paid him for his work, but I won't be making anymore videos on our channel, and, even if I wanted to, it's a clear conflict of interest."

"*Now* you're concerned about a conflict of interest?"

"I'm sorry, George. I know I'm being a hypocrite, but Congressman Bradley wants to end the wars. He can do some real good in this world."

"When we started this, I thought it was a terrible idea. I only went along with it because you were so damn persistent. But you made this into something great. We're having an impact. We're helping people."

"I really am sorry, George."

He was quiet for a moment. "Me too."

52: Julie and Debts

Julie was on her way home from the lunch shift. She glanced at the fuel light on her dashboard. It had been on for two days. She stopped at a Mobil station and pulled up to the pump. Eighty-seven octane was $3.62 per gallon. She frowned. *It was $2.50 last week.* She inserted her credit card into the pump and filled the tank halfway.

She drove home and parked in front of her townhome. Inside she found George and Max in the living room. George sat on the couch, and Max paced in front of him.

"This is bullshit!" Max said.

They turned toward Julie as she shut the door. "What's going on?" Julie asked.

"Katie screwed us," Max said. "She won't even return my texts."

Julie sat next to George on the couch. "What happened?"

"Katie took a job working for Congressman Bradley," George said. "She thinks he'll be the next president and wants to be a part of it."

"He'll be the next asshole of the United States," Max said, red-faced.

Julie sighed. "I'm sorry, guys."

"She's been taking our videos and giving them to Bradley before we release them."

"I don't understand."

"Bradley's been front-running our videos," George said, "so now it appears that we were working together."

"People are calling George a shill," Max said, his speech rapid. "Katie's the freaking shill. We should start our own channel. We could call it George 2020. That's my hashtag. You should actually run for president. We could beat them."

George shook his head. "I'm sorry, Max. It's not gonna happen."

"Come on, let's at least make a video telling everyone what assholes Katie and Bradley are."

"I don't wanna say anything bad about Katie."

Max clenched his fists. "This is bullshit, George! Why don't you ever get mad?" Max stomped up the stairs.

"Don't talk to George that way," Julie said to Max's back.

Max continued up the stairs.

"It's okay," George said to Julie. "On the positive side, Max and I fixed all your toilets."

Julie put her hand on top of George's. "I'm sorry that Katie did that. I know you liked helping people with the charities and everything."

George shrugged, ignoring Julie's comfort. "No more leaks, and, if anything goes wrong in the future, Max knows how to fix them."

"Do you want to talk about it?"

George stared at the carpet. "It's over. There's nothing to talk about." He stood from the couch. "I'm gonna clean the gutters. I think they're clogged. Last time it rained, water was spilling over. I don't want you to get water in the basement."

"Thank you, honey, but you really don't need to come here and do chores. By the way, how much do I owe you for the toilet stuff?"

George leaned over and kissed the top of her head. "You don't owe me anything."

53: George and the Protest Vote

George stood on his extension ladder, removing handfuls of leaves and debris from the front gutter. It was a breezy day in early spring. He listened to a podcast while he worked.

Gary Cook of the *Alt News Podcast* said, "China and Russia have vowed to support the rebuilding efforts of Iran and the Iranian nuclear program. Vladimir Putin had some particularly strong words for the US government. He said, 'Russia condemns the illegal bombing of the peaceful country of Iran. There will be a retaliation.' Some pundits have been asserting the possibility of a Russian military attack against the United States, but I think it's far more likely to be an economic and cyberattack coordinated with China."

George climbed down from the ladder. He raked the leaves he had pulled out of the gutter and spread them around the holly shrubs, the daffodils, and the small tree.

Gary Cook continued, "A massive amount of gold has moved from West to East over the past two decades. Not only has the Chinese central bank been hoarding gold but the Chinese government has been encouraging Chinese citizens to accumulate physical gold and silver. The Russian central bank has also been accumulating gold. I think China and Russia are preparing to sell their US Treasury holdings. This would likely cause massive inflation and ultimately the destruction of fiat currencies.

"If this were to happen, people worldwide would turn from fiat currencies to real tangible wealth. This would be the perfect climate to introduce a gold-backed yuan and a gold-backed ruble. The result would be an unprecedented wealth transfer from West to East."

"Hey, … hey, you!"

George removed his earbuds and turned toward the middle-aged man wearing a dark blue sweatsuit. He was balding with a white mustache, wire-rim glasses, ruddy complexion, and a gut somewhere between the second and third trimester.

"You can't park here." The man motioned to George's truck and trailer behind him.

George had backed up his truck and trailer in Julie's second space. The length of his rig and trailer caused the truck to sit almost in the middle of the parking lot. However, George wasn't blocking the sparse neighborhood traffic.

"I can park here," George said. "The owner gave me permission."

The man moved closer, his eyes narrowed. "The HOA owns the parking lot. We determine who and what gets parked here."

"I'll move it in a few minutes."

"If you don't do it now, I'll call the police."

George leaned the rake against the tree. "Go right ahead."

The man stood on the sidewalk with his arms crossed.

George finished spreading the leaves around the shrubs. George lowered the extension ladder and carried it toward his trailer. He nearly hit the man with the ladder. "Watch yourself," George said as the man flinched.

George parked his truck and trailer along the main road with the boats and campers of the neighborhood. He walked back to Julie's townhome. The man still stood on the sidewalk with his arms crossed.

The man pointed to the shrubs along the front of the house as George approached. "You gonna pick up those leaves?"

George stopped. "Why would I do that? It's free mulch."

"HOA rules require that all leaves must be removed."

George glared at the man. "You're Dan, right?"

"I'm the HOA president. And I know who you are. I've seen you spewin' that treasonous garbage on the Internet."

"You enjoy this, don't you?"

"I don't know what you're talkin' about."

"You enjoy having power over people. You get off on it."

"The rules must be followed. I know you don't think the rules apply to you, but I can assure you that they do. If you don't pick up those leaves, I'll fine Julie." He raised one side of his mouth in contempt.

"A lot of people watch my videos, which is really flattering. I'm always recording, because you never know what you might see. And what's really cool is how the recording devices are so small now. You can put a camera on your body as a button." George touched the black button on his flannel. It was the only black button on his shirt; the others were brown.

Dan cocked his head, like a confused dog.

"For example, the fifty million people who watch my channel would love this little exchange. A lot of these people don't like rules, and they don't like tyrants."

Dan's eyes widened. "I do not give you permission to use my image on any videos. If you do, I'll sue you so fast it'll make your head spin."

"Remember how I feel about rules."

Dan's face was taut.

"Do you know what it's like to be Internet-famous?" George asked.

Dan was silent, his fists clenched.

"It is not fun. I'll tell you that. People are crazy out there."

Dan turned on his heels and marched across the street to his townhome.

George smiled to himself, thinking about the black button he had sewed to his flannel. He didn't have a brown one in his sewing kit.

George went inside and took off his boots at the door. Julie sauntered out from the kitchen, wearing yoga pants and a long sweatshirt. Her auburn hair was pulled back in a ponytail.

"Dinner will be ready in fifteen minutes," she said as she approached. She kissed George on the lips.

He wrapped his arms around her and squeezed, causing her to giggle. He let go.

"Thank you for cleaning the gutters," Julie said. "I'm pretty sure they've never been cleaned."

"I'm pretty sure you're right," George replied.

"Were you talking to someone out there? I heard voices."

George smirked. "I met Dan."

Julie's blue eyes widened. "What did he say?"

"He complained about my truck and trailer and then the leaves I put around the holly bushes."

"Please tell me that you took care of it. He'll fine me."

"Don't worry. I took care of it."

Max bounded down the stairs, his laptop under his arm, like a book.

George and Julie looked his way.

"I'm sorry for yelling at you earlier," Max said to George.

"I understand why you're mad," George said. "Don't worry about it."

"I wanna show you something on my computer."

"We're eating in about fifteen minutes," Julie said.

Max opened his laptop on the dining room table. George and Max sat at the table and watched the video ad.

The video started with Congressman Bradley speaking at a podium. He said, "Remember what they said when we attacked Iraq? Remember that? Weapons of mass destruction and yellow cake. All of it a lie. A lie to increase their power and control over you and the rest of the world. This nation is supposed to be about freedom. We're supposed to set the example for peace and prosperity." Bradley shook his head, his hands gripping the podium, and his jaw clenched. "This isn't it." He marched off camera.

The video cut to Tehran in flames, then drone strikes in Iraq. A male voice spoke over the video. "In an era of endless war and government oppression, John Bradley is the man to drain the swamp of bullies and warmongers." The video showed Bradley onstage during his last congressional victory party. It cut to a black screen with white writing. *John Bradley 2020. United We Stand.*

Max stopped the video. "They're trying to be like you," Max said. "They're trying to take all the people who are angry with the government, all those people who were on their way to anarchism, but now Congressman Bradley's gonna convince them that they just need to vote for him, and he'll fix everything."

"I agree," George said.

"Then let's do something about it. Run for president."

George frowned. "We talked about this."

"I know, but you don't have to run to win. You could run to mess up their election and to tell people the truth."

"I wouldn't even get on the ballot."

"You could run as a write-in candidate. I did the research. Forty-three states allow write-ins. Come on, George."

George stroked the stubble on his chin. "I'll tell you what. You start your own channel, and I'll be in any videos you wanna produce. We can encourage people to vote for me as a write-in candidate, but we have to be clear that it's a protest vote."

Max smiled wide. "They're going down."

54: John and Rebuild America

John stood, staring from the window of his congressional office. Washington, DC, was gray, flurries in the air. After a quick knock on his door, Donna and Frank let themselves in.

John turned to them as they settled in the sitting area, Frank in a chair and Donna at the end of the couch. John sat on the couch, joining them for their strategy session. Donna had an iPad in her lap, Frank a pen and a notepad.

"Did you two have a nice New Year's?" John asked.

"I caught up on work," Donna said.

"I caught up on sleep," Frank said.

"Linda dragged me to a charity event," John said.

"We have the polling results for possible VPs," Donna said.

"Senator Atwell's the top candidate," Frank said. "She's the obvious choice, for obvious reasons."

"She's also my biggest competitor in the primary," John said.

"She doesn't have a snowball's chance in hell of winning, and she knows it," Frank replied.

"She's using the primary to build her base for a serious run in 2024," Donna said. "I think we might be able to convince her that she has a much better shot in 2028 after she's been VP for eight years."

"She *would* have a much better shot after being VP for two terms," John said.

"Then it'll be an easy sell," Frank said.

"She'll help us with the female vote," Donna said, "but she'll also help us with the West Coast vote, her being a native Californian."

"She's smart, and people like her," Frank said. "She has just the right mix of toughness and kindness. Not so kind that people think she's a pushover and not so tough that people think she's a bitch on wheels like ..." He winked at Donna.

"I'll take that as a compliment." Donna smirked.

Frank chuckled.

"Any skeletons?" John asked.

"She has a loser son," Donna said. "He's a wannabe actor who's been arrested three times for drug possession. He's been in and out of rehab. Other than that, she's squeaky clean. Her daughter's a fashion designer and her husband a fairly successful entertainment lawyer."

"I think we should make a deal with her now," Frank said. "We'll tell her that we'll both run tough campaigns, but we won't take shots at each other, and, when we win, she comes along for the ride *with* her supporters. Then we endorse her in 2028."

"In the VP poll, who polled second?" John asked.

Donna pursed her lips. "George Chapman, but it wasn't very close."

John blew out a breath. "Will he ever die? Maybe we should ask Katie to take another crack at him for an endorsement."

Donna shook her head. "He's been losing popularity ever since Katie left. He has some kid doing his PR. His write-in candidacy is all but dead."

"Make the deal with Atwell," John said.

Donna nodded.

"It's a good move," Frank said.

"Our latest poll shows Art with a slight lead," Donna said.

John said, "It hasn't helped that the stock market's recovered somewhat, and the president's Rebuild America stimulus program has been huge for the Republicans."

Frank adjusted his wire frames. "They're buying votes."

"There's been an uptick in the economy since Thanksgiving," Donna said.

"That's no surprise," Frank said. "They're giving fifty-year Fannie Mae loans at 1 percent, massive tax breaks, a trillion-dollar infrastructure program, and of course the green Christmas."

"The green Christmas was pure genius," John said.

"I agree," Frank said. "Republicans say they want fiscal responsibility, but, when it came down to it, they were happier than a pig in shit to receive their Christmas stimulus checks along with the rest of Americans."

"And, at six hundred dollars a pop, it only cost $200 billion," Donna added.

"The dollar has fallen 20 percent in the last few months," John said.

"I suspect one helluva hangover is coming," Frank said.

"Hopefully it comes before the election," John said.

* * *

John sat at his desk and called Donna's cell.

"Hi, John," Donna said.

"Are you still in the office?" John asked.

"I'm on my way home. My sister's in town, remember?"

"That's right. Sorry to bother you."

"Did you need something?"

"No, I just miss you."

"Me too," Donna replied. "I have some time next week."

"It's a date. See you tomorrow."

"See you tomorrow."

John hung up and pressed Katie's extension.

"Hello, this is Katie Fitzgerald."

"Katie, this is John Bradley."

There was a pause. "Congressman Bradley, what can I do for you?"

"I'd like to run a few things by you. Do you have a minute?"

"Right now?"

"When you have a moment, please come to my office."

"I'll be right there."

A couple of minutes later, Katie knocked on Congressman Bradley's office door.

"Come in," John called out.

Katie opened the door and stepped inside the office. She shut the door behind her. She wore a wool pencil skirt and a sweater. He moved from behind his mahogany desk and met Katie in the middle of the office.

Katie smiled, a pen and pad of paper in hand.

"Happy New Year," John said.

"Thanks, happy New Year to you too," she replied.

"Would you like to sit?" John motioned toward the sitting area.

"Yes, thank you," she replied and stepped to the couch, her hips rocking back and forth.

John stared at her backside, imagining the buxom beauty naked.

Katie sat on one end of the couch across from the chairs. John bypassed the chairs and sat on the middle of the couch, an arm's length away from Katie. He wore a white button-down, tie, and no jacket.

"Thank you for taking the time to speak with me," John said.

"Of course. It's an honor for me," Katie replied.

"I also wanted to thank you for doing such a great job with our social media. Donna and Grace sing your praises, but I thought I should tell you that in person."

Katie blushed. Her face was smooth and young, with little makeup. "Thank you. That means a lot coming from you."

John smiled. "Well, it's long overdue. How long have you been working here? Eight months?"

"Nine."

"So, how's Chapman doing these days?" John asked.

"I don't know," Katie replied. "I don't have contact with him anymore."

"You still follow him online, don't you?"

"I do."

"How do you *think* he's doing?"

Katie bit the corner of her lower lip. "He's losing relevance and influence by the day. He still has a cult following, but most of those people don't vote."

John grinned, his eyes squinting. "Sounds like you jumped ship at the perfect time."

Katie nodded, straight-faced.

"You know, I actually admire Chapman's idealism," John said. "In principle, I agree with anarchism philosophy, but, in practice, it doesn't work, not when you're dealing with real people and real problems."

Katie nodded again.

"I'm polling slightly behind Art now. Any ideas on how we can close the gap?"

Katie put her hand to her chest. "Oh, I'm not ... prepared. I mean, I have ideas, but I'd like to present them to you in a professional format. I'm sorry. I'm used to working with Grace and Donna."

John shook his head. "I don't want you to prepare anything. I want your unfiltered opinion."

"Okay, … well, first of all, you're behind by a single percent, and that's well within the margin of error. I think Art's rise in the polls has been the result of geopolitics and the Rebuild America stimulus program. The state of the nation come November will be half the battle. We can't control that, but we can control our narrative."

John nodded along, his eyes occasionally dipping to the sweater that stretched across Katie's chest.

"I think we're on the right track by being critical of the war," Katie said. "Tehran is in shambles. The people are rioting over the puppet president, and gas is over four bucks. I think we're on the right track by criticizing Washington and touting ourselves as the change candidate."

"We're touting ourselves, huh? Does that mean you don't believe I'm the change candidate?"

Katie blanched. "No, I totally believe you're the change candidate. I'm here because of the speech you made after we attacked Iran."

"You've told me what we're doing right. What can we be doing better?"

Katie pursed her full lips. "The design department made a video, which was a mashup of bits of your best speeches. It's set to music, and it appeals to the young. It's very powerful and very well-done—"

"I agree. It was well-done."

"But we've put very little of our ad budget toward spreading it. The older voters cost more to sway through advertising. We should be focused on younger voters, eighteen to thirty. YouTube is still kind of like the Wild West of advertising, so video views are still very cheap. And even Facebook, we can get video views for three cents. Social media marketing is cheaper than traditional marketing. I think we'd do better with more social media ads and less traditional advertising."

"You'd like a bigger budget?"

"Well, yes."

John stared at Katie, his blue-gray eyes narrowed. "I'll look at the budget and make some adjustments."

Katie raised her eyebrows. "Really?"

"Sure, why not?"

"Grace and Donna will be upset that I went over their heads."

"Let me handle them. We brought you here because you took a nobody and made him relevant in the political landscape. To top it off, your campaign was *making* money. *That* was truly amazing. But what good is it if we don't support you?"

"Thank you."

"Don't thank me, Katie. You're good at your job. I should be thanking you." He reached over and put his hand on top of hers. "I'm hoping to work more closely with you in the future."

Katie turned beet red and dropped her gaze. After a moment, John removed his hand. Katie looked up.

John sighed. "Well, Katie Fitzgerald, I'd say your career is well on its way. Hopefully you're not all work and no play. What do you do for fun? Please tell me it's not marketing."

"It's *not* marketing." She smirked and flipped her hair off her shoulders. "I guess the same things most people like to do. Read, watch movies, travel, spend time with friends."

"No boyfriend?"

She hesitated. "Not right now."

That's a lie. John raised his eyebrows. "That's surprising."

Katie cocked her head. "Why is that surprising?"

He stood from the couch with a crooked grin. "I probably shouldn't answer that question."

Katie stood.

"Thank you for talking to me, and thank you for your honesty," John said.

"You're welcome."

They shook hands, John holding on for a second longer than necessary.

55: Katie and the Change Candidate

Katie sat in the back seat of a Toyota sedan, texting.

Katie: I'm working late. I can't see you tonight. I'm sorry. ☹

Zach: That's too bad. I was hoping to see you. I'll miss you. See you tomorrow? I love you.

Katie: Definitely tomorrow! I love you too.

She stepped out of the Uber driver's car. The winter wind whipped by the stately Mandarin Oriental Hotel. She wore a long wool coat and oversize sunglasses. She debated with herself. *Maybe the glasses are too much. Who wears sunglasses in January? People up to no good, that's who. It does conceal your identity.* Katie stepped through the automatic sliding doors, her heart pounding, and the glasses still obscuring her face.

She hurried toward the elevators. The decor of the lobby was ornate with thick wooden pillars and shiny marble floors. She saw the front desk out of the corner of her eye. She willed herself not to look. *Keep moving forward.* She pressed the up arrow next to the elevator doors.

"Is there something I can do for you?"

Katie turned toward the voice, startled. A young woman with a name tag stood with a smile. Katie was speechless as she reached into the pocket of her jacket and removed a credit-card-size key. The elevator door opened.

"I'm ... just going to my room," Katie said, holding up the key. The elevator door began to close.

The woman held the door. "Very good, ma'am. Please let us know if you need anything."

Katie nodded and stepped into the stainless-steel elevator. The elevator doors closed, and Katie pressed the top floor. She fluffed her wavy brown hair. She had butterflies in her stomach, or maybe it was nausea. The elevator doors opened, and she stepped out on the top floor. She saw Agent Olson at the end of the hall. *What am I doing?* She glanced back at the elevator doors as they closed. She took a deep breath and marched toward Agent Olson. He looked away as she approached. He didn't say a word. She inserted the key. The light was red; the door still locked. *Shit.* She checked the key. It was backward. She turned around the key and inserted it into the slot. The light turned green, and she stepped into the room.

The king-size bed was made with nine pillows. A table for two was centered in the sitting area. John stood from the table. He wore slacks and an untucked button-down, no shoes. His tie and jacket hung over the chair. Her heart thumped in her chest as he approached. His face was long and oval, his chin strong. Despite the grayish-white hair, he wasn't wrinkly. He'd easily win the congressional beauty contest.

"I'm glad you're here," he said with a small, almost shy smile.

She took off her sunglasses. "I shouldn't be here. This is a mistake."

He nodded. "I understand. We don't have to do anything. We can just order some dinner and relax. They have great food here. May I take your coat?"

Katie unbuttoned her coat, and John slipped behind her and helped her out of it. She wore a little black dress with a plunging neckline and bare legs.

"Wow," John said. "You look beautiful."

Katie blushed.

John hung her coat in the closet. "Have a seat, and take off those heels. They must be killing you."

Katie stepped to the sitting area and sat on the couch. The curtains were open to a view of the Jefferson Memorial and the Tidal Basin. It was cloudy and gray outside, the sun low on the horizon. Cars and trucks used their headlights. She slipped off her spiky heels.

"Feel better?" John asked, sitting next to her on the couch.

"Yes, my feet were killing me."

"Let me help you." John reached down and put his hands around her ankles.

She stiffened.

"Relax," he said. "Lean back on the couch and put your feet in my lap."

Katie narrowed her eyes.

"Trust me."

Katie leaned back on the couch, and John put her feet in his lap. He worked her bare feet with both hands.

"That feels so good," Katie said, her eyes rolling back.

"I don't know how you wear heels all day."

"I never wore heels before this job."

"Really?"

"I was a feminist."

"You're not anymore?" John continued to hit her pressure points.

"I'm not sure what I am, but I doubt Gloria Steinem would be impressed with me right now."

"I don't know about that. You have the next president of the United States rubbing your feet."

Katie laughed.

"You hungry?" John asked.

Katie sat up. "I'm starved. My feet feel much better. Thank you."

He grinned. "I aim to please."

They ordered grilled duck breast and vanilla crème brûlée. John slipped in the champagne. They ate on the couch, plates balanced in their lap.

With empty plates on the coffee table and full bellies, John asked, "Is this what you wanted to do when you were little?"

Katie leaned back. "I don't know. I always wanted to help people. When I was in seventh grade, we went on a field trip to this strawberry farm. I saw the men picking all the fruit. I couldn't understand why someone who worked so hard could be so poor. I started this charity and raised money for them for a college fund for their kids."

"That's amazing. How old were you? Twelve, thirteen?"

"Twelve. I raised six thousand dollars and the local news made a big deal about it, but it wasn't enough for one year of college for one kid. Maybe working for you is the best way for me to help the most people. Did you want to be president when you were little?"

John laughed. "I don't think I ever had a chance to even think about it. My path was decided for me."

"What if you could have a do-over?"

John raised his eyebrows. "A do-over?"

"Yes, a do-over."

"Maybe that's what I'm doing here." John leaned toward Katie and pressed his lips to hers.

Katie felt like she was floating, buzzing from the champagne and his kiss. He unzipped her dress. She unbuttoned his shirt. He removed his button-down and undershirt. His upper body was toned. If not for the gray and white chest hair, he was built like a much younger man. His hands moved under her dress. He gripped her underwear. She lifted herself off the couch for a moment, and he slipped off her thong.

They continued to kiss, now more urgently, their tongues intertwined. His hand was between her legs. She moaned as he touched her. She fumbled with his belt buckle. He undid his belt and pulled his pants and boxer briefs down to his knees. His erection pointed toward the ceiling. Katie hiked her dress above her hips and climbed on top of the future leader of the free world. He positioned his erection as she lowered herself slowly. He groaned as his penis filled her.

John sat on the couch, his pants around his ankles, his hands gripping her round hips. Her pelvis moved like a wave back and forth, her clitoris grinding against his pubic bone, his penis deep inside her. She was breathless; her lips were full, and her eyes closed. Katie moved faster, grinding harder, her breaths more and more shallow. She exhaled heavily, moaning, as her pleasure reached a crescendo. Shortly thereafter, so did his.

56: Julie's Future Hardship

Julie drove into the shopping center parking lot. The office supply store and the financial advisors were out of business. She parked her Honda in front of the grocery store, grabbed the cloth bags George had given her, and stepped from her car. The sky was gray, making everything look black and white. The parking lot was stained with salt. She hurried to the store, hunched against the cold wind.

Inside, she pushed a shopping cart through the produce aisle. She put bananas, apples, and pears in the cart. The berries and grapes were too expensive. *Who the hell would pay $3.99 a pound for grapes?* She grabbed some lettuce, carrots, and bell peppers. She put the peppers back. They were $1.99 each. She added some radishes and sweet potatoes to her cart. *Hopefully George will bring some produce soon.*

She picked up bread, peanut butter, and jelly. Julie meandered over to the meat department. She sighed at the prices. *This is getting ridiculous.* She picked up hamburgers and chicken, but she put the fish back on the shelf. She filled her cart with canned goods. It was still cheap to eat out of a can.

Julie finished her shopping. Her cart was half full as she waited in the one checkout line with a human cashier. Most people went through the self-checkout, but she hated doing that alone. It was such a pain in the ass. While she waited, she browsed the magazines. It was mostly celebrity gossip: baby bumps, affairs, romances, and meltdowns. She recognized the serious-looking man on the cover of *Time* magazine. The title was "Our Next President?" The blurb underneath read *Antiwar Activist, Congressman John Bradley.*

The line moved, and Julie put her groceries on the conveyor belt, adding the separator at the end. Julie handed the young female cashier her cloth bags.

"I can help bag," Julie said, moving to the bagging area.

As Julie hefted a bag filled with canned goods into her cart, the cashier said, "The total is $229.90."

Julie's eyes bulged. "May I see the receipt?"

Julie scanned the receipt while an old woman next in line raised both hands in the air. No doubt late for something "important" on television. Julie dug through her shopping bags and removed the packages of ground beef. She handed them to the cashier.

"Can you take these off?" Julie asked.

The old lady in line huffed. "I ain't got all day."

The cashier took the beef. "Of course."

"I'm sorry," Julie said to the cashier.

The cashier offered a small smile. "It's no problem. The prices have been going up a lot lately."

Julie paid, loaded her car with groceries, and drove home. She grabbed the mail before hauling the groceries inside. She set the groceries on her kitchen counter and flipped through the mail.

"Damn it," she said as she saw the letter. She ripped it open.

Fairfax Woods Homeowners Association
10 Liberty Drive
Fairfax, VA 22032

February 1, 2020

Julie Welch
422 Colonial Commons Drive
Fairfax, VA 22032

Re: Parking Regulation #131

Dear Julie Welch,

On three separate occasions in the past five months, a large trailer with Pennsylvania plates has been observed parked in your parking spot. The owner of the trailer confirmed that you gave him permission to park in the spot.

Rule #131 of the HOA covenant which you signed states: *Trailers, boats, and commercial vehicles are prohibited from parking in assigned parking spots.*

The fine for this violation is $200 per occurrence. Please remit payment in the amount of **$600 paid to Fairfax Woods Homeowners Association**. You have seven days from the date listed above to pay the fine, or the HOA may be obligated to take further action as outlined in the covenant. This would include ongoing fines and a lien on the property.

It's important for residents to maintain a clean and orderly community. In the future, please refrain from parking trailers in your assigned parking spot. I look forward to you complying with this request to avoid any future hardships.

Sincerely,

Dan Gordon
President
Fairfax Woods HOA

Max bounded down the steps. Julie shoved the letter into her purse before Max entered the kitchen.

"Hey, Mom," Max said.

"Hi, honey," Julie replied.

"Yes, you went to the store. I'm starving." Max riffled through the bags, looking for something to eat. "You didn't get very much."

Julie sighed. "Everything's so expensive."

"I can help. I have money."

"I know you can, but your money is your money. My job's to take care of you, not the other way around."

"I have almost $20,000."

"We're fine. That money is yours."

57: George and Taxation = Extortion

George used the key Julie gave him to open the front door. He took off his jacket and hung it in the closet. "Julie," he called out.

"In the kitchen," she called back, her voice strained.

George stepped to the kitchen. Julie was putting canned goods on the shelves, her back to him.

"I finished earlier than I thought," George said.

She slammed the cabinet door and turned around. Her face was rigid, her mouth turned down. "Where did you park?" she asked.

"Where I usually do, along the main road." George moved closer, searching her face. "Is something wrong? You look upset."

"You can't park your trailer in front, not even for a minute."

"Did Dan do something?"

Julie's shoulders slumped. "It's okay. You just can't park in front anymore."

"Did you get a fine?"

Julie was quiet.

"Let me see the letter," George said.

She removed the letter from her purse and handed it to George.

He scanned the letter. "Shit." George grabbed her hand. "I'm sorry. This is my fault. Don't worry. I'll pay for it."

Julie shook her head. "No, I don't want you paying. It's not your fault. Dan's an asshole. If it wasn't the trailer, it would've been something else."

George shoved the letter in the back pocket of his jeans. "I'll go over to the HOA office today and take care of it. Okay?"

She nodded and hung her head, her auburn hair resting on her shoulders. "I'm sorry. I know you were helping me."

George hugged her. "It's not a big deal. I'll pay the fine. It'll be over." He stepped back and raised her chin so their eyes met. "Don't worry about it, okay?"

She nodded again.

"Is there something else?" he asked.

"We might have a problem," Max said, entering the kitchen, holding his laptop.

George turned from Julie. "What's wrong?"

Max narrowed his eyes at the scenario he walked into. "Are you guys all right?"

"Everything's fine, honey," Julie said.

Max's baby face was somber. "Did you hear about the IRS agents?"

"I haven't heard anything," George said. "I've been listening to an audiobook on the road."

"Five IRS agents were killed in their homes last night, and a bunch of demonstrations are going on."

George pinched the bridge of his nose. "This is not good. If the anarchism movement goes violent, it's over. We'll lose the moral high ground."

"There's video of the demonstration in DC," Max said.

George and Julie followed Max to the dining room. Max opened his laptop and pressed Play. The video portrayed protestors crowded on the sidewalk along two sides of the IRS building. The massive building was rectangular and seven stories tall. The exterior of the upper floors was decorated by a three-story colonnade. The protestors held up assorted signs: Taxation = Extortion, George 2020, Taxation Is Theft, Honk if You Hate the IRS, Taxation Is Free-Range Slavery, Tax Revolt 2020, and We Won't Pay.

Capitol Police officers and DC Metropolitan Police officers clashed with protestors in riot gear. Tear gas was shot into the crowd, dispersing some who held jackets over their heads and ran from the scene. Many protestors put on gas masks and pushed back against the police. Ultimately the scene devolved into a free-for-all with cops beating protestors and vice versa. Shots were fired; many protestors were arrested. Many were injured, and a few were killed.

Max stopped the video. "These tax protests weren't just in DC but also at twenty or so IRS field offices all over the country. From what I can tell from the videos, the police have been pretty aggressive in stopping the protests.

Lots of arrests and beatings. It seems like they brought in almost as many cops as protestors."

George frowned. "It's too early for a tax revolt."

"I didn't think people would go through with it," Max said. "I mean, there's been talk about this online for a month now, but I didn't think it would amount to anything."

"Neither did I," George replied. "Not enough people are on board to make a real difference. The IRS will ruin the lives of everyone who participates. They'll be arrested. Their bank accounts'll be frozen. They'll have their assets seized. We have to win hearts and minds first." George took a deep breath. "You said that a lot of cops were at these protests?"

"Yeah, tons," Max replied.

"If *we* knew this might happen, the government had to know all the specifics too. That's why they were so prepared."

"The Internet's giving you credit for the revolt. A lot of the signs mimic the 'Taxation = Extortion' video we did last month. Not to mention all the George 2020 signs."

George hung his head and rubbed his temples. He dropped his hands and looked at Max. "I need to make a video telling everyone why I'll be paying my taxes in April."

58: John Bends with the Wind

John, Donna, and Frank gathered in the sitting area of John's congressional office. They watched the flat screen on the wall. President Henry Reynolds stood behind a podium with the Great Seal of the United States emblazoned on the front. His chiseled jaw was set tight, and his large hands gripped the edge of the podium.

"The goal of terrorists across the globe is to hurt us financially. They can't fight us conventionally. We have the finest military the world has ever known." President Reynolds paused. "These tax revolts, the assassination of our IRS agents, the bombing of the Federal Reserve, currency manipulators, cyberattacks, Iran, 9/11 ... these events, these people and groups and countries are all focused on one thing—destroying us economically.

"They know that our strength *and* our weakness is our collective prosperity. They seek to destroy all that we've built—that our forefathers bled for, that our military bled for and still bleeds for. I won't stand around and watch it happen—not on my watch." The president glared at the camera. "The United States of America was founded on the ideals of democracy, equal rights, liberty, freedom, and justice for all. These are ideals worth fighting for. I know my fellow patriotic Americans agree, and I know we can win this fight, but we have to do it *together*. I'm asking all of you to support our fine soldiers. I'm asking all of you to condemn the tax protestors and the domestic terrorists. Thank you."

Donna muted the television.

John stood, pacing. "This is a fucking nightmare."

"I agree," Donna said, still sitting on the couch. "We've definitely taken a hit in the polls over the past month."

"The conservative press has been hammering us," John said, "and we're the ones who've been playing up our Chapman connection."

"It's time to change tactics," Frank said, still sitting in the chair.

John glowered at Frank. "This was your strategy."

"It's been a good strategy until now. A presidential race is a marathon, not a sprint. When the winds change, we need to bend with 'em. That doesn't mean we abandon the message. If we do that, they'll paint us as weak flip-floppers."

"What do you suggest?" Donna asked.

"We're still the antiwar change candidate that'll drain the swamp," Frank said. "We'll still defend the people's right to protest, but we're about justice and upholding the law. The first amendment grants the protestors the freedom of speech and to peaceably assemble, but they don't have the right to commit violence or to evade taxes."

John nodded. "We defend constitutional rights on the one hand and advocate for swift justice when they violate the law on the other."

"Bingo."

"We need to sever our ties with Chapman and the Anarchist movement," Donna said.

"There aren't any more ties," John replied.

Donna pursed her lips. "Katie."

"She's done a great job with our social media presence."

"She's a liability," Donna said. "Search Katie Fitzgerald and John Bradley, and you'll find a dozen articles saying that we're working with Chapman."

"I agree," Frank said. "The sooner we sever ties, the better."

"She's been here eleven months." Donna looked at Frank and then John. "According to her employment contract, we can still fire her without cause, but we need to do it now."

"Let's wait until Friday," John said.

Donna nodded. "I'll take care of it."

Frank stood from the chair. "I'll get with Grace and start refining our message." He patted John on the shoulder. "We'll be fine. We just need to stick to our guns."

"Thanks, Frank," John said, as the white-haired man exited the office.

John continued his pacing, nearing the couch, and Donna grabbed his hand.

"I miss you," she said.

John looked down on her. "I know. Me too."

She held on to his hand, her dark eyes blinking. "Maybe we can meet at the Mandarin tonight?"

He stared at the heavy makeup on her face and exhaled. "I wish. Linda was serious about expecting me home every night."

Donna let go of his hand.

"You know that's the only reason she agreed to support the race," John said.

"I know." Donna pressed out her lower lip. "We haven't been together in over a month."

"I'm sorry. I promise we'll find time next week."

* * *

John lay in bed on his back, naked. Katie straddled him, her naked body pressed against him. They were still breathing heavy. She rolled off him, a grin plastered on her flushed face.

He turned to her. "I should shower before I go home."

Katie rolled partially on to him, her head on his chest and one leg and arm draped over his body. "Stay here forever," she said.

"I wish."

"What if we met like twenty years ago? Would you have chosen me over Linda?"

"You would've been five."

"Six." She turned her head, looking up at him. "I meant, if you met me as an adult before you had kids."

"I would have chosen you over anyone," John said.

A smile spread wide across her round face. "Anyone?"

"Anyone."

He kissed her forehead, wiggled out from under her, and stood from the bed. She stared at his penis.

"Nice package," she said, grinning.

He smirked. "You want to get in the shower with me?"

"I don't want to wash you off me." She sighed. "I like to sleep with your smell."

John padded to the bathroom. He stood under the showerhead, letting the hot water rush from head to toe. He thought about what might happen when she's fired on Friday. *Would she talk to the press? Would she disclose the affair? Probably not. It would be just as embarrassing for her. She'd be the new Monica Lewinsky, forever branded a whore.*

She did sign a nondisclosure agreement. I'm not sure it would be smart to sue her if she did talk. I'd look like the asshole. Either way I would deny it. She was infatuated, but nothing happened. It would be in the press for a couple of weeks, and then it'd be gone.

The bigger problem would be Linda. She'd be a total bitch. I doubt she'd be up for all the press, which would make me look like a huge asshole. I'd have to convince Linda it's bullshit. This could be disastrous if I don't handle it properly.

I'll have Donna mention the consequences for talking about anything detrimental to our campaign. Of course Donna can't know about this either. Katie might tell Donna, but Donna will keep it a secret. We have that sex tape from Katie's douchebag ex-boyfriend. I'll tell Donna to allude to the tape as blackmail if she gets the impression that Katie might say something detrimental to the campaign.

John turned off the water and stepped from the shower. He dried himself with a towel. His cell phone chimed in the room. He wrapped a towel around his waist and exited the bathroom. Katie stood by the dresser, wearing nothing but his white button-down shirt. She stared into his chiming phone.

Katie turned, her nipples visible through his shirt. "Should I answer it?" She giggled. "It's Linda."

59: Katie's Walk of Shame

Katie knocked on Donna's open office door.

Donna closed her laptop. "Shut the door," she said.

Katie shut the door behind her.

"Sit down," Donna said, motioning to the chair in front of her desk.

Katie sat down.

"We're letting you go," Donna said matter-of-factly, her face impassive.

Katie blinked, her stomach churning, and her mind spinning. "Like, fired?"

"Yes. A generous severance package will be given, provided you abide by the terms of your nondisclosure agreement. If you breathe a single word that might be detrimental to Congressman Bradley, we *will* sue you for every penny you have, and you'll never work in this town again."

Katie showed her palms. "I don't understand. We've increased our social media traffic by 200 percent."

"Your former involvement with George Chapman has become a liability with the recent protests and deaths of the IRS agents."

"But you hired me because I did such a good job working with him."

"What was a strength is now a liability."

Katie stood, her fists clenched. "You don't have good cause to fire me. I could sue for wrongful termination."

Donna stood slowly, her skirt suit pressed and not a single strand of her dark hair out of place. "Your employment contract stipulates that, during your first year of employment, you may be terminated without recourse."

"I've been here a year." Katie's eyes were wide.

Donna sighed. "Eleven months and nine days."

"Where's John? I want to talk to him."

"He's out for the day." A tiny smirk tugged on the corner of Donna's mouth.

She's enjoying this. Katie curled her lip in contempt. "I wonder if Linda would like to know what John and I've been doing?"

Donna's mouth turned down for a split second. "I suggest you remember the nondisclosure agreement you signed."

"You're fucking him too," Katie said, shaking her head.

"I suggest you leave with a little class and dignity." Donna crossed her arms over her chest, as if she were protecting her feelings.

Katie mock-winced. "He's not fucking you anymore, is he?"

Donna narrowed her dark eyes. "I remember what it was like to be young and to think you have principles. You think you have the right to be indignant. You don't have the slightest fucking clue who you're dealing with. If you open that pretty little mouth of yours, we will ruin every facet of your life. The congressman will come out of this mess being a stud, like JFK, and you'll be another penniless whore with a sex tape on the Internet."

"What sex tape?"

"Who knows how these things come out? I think they're gross. I mean, who would video their most intimate moments? We definitely don't look our best with no makeup, jiggling flesh, and those godawful hairy armpits. It really was an unflattering view."

Katie rummaged through her mental rolodex. *Fucking Declan.*

Donna picked up her desktop phone. "Please have Chuck escort Katie from the premises." Donna marched past Katie and opened her office door.

A dark-skinned security guard appeared at the door. Katie turned on her heels and returned to her office.

"Make sure she doesn't take the laptop and get her ID badge," Donna said to Chuck.

Chuck appeared in Katie's doorway. He eyed her with his arms crossed as she packed her belongings into a cardboard box. She didn't have much: her purse, some Goldfish crackers, a framed picture of her parents, a set of gym clothes that she never used, and some office supplies.

"I need your ID badge," Chuck said.

Katie removed the lanyard from her neck and handed the badge to Chuck. She put on her coat and exited the office. The receptionist averted her eyes as Katie walked past, carrying her box, Chuck in tow. A few staffers stared as Katie was escorted from the Capitol Building.

Outside, Katie set down her box on the Capitol steps and removed her cell from her purse. It was cool, the clouds dark and heavy. She called John. It went straight to voice mail.

She said, "Please tell me this wasn't your idea. I thought you cared about me. Call me as soon as you get this."

She sent a text.

Katie: John, please tell me you didn't want to fire me. I thought we had something special. Call me.

Katie held it together on the subway ride home. She broke down in her car as she stared into her phone at the unrequited text and phone message. She sat in the driver's seat, sobbing, her head in her hands. Katie sniffed back the mucus dripping from her nose. She thought about how they had used her. She thought about how she had sold out George, how Donna had threatened her, and how John had lied to her. He had to have known it was coming. Her sorrow burned into anger. She thought about holding his phone, with *Linda Calling* on the screen. *What if I had answered?* She had stared at the number long enough to remember it. It was only a couple of digits different than his.

She sat up and wiped her eyes. She thumb-typed a text to Linda.

Katie: Thought you might want to know what your husband's been up to.

Katie forwarded the string of illicit texts between her and John, arranging meetups and expressing their affection. She attached a picture to the text—the dick pic John had sent her one month ago.

60: Julie and the IRS

Julie drove home after her lunch shift, singing along with Babyface on the radio. She flipped on her headlights. It was only three, but it was dark, the clouds threatening a downpour. The silky voice on the radio was cut, exposing Julie's off-key crooning.

A man said, "We interrupt this broadcast to bring you this very important public service announcement. Taxes must be filed and paid by April 15. Americans who evade taxes will be prosecuted to the fullest extent of the law, with prison sentences of five years and fines of $250,000. Tax evasion threatens the very fabric of our society. Your government needs your help to make sure all Americans pay their fair share. A $1,000 reward will be paid for each tip given by patriotic Americans that leads to a successful prosecution. If you know anyone who is committing tax fraud or tax evasion, please submit tips online at www.IRS.tips.gov. The website again is www.IRS.tips.gov."

Julie turned into her community. George's truck and trailer were parked along the main road with a hodgepodge of campers, boats, trailers, and commercial vehicles. She turned on her street and parked in front of her townhome. She stepped from her car and glanced at the front yard. The flower bed and tree ring were freshly edged and mulched. She smiled, thinking about George helping around the house.

She stepped to the shared mailbox—a metal box the size of an oven. Julie opened her tiny box and removed a handful of letters. She flipped through the mail as she walked home. *Bill, junk, junk, junk, bill, shit.* Julie stopped in her tracks, a wave of anxiety washing over her. She opened the letter, her fingers trembling.

Sedition

IRS Department of the Treasury
Internal Revenue Service
1111 Constitution Avenue Northwest
Washington, DC 20221

Date: March 2, 2020

Julie Welch
422 Colonial Commons Drive
Fairfax, Virginia 22032

Social Security Number: xxx-xx-3548
Tax Year: 2013-2018
Form Number: 1040 and 4070
Person to Contact: Larry Nicholson
Employee Identification Number: 256744
Contact Telephone Number: (202) 555-6322

Dear Julie Welch,

We have selected your federal income tax return for the years shown above for examination. We examine tax returns to verify the correctness of income, deductions, exemptions, and credits.

WHAT YOU NEED TO DO

Please call the individual listed above WITHIN 10 DAYS to schedule an appointment. Please call between the hours of 8:30 a.m. to 5:00 p.m., Monday through Friday.

ISSUES TO BE REVIEWED DURING THE EXAMINATION

Your examination will primarily be focused on the following issues:

1. Federal tax returns for the years 2013–2018
2. Form 4070 (tip income) for the years 2013–2018

WHAT TO BRING WITH YOU TO THE EXAMINATION

Attached to this letter is an Information Document Request that lists the items on your return to be examined and the supporting items you need to provide. Please include complete copies of your 2013 through 2018 individual income tax returns, in addition to all Form 4070s from that same time period. You should organize your records according to the issues identified above. For additional information see the enclosed Publication 1, *Your Rights as a Taxpayer*, and Notice 609, *Privacy Act Notice*.

Letter 8752 (Rev. 3-2020)
Catalog Number 84402C

Inside the envelope was a Post-it note with a handwritten message. *If you tell anyone about this audit, George will be arrested for tax fraud.*

61: George and *1984*

George sat on the edge of the bed, with Max in his computer chair. Max was still chubby and short, but, over the past two years, the seventeen-year-old had grown a couple of inches and had lost some baby fat.

"I'd like to ask your mother to marry me," George said. "How do you feel about that?"

"Are you asking my permission?" Max asked.

George nodded. "I am. Your mother loves you more than anyone in this world, and a marriage wouldn't work without you being on board."

"What does this mean for me? Would I be on my own?"

"Of course not. I'd like for you two to move to Pennsylvania with me."

"Is there enough room?"

"The earth-sheltered house is small for three people. I was thinking that you and I could fix up the cabin, and that place could be yours."

His blue eyes were wide. "The cabin would be mine?"

"It's not very big, but it's nice for one or two people. Obviously you can come up to the main house anytime you want. My Internet's not too bad, so you can still work and go to school."

Max smiled a toothy grin.

"How do you feel about all this?" George asked.

"Sounds pretty awesome to me. When are you gonna ask her?"

"I don't know. Hopefully soon. I need to get a ring. I'm pretty nervous about it."

Max smirked. "She's gonna say yes. Trust me."

George stood from the bed. "I hope so."

Max stood from his chair.

"Thanks, Max. You're a good man." George held out his hand, but Max gave him a hug. They stepped back. George had a lump in his throat. "I should get back outside. I think rain's coming."

* * *

George dumped wheelbarrow loads of mulch in equally spaced piles throughout Julie's tiny backyard. He had covered the grass with dampened cardboard, then compost, now he was working on the final layer. A podcast played through his earbuds while he worked.

"This is Gary Cook of the *Alt News Podcast*, providing vital information in a changing world. It's Friday, March 6, 2020. Today we have a very special guest speaking to us all the way from Moscow, Russia. NSA whistleblower Edward Snowden is here to discuss the recent efforts by the US government to quell the tax rebellion. Edward, welcome to the *Alt News Podcast*.

"Thanks, Gary. I'm happy to be here," Edward said.

"Yesterday I was driving home," Gary said, "and my classic rock station was interrupted with a public service announcement that threatened jail time and fines for anyone who evades taxes. There was also an offer of $1,000 to turn in your friends and neighbors for tax evasion. I'm assuming you've heard about this?"

· "I have."

"What do you think about it?"

"The dirty truth is that the laws in the United States and in many places around the world are so onerous that most people are breaking them in some way. Then it becomes a matter of what the government chooses to enforce." Edward paused. "Taxes are the lifeblood of government, so it's no surprise that tax evasion would be heavily enforced. This is just another example of the government protecting its revenue."

"What do you think about the *1984* style of enforcement by offering rewards for turning in tax evaders?"

"The US government is pitting citizens against citizens and neighbors against neighbors. To a certain extent, all governments rely on tips from citizens. The more a government relies on tips from citizens, the more divided a population becomes. All of a sudden, people are watching their backs. They don't trust their neighbors. This is a common theme of totalitarian governments throughout history."

George glanced at the clouds, heavy with rain. *I better hurry.* He raked the piles of mulch, covering the compost with an inch of shredded hardwood and leaves.

"Do you think the US tax revolt will be successful?" Gary asked.

"I suppose that depends on what you mean by *successful*," Edward replied. "The tax protestors are the early adopters of this idea that taxation is theft or, more accurately, extortion." Edward paused. "In the long run, I hope the movement will be successful, but I'm afraid there may be dire consequences for the early adopters. I think there is a possibility that the US government will make an example out of these people."

"That's my fear as well." Gary paused for a beat. "You're someone who is very aware of the surveillance capabilities of the US government. How dangerous is it to speak out against the government?"

"Historically speaking, antigovernment speech has been dangerous. In 1934, Germany criminalized political slander and libel. People were sent to prison for telling jokes. In 1917, the US Congress passed the Espionage and Trading with the Enemy Act, which criminalized antiwar speech. Hundreds of Americans were prosecuted for speaking or writing things that were considered dissent. More recently President Reynolds has used the Trading with the Enemy Act to prosecute government whistleblowers."

Edward paused again. "Freedom of speech is what we have until that speech threatens government power, then we become criminals. I think it's becoming increasingly dangerous to speak out. The NSA and the US government have access to information that tyrants of the past could only dream of. I believe they'll use that data to increase governmental power and control over the American public."

George used a diamond hoe to make a furrow one-half-inch deep along the fence line. He planted dried peas in the furrow and raked the compost and mulch over the seeds. He planted kale, spinach, and lettuce near the patio for easy picking. George planted the carrots, radishes, turnips, and rutabagas farther away from the patio. The root crops only needed to be harvested once, so their location didn't need to be convenient.

George caught a glimpse of movement in his peripheral vision. Through the sliding glass door, he saw Julie walking toward the kitchen. George leaned his rake against the wooden privacy fence, popped his earbuds from his ears, and tapped on the sliding glass door. She turned around and forced a smile.

He opened the door and stuck his head inside. "You wanna see the garden?"

She approached with a small stack of mail in hand. Her face was pale, her eyes red-rimmed.

"What's wrong?" George asked.

Julie stepped onto the back patio. "I'm just tired."

George narrowed his eyes. "Are you sure?"

She nodded.

"Why don't you take a nap? I'll take care of dinner tonight." George moved toward the edge of the patio. He motioned to the garden. "What do you think?"

"Looks like mulch," she replied.

He smirked. "It's March. Give it some time. I planted the cool season crops today. I was thinking, with the rain coming and the warm weather in the forecast, we could get a jump on spring."

"This is really sweet. Thank you." She kissed him on the cheek. "How much do I owe you for the mulch and seeds?"

He frowned. "I got the mulch for free at the landfill and brought extra seeds from home." He stared at her for a moment. "You sure you're okay?"

Raindrops began to fall.

62: John's Picture

John jammed to Def Leppard as he shut the garage door with a press of the remote. He had spent the day at his Virginia campaign headquarters, soaking up the adulation of young female staffers. Congressman John Bradley was a political rock star. The handsome antiwar activist. A modern-day JFK. He turned off his BMW, cutting the eighties rock beat. Despite the day's distractions, he had a sinking feeling in his stomach. He thought about Katie. He had deleted her text and voice message and had blocked her number. It had to be a clean break. He should call Donna to find out how it went. His phone chimed. *Speak of the devil.*

"What's up, Donna? How did it go with Katie?"

"She's gone, but we might have a problem."

"What happened?" John asked.

"I think you know," Donna said.

John furrowed his brow. "What are you talking about?"

"Don't insult my intelligence."

"I have no idea what you're talking about."

"You've been fucking Katie, haven't you?"

"That's insane. Is that what she said?"

"You know what? It doesn't matter. You can continue to lie if you like. I'll finish what I've started with this campaign, because I'm a professional, but we will not be seeing each other again outside of work."

"Donna—"

"Do you understand me?"

"Let's get together tomorrow to talk this out. I'll book a room."

"I said, it's over, and I mean it. I'm tired of being strung along. I can't believe I wasted six years with you."

"Donna—"

"I have to go."

"Don't go. Talk to me."

"I'm going out to dinner with Jake."

"Agent Barnes?"

"Good-bye, John."

"Donna." The line was dead.

John hung his head over his steering wheel. After a moment he trudged inside. It was quiet. The kitchen was clean, no sign of dinner being made or having been eaten.

"Linda?" John called out.

"In the dining room," she replied.

John set his briefcase and keys on the counter and walked to the dining room. Linda sat at the head of the table, her phone in front of her, a wad of tissues in hand. Normally she had beautiful skin, like Snow White with a bit of strawberry, but, when she was upset, it showed with blotchiness, puffy eyes, and even hives on her chest. She was definitely upset.

"Where is everyone?" John asked.

"The kids are with my parents," she replied, her voice trembling.

"What's wrong?" John winced, not sure if he wanted to know the answer.

"Sit down, and I'll show you."

John sat in the seat kitty-cornered from her. He scrolled through the possibilities in his mind, but, given the timing, it had to be Katie.

She picked up her phone and pressed the button on the side, waking it up. She swiped right and slid it across the table toward John. He picked it up and looked at his penis on the screen.

John dropped the phone. "Jesus, Linda, that's disgusting. Who the hell's sending you dick pics?"

She clenched her fists, her eyes like lasers. "Your girlfriend, Katie Fitzgerald."

John exhaled. "I see what this is about. Donna fired her today because she was unproductive. Donna told me that Katie had made threats. She said something like, 'I'm going to make him pay.' That's what this is, Linda. A disgruntled former employee."

"It's your penis."

John picked up the phone again. "It can't be." He examined the picture. "Shit. I'm so sorry, honey—"

"I'm leaving you."

"I never touched her."

Linda glared at John. "Then why does she have a picture of your penis?"

"She must've got it from Agent Olson or Barnes or one of the other guys."

She raised both hands. "Do I even want to know?"

"Look. It's really embarrassing and stupid. During the congressional campaign, I was hanging out with the Secret Service guys late one night. One of our donors had given us a nicely aged scotch. We drank too much, and one of the guys thought it would be funny to send dick pics to his girlfriend, except he wanted to send a picture of another guy's penis, to see if she knew what his penis looked like. The other guys thought it was funny. So we all traded these pictures. I knew it was a stupid idea, so I sent the picture to myself, because I didn't want you to get it. I was trying to bond with the guys. They think of me as their boss. I guess I just wanted to be one of the guys for once. I'm really sorry, Linda. It was incredibly stupid."

She narrowed her eyes. "Do you still have the message and picture on your phone?"

"I deleted it a long time ago. I didn't want anyone to find a penis picture on my phone. Knowing what's possible to be hacked makes me paranoid. I'd be painted as the gay politician on the down-low. The press would have a field day."

"I've been thinking about what to do about this for the past four hours. Do you want to know what I decided?"

John reached for her hand, but she snatched it away. "I know this must've been really upsetting. I'm so sorry."

"I decided that I would give you another chance if we went to counseling and you told the truth."

"I don't think we need counseling. It was a stupid prank. If someone found out we were going to couples counseling, it'd be plastered all over USN."

Her eyes filled with tears. She pointed a shaky finger in his direction. "You're a liar."

John showed his palms. "What are you talking about?"

Linda snatched her phone from the table, tapped on the screen, and slid it back to John. He picked it up and looked at the text string between him and Katie arranging meetups and expressing their affections.

Tears slipped down her face. "How stupid do you think I am?"

"I've never seen these texts before in my life," he said.

She stood from the table and grabbed her phone from his hand. He stood.

She sniffled and wiped her tears on the sleeve of her sweater. "You have three seconds to tell me the truth, or, so help me God, this marriage is over, and I'll release this filth to the press."

"Linda, be reasonable. She must've hacked my phone somehow."

"One."

"Don't you see what's she's doing?"

"Two."

"Linda, please."

"Three. We're finished."

Linda turned and marched toward the stairs. John followed. At the bottom of the steps was a suitcase. She grabbed her luggage and rolled it past him. John grabbed her by the upper arm.

"Take your hands off me," she said.

He let go. "Where are you going?"

"To my parents. I can't stand the sight of you. You make me sick."

John hung his head. "I make myself sick. Please don't go. I have a problem, and I need help. I need you. Please, Linda. We can go to counseling."

Linda shut her eyes for a moment. "How long were you having an affair with her?"

"For about a month, but it's over."

She exhaled. "I don't trust you, but it's more than that. I don't even like you. I'm tired of pretending."

"We'll go to counseling. We'll fix it. What about the kids? They'll be devastated."

"It's over."

"I can't win without you. No way in hell the American people would elect a divorcee."

She shook her head. "You're unbelievable." She marched past the dining room, into the kitchen, rolling her suitcase behind her.

John stopped her in the kitchen, his hand on her wrist. "This isn't about me. This isn't about you. If Art's elected, you know what he'll do. I'm trying to stop the wholesale slaughter of millions of people."

"You can't put that on me."

"I'm not trying to put anything on you. These are the facts. You leave me before the election, the Republicans win, and the endless wars continue. If you stay, I win and put an end to the wars. I'm asking for eight months. That's all. If you still feel the same after the election, I won't contest the divorce."

She stood up her suitcase and parked it. "Damn you, John."

63: Katie Comes Clean

The lock turned, and Zach pushed into Katie's condo, lugging his suitcase. Katie stood from the couch.

"Hey," Zach said with a smile.

Katie forced a smile and approached her boyfriend. "How was the flight?"

"It was fine." He left his suitcase by the door and turned his attention to Katie. He pecked her on the lips and wrapped her up in an embrace. "I missed you," he whispered in her ear.

She pulled back. "I need to tell you something."

His eyebrows arched. "Okay."

They sat on the couch. Katie bit her lower lip. Zach was ten years older than her, but he looked young with his baby face, small stature, and disheveled dark hair.

"I had an affair with Congressman Bradley," Katie said, ripping off the metaphorical Band-Aid.

Zach's eyes widened. "When?"

Katie looked down. "For the past month."

"I don't understand. I thought things were good between us."

She looked up. "They are. They were. I'm so sorry, Zach. You don't deserve any of this."

He rubbed his eyes and pinched the bridge of his nose. "So, that's it. We're finished?"

Katie's eyes moistened. "I hope not. It's up to you. I was an idiot, but I love you. I don't think I really knew that until now."

He stood from the couch. "It's too late." He removed Katie's house key from his key ring, set it on the coffee table, and marched toward the door.

Katie chased after him. "Please don't go."

He turned at the door, his hand on his suitcase. "I know I'm not the type of guy who girls dream about, but I won't stick around just because I can't do any better. I'd rather be alone."

"I'm sorry." Tears slipped down Katie's cheeks. "Please stay."

He opened the door and hurried to the green rental car parked next to her SUV. She stepped on to her stoop, willing him to change his mind, to come back. Puddles had accumulated in the parking lot from two days of rain. The sun pierced the clouds. Under normal circumstances, she would have laughed at the color car he always requested. He loved the movie *Meet the Parents*, and there was a bit with Ben Stiller, a green rental car, and Robert De Niro saying, "Well, they say geniuses pick green." These are the goofy things you learn about someone after a nearly two-year-long relationship.

Zach sped out of the parking lot, and Katie trudged back inside. She curled up in bed and sobbed. She sobbed for Zach, for John, for who she'd become. She eventually fell asleep.

* * *

Katie awoke to a darkened room. She felt for her glasses on the bedside table, grabbed them, and put them on. She staggered to the bathroom, flipped on the light, and stared at her reflection. Her eyes were red-rimmed, her face washed out, and her light brown hair tousled. She sat on the toilet and peed. Sitting there, she thought about what George had said to her the last time they talked. *You made this into something great. We're having an impact. We're helping people.* There on the toilet, she had an epiphany.

She washed her hands, hurried to the living room, and picked up her phone from the coffee table. It read 8:34 p.m. She pressed her George contact. It rang half-a-dozen times and went to voice mail. She went back to her room, threw on a sweatshirt and jeans, and hurried to her car. *He might be at Julie's.* Katie's condo was in northern Virginia, not far from Julie's townhome. Katie drove across town and parked in a visitor's spot. She glanced in the rearview window and tried to fix her hair. *Screw it.* She stepped out of her SUV, marched to the townhome, and knocked.

Julie answered the door. "Katie, what are you doing here?"

"Is George here?" Katie asked. "I really need to talk to him."

"Come in."

Katie stepped inside. George approached them.

"Katie's here to see you," Julie said to George. "I'll be in the basement. I have some laundry to do." Before leaving, Julie turned to Katie. "It's nice to see you, honey."

"This is a surprise," George said.

"I know. I need to talk to you." Katie chewed on her lower lip.

"Why don't we sit?"

They sat at opposite ends of the couch. George wore jeans and a sweatshirt. He had a dark five-o'clock shadow.

"I was fired," Katie said.

George exhaled. "I'm sorry to hear that. I'm sure you'll find something else."

"I know what I did to you and Max was really messed-up. I'm sorry. I really am."

"I appreciate that."

"I left because I didn't think we would make as big an impact as Bradley's campaign. I thought I was doing the right thing, but I was just feeding my ego. I wanted people to think that I was someone important and successful, not some political wannabe YouTuber who people only watched to see cleavage. But you were right. We *were* making an impact."

"Not so much anymore."

"We can again. And I think we can change the world."

"You've lied to me twice now."

Katie nodded. "You're right, but don't let my stupidity ruin all the good we could do. How many states have you done the paperwork for with the write-in campaign?"

"I have no intention of doing any paperwork. It's a protest vote."

"If we do the paperwork, it'll have a bigger impact, and it'll be more likely to scare the establishment. I can do it for you. It's not too late. There are thirty-three states that require paperwork and forty-three states that accept write-in candidates."

George shook his head. "Even if it were possible to win, I won't take the job. That's not the point anyway. The point is to—"

"Tell people the truth?"

"That was the idea, but I'm not sure people really want the truth. Mostly people wanna believe what they already believe."

"The more politically relevant we become, the more receptive people will be to the message. You've said that voting influences people to engage with the system and support it. What if they voted for *you*? Maybe they'd be more engaged with the ideas of real freedom and a nonviolent society."

"We were a long way from political relevancy before you left, and now we're barely a blip on the radar screen."

"You're more politically relevant than you realize. We did some polling to find the most popular VP candidate for Bradley. Senator Atwell from California was number one, but you were number two. With my contacts, I can revive the George 2020 campaign. Who knows? We might get into the debates. Don't you want the chance to put those lying pieces of shit in their place?"

"I don't know if I can do that." George stared at the carpet for a moment. "One-on-one or on video I can do, but, in front of an audience, that's not my strong suit."

"What do you mean?"

"I have stage fright."

"We'll work on it. There are therapists for stuff like that."

"I've been to therapy."

"We may never get into the debates anyway." Katie pursed her full lips. "You know? I used to get hundreds of emails every day from people saying that you changed their life for the better. Please, George. I need this."

George rubbed the stubble on his chin. "I have three conditions. Max has to agree. Also, the same agreement we had about profits over $100,000 going to charity stays in effect. And no more lies. If you have anything else to tell me, now's the time."

Katie winced and said, "I had an affair with Congressman Bradley."

"I don't need to know about that."

"You do because I want to go public."

"Katie." George shook his head. "Why? It'll be a circus."

"Bradley used me and threw me away when it suited him. This would ruin his campaign."

"I don't think that's what'll happen. They'll say you're lying, and people'll believe 'em."

"I have proof, and, if I explain what happened, women will understand. I might destroy his biggest advantage, the female vote. Think about it. More women are Democrats already, and he'll have the female vote with Senator

Atwell as his VP, unless I tell people who he really is."

"I don't know, Katie. Ultimately it's your decision. I would strongly recommend that you sit on this for at least a month and think about it, because, once it's out there, you can't get it back."

"Okay, I'll give it some time."

"I think that's smart."

Katie stood from the couch. "I guess I need to talk to Max."

George stood.

As if on cue, Max descended the stairs. His blond hair was combed forward, and his eyes were narrowed behind his wire-rim frames. Max stood eye-to-eye with Katie.

"Hi, Max," Katie said, smiling.

Max crossed his arms over his chest.

"I'm really sorry about what I did to you and George."

"You're a sellout," Max said.

Katie nodded. "You're right. I sold you out. I don't have an excuse for what I did. I'm sorry." She took a deep breath. "I was hoping that we could work together again."

He shrugged. "You don't need me. You need George."

"I do need you. It's not the same without you. You, me, and George— we're a team."

Max looked at George, then Katie. "George said he won't do it without me, huh?"

She smiled. "Something like that."

"At least you're telling the truth now." His smirk turned into a grin.

64: Julie's a Criminal

Larry shut the door behind them.

Julie's stomach churned. She was dressed in an oversized sweater and a long, loose skirt—the least sexy outfit she had. She wore no makeup. She did brush her hair. If she had a bonnet, she could pass for Amish. She started to sweat under her arms and between her breasts.

"Have a seat," Larry said, motioning to the cushioned chair in front of his desk.

He sat behind his wooden desk. Julie sat across from him, balancing a stack of tax returns and 4070 forms on her thighs. Larry typed on his laptop as if she wasn't there.

"Why are you doing this?" Julie asked.

He ignored her and continued to type. He moved his laptop to the side and leaned his elbows on the desk. He looked powerful in his suit—like the man who attacked her, not the one she thought was so gentle and self-deprecating.

"Why do you wait tables?" he asked.

"To pay my bills."

"I do audits to pay *my* bills."

Julie gripped the stack of files in her lap, her knuckles turning white. "But why now? We broke up two years ago."

"For the record, it was one year and nine months ago."

Julie scowled. "Why are you so fixated on me?"

He chuckled. "Don't flatter yourself. I have a girlfriend."

"Are you referring to that beach picture you sent me out of the blue? I blocked your number by the way."

Phil M. Williams

He furrowed his brow. "Hmm, ... oh, you must be talking about our trip to Turks and Caicos. That picture accidentally went out to my entire contact list. It is interesting that it bothered you so much that you'd block my number."

"Cut the bullshit, Larry. Why am I here?"

"The United States is in crisis. In the past few months, terrorists have killed IRS agents. People are refusing to pay their taxes. Domestic terrorists, like your boyfriend, have made my life very unsafe. Do you think I should sit back and do nothing?" He paused, waiting for a reply that never came. "As a patriotic American and an IRS agent, it's my duty to audit anyone who I feel is breaking the law, especially those with ties to domestic terrorism."

"I'm not breaking the law."

"On the contrary."

"I sent all your stupid paperwork, and I have the copies right here. I filed everything, like I was supposed to." She smacked her hand on top of the stack of files in her lap.

"That's my evidence. You see, Julie, I cross-referenced your bank account with your stated income over the six years from 2013 to 2018, and it seems that you made quite a bit more money than you were claiming. I'm surprised actually. Most waitresses spend their cash tips, but you deposited them in your bank account and claimed a total of $31,760 less than you actually made in those six years."

Julie's mouth was dry as she searched her mind for an explanation. "My sister and my mother, ... they gave me money. I don't think gifts are taxable."

He nodded, his receding hairline shiny in the fluorescent light. "Nice try. I found three personal checks that you deposited—two from your sister and one from your mother. These checks amounted to less than $3,500. I didn't count them in the $31,000 total."

"They didn't always give me a check. A lot of times they gave me cash."

A toothy grin spread across his face. "It's settled then. I'll just need to audit your mother and sister to be certain. What would they say if I called and asked them?"

Julie hung her head. "I don't know."

"Would you like me to forget that you just lied to a federal agent?"

She nodded.

"All right then, let's stick with the truth from now on. With penalties and

346

interest, your total due comes to $9,120.96."

Julie's heart thumped in her chest. "I can't afford that."

"You can apply for a short-term extension or a payment plan, but the IRS isn't granting very many of these lately, given the revenue shortage."

They were quiet for a few seconds.

"I could've gone to the police after what you did," Julie said.

"You mean, when you invited me to your bedroom and assaulted me?"

Julie's face was taut. "You tried to rape me, you piece of shit."

He shook his head slowly. "You might want to keep it down. Making false accusations to try to blackmail a federal agent is a felony and a much worse crime than tax evasion."

"Fuck you."

He sighed as if he were dealing with a petulant child. "I guess we're done then. They won't come for you immediately, but you can rest assured, they will come for you. In the meantime, I need to start working on Chapman's audit. Self-employed, antigovernment Anarchist. You and I both know he's not paying all his taxes."

Julie hung her head, a lump developing in her throat. *Don't you cry in front of him.* She swallowed and lifted her head. "What do you want from me?"

"First, you're going to shut up and listen. Do you understand?"

Julie nodded.

"Women like you can't see a good thing when it's right in front of you. You spend high school chasing the popular assholes who treat you like garbage. You spend your twenties dating and marrying the same type of guy. You have kids that turn out to be idiotic assholes just like their parents."

Julie's eyes were glassy.

"The asshole husband gets tired of you when you hit the wall in your thirties. In your case he was so tired of you that he put a bullet in his brain."

A tear slid down her face. She wiped her eyes with her sweater sleeve. "Fuck you," she said barely audible.

"What was that?"

Julie clenched her jaw but didn't say anything.

"You're probably wondering how I found out. Working as a federal agent gives me access to massive amounts of information." He smiled wide. "So, after your husband checks out of heartbreak hotel, then you're finally interested in the nice guy. But you're ruined now. Just a used-up whore. And us nice guys are supposed to be so grateful for the sloppy seconds." He cackled to himself. "I bet more like sloppy sixteenths. This isn't high school anymore, and you're not hot anymore. Maybe you should have made better choices when you were young, and you wouldn't be a single mother, with no money and a massive IRS debt."

Tears streamed down Julie's cheeks.

He huffed. "When all else fails, cry, right? It might work with speeding tickets, but it won't work with me. I see who you really are." Larry adjusted his black-rim glasses, picked up a sealed envelope from his desktop, and held it out toward Julie. "Your itemized bill."

Julie snatched the envelope.

"I'd make sure your 2019 tax return is in order," he said with a crooked grin. "Once you're on the radar, we won't let you fall through the cracks again."

Julie stood, cradling the files. "You're a pathetic excuse for a human being." She turned on her heels, opened the door, and left the office.

"Say hi to George for me," he said to her back.

* * *

Julie parked along the street in front of the stone mansion. A landscaping truck and trailer was parked in the driveway. Brown-skinned men in matching sweatshirts pushed wheelbarrow loads of mulch to the flower beds. Birds chirped and daffodils popped out of the earth, early harbingers of spring.

She called George.

"Hey, Julie," he said.

"Hi, honey. Are you driving?" she asked, her cell pressed to her ear.

"Yeah, I'm in Georgia, near Atlanta. Are you okay? You sound off."

"I'm fine. I'll let you go. I don't want you talking and driving. I love you."

"I love you too. I'll call you tonight."

Julie disconnected the call. Her sister, Summer, exited the mansion. Julie took a deep breath, stepped out of her car, and walked across the lush green lawn. It was green a bit earlier than was natural. No doubt the result of chemical fertilizers.

"Hi, sis," Summer said, walking toward Julie.

They met in the middle of the lawn.

"Thanks for making time to meet me," Julie said.

"Of course." Summer narrowed her eyes at Julie's ensemble. "What are you wearing by the way? You look homeless."

"I might be soon," Julie said under her breath.

"What was that?"

"Nothing."

"Would you like to come in for some tea? I picked up some great herbal tea from the farmer's market last weekend."

"That would be nice."

Julie followed her sister across the lawn toward the front door. Summer wore yoga pants and a fleece top from Athleta. Summer had encouraged Julie to shop there for her workout clothes. "I know it's expensive," she had said, "but they last forever. You have to buy quality." Julie still shopped at T.J. Maxx.

Summer stopped next to an older man pushing mulch around with a rake. "What time will you be done?" Summer asked, her hands on her hips. "My husband will be home in an hour, and you're blocking the garage."

"We're almost done," the man replied with a heavy accent.

Julie glanced at the freshly mulched flower bed of boxwoods, pink blooming camellias, and a Japanese maple. "Looks nice," Julie said to the man.

He smiled, a single gold tooth glittering in the sun. "Thank you."

Julie followed Summer inside. The foyer consisted of three stories of open air, a marble floor, and a hand-painted mural of a vineyard on the wall. They passed the spiral staircase and the cavernous living room on the way to the kitchen.

The kitchen was filled with massive stainless-steel appliances and a center island with a built-in grill. Summer filled the teakettle and placed it on the gas burner. They sat at the round kitchen table for four. Summer's makeup was flawless, and her blond hair was highlighted and coiffed.

"What are you doing today?" Julie asked.

Summer groaned. "I've had the landscapers here since seven. They'd mulch the grass if I didn't watch over them. I still need to work out, go to the store, and make dinner."

"Sounds like you have your hands full."

"So how's George these days?" Summer raised one side of her mouth in contempt. "Is he still raging against the machine?"

"Don't do that."

Summer showed her palms. "Do what?"

"You know what. You're making fun of him. You barely know him."

"You're right. I don't know him. You've only brought him here like twice. How long have you two been dating?"

"It'll be two years this summer."

"Exactly. And, when he was here, he had a holier-than-thou attitude. I mean, who digs out of the trash can to save plastic?"

"That doesn't make him holier than thou."

"Jason thinks he's an asshole."

Julie frowned. "Why?"

"Jason thinks he has all these ideas just to shock people and make himself feel bigger. He can't make it in the real world, so he has to criticize everyone who's successful."

Julie shook her head. "That's total bullshit. I can't believe you'd say that."

Summer sighed. "I'm just telling you what Jason thinks."

Julie exhaled. "If you two hate him so much, why do you care if I bring him over or not?"

"I didn't say that we hated him. I'm just worried that he's not good for you."

"I love him."

Summer looked away. The teakettle spit and screamed. She stood and tended to the tea. Julie followed.

"He's a good person," Julie said. "Max likes him, and Max hates everyone."

"Mom doesn't like him either."

"That's because she agrees with everything you and Jason say."

Summer dropped a teabag in a steaming mug. "Max likes him because Max believes in the same nonsense. You know, if you search *George Chapman* and *cult* in Google, you'll get tons of articles that say he's a cult leader."

Julie pinched the bridge of her nose for a moment. "That's ridiculous. He's not a cult leader. He doesn't take money from anyone. He doesn't even make any money from his videos."

Summer picked up the mugs. "He's a great guy then. My mistake." She took the mugs to the table.

"Don't patronize me," Julie said, returning to the table.

"What do you want me to say? That I like him when I don't?"

"Fine." Julie shook her head. "You know he's never said one unkind thing about you or Jason."

"Like I said, I guess he's a great guy." Summer rolled her eyes. "Why are you here anyway? I know it's not because you're interested in *my* life."

Julie took a deep breath. "I'm in a bind. I've been audited by the IRS. They hit me with a bill for"—Julie winced—"$9,000."

Summer stared into her tea, pressing her teabag against the edge of the mug with her spoon.

"I picked up two more shifts, but tips are lower, and, with this inflation, my grocery bill is sky high, not to mention gas."

Summer glanced up from her tea, her face impassive. "I haven't noticed all this inflation everyone talks about. Our bills are pretty much the same."

"Yeah, because you don't spend the bulk of your income on food and gas."

"I have four people eating in this house and three vehicles."

Julie rubbed the back of her neck. "I need a loan. I can't ask Mom. It's too much."

"How much this time?"

"Eight thousand."

Summer gasped. "We're just starting to put the pieces back together since the stock market crash. This whole thing was a lesson to us. We're trying to be more careful with our money. We're cutting back on everything."

"Please, Summer, I'll lose my home. I could go to jail."

"Somehow I doubt that. Why don't you ask George? He's such a great guy, I'm sure he'll help you out."

"He doesn't have much, and his ex-fiancée stole his money. I don't want him to think that I'm like her."

"Why don't you ask Max? He's been bragging about all the money he's been making with those anti-American videos."

Julie clenched her fists. "Max said he was saving up for a truck after Jason asked him what he had been doing. That's hardly bragging. And would you want to borrow money from Heather or Abby?"

"Maybe you should cut back on your spending or stop playing house with George and get a second job. You're an adult. You need to learn to handle your own finances."

"A second job? I'm already working sixty hours a week and Max still needs me. I'm neglecting him as it is."

Summer shrugged. "I don't know what to tell you."

"You're not going to help me?"

"I can't keep throwing good money after bad."

"You've helped me twice, and I've been paying you back. I owe you $1,960. I'm not ungrateful, but you act like you've given me a fortune."

Summer shook her head. "Paying me back? It's not even worth my time. You send me these checks for like twenty dollars. Then I have to fill out the check and take it to the bank. When it's all said and done, you've cost me more than twenty dollars of my time."

Julie stood from the table. "Forget it. You'll get the money I owe you." Julie stomped toward the front door.

65: George, You Gotta Do Your Thing

George drove through Buckhead, a suburb of Atlanta, Georgia. He passed stucco and brick mansions with five-car garages and manicured landscapes with formal hedges, palm trees, crepe myrtles, and magnolias. A mixed hardwood and pine forest provided a buffer between the estates. The hardwoods were free from foliage, but some were starting to bud.

"You have arrived at your destination," Miss GPS said.

George turned into the circular paver driveway and parked on the edge, leaving enough room for another vehicle to pass. He gazed up at the house that looked more like a hotel. The redbrick estate had columns framing the front door, a wraparound porch on the second floor, and four chimneys. George glanced at the clock on his radio. It read 1:48. He hopped out, stepped to the front door, and rang the doorbell. No response. He rang the doorbell again but still no response. *I am a little early.*

He returned to his truck and listened to a podcast through his earbuds.

"We've had protests popping up all over the country," Gary Cook said. "Protests against police brutality, antiwar demonstrations, the tax revolts, and now we have the upcoming Million Mask March. The common thread is that all these demonstrations are antigovernment. People are waking up, and they're using the Internet to connect, but the US government won't simply go quietly into the night. They'll fight tooth and nail to hold on to their power. I'm afraid this could get bloody."

George turned to the tapping on his window. A gigantic black man grinned with bright white teeth. George popped his earbuds from his ears and stepped from his truck. The man was muscular and insanely tall.

"You're George Chapman," he said.

"Yes," George replied, looking up at the man. "I have your Triumph for delivery."

"I can't believe it. I just saw you on Instagram."

George nodded. "I have a few videos out there."

They walked to the back of the trailer.

"Come on now. It's not just a few videos. You're the real deal. No need to be humble. I sure as hell ain't humble."

George opened and lowered the trailer door that doubled as a gate.

"Do you know who I am?" the man asked.

"I'm assuming you're Bernard Brown. At least that's what the paperwork says."

"Downtown Bernie Brown?"

"I'm sorry, Mr. Brown. I'm not sure what you're referring to."

Bernard laughed, a deep masculine laugh. "Don't you watch sports? I'm the second coming of Lebron James. I play for the Atlanta Hawks."

"I'm sorry. I don't follow sports."

He clapped a massive mitt on George's shoulder. "That's okay."

Bernard's hand was heavy on his shoulder. George moved away from the man, stepping inside the trailer. George unhooked the Triumph Thruxton. It was a modern classic, a sport bike with classic styling but modern technology. The 1200 cc beauty had shiny spokes, a single seat, and dual exhausts.

George rolled the bike from the trailer and parked it in front of the man. Bernard threw his leg over and sat on the motorcycle. He looked like an adult on a kid's bicycle. The only thing missing was the training wheels.

"What do you think?" George asked.

"It's a bit small for me," Bernard replied.

George cringed, thinking about dealing with the return.

"It ain't for me though," Bernard said. "A friend of mine. He lost his job and his car. I'm helping him out."

"You're a good friend."

Bernard shrugged. "I make enough to buy this bike in about a minute and a half on the court. It would be like you buying your friend a cup of coffee."

"It's still nice."

"Oh, shit. I gotta show you something. It'll just take a minute."

Bernard led George to the side of the house and the ten-car garage. One of the ten doors were open. Bernard didn't store junk in his garage. There were ten cars. A Range Rover, a Cadillac Escalade, two BMWs, an F-250 pickup, a vintage Cadillac convertible soft top, a Mercedes, a Lamborghini, a Porsche 911, and a red Ferrari. He bounded toward the Ferrari. It was backed into the garage, the nose pointed out.

"Check this out," Bernard said, motioning toward the back of the Italian sports car.

"It's a nice car," George replied.

Bernard had a crooked grin. "No, come over here and check out the bumper."

George walked to the back of the vehicle. A single bumper sticker defaced the $350,000 automobile. It read George 2020. George and Bernard laughed.

"How do you fit into this thing?" George asked.

"I gotta special seat, but it's still tight." Bernard reached into the pocket of his sweatpants. "We gotta take a selfie."

Before George could protest, the seven-foot-tall man held out his phone with his arm around George. After a series of photos, Bernard checked his phone.

"I gotta couple good ones," Bernard said. "Being famous is a trip, huh?"

"I guess you could say that," George replied as they walked toward George's truck.

"I gotta George 2020 T-shirt. I'm gonna wear it during warmups."

"That might not go over real well."

Bernard cocked his head and rapped George on the back. "You gotta do your thing. You can't worry about the haters."

* * *

George stopped for gas near the border of Georgia and South Carolina. Diesel was $4.63 per gallon. The pit stop cost George $185. After refueling, he parked his truck and went inside the gas station to use the restroom. On the way out his phone chimed. He fished his phone from the front pocket of his jeans.

"Hey, Katie," George said as he walked to his rig.

"I have something big, no huge actually." Katie spoke rapidly. "I was contacted by an organizer for Anonymous. They want you to be the featured speaker at the Million Mask March on April 15. There may actually be over one million people there. The theme is the tax revolt."

"I've already said that I wasn't participating in the tax revolt." George climbed into the cab of his truck and shut the door.

"I told them. They still want you to speak. They think you'll draw a large crowd."

"I'm not a good public speaker."

"We'll come up with a speech, and we'll practice. Worst case scenario, you can get up there and read it off a piece of paper."

George exhaled. "I'm not comfortable with this."

"This is huge. We have over a month to prepare. You'll be ready. I promise."

"If I'm not?"

"Then people won't hear your speech. That wouldn't be the end of the world."

"All right."

66: John and That's How They Getcha

John, Frank, and Donna sat in the sitting area of John's congressional office. A commercial played through the flat screen on the wall.

"WNN wants a comment immediately afterward," Donna said to Frank, as if John were invisible. "I'd be nice if we had the president's speech ahead of time."

Frank said, "I'd bet dollars to donuts, it's gonna be about patriotism, American exceptionalism, and paying your taxes."

John nodded.

"This tax revolt might have legs," Frank added.

"We'll see after tax season," John said.

"Chapman's seen quite a spike in popularity. Not sure if it's the tax revolt or because Katie's back in the saddle."

John frowned at Frank. "For the record, I was the only one with reservations about firing her."

Donna glowered at John. "It had to be done. I think you know that."

President Reynolds appeared on the flat screen. The president sat behind his shiny desk in the Oval Office, flanked by an American flag and a blue flag with the eagle crest that formed the Great Seal of the United States. Behind him was a cabinet with framed pictures of his family. President Reynolds was somber, his face drawn. His blond-gray hair was cut military short, his hands clasped on the desk as if he were praying.

"Toward the end of my military career, I was deployed to Iraq," President Reynolds said. "This wasn't my first time in a war zone or even my first time in Iraq. I had been a captain during Desert Storm. I was scared that first time. There had been a lot of talk about Saddam using chemical weapons. On my second deployment to Iraq, I wasn't afraid. That's not because I was some tough guy. I was a colonel. I knew I wouldn't be anywhere near danger. The danger would be for the enlisted men and lieutenants.

"One of the men under my command was Corporal Edgar Ramirez, a medic. In 2004, he was part of a convoy hit by an IED left by insurgents. Corporal Ramirez did his job that day, saving the lives of two of his fellow soldiers. He also saved the lives of two Iraqis who were in the wrong place at the wrong time. A father and his nine-year-old daughter. Corporal Ramirez didn't give better care to the Americans. His best efforts were given to the Americans and the Iraqis alike.

"A few years later, Corporal Ramirez was now Sergeant Ramirez, and he was on his second tour in Iraq. He was part of another convoy when another IED detonated. This time it was *his* Humvee that was hit. The blast ignited the fuel tank and engulfed the vehicle in flames. Three of the four men seated inside were knocked unconscious by the force of the blast. Sergeant Ramirez was conscious and on fire.

"Somehow he managed to crawl from the burning wreckage. Despite severe burns, he pulled a soldier from the back seat and dragged him to safety. Then he went back to the burning Humvee. His uniform caught fire as he pulled the driver from the wreckage. At this point, help had arrived to evacuate the driver from the scene. Sergeant Ramirez no longer wore a stitch of clothing. He had his body armor and his helmet, but the rest of his uniform was in ashes or seared to his skin." President Reynolds paused, nodding his head slightly, his masculine jaw set tight.

"He went back for the third time to remove the last soldier in the Humvee. Two of the three men who Sergeant Ramirez removed from that inferno are alive today. Sergeant Ramirez suffered second- and third-degree burns over 80 percent of his body. He died in an army hospital two weeks later." The president's eyes were glassy. "Before his death, he was asked why he kept going back to the burning vehicle. He said, 'They would've done the same for me.'" President Reynolds paused again, letting the sergeant's words sink in.

"The United States of America is still the shining light of freedom, liberty, and prosperity to the world. But we're at a crossroads. We haven't been this divided since the Civil War. Domestic terrorists are using alternative media and the Internet to spread antigovernment propaganda. Well-meaning

Americans are being brainwashed and duped into following those who only wish to tear down this great country we've built—that our parents and grandparents and great grandparents have built.

"My father used to say, 'That's how they getcha.' He was referring to anything that was too good to be true or a con. This Anarchist movement is exactly that. I would love it if we could have this wonderful society that we all enjoy and not actually have to pay for it. That would be great, but we live in the real world where prosperous, safe, and peaceful societies require government to ensure that society remains so.

"I know times have been tough. It's the tough times when we need each other the most. We need to stick together and pick each other up when we fall. If we stand together, we can weather any storm.

"We're two short weeks from April 15. When you're doing your taxes, when you're writing those checks, when you feel burdened by the shared sacrifice, I hope you think about Sergeant Ramirez. I hope you think about the ultimate price he paid, so we can live in the greatest country the world has ever known. I'm confident that we'll do the right thing ... *together.*"

Donna muted the flat screen. "We have about fifteen minutes to craft a statement."

"I think I have to stick to the talking points," John said. "People are upset and falling prey to Anarchist propaganda because the current regime has screwed things up so badly. I could talk about the economy, the growing wealth gap, inflation, high gas prices, high food prices, and the endless wars and dangers that our servicemen and women have been subjected to."

Frank nodded. "That's good. It would be a nice touch to add that the US government needs to earn back the trust of the American people. Emphasize the greatness of Americans, and that our government needs to reflect that greatness."

67: Katie and There's Only Now

"**A**re you sure you wanna do this?" George asked through the phone. "Once it's out there, you can't get it back. Your parents'll see it—your future husband. I don't want you to do something that you'll regret later because you're angry."

Katie paced in the living room of her condo. "I am angry. I'm still just as angry as I was a month ago, when you said I should wait and think it over."

"Obviously I can't stop you from posting this. It's your channel." George paused. "His kids will see it."

Katie frowned. "Maybe they should know what a cheating piece of shit their father is."

"They're innocent in all this. I think you know that."

Katie spewed a breath. "I won't talk about the affair, but everything else is fair game."

"Bradley's a snake," George said. "You know that better than me. He'll do everything he can to discredit you. The lawyer said that, with the nondisclosure agreement you signed, he could sue."

"The lawyer also said that it was unlikely he would sue, and *I* have grounds to sue for wrongful termination. I don't think he'll sue. It would make him look like a bully."

"Maybe it's best not to poke the hornet's nest."

"I don't care what happens to me—"

"I do. I care."

Katie was quiet for a moment. "What pisses me off is that he sold me a lie, and I bought it. I ruined my relationship with Zach, and I sold you out. I did all those things because I believed in him and his campaign. Looking back on it, it's so obvious now, but, when I was in it, it was like I was blind." Katie shook her head. "He doesn't actually care about ending the wars. It's a political stance that he thinks will help him get elected. That's what it's all about. He has no standards, no morals. I rationalized it by telling myself that the ends justify the means. I was stupid and vain and a total cliché. The young staffer chasing after the handsome politician."

"We all do things that we regret. Forgive yourself, don't make the same mistakes, move on, and be a better person. Don't let Bradley have any more power over you."

"You're right. I know you're right, but what kills me is people continue to love and support him. It's all a lie." Katie took a deep breath. "I'll send you a copy before it goes live."

"Katie."

"Don't worry. I can take whatever they can dish out." Katie disconnected the call.

She went to her room and removed her sweatshirt and T-shirt. She put on a bra, a camisole, and a sweater, but didn't change her sweatpants. Katie went to her office, started the camera, sat behind her desk, and told the truth.

"A year ago, I left the George 2020 campaign to be the head of social media for Congressman John Bradley. They promised that I would be the White House press secretary if he won the presidency. For a longtime Democrat, it was a dream come true. I left George for the opportunity, but also because I thought that Congressman Bradley was the best chance we had to stop the endless wars. I wanted to be a part of that.

"Like many women out there, I was enamored with Congressman Bradley's charm and charisma. I thought he was the second coming of JFK. I thought that, if he became the next president, he'd make a difference. I'm here to tell you that he's no different. Prior to my defection, the Bradley campaign tried to buy George Chapman's endorsement with a cabinet position. George said no."

Katie took a deep breath. "I gave Congressman Bradley access to George's videos and blog posts *prior* to their release. They ran similar, but less extreme versions of the material, effectively front-running George's content and increasing support from the disaffected in our society. People figured out the ruse, and George was accused of working with the congressman. This was entirely my fault." Katie stared into the camera. "I'm really sorry.

"People are angry, and they have every reason to be. Congressman Bradley's con is to make you believe that a vote for him is a vote for change and peace. Like all politicians do, he's placating us. He may bring home soldiers, but he'll replace them with government contractors who cost ten times as much. He'll grow the size and power of government just like every one of his predecessors.

"I've been behind the scenes of the Bradley campaign, and I can say with 100 percent certainty that they don't have any standards or morals. The congressman spends most of his time begging for money from donors, donors who his presidency will be beholden to. Policies and platforms are determined wholly based on whether or not it improves the congressman's electability. They poll everything to craft the perfect stance, the perfect statement to propagandize the public. Don't fall for the trick. The Democrats and Republicans are two sides to the same coin. It's time to let go of this false dichotomy and support someone who deserves our support and our respect. When you go to the polls this November, tell them all to go to hell and write in George Chapman."

Katie turned off the camera, grabbed her cell, and returned to her desk. She tapped her Zach contact.

"Katie," he said.

"I know you probably don't want to hear from me," Katie replied, "but I need to talk to you."

"I'm listening."

"I miss you."

"Don't."

"I'm working with George again."

"I know. You guys are all over the Internet. I'm happy for you. The new material's been excellent."

"Thank you." Katie paused. "I'm working on a video about Congressman Bradley. I need help finding some information for the video."

"Okay."

"Information that's off the beaten path."

"I don't know what you're asking."

"Do you know someone who's really good with computers and finding information, information that people don't want to be found?"

"First of all, you need to stop talking. Do you have a piece of paper and a pen?"

She removed a stack of Post-it notes from her desk drawer and a pen. "Yes."

"Write the first letter of my favorite color."

"Why?"

"Just do it."

"Okay, first letter of your favorite color."

"The first and second letter of the restaurant we went to on our first date. Do you remember the place?"

"I remember. The local—"

"Don't say it. The first two letters of my childhood pet's name. Do you remember his name?"

"Yes."

"The first letter of your favorite dessert. The one I made you for your birthday."

"Yes."

"The first letter of the first name of the woman you consider your mother. Her real name."

"Before she changed—"

"Don't say any more. You got it." He paused. "You should have seven letters. Add a 202 and call me from a burner phone."

Zach disconnected the call.

Katie went to a convenience store, purchased a prepaid cell phone with one thousand minutes and returned to her condo. She dialed the number that corresponded to the letters Zach gave her.

"Katie," he answered.

"What's with all the cloak and dagger?"

"They listen to everything. You know that. This is an encrypted phone. I'm going to have an encrypted phone delivered to you, and a guy by the name of Glen will call you. He can help you."

"Is that it?"

"Why couldn't you just tell me that over the regular phone?"

"The NSA has software that tallies everything you say and do on the Internet, on cell phones, landlines."

"So what? They've had that for at least a decade."

"This is different. They're using it to rate a person's threat to the government. So, if you say something like 'encrypted phone,' it adds to your threat level, and, if you rate high enough, they'll take you out."

"What do you mean, 'take you out'?"

"They'll arrest you."

"On what charge?"

"That's the power of the software. Not only will it identify threats, it finds laws that the person has broken. So, if you bought medication online without a prescription or posted a picture of yourself with a joint, or a million other things that are illegal, you could be arrested. The program finds a crime for 92 percent of people."

"This is how they'll crush dissent."

"Be careful. Tell George to be careful. Whatever you do, don't break any laws."

"How do you know all this?"

He was quiet.

"This is Armor Software," Katie said. "You fucking developed it."

"It's not what you think."

She shook her head. "I can't believe you."

"Things aren't as they appear. I'll send the phone tomorrow. I've already said too much. I have to go." He disconnected the call.

68: Julie's Debt Slavery

Julie sat at the dining room table with her checkbook open and her outstanding bills spread out in neat rows and columns. They were organized by due date and importance. The IRS bill was at the top left. Eight hundred dollars per month for the next twelve months. *Thank God they gave me a payment plan.* Her second-most-important bill was her mortgage. *If I pay the mortgage and the IRS, I'm broke. I can't pay for health insurance, the power bill, groceries, gas. I can't even pay the minimums on my credit cards.* She hung her head and rubbed her temples. *Maybe I could pay my mortgage with a credit card. Then I can pay the minimum on the credit cards, but that'll just raise my minimum payments, and I'll be in the same boat next month, only worse.* She shook her head. *I'm going to lose this house. There's no way around it. Can we even get an apartment with bad credit?*

There was a knock at the door. Julie looked at the door from the dining room. The dead bolt turned. *George.* She stood, collecting her bills as George entered the townhome carrying a suitcase and a cloth grocery bag.

"Hey," he said, spotting her at the dining room table.

Julie shoved the bills into an overstuffed folder.

He stepped across the family room to the dining room. "What are you doing?" he asked.

"You're back early." Julie shoved her checkbook into her purse, not making eye contact.

He stood his suitcase upright and let go. "Yeah, I thought I'd surprise you. I brought some things for dinner." He held up the cloth bag and set it on the table.

Julie stood and gave George a quick hug.

"I wanna talk to you about something over dinner," George said.

"I picked up a shift tonight. Sonya called in sick."

"Oh."

"Sorry." She glanced at his attire. He wore dress pants and a button-down shirt. His lips were pressed together. "Why are you so dressed up?" she asked.

"I wanted to make you a nice dinner. I thought you'd be off. What about Sunday?"

She shook her head. "I'm working the dinner shift the next three nights. The next night I have off, you'll be back on the road." She paused for a moment. "What did you want to talk about?"

"What were you doing?"

Julie glanced at the overflowing folder on the table. "Oh, I was paying bills."

George narrowed his dark eyes. "What's going on?"

"Nothing." She looked away.

"You sure about that?"

"It's fine."

"What's fine? I didn't know we were talking about something specific."

She pinched the bridge of her nose. "I'm dealing with it, okay? I'll figure it out."

He furrowed his brow. "Dealing with what?"

"I don't want you to be involved."

"I'm involved whether you tell me or not."

"Fine, but it isn't your problem. I'm handling it." She sat at the table.

George sat kitty-cornered from her.

"If I were you, I'd look for a new girlfriend." She sighed, her shoulders slumped. "My finances are a disaster. I'm going to lose this house."

"Can I take a look?" he asked, motioning with his chin toward the file.

"If you want."

He grabbed the file and flipped through the bills.

A few minutes later, Julie asked, "Do you want something to drink?"

"No thanks," George replied, engrossed in her finances.

Julie went to the kitchen, poured a glass of water, and returned to the dining room. When she sat down, George held up the IRS bill.

"You were audited?" he asked.

Julie nodded.

"Larry?"

She nodded again.

His jaw tightened. "Damnit." He shook his head. "Are you okay?"

"I'm fine. I didn't report some tips."

"Why didn't you tell me?"

"He said he'd arrest you for tax fraud. I didn't want anything to happen to you."

"My taxes are fine. Don't worry about me. I'm worried about you."

"I'm fine."

"You keep saying that."

She looked away.

"You bought this house in 2007 at the peak of the housing bubble," George said, "and, with the interest-only loan, you don't have that much equity. After you factor in real estate fees and the current comps, you're probably upside down." George took a deep breath. "There's no point in paying your mortgage."

A tear slipped down her cheek.

He leaned toward her and kissed her cheek, erasing the tear. "I would like for you and Max to come live with me in Pennsylvania. I have a decent Internet connection, so Max would be fine to work and go to school. There aren't very many jobs, but I could take care of you until you find something. Maybe you could take some time off to figure out what you wanna do."

She pecked him on the lips and squeezed his hand. "That's really sweet of you, George, but this is partly why I didn't want to tell you about my financial issues. I knew you would try to fix everything for me. I need to stand on my own."

"I need you, Julie. It's okay if you need me too. You can count on me. I promise I won't let you or Max down."

"I know that, and I love you for it." She motioned toward the stack of bills. "What do I do with this mess? If I move in with you, I won't be making much money."

"Well, first, stop paying your mortgage and the credit cards. It'll probably take at least two years for the bank to foreclose, so we have plenty of time to plan the move. In the meantime, you can save your money and put it toward the IRS bill. You can't default on that."

"I've always paid my bills. It doesn't feel right."

"It's a strategic default. Businesspeople do it all the time. Our economic system is designed for us to take on more debt every year in perpetuity, to make us work harder and harder for less. Meanwhile the banks own more and more."

Julie rubbed her temples.

"What's wrong?" George asked, his eyebrows arched. "I thought you'd wanna move in with me, but you don't seem very happy."

She forced a smile. "I'm sorry. I want to move in with you. It's just ... I feel like a failure."

"You can only be a failure if you give up."

"We need to talk to Max about it." She glanced at the clock on the microwave and stood from the table. "Can we wait to tell Max tomorrow? I'm going to be late for work."

"He's already on board."

Julie furrowed her brow. "How does Max know?"

"I wanted to talk to you about this over dinner, but I don't wanna wait anymore." Still sitting, he reached into his breast pocket. "I love you, Julie." He held out his open hand. In his palm was an antique silver ring, the band etched with vines and flowers. "Will you marry me?"

Her eyes were glassy, and her mouth was open as she plucked the ring from his hand. She cocked her head, gazing at George. "The nice clothes and the dinner?" She put her hand to her chest. "I ruined it."

"A fancy dinner's not gonna change how I feel." He stood from the table.

"Max already knows?"

"Yes, and he's happy for us."

"Are you sure you thought this through?" she asked. "If we get married, I'll destroy your credit."

"Doesn't matter. I don't plan on borrowing any money."

She placed the ring on her left ring finger and smiled wide. "I love you."

He wrapped his arms around her, squeezed, and lifted her from the floor.

69: George and the Death of Money

"It's really good, Katie," George said into his cell phone. He stood on Julie's back patio. "This could do some serious damage to their campaign. Where did you find the information?"

"I can't say," Katie replied. "There's something else. Umm, you haven't committed any crimes, have you?"

"Probably—since about four thousand federal criminal laws and another three hundred thousand regulations carry criminal penalties. That doesn't include state and local laws, codes, and ordinances. The average American commits three felonies a day."

"You can't be like the average American. You have to be careful. The government is looking for a reason to arrest people like us. We have to be squeaky clean."

"Where's this coming from?"

"I can't say over the phone."

"Governments have always used the law to silence detractors."

"We have to be careful and aboveboard. Did you file your taxes yet?"

"I sent my return a few weeks ago."

"Okay, good. I'll talk to you later." She disconnected the call.

George slipped his earbuds into his ears and played a podcast on his phone. He returned to the garden, plucking loose-leaf lettuce and unearthing radishes. It was chilly, upper fifties, the perfect weather for cool season crops.

"This is Gary Cook of the *Alt News Podcast*, providing vital information in a changing world. It's Saturday, April 4, 2020. The pace of change is quickening. Unemployment is in the double digits, and that's the official statistic, which we know is a rigged number. The unemployment rate only takes into account those who are currently receiving unemployment compensation. It doesn't count people who have been fired, quit because of a medical condition, people who've run out of benefits, or the self-employed who don't pay unemployment taxes to cover this eventuality.

"We had a massive stock market crash that took the S&P 500 from 2263 down to 755. Americans saw their pensions and stock portfolios cut by two-thirds. Since then we've had the Rebuild America stimulus program which provided fifty-year Fannie Mae loans at 1 percent, massive tax breaks, a trillion-dollar infrastructure program, and the green Christmas, where every single American received $600. This was on top of the Federal Reserve engaging in further quantitative easing by purchasing distressed assets and some believe by directly propping up the stock market. This intervention has whipsawed the S&P to 1467, but, in the process, we've seen some nasty inflation.

"Today we have the famed Austrian economist Wilson Dyer to talk about what's happened and where the economy is likely to go in the future. Welcome to the *Alt News Podcast*, Wilson."

"Thanks, Gary. I'm happy to be here," Wilson replied.

"Could you give us a rundown of how we got into this mess and where we're likely to go from here?"

"In the 2008 crash, the central banks of the world bailed us out with 0 percent interest rates and quantitative easing, which is just a fancy term for creating money out of thin air. Back then it appeared that the central banks had saved the day and had righted the ship. The truth of the matter is they simply kicked the can farther down the road, making the problem larger for the future. We didn't deal with the heavy debt loads or the bubbles in various asset classes, notably government bonds.

"In 2018 and 2019, we had another stock market crash and a massive deflationary wave. The central banks of the world compensated for this by creating stimulus programs and engaging in more quantitative easing and even direct-asset purchases. They couldn't lower interest rates like they did in 2008 because rates were already very low. Essentially they're fighting deflation with money creation. Now we're in the midst of what many people are heralding as the beginning of the recovery. These people point to the stock market recovery, but what they fail to mention is the inflation that's been created and the danger of the destruction of fiat currencies.

"All this money creation has helped the stock market, but the world economy is not growing in response. People, companies, governments, and banks around the world have parked their money in fiction, in digits on a computer screen. They've invested in overvalued companies, overpriced houses, and broke governments. I think people are starting to realize the value of tangible things, things like oil and gold and food. This money is starting to slosh into commodities, driving up the price of everything we need. Basically we have too many units of currency for the real things in existence. We've already seen double-digit inflation, which hasn't been seen since 1981. Of course I question the government's numbers. They don't count food and energy, and, with their hedonic adjustments, we know it's fiction. My educated opinion is that, in the past year, we've had 30 percent inflation."

"We've seen gas prices double in the past twelve months," Gary said. "Food prices are up at least 30 percent."

"I think it'll get worse before it gets better," Wilson said. "If the central banks aren't careful, they might see the destruction of the currency itself."

70: John's Regret

John, Frank, and Donna sat on the couch in John's congressional office, huddled around the laptop, their mouths open. Donna paused the video on a flow chart image. They followed the lines, denoting the flow of money from defense contractors, bankers, and oil companies to shell corporations, and finally to Congressman Bradley's campaign coffers.

"This is a fucking disaster," John said.

"And it's correct," Donna said, as she finished reading the chart. "This is *not* good."

John stood and paced in front of the coffee table. "It makes me look like any other lying politician." John stared at Frank. "How bad do you think this'll hurt?"

Frank sucked in a breath. "Most people who've already decided to vote for you won't change their mind. For better or worse they're already married to their choice."

"Via confirmation bias?" Donna asked.

Frank tipped his block-shaped head to Donna. "Yes, ma'am. If they see this, they'll seek out information that counters it, or they'll simply rationalize it. Ultimately they won't care that the antiwar candidate received donations from defense contractors. Where it'll hurt is with the undecideds, and we need them to win."

John rubbed the back of his neck. "We could sue her. She did sign the NDA."

"Did she say or present anything in the video that's untrue?" Frank asked.

"There were some opinions."

"You're a political figure. People can voice their opinions."

372

"The NDA explicitly forbids exactly what she did," Donna said.

"Okay, let's say we sue her," Frank said. "Her parents are wealthy, but she's not. Best case scenario, we bankrupt her. Court records will show that she lost the lawsuit, not because what she said was untrue but because of the NDA. We'll make a martyr out of her and look like bullies in the process."

"We can't do nothing," John said.

"That's not what I'm suggesting. We attack her credibility. People have a tough time separating the message from the messenger. If we destroy the messenger, the message is bound to follow."

"This might be more complicated than you think," Donna said to Frank. She looked at John. "He needs to know."

John nodded with a frown.

Frank rested his hands on his gut. "I'm all ears."

John took a deep breath. "I had an affair with her. For about a month."

"That does complicate things," Frank said. "Hell hath no fury like a woman scorned." He paused. "Does she have any evidence of the affair?"

"Text messages between us," John said.

"How dirty are they?"

"They're pretty bad."

"Any penis pictures?"

John cleared his throat. "Unfortunately."

"The $64,000 question is, why didn't she release that evidence?" Frank said. "She could have blown us out of the water."

"Maybe she doesn't want it to come out any more than we do," Donna said. "Maybe there's a boyfriend. Maybe she's worried about what her parents will think. Maybe she doesn't want to be the next Monica Lewinsky."

"Maybe she's waiting to release it closer to the election, when it'll do the most damage." Frank shook his head and looked at John. "Are there any others?"

Donna looked away.

"No," John said.

"Okay, that's good," Frank said. "If it's more than one, it becomes much more difficult to deny."

"She has proof," Donna said.

"All we need is plausible deniability. Remember what I said about people not being able to separate the message from the messenger. We need to destroy her credibility before she releases evidence of the affair." Frank looked at John. "Does Linda know?"

"Yes," John said.

"Will she stand by you in public?"

"We have an agreement."

Frank nodded. "Good."

* * *

John entered his home through the garage, carrying a bouquet of flowers and his briefcase. The kitchen was clean and sterile. He stepped past the kitchen into the family room. Bobby lay on the couch, watching the American Heroes Channel, formerly the Military Channel. A World War II tank battle was on the screen. Bobby's ten-year-old body was long and thin, his strawberry hair tousled and still wet from the shower.

"Hey, bud," John said.

"Hey, Dad," Bobby replied.

"Where is everyone?"

"Ellen's probably at Tyler's. Charlotte and Mom are upstairs."

John approached the couch and put his hand on Bobby's shoulder. "Don't stay up too late."

"I won't."

John put his briefcase in the office and climbed the spiral staircase. He knocked on Charlotte's door.

"Come in," she said.

Inside, Charlotte sat at her desk, a textbook open, and a boy band crooning through her iPod speaker dock. She turned from the text. Her face was round and chubby, her arms beefy.

"Hey, honey," John said.

"Hi, Dad."

"I was just checking on you. You okay?"

She shrugged. "I'm fine. I have a lot of homework." She glanced at the flowers. "Those for Mom?"

"Yes." John approached his daughter. He bent over and kissed her on the forehead. "You're a hard worker. I admire that about you."

She blushed. "Thanks, Dad."

John plucked a rose from the dozen and handed it to Charlotte. "Don't work too hard."

Charlotte smiled briefly. "Good night, Dad."

John shut his daughter's door and stepped to his bedroom. Linda was in bed, reading a novel. Probably chick lit. She didn't acknowledge his presence. John moved alongside the bed near her. She looked up from her book. Even without makeup, her skin was still flawless. Her straight blond hair hung to her shoulders.

"I brought you some flowers," John said.

"Why?" she replied.

"I thought you'd like them."

She scowled. "Throw them away."

"Linda."

"They might look pretty, but you and I both know they're already dead."

John sighed and sat on the edge of the bed. "I wish I could go back and fix this. It was the biggest mistake of my life. I'm so sorry, Linda."

She set her book facedown on her lap. "What do you want from me?"

"I want us to be like we used to be."

She gripped the comforter. "You think I don't want that?" She shook her head, her face taut. "You broke us."

"I'm so sorry. Tell me what to do, and I'll do it." His eyes were glassy.

"There's nothing you can do."

71: Katie and We Are Anonymous

Katie was slack-jawed as she watched the video on her laptop. On screen, Lisa Kelly of WNN spoke behind her news desk.

"Katie Fitzgerald, former staffer to Congressman Bradley and current campaign manager for George Smith Chapman, is under fire today from one of her former professors from UC Berkeley. Here with us today is Dr. Sergio Davila."

WNN cut to a balding swarthy man, with an athletic physique. The screen was now divided in half, with the professor on the right and the blonde news anchor on the left.

"Welcome, Dr. Davila," Lisa Kelly said.

"Thank you, Lisa," Sergio replied.

"Katie Fitzgerald was in your journalism class in the spring semester of 2012. Is that correct?"

"Yes, she was."

"Can you describe your relationship with Ms. Fitzgerald?"

"It was a typical teacher-student relationship. She was a bright student, very argumentative and passionate in debate, but she didn't always complete her assignments."

"What grade did she earn in your course?"

"She earned a D."

Lisa nodded. "Can you tell us why you gave her an A?"

Sergio swallowed. "She blackmailed me. She told me that she'd report me for sexually assaulting her if I didn't give her an A."

"Did you ever touch Katie Fitzgerald?"

"Never."

"Then why give in to her demands?"

"I was new to UC Berkeley. A charge like that, even if unfounded, can ruin your career. It ends up being her word against mine. It was much easier to give her what she wanted and to move on with my life."

"Then why come out now? Why not keep it a secret?"

"For the past eight years, I've regretted that I acquiesced to Ms. Fitzgerald's demands. I no longer work in academia, so I no longer fear the loss of my career. As a freelance journalist, the first principle in ethical journalism is to seek truth and to report it. I'd like the public to know that Ms. Fitzgerald will manipulate and distort the truth to further her agenda."

"Thank you, Dr. Davila."

Katie stopped the video. She typed her name into the Google search bar and scanned the latest articles:

"Katie Fitzgerald Blackmailed Professor"

"Is Katie Fitzgerald a Con Woman?"

"Katie Fitzgerald Arrested for Shoplifting"

"Katie Fitzgerald Sex Tape"

She clicked on "Katie Fitzgerald Sex Tape." She was greeted by three popups of half-naked women begging for private chats. Katie clicked the X on each of the popups. Her heart raced as she clicked on the video. Donna was right. It was an unflattering view. There she was grunting, no makeup, hairy armpits, flesh jiggling, and breasts swaying, with Declan behind her, pumping and adding his own grunts. His head was conveniently cutoff at chest level.

Katie closed her laptop, nauseated. She ran to the bathroom and deposited her lunch into the toilet via throat-burning chunks. She flushed and sat against the wall, her legs on the cold tile. *I wonder how much they paid Declan and Davila.* She staggered to her feet and rinsed out her mouth.

She returned to her office, picked up her cell, and tapped her George contact.

"Hey, Katie," George said.

Katie paced in her living room. "Did you see Sergio Davila?"

"Who's Sergio Davila?"

"He was one of my journalism professors from UC Berkeley. He's claiming that I blackmailed him. He said I threatened to tell the administration that he sexually assaulted me if he didn't give me an A." Katie huffed. "I was a straight-A student. Why the hell would I blackmail a professor?"

"They're trying to inject reasonable doubt. If they can discredit the messenger, they can discredit the message."

"There's more—articles about an arrest I had for shoplifting. It's true. I did shoplift. I was nineteen and stupid."

"People do stupid things when they're young."

"There's a sex tape."

"Sex tape?"

"They released a sex tape from an old boyfriend."

"I'm sorry, Katie."

Her eyes watered. "I don't know what to do."

"We can hire a lawyer and send takedown notices."

"It's too late. It'll be out there forever." Tears slipped down her cheeks. "Donna threatened me with the video." Katie sniffled. "I didn't think they'd use it, especially since I didn't talk about the affair."

"The video you made damaged their campaign. It made Bradley look like the hypocrite he is. I think they're desperate."

Katie wiped her face with her sleeve. "I might as well talk about the affair. What do I have to lose at this point?"

George took a deep breath. "I don't think it's a good idea. It'll hurt them, but it'll also hurt you. Maybe everything about you shouldn't be on the Internet."

"What the hell am I supposed to do then?"

"I still think we should send takedown notices for the tape. It may not eliminate it, but it'll lessen the exposure. Tell the truth about the shoplifting, and we'll fight this Sergio guy with facts. We'll expose them for the liars they are. Do you have your transcripts?"

"Yes."

"We can publish your transcripts and ask the same question you posed. 'Why on earth would you blackmail a professor for an A when you were already a straight-A student?' We can also do some research on the professor. He probably has a shady past if he's willing to lie for what I presume is money."

"I could go to San Francisco and confront him. We'd have to hire a cameraman in California. It'd be a viral video. People love confrontations."

"That's up to you."

Katie sighed. "Let me think it over, and I'll call you back."

"We'll figure it out."

"Thanks, George." Katie disconnected the call.

Katie set her phone on the coffee table. She went to her bedroom, put on sweats, sneakers, and a baseball hat. She stepped outside and took a deep breath. It was sunny, the air crisp. Daffodils and pansies bloomed in the flower beds of her condo community. She powerwalked along the asphalt path that circled her neighborhood. An old lady walked her puffball of a dog. The path meandered through a stretch of woods where birds chirped and squirrels rustled in the leaves.

She returned to her condo an hour later with a sheen of sweat and a clear head. She took off her sneakers, went to her office, and picked up her phone. She had a message and a text from George.

George: It looks like someone did our work for us. **Link.**

Katie clicked the link. A man dressed in all black appeared with a Guy Fawkes mask. His voice was digitized.

"Greetings, we are Anonymous," he said. "This is an open message to you, John Bradley. We know what you and your people stand for. We do not forget, and we do not forgive. We are tired of your lies, and we are tired of your political games."

The flow chart that Katie made appeared on the screen. "You claim to be the antiwar candidate, yet you are bought and sold by defense contractors and bankers. This information was so damaging to your campaign that you attempted to defame the person who published it." The video cut to a picture of Dr. Sergio Davila, with the headline that read "Professor Blackmailed by Katie Fitzgerald."

The video showed the masked figure. "Your lies can't protect you anymore. We are everywhere, and we know everything." An email appeared on the screen.

From: FrankWhitehead@JohnBradley.house.gov
To: JohnBradley@JohnBradley.house.gov

Subject: Katie Fitzgerald

John,

I've located a former professor who will say what we need him to say.

Frank

The video cut to another email.

From: JohnBradley@JohnBradley.house.gov
To: FrankWhitehead@JohnBradley.house.gov

Subject: Re: Katie Fitzgerald

Make sure payment is untraceable.

The man in the mask appeared on the screen. He said, "John Bradley, we will continue to expose you as the hypocrite you are. We are Anonymous. We do not forgive, and we do not forget. To all the current and future Zionist puppets in the White House, expect us."

72: Julie's Dirty Mouth

Julie pressed the doorbell of the stone mansion. Summer opened the front door that was fit for a giant. Julie stood in her black pants and white polo from the lunch shift.

"Come in," Summer said.

"I'm not here to visit," Julie said.

Summer put her hands on her hips. "I can't loan you any money."

Julie held out an envelope. "This is for you."

Summer opened it and glanced inside. "What's this?"

"The money I owe you plus 10 percent interest. Thank you for helping me."

"Where did you get this?"

"I'm not paying my house payment and credit cards anymore."

Summer's jaw dropped. "Why would you do that?"

"It's called a strategic default."

"You can't just not pay your bills." Summer thrust the envelope back toward Julie. "I don't want your money."

Julie crossed her arms over her chest, ignoring the envelope. "Last time I was here, you said I needed to handle my own finances. That's what I'm doing."

"You'll lose your home, your credit."

Julie nodded. "Not your problem."

"Are you mad that I didn't give you any money?"

"No, I'm glad you didn't. I'm done discussing my finances with you."

"You're mad."

"I should go." Julie turned on her sneakers and marched toward her car.

"Come back," Summer said from the doorway. She wasn't about to chase Julie in her socks.

Julie turned halfway to her car. "I'm not mad."

Julie drove home with the visor down to block the afternoon sun. As she approached her parking spot, she saw Dan standing on the sidewalk in front of her townhome. She thought about going somewhere, anywhere to avoid him. She parked, and he was in her face as soon as she stepped out of her Honda.

"You're behind on your HOA dues again," Dan said, standing in the narrow aisle between Julie's Honda and her neighbor's pickup. "You said it wouldn't happen again."

Julie slammed her car door. "Can you move, please?"

Dan smirked, his face ruddy. He edged aside. As Julie slipped past, he brushed his gut against her. Dan followed her to the front door. "The HOA'll put a lien on your house," Dan said. "You'll lose this place."

Julie turned her key in the dead bolt. "That's fine with me. There's no equity."

Dan huffed. "You're gonna pay, one way or another."

"Leave me alone." Julie pushed inside. Dan followed her. "What are you doing?"

Dan shut the door behind him. "You don't care about this house. You shouldn't care who comes in."

"Get out of my house." Julie pointed toward the door.

"Now you care about your house?"

"My fiancé and my son will be home soon." In reality, they probably wouldn't be home for many hours. George had a day-trip delivery, and Max wanted to tag along.

"Oh, *fiancé*, look at you." He chuckled. "That why you're a deadbeat now? This Chapman fella got you believin' his nonsense? This is the problem with Americans today. They think they can have somethin' for nuthin'. This country was built on hard work and savin'. People like you and your fiancé who think they're above the rules are destroyin' this country."

Julie crossed her arms. "Are you finished?"

"You gonna write me a check?"

"Get out before I call the police."

"I still know some Fairfax County Police officers. You think they're gonna arrest a retired officer? You invited me in. As soon as I told you about the bill, you got mad and called the police."

Julie froze, her heart pounding.

Dan looked Julie up and down, his eyes settling on the bare skin between the V of her polo. "Your fiancé ain't gonna be back soon, is he?"

Julie was silent.

"I could make this go away for you." He grinned, his white mustache spreading across his face.

Julie moved past him and opened the front door. She pointed outside. "Get the fuck out!"

His grin receded, and he clenched his jaw. "You kiss your mother with that dirty fuckin' mouth? I got somethin' dirty for that mouth." He grabbed the crotch of his sweatpants and adjusted his penis.

Julie reached into her purse, retrieved her phone, and dialed 9-1-1.

"Nine-one-one, what is your emergency?" the female operator asked.

"There's a man in my house, and he won't leave," Julie replied. "Please send help."

Dan crossed his arms and remained planted.

"Is anyone hurt?" the operator asked.

"No, but I'm afraid he might hurt me. His name is Dan Gordon, and he lives across the street from me. He barged into my house. He threatened me, and he won't leave."

"According to our records, your name is Julie Welch and your address is 422 Colonial Commons Drive, Fairfax, Virginia. Is that correct?"

"Yes, please send help," Julie said.

Dan glared at Julie with his hands on his hips.

"Help is on the way, Julie. I'll stay on the phone with you until the police arrive."

"Fuckin' bitch," Dan said as he left the house.

Julie slammed the door and turned the dead bolt.

Eight minutes later, a police cruiser parked in front. "They're here," Julie said to the operator. "Thank you for staying on the phone with me."

"You're welcome, Julie," the operator replied.

She opened the front door as two officers marched toward her. One cop was young and heavyset; his name tag read Officer Boyer. The other was middle-aged and tall; his name tag read Officer Clifton.

"Julie Welch?" Officer Clifton asked.

"Yes," she replied.

"We have a report of a man who refused to leave your home. Is that correct?"

"Yes, sir. My neighbor, Dan Gordon."

"Where is Mr. Gordon now?"

"He went home." She pointed across the parking lot. "He lives over there, where that green truck is parked."

"Did he touch you?" Officer Clifton asked.

"No, but he was threatening me in a disgusting way."

Officer Clifton blew out a breath. "You're gonna have to be specific, Mrs. Welch."

"I told him to get the F out."

The cops glanced at each other.

"This was after I had asked him to leave multiple times," Julie said. "Then he said he had something for my dirty mouth, and he grabbed his crotch."

"What did he say he had for your mouth?" Officer Clifton asked. "Please be specific."

"He didn't say exactly."

Officer Clifton sighed. "So he did leave. He didn't touch you, and he threatened you by grabbing his crotch?"

"Yes."

"What would you like us to do?"

"Arrest him."

"He hasn't committed a crime."

"He broke into my house."

"Is there evidence of forced entry?"

"Like a broken lock?" Julie asked.

"Or a broken window or doorjamb."

"He pushed in behind me as I was coming inside."

Officer Clifton hiked his duty belt. "In the future, I'd suggest that you don't let someone get that close to you when you're entering your home."

Julie knitted her brow. "Is that it?"

"We have to have evidence of a crime before we can do anything."

"Aren't you going to talk to him?"

"I can talk to him," the younger cop said.

Officer Clifton glowered at his partner, then turned to Julie. "We'll talk to him. In the future, be more careful about who you let into your home."

The officers marched across the parking lot to Dan's home. Dan stepped out on to his stoop as if he was expecting them. Julie watched the conversation from her stoop. Officer Clifton was relaxed with Dan, almost jovial. The younger officer was stiff by comparison. After a couple of minutes, Officer Clifton shook Dan's hand. As the officers returned to their cruiser, Dan waved at Julie.

Julie went back inside and turned the dead bolt. She sat on the couch, her eyes wet. Her fingers shook as she tapped the George contact on her cell phone.

She told George what had happened.

"Go to your mother's," George said. "Max and I are on our way. We'll be there in three hours."

Julie nodded, her face wet with tears. "I don't feel safe here. I can't be here anymore."

"We can move to Pennsylvania now. We'll come back for the bankruptcy hearing."

73: George and the Million Mask March

George and Katie stood onstage, the Lincoln Memorial behind them, the largest reflecting pool in DC in front of them. Masked marchers filled every square inch of the National Mall's 146 acres. Men and women wore Guy Fawkes masks, some covering their faces; many others wore the masks on the backs of their heads. Taxation = Theft was the most popular sign, but also many George 2020 signs were held by marchers. A few marchers wore earpieces, had short hair, and were clean-shaven. They wore the jeans, T-shirt, and the mask of the average marcher, but their clothes were too new, too perfect. Uniformed cops in riot gear amassed at the edges of the crowd.

"We went over the $100,000 cap today," Katie said to George. "Ad revenue's been good, but the donate button's on fire. We need to make a decision on charities."

George felt nauseated as stage fright hit him full force. He glanced at the typewritten speech in his hand.

"You okay?" Katie asked.

George shook his head.

"You'll be fine. Your practice run was great."

"You were the only one watching."

"You know what I do when I'm nervous?"

George glanced at Katie.

"I distract myself," she said. "How are Julie and Max settling in?"

"Max and I still have some work to do, but the cabin's in good shape. Max really wanted to be here, but Julie was worried about arrests and violence. I asked her to stay home too, for the same reasons."

"It's been peaceful so far."

"So far." George pointed to his left, toward Constitution Avenue. "Check out the cops in riot gear."

Katie looked at the armored cops.

"I think they know something we don't," George said. "I've also seen quite a few undercover agents among the crowd."

"That's to be expected," Katie said. "They don't want this getting out of hand."

"Maybe they do."

Katie frowned. "Let's hope not."

A bearded man with a Guy Fawkes mask on the back of his head approached. "You're on in sixty seconds," the man said.

"Thanks," Katie replied.

"Based on the crowd size, we think we have a little over two million people," the man said. "The biggest crowd DC has ever seen." He flashed a grin and checked his watch.

George's stomach churned. He felt dizzy.

The bearded man turned to George. "You're on." He motioned toward the empty podium.

George swallowed the bile that had risen from his stomach. He was sweating even though it was a comfortable sixty-two degrees. He staggered to the podium as if he were three sheets to the wind. With a shaky hand, he placed his typewritten speech on the podium. The crowd cheered. After a long minute, the cheers quieted, and George looked down at his speech. He opened his mouth, but nothing came out.

He swayed back and forth, his vision fuzzy. He heard two pops that sounded like firecrackers with more bass. George fell to the stage, clutching his chest, near his armpit. A collective panic rose among the crowd. Two more pops sounded as screams and shouts followed, with people running and trampling each other, causing more screams and shouts. Two men lay lifeless near the stage with masks on the backs of their heads and earpieces dangling from their ears.

Katie was on the stage floor next to George. "Help!" she said. "He's been shot!"

A handful of men approached the scene. Katie's eyes bulged as she recognized one of them.

"Zach?" Katie said.

"Katie," Zach replied.

A clean-cut thirtysomething male knelt beside Katie and George. "I'm a nurse. Lemme take a look," he said to Katie.

Katie nodded at the nurse.

"George, my name's Alan, and I'm gonna take care of you."

George lay on his side, groaning, his gray T-shirt stained with blood on his back, but less blood on the front.

"I need scissors," Alan said to the group that surrounded them, "and clean gauze or at least a clean cloth. We have to get him to the hospital. We need an ambulance."

A handful of men dispersed, screaming for a first aid kit. Two minutes later, a skinny man with a scraggly beard and glasses returned with a shirt, another man with scissors.

"The lady I got this from said the shirt's clean," the skinny man said.

"It's a gnarly scene," the other man said, handing the scissors to Alan. "Some dead people out there that look trampled."

Alan cut the clean shirt into two pieces, one larger than the other. He cut off George's T-shirt. He folded the pieces of clean shirt and applied the larger one to the exit wound, eliciting a grunt from George.

"Apply this to the entry wound," Alan said to Katie, handing her the other cloth.

Katie was unresponsive.

Zach knelt next to George, grabbed the cloth, and applied pressure to the entry wound.

"Where's the ambulance?" Alan called out.

"I didn't see any ambulances," the skinny man said. "Should I get my van? It's parked a quarter-mile from here?"

Katie stared at the skinny man, her head cocked. *His voice sounds familiar.*

"Can you get it here through the crowds and the blockades?" Zach asked.

"It might be fifteen minutes or so," the skinny man said.

"Hurry," Alan said.

The skinny man ran toward Twenty-Third Street.

"That's Glen, isn't it?" Katie asked Zach. "The man who went to get the van."

Zach nodded, his hands still on George. Glen was the hacker who had helped Katie find the origins of John Bradley's campaign donations.

"We're gonna need a stretcher," Alan said to the group of men. "We need sturdy poles and support material."

"What kind of support material?" one of the men asked.

"A tarp, rope, a couple jackets, backpacks, even a roll of duct tape would work."

A few minutes later, men returned with two Gadsden Don't Tread on Me flags attached to sturdy poles, and another man returned with three sturdy backpacks. The men put together a makeshift stretcher.

Shortly thereafter Glen honked as he drove across the grass and through what remained of the crowd. The stage was the eye of the hurricane. Most marchers had fled the area after the gunshots, pushing against the police on the perimeter of the National Mall. The few remaining loitered, gawked, and took pictures and videos of the scene. Glen parked near the stage steps.

Alan and Zach placed George on the makeshift stretcher and carried him down the steps. George grunted in pain with each jostling step. The back of the van had a computer workstation and a carpeted floor. They placed George and his stretcher on the carpet. Alan and Katie got in the back with George. Zach rode in front with Glen.

Glen drove on grass for a minute. He drove slowly through the crowd, honking incessantly. Searing pain shot through George's wounds as Glen drove off the curb on to the pavement.

"Shit," Glen said. "The cops have Twenty-Third Street blocked."

"Keep going," Zach said. "What are they gonna do? Shoot us?"

"They might."

Zach climbed out of the slow-moving van.

"Where's he going?" Katie asked.

"To the blockade," Glen said. "He'll explain to the cops, so we can get outta here."

The van stopped. They waited, the minutes ticking away.

George shut his eyes and pictured Julie.

"Step out of the vehicle with your hands up," a man said through a bullhorn.

George's eyes popped open.

Glen put the van in Park and stepped from the van with his hands up.

The van's rear doors opened, and three M-4 carbines pointed at Katie, Alan, and George.

"Put your hands up," a police officer said.

Alan and Katie put up their hands. George didn't even try.

"We need to go to the nearest hospital," Katie said.

"Step out of the vehicle," the police officer said.

Alan and Katie exited, leaving George on the floor of the van.

"We have a gunshot victim," one of the cops said into his mike.

"That's George Chapman," another cop said.

"He'll die if he doesn't get to a hospital," Alan said.

A few minutes later Zach, Glen, Katie, and Alan returned to the van. They were moving again. A siren wailed, and lights flashed. The van moved faster.

"You'll be fine," Katie said, squeezing George's hand. "Hold on, okay? We have a police escort. We're almost there."

"Julie," he said, delirious.

74: John and *Manufacturing Consent*

"The shooting of Anarchist leader George Smith Chapman has sparked riots nationwide," WNN newscaster Lisa Kelly said.

John, Frank, and Donna watched the television in John's congressional office. WNN cut from Lisa Kelly to footage of burning cities across the nation, the looting of box stores, and overturning high-end cars by groups of young men.

Lisa spoke over the images. "President Reynolds has declared a national emergency." They cut to images of police clashing with protestors. "Sixteen states have activated their National Guards to help overwhelmed police departments quell the riots."

WNN showed Lisa Kelly again, her face somber. "We have domestic terrorism expert Victor Bullard to discuss the current status of the Anarchist movement. Victor, welcome." WNN cut to Lisa and Victor sitting across from each other at a glass table. They were polar opposites, Lisa the leggy ice queen with thin limbs, Victor the stocky olive-skinned man with dark hair.

"Thanks, Lisa," Victor said.

WNN cut to Lisa. "Early reports suggest that the shooting of George Chapman was from inside the Anarchist movement. What is the status of the movement now, with the shooting and subsequent rioting?"

WNN showed Victor. "The Anarchist movement has always been fractured and divided. Many different sects claim to be Anarchists, and, if you listen to them, you'll find that they often hate each other more than they hate the government. The two largest sects are the anarcho-capitalists and the anarcho-communists. To my knowledge, George Smith Chapman has never said he was a member of either of these sects, but his rhetoric is clearly on the side of the anarcho-capitalists."

They cut to a shot of Lisa and Victor. "What's the difference between the two sects?" Lisa asked.

"The major difference is the anarcho-communists don't believe that property should be owned, whereas the anarcho-capitalists believe in private property rights."

"To my knowledge, both of these sects would like to eliminate government. Is that correct?"

"Yes," Victor replied. "They both believe that people shouldn't be subjected to a ruling class, whether that be a government or a king. They consider this subjugation to be violence against the people, even if the governed consents, as we have in the United States with voting rights and representative democracy."

"It's hypocritical to oppose violence, then riot and loot and steal, causing billions of dollars' worth of damage."

Victor nodded. "I agree."

John muted the television and set the remote on the coffee table. "Does our strategy change if Chapman survives versus his death?"

"If he dies," Donna said, "we embrace his ideals and criticize the movement for their violence and impracticality."

"If he lives?" John asked.

"If he lives," Frank replied, "we embrace his ideals and criticize the movement for their violence, impracticality, and, I would add, their destructiveness and disrespect for law and order."

"Am I the only one not buying the official story?"

"They haven't said much yet," Donna said.

"He was shot four hours ago," John said, "and the media already has experts lined up to tell us how someone inside the movement did this. I think they're pushing a narrative. Also the tax revolt had already started when Chapman was shot. How can they blame the shooting of four hours ago on the riots already underway in much of the country?"

"The shooting threw some gasoline on the fire," Frank said, "but you're right. The pieces were already in place for the riots. Could've been a CIA hit."

"That's what I'm thinking. If they can blame one of the Anarchist sects, they can create more infighting. Textbook divide and conquer. I almost feel bad for the guy."

"Either way this is good for us. If it was an inside job, the Anarchist movement loses credibility, and we can pick up Chapman's supporters. If it was a CIA hit, that's even better for us, because people'll be madder than a junkyard dog at the current administration."

"After this Chapman might quit," Donna said.

"If he survives," John replied.

Breaking News flashed across the flat screen. John grabbed the remote and turned up the volume.

Lisa Kelly spoke over footage of the FBI escorting a young man in handcuffs. "The FBI has arrested three men in connection to the shooting of George Smith Chapman. Anthony Calhoun ..." A picture appeared of a young man with a mop of dark hair and a T-shirt portraying a hammer and sickle. "Luis Cabrera and Ross Blevins." They cut to an of image of Cabrera with his brown skin, bushy beard, and T-shirt featuring the face of Che Guevara. WNN showed Blevins posing with an AK-47.

"There it is," John said. "So goddamn predictable."

WNN cut to Lisa Kelly. "These men are part of a group called the Maoist Worker Party. The FBI found social media posts bragging that the group would kill George Chapman at the Million Mask March."

WNN showed the Facebook posts. The expletives were obscured. Anthony Calhoun wrote, *If Chapman steps foot onstage at the Million Mask March, I'll put a ****ing bullet in his brain. ****ing Ancap.*

A Facebook reply from Luis Cabrera read *Chapman's a ****ing corporate shill. You go for the head. I'll take the heart.*

Ross Blevins wrote, *I only need one shot for one kill.*

75: Katie and Off Center

"This is bullshit," Katie said, watching WNN and the breaking news. "It's divide and conquer propaganda."

A chorus of jeers rose from the waiting room crowd.

George Washington University Hospital was filled with protestors waiting for friends injured by trampling or clashing with police. Zach and Glen flanked Katie.

"We're going to the office," Zach said to Katie. "I'd like to see if we can find any information on the shooter or shooters."

"Do you believe this?" Katie asked, gesturing toward the screen.

Zach tilted his head. "We'll talk later. Use the phone I gave you."

"It's been over three hours. What's happening with him?"

"If he was gone, I think we'd already know about it. Call me after you talk to the doctor."

Zach and Glen started for the exit. Katie grabbed Zach's hand.

"Thank you for helping George," Katie said, glancing at Zach and Glen. "Both of you."

Zach squeezed her hand for a moment and nodded.

"May I talk to you for a minute ... in private?" Katie asked, her eyes flicking to Glen.

Zach and Katie moved to a lonely spot at the end of the long hallway.

"You and Glen are Anonymous hackers," Katie said in a hushed whisper.

Zach shrugged. "I don't know what you're talking about."

Katie put her hands on her hips. "Cut the shit, Zach."

"The less you know, the better. I have to go." Zach joined Glen, and they left the hospital.

Katie returned to the waiting room and found an empty seat in the corner. Fans approached her periodically to offer encouragement and condolences. Her phone chimed. She swiped right. "Where are you?" Katie asked.

"Maryland, stuck in traffic," Julie replied. "Have you heard anything?"

"Nothing."

"My hands are still shaking."

"If he was gone, I think we'd already know about it. Based on where the wound was, I don't think the bullet hit any vital organs, and he was conscious for most of the van ride."

"I can't believe this happened."

"I know."

"I should save my cell battery. Call me if you hear anything. Hopefully I'll be there soon."

"Be careful." Katie disconnected the call and shoved her cell phone into the pocket of her windbreaker.

Half an hour later, a doctor entered the waiting room.

"Katie Fitzgerald," he announced.

All eyes were on Katie as she approached the doctor. He led her to a more private area in the hall.

"Mr. Chapman lost a lot of blood," the doctor said.

Katie was nauseated and dizzy.

"He was given a transfusion, and we repaired what we could, but he'll need surgery to repair the damaged tissue. He'll probably have some limited movement in his left pectoral—"

"He's okay?"

"He'll be fine," the doctor said. "I scheduled him for surgery the day after tomorrow. After the blood loss I didn't want to put him through any more trauma today—"

"May I see him?"

The doctor led Katie to George's trauma room. The room was dimly lit with two beds. A man dozed in the first bed, his head wrapped in a bandage. George was in the second, hooked up to an IV. He was pale with dark circles under his eyes. He smiled as Katie approached. She hugged him, careful to stay away from the bandaged side of his body.

She pulled back, her eyes glassy. "You're running out of lives."

"Did you call Julie?"

"She's on her way."

"Is it safe?"

"Reynolds declared a national emergency."

"I need to talk to her. Do you have your cell phone?"

Katie removed her cell from the pocket of her windbreaker. She pressed her Julie contact and frowned at her phone. "No cell service."

"I don't want her coming here. It's dangerous."

"I'll keep trying, but I guarantee you that she won't listen to either of us."

"I know." After a moment, he said, "Thank you, Katie."

"It's just a phone call."

"For saving my life. I remember you holding my hand, and I remember Zach. Was there an Alan? And another man?"

"Glen."

"Where are they? I'd like to thank them."

"They waited for a few hours, but they're gone."

He nodded, his head barely moving.

"How are you feeling?" Katie asked, sitting in the chair next to him.

"Not great, but I'm not sure if it's the bullet or the fact that I didn't sleep a wink last night."

"Nerves?"

"Yeah. That bullet actually saved me from humiliation. I do believe I was going down before I was shot."

"You fainted?"

"Yeah. I wonder if that's why they didn't get me dead center."

76: Julie and the Trauma Room

Even with the traffic jams and accidents, Julie made progress. She listened to her car radio on pins and needles, hoping to hear that George was okay but fearing he wasn't.

"We've had reports of nearly one hundred deaths and thousands of injuries across the country," the male newscaster said. "Three of the reported deaths have been police officers killed in the line of duty. Mass arrests are being made across the country to stop the violence and damage to property. Unless you are a first responder, please stay indoors. A nationwide curfew is in effect at 9:00 p.m.

"The FBI arrested three men in connection with the shooting of George Smith Chapman. Anthony Calhoun of Gaithersburg, Maryland, and Luis Cabrera and Ross Blevins of Silver Spring, Maryland. The three men are members of an Anarchist extremist group called the Maoist Worker Party."

Julie drove on K Street. The lower windows of the high-rise office buildings were broken. Buildings and cars were decorated with anarchy symbols. Protestors dressed in all black with bandanas over their faces, threw rocks and bricks, lit fires, and overturned expensive cars. A limo was in flames, brightening the shade, as the late afternoon sun dipped below the buildings. One side was spray-painted with a message to President Reynolds: *Fuck you, Hank.*

Julie moved slowly through the carnage. She flinched as a protestor smacked her car window. The crowd increased as she drew closer to her destination. According to her old Garmin GPS, she was one mile from the hospital. More hands smacked her car. She stopped her vehicle as protestors surrounded her. A young man jumped on her hood, holding a brick. When he reared back to throw the brick through her windshield, Julie cowered and covered her head. She anticipated a crash that never came. When she looked up, he was gone.

She parked along the curb—no doubt illegally—and stepped from her old Honda. She was thankful for her jeans and sneakers but not thankful for her baby-blue fleece in a sea of black. In front of her, the crowd screamed and hollered, a collective madness infecting them. Julie slung her purse across her chest and pushed through the melee.

Young men threw bricks at anything glass on ground level. Others spray-painted messages on offices, storefronts, cars, and bus stops. *Taxation = Theft. Fuck the 1%. George 2020.* Julie turned right on Nineteenth Street, looking for a detour, finding much less foot traffic now. She turned left on L Street, walking perpendicular to K Street. With room to run, that's what she did until she reached Twenty-First Street. From here, it was a short, unfettered distance to George Washington University Hospital.

Inside the hospital, the black-clad protestors were subdued, the mass hysteria broken by cold fluorescent lighting, the reality of immortality, and the constant watch of uniformed security guards. Julie approached the information desk.

"I'm here to see George Chapman," she said to the dark-skinned woman.

She snapped her tongue off the roof of her mouth. "You and about a thousand other people."

"I'm his fiancée."

The woman stared at Julie, her eyes narrowed. "Name?"

"Julie Welch."

The woman checked her computer. "Do you have ID?"

Julie opened her purse and fished out her license for the woman.

The woman looked at the ID, then Julie. "We closed off the trauma rooms," the woman said. "These damn protestors. We're only letting approved visitors up there. Have a seat, and I'll call you when I get an escort down here."

Trauma room. Julie was afraid to ask.

Twenty minutes later, a security guard escorted Julie to George's trauma room. The security guard gave her a nod, and she entered the darkened room. A man with a bandage around his head lay in the near bed, and Katie sat next to George in the far bed.

Julie's gaze met Katie's, and Katie stood and stepped aside. Julie approached, searching George's face and body, assessing the damage. He was pale with dark circles under his eyes. The left side of his body was bandaged. He was hooked up to an IV and a heart monitor. George smiled in her direction.

Julie burst into tears as she neared his bedside. "Can I hug you?" she asked.

"Just stay away from my left side." George wrapped his right arm around Julie as she hugged him.

"Are you okay?" she breathed, her mouth inches from his ear.

"I need surgery to repair some tissue damage, but I'll live."

"I thought I lost you," she said, tears slipping down her cheeks.

"I'm not going anywhere."

77: George and the Safe Act

George lay in his hospital bed, recovering from surgery. Julie and Katie sat near him as they watched the news on the television.

An older Asian woman was on the screen in front of her looted and vandalized store. "We lost everything," she said. "Why did they do this? We're not the government. The Anarchists don't care about this country. They just want to destroy it."

Next to her was a thirtysomething reporter. "This is Wayne Huffman reporting from New York City."

WNN showed Lisa Kelly. "Thanks, Wayne." Lisa turned to the camera. "In the wake of the 2020 riots, property damage estimates are over five billion dollars and rising. Stay tuned for President Reynolds, live from the Oval Office."

WNN cut to a commercial.

A few minutes later, President Reynolds appeared on the television. The president sat behind his shiny desk in the Oval Office. President Reynolds glared, his jaw set tight. His hands were clasped on the desk as if he were praying.

The president said, "I won't sit idly by while this country that I swore an oath to protect is torn to pieces by the cowardly actions of antigovernment radicals and terrorists. I can assure you that these extremist groups will be vanquished from this country. The United States of America has always been a nation of law and order, and it will to continue to be so.

"This afternoon congress passed the SAFE Act, and I signed it into law. The Safe for Everyone Act allows for instantaneous issuance of electronic warrants and indictments based on criminality identified from online investigations. These documents will be analyzed and signed by virtual judges and virtual grand juries. The SAFE Act will increase arrest speeds, lower costs, and eliminate human errors. We live in a world where information travels at the speed of light and where rapidly changing technology is used for good and evil alike. No longer will terrorists slip through our fingers because our laws are slower than technology. Thousands of domestic terrorists will be removed from the streets in the coming weeks with these instant electronic warrants and indictments.

"The SAFE Act also shuts off the spigot of dirty money being used to fund terrorism. Cryptocurrencies have been used to launder money and to fund terrorism. The SAFE Act bans private cryptocurrencies, effectively cutting off the main source of illegal banking and money laundering for terrorists and criminals. In thirty days, banks and private cryptocurrency exchanges will no longer be allowed to exchange US dollars for cryptocurrency and vice versa. It is now unlawful for any US business to accept payment in a private cryptocurrency. It is now unlawful for Americans to *use* any private cryptocurrency. You have thirty days to exchange your cryptocurrency for dollars."

President Reynolds paused for a moment, glowering at the camera. "I won't let this country be torn apart by domestic terrorism. That's a promise. Know this. If you're engaged in domestic terrorism, we're coming for you."

WNN cut to Lisa Kelly.

George turned off the television. "I can't watch this crap anymore. This is bad. We could wake up a week from now with warrants for our arrests signed by computer judges programmed to sign whatever they want signed."

"I'll talk to Zach about it," Katie said. "He might be able to find out if we're in danger. Speaking of danger, I think we should hire a security team to protect you in the future."

"The future?" Julie said, scowling. "It's over. How many times does he have to be shot before you get the message?"

"We'll hire the best security team we can find."

"I don't want you to do this anymore," Julie said, turning to George.

"I don't know if I want to either," George said, "but this is bigger than what I want. The government is using the riots to exert more control. This could end in a civil war."

Julie nodded, her face neutral.

"We'll be more careful," Katie said to Julie.

"No more speeches outside like that," Julie replied.

"That's fine." Katie looked at George. "George?"

"You know how I feel about public speaking," he said.

Katie's phone chimed. She swiped right. "Zach." Katie nodded, listening. "I'll call you back." She disconnected the call and looked at George and Katie. "Anonymous posted a video of the shooting."

Katie placed her laptop on George's overbed table. They huddled around the laptop and watched the video.

A man dressed in all black appeared with a Guy Fawkes mask. "Greetings, we are Anonymous," he said in a digitized voice. "This is an open message to the US government and the mainstream media. We know what you did, and we know about your lies. We do not forget. We do not forgive. On April 15, the CIA engineered an assassination attempt on George Smith Chapman. The FBI arrested patsies affiliated with an anarcho-communist group, and the media trumpeted the propaganda, spreading the misinformation like a virus."

The video cut to footage from April 15 at the Lincoln Memorial. The video was taken from the stage. George staggered to the podium. Approximately two hundred yards away was a boom lift extended into the air just above the tree line. The video paused, and a red circle marked the camouflaged bucket lifting a man skyward.

The digitized voice spoke over the images. "The bullet that hit George Smith Chapman was fired from this boom lift. Notice the muzzle flashes."

The video continued in slow motion. George swayed, and a muzzle flash appeared from the bucket and then another. George was on the ground, and the crowd was in a panic.

The video cut to a different camera angle—from someone in the crowd. The camera shot was close to the stage—fifty feet away. A man with an earpiece and a short military haircut pointed a handgun at George. Another man grabbed the shooter's arm, causing two errant shots. A group of men, with their faces blacked out, wrestled the gunman to the ground and stomped him with heavy boots.

The digitized voice explained the footage. "This CIA agent intended to finish the job if the sniper in the boom lift were to fail. Notice the military haircut and the earpiece."

The video presented street camera footage of the boom lift in the distance as it retracted from the tree line. A man dressed like a protestor exited the bucket and carried a long case with him to the street. He was picked up by a black Chevy Suburban, and the SUV raced from the scene.

The digitized voice spoke over the video. "The assassin in the boom lift made his getaway in a common government vehicle. This man also had an earpiece and a military style haircut." The man in the mask appeared on the screen. "We are Anonymous. We are everywhere. We do not forgive. We do not forget. To all the liars in government and the media, expect us."

78: John and Decision 2020

John stood behind the stage backdrop, waiting for his cue. He listened to the intro by Corrinne Stevens.

"Good evening from Syracuse University. I'm Corrinne Stevens, anchor for US News. It's Monday, September 28, and I want to welcome you to the first presidential debate. The participants tonight are Arthur Coleman and John Bradley. This debate is sponsored by the Commission on Presidential Debates, a nonpartisan, nonprofit organization. The commission drafted tonight's format, and the rules have been agreed upon by the campaigns. The fifty-minute debate is divided into ten segments, each five-minutes long. At the start of each segment, I'll ask the same lead off question to both candidates, and they will each have up to two minutes to respond.

"The questions are mine and have not been shared with the commission or the campaigns. The audience here in the room has agreed to remain silent so that we can focus on what the candidates are saying. I *will* invite you to applaud as I welcome the candidates. Democratic nominee for president of the United States of America, John Bradley."

John received his cue and strutted onstage to a thunderous applause. He waved to the crowd.

"Republican nominee for president of the United States of America, Arthur Coleman," Corrinne said.

Art Coleman received a similar applause as he approached center stage.

John shook hands with Art and said, "Good luck."

Art nodded. "You too, John."

The candidates were all smiles as they shook hands and greeted Corrinne before taking their places behind their podiums.

The stage was a sea of blue. Blue carpet with red trim and white stars. The backdrop was the same blue with more red trim and white stars. Dead center of the backdrop was the eagle emblem that represented the Great Seal of the United States. The podiums were blue, both facing the audience and also tilted toward the opposing candidate.

Corrinne Stevens sat front and center at a desk, just offstage. Her face was flawless with heavy makeup, and her dark hair was highlighted with a bit of brown.

John thought she looked librarian hot with her dark-rim glasses. *Too bad she's a Republican.* John glanced at Linda and the kids in the front row. He waved and smiled.

Once the applause dissipated, Corrinne said, "We will focus on the issues that voters tell us are most important to them, and we'll press for specifics. Candidates, we look forward to you articulating your policies and positions, as well as your visions and your values. Let's begin.

"Congressman Bradley, ninety-seven people died during the tax riots last April, with property damages estimated at 5.7 billion dollars' worth across the country. As president, how would you stop this from happening in the future?"

"First, I voted in support of the SAFE Act," John said, "and, if we had a repeat of last April, I would have the power of the SAFE Act to arrest rioters and looters immediately. But the SAFE Act is only treating the symptom. People are rioting because they're upset, disappointed, and disillusioned with the direction the Republicans have taken this country over the past eight years. In addition to enforcement, I would focus on returning the United States of America to a government for the people and by the people. My attorney general would investigate and bring charges on corrupt politicians. I'd close the tax loopholes that the wealthy and connected exploit to the detriment of the common man. By creating policies for a fairer country, the impetus for protest would be lower and much less volatile."

"Secretary Coleman, as president, how would you stop protests from causing the tragic loss of life and costly property damage that we endured during the tax riots?"

"First, I'd like to thank Syracuse University for hosting," Arthur said, "and I'd like to thank you, Corrinne, for moderating."

Corrinne smiled. "You're welcome, Secretary Coleman."

Arthur "Art" Coleman wore a dark suit over his massive frame. He could pass for a retired NFL linebacker. His tight curls were white, and his skin was light brown. He was a dream for the Republican Party—a former general who was brilliant, conservative, and, most important, black. The Republicans could finally tell people to get off welfare and get a job without being called a racist.

"I worked very closely with President Reynolds on the SAFE Act," Arthur said, "and I think Congressman Bradley and I agree on its effectiveness. I disagree that the riots are a symptom of justified rage against the government. A very small percentage of our population participated in the riots, but, if just one in one thousand participate, it can be quite disastrous. I disagree with the congressman's attempts at appeasement of these antigovernment terrorists. We have the most advanced and effective law enforcement in the world. As President, I would use the SAFE Act and the Espionage and Trading with the Enemy Act to prosecute these terrorists and to put them behind bars where they belong. Make no mistake. The majority of Americans are good, patriotic, God-loving people, but these antigovernment radicals seek to destroy all that we've fought for. I refuse to give them an inch."

"Secretary Coleman, do you agree with the recent policy allowing the tax protestors to pay their taxes and penalties to avoid prison sentences?" Corrinne asked.

"Ideally these tax protestors should go to prison, but it was a tough choice. Almost one million people were arrested for tax evasion. We have massive overcrowding of our prisons plus revenue and budgetary issues caused in part by the tax revolt. I believe it was the right decision, but, as president, I would be more proactive in heading off issues like these at the pass. I think increasing the penalties for tax evasion would serve to discourage this behavior in the future."

"Congressman Bradley, same question," Corrinne said. "Do you agree with the recent policy allowing the tax protestors to pay their taxes and penalties to avoid prison sentences?"

"Again the GOP is treating the symptom," John said. "The tax evaders broke the law, and they should be punished to the fullest extent of the law, but I refuse to believe that those million Americans are all antigovernment terrorists. The people are telling us to clean up our act and to do what's in the people's best interests, not simply our own. I intend to do what's in the people's best interests, and I fully expect tax receipts to return to normal."

"Congressman Bradley," Corrinne said. "Over the past two years, we've had rising unemployment, a sagging economy, and high inflation. As president, how would you tame inflation and increase growth and employment?"

"We spend one trillion dollars a year on militarism, which is more than the next eight countries combined." John paused, letting his point sink in. "As president, I would stop the wars and bring home our heroic soldiers. I'd use the money saved to alleviate poverty, provide debt relief for college loans, and to continue to rebuild our ailing infrastructure. I'd institute tax breaks for the middle class and tax hikes for companies and the wealthy. It's proven that, if you put more money in the pocket of the middle class, they will spend it at home, helping their local economies, thereby increasing jobs. If we put more money in the hands of the wealthy, it doesn't help the overall economy. It might help Tiffany's and jet-leasing companies, but it doesn't help the middle class, and it's the middle class who's the heart and soul of this country."

"Same question, Secretary Coleman," Corrinne said. "As president, how would you tame inflation and increase growth and employment?"

"We need tax relief for all Americans," Arthur said. "The congressman's correct. Tax breaks have proven to stimulate the economy, but you might want to dig a little deeper into the congressman's tax plan. What he considers wealthy—households earning over one hundred thousand dollars—is barely scraping by in many areas of the country. I agree that we can trim the military budget, but it would have to be done with care and gradualism so as not to endanger the lives of our soldiers or the burgeoning democracies in the Middle East. Furthermore I'd like to continue with President Reynolds's very successful Rebuild America stimulus program. This stimulus program is the only reason we're not in a global depression at the moment."

"Secretary Coleman," Corrinne said, "we've seen increasing amounts of soldiers and military hardware deployed to Iran. The original plan called for bombing only. Do you plan to expand the war in Iran?"

"We have a democratically elected president in Iran. We've helped the Iranian people repair vital infrastructure damaged in the invasion. We've protected the oil fields. During my presidency, we will be removing our troops, but we will do it prudently and judiciously. Total and immediate removal would result in a failed state. ISIS would take over the oil fields and sell oil on the black market to fund their operations. Our continued support and prudent drawdown of troops will result in lower oil prices and a Western-friendly democracy in the heart of the Middle East."

"Congressman Bradley," Corrinne said, "we've heard your plan for putting an immediate end to foreign wars. How do you respond to Secretary Coleman's assertion that Iran would become a failed state if we withdrew?"

"Iran's already a failed state," John said, shaking his head. "It's already another quagmire, like Iraq and Afghanistan. ISIS moved into Iran after the invasion—"

"We want George," someone from the crowd called out.

John smirked.

Then another. "We want George."

They were chanting now—five people, standing and shouting in an audience of one thousand. "We want George. We want George. We want George."

USN cut to a commercial break. The chanting continued as police officers stormed the stands, wrangling the unruly. They were handcuffed and removed from the premises.

After the commercial break, Corrinne spoke to the camera. "Welcome back to Decision 2020, the first presidential debate. We'll pick up where we left off with Congressman Bradley. Congressman, would you like to finish your comment on Iran?"

"Iran's another disaster in the Middle East," John said. "There's nothing else to say."

"We'll move to the next question then. Congressman Bradley, Americans have struggled with high gas prices and high energy bills. As president, how would you handle the energy crisis?"

"First, we need to transition from the dirty fuels of the past to a clean renewable energy future—"

"Fucking liars," someone from the crowd shouted.

"We want George," someone else from the crowd shouted.

John showed his palms.

The chanting started again. This time, at least fifty people chanted, "We want George. We want George."

USN cut to another commercial break. Pandemonium reigned in the audience, with police officers struggling to catch the protestors. Some of them were accosted and restrained by civilians in the audience. Fifteen minutes later, the rabble-rousers were hauled away in handcuffs, and the audience was quiet again.

A producer walked onstage with a microphone. "I'm sorry," he said, "but, because of the outbursts, we will finish this debate without an audience. I ask everyone to exit through the rear, starting with the back rows."

79: Katie and PewDiePie

Katie read the statistics on her screen with a wide smile.

George Smith Chapman Campaign 10-1-2020
Prior totals + September = New Total

Social Media
YouTube Subscribers: 33.1 + 4.1 = 37.2 million, Rank #3
Facebook Followers: 57.3 + 6.2 = 63.5 million
Twitter Followers: 67.1 + 7.9 = 75 million

Email Marketing
Newsletter Subscribers: 5,121,236 + 955,902 = 6,077,138
Virtual Volunteers: 0 + 43,378 = 43,378

Financials
Ad Revenue: $257,880 + $98,126 = $356,006
Incoming Donations: $8,491,207 + $10,755,190 = $19,246,397
Total Revenue: 19,602,403

Expenses: $143,311 + $44,646 = $187,957
Outgoing Donations: $6,161,385 + $2,255,436 = $8,416,821
Total Expenses: $8,604,778

Net Income: $10,997,625

Katie thought about the past six months, the six months since the shooting which had propelled George to superstardom. He was a household name now, a polarizing figure, loved or hated, depending on who you talked to. Young people mostly loved him. The young were always happy to piss off their parents. Predictably George was hated by government employees: teachers, police officers, soldiers, and bureaucrats. Unpredictably veterans gave more money to George than any other candidate. Those vets had been to the circus and had seen the magician's tricks.

The campaign rented the condo next to Katie's for George and Julie. Max worked remotely from George's Pennsylvania house. Julie drew a modest salary for her work on the campaign. George spoke to small groups to replace his trucking income. He still couldn't speak to large crowds. He received regular death threats, but they never materialized, and Katie and George had hired an excellent security team.

Katie glanced at the time on her laptop—12:58. She printed two copies of the report. She grabbed her phone and thumb-typed a text to George.

Katie: Meeting in one minute. I'm coming over.

She grabbed the copies of the report from the printer and stepped outside. It was cloudy and breezy. The parking lot of her condo community was half empty. *It's finally starting to feel like fall.*

She waved at the man in the dark SUV, walked to the condo next door, and rang the doorbell. A muscled man in cargo pants answered the door with a handgun holstered on his hip. He stepped aside, allowing Katie to enter.

"Ms. Fitzgerald," he said with a nod. He shut the reinforced door and turned the dead bolts.

"Why can't you call me Katie?" she asked. "Come on, *Shawn.* See what I did there?"

"Ms. Fitzgerald." He nodded again, this time with a hint of a grin.

"Leave him alone," Julie said, emerging from the kitchen. "I finally got him to sit down."

Shawn sat at the card table near the front door with an open laptop displaying various camera views on split screens.

Katie walked through the living room toward Julie.

"Did you want some tea?" Julie asked. "We also have leftovers from lunch."

"I'm fine, but thank you."

"It's good," George said from the dining room. "Lemongrass and mint."

"Actually I would like some tea if it's not too much trouble," Katie said to Julie.

"The kettle's still warm," Julie replied.

"I'd like you to join George and I for the meeting. I have huge news."

"Okay, I'll be there in a minute."

Katie sat across from George at the dining room table and handed him one of the reports. He shut his laptop.

"These are preliminary numbers," Katie said. "The accountant still has to go through them."

George glanced at the bottom line, his eyebrows arched. "Is this right? We had more donations in September than our year-to-date total?"

"The election's in five weeks. People are giving money to their chosen candidate. Every day more and more people think *you're* their candidate."

George rubbed the stubble on his chin. "People are generous. I hope we can put it to good use."

"I know it seems like a lot of money, but it's only a fraction of what Bradley and Coleman are raising."

"Julie's gonna be busy."

Julie set a cup of tea in front of Katie. She glanced at the page before George as she slid into the seat beside him. "I knew we were having a good month with donations but ... wow."

"It worries me having this much money in the bank," George said. "I wouldn't be surprised if a bank holiday is declared at some point, with depositors forced to bail out the banks, like Cyprus in 2013."

"We can start allocating the donations weekly instead of monthly," Katie said. "That'll keep our balance much lower."

"Let's do that."

"What's a virtual volunteer?" Julie asked, her eyes on the report.

"That's new," Katie said. "Basically it's a list of tasks that anyone with an Internet connection can perform to help boost our reach, exposure, and influence. The best part is the volunteers require no supervision or infrastructure, which means no cost. We've gamified it by awarding virtual badges for completing tasks."

"What kind of tasks?"

"Most of them involve sharing our information with their social circles. The more difficult tasks involve influencing a certain number of people to sign up to our newsletter, subscribe to our YouTube channel, or follow us on Facebook and Twitter. The most difficult one involves creating original content in support of George and his ideas. We've had some amazing content come in. Videos, artwork, blog posts."

"Wow, thirty-seven million subscribers on YouTube," Julie said, still reading the paper. "It says we're number three. Who's ahead of us?"

"We're behind Justin Bieber and PewDiePie," Katie replied with a mock frown.

"What's PewDiePie?"

"He's a Swedish comedian and video game commenter."

"I'm worried about allocating this amount of money to our charities," Julie said. "I've picked very lean charities with low overheads, but they're mostly small organizations. I'll have to find and vet some new charities to put that kind of money to good use."

"Maybe we can poll the donators to find out how they think we should use the money?" George asked.

"I like that idea," Julie said.

"We could do that," Katie said. "Or we could save the money and make a serious run in 2024. I bet we'd win."

George shook his head. "This is a one-time deal. You know that. Three bullet holes are enough for me. Besides, this was never about getting elected."

"It might happen without your consent."

"Well, as my VP, you'll get the booby prize." George smirked.

"I'm serious. You're set up as a write-in candidate in forty-three of the fifty states. I think there's a very good chance you'll win the popular vote in Idaho and New Hampshire. If I can get you into the debates, who knows?"

"Thankfully that'll never happen."

80: Julie's Story

"It really is amazing what you're doing on a shoestring budget," Julie said into her cell phone.

"It's not unlike what you and George are doing with his campaign," the man replied.

"Thank you. That's very kind. You should receive a check from us in the next week or so."

"I can't thank you enough, Julie. Good luck in November. We'll be pulling for you guys."

"You're very welcome. Keep up the great work. I'll be in touch."

"Bye."

Julie disconnected the call and set her cell on the wooden desk. The doorbell rang. Shortly thereafter, she heard Katie talking to George in the kitchen. Then there was a knock at Julie's door.

"Come in," Julie said.

Katie entered the tiny office of the Virginia condo. She was dressed casually in jeans and a fleece, her long hair in a ponytail. She smiled.

"Hi, Katie."

"Max just sent me a pretty spectacular animated video spoofing the debate," Katie said. "It's hilarious. I emailed it to you."

"Sorry, I haven't even looked at my email yet." Julie brushed her auburn hair from her eyes.

"He seems to really like living at George's place in Pennsylvania."

"I would've preferred he came down here for the run up to the election, but, with his girlfriend and his cabin, he does love it there. It is nice that he's doing the chores while we're away." Julie sighed. "He said I need to stop treating him like a baby. Maybe he's right. He is eighteen."

"Well, his work just gets better and better." Katie sat in the chair in front of the desk. "Have you had any luck allocating the donations?"

"I found a fantastic charity called First Responders for Peace. They have a network of EMTs and former military medics. They go to war zones around the world, giving aid to the civilians caught up in the fighting. They risk their lives for free. They're all volunteers. Some of the money we donate goes to their transportation, setup, and equipment, but most of it goes directly to the people in need in the form of medical supplies, water purification, and food."

"Sounds fantastic."

"I think they are."

Katie said, "So the real reason I stopped by is to ask if you'd appear in a microdocumentary I'd like to produce."

"What's it about?"

"You and your relationship with George."

"Me?" Julie put her hand to her chest.

"We need more female supporters. Sixty-eight percent of our followers are male. Bradley's winning in the polls because he dominates the female vote, especially with Atwell as his VP. I think your story is fascinating, and it'll resonate with women. Also people want to know more about George. It'll be good to show who he really is behind his encyclopedic brain."

"I don't know. Did you talk to George about it?"

"He said it was up to you, and he asked me not to pressure you. His exact words were, 'Please don't pressure her like you did me.'"

Julie laughed.

* * *

Julie stared into the lens, wearing her best T.J. Maxx sweater. Katie was behind the camera.

"Talk about how you and George met," Katie said, "and anything else you want to share about your relationship. Don't worry about mistakes. That's what editing's for."

Julie's heart pounded, her sweater suddenly too warm. She nodded at Katie. "I met George through my son, Max, who was being bullied at school and had injured his head. He ended up in the same hospital room as George, who had just been shot in Congressman Bradley's campaign headquarters. Max didn't have many friends or anyone who understood what he was going through. I'm embarrassed to say that I didn't understand how he felt. George had dealt with his share of bullying as a kid, and he recognized that Max was struggling. George was kind to Max at a time when he really needed it. They became friends in that hospital room.

"I was concerned about Max having a forty-year-old friend, but I didn't think they'd have much contact. George delivered motorcycles back then. I'm assuming he'll go back to that after this is over. Anyway, he was in town, and Max invited him over for dinner. I was dating an IRS agent at the time." Julie frowned. "The irony of this isn't lost on me. The IRS agent, who we'll call Larry, seemed like a nice guy, but what did I know? I hadn't dated since my husband had passed away—eight years ago at the time. At dinner, Larry was terribly rude to George, but George handled it like he handles every-thing—with class."

Julie took a deep breath. "One night Larry tried to sexually assault me, and I kneed him in the groin, dropping him like a sack of potatoes, as George would say." Julie looked down for a moment, then back to the camera. "I was devastated and scared. I was an emotional wreck. Out of desperation, I contacted George. I'm not sure why I did it, because we weren't close, but there was something honest and kind about him. He listened to me and stayed with me on the phone until I fell asleep.

"We were friends before we began a romantic relationship. Apparently Max told George that he was in danger of being stuck in the friend zone forever if he didn't make a move." Julie smiled briefly. "I still remember the first time George held my hand. I had that electric feeling you get when someone you care about shows that they feel the same way. The more I know George, the more I love him, and the more I need him in my life.

"I worry terribly for his safety. To so many people out there, he's just a symbol—a symbol to idealize or to tear down, depending on your politics. But to me, he's my fiancé, the man I love, and a friend and father figure to my son. After the shooting in DC, I wanted him to give all this up. When I asked him why he still wanted to continue with the campaign, he said, 'It's not about me.'"

81: George and Attack Ads

George sat at the dining room table, watching the WNN report on his laptop.

Lisa Kelly sat behind the news desk and said, "In past elections, we've had over one million people involved in counting and processing presidential ballots. With the possibility of millions of write-in votes for George Smith Chapman, this election will be much more complex. To combat the possibility of fraud and human error, a special software will be deployed to scan the ballots. This software can recognize cursive and manuscript handwriting, although many polling stations will provide preprinted stickers for Chapman voters."

George's cell phone buzzed. He closed the video and checked the text.

> **Max:** I'm not sure if you've seen this, but you should look at it. It's total BS. <u>Link</u>

George clicked the link and pressed his earbuds into his ears. It was a recently posted video from US News. The video was entitled "George Chapman's Childhood Friend Drops Bombshell!" George clicked Play. *HH Live with Hugh Henderson* was scrawled across the screen. Hugh shook hands with his guest. They sat across from each other at a round wooden table. The background was staged with a bookshelf and floor lamps.

The camera zoomed in on the dapper and dark-haired Hugh Henderson.

"Today on *HH Live* we have childhood friend of George Smith Chapman, Dusty Leach. Welcome Dusty."

The camera cut to Dusty. He was a portly fortysomething. "Uh, thanks."

HH Live cut back to Hugh and his tailored pin-striped suit. "So, Dusty, you were childhood chums with George Smith Chapman?"

The camera showed both men now. "We were neighbors up the mountain, just outside Minersville, PA. We went to middle school and high school together. It was a small school. Everybody knew each other."

"You weren't friends?"

"George didn't have any friends. I suppose I was the closest thing because I didn't do nuthin' to him. But we didn't hang out or do things together."

"Was George bullied at school?"

"Yeah, he didn't have no money, like me."

"Is that why he was bullied?"

"No." Dusty shook his head. "Nobody was rich. He had some problems with his face, you know zits and stuff, and he didn't always have soap and running water at his house, so he was dirty. He smelled sometimes."

"Did you spend much time with George?"

"We were neighbors, so I tried to be a good neighbor and stuff, but he mostly kept to himself."

"Mostly?" Hugh raised his dark eyebrows. "Was there a time when he didn't keep to himself?"

The red-faced man swallowed, his Adam's apple bobbing up and down. "There was this boy with him sometimes. The boy was younger, like eight or nine, lived near George and me. I don't wanna say his name. I doubt he'd want me talkin' about this."

"How old was George at the time?"

"Sixteen."

"What happened between George and this boy?"

"Rumor was that George was touchin' the boy, and the dad found out about it and beat George pretty bad."

"Did you witness George doing anything inappropriate with the boy?"

"It was weird. He never hung out with nobody, but then he's gonna be around some young boy? It was just weird."

"But did you see George do anything inappropriate with the boy?"

The man swallowed again. "I saw him touch the boy."

Hugh leaned forward. "Dusty, I need you to be specific. What part of the boy's body did George touch?"

Dusty looked down. "His penis."

George stopped the video, removed his earbuds, and tapped his Katie contact.

"We might have a problem," George said in lieu of a greeting.

"I know," Katie replied. "I just saw it. I'll be over in a minute."

George hung his head and rubbed his temples. He trudged to the office and knocked on the open door. Julie looked up from her laptop with a smile.

"Hey, you," she said. "You ready to go to bed?"

"We have to talk about something," George said, his brow furrowed.

Her smile receded. "Okay. What's wrong?"

"Katie's coming over."

"More attack ads?"

George nodded. "This one's really bad."

The doorbell rang. Shawn opened the door for Katie. George, Julie, and Katie sat at the dining room table. They played the video for Julie.

"They have no shame," Julie said.

"They don't," Katie agreed.

Julie put her hand to her chest. "Oh, my God. In the documentary, I said that I was concerned about Max being friends with a forty-year-old man."

"It's fine," Katie said to Julie. "We're still in the editing stages. We can take it out." Katie turned to George. "We need to know if any of that's true."

"They twisted the truth," Julie said.

"Most of it's true," George said. "Dusty was my neighbor. He was a nice-enough guy. The bullying, my hygiene, my clothes, and my acne—that's all true."

"None of that is your fault or anything to be ashamed of," Julie said, her face taut.

"It's okay," George said, squeezing Julie's hand. "The boy's name was Joey Ebersole. His home life was a lot like mine. Single mom and a parade of boyfriends. He used to hike with me up the mountain. Anything to get out of his house. He didn't have many friends either.

"We were hiking in the late fall, and we got back just after dusk. The days were getting so short. Usually we parted ways at my house, and he walked the rest of the way to his by himself. This time I walked him to his house because it was dark. We weren't concerned about being late. Nobody seemed to care what time he came home. I'd never even met his mother. She must've been coming down from her high, because she was hysterical. We could hear her carrying on as we approached the house from the trail above.

"Her boyfriend saw us coming down the trail and stalked toward us with a flashlight pointed in my face. He started questioning me about what I was doing with Joey. I tried to tell him that we went hiking. He kept calling me a liar and a faggot and asking me why I was hanging around a little kid. I pleaded with him. Joey told him that we were hiking. The boyfriend told Joey to go inside.

"When Joey left, I knew something bad was gonna happen. He was a big guy. Bloodshot eyes. Smelled like alcohol. He had one of those big heavy flashlights, and he beat me with it until I stopped moving." George closed his eyes for a moment, his face contorted as if the memory caused him physical pain.

"Joey must've heard my screams. He must've begged his mother to help me. I don't remember getting to the hospital, but someone dropped me on the pavement in front of the emergency room. I spent a couple days in the hospital. My mother pretended to care and played the part of the worried parent. The last thing she wanted was the state looking into our house.

"I never told who did it. I was too afraid. But word got around anyway. I guess the boyfriend had been telling people that I liked little boys and bragging that he taught me a lesson. People already thought I was weird, so the small-town gossip spread without much scrutiny. There were a few instances after that of people throwing things at me and threatening me. I stopped going to school. I stayed away from Joey, and he stayed away from me." George blew out a breath. "I needed to get away from that town, my mother, her boyfriends, everyone. I couldn't stand it anymore.

"That winter, we had a lot of snow, and I worked for a landscaper shoveling sidewalks. Most of his work was thirty minutes away, but he lived near me, so he'd pick me up. He was a nice guy. In the spring, he taught me the ropes and let me drive one of his trucks home. I found a basement room for rent near the jobsites, and I left home. That was it. I never saw Joey again, and I never saw my mother again."

"I'm sorry, George," Katie said.

George nodded.

Julie squeezed George's hand. She wiped her eyes with the back of her hand. "I've heard this before, but it still upsets me."

"It's something I'd like to forget." George looked down for a moment. "Of course that's my gift and my curse. I never forget anything."

"It'll be easy enough to debunk this Dusty guy," Katie said. "This could actually be really positive for us."

Julie frowned at Katie. "It's not always political."

"Hear me out. If we can find Joey Ebersole, I bet he'll tell the truth. I bet Anonymous is hacking this Dusty guy's account right now. I bet they find a large sum of money that he received recently. It's another example of the depths that government will go to protect their power. The attack ads from the Coleman campaign and now this. I think they're desperate."

George shook his head. "I don't think so. Coleman's been running attack ads calling me a terrorist for the past week and now this interview. And WNN had a huge piece on Somalia, asserting that the United States will be like Somalia if the Anarchist movement achieves their goals. So we're seeing a heavy dose of propaganda against me specifically and generally about anarchism. But it doesn't make sense. Why would Coleman acknowledge me at all? The polls have me at 6 percent of the popular vote. I'm not a threat. I'm not taking Republican voters. I'm mostly getting first-time voters, Libertarians, and a few Independents."

"Six percent is huge for a write-in candidate," Katie said. "Ross Perot in '96 was the last third-party candidate to get more than 5 percent of the popular vote."

"I still don't see the upside for Coleman."

"They'll praise Coleman for his patriotism," Katie said. "The average Republican hates you."

"But those people are gonna vote Republican whether Coleman comes out against me or not. Why alienate those people who are sympathetic to our cause? There's a reason why Bradley's winning. He's been able to walk that line. People think they can get change and freedom in a less extreme package with Bradley. Coleman had been careful not to be too critical of me until just this week. What happened?"

"Or what *will* happen?" Julie asked.

82: John and the Train's Leaving the Station

John sat behind his dark wooden desk, Donna in one of the leather chairs across from him.

"Either Art made a huge mistake or he knows something we don't know," John said.

"Frank's mining his contacts to see what he can find out," Donna replied.

"I know Art's not that stupid," John said. "It's obvious that this 'friend' of Chapman's from high school is lying." John threw up air quotes when he said "friend." "Give it a few days, and they'll find the truth."

"And Art will be the one who looks bad. This could be good for us."

John shook his head. "It's too easy."

"I should get back to work." Donna stood.

She was different. She still looked beautiful and competent—fit body, skirt suit with heels, and her dark hair in a tight bun, but she didn't look at John with the same dilated pupils and glances held a bit too long.

Donna turned to leave.

"Don't go," John said.

She faced John but didn't sit. "Is there something else?" Her face was expressionless.

"No, I, uh, wanted to know how you're doing."

"I'm doing fine."

"How's Agent Barnes?"

She crossed her arms. "Let's not do this, John."

"We can't be friends?"

"Is that really what you're after—friendship?"

John smiled wide. "You know me better than anyone."

"Is that it?"

"Do you feel the same for Jake that you did for me?"

"It's not the same," Donna said. "It's completely different. He doesn't have a wife. We actually have a future."

"I miss you. Don't you miss me? You've always been the one I want. If it wasn't for my responsibilities—"

"Stop."

There was a knock. Donna marched to the door and opened it. Frank barreled into the office. Donna shut the door behind him. The three of them stood around John's desk.

Frank said, "My source at the FBI told me that they're gonna arrest Chapman."

"For what?" John asked.

"I don't know. The only thing I know is that he's been identified as the number one domestic terror threat on their new software."

"The crime matters. If he's arrested for pot or something nonsensical that most Americans do, it'll just make him more of a martyr."

"What if it's treason?" Donna asked.

"Then we need to distance ourselves from Chapman and condemn him as a terrorist," Frank said. "Art's already on the train. We might wanna hop on before it leaves the station."

"I might be able to find out what the charges'll be," John said. "Give me a few hours."

* * *

John sat across from Adam Doyle in a secluded booth. The lighting was dim, the restaurant mostly empty. It was in between lunch and dinner.

"What can I do for you, Congressman?" Adam asked, his face blank.

"You hungry? I'm buying." John smiled.

"I don't have much time." Adam's pale face was haggard, his red hair disheveled.

"Down to business then." John leaned forward, his elbows on the table. "You and I both know that George Chapman will be arrested before the election. I need to know the charge."

Adam was quiet.

"I'm actually a little hurt," John said. "I'm supposed to be your friend,

423

yet Art Coleman knows something that I don't know—something that came from you."

"I didn't tell him anything. As secretary of state, he has access. President Reynolds has access."

"If I were you, I'd stay neutral and back both horses. I'm a loyal guy, Adam, but I'm also a vindictive one. When I win, I'll remember my friends, but I'll also remember who fucked me." John glared across the table.

Adam rubbed the back of his neck. "I don't know what the specific charge will be. My company helps with maintenance and updates, but the NSA has control. I can tell you that it'll be something bad enough to destroy his reputation."

83: Katie, Big Brother's Coming

Katie and George stood in the living room of her condo, watching her television. Congressman John Bradley was on the screen behind a podium with multiple microphones attached.

"There's freedom of speech in this country," John said, "but there's also hate speech, and there's speech that incites violence and endangers people. You can't shout 'Fire' in a crowded theater. Obviously this speech endangers people. George Chapman's rhetoric and speech are inciting violence, and I condemn him as a domestic terrorist. I believe there's a strong case to be made for his arrest under the Espionage and Trading with the Enemy Act." The congressman paused, his large hands gripping the edge of the podium. "I can take a few questions."

John pointed to a fortysomething man. "Seth."

"Until today, you've been a supporter of George Chapman's constitutional right to free speech. Why the sudden change?"

John scowled at the reporter. "There hasn't been a change. I support everyone's right to free speech, but, when that speech incites violence, it's no longer protected by our constitutional right to freedom of speech."

Katie muted the television and set the remote on the coffee table. "Bradley's falling in line with Coleman."

"I figured it was coming," George said. "They must be planning to arrest me."

"On what charge?" Katie asked.

"Maybe the Trading with the Enemy Act, like Bradley said. I'm sure they can find something."

"People will go crazy. They're risking massive riots. I think they know that."

"Maybe it'll give them a reason to arrest all the Anarchists and put an end to this movement once and for all."

Katie's phone chimed. She removed it from the back pocket of her jeans. "It's Zach. Can you give me a minute?"

George nodded, and Katie swiped right.

"Where's the phone I gave you?" Zach asked, without a greeting.

"It's in my room, powered off," Katie replied.

"Call me from that phone right now." Zach disconnected the call.

Katie looked at George, her eyes wide. "He wants me to use the encrypted phone."

"Do you want privacy?" George asked.

"No, it's probably about you. Wait here."

Katie rushed to her bedroom and retrieved the encrypted phone from her bedside table. She powered on the phone and returned to George and the living room. She took a deep breath, glanced at George and called Zach.

"Listen carefully," Zach said. "You need to destroy every hard drive that you and George have. Phones, tablets, laptops, desktops—everything."

"Why? Are the Feds planning to arrest George?"

"Yes. He's number one on their domestic terror threat list. You're on the list too. Take out the hard drives, smash them to pieces, then scatter the pieces in the Potomac. Do the same with your backups. Do you have a cloud backup?"

"Yes."

"You need to get rid of that too. Make sure they scrub everything from the backup—the current and the historical backups."

"I can't do that," Katie said, her voice higher than usual. "We're running a presidential campaign with our computers. There's nothing illegal on our computers."

"Are you sure about that?"

"Well, no, but, if there *is* something, it's some obscure violation that'll just piss people off and prove our point that the government's tyrannical."

"They can plant evidence. Get rid of it all. Now."

"We have good cybersecurity."

"It doesn't matter. Get rid of it all, and do it now. Trust me. I have to go." Zach disconnected the call.

Katie sat on the couch, gripping the phone.

George approached, still standing. "He told you to get rid of the computers."

Katie nodded, her head hanging. She looked at George. "And phones and backups. All that work."

George sat next to her on the couch. "I think I know what they're planning. If I'm right, Zach's right."

84: Julie and the No-Knock Raiders

Julie, George, and Katie followed Zach's advice. They removed the hard drives and sim cards from their laptops, phones, and tablets. George smashed them on the concrete, collected the pieces, and took them to the Potomac River. Katie contacted Carbonite, and they assured her that their backups would be erased by the end of the day.

Julie and Katie sat at the dining room table with nothing to do but wait for George to return from the Potomac.

"The videos are still stored on YouTube," Julie said. "We still have our Facebook and Twitter followers, and AWeber has our subscribers."

Katie nodded, her brow creased. "I know. That's not what I'm worried about. I keep thinking that, even if they can't plant the evidence on our hard drives, who's to say they can't plant the evidence some other way? How easy would it be to drop a flash drive, then pick it up?"

Julie closed her eyes for a moment. "I know."

"They're here," Shawn called out from the front window.

Julie and Katie moved from the dining room to the living room. Shawn peered out the front window, a handgun holstered on his hip.

"It's the FBI," Shawn said.

"I think you should hide your gun," Julie said to Shawn. "I don't want them shooting you and justifying it because you have a gun."

Shawn turned from the window, his face taut. "Ma'am, they can take my right to bear arms, but I won't give it away." He went back to the window. "Shit, it's SWAT, and they have a door knocker." He turned to Julie and Katie. "Do you want me to open the door? Otherwise they'll bust it down."

"Open it," Julie said.

"You two should put up your hands and *do not drop them, even an inch.*"

Julie's heart pounded as she and Katie raised their hands. Shawn opened the door to shouts of "Get down! On the ground." A single-file line of SWAT agents poured into the condo, each one identical to the other. They were dressed in dark blue, with helmets, goggles, and their faces covered like ninjas. Four agents approached Julie and Katie, pointing M-4 carbines at them.

An agent shouted, "Clear," from the office.

Julie's and Katie's hands were forced behind their backs, and they were handcuffed. The metal bit into Julie's wrists.

"Do you have any weapons on your person or anything that might stick me?" an agent said to Katie.

"No," Katie replied. "Are we being arrested?"

Katie was searched without a response to her question.

"Do you have any weapons on your person or anything that might stick me?" another agent said to Julie.

Julie was paralyzed with fear.

"Do you have any weapons on your person or anything that might stick me?" the agent said louder and faster.

"No," Julie replied, her eyes glassy as the man ran his hands over her body—over her chest, up and down her legs.

"Did you enjoy that?" Katie asked the agent. "Piece of shit."

Another agent said to Julie, "We have an electronic warrant to arrest George Smith Chapman. Where is he?"

Julie sniffled, tears slipping down her cheeks. "I don't know."

"Electronic warrant?" Katie asked, incredulous. "Are you serious? What's the charge?"

"Possession of child pornography," the agent said. "We also have an electronic warrant to search this location, next door, and your vehicles for electronic devices to be included, but not limited to, computers, tablets, laptops, and phones."

Julie and Katie were released from their handcuffs, given copies of the search warrant, and forced outside. They stood on the sidewalk as dozens of agents in dark suits or blue windbreakers searched the two condos and Katie's SUV. Shawn and his partner, David, approached.

"Are you two okay?" Shawn asked.

"We're fine," Katie said.

Julie, Katie, and the bodyguards stood, helpless, as they watched the agents invade the homes, and emerge with laptops and tablets without hard drives.

Julie was thankful that she wore her fleece. A cool breeze blew through the community, and the clouds were heavy with rain. "They'll take George," Julie said.

"We'll bail him out," Katie said. "Don't worry." She leaned forward and whispered in Julie's ear. "I hope Carbonite finished the deletion."

"Me too."

Julie stared toward the community entrance as her Honda crept into the neighborhood. "He's back," Julie whispered to Katie. "Don't turn around. He stopped the car. He's driving toward us now. They see him."

Katie and the bodyguards turned around and watched as the SWAT team surrounded the Honda. George stopped the car and stepped from the vehicle with his hands up. He was surrounded and forced facedown on the asphalt. An agent pressed his knee into George's upper back, as he was cuffed. Julie ran toward the scene.

Shawn stopped her in the middle of the parking lot, holding her shoulders firm, but careful not to hurt her. Katie took over and wrapped her up in an embrace. "Don't give them an excuse," Katie said.

Julie watched over Katie's shoulder as George was searched and stood up. His legs were shackled; a chain was placed around his waist and attached to his handcuffs. He was forced into the back of a van outfitted with a metal cage.

85: George and the Empire Strikes Back

George sat on the built-in metal bench as he rode in the back of the van. He was fastened with a locked seat belt. The cage was partitioned, so it was very narrow—barely enough space for a man. He tried not to move because, each time he did, the metal bit into his wrists and ankles. There was a metal grate in front and in back, offering a limited view of the scenery. A couple dark SUVs were in front and behind the van.

They drove against traffic to Washington, DC. Their destination—the FBI field office—was an eight-story building with a marble facade. Inside, George was fingerprinted, photographed, and placed in an interrogation room with a two-way mirror. He sat on a metal chair, his hands attached to the chain around his waist and confined to his lap, cameras pointed down at him.

Two agents entered the room, one male and one female, both probably in their forties.

"Mr. Chapman," the female said, holding a file in her hand. "I must say that I'm surprised to see you. Aren't you the guy who says morality is above the law?"

George was silent.

The female agent was small, athletic, and overly tan. She had a brown pixie cut and wore a dark pantsuit. She slapped the file on the desk and sat across from George.

The male agent shook his head. "It's a crying shame. There are no heroes anymore." He unbuttoned his dark jacket and also sat across from George. The man was barrel-chested, his bald crescent cut tight to his scalp.

"I'm Agent Avery, and this is Agent Dodson," the woman said. "We can make this as painless as possible, or it can be ..."

"Unpleasant," Dodson said.

Agent Avery smirked at Dodson. "That's an understatement." She turned her gaze to George. "The whole world already knows that you're a pedophile, arrested for kiddie porn. Do you know what happens to pedophiles in prison?"

George remained expressionless.

"Agent Avery asked you a question," Dodson said.

"I'd like a lawyer," George said.

Agent Avery laughed. "And I'd like a beach house and a seven-figure bank account."

"Don't worry, George—is it okay if I call you George?" Dodson waited a beat for a response that never came. "Don't worry, George. You'll see an attorney before your arraignment and bail hearing."

"When's my arraignment?" George asked.

Dodson and Avery laughed.

"Do you know what time it is?" Avery asked Dodson.

Dodson checked his watch. "Half past four."

"Time goes"—Avery snapped her fingers—"just like that." She turned her attention to George. "The problem with being arrested on a Friday afternoon is you get stuck in a holding cell for the weekend."

"That sucks," Dodson said. "Don't worry. We'll keep you safe and sound until Monday."

"I'm not sure we can do that," Avery said. "He's supposed to be transferred to the detention center."

Dodson winced. "You definitely don't wanna go there with a kiddie porn charge. And you're famous." The bald man shook his head. "You'll be the target of every criminal who's trying to build his rep."

George hung his head.

"Which is pretty much all of them," Avery added.

"There is a way we could keep him from going to the detention center," Agent Dodson said. "Hell, we could keep him out of prison altogether."

"You could walk out of this relatively unscathed, George. All you have to do is one thing."

George lifted his head. "Confess."

"That's right," Dodson said. "You confess to possession of child pornography, and we can guarantee no prison time, *and* we can guarantee your safety this weekend."

"On the other hand," Avery said to George, "if you wanna fight the system …" She sighed. "Did you know that the maximum sentence for possession of child pornography is ten years in prison?"

"That's hard time," Dodson said.

"Given the mountain of evidence we have"—Agent Avery patted the file folder—"I'm sure they'll have no problem locking you up for a decade."

George huffed. "Let me get this straight. I plead guilty to possession of child pornography, and I don't do any jail time, but my reputation is ruined and I'm on a sexual offender list for the rest of my life."

"You'll be on that list either way," Dodson said. "This deal is real, George. It'll be in writing. If you agree, you won't do a second of jail time. You can have your lawyer look it over before you sign."

George leaned back in his chair. "Did you know that in 2016, 90 percent of criminal cases were never tried in court. The defendants took plea bargains instead."

"That's the way the legal system works," Avery said.

"It was 88 percent in 2017, and 82 percent in 2018, 76 percent in 2019, and this year it's 71 percent and trending downward."

Avery frowned with deep creases around her mouth. "What's your point?"

"My point is, I'll make bail, and it'll take forever for you guys to try my case because courts are backlogged three and a half years. That'll give me and the millions of hackers out there plenty of time to figure out how the NSA or the FBI sent this shit to my computer. Then what?" George shrugged. "There won't be a jury in America that'll say I'm guilty."

Avery opened the file and slid it across the table. There was a naked picture of a prepubescent boy with a middle-aged man. George turned his head.

"I'm pretty sure they'll move you to the front of the line," Avery said.

"I'll take my chances," George said.

"This is a one-time offer," Agent Dodson said.

"Don't be stupid, George," Avery said.

"Like I said, 'I'll take my chances.'"

"It's your funeral," Dodson said.

Agent Avery shook her head. "I thought you were supposed to be smart."

The agents left the room. They were replaced by five jackbooted agents. George shuffled with his escorts to the elevator, the metal cuffs digging into his wrists and ankles.

He was taken to the basement parking lot, where a van idled with one of the rear doors open. It was identical to the one he had ridden in earlier, with the partitioned cage. George was forced into the narrow metal cage. He sat on the metal bench and was restrained with a locked seat belt.

An agent shut the cage and slammed the rear door. They moved slowly at first as they inched their way out of the city during rush hour. George looked through the metal grated back and front windows. Dark SUVs were in front and behind them. He had to pee. His wrists swelled from the pressure of the handcuffs, making them tighter and more painful. George closed his eyes and thought about Julie.

After an hour or so, the caravan stopped. Then they moved slowly through open metal gates. The detention center was a compound of three connected brick buildings. The tallest was eight stories, and, if it wasn't for the sparse windows, it resembled a low-rent apartment building. The other two buildings were shorter and wider, with the same dull reddish-orange brick.

A handful of FBI agents and detention officers escorted George inside. He shuffled his way through a metal detector and through a heavy metal door labeled Intake. In the intake room, he was searched again. George rubbed his wrists as the handcuffs and leg cuffs were removed. He was made to strip, to open his mouth, and to lift his tongue.

"Bend over, spread your ass cheeks, and cough," the chubby guard said.

George complied, in a fog, trying to disassociate himself.

"Stand up, turn around, and lift your scrotum."

George complied.

He was given a pair of underwear, socks, a T-shirt, slip-on canvas shoes, and brown pants and a shirt that resembled hospital scrubs. George dressed quickly. He was handcuffed again, his hands in front, no leg irons. Four detention officers took him to an elevator. They rode the elevator to the top floor. Two men were in front of George, two men were behind. Nobody spoke; all eyes were forward.

The elevator doors opened, and George was led down a brightly lit corridor with metal doors on both sides with small, but thick Plexiglas windows. The detention officers stopped, and one opened a door. George gagged on the smell of feces and urine. Two of the officers covered their faces. The other two shoved George inside and shut the door behind him.

George turned around and looked at an officer through the window. "Please give me something to clean the cell."

The officer stared impassively.

"At least take off these handcuffs," George said.

The detention officers left without a response.

"Don't leave me like this," George called out to deaf ears.

George turned around. Two metal bunks were attached to the wall without mattresses, blankets, or pillows. He approached the stainless-steel toilet and attached sink. The toilet, the floor, and the wall near the toilet were smeared with black feces. A puddle of urine stood in one corner of the cell. He stepped around the feces carefully and peered inside the toilet bowl. Not a drop of water was inside. It was filled with clumped feces, an amalgamation of filth the size of a man's foot. He pressed the button on the top of the toilet to flush, and nothing happened. He tried the sink. No water.

George peed on the clumped feces in the toilet, resisting his gag reflex. Afterward he moved to the corner of the lower bunk, as far away from the toilet as possible. He looked at the bunk above him and wondered if he'd get a roommate.

Time stood still. With no windows to the outside, George had no idea what time it was. After what felt like hours, the fluorescent lights clicked off. It was dark but not pitch black because of the hall lights. George lay faceup on the metal slab, his swollen and bound wrists throbbing in pain. Between the smell and his aching body, sleep was impossible. After a few minutes, his back, butt, and head ached from the hard metal. George adjusted his position to relieve the pain, and, a few minutes later, something else ached.

The door clicked and opened. George felt a surge of optimism. *I'm getting out of here.* Three men entered the cell, and the door shut behind them. George stood from the bunk, adrenaline coursing through his veins.

They were all big men. Dark skin, dark jumpsuits, and actual shoes with shoelaces given to the longer-term prisoners. The middle one was the largest with tree trunks for legs and anacondas for arms. He stood with his arms crossed, clearly in charge of the room and everyone in it.

"Damn, it smells like shit in here," one of his underlings said.

George calculated his options. *No hands. No weapon. No help. Outsized. Outmanned. I have to take out the guy in charge. There's no other way out. But how? Any one of these guys can kill me.*

"You like to fuck little boys, faggot?" the leader asked.

George was silent.

"Yeah, he do," an underling said. "Look at this punk-ass bitch."

"I'm innocent," George said.

The men laughed. "Every motherfucker in here says that shit."

The leader unbuttoned his jumpsuit. The white T-shirt underneath brightened the scene. He removed his arms and let the jumpsuit fall to the floor. The massive man stood without underwear, stroking his erect penis. "On your fuckin' knees, faggot," the leader said.

George's heart pounded in his chest as he sank to his knees.

"Do it good, or I'll fuckin' kill you." The massive man palmed George's head. "Open up, bitch."

George opened his mouth. As the man shoved his penis inside, George bit down with the force of a pit bull. Warm, metallic-tasting blood slid down his throat. The massive man shrieked and clubbed George repeatedly on both sides of the head. George released and stood, the henchmen already on him. The massive man was wide eyed as he held on to his bloody penis—the head barely attached. One of the henchmen had George in a chokehold and the other took shots that left George breathless. They let go and George fell to the floor, gasping. On the ground now, the two underlings kicked and stomped him. George covered his head with his bound hands to protect himself from the onslaught.

The leader screamed, his voice in an octave much higher now. "Guard! Guard! Open up!"

A henchman straddled George with his hands around George's neck again. They locked eyes, George wide-eyed with terror, the henchman's bulging with rage. The other man controlled George's legs. George flailed and bucked impotently. He was drifting out of consciousness. His pants and underwear were removed. The hands let go of his neck and George gasped for air. He was turned over, flat on his stomach. Knees were ground into George's upper back and hands were around his neck again, shutting off his air supply. George tried to buck and push himself up, but the man was too heavy.

George was dizzy and weak from lack of oxygen. There was spitting. George's legs were spread.

"Yeah, you like that, fuckin' faggot," the man said as he entered.

"Get some. Tear that ass up," the other man said to his partner. He leaned forward, his hands still tight around George's neck. He whispered in George's ear. "You got HIV now, faggot."

George blacked out.

* * *

George awoke on his back, naked from the waist down, the fluorescent light blinding, his entire body in agony. One eye was swollen shut. His wounded neck protested with every millimeter of movement. He smelled like urine. His mouth tasted bitter and salty. He spat on the floor. It was wet underneath him. He grunted as he rolled on his side, a shooting pain emanating from his ribs. He looked behind himself to confirm what he already knew. His rectum and inter-gluteal cleft were stained with blood.

86: John's a Fresh-Fucked Fox in a Forest Fire

John glanced up from his laptop at the knock on his open door. He motioned Frank to come in and said, "Shut the door, please."

Frank sat across from John in the Spartan campaign office. The walls were stark white; the desks were pressboard. Frank pushed his wire-frame glasses up his bulbous nose. His white hair was feathered and parted to the side.

"The early numbers look good," Frank said, handing a piece of paper to John.

John skimmed the paper, his eyes like saucers. "What's the margin of error?"

"Two percent."

"This has us up by 3 percent."

"I didn't want to spend a fortune on this poll. I just wanted to get a feel for how Chapman's arrest affected us. I'd like to do a more-thorough poll after he's been arraigned on Monday. A fair amount of Chapman's people are jumping ship to us or dropping out altogether. He does still have a strong core of people who are shouting his innocence."

"They can shout all they want. No coming back from a charge like that." John smiled wide. "It's looking pretty good, huh?"

"That's an understatement." Frank grinned. "You're hotter than a fresh-fucked fox in a forest fire."

John and Frank laughed.

John settled down, his face turning serious. "Not to put a damper on the good news, but I do have something serious to discuss with you."

Frank sat up a little straighter. "I'm all ears."

"After the election, win or lose, I want Donna and Agent Barnes gone."

Frank nodded.

"I'm telling you now, so you can start making arrangements for a smooth transition, especially when it comes to Donna. Obviously it's advantageous for us that she doesn't know what's coming. The last thing we need is her trying to sabotage the campaign."

"I'll be discreet. Hell hath no fury like a woman scorned."

87: Katie and the Arraignment

The courtroom was packed. The walls were dark wood, with marble columns interspersed. The furniture matched the walls—attorneys' desks, the judge's bench, and the jury box—all dark, glossy mahogany. Katie, Julie, and Max sat near the front, in a wooden pew similar to a church. Katie and Julie wore skirt suits and dark tights, Max a dark suit. George's lawyer, Harry Burkett, sat next to Katie and the aisle. Two dozen court officers were placed around the room.

The crowd was silent as the clerk said, "Case number oh-four-dash-three-eight-two-four, the *State versus George Smith Chapman*, thirty-seven counts of possession of child pornography."

George was ushered into the courtroom by two court officers. He shuffled and moved gingerly, his legs and hands bound. He wore a brown prisoner uniform. His left eye was black and blue and swollen shut. His ears were swollen. He had a ring of bruising around his neck. Julie covered her mouth and stifled a sob. Max squeezed her hand.

Harry stood from his seat, moved through the swinging gate, and joined his client in front of the judge. Harry was a pudgy man with gray hair and a gray goatee.

The white-haired woman glared down from the bench. "In the matter of the *State versus Chapman*, Mr. Chapman, how do you plead?"

George raised his head. "Not guilty, ... Your Honor."

The judge turned to the prosecuting attorney. "I'll hear from the State regarding bail."

A lanky man with salt-and-pepper hair rose from the seat behind the prosecutor's table. "We have thirty-seven pieces of child pornography obtained via an electronic warrant. Mr. Chapman disposed of the hard drives in an attempt to conceal his criminality. We obtained the evidence through his cloud backup, all well within the legal parameters of the warrant."

"Liar!" a man from the audience stood. "The evidence was planted!"

The judge pounded her gavel.

Four court officers converged on the man.

"It was planted," the man said as he was forcibly removed. "Liars."

The crowd spoke in hushed whispers, creating a buzz.

"Order," the judge said, pounding her gavel again.

The crowd quieted. The judge flipped through the pictures in the file, her face twisted in disgust. She turned back to the prosecuting attorney. "Mr. Davis, does the state have a recommended bail amount?"

"We're recommending bail to be set at $500,000," the prosecutor replied. "Mr. Chapman is a well-known advocate for the destruction of the US government and is affiliated with terrorist organizations such as Anonymous. He is a danger to the public and a flight risk."

The judge turned to Harry. "Mr. Burkett?"

"Mr. Chapman is not a flight risk," Harry said. "He doesn't have a passport and has never been out of the country. He has no prior criminal record, and, if you haven't noticed, take a look at his face and neck. The State poses a far greater risk to Mr. Chapman than Mr. Chapman does to the State or the public. Furthermore, a $500,000 bail is ludicrous given the charges."

The judge frowned. "I'm inclined to agree that $500,000 is excessive, but we are talking about children. I'm setting bail at $100,000, and Mr. Chapman is not allowed within five hundred feet of any school, day care center, or youth sporting event." The judge glowered at George. "Mr. Chapman, if you so much as breathe near a child, you'll be remanded so fast it'll make your head spin. Do you understand?"

George was silent.

"Do you understand?" she repeated.

"Yes, … Your Honor," George replied.

George was taken from the courtroom by two court officers.

Harry returned to Katie, Julie, and Max. He extended his hand. "Let's get him out of here. He needs to go to the hospital."

A half hour later, Katie paid George's bail.

88: Julie and Picking up the Pieces

George exited the holding area in the jeans and black fleece he wore last Friday. He was pale and moved with the speed of an octogenarian.

Julie hugged him gingerly. "What did they do to you?" Julie whispered, her voice catching.

"I was beaten. I need to go to the emergency room," he said in her ear.

She kissed him lightly on the cheek. "We're leaving now." Julie turned to Katie, Max, and Harry. "Let's go."

"I'll deal with the media," Katie said. "It's a madhouse out there." Katie squeezed George's hand. "I'll see you at the hospital." She hurried toward the madness.

"My car's out back," Harry said.

Max and Harry supported George as they made their way to the elevator and finally to the alley behind the courthouse. Julie held the doors. George lay in the back of Harry's BMW, covered by a blanket. They drove through reporters and demonstrators. Protestors wearing black bandanas over their faces smacked the car windows and shouted.

"Capitalist pig!"

"Fascist!"

Various signs read Chapman Child Molester, Death to Pedophiles, George for Prison, The Truth Will Be Revealed, George Is Innocent, and The State Lies.

Once they were through the crowd, Harry raced to the nearest hospital. He parked in front of the emergency room. Julie and Max helped George out of the car and inside. Harry went to park his car.

A triage nurse took one look at George, put him in a wheelchair, and took him to an exam room. Max stayed in the waiting room; Julie walked alongside the wheelchair. George ended up in a hospital bed on wheels with a shower curtain–like wall around him for privacy.

"What happened?" the nurse asked as she took his vitals.

"I was in a fight," George replied.

"Can you tell me what hurts?"

"My ribs, my neck, my wrists."

"How about that eye?"

"It looks worse than it feels."

The nurse finished recording his vitals. "The doctor will be right with you." The nurse exited the curtained "room."

Julie held George's hand, trying not to break down. "Is there anything I can do?" she asked.

George looked at Julie, his eyes wet. "When the doctor comes in, I need you to give me some privacy."

Julie put her hand to her chest. "You want me to leave?"

"Just for a little while. I need privacy with the doctor."

"Why?"

"Please."

"What happened?" She stroked his forearm.

He looked away.

"Talk to me, honey."

"Please. I can't." A tear streaked down his cheek.

89: George and Broken

Katie weaved her SUV through the morning traffic on the way home from the hospital.

"You look a lot better," Katie said, glancing in the rearview mirror.

After spending the night in the hospital, George did look better. His color had returned. He still had bruising on his neck and a shiner, but he could open his eye now. He had three fractured ribs that still made movement very painful.

"He does," Julie said from the back seat, where she held hands with George.

George gazed out the window in a fog.

"I brought some produce down," Max said from the front passenger seat. "I'm pretty sure I harvested everything at the right time."

"Thanks, Max," George said, his face empty.

"Of course."

George continued to stare out the window, disengaged from the conversation.

"Are you okay?" Julie whispered to George.

George turned to Julie and nodded. "I'm fine." He went back to the window.

Katie, Max, and Julie talked about the status of the campaign and the latest conspiracy theory about George. They'd dropped from 6 percent of the popular vote to 3, and the latest conspiracy theory claimed that John Bradley and Art Coleman had worked together with the FBI to discredit George. It was long on hyperbole and speculation but short on evidence.

They passed a Mobil station. Regular gasoline was $5.19 per

gallon. Brown-skinned men looking for work lined up outside a Home Depot. Their condo community center had a banner hanging that read Vacancies! First Month Free!

Julie and Max helped George into their condo and into bed. Max had shed much of his baby fat, and his arms flexed with muscle as he helped George. Good food and hard work had had a positive effect on him. Max left his mother alone with George.

"Did you want something to eat?" Julie asked.

"I wanna sleep," George replied.

"I'm here if you want to talk," Julie said, caressing his forearm.

"I know."

90: John's Home

John entered his kitchen from the garage. He set his bag of groceries on the center island but held on to the bouquet of roses. The television blared from the family room. John walked toward the noise. "Hey, bud," John said to Bobby.

Bobby looked up from the World War II footage and pressed Pause on the DVR. He knitted his brow, his light eyebrows barely visible. "What are you doing home so early?"

"I wanted to surprise your mother. Where is she?"

"She went running."

"Your sisters?"

"Charlotte's in her room, and Ellen's probably with Tyler."

John exhaled. "Well, don't go anywhere because I'm making homemade pizza for dinner."

"Cool." Bobby pressed Play on the DVR, resuming the carnage caused by the Luftwaffe.

John returned to the kitchen and placed the roses in a water-filled vase. The garage door rumbled as it opened. It rumbled again as it closed. Linda entered the kitchen, her blond hair dark with sweat. She looked fit in her running pants. John smiled at his wife, taking in her subtle curves and angelic face. Linda ignored him and grabbed a bottled water from the fridge. She shut the fridge, twisted the cap, and took a long drink. She placed the half-empty bottle on the center island and glared at the roses.

John moved into her personal space. "You always look great in your workout gear."

She gestured to the roses, straight-faced. "You get a new girlfriend?"

John smirked. "Will you be my girlfriend? We could go steady."

She rolled her eyes. "What are you doing home so early?"

"I thought I could make dinner. I bought stuff for homemade pizzas."

Linda glanced inside the grocery bag. "You should've called me. We need milk for breakfast tomorrow."

"I can go by the store after dinner."

She sighed. "If you want."

John reached in the inside pocket of his suit jacket and removed a narrow felt-covered box about six inches long. "This is for you."

Linda took the box and opened it. The tennis bracelet sparkled with gold and diamonds.

Charlotte entered the kitchen. "Hi, Dad."

"Hey, sweetheart," John replied.

Charlotte looked much older than her fourteen years. She was curvaceous and forty pounds overweight. Her V-neck T-shirt left little to the imagination. "What's that?" she asked, looking at the bracelet.

"It's a gold and diamond tennis bracelet that I picked up for your mom," John said. "The jewelry store was cleaned out. Gold has gotten really expensive."

Linda shut the box and tossed it on the center island. "Take it back."

"I'll take it if you don't want it," Charlotte said.

"Charlotte, could you give your mom and I a minute alone?" John asked.

"You're gonna fight, aren't you?"

"No, we're fine."

"Whatever." Charlotte went upstairs.

With Charlotte out of earshot, John said, "I'm trying here. I really am."

"I told you I'd stick by you through the election, but after that I'm done. Nothing's changed."

John pinched the bridge of his nose and looked at Linda. "I want things to change. I want you. I know I screwed up, but I'll do anything to make it up to you."

"I'm going to take a shower."

John showed his palms. "That's it?"

"What do you want from me? You asked me to support you through the election, and that's what I'm doing."

John shook his head. "Get Charlotte some conservative clothes. The Internet'll eat her alive with those tight shirts."

91: Katie and Patsies and Martyrs

"Have you found anything?" Katie asked through the encrypted phone. "We're working on it," Zach replied. "There's been some cybersecurity upgrades. I'll let you know when we have something."

"The natives are restless. Hurry."

"I will." Zach disconnected the call.

Katie set her phone on her desk and scrolled through the comments of the last video George recorded before he was arrested.

> **Libtard Hater:** Why can't we have any real heroes? A fucking pedophile, that's just fucking great.

> **View all 674 replies**

> **Marxist Light:** I knew it. The poster child for ANCAPS fucks little boys. LMAO.

> **View all 890 replies**

> **Joe Treadwell:** Goddamn, people are stupid. The CIA tried to kill the man. The NSA has access to everyone's computer. You think they can't plant that shit?

> **Ophelia Ahearn**: It's not always a government conspiracy.

> **View all 183 replies**

> **Phil Kershaw**: I actually liked the guy. Another corrupt politician. So disappointed. ☹

Katie sighed and shut her laptop. A camera set on a tripod pointed at her desk. She powered it on, pressed Record, and returned to her desk.

She stared into the camera and said, "Thank you to everyone who donated to the George Chapman Legal Defense Fund. More important than the money is the loyalty and affection it shows for George. We had enough to make bail, and we believe we will have enough if and when George goes to trial. Any leftover funds will be disbursed to our approved charities.

"We're still compiling evidence to prove George's innocence. I know George is innocent, but I'm not asking you to take my word for it. I'm simply asking you to reserve judgment until we have all the facts. Please think about what we already know. George Chapman was shot by agents of the CIA. Immediate arrests were made and blame was placed on Anthony Calhoun, Luis Cabrera, and Ross Blevins of the Maoist Worker Party. All three of these men have verifiable alibis for their whereabouts at the time of the shooting. Despite no credible evidence beyond threats made on social media, these three men are being held in federal prison without bail. With the current backlogs of our legal system, their trial isn't set to begin until late 2023.

"If the CIA and the US government are willing to assassinate an American citizen for exercising his right to free speech, what's to stop them from defaming his character? Edward Snowden has already proven that the NSA has unrestricted access to our computers and phones. Planting child pornography and destroying a man's character is far more effective than making him a martyr. Please don't fall for the lies and propaganda. Please wait for the facts. Thank you."

92: Julie and PTSD

George thrashed in bed. Julie propped herself up, her eyes adjusting to the darkness. George was hyperventilating. Julie shook him lightly.

"Wake up, George. Wake up."

George pushed her away. "Help," he said. "Help me! Help me!"

"Wake up, George," she said as she moved closer.

His eyes fluttered. He stared at Julie; his breathing slowed.

"You were having a nightmare," Julie said, caressing his hand.

The knock at the door caused George to flinch.

"Are you guys okay?" Max asked through the door. "I heard George calling for help."

"Everything's fine, honey. Go back to bed."

"Are you sure?"

"Positive."

"Okay," Max said, still unsure.

"They were right here," George said. He lay on his back, shirtless, covered in a thin sheen of sweat.

Julie grabbed the towel from the bedside table and dried him. "You've had nightmares the past two nights now. You have PTSD. I know the symptoms."

"I know. I'm sorry."

Julie shook her head. "You have nothing to be sorry for. You've been through a terrible ordeal." She pecked him on the lips and lay facing him on her side, her head sharing his pillow. "We need to get you some help. If I make you an appointment to see someone, will you go?"

He nodded.

"I'm really worried about you," Julie said. "I feel like this election is too much right now. You say the word, and I'll tell Katie, 'It's over.'"

"It'll be over soon enough," George said, staring at the ceiling. "Three weeks."

"I'm looking forward to our lives having some sense of normalcy. I'm looking forward to marrying you." She lifted her head and kissed him soft and slow. She smiled as she pulled back. "Mostly I'm looking forward to spending the rest of my life with you."

His eyes were glassy.

Her smile evaporated.

He shook his head. "I can't."

"You can't what?" Julie asked with a furrowed brow.

"I can't marry you." He turned away from Julie and wiped his eyes.

Julie sat upright, her eyes wide. "Honey, you have to talk to me."

He sat up and shook his head.

She moved closer to him and held his hands. "Whatever it is, we'll deal with it together."

He rubbed his eyes with his thumb and index finger. "I'm ruined."

"You're not. We'll prove how you were framed."

He shook his head. "I don't care about that."

"Then what, honey?" She inched closer, her eyes searching his. "I need you to talk to me so I can help you."

He hung his head, staring at the bed as he said, "I have an HIV test in a few weeks." He cleared his throat. "There's a good chance … I've been infected."

Julie put her hand to her chest, slack-jawed. "The men who attacked you … they …"

George nodded his hanging head. "I can't forget. Not one detail."

Julie wrapped her arms around him. His body jolted as he sobbed, his face in her neck. A lump was lodged in her throat. She tried to hold the dam, to stop the flood, to be strong for George, but it was too much.

93: George and Cruelty

George was awakened by the smell of bacon. Shortly thereafter Julie entered their bedroom with breakfast on a tray.

"Good morning," Julie said, smiling.

George sat up in bed. "Smells good."

"I thought you might be hungry." Julie placed the tray in George's lap.

"Do you want some?"

Julie smiled again. "I already ate."

He looked at Julie. "Thank you."

"It's just breakfast."

"For everything."

She bent over and kissed him. "I love you." She stood, her hands on her hips like Wonder Woman. "I'm going to get my tea, and I'll sit with you."

He nodded and turned his attention to the scrambled eggs with caramelized onions, bacon, toast, raspberries, and herbal tea.

A couple of minutes later, the doorbell rang. George listened, his stomach churning his breakfast. He relaxed as he heard Katie's voice. George resumed eating his breakfast. Outside the bedroom door, he heard Katie and Julie talking in hushed whispers.

"There's a video that you and George should see," Katie said.

"Give him some time," Julie said.

"I don't want him to see this on the Internet without preparation," Katie said. "Or *you* for that matter."

"Maybe tomorrow. He needs a break from all this, and so do I."

"Do you know what really happened?"

"Yes."

"All of it? What they did to him?"

"Do you?"

"It's on the video."

Julie gasped. "Oh, no."

"Julie," George called out. Julie opened the bedroom door. "I wanna see it."

Julie frowned at Katie, then looked at George. "I don't think this is a good idea."

"I read that if you relive a trauma over and over again, you can become desensitized to it."

Katie entered the room with red-rimmed eyes, her iPad in hand. Julie was right behind her with her herbal tea. George moved the tray from his lap to the bedside table.

"Did you watch it?" George asked Katie.

"There's been an outpouring of support for you," Katie replied. "We've had over a million dollars in donations come in since—"

"Did you watch it?"

"Not the part," Katie said, dropping her gaze. She looked up. "It exonerates you. People are irate that they did this to you. I don't want to sound crass, but this is huge for the campaign."

Julie shook her head. "Katie, don't."

"Sorry." Katie handed the iPad to Julie. "You two watch it. I'll be in my condo if you want to talk." Katie hugged George and whispered in his ear. "I'm so sorry." Katie left the room.

Julie sat on the edge of the bed, next to George. She opened the iPad and played the video on the screen.

A man dressed in all black appeared, wearing a Guy Fawkes mask. "Greetings, we are Anonymous," he said in a digitized voice. "This is an open message to the CIA, NSA, FBI, the puppet President Henry Reynolds, and his Secretary of State Arthur Coleman. We know what you and your people stand for. We do not forget, and we do not forgive. We are tired of your lies, and we are tired of the evil you represent."

The video moved closer to the man, showing him from the shoulders up. "We know that you're afraid of men like George Smith Chapman and the thousands of freedom fighters who you've rounded up with the SAFE Act." The video cut to footage of various activists being removed from their homes by the FBI. This went on for six minutes.

The video showed the masked figure again. "We know that child pornography was planted on George Chapman's computer by the NSA. Your lies can't protect you anymore. We are everywhere, and we know everything." An email appeared on the screen.

From: ADMLewisSCoffey@NSA.gov
To: MichaelHewitt@FBI.gov

Subject: George Smith Chapman

Director Hewitt,

Evidence is implanted. Operation Discredit is ready for search, seizure, and arrest. Move immediately as we expect a warning to reach Chapman shortly.

This email is encrypted but destroy immediately, using proper protocols. We believe there to be information leaks that we cannot pinpoint.

Admiral Lewis S. Coffey
Director of the National Security Agency

The video showed the masked man. "You tried to kill George Chapman and blame it on a group of patsies. This failed attempt only solidified our resolve against the criminal enterprise called the US government. Outright murder would only serve to martyr him now, so you tried to discredit the man with the foul stench of a child predator. But that wasn't enough. You wanted to punish him in the most inhumane way possible. You wanted to break him. What you are about to see is disturbing."

The video cut to footage of the hallway of the detention center. Twelve guards escorted three prisoners to a prison cell. They uncuffed the three prisoners and opened the cell door. The video showed the inside of the darkened cell. It was dim, the only light coming from the hall, but the video was clear. There was no audio. George shot out of the bunk, his hands bound in front of him.

"I'm sorry," Julie said, standing from the bed. "I can't watch it." She hurried from the room.

The video showed George on his knees. Genitals were blurred, but the movements left little to the imagination. It showed the massive man in terror, holding his blurry, bloody stump of a penis. The guards let the massive man out of the cell, while the other two men pummeled George into submission. George was stripped, strangled, and raped. One of the men whispered something in George's ear.

Without sound on the video, and the man's mouth obscured by George's head, the world wouldn't know what he had said. George, on the other hand, couldn't forget. *You got HIV now, faggot.* Afterward the two rapists turned George over on his back. This was the first definitive view of George's face. The men peed on his body, his face, and in his mouth.

George, watching himself, was agitated, fists clenched, heart pounding, sweat beading.

The video cut to the morning, the cell bright with fluorescent light. George lay on his back, naked from the waist down, his genitals blurred, and his eye swollen shut. Shit stains covered the walls and floor near the toilet. Finally, mercifully, the video cut to the masked man.

"People are waking up to your evil ways. No longer will the American people bow to your feet and call you heroes. No longer will the American people think their government is for the people and by the people. We are Anonymous. We do not forgive, and we do not forget. Expect us."

94: John and the Second Presidential Debate

John stood behind the stage backdrop, waiting for his cue. He watched Lisa Kelly on the monitor. She sat behind a desk in front of the stage, wearing a black dress and a heap of makeup.

"Good evening. I'm Lisa Kelly with WNN. I'd like to welcome you to the University of Kansas in Lawrence and the second presidential debate between Arthur Coleman and John Bradley, sponsored by the Commission on Presidential Debates. Tonight's debate will be in a town hall format which gives voters an opportunity to ask the candidates questions directly. I may ask follow-up questions, but this night belongs to the voters in this room and the voters across the country at home.

"The people on this stage were chosen by the Gallup Organization. They're all from the Lawrence area, and they told Gallup that they haven't committed to a candidate yet. They each came here with questions they wanted to ask, and I saw these questions for the first time this morning. My team and I from WNN are the only ones who have seen the questions. Both candidates will have two minutes to respond to each audience or online question. We hope to get to as many questions as we can, so we've asked the audience not to slow things down with any applause, except for now."

Lisa Kelly smiled, her teeth bright white. "Ladies and Gentlemen, the Republican nominee for president Arthur Coleman and the Democratic nominee for president John Bradley."

John was given his cue by a pretty young thing. He winked at her and strutted to a muted applause from the forty voters onstage. John smiled and waved at them, then smiled and waved at the empty seats in the auditorium. He shook hands with Art center stage, then took his place behind his podium. The Commission on Presidential Debates had decided against a crowd. WNN had filmed the crowd yesterday, to be dubbed in. That was probably a smart move. The protesters outside had to be controlled by the National Guard. The last thing they needed was another debate ruined by protestors in the audience.

The stage and backdrop were covered in Smurf-blue and accented with white stars, red stripes, and of course the eagle crest that formed the Great Seal of the United States.

John made eye contact and nodded at the undecided voters seated onstage. They were arranged on each side of the stage, sitting in padded wooden chairs on three tiered rows. *What a bunch of old fat fucks. I bet not one person is under forty on this stage. Is this the best Kansas has to offer? Probably.*

These people *were* essential. It was a town hall debate after all. They had passed exhaustive background checks. No shenanigans were expected with this crowd.

John waved at his family in the VIP seating just offstage. The kids waved back, Charlotte and Bobby smiling, Ellen reserved—still pouting from John's reprimand for making fun of a waitress. Actually it wasn't a problem that she had made fun of a waitress. The problem was that someone had recorded it. Linda looked through John, impassive. He hoped the cameras didn't pick up on her thinly veiled displeasure. Art Coleman was to his left, behind an identical podium, waving at his family.

The applause dissipated, and the candidates turned their attention to the moderator. "Thank you very much for being here," Lisa said. "We'll begin with a question from one of our town hall members. Secretary Coleman, you won the coin toss, so you'll go first. Our first question comes from Pamela Yarborough."

A short white woman with brown hair and pudgy arms stood from her seat. Secretary Coleman approached her, a microphone in hand. She spoke into her mike, reading from the card and never lifting her gaze. "Secretary Coleman and Congressman Bradley, I've been following your campaigns for the past three months and not once have I heard your definitive stance on abortion. You both dodge the issue. I would like to know if you are for or against abortion. Thank you." She sat in her seat.

Secretary Coleman nodded. He looked sharp in his dark suit and red power tie. His tight curls were the color of dirty snow. "Is it Mrs. Yarborough?" he asked.

Pamela nodded.

Arthur smiled. "Mrs. Yarborough, you're absolutely right. I haven't stated my position definitively. This is not out of malice or avoidance. This campaign has been particularly concerned with other issues, such as the war and the economy. My stance on abortion is that it should be illegal. I am an advocate for legal abortions when medically necessary to protect the health of the mother. I do believe a child to be a life at conception. If you asked any pregnant mother-to-be if that child growing in their belly was a life, I think we all know what the answer will be. Does that answer your question, Mrs. Yarborough?"

The woman nodded with a grin.

Arthur returned to his podium.

"You have two minutes, Congressman Bradley," Lisa said.

John strutted toward the woman. "Mrs. Yarborough, do you have children?"

"Yes, two boys," the woman replied.

John smiled. "I have two girls and a boy. I'm proud to say that they're here today." He motioned toward his kids. "I think it's safe to say that you and I know the greatest joy in life, which is being a parent and raising children."

The woman nodded enthusiastically.

"I do not think abortion is a good thing. I think it must be about the most traumatic thing a woman may choose to do. I think we should provide women with education and support, so we can limit abortions to the absolute minimum. Having said that, I do not think that I should have the power to legislate what women do with their bodies. What's next? Do I ban contraception? Women have fought long and hard in this country for equal rights. I don't intend to go backward."

The woman was frowning.

Fucking cow. John returned to his podium.

"We have a question from the Internet," Lisa said. "Tessa Baker from Florida says, 'The price of gasoline is well over five dollars now. My electric bill is double what it was a few years ago, and my grocery bill is sky-high. What do you plan to do about this inflation?'" Lisa looked at John. "Congressman Bradley, you have two minutes."

"Thank you, Tessa," John said, standing behind his podium. "I appreciate your question, and I understand your concerns. I won't sugarcoat it. You're absolutely right. Inflation has been awful under President Reynolds and the Republican-controlled congress. They've overspent on warfare and underspent on things we need, like renewable energy. As president, I'll eliminate the endless wars, saving nearly one trillion dollars a year. I'll use the surplus on renewable energy produced at home and to help Americans who are suffering and struggling. We'll have cheaper energy, more jobs, no war, and food for Americans in need. There's absolutely no excuse for the richest country in the world to have people starving."

"Secretary Coleman," Lisa said.

"Mrs. Baker, many factors create inflation," Arthur said. "It's not nearly as simple as the congressman professes. The war in Iran has contributed to the spike in gas prices, but worldwide supply and demand is the main culprit. With Iran under control now, we expect fuel prices to regulate. If we were to simply end the war, as Congressman Bradley suggested, it would result in destabilization, and four million barrels of oil per day would be wiped off the world market. Our efforts in Iran have made a bad situation better, not a bad situation worse. As far as renewable energy, I'm all for supporting cost-effective solutions that can compete in the free market. Unfortunately renewable energy isn't a magic cure for our energy woes. It is far more expensive than traditional sources. As president, I will work to reduce the cost of renewable energy. At the same time I will help our domestic energy companies provide the energy we desperately need at competitive prices." Arthur nodded at Lisa.

"Our next question comes from one of our town hall members," Lisa said. "Leonard Brock."

Leonard stood from his seat, barrel-chested and balding. He read from his card. "Secretary Coleman and Congressman Bradley, how do you explain your attack ads on George Chapman right before—" His microphone went dead. The man shouted, "Right before he was arrested on fake charges. You knew they would discredit him!"

WNN cut to a commercial.

A handful of police officers stormed the stage.

Leonard moved toward the candidates. "You knew!" He was tackled. On the ground, center stage, Leonard shouted, "You're both full of shit!"

95: Katie and the Opportunity

Katie sat at her desk, typing on her laptop. Her cell phone chimed. It was a number she didn't recognize so she sent it to voice mail. *Damn telemarketers.* She went back to her laptop. The phone chimed again, same number. She scowled and sent the call to voice mail again. She turned her ringer to Vibrate and went back to her work. Her cell vibrated across her desk, just as annoying as the chime. It was the same number. She swiped right.

"What the fuck is your problem?" Katie asked.

"Is this Katie Fitzgerald?" the man asked.

"I'm so sick of telemarketers. I'm on the Do Not Call List, yet you continue to call."

"This is Mike Downs, Co-Chairman for the Commission on Presidential Debates."

Katie knitted her brow. "Who?"

"Mike Downs, Co-Chairman for the Commission on Presidential Debates."

"You're Mike Downs?"

"Yes, ma'am."

"Bullshit."

He laughed a hearty laugh. "I've just replied to one of the many emails you've sent me over the past few months, so you can verify my identity."

Katie checked her email and found one from MikeDowns@CPD.org. She was slack-jawed and speechless. It was an invitation to the final debate.

"Are you still there?" Mike asked.

"Yes," Katie replied.

"We're hosting the final presidential debate at the University of Southern

California. We'd like to extend an invitation to George Smith Chapman. We'll provide hotel accommodations and airfare via a private jet."

"Why? Why now?"

"Well, we try to listen to the people. The people want to see George debate, and, quite frankly, so do I."

What a load of bullshit. "Will there be an audience?"

"We expect to pack the Galen Center. It'll be about ten thousand people."

"What if we wanted to debate without an audience?"

"Not an option. After the audience debacles we've had, we're trying to give them what they want. If he won't debate with an audience, we'll make sure the audience knows that the invitation was rescinded."

"Need I remind you that George was shot the last time he appeared in front of a large audience?"

"We'll have metal detectors at the entrances and heavy security. Furthermore, given the current climate, Congressman Bradley and Secretary Coleman have more to fear than Mr. Chapman."

"I'm assuming you'll send me the rules and specifics for the debate."

"Does that mean he'll participate?"

"Will George receive equal airtime to Coleman and Bradley?"

"The rules apply equally to all."

"Send me the specifics, and I'll talk it over with George."

"Will do. Thank you, Miss Fitzgerald."

"Thank you." Katie disconnected the call, rose from her chair, and ran from her condo.

David's eyes widened as he saw Katie exit in a hurry.

"I'm fine," Katie said to him as she hurried past.

She banged on George's condo. Shawn opened the door, and Katie rushed inside.

"What's wrong?" Shawn asked.

"Nothing," she replied over her shoulder. She found George, Julie, and Max, eating lunch at the dining room table. The three of them looked at Katie and her crooked grin. "We've been invited to the final presidential debate in two weeks."

"Holy shit," Max said.

"Language," Julie said.

George hung his head.

"Did you hear me?" Katie asked. "You're in the debate. This is huge. They'll fly us to California on a private jet and put us up in a hotel."

George exhaled and looked at Katie. "I can't do it."

"Yes, you can."

George shook his head. "How big is the crowd?"

Katie cleared her throat. "Only nine thousand or so."

"They'll pack that audience with Bradley and Coleman supporters," George said.

"You'll win 'em over."

"It's a trap. They know I have stage fright."

"Not necessarily."

"Everyone who saw my attempted assassination on video saw me pass out. Read the comments. They noticed."

"I'll get you the best stage-fright therapist in the country," Katie said. "We can practice. We'll do mock debates with huge crowds. I bet people would pay to attend."

"It's too much, too soon," Julie said.

"It can be done," Katie said.

"In two weeks?"

"This is about humiliating me," George said. "People've been protesting, especially since the Anonymous video. It's a brilliant plan actually. They give the public what they want, knowing that I'll freeze and show how unfit I am to lead. Even if I don't freeze, I guarantee you that Bradley and Coleman already know the questions. I'll be going in blind."

"But you don't need to know the questions ahead of time," Max said. "You have a freaking computer for a brain."

"Max is right," Katie said.

"You can do it, George. I know you can," Max said.

George rubbed his temples.

"If we don't debate," Katie said, "they'll make sure the world knows that we turned down the invitation."

George hit his fist on the table, rattling the plates. "I don't care what the world thinks." George stood from the table and marched outside, slamming the front door behind him.

Wide-eyed, Katie and Max watched him leave in stunned silence.

"I've never seen him so angry," Katie said.

Julie glowered at Katie. "He's not a robot. How do you think he should act after what he's been through?"

"I'm sorry."

"He needs more time. He just started therapy."

"There isn't more time." Katie took a deep breath. "This is bigger than what happened to him. He has a chance to tell the whole world the truth. He may not think he can handle the debate now, and maybe he can't, but he'll regret it for the rest of his life if he doesn't try."

Julie blew out a breath and stood from the table. She looked at Katie with her jaw set tight. "I'll talk to him, but, if he says no, that's it." She marched out the front door in search of George.

"Do you think he'll do it?" Max asked.

"He'll come around." Katie stood and started for the door.

"Where are you going?"

She turned to Max. "To rent a theater and to find the best stage-fright therapist in the country."

* * *

Katie sat in the front row of the rented theater, Julie on one side; Dr. Joyner, the stage-fright specialist, on the other. They had packed one thousand people inside. George stood onstage behind a podium, pale and shaking like a leaf. Stand-ins for Bradley and Coleman stood behind the other podiums. The Coleman stand-in spoke to the audience.

"Anarchism might be a great idea in theory," fake-Coleman said, "but without the US government, nobody would deter, arrest, or prosecute burglars, child molesters, rapists, and murderers. Nobody would protect the American people from terrorism or invasion. Anarchism is a quaint utopian idea but has no business in serious political discourse."

Katie thought, *Damn, this guy's good.*

The moderator sat at a desk front and center, just offstage. She was a dead ringer for Corrinne Stevens, the future debate moderator. She said, "Mr. Chapman, you have two minutes to respond."

George's face had gone from pale to green.

I think he's going to puke.

George turned and walked offstage. You could've heard a pin drop, but what you heard instead was George retching. Katie, Julie, and Dr. Joyner stood from their seats.

Dr. Joyner was a thin, swarthy man with a full head of gray. "Julie, would you stay here, please?" he asked.

Julie sat down. "Okay."

Dr. Joyner continued. "When George comes back out, smile at him and nod with him as if you're having a conversation."

Julie nodded, her brow furrowed.

Katie approached the moderator. "Tell the audience to please wait patiently. That George will return shortly."

The moderator made the announcement as Katie and Dr. Joyner hurried backstage. George was bent over a trash can. He spat and stood.

"You okay?" Katie asked.

He shook his head. "I can't do this."

"You can," Dr. Joyner said. "The fact that you're throwing up just means that we've set up a good practice test—"

"One I'm failing." George moved to the water fountain along the wall and rinsed his mouth.

When George turned around, Katie handed him a container of Tic Tacs.

"Thanks," he said as he tapped a handful of Tic Tacs into his palm. George popped the mints into his mouth and handed the half-full container back to Katie.

"Remember, the key to overcoming stage fright is to prepare, practice, and breathe," Dr. Joyner said. "You're prepared, and we're practicing. Now do your breathing exercises."

George lifted his arms over his head and took slow deep breaths. Then he put his hands on his lower back, pushed his hips forward, and took more deep breaths. He stood up straight, his color returning.

"Feel better?" Katie asked.

George ran his hand through his dark hair. "The breathing exercises help, but I can't tell an audience, 'Hey, hold on while I activate my hypothalamus to trigger a relaxation response.'"

Dr. Joyner chuckled. "When you go back out there—"

"What do you mean, go back out there?" George's dark eyes were wide. "I'm done for today."

"Listen, George. Just try one thing. If it doesn't work, we'll call it a day."

George nodded.

"When you go back out there, look at Julie and only Julie. Answer the questions, like you're having a conversation with her."

"You're supposed to look around when you're giving a speech."

"Don't worry about that right now," Dr. Joyner said. "Talk to Julie. Don't worry about anyone else."

George frowned.

"Just try it. Take whatever time you need here, then come back out and talk to Julie."

Katie and Dr. Joyner went back to the audience and sat next to Julie. The audience whispered to each other, but not a single soul left.

"Is he okay?" Julie asked Dr. Joyner.

"He's fine," Dr. Joyner replied.

"What did you tell him?"

"I told him not to worry about all these people, to just talk to you."

Julie raised her eyebrows to Katie, as if to say, *Where did you find this quack?*

Katie lifted a shoulder in response.

George returned to his podium, and the audience gave him a standing ovation. After a moment, they sat and quieted.

"Mr. Chapman," the moderator said, "would you like Secretary Coleman to repeat his argument?"

George opened his mouth, but nothing came out. He hung his head and pinched the bridge of his nose. He stared at Julie; she smiled and nodded her encouragement. Finally he spoke, his voice shaky. "No, thank you. Secretary Coleman said, 'Without the US government, nobody would deter, arrest, or prosecute burglars, child molesters, rapists, and murderers. Nobody would protect the American people from terrorism or invasion.'"

George paused and looked away from Julie for the first time. "Let me get this straight. We need the US government to rob us, to imprison us, and to send us to war to keep us safe?"

96: Julie and the Test Results

Julie sat on the couch in the waiting room, responding to a text from Katie.

Julie: That's great news!!!!! I'll tell him.

It was more of a sitting area than a waiting room. There was no receptionist. It was quiet except for the grandfather clock ticking in the background. George was seeing a therapist who practiced out of her home. With the media and the paparazzi now documenting his every move, he had chosen an especially discreet therapist.

George showed marked improvement over the past few weeks. Therapy had undoubtedly helped. He still had nightmares, but they were less frequent. The HIV test still hung over them like the Sword of Damocles. It was a secret only Julie and George's doctors knew about.

The office door opened. George appeared with his therapist, Ivy. Julie stood and walked across the Oriental rug toward them. Ivy was a bit of a hippie with her long skirt and beaded jewelry.

"Same time next week?" Ivy asked.

"I'll see you then," George replied.

"Hi, Julie," Ivy said with a wave and a smile.

Julie and George exited the house. As they were walking to the car, Julie said, "I have some great news."

"Yeah?" George replied.

George climbed into the driver's seat of the Honda, Julie in the passenger's seat.

"Katie texted me while you were talking to Ivy. The state dropped the charges against you, and the prison guards and inmates have been indicted."

George shook his head. "They didn't drop the charges because it's the right thing to do. They dropped the charges because they want this thing to go away." George gripped the steering wheel, his knuckles white. "Those prison guards and those inmates were told to do what they did. They're scapegoats. If anyone cared about justice, the people who ordered the attack would've also been indicted. The state's just trying to convince the public that the legal system's fair. It's not."

"You're right, but it is good that they'll pay for what they did."

George scowled. "It doesn't change a damn thing."

"I'm sorry, honey."

George exhaled heavy. "You're right. It is good that they dropped the charges. I'm just worried about the test."

"What did Ivy say about it?"

"She said that, even if it's positive, many people live for decades with HIV. She wants me to call her after we get the results."

From Ivy's home office, they drove to the hospital.

"I feel like I'm ninety, shuttling from doctor's appointment to doctor's appointment," George said.

Julie put her hand on his leg. "It won't be forever."

They drove through the suburban sprawl. Julie gazed out the window, admiring the orange, yellow, and red leaves of the occasional maple, oak, or hickory. She turned back to George.

"Have you made up your mind on transportation to the debate? Katie mentioned that the private jet's still an option."

"I don't wanna accept anything from them. If you wanna go on the private jet, you're welcome to."

Julie frowned. "There's no way I'm going on that jet without you." She pursed her lips. "I am worried about your safety. Shawn and David think it's a terrible idea to fly coach."

"I think we're both far safer with lots of civilians around us. The more witnesses the better. We'll have five guys with us for security."

George parked in the hospital lot.

Julie squeezed his thigh. "Whatever happens, we'll deal with it."

He nodded, gazing out the windshield.

"Try to think positive," Julie said.

George undid his seat belt. "Let's get this over with."

* * *

Julie sat next to George, across from the doctor. She held George's hand in anticipation. The Japanese doctor sat behind his desk, his hands clasped together. He glanced at the paperwork in front of him. The doctor looked at George, straight-faced. Julie's stomach clenched, anticipating the metaphorical gut punch.

"Mr. Chapman, your STD screening looks very good," Dr. Kushida said.

Julie's shoulders slumped; her face relaxed.

The doctor continued. "You tested negative for chlamydia, gonorrhea, syphilis, herpes, and hepatitis." The doctor paused. "As you know, HIV is a little trickier to test only a few weeks after the possible exposure. We tested your blood with a viral load test. The viral load test looks for HIV DNA directly in your blood as opposed to the combined antibody and antigen test which tests for a protein produced by your body in response to the virus. I'm very happy to tell you that we did not detect the HIV virus in your blood."

Julie breathed a sigh of relief and smiled.

George nodded, his face neutral.

"This is excellent news," Dr. Kushida said, "but we're not out of the woods yet. Viral load tests are not as effective at diagnosing HIV as the combined antibody and antigen test. We need to test you again at one month from exposure. At that time, we'll test for the protein response. This will give us a 95 percent accuracy. Then we'll test again at three months. In the meantime, continue to take your medication."

"If I test negative at one month and three months, will you be certain that I'm not infected?" George asked.

"Yes, 100 percent certain," the doctor said.

"You said that the one-month test is 95 percent accurate. How accurate is the viral load test?"

"It's not an approved HIV detection test, but I've seen 80 percent accuracy."

"So, there's a very good chance he's *not* infected?" Julie asked.

"It is likely that he's *not* infected," the doctor said, "but I cannot say with certainty at this time. Do either of you have any more questions?"

"I don't," George said, glancing at Julie.

Julie shook her head.

"Thank you, Dr. Kushida." George stood from his seat.

The doctor stood, and they shook hands over the desk. "You're very welcome."

"Yes, thank you, Doctor," Julie said, standing, shaking hands with the doctor too.

"Good luck this Saturday," Dr. Kushida said to George.

George smirked. "Thanks, I'm gonna need it."

In the hospital hallway, Julie hugged George. He squeezed tight, with the force of a formerly condemned man.

"I'm so happy for you *and* us," Julie said, as they disengaged.

His face was stoic.

"Aren't you happy?" Julie asked.

"I am, but I'm tempering my enthusiasm," George replied. "Like Dr. Kushida said, 'We're not out of the woods yet.'"

"Are you sure that's it?"

He paused for a moment. "I'm nervous about Saturday."

"You were really relaxed in the last practice debate. You'll be great."

He exhaled. "Everyone says that, and I appreciate it, but I might not be great. I might be terrible. I might projectile vomit on the people in the front row. Better yet, I'll aim for Congressman Bradley."

Julie laughed, covering her mouth. "I'm sorry. I know it's not funny."

George chuckled. "I suppose it is."

"Whatever happens, I love you."

George hugged her again. "I love you too."

97: George and Percy

"Are you nervous?" the man asked.

George and Julie were in a 747 airliner, sitting in the front row of coach. Shawn, David, and three other security guards stood nearby, scanning the passengers as they boarded and stowed their luggage.

George smiled at the man and his wife from the aisle seat. "Nervous would be an understatement."

"Well, good luck," the man said.

"We're gonna vote for you," the wife said.

"I appreciate that," George said.

The man turned and glanced at the crowd queueing behind him. "We should let these other people talk to him," he said to his wife.

A dark-haired woman approached. "Oh, my God, my husband would freak out! He loves you. I prefer Congressman Bradley." The crowd behind her booed. She turned around with a scowl. "It's still America, right? I can like whoever I want." She turned back to George. "Will you sign my ticket stub?"

After signing the ticket, George was mobbed in all directions. He posed for pictures with his fellow passengers. He shook hands; he received hugs and kisses on the cheek. George said thank-you at least one hundred times. Julie was also mobbed, answering questions in his stead, with many inquiries about the status of their relationship.

"Where did you two meet?"

"Are you married?"

"Engaged?"

"How did he propose?"

"Oh, that's so sweet."

"My boss hates George. He says he's trying to destroy the government. I said, 'That's right. He is.'"

George was occupied by a bodybuilder with a fanny pack and loose cotton pants.

"They're both a-holes," the bodybuilder said. "They don't know what it's like for regular people in this country. You got my vote."

"Thank you."

A young couple with a five-year-old girl approached. The girl had pigtails, a pink backpack, and a worn teddy bear.

"Mr. Chapman, we just wanted to wish you good luck," the father said.

"Thank you. Please call me George."

"I'm Craig, and this is my wife, Belinda." George shook hands with the man and his wife. "And this is Lizzie," Craig said with his hand on his daughter's shoulder.

"That's a nice-looking bear you have there," George said to the girl.

The girl looked at her bear, then to George. "You can't have him," Lizzie said. "He's my protector."

George and Julie laughed.

"It's good to have a protector," George said. "He's my protector." George pointed to Shawn, standing with his arms crossed.

Lizzie looked at Shawn with narrowed eyes. "He looks mean."

"He's just a big teddy bear."

Shawn struggled to restrain his grin.

Lizzie turned to her mother. "He can have my new bear." She shrugged off her little backpack and unzipped it on the floor. She removed a small stuffed bear the size of a man's fist and handed it to George.

"Is this for me?" George asked.

"His name's Percy. My daddy said you're scared of stages. Percy will protect you from the stages."

Julie, Lizzy's parents, and the crowd tried to contain their laughter. Smart phones recorded the exchange for posterity.

George smiled at the girl. "This was very nice of you, Lizzie. Thank you. I think you're right. I think Percy will protect me."

"I'm right a lot, you know."

"I hope you are."

"You have to kiss Percy, so he knows that you love him."

Camera phones clicked as George kissed the bear.

Stewards and stewardesses herded the crowd. "Please find your seats," they said.

The loudspeaker clicked on. "This is Captain Buckley speaking. Please take your seats. We'll be taking off shortly. I'm sure Mr. Chapman needs his rest. As your captain, I can't publicly support any one candidate, but, as an American citizen, I will say one thing." The pilot paused. "George 2020."

The passengers cheered.

98: John and Slicker Than Deer Guts

"This has been disastrous," John said.

Frank nodded. "Chapman's slicker than deer guts on a doorknob."

John opened his mouth and shut it. *I really don't need your fucking redneck wisdom right now.*

The two men gathered in the sitting area of John's suite at the Four Seasons in Beverley Hills. They sat across from each other at a round table, John's breakfast between them, half-eaten, and getting cold.

"That goddamn video," John said. "How the hell did they get footage from the detention center? And the email from Coffey to Hewitt? If the head of the FBI and the NSA don't have privacy, none of us do."

"At some point there'll have to be mass arrests," Frank said. "Otherwise this country could go up in smoke."

"We should've stayed out of it." John shook his head, scowling. "We should've stuck with our original plan, but we jumped on the bandwagon with Art and the negative campaigning against Chapman, and now we look like we were in on it."

"Hindsight's twenty-twenty. We're still neck and neck with Art. I suspect this debate'll put us over the top."

John huffed. "The questions are biased in favor of Art."

"Technically they're meant to be biased against Chapman, but, yeah, they are slightly more favorable to Art, but he doesn't have the charisma you do. He's too stiff with the audience, too out of touch. We'll be fine. Just don't go negative with Chapman. It'll make you look like a bully. And he has the sympathy of the nation right now."

99: Katie and Game Time

Katie paced in the training room of the Galen Center. The room would normally be filled with college basketball stars getting their ankles taped, but today it was the waiting area for Team Chapman. Bradley and Coleman were in the home and visiting locker rooms. George lay on the training room table, fully dressed in the first suit he'd ever owned. A towel was over his face to block out the harsh fluorescent lighting. Julie sat in the chair next to him, Dr. Joyner on the other side of him. Julie looked like she was in mourning, with her black dress and her face twisted in sympathetic anguish.

"He was around all those people at the airport and on the plane," Julie said to Dr. Joyner. She turned to George. "George, honey, is it sickness or nerves?"

George removed the towel from his face. He was pale. "It's nerves."

"George, you need to get up and do your breathing exercises," Dr. Joyner said.

Katie approached the end of the table. "You've been killing it in the practice debates. You'll be fine."

"That was a thousand people who liked me," George said. "This is ten thousand who don't." He placed the towel back over his face.

Max entered the room, holding a bottled water. He handed it to Julie. Max looked sharp in his dark blue suit, his blond hair jelled.

"Do you want some water?" Julie asked George.

"I might throw it up," George replied.

"I have something to show you, in private," Max whispered to Katie.

"We'll be right back," Katie said.

Katie led Max to the training room office and shut the door.

"What's up?" Katie asked.

Max tapped on his phone and handed it to Katie. "Read it," he said.

A WikiLeaks article entitled "Final Debate Rigged." Katie skimmed it. John and Art had received the questions ahead of time. *We figured that much.* The questions are biased against George. *That too.* The audience was chosen by the DNC and the RNC. *That too.*

"There's nothing in this article that we didn't expect," Katie said.

"You don't think we should show George?" Max asked.

"We can't do anything about it so why bring it up."

"He might wanna know."

"He's hanging by a thread. Why make him more upset for no reason?"

"Okay."

They returned to George, Julie, and Dr. Joyner. George was still flat on the table, the towel over his face.

"Is everything all right?" Julie asked.

"Everything's fine," Katie replied.

A young man wearing a headset entered the training room. "Two minutes," he said and left the room.

"Time to get up," Dr. Joyner said to George.

George removed the towel from his face. He was still pale, with dark circles under his eyes. He sat up with the speed of an octogenarian. George removed his jacket. "Is it hot in here?" he asked.

"A little," Katie replied. "It's from the whirlpool."

George removed his tie.

"What are you doing?" Katie asked.

"Taking off my shirt," George replied. "I'm starting to sweat through."

"We don't have an extra shirt."

"He can have mine," Max said.

"Thanks, Max," George said.

Max removed his jacket, tie, and button-down. He took off his T-shirt and handed it to George. Max dressed without an undershirt. George removed his sweat-ringed T-shirt and replaced it with Max's clean shirt. George slid off the table. He was wobbly on his feet as he dressed.

"Do your exercises," Dr. Joyner said. "You've prepared. You've practiced. Now you just have to breathe."

George raised his arms and took slow deep breaths.

"Remember, Julie will be in the front row," Dr. Joyner said. "All you have to do is talk to her."

George pushed his hips forward, his hands on his lower back. He took more deep breaths.

The young man with the headset opened the door again. "It's time," he said.

"We'll be right in front," Katie said. She hugged George for a moment. "You'll be great. I know it."

George forced a smile.

"You're ready," Dr. Joyner said.

George shook the doctor's hand.

"Good luck, George," Max said.

George extended his hand to shake, but Max hugged him. George patted him on the back. Max let go and stepped aside for his mother.

Julie hugged and kissed George. She whispered in his ear. He kissed her cheek and whispered a response.

Julie let go, and George trudged toward the door. The young man in the headset whisked him away.

They accosted Dr. Joyner.

"Why is he such a mess?" Julie asked.

"He hasn't been this bad since the first practice debate," Katie said.

"Is he gonna be okay?" Max asked.

Dr. Joyner shrugged. "I don't know. The stakes are higher, so the anxiety's higher."

100: Julie and the Surprise Guest

Julie, Katie, and Max were escorted into the arena. Julie gazed upward at the stadium seating and the massive four-sided video screen hanging from the ceiling. They were escorted toward the stage.

Like the previous debates, the stage was a sea of blue. Blue carpet with red trim and white stars. The backdrop was the same blue with red trim and white stars. Dead center of the backdrop was the eagle emblem that represented the Great Seal of the United States. Three podiums were set up this time, evenly spaced across the stage and facing the audience. Another massive video screen hung from the rafters above the backdrop. A desk was positioned in front of the podiums for the moderator. American flags, the size of Greyhound buses, hung from the set and framed the stage.

Julie, Katie, and Max were ushered to the front row. The first two rows were roped off and patrolled by police. The VIPs smiled and laughed and talked, shaking hands, congratulating themselves, and patting each other on the back. Julie recognized former president, Will Bradley. He spoke with Susan Sarandon and Tim Robbins. She recognized Congressman Bradley's wife and kids and Secretary Coleman's family from the first two debates.

The front rows were crawling with celebrities. Oprah Winfrey, Matt Damon, Arnold Schwarzenegger, Sean Penn, Roseanne Barr, and Charlize Theron. Jennifer Aniston was smiley as she talked to Angelina Jolie. But one man didn't fit in. He was sitting front row center, wearing a cheap suit, with nobody to talk to.

Julie and Max took their seats, while Katie mingled with the glitterati. Julie stared across the front row at the side of the old man's head. He had a whitish-gray buzz cut, wire glasses, and a square jaw. *Where have I seen him before?*

Julie turned to Max. "Do you know who that man is over there? The one sitting by himself with short white hair?"

Max looked at the man for a moment. "He looks familiar." Max's eyes widened. "Uh-oh."

"What?"

"If I tell you who he is, will you promise not to freak out?"

"I won't freak out. Who is he?"

"I think that's George's dad."

Julie's eyes were like saucers. "That son of a bitch." She stood and marched toward the man.

"Mom," Max called out in vain.

Julie stood over the retired colonel. He looked up at her, his wrinkled brow creased, and his eyes narrowed.

"What do you want?" he asked.

Julie pointed in his face. "You're a low-class, poor excuse for a human being, you know that? You don't deserve a son like George." The nearby glitterati were slack-jawed. Julie turned on her heels and marched to her seat.

"Who the hell do you think you are?" Colonel Chapman said to her back.

Max smirked at his mother as she sat down. "I thought you weren't going to freak out?"

"It needed to be said," Julie replied.

Katie sat next to Julie. "Who were you yelling at?"

"George's dad is over there. Probably the last person George wants to see."

"Shit. Maybe George won't see him."

The Galen Center was filled to capacity. A man spoke to the crowd through the audio system. "The final presidential debate will begin shortly. Please remember, no signs are allowed. Also please refrain from applauding, booing, or heckling during the debate. Anyone caught disturbing the debate will be promptly removed from the premises without a refund. Thank you."

Corrinne Stevens appeared on the large screen above the stage. She wore a blue gown that hugged her curves just enough to hint at her femininity. Her face was flawless with heavy makeup, and her dark hair was highlighted with a bit of brown. She sat at the desk in front of the podiums and adjusted her black-rim glasses.

Corrinne's voice emanated from the sound system. "Good evening from the University of Southern California and the Galen Center. I'm Corrinne Stevens, anchor for US News. I want to welcome you to the final presidential debate. The participants tonight are Arthur Coleman, John Bradley, and George Smith Chapman."

A few whistles came from the crowd as George was mentioned.

"This debate is sponsored by the Commission on Presidential Debates, a nonpartisan, nonprofit organization. The commission drafted tonight's format, and the rules have been agreed upon by the campaigns. This debate is ninety-minutes long. Each candidate will be given two minutes to answer questions and an additional two-minute rebuttal if the candidate so chooses.

"The questions are from a nationwide poll and have not been shared with the commission or the campaigns. The audience here in the room has agreed to remain silent so that we can focus on what the candidates are saying. I *will* invite you to applaud as I welcome the candidates. Republican nominee for president of the United States of America Arthur Coleman."

The crowd applauded. Secretary of State Coleman marched onstage from behind the backdrop. He waved at the crowd and his family with a wide smile.

Corrinne said, "Democratic nominee for president of the United States of America John Bradley."

The crowd applauded louder. Congressman Bradley strutted onstage, relaxed and at ease in tinsel town with his movie-star good looks and liberal populace. He waved at his family in the front row, then the crowd.

"And write-in candidate George Smith Chapman," Corrinne said.

Some whistles and shouts were heard, but the applause died down to a trickle when George didn't appear. Ten thousand people chattered about his absence. Julie looked at Katie. Katie shrugged. Finally George staggered onstage, looking ill, his eyes on the blue carpet. The crowd quieted as George met his competitors center stage. The candidates shook hands. They walked to their assigned podiums. Coleman was on the right, Bradley on the left, and George smack dab in the middle.

George held on to the edge of the podium with white knuckles, glaring at his father.

"Shit, he sees him," Katie said to Julie.

"How could he not? He's right in front of him," Julie replied.

"Secretary Coleman," Corrinne said, "you won the predebate coin toss, so you'll go first, followed by Congressman Bradley, who won the second coin toss. Let us begin." Corrinne paused and read from the stack of cards in front of her. "Please identify the cause of the energy crisis, and, as president, what will you do to remedy it?"

"Energy isn't simply about geology and science," Coleman said. "Energy is also about geopolitics. Much of the recent gas spike is because of OPEC lowering production to boost their profits. It's greed pure and simple, and I can assure you that my administration will apply the proper pressure to get those pumps flowing.

"In the early twenty-tens our domestic oil drillers saw a resurgence with shale oil and horizontal drilling. This is waning now because of heavy regulation. I will continue to support our domestic oil and gas drillers by opening vast territories of untapped energy from the Arctic to the vast tracts of offshore oil that's been off-limits. I will release the handcuffs from our innovative energy companies so they can provide the energy and jobs this economy so desperately needs."

"Congressman Bradley," Corrinne said, "same question. Please identify the cause of the energy crisis, and, as president, what will you do to remedy it?"

John smiled at the moderator. "Thank you, Corrinne." He surveyed the crowd for a moment. "Secretary Coleman's stuck in the past. First of all, much of the current crisis can be blamed on the constant wars in the Middle East. My first priority as president will be to end the wars and bring our brave soldiers home. Second, fossil fuels are a nonrenewable resource. We all know this. It's not controversial information, yet we continue to be hooked on dirty nonrenewable fuels. Why? Because we continue to give big oil and gas massive subsidies. Because our politicians are bought and paid for."

Bradley glanced at Secretary Coleman. "The Republicans will continue on our current path, which is clearly not working. Well, it's working for big oil and gas but not for the average person. I'm an advocate for supporting our domestic energy companies of the future—clean renewable energy, like solar and wind and geothermal. Electric car and battery technology companies like Tesla. We can't move forward if we continue to subsidize the past."

"I'd like to use my rebuttal," Coleman said.

"It's your rebuttal, Secretary Coleman," Corrinne replied. "You have two minutes."

"Congressman Bradley is incorrect in his assessment," Coleman said. "The war in Iran has had little effect on domestic oil supplies. Prior to the invasion, most of the Iranian oil was sold to China. Now more Iranian oil is flowing West. Second, all of our domestic energy companies are vital to our economy and way of life. I'm a big supporter of renewable energy, but I'm also a realist. Our economy has a tremendous appetite for energy, and we need all forms of energy. Furthermore, let us not forget that 80 percent of our energy is derived from oil, gas, and coal. *Eighty percent.* Solar, wind, and geothermal are still under 3 percent. I agree that we need to build our renewable energy infrastructure, but it won't happen freezing in the dark."

"I'd like to use my rebuttal," Congressman Bradley said.

"Why won't they let George talk?" Julie asked Katie.

"It's the format," Katie said. "If their statement's challenged, they can use their rebuttal immediately. I suspect they'll try to ignore George."

"In 1977, a watt of solar cost seventy-six dollars," Congressman Bradley said, "but today it's forty-eight cents. A gallon of gas was sixty-two cents in 1977. We all know it's quite a bit more expensive today." The crowd applauded.

"Please hold your applause," Corrinne said.

The crowd quieted.

Bradley continued. "Secretary Coleman's right that renewable energy still makes up a small portion of our energy sources, but he's missing the big picture. Solar power made up 41 percent of the *new* electricity generated last year. Clearly, renewable energy is the future. What are we waiting for?"

"Mr. Chapman," Corrinne said, "you have two minutes to tell us the cause and the solution to the energy crisis."

George stood there, gripping the podium. It looked like a strong wind could blow him over. He opened his mouth, but nothing came out.

Come on, honey.

George looked around the arena in a fog. He looked at Corrinne and his father just beyond her. He looked at Julie. She smiled.

"Mr. Chapman, do you forfeit this question?" Corrinne asked. "Mr. Chapman?"

George looked down at the podium, silent.

101: George and the Debate

George gripped the podium, woozy with ten thousand eyes on him. Bile rose from his stomach. He swallowed the hot bitterness. He stared at his father and felt nothing—not disdain and certainly not love. He found Julie. She smiled, her blue eyes filled with empathy. He remembered the last thing she said to him, the whisper that was their bond. *Whatever happens, I love you.*

"Mr. Chapman, do you forfeit this question?" Corrinne asked.

George thought about the people on the flight and in the airport. He was an imperfect messenger but their messenger nonetheless.

"Mr. Chapman?" Corrinne said.

George reached into the inside pocket of his jacket and placed Percy, the tiny teddy bear, on the podium facing him. The crowd laughed as the massive screens showed the bear.

"Mr. Chapman, do you forfeit this question?" Corrinne asked again, a hard edge to her voice.

George looked at the moderator. "No." His voice was shaky. "I'm just getting my bearings. ... This is Percy, by the way." George patted Percy's head. The audience laughed again. "Thank you, Lizzie, if you're watching." His eyes flicked to Julie, then back to Corrinne. "As you may know, I have terrible stage fright." His voice was steady now. "Of course that was the point, right? To humiliate me or anyone who stands up to those in power. That's why my father's sitting in the front row, right?"

"Mr. Chapman, you've already wasted over a minute."

"My father left when I was six," George said, glaring at the colonel. "The only thing I remember about him were the beatings."

The video screens showed his father. The crowd booed. The colonel clenched his jaw. The screens cut to Corrinne.

"Please refrain from booing." Corrinne looked at George, her face blank. "Mr. Chapman, your two minutes are up. We're moving on to the next question."

"I didn't get my rebuttal," George replied.

Corrinne narrowed her eyes for a split second. "You have two minutes."

"The world burns an Olympic-size swimming pool of oil every fifteen seconds." George nodded. "Think about that. An Olympic-size swimming pool of oil every *fifteen seconds*. Human beings have already exploited the easiest-to-obtain resources from this planet. We've drilled the lightest oil from the shallowest wells from West Texas to Saudi Arabia. We've burned the best anthracite coal with the highest energy content. We've exploited the richest mineral deposits. We've picked the low-hanging fruit so to speak. What's left?" George showed his palms, then rested them on the edges of the podium.

"What's left is expensive-to extract energy and expensive-to-extract minerals. Deepwater drilling, horizontal drilling, tar sands, and mines that stretch two miles beneath the surface. In 2009, the *Deepwater Horizon* drilled what, at the time, was the deepest well ever drilled at 35,000 feet. That's over *six miles* deep. It was an amazing feat of engineering, but why would British Petroleum risk their capital and the men who worked that rig if they could drill a well on land or in shallow water? They did it because the easy wells have already been drilled.

"Look. The energy crisis isn't a problem to be solved by government. The Republicans talk about lifting regulations, and the Democrats want to sell you on the idea that we'll be driving solar-powered cars to Walmart. Neither of them talk about the real problem of declining ore grades, declining energy returned on energy invested, and an economy that pushes growth at all costs, leading people to be overly consumptive, materialistic, and indebted, not to mention the environmental destruction. And for what? So bankers can continue to profit, and Wall Street can hit their quarterly earnings projections, and the government can increase their power and control over you.

"The solutions come with a rejection of materialism and a reconnection to nature—"

"Mr. Chapman, your time's up," Corrinne interjected.

"We need conservation, local food, local manufacturing, walkable communities and cities, earth-sheltered housing, rocket mass heaters, rail—"

"Mr. Chapman."

"Microhydro, wind, solar, a rejection of thin-air money, a rejection of Wall Street, a rejection of government, and an investment in our communities."

The crowd applauded.

"Please hold your applause," Corrinne said. "Mr. Chapman, your time's up."

102: John and Antiwar?

"Congressman Bradley," Corrinne said, "the invasion and occupation of Iran has been a controversial issue over the past year and a half. As president, how do you plan to manage the Iran War?"

"Thank you, Corrinne," John said. "That's an important question. I've been an outspoken critic of our militaristic adventures in the Middle East for quite some time. We spend over one trillion dollars a year on our military. That's a trillion with a *T*." John nodded. "We spend more on our military than the next eight countries *combined*. We have allies to the north and the south, and oceans between us to the east and west. This excessive militarism isn't necessary to keep us safe. As president, I *don't* plan to manage the Iran War." John paused, surveying the audience. "I plan to bring our troops home."

The crowd cheered. Corrinne waited for the applause to dissipate.

"Mr. Chapman, same question," Corrinne said. "You have two minutes."

George said, "The only reason Congressman Bradley's talking about bringing the troops home is because he thinks it'll get him elected. If Bradley were actually antiwar, why has he voted to approve the defense budget every single year he's been in congress? Then he has the arrogance to complain about defense spending."

John was pokerfaced. *Motherfucker.*

"Iran's not about nuclear weapons," George said, staring at Julie. "Just like Iraq wasn't about weapons of mass destruction. Iraq, Libya, Syria, Iran, they've all been about the petrodollar. In 1971, Nixon took us off the gold standard because he was overspending on warfare and welfare, and countries worldwide were exchanging their depreciating US dollars for appreciating gold, thereby draining the US vaults. Without gold backing, what would provide demand and, therefore, value to those infinite dollars being spent domestically and abroad? The petrodollar.

"In 1974, then Treasury Secretary Simon, President Nixon, and Secretary of State Kissinger convinced Saudi King Faisal to sell Saudi Arabia's oil only in dollars and then to recirculate his dollar profits into US treasury securities. In return, the US government offered military protection and weapons. With the Saudis on board, the other oil-producing nations wanted in. A year later, *all* of OPEC had agreed to the same deal.

"The petrodollar system has brought tremendous wealth and power to the United States and the central bankers. It's vital to the interests of the US government. Saddam Hussein referred to the US dollar as the 'currency of the enemy' and in 2000 began selling Iraqi oil in euros. We all know what happened next.

"Former Libyan leader Gaddafi proposed a gold-backed dinar to be used in Africa. His plan was to stop selling oil in US dollars. Ultimately Gaddafi was killed, and Libyan oil is still sold in dollars.

"Bashar al-Assad of Syria dropped the dollar for the euro in 2006. The US-backed anti-Assad rebels and the US military bombed Syria in 2017.

"Iran created the Iranian Oil Bourse in 2005 and stopped accepting US dollars in 2007. In November of 2018, Iran went too far when they entered into an agreement with Iraq to sell Iraqi oil on the Iranian Oil Bourse, outside of the US dollar of course—"

"Times up, Mr. Chapman," Corrinne said.

"I'd like to use my rebuttal," John said.

"Congressman Bradley, you have two minutes."

John surveyed the audience. "It's easy for Mr. Chapman to sit on his high horse, reading conspiracy theories on the Internet, and spewing these lies for shock effect. While he's been trolling the Internet, I've been doing the real work of governing this great country."

John nodded. "I did approve the defense budget, not because I approve of the wars but because I knew that the wars would happen with or without my approval. I didn't want our soldiers to go to war without the equipment they needed to be as safe as possible. These are the hard choices I've had to make as a congressman. These are the choices that keep me up at night. What hard choices has Mr. Chapman had to make? He lives alone, has no children, a nomadic job. He's completely detached from reality and, therefore, sees these extremely important situations as black and white, when in reality there are multiple shades of gray." John paused, scanning the audience.

"If you elect me in November as president of this great country, you have my word that I *will* bring our troops home."

The crowd cheered. Corrinne again waited for the cheering to subside.

"Secretary Coleman," Corrinne said, "same question. As president, how to you plan to manage the Iran War?"

"Thank you, Corrinne," Coleman said. "I'm the only candidate on this stage that actually has experience with Iran. Mr. Chapman is completely out of his depths, and Congressman Bradley is misinformed on the disastrous results of a military withdrawal from the Middle East. Iran is stable because of the diligent and heroic efforts of our military men and women. It would be a great disrespect to the thousands who have lost their lives in service to this country and to those countries abroad to simply walk away before a stable democratic government has been established. Not only would it be a great disrespect, it would be irresponsible and highly dangerous."

Secretary Coleman used his hands to emphasize his points. "Without our protection, millions of barrels of oil would be controlled by terrorists, who would use the revenue from the oil sales to finance a wave of global terrorism unlike anything we've ever seen. At best, we'd see a major increase in terrorist activity. At worst, we'd see a complete breakdown of society, with millions of civilian casualties.

"As a veteran of the Gulf War, I know the realities of war. I desperately want peace, and I'm the only one on this stage who's willing to fight for it."

"I'd like to use my rebuttal," George said.

"Mr. Chapman, your rebuttal," Corrinne said.

"Secretary Coleman's fear-mongering," George said, glaring at the white-haired ex-general. He turned back to Julie. "The US government began the War on Terror on September 11, 2001. Between 2001 and 2014, there's been a 500 percent *increase* in terrorism fatalities. Clearly war creates more terrorism. This statistic appeared in *The Guardian* on November 18, 2014. I suspect it's even higher now. An organization called the Institute for Peace had been indexing and publishing global terrorism fatalities. They are no longer operating. I don't know for sure, but I think they were shut down for distributing *inconvenient* statistics." George clenched his fists. "This is what government propaganda does. It makes you afraid, so you'll support these wars. The biggest threat to the American people is the American government and the Federal Reserve." George paused, looking from Julie to the crowd.

"I'd like to recite a quote from US Marine Corps Major General and two-time Medal of Honor Recipient Smedley Butler. He said the following about war." George took a deep breath.

"'War is a racket. It is possibly the oldest, easily the most profitable, surely the most vicious. It is the only one international in scope. It is the only one in which the profits are reckoned in dollars and the losses in lives. A racket is best described, I believe, as something that is not what it seems to the majority of the people. Only a small inside group knows what it is about. It is conducted for the benefit of the very few, at the expense of the very many.'"

John watched George's dad stand and march for the exit. *What a fucking disaster.*

* * *

At the conclusion of the debate, the candidates moved to center stage. Art and John waved to the crowd with big grins as if their faux excitement could camouflage their debate debacles. They shook hands and exchanged pleasantries. George was off to the side, his face expressionless. John approached, with his movie-star smile. He looked down on George from his lofty six foot two perch.

John extended his hand. George crossed his arms over his chest, his face still blank. The crowd roared at the slight. John turned, smirking, and presented his palms to the audience. The audience laughed.

John turned back to George. "You'll never win," John said through his plastered smile.

"That's the first true thing you've said tonight," George replied.

"You've torn this country in two. That's on your conscience."

George was unresponsive.

John moved closer, his back to the cameras. He turned off his mike, still smiling.

George turned off his mike. "It's a booby prize."

"What?" John asked.

"The presidency. It's a booby prize. It's the captain's seat on the *Titanic*."

John said, "This is as good as it gets for you and everyone you care about. It's all downhill from here."

103: Katie and It's Never the Same

George entered the training room, the roar of the crowd behind him and a smile on his face. Julie hugged him. Max and Katie joined in, making it a group hug. After a moment, they separated.

"That was badass," Max said.

"You just made the two best politicians in America look like fools," Katie said, "and you did it with the truth."

"I'm so proud of you," Julie said.

"Did they show the entire debate on television?" George asked. "I kept expecting them to stop it."

Katie said, "According to the Internet, certain markets experienced some blackouts, but WNN did run it in its entirety."

* * *

Katie hurried into George and Julie's condo. George was outside, on the tiny deck. Katie opened the sliding glass door and joined him. The fall air was crisp, the sun shining. The deck and railing were littered with potted plants. George clipped and harvested herbs.

"Hey, Katie," he said, holding a pair of scissors and a basket of herbs. He wore a sweatshirt and jeans.

"You have to look at this," Katie said, thrusting a piece of paper in his direction.

He set the basket and scissors on the deck and took the paper. His dark eyes scanned back and forth. He looked at Katie. "This can't be right."

A smile spread across Katie's face. "It is."

"How did this happen?"

"I think with what happened to you"—Katie looked down for a

moment—"people empathized, and they're angry." Her voice turned upbeat. "And the debate was huge of course."

"I still can't believe it."

"Believe it. You're within the margin of error to win the popular vote."

George pursed his lips. "Even if that were to happen, we can't win where it counts."

"The electoral college." Katie shook her head. "I think you'll have some electors that'll vote against party to vote for you."

"Not all states allow it."

"It's still huge. You know, if we went to the Libertarian Party, you'd be a shoo-in for president in 2024."

"This is it for me. You know that."

"We'll see about that. I can be pretty persuasive."

George frowned, his hands on his hips.

Katie flashed her palms in mock surrender. "Fine, I'll let it go … for now. On another note, I was thinking about renting an arena for an election-night celebration. We could easily book five thousand seats."

George's face softened. "I'd like to go home."

"Oh." Katie's mouth turned down.

"I'm sorry, Katie. I've had enough. Julie and I are going to the Poconos during the election. Then we're going home."

"That's it? You're not coming back?"

"The lease on this place is up at the end of the month. I wanna marry Julie, and I wanna go back to my life."

"Oh, … I just thought there'd be more."

"I know. I'm sorry."

Her eyes were brimming with tears. "What about all the people we've helped?"

"You and Max will continue to help them. I'll still appear in your videos, but I don't wanna run again."

"It won't be the same."

George hugged Katie. "It never is."

104: Julie and Election Night

Julie and George lay together on the couch, kissing. A log crackled in the cabin fireplace. She moved her hand under the waistband of his flannel pajama pants.

"We can't," he said, removing her hand from his crotch.

They sat up, breathless.

"We have condoms," she said.

"I know, but you heard the doctor. That test is only 80 percent reliable. If something happened with the condom, and I end up being positive, I'd never forgive myself. It's just a couple more days."

She pressed out her lower lip. "It feels like it's been forever."

"I know. Trust me. I know."

She sighed. "Are you hungry?"

"I'm still full from dinner. You?"

"No." She smirked. "We could watch the election."

"I thought the whole point in coming here was to get away from the election."

"Aren't you curious?"

He mock-frowned. "Yes."

She smiled, grabbed the remote from the coffee table, and turned on the television. Election coverage was on almost every channel. She settled on WNN because of the "Does Chapman Have a Chance?" headline scrawled across the bottom of the screen.

Corrinne Stevens sat at a glass table, her luscious legs in full view. Chairman of the RNC Ken Osborne and political strategist Alex Cooley sat across from her. Ken was red-faced and white-haired. Alex was swarthy and in his mid-forties. Neither man held a candle to Corrinne in the looks department.

"I predicted a huge divergence in the preliminary polls to the actual polls," Ken said, "and that's what we're seeing as the numbers come in. Chapman's somewhere around 17 percent, which is absolutely fantastic for a write-in candidate but nowhere near the 33 percent he was projected to garner after the debate."

"This is crap," Julie said.

George stared at the screen.

Ken continued. "Many of Chapman's supporters are first-time voters. First time voters often say they're planning to vote, then they don't. Many aren't even aware that you have to register."

"For presidential elections," Alex said, "you *can* register in person the day of, but it's another barrier. It's also simply easier to check a box than to write-in someone's name. I think the Chapman phenomena has worn off. Most people are thinking rationally now, and that's showing up in the poll results."

George rubbed his temples. "They might've rigged the election somehow."

"I should call Katie," Julie said, grabbing her phone from her purse.

"So much for getting away from it all."

"I don't have to. I can leave my phone off."

George frowned. "No, go ahead."

Julie turned on her phone. She had a slew of texts from Katie and Max, and a couple of messages. She read her texts.

"Max thinks it was rigged too," Julie said. "They're trying to figure out how."

George stood from the couch. "Do you mind if I go to bed?"

"Really? We have to find out—"

"I think I get the gist. I'm tired of politics—the lying, the propaganda, the backdoor deals."

Julie raised her eyebrows. "Are you okay?"

"I'm just tired. I haven't slept well the past few weeks. I think it's starting to hit me."

"Do you mind if I watch it?"

George shook his head. He bent down and kissed her on the lips. "Good night."

"Good night, honey. I'll keep the volume low."

105: George and the Faithless Electors

George's eyes fluttered. His vision adjusted to the darkness of the bedroom. The bedside clock read 2:43 a.m. The television murmured on the other side of the wall. He closed his eyes and tried to go back to sleep, but he was restless. He thought about the test, and the relief he and Julie would feel when it was negative. He tried not to think about the alternative. He thought about the threat from Bradley. *This is as good as it gets for you and everyone you care about. It's all downhill from here.* George thought about the election and the futility of politics. *The real fight's in the minds of the people.*

He was wide awake now. George rolled out of bed and padded to the living area of the cabin.

Julie was texting and watching the election results. She looked up from her phone. "The results are in," Julie said, scowling. "I thought about waking you up. A lot's happening."

"Do I even wanna know the results?" George sat down on the couch next to Julie.

Julie kissed him on the cheek. "I'm so proud of you."

"That bad, huh?"

"Not necessarily. It's complicated." Julie pursed her lips. "Nobody won."

George laughed. "What do you mean, *nobody won?*"

"Well, Bradley won the popular vote by one percentage point, but he only had 268 electoral votes, and Coleman only had 266." Julie grinned.

"The Idaho electors voted for me?"

"They did. The Republicans are pissed because they were supposed to vote for Coleman."

"That would have given him 270. No wonder they're pissed. Faithless electors. Congress will have to elect the president."

Julie nodded. "The electors said that they voted for you because they believed you won the popular vote in Idaho."

"Did I?"

"No, but—"

"How many votes did I get overall?"

"You had more write-in votes than anyone in history. Something like forty-five times what Nader had in '96."

George did the math in his head. "I only got thirty million votes?"

"Twenty-nine-point-two-five million." Julie winced. "But you were right about the election-rigging. There are people everywhere saying that the election was rigged against you. Not just people on the Internet but people in charge of the polling stations. They claim the machines were set up to count your votes as .5 instead of 1.0. They say that's the reason for the claimed low-voter turnout. I think they're on to something because the voter turnout *was* really low."

"How many people voted?"

"One hundred forty-three million."

George sat up straight. "That is a good bit lower than the 160 million they projected, but the 2016 election was 137 million. It is in line with that. Maybe all those new voters didn't show up."

"But the exit polls said they did," Julie said.

George grabbed the notepad and pen from the end table. He scribbled the following with Julie reading over his shoulder:

> 29.25 million votes claimed for me
> 143 million voters total
> If rumor is correct, should be 58.5 million votes for me
> 58.5 – 29.25 = 29.25 additional voters
> Actual total voters = 143+29 = 172 million
> 58.5/172 = Roughly 34 percent of the vote for me
> Libertarians and Green Party probably had 1 percent
> If D and R split evenly, they would have 32.5 percent each.

George looked up from his calculations, wide-eyed.

"You should've won the popular vote," Julie said.

106: John and a Snowball's Chance in Hell

"It's done," Frank said, shutting the door behind him.

They were in John's dingy campaign office, complete with a pressboard desk and eggshell-colored walls.

"How'd she take it?" John asked, sitting behind his desk.

"She's madder than a wet hornet," Frank replied, as he plopped into the wooden chair opposite John.

"Is she still here?"

"Agent Olson escorted her off the premises."

"And Agent Barnes?"

"He's been reassigned."

"Good," John said.

Frank had a crooked smile. "How does it feel?"

"How does what feel?"

"To get everything you want?"

John frowned. "Nothing's been decided yet."

"Come on, John. I think we can stop and smell the roses. Shoot, we *should* stop and smell the roses. Once you're elected, we're gonna have our hands full."

"Do you think there's any chance congress will elect Art?"

"With a Democrat majority? Not a snowball's chance in hell."

"What about Chapman and the recount?"

"The chance of a recount is slim to none, and slim just left town."

"Do you think Chapman won the popular vote?"

"Does it matter?"

"I don't know." John exhaled. "I had ideals, … principles. Now I have obligations."

Frank groaned as he stood from the chair. "You ran a good race, John. You earned the win."

"Thanks, Frank."

Frank nodded and exited John's office, shutting the door behind him.

John's phone buzzed. He read the text.

Donna: I voted for Chapman.

107: Katie and the Controlled Demolition

Katie paced in her living room as she spoke to George. "This is the deal. Credible whistleblowers claim that the new software they used to count the ballots counted your votes as .5 instead of 1.0. The polling stations had to run the software to report the votes, but some of the polling stations counted the ballots by hand after running the software, and they found the irregularity. Six polling stations reached the same finding. It's a freaking disaster of epic proportions for the government. People are threatening mass riots if there's not a recount."

Katie ignored the incoming call from her dad.

"If they did this, you can guarantee there won't be a recount," George said. "If they didn't, they'll do the recount, and it won't change a thing."

"You and I both know they did this, which means you should've won the popular vote," Katie said.

"This was never about winning the election. It was about showing people the true nature of government. This voter fraud is another great example. Maybe people will finally realize that elections aren't about giving us choice. They're about making us think we have a choice and making us think we consent to be governed—that somehow *we* are the government."

"You don't want to fight this?"

"No, and we need to make it clear that rioting isn't the answer."

"You'll need to send that message quick. People are seriously pissed."

"I'll send it to you by the end of the day."

Katie sighed. "All right. I'll talk to you later."

Katie disconnected the call. She tapped *Dad* on her recent call list.

"Katie," Peter Fitzgerald said.

"Hi, Dad," Katie replied. "I saw that you called."

"I'm proud of you. It really is amazing what you've accomplished with Mr. Chapman."

"Thanks, Dad, but we didn't win."

"Ah, *winning*. I imagine it was never about winning."

Katie exhaled. "I guess not, but ... I still wanted to win."

"I understand, but I do believe Mr. Chapman made his point loud and clear. Hearts and minds are more powerful than the presidency."

"Thanks, Dad."

"Believe it or not, I didn't call to talk politics. I have some important news that you should hear."

Katie sat on her couch, her phone pressed to her ear. "Are you okay?"

He chuckled. "I'm perfectly fine." He paused for a beat. "Your mother and I are moving to Switzerland. We've put the house on the market. We'd like you to come with us."

Katie knitted her brow. "Switzerland? When?"

"After the new year. We've priced the house to sell, so we expect we'll meet that deadline."

"But Switzerland?"

"The United States may be a very dangerous place in the near future. For that matter, the world may be a very dangerous place in the near future. The financial system is coming apart. In reality, it collapsed a long time ago, but the losses haven't been recognized. The music is about to stop, with a lot more dancers than chairs."

"How do you know this?"

"It's a controlled demolition by the banks really. The fiat currency system is long overdue for a reset."

"Controlled demolition?"

"They had planned to transition over the next decade, but, with the current instability, they're afraid if they wait, there'll be unnecessary carnage—"

"They're afraid of losing their control."

"I'm sure you're right," Peter said, "but they don't want the world in flames. Of course they can't control everything, but the plan is, two years from now, the world will return to a gold exchange standard. Gold money will be spent digitally in fractions using block chain technology as a ledger to eliminate fraud."

Katie shook her head to herself. "So the rich and connected buy all the gold and ride out the apocalypse in Switzerland? What happens to everyone else?"

"Ultimately it'll be a much more equitable system."

"Equitable? Are you serious? Sounds like the people in power are getting a nice advantage in this *equitable* system."

"The regular people who've been paying attention will profit greatly from the transition."

Katie scowled, her free hand clenched into a fist. "This isn't a transition, *Dad*. This is a controlled demolition, *remember*?"

"I don't know for certain what will happen. This is what I know from the information I have. I don't have the power to stop or influence this. I'm simply recommending that you step off the tracks because a train's coming."

"I can't go to Switzerland. My business is here."

"Most of your work is online, isn't it?"

"I'm not leaving."

108: Julie and the State Specializes in Violence

Julie was in the cabin, pacing, her cell phone to her ear. "You're not coming to my wedding?"

"Jason and I don't think it's safe to be near George," Summer said. "Mom agrees."

"You can't be serious," Julie replied.

"How many times has he been shot? Who knows? Someone might plant a bomb at the reception."

"You and Jason have never liked George."

"This isn't about whether we like him or not. It's about the safety of our girls."

"Fine." Julie disconnected the call.

George sat on the couch, a pad of paper in his lap, and a pen in hand. He looked up from writing his speech. "Summer and Jason aren't coming?"

Julie plopped down on the couch next to George. She shook her head. "My mom's not coming either. How can they do this to me?"

George squeezed her hand. "I'm not taking her side, but she does have a legitimate reason to be afraid."

"She's never been supportive of us."

George turned to Julie. "She doesn't have to be. We're supportive of each other, and we have Max and Katie."

Julie smiled small. "And 58.5 million Americans."

George nodded with a grin. "Yeah, them too." His grin receded. "I'm starting to have second thoughts."

"That's not funny," Julie replied.

"Not about us being together. About us being married by the state."

Julie frowned. "That doesn't leave us many options."

George stood and walked into the bedroom.

"Where are you going?" Julie asked.

"I'll be right back." George returned with a felt-covered ring box and sat back down next to Julie.

Julie furrowed her brow.

"I love you," George said. "You know that. I wanna be with you for the rest of my life. You're already the sole beneficiary of my will. We already have a joint bank account. We're already living together. Why do we need the state to say we're married? I believe we're already married. A piece of paper won't change how I feel."

George opened the box. Inside were two silver wedding bands. He placed the thicker of the two on his left ring finger. Julie looked at George for a moment and placed the thinner ring on her left ring finger.

Julie was quiet, looking at her left hand.

"If you still want to go to the Justice of the Peace next week, we can," George said.

Julie stared at George, thinking about his incarceration and the attempted assassination.

"Julie?"

"The wedding isn't important to me. You are," Julie said. "After everything you've been through, and everything we've been through, I don't want the state anywhere near our marriage."

* * *

Julie stood behind the camera in the rented cabin. George sat on a chair in front of the stone fireplace.

George continued. "I have no desire to use the violence of the state to enforce my values and views on others. A vote for me was a vote in protest, a message to the powers that be that we know and understand the true nature of government. We see the chains that bind us and the lies that propagandize us in this modern form of slavery.

"It shouldn't be a surprise to us that the elections are rigged. It proves our point that government is a violent, immoral institution. But rioting isn't the answer. Violence isn't the answer. We are a movement of nonviolence. Violence is the specialty of the state.

"A few years ago the vast majority of Americans believed the power of their government to be legitimate. That's the purpose of thirteen years of government schooling, nonstop bombardment of propaganda in the media, and the constant drumbeat coming from our culture—to legitimize the illegitimate."

George stared into the camera, his dark eyes clear, his face stubbly. "The tide is turning. People are waking up to the fact that all government authority is illegitimate, that the fictional entity called government doesn't have the moral authority to kill, steal, kidnap, cage, extort, or assault any more than we do. We don't need a violent revolution. We'll simply walk away. We'll stop supporting the beast with taxation and debt money. We'll stop sending our young men to fight in their wars. We'll withdrawal our consent. This day is coming soon but not yet."

109: George and Negative's Positive

The sign read Dr. Roberts and Associates. George parked Julie's Honda Civic in the lot under an old oak. His cell phone rang. He glanced at the phone and sent the caller to voice mail.

"It's Katie," George said, looking at Julie. "I'll call her afterward."

Julie covered his hand and squeezed. "Are you ready?"

George looked at the door to the doctor's office, then back to Julie. "No."

"Think positively. There's a much higher chance that it'll be negative."

"You're right." His phone buzzed. He picked it up again. "Katie sent a text."

> **Katie:** I have something important to talk to you about. Congress voted. Bradley won. No surprise. That's not the important thing. My parents are moving to Switzerland. My dad said that the banks are planning a controlled demolition of the economy. They're planning a gold exchange standard. He thinks the transition could get ugly. Call me, and I'll give you the specifics. I'm working on a video to warn people.

"What's wrong?" Julie asked.

George set his phone in the cup holder. "Congress elected Bradley."

"That's no surprise."

"And Katie's parents are moving to Switzerland."

"Switzerland? Why?"

"Her dad told her that the banks are planning a controlled demolition of the economy. I'm assuming they're moving because it might become dangerous here."

"What do you think Katie's dad meant by a controlled demolition?"

"I'll have to talk to her about the specifics, but I assume it means that they'll stop propping everything up with thin-air money. Potentially this could be very bad."

"How bad?"

"I don't know for sure, but we might see another stock market crash in real terms, massive inflation of the currency, pension failures, and the average American having their wealth and purchasing power go up in smoke."

"We need to warn people."

"Katie's working on it. Unfortunately I don't think a warning will make much of a difference."

"Why not?"

"We've been warning of the possibility of an economic crash for years now. Some people probably took steps to prepare, but, to most, it doesn't seem real. People are stuck in normalcy bias. For the most part people are well-fed, and even those without jobs have basic comforts. They think the future will be just like the past, because, in their experience, for the most part, it has been."

Julie nodded. "Do you want to call Katie now? We have a few minutes."

"No, it'll be a long conversation." He stared at Julie for a moment. Her auburn hair looked brown in the shade of the oak. She had faint dark circles around her eyes. She was still beautiful with high cheekbones, full lips, and a mostly wrinkle-free face, but the shooting, the rape, the death threats, and the false accusations had taken a toll.

"I haven't been getting enough sleep," she said, suddenly aware of his gaze. "I know I look terrible—"

"You look beautiful. I was thinking that I'm lucky to have you."

They leaned toward each other and hugged. "I love you," she whispered in his ear.

They separated, and George took a deep breath. "We should go in."

They entered the doctor's office, headed toward the chest-high reception counter and a heavyset woman behind a computer screen.

"Hello," the woman said. Her eyes widened in recognition. "Are you—"

"I'm George Chapman, and I have an appointment with Dr. Roberts at three."

"I saw your name on the appointments, but, ... well, Chapman's a common name."

"That's true," George replied.

"I just saw on my home page that John Bradley is our new president."

"I heard."

"I voted for Bradley. I just felt he was stronger on women's issues and health care. Maybe next time you should pay more attention to those issues."

"There won't be a next time," George replied, his face blank. He added his name, signature, and the time to the sign-in sheet on the counter.

"Are you a new patient?" she asked.

"No."

"Do you have the same insurance?"

"Yes."

She smiled. "Have a seat, and we'll call you when he's ready for you."

George stepped to the empty waiting room and sat next to Julie. She was perusing a *Time* magazine. She tilted the cover to reveal George's face. The caption read, Domestic Terrorist?

George smirked. "I was upset when that came out, but now I'm starting to think it's a compliment. By the way, the receptionist said she voted for Bradley."

Julie shook her head. "Women do seem to love him."

"She felt he was stronger on women's issues and health care."

Julie laughed.

A few minutes later, George and Julie were taken to Dr. Roberts's office.

Dr. Roberts stood from his desk. "Mr. Chapman," he said, his hand outstretched. George and the doctor shook hands.

Dr. Roberts was short and bald, with a crescent moon of white hair and a scrunched face. His expression was neutral.

"Mrs. Chapman," he said to Julie.

Julie shook his hand.

They all sat, Dr. Roberts behind the walnut desk, his framed degrees on the wall above him, and George and Julie in the padded wooden chairs in front of him.

"I received the results from your antibody and antigen test," Dr. Roberts said, his face impassive. "Your body produced the protein response indicative of being HIV positive."

Julie gasped, her eyes like saucers. "But the viral load test was negative."

"The viral load test was done only a few weeks after infection. It's only 70 to 80 percent accurate."

"This test could be wrong," Julie said.

"It's very rare to have a false positive on the antibody and antigen test," Dr. Roberts said.

"But it's possible?" Julie asked.

"Yes, but highly unlikely." Dr. Roberts looked from Julie to George. "I know it sounds disastrous, but antiretroviral therapy is very effective in slowing the progression of HIV and protecting your immune system. It's not uncommon to live with HIV for many decades."

George was in a fog, the doctor's words sucking the oxygen from the room. His chest was tight, constricting his breathing. George unbuttoned his flannel shirt.

"I'd also like to test Mrs. Chapman," Dr. Roberts said.

"Can we still have sex?" Julie asked.

"You'd want to avoid high-risk sex, such as anal sex, but, with the proper use of a condom and the antiretroviral drugs, it is possible to have a healthy sex—"

George hurried from the room, his flannel shirt open, exposing his T-shirt. He spilled into the parking lot and sucked in the fall air. He was under the oak tree, his hands on his knees. Julie approached, her eyes glassy. He stood, and she hugged him, tight.

"They took everything," George said, still holding on to Julie. "I just wanted you."

"You still have me," she replied. "I'm not going anywhere."

110: John's Party

The crowd cheered, shaking their signs: Bradley-Atwell 2020, United We Stand, Bradley 2020, Drain the Swamp, and a couple of smuggled in George 2020 signs. The auditorium crawled with secret service agents. The Chapman supporters were quickly ejected.

President John Bradley was center stage, behind the podium. Behind him were Linda and the kids, Vice President Rebecca Atwell and her family, Frank and his wife, Grace and her husband, and a handful of secret service agents. John waved and smiled, waiting for the crowd to quiet. He turned and smiled at his family. Linda's forced contentment made her look guilty. *The Internet will have a field day with Linda memes tomorrow.* He turned back to the crowd. They were mostly quiet now, just a couple of spontaneous yelps from people who wished to be recognized as special snowflakes.

"Thank you," John said. "Thank you. We did it!" John shook his fist in celebration.

The crowd cheered some more.

John waited again for the cheering to subside. "I spoke with Art just a few minutes ago, and he wished me good luck. Art Coleman is a great American and a great man. We may not agree on political policy, but I admire his devotion to this country. I'd like to thank him for running a tough and honest campaign.

"I'd like to thank my family." John motioned toward his family behind him. "My beautiful wife, Linda, the best kids a father could ever hope for, Ellen, Charlotte, and Bobby. I love you."

The crowd applauded.

John continued. "I'd like to thank my vice president, Rebecca Atwell.

Together I know we can make a difference. I'd like to thank my friend and campaign manager, Frank Whitehead."

Frank waved at the crowd.

"I'd like to thank Grace Levy, my director of public relations, and now my White House chief of staff."

The diminutive woman waved, grinning ear-to-ear.

"But most of all," John said, "I'd like to thank you, the voters, because this victory isn't about me. It's about all of you. After eight years of Republican reign, we're ready for change. The United States is divided. This campaign showed exactly how divided we are as a people. You might be a Democrat or a Republican or a Libertarian, but you're an American first. This is the *United* States, and I plan to keep it that way."

The crowd hailed and shook their signs in a mass hysteria of optimism.

111: Katie and Get Out of Dodge

Katie sat on her couch, typing on her laptop, the television on in the background. She looked up at the television. On screen, USN anchor Corrinne Stevens sat at a glass table across from RNC Chairman Ken Osborne.

The white-haired man said, "The first few months of John Bradley's presidency has been an unmitigated disaster. Since he's been in office, we've had a spike in unemployment, crime, and the worst inflation since the Civil War."

Katie's cell phone chimed. She muted the television and answered her phone.

"Where are you?" George asked.

"I'm still at home," Katie replied into her cell. "I'm finishing a few things."

"You should have left hours ago!"

"I know. Our tax slavery videos from last April are going viral again. I reposted them on social media, and I'm checking over the interview with the guy from the Congressional Budget Office. I still can't believe they only have half the tax revenue that they did at this time last year. I know we're in a depression—"

"Katie, we'll talk about it when you get here. You need to get moving."

"I just have to stop by the bank, and I'll be on my way."

"You still have money in the bank?"

"They've had a cash withdrawal limit for the past month. I've been withdrawing the maximum every day. I only have about a thousand dollars left."

"I'm hanging up. I expect you to leave *now*."

"Yes, *Dad*."

George disconnected the call.

Katie posted the interview with the guy from the CBO. She closed her laptop and shoved it in her laptop bag. Katie carried boxes and suitcases to her SUV. The parking lot of her community was half empty. Many neighbors had already left in anticipation of the Tea Party. DC was considered ground zero, and northern Virginia was too close for comfort.

Katie locked her condo and climbed into her SUV. Her cell phone chimed. She picked up.

"Katie," Zach said.

"It's been a long time," Katie replied.

"Do you still have the phone I gave you?"

"Yes."

"Turn it on and call me back." Zach disconnected the call.

Katie removed the encrypted phone from her laptop bag, powered it on, and called Zach.

"I don't have a lot of time," Zach said. "I'm assuming you're someplace safe."

"I'm on my way to George's," Katie replied.

"Christ, Katie—"

"I know."

"Be careful on the drive. It'll be slow going. When you get there, stay there. Something's happening, and I think things could get very dangerous, especially for people like you and George."

"Are we a target? Should we not stay at George's?"

"It's remote, isn't it?"

"Yes."

"It should be perfect for now. I'll let you know if and when that changes. I need you to text me his address, in case I can't contact you via phone or Internet."

"I'll send you the GPS coordinates. His street address doesn't show up on GPS."

"Be careful, Katie. I have to go."

"Wait. What's happening? Is it the banking crisis? The Tea Party?"

"It's a lot bigger than that. It's better you don't know at this point. Look. I have to go."

"What's bigger than that?"

"Be careful." Zach disconnected the call.

She texted him the GPS coordinates.

Katie drove to a nearby shopping center. The grocery store was packed, as if there was a pending ice storm. The gas station had lines seven cars deep at every pump. The price at the pump was $11.78—for regular. A spray-painted plywood sign read LIMIT 5 GALLONS. Thankfully she had listened to George and had a full tank. A line snaked outside of Katie's bank. *Shit.*

Katie found a spot toward the back of the lot. She stepped from her SUV, locked it, and marched toward the bank. It was sunny and warm, the spring flowers in full bloom. She cut between a row of cars and was startled by two teenagers crouched next to a Volkswagen. She sucked in a breath and put her hand to her chest. They were siphoning gas.

One was still, like a rabbit with wide eyes; the other had the look of a predator. He stood, his hood up. Katie turned on her sneakers and walked around them. The teens went back to their business. Katie gazed through the window of her bank. It looked like a line for a Disney attraction with ropes forming a one-way maze. The front door was propped open. A sign taped to the door read:

All Branches and Internet Banking Closed
Thursday 4-8-2021
Friday 4-9-2021
Saturday 4-10-2021

All branches and Internet banking to reopen Monday 4-12-2021. We apologize for any inconvenience.

"Fuckin' $250 maximum *and* they're closed tomorrow," a man in line said. "They're gonna gimme my fuckin' money."

"Did you say $250 maximum?" Katie asked the man.

"Yeah. They're only letting us withdrawal $250," the man said.

"It was $500 yesterday."

"That was yesterday."

Katie hurried back to her SUV, $250 wasn't worth the wait. She sped from the lot toward 495 North. The backup started miles from the exit. The congestion was a combination of overpopulation, rush hour, and get-out-of-Dodge traffic. It was a slow-crawling cocktail of starts, stops, honks, and the occasional angry hand gesture. It was warm enough that many people had their windows down, their music blasting to the dismay of others. Katie kept her windows up, her music down, and her eyes on the road. She didn't want to be a victim of the road rage bubbling around her.

She changed her satellite radio station from Alt Nation to DC Traffic and Weather.

The female newscaster said, "With one week until tax day, commuters and long distance travelers have merged to create massive gridlock around the nation's capital. The sudden rationing of gasoline and limits on banking withdrawals has spurred many to rush to their destination a week ahead of the Tea Party, which has been estimated to be the largest demonstration in the history of the United States."

* * *

A few hours later, she was still on 495, the traffic deadlocked. She cut her engine to save fuel. They hadn't moved an inch in fifteen minutes. Katie grabbed her phone from the center console and tapped her George contact.

"Shit," she said to herself. *Cell tower must be down.* She listened to WNN now.

"Trading has been halted on Wall Street," the male newscaster said, "with the S&P 500 down 6 percent before the suspension. Trading is expected to resume tomorrow. Fears over the future and the upcoming Anarchist-sponsored Tea Party spurred the heavy selling pressure.

"The US Treasury market was also in turmoil, with yields spiking to new highs, at the same time the dollar index has dropped to new lows. Meanwhile, trading was halted at the COMEX and NYMEX with most commodities hitting their limit-up thresholds. President Bradley said the following in response to the ongoing financial crisis."

WNN cut to President John Bradley's voice. "We're surrounded, and we're under attack. Our way of life is under attack. Our freedom is under attack. These domestic terrorists—these Anarchists—are doing exactly what terrorists do. They're causing fear, and that fear is behind the sell-off on Wall Street.

"Chinese currency manipulators are flooding the world with dollars, reducing our purchasing power and increasing borrowing costs for the US Treasury. In addition to the Chinese, we have Russian hackers hired by the Russian government to artificially inflate commodity prices."

President Bradley paused for a moment. "We may be down, but we're certainly not out. We *will* defend the dollar against the Chinese currency manipulators. The dollar has been the world's reserve currency for over seventy years. I don't see that changing anytime soon. We *will* stabilize energy prices and agricultural commodities. I won't stand idly by while everyday Americans are forced into poverty by international and domestic terrorists. We *will* stand together as Americans. Thank you and God bless America."

The car in front of Katie began to move. *It's about time.* She started her SUV, drove a bit, accelerated to 15 mph, then stopped again. *Damn it.* There were shouts behind her. In her rearview mirror, two men fought on the asphalt of 495. Traffic moved again. Cars skirted the skirmish behind her, more interested in getting to their destination than watching bare-knuckle brawling.

Katie merged right and took the next exit. She'd take an alternate route. Thankfully her GPS still functioned. It was slow going through the suburbs of northern Virginia but better than the stop-and-go tedium of the highway. Traffic lightened as she drove north through Maryland. Here on the backroads near the Pennsylvania border she noticed the poverty. Houses with caved-in roofs and unkempt lawns adorned with stripped husks of cars in the front yard, foreclosure notices on the doors, and skinny animals roaming about.

The United States was rusting from the inside out.

112: Julie and Confidence Currencies

"This is Gary Cook of the *Alt News Podcast*, providing vital information in a changing world. I'm streaming this podcast live on Wednesday, April 7, 2021. There've been reports of cell phone and Internet outages across the country. There are conflicting reports for the outages, many blaming domestic and international cyberterrorists and a few blaming the US government, citing their desire to limit communication ahead of the Tea Party."

Julie, George, Max, and Max's girlfriend, Daisy, sat around the table, listening to the broadcast on a laptop. George spun his silver wedding band around his finger with a thousand-yard stare.

He's worried about Katie. Julie put her hand on top of George's and squeezed. "Try not to worry," Julie whispered.

George nodded.

"In *The Sun Also Rises*," Gary said through the laptop speaker, "Hemingway wrote about going bankrupt slowly, then all at once. This aptly describes the situation we face today in the United States—and around the world for that matter. It's been a slow drip over the past few decades, but the reckoning has reached warp speed of late.

"In 2018, the inflation rate was around 4 percent in the United States. This was double the Fed's initial target inflation rate of 2 percent. In 2019, the Reynolds administration introduced the Rebuild America stimulus program, which was nearly unanimously approved by congress. With the wars, the stimulus program, and the massive growth of government, the Federal Reserve fired up the digital printing presses to pay for what couldn't be paid for through direct taxation, which was quite a lot. In 2019, the inflation rate hit double digits for the first time since 1981. Then in 2020, the US government stopped publishing inflation rates, but many pundits put that number somewhere between 30 and 60 percent.

"In January of this year, China announced that they'd been a net seller of US Treasuries for many years. As is customary in Chinese diplomacy, there was an air of secrecy, as *many years* is unspecific, and no amounts were given. Chinese President Xi Jinping did give a rationale for the US Treasury dump. He said, 'The United States is a dying superpower, stretched too thin with too many wars. Tax receipts are too low, and spending is too high. They cover these shortfalls with an increase in the currency, devaluing our investments in US Treasuries. It is prudent for the Chinese government and the Chinese people to look for safer investments.' On the heels of the Chinese announcement, Russia announced that they will only accept gold for their oil and gas.

"Then just last month, China was at it again when they shocked the world with a plan for a gold-backed yuan. Russia again followed China and announced similar plans for a gold-backed ruble. Commodities have been in a massive bull market for the past few years, but the Chinese and Russian announcements sent commodity prices soaring. Trading at the COMEX and NYMEX have been halted on eight separate occasions as limit-up parameters have been triggered.

"It is estimated that inflation was a blistering Zimbabwe-like 70 percent last month. Americans are literally going broke all at once. The US dollar isn't the only currency in trouble. Fiat currencies around the world have seen massive devaluations against real tangible things. These currencies require the confidence of those who use them. Without confidence, there's no value. People around the world have lost quite a bit of confidence in fiat currencies.

"Last week, ironically on April 1, OPEC announced that temporarily they would not accept any currency in trade for oil. All oil trades would be settled in gold or a basket of commodities. Despite the date, this wasn't meant to be funny, although there was a bit of irony in their announcement. The OPEC announcement said that the move was temporary. In 1971, Richard Nixon said, 'I have directed Secretary Connally to suspend *temporarily* the convertibility of the dollar into gold or other reserve assets.' *Temporarily* in that case meant *forever*. The suspension of the gold standard by Nixon led to the petrodollar deal between the US and OPEC. I believe OPEC's use of the word *temporary* means that the petrodollar is finished forever. If that's the case, it's likely to be the death knell for the US dollar.

"Throughout this crisis, the mainstream media has been in the background, spewing US government propaganda. Blame for the crisis has been squarely placed on OPEC, China, Russia, Anarchist domestic terrorists, international terrorists, cyberterrorists, and currency manipulators. Essentially anyone *but* the US government. My opinion is that the media has been softening us up, placing blame on others, so we'll rally behind our government against the evil foreigners and terrorists. The truth of the matter is that the biggest threat to any people is usually their own—"

The podcast stopped.

"Did we lose the Internet connection?" George asked.

Max checked the connection on his laptop. "No connections available," Max said. "Our neighbor's Internet's out too."

"No phone either," Julie said, checking her cell.

"Hopefully Bradley won't say it's *temporary*," Max said, frowning.

George said, "With the Tea Party next week, an Internet and phone blackout would drastically reduce the number of protestors."

Daisy stood from the table. She was thin, with birdlike features, her hair braided into two ponytails.

"I should go home," Daisy said. "My parents might be worried."

Max stood. "I'll walk you."

"Be careful, you two," Julie said.

"Please stay away from the road," George said. "People are afraid right now, and scared people do stupid things."

"We'll take the trail," Max said. "I'll be back before dinner."

After Max and Daisy left, Julie said to George, "This bank holiday, the gas rationing, now the Internet and phones are out—they're preparing for something big, aren't they?"

George nodded. "I think so."

113: George and the Visitor

George was in his bathroom as he popped an antiretroviral pill and washed it down with water. The pill bottle was mostly empty. He had tried to stockpile the medication, but the recent shortages made that impossible. He placed the pill bottle behind the mirror that doubled as a cabinet. He marched to the living room, his Glock holstered to his hip. Julie and Max sat at the table, talking.

"Something's not right," Julie said to George. "She should've been here by now."

"I know," George replied.

"Maybe she ran out of gas?" Max said.

"That's what I'm afraid of—her being stranded." George blew out a breath. "But something else has been bothering me all day."

Julie furrowed her brow.

"I'm not sure we're safe here," George said. "I think at some point there'll be a warrant for my arrest and possibly yours as well." He looked at Max. "I'm sorry, Max. I'm not trying to scare you, but you're eighteen, and you've become an influential activist in your own right."

Julie went pale.

"Shit," Max said, his eyes wide in recognition.

"But the government has to be in disarray at this point," Julie said. "I can't imagine they have time to make arrests with everything that's going on."

"Maybe," George said, sitting at the table. "Let me walk you through my reasoning, and you can tell me what you think." He paused for a beat. "We know the banks were planning a controlled demolition of the economy, but I think things have gotten out of control and are happening faster than the

Fed and the US government anticipated. The question then is, what's likely to happen now?"

"A new currency," Max said.

"I agree," George said, "but how will they get the American people to accept it after the dollar goes up in smoke?"

"They'll be so scared that they'll beg for a solution—any solution," Julie said.

George nodded. "What about the people who oppose the new currency? What about the Anarchists? They appear to be correct at the moment. What's to stop people from saying, 'Screw it. We're done with government'?"

"Brute force?"

"That seems likely. The US government has the biggest military and police apparatus on the planet. I can't imagine they won't use it."

Max winced. "This is bad, isn't it?"

"Potentially," George replied.

"So they go around and arrest anyone who opposes the government?" Julie asked.

"If I was on the other side, and I was sociopathic," George said, "I'd round up all the Anarchists and anyone else who was antigovernment during this communications blackout and dispose of them quietly. After that, I'd monitor communications via the Internet and phones and remove anyone else conspiring against the government. To pay for the capture and disposal, I'd take these people's property and wealth."

"Whoa, George, that's pretty dark," Max said. "You really think they'd do that?"

"I know they would."

"Are there even enough cops to do it?"

"Probably not, but they could use the National Guard. Who knows? Maybe they'd use active duty military too."

"Do you really think US soldiers or police officers or whoever they tell to do this would take people away, like Nazis taking Jews?" Julie asked.

"Americans are programmed to follow orders," George said. "The Stanley Milgram experiments proved that most will electrocute someone to death simply because someone in authority told them to do so."

"Times are changing," Julie said. "I've seen so much support for a stateless society. I think there'll be too much dissension to pull it off."

"I think they'll try. Whether they're successful or not remains to be seen."

"What do we do?" Max asked. "Go to Canada?"

"I don't know," George replied. "I do agree with your mother that they're probably too busy with the crisis right now, but soon they'll turn their attention to people like us. I would imagine that I would be enemy number one."

"We need to get out of here."

"It's not exactly safe on the road either. I was thinking that we should figure out an escape plan, for if and when the time comes."

"We have the driveway alarm, but it doesn't give us much time to get away," Julie said.

"I agree," George replied. "We could dig it up and move it out on the road. There's only one way in, and traffic's been nonexistent, so there wouldn't be too many false alarms."

"Where would we go?" Julie asked.

"There's an old campground about thirty-five miles from here. A hunting camp would be better, but I don't know of one we can use."

"Daisy's dad hunts. Maybe he has a camp. I can ask him."

George turned to Max. "That's a good idea. Do you think he'd let us hide your truck and our travel bags in his barn?"

"I don't see why not," Max replied. "The barn's empty right now."

The driveway alarm chimed, and the digital voice said, "Alert sector one. Alert sector one."

George looked at Max and Julie. "It must be Katie." *What if it isn't?*

George hustled outside, into the darkness. He moved through the wooded trail, barely lit by moonlight. Headlights crept up the driveway toward Max's cabin. George took cover behind an oak at the edge of the trail. It was an SUV, but he couldn't tell if it was hers. The engine and headlights were cut. The door opened and shut.

"It's me," Katie called out.

George took his hand off the butt of his Glock and turned on his flashlight. They met near the cabin.

"Are you all right?" George asked.

Katie hugged him. "I'm fine," she said over his shoulder. "A little sore from sitting for eight hours."

They disengaged. "I'm glad you made it. I was worried."

"Me too."

Max and Julie approached from the trail, flashlights bobbing in the dark. They hugged Katie.

"Why don't you help Katie with her stuff," Julie said to Max.

"I can get it," Katie said. "I just need my suitcase for now."

"I got it," Max said, walking to the SUV.

"It's in the back seat."

"You'll stay in Max's cabin," Julie said to Katie. "He'll be on our couch at the main house. I hope that's okay. Max and George fixed it up really nice."

"Sounds great," Katie said. "Thank you for letting me stay."

"Of course, honey. You're welcome anytime."

Max approached, lugging the suitcase. "Did you pack your whole house in here?"

"It's my shoes, smartass," Katie replied with a crooked grin.

They entered the cabin and turned on the light. It was a single room with a kitchenette, a tiny bathroom and shower, a living room, a fireplace, and a double bed. Max set her suitcase by the bed. Katie plopped down on the couch. Her eyes were bloodshot, her brown hair disheveled.

"Are you hungry?" Julie asked. "We have leftovers from dinner."

"I'm fine," Katie replied. "I ate an hour ago."

"I'll make you a nice breakfast tomorrow. Max's girlfriend raises chickens, and she supplies us with fresh eggs."

"I wanted to talk to you guys about something."

Julie sat on the end of the couch, George and Max on the chairs.

"Zach called me earlier," Katie said. "He said that things may get dangerous for people like us. I tried to get him to elaborate, but he had to go. He said we should be safe here for the time being. He said he would contact me if that changed. He didn't actually say that we might be arrested, but that was the impression I got. I thought about it on the drive up here, and it makes sense to me that they would make mass arrests. It may be why the Internet and phones are out."

"We were thinking the same thing," Julie said.

"Zach also asked for the GPS coordinates of your house," Katie said.

"Did you give him the coordinates?" George asked.

"Yes. I guess I should've asked, but he warned us before, and I trust him."

"If *you* trust him, I trust him. I'm pretty sure the US government can find this place with or without your coordinates anyway."

"How will he warn us with no phones or Internet?" Julie asked.

"Now that I think about it," Katie replied, "I can't remember if he said he *would* warn us or he would *try* to warn us."

"We've been discussing an escape plan, just in case."

114: John and the Cabinet Meeting

President John Bradley sat at the head of the massive oval table with twenty cabinet members. Other relevant, but less important personnel sat in chairs along the wall. They weren't high enough on the White House food chain to earn a seat at the table. Each person at the table had a glass of water, a coaster, and an open binder.

"Where's Blake?" John asked.

A thin man with round eyeglasses stood from the wall. Blake Robinson was the head of the FCC.

"Yes, Mr. President," Blake replied.

"What's the status on the Internet and phone blackout?"

"The major carriers have already complied. There have been a few holdouts from small ISPs, citing the move as unlawful."

John turned to a middle-aged man with a receding hairline and a large nose. "Attorney Davidson, correct me if I'm wrong, but this blackout is perfectly legal."

Scott Davidson was the attorney general. "The 2018 Protecting Cyberspace and Telecommunications as a National Asset Act grants the executive power to suspend Internet, cell service, cable, and landlines."

John turned back to Blake. "How many holdouts are there?"

"Most of the country is without Internet or phone right now but ..." Blake's eyes darted right and left. Everyone at the table stared at him. "The problem is that there are over eight thousand Internet service providers and over one hundred cell carriers and phone companies. We're working from the top down. The biggest companies have already complied. Verizon, Comcast, AT&T, Sprint, CenturyLink, Frontier—"

"What percentage of the country has been turned off?" John asked, scowling.

"I'm not sure of the exact—"

"A ballpark estimate, Blake."

"At least 98 percent."

"You should've led with that," John said.

Blake skulked back to his seat.

John turned to the white-haired man to his right. "Secretary Humphrey, what's the status on gasoline and diesel?"

Carl Humphrey was the Secretary of Energy and the former CEO of Unico Oil & Gas. "With people hightailing it out of the cities, there's a shortage right now. A lot of stations are dry, and the rest of them are rationing. A backup of tankers in the Gulf of Mexico wait to be offloaded. I think it's a mistake to make them wait any longer. Grocery stores are already bare. Refineries need inventory."

"How long does it take for crude to be refined and delivered to a gas station?" John asked.

"Twelve to twenty-four hours for the refining," Carl said, "then it could be anywhere between one day to three weeks for the trucks and pipelines to disperse the fuel."

"It could be as little as two days then."

"It rarely is."

"We'll let the tankers offload after tax day. I want to restrict movement and communications during the protest."

"You're gonna have a lot of hungry, pissed-off people."

"We already have that." John took a sip of water and turned to the director of the FBI. "Director Hewitt, do we have the arrest list?"

Director Hewitt had dark hair and bags under his eyes. "We do," Hewitt said. "We've identified 3.3 million people, the top 1 percent of people who are most likely to pose a threat."

"How many of them can we arrest, and when can we arrest them?"

"We've begun reaching out to state and local law enforcement, and they are willing to make the arrests, but it's a numbers game, and we simply don't have enough officers and agents to make three million arrests. It could take two years."

John glowered at Hewitt. "Two years? We don't have two years. How many can we arrest in the next month?"

"Maybe one hundred thousand."

John shook his head. "That's not good enough." He turned to a fit man with a military style haircut. "Secretary Gates, can we spare military personnel to help with the arrests?"

Secretary of Defense Doug Gates was a former marine general and former CEO of the defense contractor, Allied, Inc.

"We have 240,000 army and marine corps reserves. About 100,000 of them are at home, twiddling their thumbs. Not sure about the legality."

"Attorney Davidson," John said, glancing at the attorney general.

"The National Defense Authorization Act allows for US citizens to be arrested and detained by the armed forces," the attorney general said.

John looked at the FBI director. "Director Hewitt, with an additional one hundred thousand men, how many arrests can we make in the next month?"

"It's difficult to say," Hewitt replied. "It depends on how many resources are expended on each name."

John glowered at Hewitt.

"I think we can arrest at least three hundred thousand," Hewitt said.

"How many of the three hundred thousand would have legitimate charges?"

"Almost all of them now. The NSA and Armor Software have upgraded the crime detection component of the software to include people breaking copyright laws by illegally streaming movies or downloading music."

"What about detention? I know the jails and prisons are already overcrowded."

"In my opinion, that's more of a logistical hurdle than the arrests," Hewitt replied.

"How many people are incarcerated now?"

"Two and a half million."

"How much capacity do we have?"

"Officially, none," Hewitt said. "Unofficially, we might squeeze in another hundred thousand."

John showed his palms. "Anyone have any ideas?"

The Secretary of Homeland Security Isaac Quarles spoke. "We could release a few hundred thousand nonviolent offenders."

John nodded. "Any downside to this idea?"

The White House Chief of Staff Grace Levy said, "Even if the public becomes aware of the release, I believe it would be positive. Most people are against prison time for drug use, especially marijuana."

"Let's release the marijuana users first," John said.

"Yes, Mr. President," Hewitt replied.

"How would resources be allocated for the arrests?" John asked.

"We would concentrate on the top four hundred thousand," Hewitt said. "Obviously more resources would be allocated to the number one slot than someone at two hundred thousand. We're still working on the details, but the goal is to arrest 100 percent of the top ten, 98 percent of the top one hundred, 90 of the top one thousand, and so on."

"Keep me updated."

"Yes, Mr. President."

"Does anyone have anything to add?" John glanced around the table.

"Mr. President," Admiral Coffey said.

Admiral Coffey was the director of the NSA, commander of the US Cyber-Command, and chief of the Central Security Service. He wore his naval dress blues.

"Admiral," John said.

"We've war-gamed our current scenario," Admiral Coffey said. "In the simulation, the lack of communication and fuel reduced the projected numbers for the Tea Party protest by 84 percent. We expect the protests to be largely impotent. However, a potential problem with the arrests was highlighted. Many of the arrestees fought back. The simulation found that there is sufficient anger among the public that these arrests could trigger a revolution."

"In your simulation, did the arrestees know they were to be arrested?"

"We tried it both ways. The likelihood of resistance was much higher if they were aware of the pending arrests."

"Then we have to keep this under wraps, and, when we start making arrests, it has to be done very quickly."

"With all due respect, Mr. President, I think the arrests will only antagonize the enemy and build more sympathy for their cause."

John clenched his jaw. "Their cause is the *elimination* of the US government." John looked around the room. "That elimination includes everyone in this room. We're on the brink of becoming a failed state." John glared at the admiral. "One reason that we're on the brink of a revolution is because we've been hacked and exposed on the Internet. We've lost the war of information. The NSA is a big part of the problem."

The admiral held his head high, despite the admonishment.

John continued, glancing at his cabinet members. "We've been one step behind because we're too big and too slow to act. The men and women on that list are traitors and terrorists. It's about time we treated them as such."

The room was dead silent. John turned the page in his binder. Then everyone else did, breaking the silence with an echo of paper shuffling.

"The biggest reason we're in this predicament is because we're in an inflationary depression," John said. "Like Clinton's campaign strategist said in '92, 'It's the economy, stupid.' We can't simply arrest our opponents. We also have to fix the economy or at least show some measured improvement." John looked at the serious-looking man to his left. "Secretary Moody, what's the status on the banking sector? Will banks reopen as scheduled?"

Secretary of Treasury Walter Moody wore wire-rim glasses, a perpetual scowl, and his receding hair slicked back. "We're working on recapitalizing the banks and providing additional cash for the reopening. I think we should extend the bank holiday a few additional days. It's possible there'll be a run on the banks when we reopen. We can set withdrawal limits, but money is likely to be spent quickly, speeding up velocity, thereby increasing inflation."

"I don't have a problem extending the bank holiday, as long as it doesn't outlast the Internet blackout," John replied. "What about the new currency? When will it be introduced, and what effect will it have on the economy?"

"The original plan was a gradual introduction of a gold exchange standard to be completed in 2026," Secretary Moody said. "The Chinese and Russians forced our hand with their gold-backed currencies. The Fed hopes to implement the gold exchange standard in December of this year. The United States has enjoyed an exorbitant privilege, having the reserve currency for nearly eighty years. That time has come to a close. The gold exchange standard will stabilize the economy and eliminate booms and busts. Gold money will be spent digitally in fractions using block chain technology as a ledger. This will eliminate fraud and tax evasion." Moody paused for a beat. "The downside is there's a reckoning with the introduction of the new currency. The losses, the derivatives, the bubbles, the malinvestments that have metastasized under the fiat dollar, well, ... those losses will be accounted for."

John pinched the bridge of his nose. "Are you suggesting the economy won't improve with the new currency?"

"It'll improve but from a much lower level."

115: Katie and Resist

The driveway alarm chimed, and the digital voice said, "Alert sector one. Alert sector one."

Katie's eyed fluttered and opened, but she couldn't see. She panicked, her breathing elevated.

Another chime rang out, and the digital voice said again, "Alert sector one. Alert sector one."

Katie saw the outline of the white lampshade next to the bed. She fumbled around the lamp and flicked the switch, illuminating the cabin. This was her tenth night in Max's cabin, but she still wasn't used to the pure darkness of the wilderness.

Her heart was pumping as she dressed in the clothes she had set aside specifically for this occasion. She laced up her boots, grabbed her flashlight, and turned off the lamp. She hurried outside and ran up the path through the woods toward George's house. She was able to navigate by moonlight, so her flashlight was dark. The throaty rumble of vehicles and crunching gravel cut through the quiet.

Leaves rustled uphill under heavy footsteps. The footsteps approached—rapidly.

"Katie," George said as he hustled down the trail.

"I'm here," Katie said.

George had an AR-15 slung across his chest and pointed down. "I tried to radio you, but there was no response."

"Sorry. I forgot to turn on the walkie-talkie. I heard trucks coming up the road."

They ran through the woods to the meadow. They skirted the edge of the meadow as they passed the earth-sheltered house and greenhouse. The wildflowers and grass were knee high and wet with dew. George looked back periodically to make sure Katie was still behind him. Near the top of the hill, they entered the woods again through a rough game trail. They stopped, just inside the wood line. George struggled to catch his breath, his face ashen in the moonlight.

"Julie, Max," George said, his breath heavy.

They emerged from behind an old hickory. Max holstered a Glock handgun. Katie had her hands on her knees, nearly hyperventilating.

"That's … a … big … hill," Katie said between breaths.

"Katie said she heard trucks coming," George said.

Katie stood upright, her breath regulating. "It could be Zach."

"At this hour? I doubt it. We need to get out of here."

"It's not like they can call," Julie said, then stared at George. "Are you okay? You look pale."

"I'm fine," George replied.

Julie put the back of her hand to his forehead. "You're hot."

"I feel fine. Let's go."

The walkie-talkie on George's hip crackled. Someone said, "Katie, George?"

George raised his eyebrows to Katie. "Where's your walkie-talkie?"

Katie's face felt warm with embarrassment. "Sorry. I left it in the cabin."

"Katie, George?" the man asked again.

Katie breathed a sigh of relief. "That's—"

"This is Zach," the man said. "We need to talk to George."

George removed the walkie-talkie from his belt and spoke into the receiver. "Who's *we*?"

"Anonymous," Zach replied. "We need your help, and you need ours."

"We're on our way." George turned off the walkie-talkie. He looked at Katie, Julie, and Max. "I'm not sure I trust this."

"I know Zach," Katie said. "He wouldn't lie. I was the liar in our relationship."

"I should check it out first," George said.

"We're not letting you go down there by yourself," Julie said.

"If you're going, we're going," Max said.

"You worry too much," Katie said.

They hiked down the hill past the house through the wooded path. George stopped at the edge of the path. Five black SUVs, a box truck, and fifteen men with M-4 carbines formed a perimeter. The headlights of the rear SUV lit the area. Zach was nowhere in sight.

"Can I worry now?" George whispered.

"I'll be right back," Katie replied. She walked from the woods into the open.

"Katie, wait."

Katie walked toward the cabin. "Zach," she called out.

The men with rifles turned toward Katie's voice, but their weapons still pointed downward. Zach opened the back door of one of the SUVs and exited the vehicle. He stepped toward Katie and wrapped her in a tight embrace. After a moment he let go. They stood eye to eye. He still had that baby face that made him look twenty-one instead of thirty-eight. Who couldn't trust a face like that?

"Where's George?" Zach asked.

Katie shrugged. "Can he trust you?"

"This isn't about me."

A small red-headed man exited the SUV.

"Who's the leprechaun?" Katie whispered to Zach.

"My boss from Armor Software. He's on our side."

"Katie Fitzgerald," the man said as he approached. "I'm a big fan of your work. I'm Adam Doyle." He extended a freckled hand.

Katie shook his hand. "What are you doing here?"

"We need to talk to George."

Katie scanned the area, then narrowed her eyes at Adam. "I want all your men to put their weapons in one of these trucks, and I want the keys. Then I want all of them to get in another truck like it's a clown car. I want them to stay in there while we talk."

Adam cocked his head. "Are you serious?"

"How many times have you been shot?"

Adam didn't respond.

"George's been shot three times. For all I know, you guys are here to finish the job."

Adam pursed his lips, the wheels turning in his mind. He turned to Zach. "Tell the guys to put their weapons in the lead truck, bring me the keys, then to pile in the rear truck."

Katie watched with her hands on her hips as the men placed their weapons in the lead SUV. One of the men tossed the keys to Zach and joined the others as they squeezed into the rear vehicle. Zach handed Katie the keys. She locked the lead SUV with the key fob. Katie smirked as the men jockeyed for real estate inside the rear SUV.

"Happy?" Adam asked.

Katie nodded. "George," she called out. "It's safe. They want to talk to you."

Thirty seconds later, George appeared from the darkness, his rifle pointed down. Adam stepped back, his wide eyes glued to the AR.

"George, you remember Zach, my favorite ex-boyfriend," Katie said, with a wink to Zach, "and this is his boss, Adam Doyle."

George shook their hands and said to Zach, "It's nice to see you again."

Adam's posture relaxed. "We're here for two reasons," Adam said. "First, we need you to record a message. Second, we're here to protect you from arrest."

"How do you plan to broadcast a message?" George asked. "As far as I know, Internet and cable are still out, and the one radio station still broadcasting is spewing nonstop propaganda."

"The government forced ISPs, and cable and phone providers to shut off their services to subdue the Tea Party. The providers are turning on limited services tomorrow. Basically it'll be news propaganda, some limited mindless entertainment, and, most important, spotty cell service. We've hacked the Integrated Public Alert and Warning System to access the available platforms."

Katie knitted her brow. "The integrated what?"

Adam said, "It's the Emergency Alert System, National Warning System, Wireless Emergency Alerts, and NOAA Weather Radio, all under a single platform. We'll send a text, a radio message on all channels, and a television message to increase our odds of reaching more people. The downside is it will be audio only. On television, it's just a blue screen that says Emergency Alert."

"Why not deliver your own message?" George asked.

"Because people trust you. They know your voice and we're, well, *anonymous*."

"What's the message?" Katie asked.

"Mass arrests are coming," Adam replied. "The government's goal is to arrest three hundred thousand people identified as a threat to them. There's a ranking algorithm, and they'll be expending more resources for the top people, such as yourself."

"This is your fault," Katie said, glaring at Adam. "It's your fucking software."

Adam was calm. "Yes and no. The software had to work to gain access."

"Access to what?" George asked.

"The goal was to crash the banking system, to wipe out all the debts, and to destroy government currencies. This is a worldwide initiative called the Debt Jubilee. We have to break the chains of debt money and taxation if humanity is ever to be free."

"The Tea Party was just a distraction," Zach said.

Adam nodded. "We sent malware to the central banks and banks in the United States and around the world through the Armor Software program. With all the chaos of the Tea Party, we had hoped to deliver electromagnetic pulse generators to bank server farms across the globe. The crown jewel was the Bank of International Settlements in Basel, Switzerland. Unfortunately we were unsuccessful. The malware caused quite a bit of damage, but, with movement and communications restricted, the Tea Party diversion was ineffective, and the EMPs went mostly undelivered. A lot of our people were arrested. We expect the bank holiday to continue for another few weeks because of our attacks, but we didn't achieve our goal."

"We had hoped to eliminate the power the governments and banks have over us without firing a single bullet," Zach said.

"That brings us back to the message and why we're here," Adam said. "We need to warn people of the arrests because—"

"You want them to resist," George said.

116: Julie and the Message

Julie, Katie, Max, George, Adam, Zach, and Gideon crowded around the kitchen table. Gideon was their head of security—a bearded man in his mid-thirties with massive tattooed arms.

"Are we sitting ducks here?" George asked.

"Fuel is still spotty out there," Adam said, "and we'd probably end up someplace far more vulnerable if we left. This place is actually far better than I anticipated. You're off grid with spring-fed water and stored food."

"We can defend this place," Gideon said. "There's only one road in and one road out. The terrain is rough, and we have the high ground."

"What's to stop them from sending a drone up here and bombing us off the map?" George asked.

"We have intel that they won't use drones," Adam said. "They're worried about losing all support from the populace. Drone bombings have been unpopular overseas. Drone bombings in the states would be a PR disaster. They're trying to make the arrests as if they're legitimate arrests of criminals."

"What if they send an overwhelming force?" George asked.

"You have to remember," Adam said, "we essentially have them wired. If they're planning a huge force, we'll know about it ahead of time."

Without a word, Julie stood from the table and walked outside. It was dark, the moon a small crescent. Men carrying carbines were stationed strategically around the perimeter of the property. The door opened and shut behind her. She turned.

"You okay?" George asked.

Julie shook her head. She glanced around to make sure the men were out of earshot. "I don't like all these guns and these mercenaries."

"They're here to protect us."

"You're supposed to be against wars, the police state—any violence for that matter. Now you're going to war?"

George moved closer. One side of his face was illuminated by the house, the other half, dark. "I'm not going to war. The war's coming here."

Julie exhaled heavy. "It's violence."

"People have a moral right to protect themselves against aggressors. Was it ethical to knee Larry in the groin when he tried to rape you?"

Julie glowered at George. "That's not the same thing."

"It's not?" George showed his palms. "It's *exactly* the same thing. Do you wanna talk about what happened to me when I was arrested?" George visibly shook, his fists clenched. "The only difference was I wasn't able to successfully defend myself. You were. Not a day goes by that I don't wish I could've stopped it." He stalked toward the dark woods.

Julie followed. "George, wait." She grabbed his hand.

He turned around, his eyes wet. "I won't go back to their cage. I'd rather die on this mountain."

* * *

Sunlight shone through the south-facing windows. Adam fidgeted, his knee bouncing in his seat. Zach sat next to him, checking his phone. Julie, George, and Max also sat at the table, anxiously awaiting the message. They all wondered the same thing. *Did it work?*

Everyone's cell buzzed and chimed. Immediately people checked their phones.

"That's it," Adam said.

Katie turned up the radio on the kitchen table.

A digital voice made the introduction. "This is a message from George Smith Chapman."

"Good evening," George said through the radio speakers. "I wanted to talk to you about our current situation—how we got here and how we can fix it. First, it's about the money. It's always been about the money. The money isn't simply a medium of exchange. It's been used to control us and to steal from us. You see the money is debt, and the debt is money. Without debt, there would be no money. Our system requires more of us in aggregate to be indebted every single year in perpetuity, or the system collapses. If we don't borrow enough, no problem. Our government is happy to pick up the slack.

What do they care? It was never about repayment. It's about stealing our labor, our wealth, and our freedom in the most insidious, ingenious scheme ever created.

"Voltaire said, 'Paper money eventually returns to its intrinsic value—zero.' Today it's digital money, and this dying debt-based monetary system is headed for its intrinsic value. You're probably wondering what that means for you. I suppose that depends on who you are. You can bet the connected knew this was coming and moved their wealth into tangible real things. For the unconnected, it means that much of the wealth you thought you had just went up in smoke, and the standard of living for the average American is now much lower.

"Over the next few weeks and months, prepare yourself for the steady barrage of propaganda blaming terrorists and hackers and Anarchists and Russia and China and numerous other boogeymen. Don't believe it. This was supposed to be a controlled demolition by the central bankers that spiraled out of control because of China and Russia's gold-backed currencies. The blame for this tragedy can and should be squarely placed on the US government, the Federal Reserve, and the world's central banks.

"I know this is infuriating and scary and depressing, but crisis also brings opportunity. We may not have our digital wealth, but we still have our families, our homes, our factories, our properties, our farms, our businesses, our communities, our skills, and we have a once-in-a-millennium opportunity to be free, to shed ourselves of the biggest leeches in society—the government and debt-based money. Without the leeches sucking the lifeblood from our souls and our wallets, we can be free and healthy and happy and prosperous.

"The question then becomes how. How do we defeat the biggest empire and the wealthiest group of bankers the world has ever known? It's really quite simple. We resist. We say no.

"In the next few weeks, the US government is planning to arrest three hundred thousand people—people who were identified as threats by software that tracks and records all Internet, cellular, and banking activity. Charges will be brought for their arrests. It'll be lawful according to *their* rules, but the dirty secret is that they can find so-called criminal activity for 98 percent of us. Everything from purchasing drugs online without a prescription to evading sales tax on Internet purchases to illegally downloading music and movies. And if you're one of the 2 percent without criminal activity, they'll simply manufacture a charge. I'm proof of that.

"When the police and the military and the FBI show up on your doorstep, we must defend ourselves. We must resist. Brothers and sisters, families, friends, neighbors, communities, human beings—we must resist together. By resist, I mean resist by force. The US government plans to kidnap us from our homes because we threaten their power to rule us. Our resistance is self-defense, pure and simple. I don't make this request lightly, but I believe, if we comply like docile cows, we'll die like docile cows. This fact is born out of the ghastly history of government democides that have claimed the lives of nearly three hundred million citizens in the last century.

"In addition to the US government, we must resist the Federal Reserve. At some point in the near future the Federal Reserve will unveil a new dollar with the promise that it'll fix the economy, that it'll bring jobs and wealth. Don't believe it. It's simply a reset of the old rigged game, where they continue to profit off our backs. There are free market solutions to money. Use one of them instead.

"Human beings aren't meant to be chained and mind-controlled. We're meant to be free. If we can resist the arrests and trade with money of our choosing, we'll have our freedom."

George on the radio paused. "If you're an enforcer for the government—a police officer, a soldier, or a federal agent, I implore you to walk away from the criminal enterprise that employs you. Don't turn your rifles on your friends and neighbors. We have the moral right to resist, and we have over three hundred million guns. Come and get us at your own peril."

117: George and the Best Defense

George, Gideon, and Adam walked through the forest, the rumble of a miniexcavator in the foreground. Adam and the militia men wore identical green camouflage pants, brown boots, and green T-shirts. It was shady under the closed tree canopy. One man leaned on a shovel, watching the tracked excavator make short work of the digging.

"How are you doin', Nelson?" Gideon asked.

Nelson was in his late-twenties, wiry, and short with a scruffy beard. "Beats the hell out of hand diggin'," Nelson said, "especially with all these damn roots." He turned to George. "Your neighbor saved us two days of diggin', at least."

George nodded. "I'd rather we be ready a week early than a minute late."

"I'll second that," Nelson said.

"Make sure the hole's armpit deep," Gideon said, gesturing with his tattooed arms. "Two M4s' wide by two Kevlars. I want interlocking sectors of fire, grenade sumps, elbow holes, and overhead cover. We'll bring you sandbags and plywood with the tractor. Make sure you cover those sandbags and the roof with native cover. Logs, rocks, branches, leaves."

Nelson nodded. "Do you want me to clear a field of fire?"

"Maybe a few of the small trees," Gideon replied, "but don't leave a stump sticking from the ground, and, if you do any work beyond our fighting positions, do not leave a trail. We need the element of surprise, or we're all dead."

"I have a couple chainsaws in the garage," George said.

"Thanks, George," Nelson said, sticking his shovel in the ground. "I'll grab 'em now."

Gideon took George and Adam to another nearby fighting position, one further along but smaller, built for only one person. A man dug a trench at one end of the hole. The hole was armpit deep, the floor sloping toward the trench.

"He's digging a grenade sump," Gideon said. "If a grenade's tossed in, it'll roll into the trench."

"How many fighting positions are you digging?" George asked.

"Four two-man positions and four one-man positions," Gideon said. "I'd like to have fallback positions, but we'd have to dig the positions in the meadow. I'm not sure we can conceal those positions well enough without tree cover. I'm afraid we'll lose the element of surprise."

They hiked deeper into the woods. There a swarthy man dug a series of boot-size holes. A wheelbarrow was filled with the spoils of earth. Gideon gazed at the holes, his hands on his hips.

"Freddie," Gideon said.

Freddie looked up, still working the spade. "Gideon."

"Freddie's making cartridge traps," Gideon said to George and Adam.

Adam stepped away, tapping a text on his phone.

"I set one up where I started, just to make sure my size was all right," Freddie said. "It's not covered if y'all wanna take a look."

George and Gideon followed the holes uphill. They peered inside the first hole to find a small square of wood with a shotgun shell encased in a piece of bamboo.

"We'll cover these with netting and then leaves," Gideon said. "When someone steps on the hole, it forces the round onto a nail that's against the firing pin. The round goes off, and they have a soldier who can't walk, and one injured soldier slows the whole operation. I thought about using larger pits and punji sticks, but I think they'd notice the disturbed ground. It's hard to conceal that much digging. These traps are very simple, don't involve too much digging, and are easy to conceal. We'll put in as many as we can, maybe a few hundred."

"What about afterward?" George asked. "I don't want someone ten years from now getting their foot blown off."

"Don't worry," Gideon said, "Freddie'll make a map, and he'll have a count before he conceals anything. We will have to stay inside our perimeter once he starts concealing the traps. If we can cause at least one casualty on the assault team before they reach our fighting positions, it'll be a huge advantage."

Adam joined them again as they trekked down the mountain to the cabin. Most of the black SUVs were already stashed in Daisy's family barn. Only one remained, with the box truck. They hiked down the driveway to the gravel road.

Gideon pointed along the deserted access road. "They'll secure this road. That's a given, and I wouldn't be surprised if they set up a QRF on this road a mile or two from here. Or the QRF might fast-rope off a CH-47." He looked at George. "A CH-47 is a tandem rotor heavy-lift helicopter."

"What does QRF stand for?" George asked.

Adam tapped his phone again.

"Quick reactionary force," Gideon replied. "If things go bad for the assault team, which I certainly hope it does, they'll send in the backups, which will be the QRF."

"How many men would be in the QRF?" George asked.

Adam put his phone in his pocket.

"We don't have any intel yet," Gideon replied, "so we're speculating, but I'd guess they'd use a platoon of army Rangers, which would be thirty men."

"I don't think they'll have that many men to spare," Adam said.

"I hope I'm wrong." Gideon glanced at George. "I'm sorry, George, but you're a high-value target. Shit, you're *the* high-value target. I'm nearly certain that they'll send at least four Delta assault teams, a platoon of Rangers to provide security, and another platoon for the QRF, and, even if they don't use artillery or air strikes because we're on US soil, they'll have drones in the sky watching everything."

George pinched the bridge of his nose. "So, sixty army Rangers plus the Delta Force assault teams?"

"At a minimum," Gideon said.

"How many men are on the Delta assault teams?"

"They use small teams of three each."

George turned to Adam. "You seem awfully calm about this."

Adam looked down for a moment, his pale face turning crimson.

George clenched his fists. "You're leaving, aren't you?"

Adam rubbed the back of his neck. "We have intel that they're sending recon and drones to surveil us—"

George glowered at Adam. "How long have you known?"

"I just found out. If I don't leave now, I'll be stuck here." Adam paused for a moment. "Look, George. We're both leaders of this movement. It's not smart for us to be in the same place at the same time. I'll leave most of the guys here."

George shook his head. "You're not even on the list, are you?"

Adam was quiet.

"It's your software. Of course you'd fix it to not implicate yourself. You had me read a statement telling people to resist, and you're gonna run away?"

"I didn't have to twist your arm to make that statement. Most of it was *your* words. Resisting's the right thing to do. I think you know that."

"It's a no-win situation for people," George said. "Self-defense is a right you hope never to exercise."

Adam looked up at George. "We can still fix this."

George shook his head. "No, we can't. It's not up to us anymore. It's up to the three hundred thousand people on your list. You drafted those people into a revolution, and I lit the match." George glanced up his driveway, toward Adam's SUV. "You better get moving."

Adam showed his palms. "George, I'm sorry."

George turned to Gideon as Adam walked back to the cabin.

"I thought you knew," Gideon said.

"No, I didn't." George stared down the road, then looked at Gideon.

Gideon was a big man, tall and muscular. He had a bushy beard and thick dark hair under a baseball cap that read Infidel.

"Does everyone know what we're up against?"

"For the most part."

George nodded. "That's good, but we should have a formal meeting, give people a chance to leave if they want."

"I think most of the guys know why they're here."

"Why are *you* here?" George asked. "I figured you were here to protect Adam, and I was just part of the package, but he doesn't really need protection, does he?"

"No, he doesn't. We're here by choice. We're all grunts and jarheads who've been used up and lied to. Seven of us served in the same SF detachment. We saw some shit in Afghanistan—poppy fields, the drug trade, and the CIA ..." Gideon shook his head. "Let's just say it was obvious to us that it was never about freedom or protection. The seven of us got out as soon as our enlistment contracts were up. I started protesting the war with these guys, and we formed a militia group. Then we got hooked up with Anonymous, eventually with Adam, and now we're here." Gideon nodded, the wheels turning in his mind. "I think this is the first time that we're actually fighting for freedom."

"Thank you for protecting my family," George said, extending his hand.

They shook hands. Gideon had a hint of a smile.

George took a deep breath. "If we repel the assault—"

"*When* we repel the assault," Gideon said.

"When we repel the assault, how do we handle the QRF?"

Gideon gazed at the ridge in the distance and grinned. "Like the Taliban."

118: John and Losing Control

Secretary of Homeland Security Isaac Quarles was thin and bald with a crescent of white hair. He spoke to President John Bradley and the cabinet members.

"Grocery stores are still mostly bare, and so are gas stations," Secretary Quarles said. "Thousands of reports confirm violence at grocery stores, gas stations, and convenience stores. Police are operating at a limited capacity. Many officers have elected to stay home and to protect their families. Anecdotally crime has spiked, but we don't have official statistics. There've been reports of communities banding together and forming armed neighborhood watches."

John sat at the head of the massive oval table with the twenty cabinet members. His face and body were taut as he listened to the disaster that he presided over. He turned to the secretary of energy.

"Secretary Humphrey," John said, "When can we expect gas stations to be refueled?"

Carl Humphrey raised one side of his mouth in contempt. "I believe I made it clear that it was a mistake to block those tankers. I also made it clear that refineries can process and deliver fuel in two days under perfect conditions, but I thought it would take much longer, which it has. Having said that, as of today, fuel is flowing through the pipelines, and the trucks are beginning to run now, but it's sporadic and at a lower volume."

"I'd like to release fuel from the strategic reserve," John said.

"Mr. President," Secretary of Defense Gates said, "I think it would be a mistake to release the strategic reserve for civilian use."

"It won't help the immediate problem," Secretary Humphrey said. "That fuel's crude oil. It still needs to be refined."

John nodded.

Humphrey continued. "The biggest problem is that fuel is damn expensive in dollar terms, and, with the banks still shuttered, people are only accepting cash, barter, precious metals, and illegal cryptocurrencies." Humphrey pointed at John. "You're damn lucky this April's been warm."

John looked away for a moment, then at the secretary of the treasury. "Secretary Moody, when will the banks reopen?"

"The banks should be reopened in a couple of days," Moody said. "With the cyberattack, we've had to restore the entire system. The Federal Reserve has moved up the timeline for the new currency. Given the dire state of the world economy, we need a stable reserve currency, and we need it now. They're planning for the Fourth of July. It can be sold to the public as a new Independence Day. Cryptocurrencies and gold are very popular with the antigovernment crowd. Giving them a gold-backed currency with block chain technology may be one way to suppress the dissent and give them what they want." Secretary Moody took a sip of water.

"I agree," John said.

"We've restocked the banks with fresh currency for the reopen," Moody said. "We're expecting the currency velocity to increase rapidly, given the pent-up demand and loss of confidence. We will withstand the expected bank runs, but this will be at the expense of the purchasing power of the dollar."

John clenched his jaw for a moment. "More inflation?"

"Yes, and we expect it to accelerate."

"What does that mean? Are we talking about wheelbarrows full of money? Zimbabwe-style inflation? What?"

"It's impossible to say, but we might see prices rise a few hundred percent in the next few months."

John blew out a breath. "Will this new currency fix the problem?"

"Yes."

"Then we just have to survive the next two and a half months." John looked at the director of the FBI. "Director Hewitt, what's the status on the arrests?"

"We're issuing electronic warrants as we speak," Hewitt said. "We expect to begin making arrests tomorrow and for the next week or so. It would be advantageous for the mission if we had more time for reconnaissance."

"Do we have the manpower to surveil before making arrests?" John asked.

"If we had more time."

"In case you haven't noticed, Director Hewitt, this country's falling apart. With Internet and communications operable, the antigovernment activists are gaining momentum. Every day that we wait is another day that they spread their propaganda and enlist more domestic terrorists."

"Yes, Mr. President."

John looked at the director of the NSA. "Admiral Coffey, have you found George Chapman?"

"Yes, Mr. President," Coffey replied. "We have cell phone records that indicate he's at his residence in central Pennsylvania. We have a drone en route to confirm and to provide reconnaissance. I would like to reiterate that I believe these arrests will be disastrous. These people are ready and willing to resist. There are over three hundred million guns in this country. Our police officers and even the reserve military units may not have the resolve to make arrests under such violent resistance. I think it would be prudent to wait until the economic situation stabilizes to make the arrests. If you waited a few months, people will be far more complacent."

"Until they're warned again," John said. "We've forgotten what *classified* means in this country." John leaned forward, his elbows on the table. "We don't wait for terrorists. George Chapman committed cyberterrorism and incited nationwide domestic terrorism with his hack of the Integrated Public Alert and Warning System and subsequent message of violence. Need I remind everyone that he endorsed killing police officers, federal agents, and soldiers? We're not arresting him for downloading music. He's a confirmed terrorist." John turned to the secretary of defense. "Secretary Gates, do you have an update on the assault on the Chapman residence?"

"We have four Delta teams for the assault," Gates said, "and two platoons from the 10th Mountain Division for security and QRF. We have drones for surveillance and Blackhawks for fast-roping the assault team into the mountains, but we'd be far more secure with authorized air strikes."

"Need I remind you that we are on American soil," John said. "If we bomb Chapman's residence, there's no going back for this country. We are then in a war against our own citizens. People will accept arrests. They'll accept that these people are criminals, but they won't accept bombing Americans like we're in the Middle East."

119: Katie and Triple-Tapped Bull's-Eyes

Katie was in the garage, a face in the crowd, along with Julie, Max, Zach, Adam, and the fifteen-man security detail. George stood in front of a dry erase board with a hand-drawn map that detailed their strategy. He looked pale and haggard as he addressed them.

"First, I want everyone to know how grateful I am that you're here. Thank you," George said. "Without you, my family's odds of survival are very low in my opinion. Having said that, this is still very dangerous. Gideon and I spoke earlier, and I know many of you are aware of the dangers, but I'd like Gideon to detail it one more time, and, if anyone wants to leave with Adam, you are of course free to go." George nodded to Gideon and joined the crowd.

Gideon took George's place at the dry erase board. "Thanks, George." Gideon cleared his throat. "I'm not gonna bullshit you. None of us have been in this position before—facing an enemy with superior technology, numbers, support, and weaponry. We don't have intel yet, but, given that George is probably their number one target for arrest, and Katie, Julie, and Max are all high-value targets, I expect four three-man Delta teams for the assault. I also think they'll have a platoon of Rangers for security and another platoon for the QRF. They'll have drones for surveillance. I don't think they want to use air strikes on American soil, but it's always a possibility." Gideon paused, making eye contact with the guys, one-by-one. "If you're thinking they might not kill Americans on American soil, I can guarantee the Delta guys will shoot to kill without hesitation." Gideon paused for a moment and glowered at the audience. "That's what we're dealing with. If you don't wanna be here, get your shit and leave, because, if you're not willing to die on this mountain, you shouldn't be here."

A few guys looked at each other and spoke in hushed tones.

Adam spoke to Zach. "I'll keep you updated when we have new intel." Adam turned to the crowd. "Good luck, everyone. Be safe." He exited the garage. Three men followed him.

Two men were arguing. "Fuck this. I'm leaving," one of them said and marched for the door. The other picked up his bag and stepped to the door, his head bowed.

"Anyone else?" Gideon asked.

Another young man grabbed his gear and hurried for the door.

Gideon shook his head. "Is that it?" He paused, surveying the crowd.

Katie counted the remaining people. The numbers had dwindled from twenty-one to fourteen.

"Let's get a head count," Gideon said.

"We have fourteen," Katie replied.

Gideon stroked his beard, his face in anguish. "Fuck," he muttered under his breath.

George looked like he was going to throw up.

"What's wrong?" Katie asked.

"We need fourteen people, minimum," George said.

"We have fourteen."

"I hadn't planned on you three"—Gideon motioned to Katie, Julie, and Max—"having to …"

"Fight?" Katie asked.

"Yes, ma'am," Gideon replied.

"Correct me if I'm wrong, but we're high-value targets."

"Yes."

"Then they're trying to kill us."

"Yes."

"Maybe we can change the plan," George said.

Gideon hung his head for a moment. "We have to have at least one person on the ridge to detonate the IEDs and provide surveillance from the road, but I much prefer two. If someone falls asleep, we're dead. We have fighting positions for twelve people, and that's a minimum. If we had the numbers, I would've doubled that. If we don't have all those positions covered, we'll have gaps in our sectors of fire."

"Then we'll fight," Max said.

"No, you won't," Julie said.

"I'm not a kid anymore. They're trying to kill me too."

"You're only eighteen years old."

Max crossed his arms over his chest. "Old enough to join the military without a parent's consent."

Max looked like he could join the military. He still had a baby face, but he had a little stubble on his chin. He was stocky, his arms and chest defined from working on the homestead and helping Daisy on her parents' farm.

"Max, please," George said.

"You know I'm right," Max replied.

"It'll be safer on the ridge," Gideon said, "and it doesn't matter if you can shoot. It's not as safe as hiding out at the Baxters' farm, but much safer than manning a fighting position. They just have to press the buttons and make it to the rally point."

"My mom and Katie can go to the ridge," Max said. "I'll take a fighting position."

"Absolutely not," Julie said. "I'll take a fighting position."

"I'll take a fighting position," Katie said.

"Have any of you fired a rifle before?" Gideon asked.

"George taught me how to shoot a handgun," Max said.

"I was an archer in prep school," Katie said. "A very good one."

"Julie?" Gideon asked.

"I don't like guns," Julie replied, barely above a whisper.

"It's okay," Gideon said, approaching Julie. "We need you to be on that ridge. Will you be able to detonate those IEDs?"

"Yes."

"We should have a contest for Katie and Max," said Freddie, the swarthy man in camo. "We'll train 'em up on the M4—safety, marksmanship, breathing, malfunctions, reloading, the works. Then we'll see who's better."

* * *

The makeshift range was set up under the tree canopy but in an area relatively clear of brush and small trees. It wasn't ideal, but they didn't want to be seen by possible overhead surveillance.

"Range is hot," Freddie said. "Make ready. Three rounds in circle A, and three rounds in circle F."

Katie pulled the charging handle on her M4. She stood in an isosceles stance, her rifle pointed down a few feet in front of her.

"Engage the target," Freddie said.

Katie raised the rifle and flipped the safety off with her thumb as she did so. The stock was tight to her shoulder, her eyes and face close to the red dot sight. She fired three rounds dead center of the circle marked A, then three more rounds in the circle marked F. Max was still firing when she dropped her empty mag to the ground and flicked on the safety.

"Cease fire," Freddie said. "Weapons on safe."

Freddie and Gideon checked that the rifles were on safety, and they walked toward the targets alongside Katie and Max.

"Goddamn, girl," Freddie said, looking at Katie's target. "You're like that Katniss Ever—whatever her name is." Freddie turned to his co-instructor. "Gideon, check this shit out."

Katie's target had two tiny clusters of triple-tapped bull's-eyes.

120: Julie and the Plan

Julie stood among the group, between George and Max. George had dark circles under his eyes and pale skin. *He says he's fine, but the evidence written on his face says otherwise. One life-threatening crisis at a time please.* Gideon stood at the whiteboard, the remaining thirteen defenders huddled close, their attention astute.

"I guarantee the attack will come at night," Gideon said. "They think they own the night. They don't know we have NVGs or image intensifiers, so they'll come in here lit like Christmas trees. When they use image intensifiers, and they think the enemy is in the dark, they'll attach infrared strobes, which are tough to spot in darkness but will pop with night vision. They use it to avoid friendly fire. It'll be an advantage for us because we'll see them coming."

Gideon pointed to the hundreds of small squares just beyond the fighting positions. "Three hundred cartridge traps surround us. Do not venture beyond the fighting positions without Freddie or myself and the map. I believe the assault will likely trigger at least one, possibly more if they come in from multiple directions. I expect the Delta assault team to fast-rope in off a Blackhawk at least a mile from here. I think the main assault will come from the west with at least two Delta teams, and they'll send another team from the north and another from the east. I think they'll leave the south open, to encourage us to take the obvious escape route through the road. Of course they'll have that road locked down with their security platoon."

Gideon pointed to the north-facing two-man fighting position. "George and Katie, you'll be here. This position is closest to the game trail for escape, and Freddie and I will be in holes on your flanks." Gideon pointed to the eastern two-man fighting position. "Zach, you'll be with Nelson here. I've put our most experienced guys on the west fighting positions, where I think the main assault will occur. We must repel the initial assault at all costs. If we don't, it's over." Gideon surveyed the group, unblinking.

"When we repel the initial assault, they'll send in the QRF. I believe they'll send the QRF from the road. Julie and Max, you'll be in the hidey-hole on the ridge. Remember your marker is that busted refrigerator on the side of the road. As soon as you see the first truck pass the fridge, push the button marked Road. That'll detonate the daisy chain buried in the gravel road. Ideally we'll disable multiple vehicles, causing a traffic jam on the narrow road. Likely they'll send the remaining QRF on foot, along the ditches on both sides of the road. When the first man nears the front of the wrecked convoy, press the second button labeled Ditches. That'll trigger the daisy chains buried in the ditches." Gideon moved closer to Julie and Max. "Do you two have any questions?"

"What does the detonator look like?" Julie asked.

Gideon turned to a wiry man with thick dark-rim glasses. "Lincoln."

Lincoln stepped toward Julie and Gideon. He removed a garage door opener from his camo cargo pants. There were two buttons, each labeled by Sharpie on athletic tape.

"It's just a garage door opener," Lincoln said, showing Julie, with Max also looking on. "It'll give us near-instant detonation. Not as good as direct-wired but still pretty good."

Lincoln held on to the detonator.

"As soon as the QRF has been repelled, we need to evacuate to the north through the game trail. We'll rally behind the overturned oaks that y'all saw yesterday. We'll wait five minutes, and then we're gone. If you miss the rally point, you'll have to meet us at the second rally point near the Baxters' farm. Does everyone remember the spot?"

There were head nods, and some said, "Yes."

Gideon continued. "When we get to the Baxters', we'll resupply, and four of us will drive the SUVs in opposite directions as a diversion. Raise your hand if you volunteered to drive."

Freddie, Nelson, and two other men raised their hands.

Gideon nodded at the men. "The rest of us will provide protection for the twenty-six-mile hike to the hunting cabin. Mr. Baxter recommended this cabin because the owner died recently and isn't connected to Mr. Chapman or Mr. Baxter. We're relying on his silence, but we have no other choice."

"He would never say anything," Max said.

"I agree," George said.

"Let's hope not," Gideon replied.

"Daisy's dad would never do that," Max said quietly to Julie.

"I know," Julie whispered.

"Remember, the code word is *shit show*. Any questions?" Gideon asked.

The group shook their heads. A few said, "No."

Zach's encrypted phone buzzed. The group looked at him wide-eyed, as he fished his phone from his pocket. He read the text.

"It's from Adam," Zach said, still reading. "The arrests have started. There's already been reports of armed resistance. An attack is planned here tomorrow night and possibly on-the-ground recon tonight. Drone for surveillance. The force is almost identical to what we've been preparing for. Four Delta teams and two platoons for security and QRF, but they're from the 10th Mountain Division in Fort Drum, not Rangers. Assault team fast-roping in to the west." Zach looked up from his phone. "That's all it says."

"Does it say where the QRF's coming from?" Gideon asked.

Zach checked his phone again. "No."

Gideon stroked his beard for a moment. "Everyone, except George and Katie, needs to be in position in the next hour." Gideon pointed to George, then Katie. "Remember, you two. Just act normal tonight and tomorrow. Keep the lights on in the main house until 2200 hours. Tomorrow set the timer for the lights to turn off at 2200, and at dusk get to your fighting position." Gideon glanced around the group. "For the rest of you, shit, eat, do what you need to do, because—for the next thirty-six hours—we need to remain hidden. You are not to leave your holes for anything. When you have to piss, use the grenade sumps. When you're hungry or thirsty, you only get what you bring to the hole. Got it?"

121: George and the Assault

George scanned the forest, looking through the porthole of his fighting position. It would be pitch dark if not for the night vision goggles attached to his helmet. The image intensifier made everything look dull green and black. Katie was on the opposite end of their hole. The plywood roof was covered with branches and leaves. The sandbags raised the roof enough to provide portholes. Stones and branches scavenged from the forest obscured the sandbags. The men had been careful to haul stones from inside their position. Gideon was paranoid that the Delta guys would notice if the area was disturbed as they made their assault.

George's heart pounded at the sight of movement. He grabbed his rifle and looked through the sights. He relaxed and set down his rifle. It was a fox. Even it bounded away as if it knew it shouldn't be here. George wanted to ask Katie if she saw it, but they were supposed to maintain noise discipline. They'd been on high alert for hours. It was exhausting, the calm and the quiet, like a chilling horror scene right before the murder, except the creepy music and anticipation lasted four hours, instead of forty seconds.

His eyes felt heavy. It had to be past one. For a split second, a light appeared in the distance, just a tiny blip, then it was gone. *Am I seeing things?* A single shotgun blast pierced the air. George grabbed his rifle, his heart racing and his stomach churning. *That had to be a cartridge trap.* He flipped the safety to fire. Another shotgun blast came, followed by a barrage of rifle fire.

The blinking light appeared again, closer. It was a man moving quickly, then another. George aimed for the lower neck, just above the body armor. He fired three shots, the noise deafening. The man dropped; the other moved behind a tree. Katie was firing now. George aimed for the down man, knowing that they never leave a man behind. George waited for the second man to help his comrade. The second man low-crawled toward the body. He crouched and tried to drag the dead or injured man behind a tree. George lit up the second man with another burst of fire. The second man dropped in a heap.

"Get down!" Katie said.

Her voice sounded like they were in a tin can. George looked to his left. Katie kicked at a grenade. George threw himself to the ground and covered his head. Then came the explosion, dirt and debris raining down on him.

122: John and the Situation Room

President John Bradley and the National Security Council sat at the rectangular table in the White House Situation Room. They leaned toward the massive screen, watching and listening to the assault. The screen was split into twelve, each one a camera and mike for each Delta operator. Like a first-person shooter game, they saw what the Delta operators saw, an NVG-enhanced green-and-black forest.

A single shotgun blast was heard and then a grunt. One Delta operator on the ground.

"Cartridge trap," a Delta operator said. "Watch your step—"

Another shotgun blast came, followed by a barrage of automatic gunfire. Muzzle flashes emanated from low piles of brush and leaves and rocks. Three more operators were on the ground.

"Contact!" a Delta operator said. "Turn off the strobes. They have NVGs."

The Delta operators returned fire. Two operators tossed grenades into the fighting positions. One operator was shot as he did so. The grenades exploded; the roof blown off one fighting position, the other still intact. More muzzle flashes brought another Delta casualty.

"Abort," Colonel Erickson said through the laptops on the table. The colonel broadcasted from the command outpost.

"Abort," the remaining Delta operators echoed.

"Goddamn it," John said.

"Requesting air support," Colonel Erickson said.

Joint Special Operations Commanding General Webb said, "Mr. President, requesting authorization for an air strike."

"No air strikes," John said.

"Mr. President, if we send in the QRF, they are likely to suffer further casualties."

"This was discussed. No air strikes."

"Negative on air support. Activate the QRF," General Webb said to the laptop microphone and Colonel Erickson.

"Activate the QRF," Colonel Erickson said. "Be advised the area is booby-trapped with cartridge traps and there are camouflaged fighting positions."

123: Julie and the IEDs

Julie and Max were in their hole on the ridge above the gravel road. Julie watched the road through the porthole, her NVGs painting the scene green and black. Max also watched, the detonator in hand, his rifle leaning against the earthen wall. Julie's eyes were heavy. Max had kept watch last night, and he had slept all day, but Julie hadn't slept at all the previous night. She'd never tried to sleep in a dirt hole before.

A single shotgun blast sounded in the distance.

Julie flinched.

"They're here," Max whispered.

Another shotgun blasted in the distance, followed by a barrage of gunfire. Julie closed her eyes, thinking of George and Katie and the men she barely knew.

She heard the thud of an explosion, followed by another, then more gunfire.

"They'll be coming soon," Max whispered.

Julie opened her eyes. The gravel road was desolate.

"Do you think they stopped the assault?" Julie asked, her voice barely audible.

"Probably ... I hope so," Max whispered, not looking away from the road.

"I love you, and I'm sorry that you're here—"

"Don't, Mom. I'm here because I wanna be. You know what they did to George."

"I know."

"And now he's sick because of them."

"He's fine."

Max frowned. "Stop, Mom. I know he's HIV positive. I saw the antiretro-viral drugs in the medicine cabinet. Why didn't you guys tell me?"

Julie exhaled. "He didn't want you to worry."

"He looks awful, so I'm worried. His pill bottle's empty, by the way. He's out of medication, isn't he?"

"We'll get him his medicine as soon as possible."

The rattle and hum of diesel engines could be heard and was getting louder. No headlights appeared, but Julie saw the convoy of Humvees approaching rapidly, dust and gravel spilling from their tires. As soon as the lead truck passed the abandoned refrigerator, Max detonated the daisy chain of explosives on the road. The mountain shook, and the road was obscured by a cloud of stone dust.

"Holy shit," Max said, his voice muffled.

"Are you okay?" Julie asked, her ears ringing.

"I can't see the road. Should I blow the ditches?"

"Wait a minute. Let the dust settle."

Max picked up the walkie-talkie to call Gideon. "Maybe I should ask Gideon."

"Gideon said to only use that in an emergency. Just wait."

They waited as the stone dust fell to the ground, covering men and machines in a film of gritty powder. The convoy was stopped dead, eight Humvees in a pileup. One vehicle was on fire, and all but two were rendered inoperable. One Humvee tried to pull off the road but was wedged between the trees tight to the roadside and the wreckage in front and behind them. Men exited the vehicles, dazed and disoriented. Some were screaming; others barked commands. Bloody bodies were pulled from the wreckage. More Humvees approached from behind. Additional men rushed the scene.

"My God," Julie said, horrified at the destruction.

"There's more men," Max said. "I have to blow the ditches."

"Wait. Let them get their injured."

"Mom, we have to go."

"A few more minutes."

Julie watched, her mouth still open as bodies were carried over shoulders and on stretchers and placed into Humvees. A few men fought the vehicle fires with extinguishers. Screaming and pleas for help continued, the human suffering spread over the road.

Phil M. Williams

A few minutes later fresh soldiers—soldiers with clean uniforms—hurried past the marooned convoy along the ditches.

"When they get to the lead vehicle ..." Julie said.

Max nodded, his finger hovering over the detonator.

Julie crouched down in the hole and covered her head and ears. Max pressed the button, detonating the daisy chains in the ditches.

124: George and Katie

"Katie," George called out, still crouched in their hole. Another explosion went off nearby and then more gunfire.

Katie was in a heap, six-feet away.

George's ears pounded, his voice sounded muffled. He flipped up his NVGs and crawled to her. He touched her back. "Katie." He turned her over.

Her head lolled to the side. Her face was a bloody mass, completely unrecognizable. Blood covered her neck and chest.

George's hand shook as he pressed his fingers to her neck. No pulse. George cradled her bloody body to his chest, his eyes brimming with tears. He rocked her like a child, tears clearing paths through the dirt on his face. "I'm sorry, Katie. I'm so sorry."

The gunfire ceased. There was another explosion, this one in the distance, from the direction of the gravel road. George dragged Katie out of the fighting position through the rear crawl space. He kneeled in front of her body.

"Shit show," Gideon said as he approached. "Are you all right?" Gideon flipped up his NVGs and looked at Katie's body. "Fuck. I'm sorry, George."

"She saved my life," George said, still on his knees, "but I'm already dead."

"We have to go," Gideon said. "They just detonated the road."

"Is everyone else okay?"

"We lost two, Neil and Darren."

George nodded. "I'm sorry, Gideon."

"We have to go—now."

George stood, bent over, and tried to hoist Katie.

Gideon put his hand on George's back. "Let her be, George. We can't take the bodies."

George knelt beside her, took her hand in his, and squeezed. He stood; Gideon's head was bowed in respect. George grabbed his rifle from the fighting position, and he and Gideon crept to the rally point.

As they approached the game trail and the overturned oaks, Gideon whispered, "Shit show."

"We're here," Freddie whispered back.

George and Gideon slipped in a narrow opening between the trees. Inside, seven guys were huddled with full battle rattle.

"Where's Katie?" Zach asked.

George shook his head. "She's gone."

Zach took a few steps away from the group. He kneeled by himself, his head bowed. He didn't make a sound, but his eyes overflowed with tears.

They waited for Julie and Max. The men were antsy to leave the war zone.

One man whispered, "We're sitting ducks."

"They should've detonated the second daisy chain by now," George whispered to Gideon. "Maybe we should radio them."

"I don't wanna break radio silence unless we're sure it's an emergency," Gideon replied.

"I'll go get them, then."

"You're not going anywhere. Give 'em a couple minutes. If they don't show, I'll get 'em."

The men smiled as the second charge blew.

125: John and from Bad to Worse

The screen switched from the Delta operators to the team leaders of the QRF. President John Bradley and the National Security Council watched the split screen as the men of the 10th Mountain Division sped along the gravel road in an eight-vehicle convoy.

There was an explosion, some screens immediately going black, others obscured with dust. Groans and screams and wailing transmitted now. John and the National Security Council watched the screens, silent, their mouths agape.

"Mr. President," General Webb said, breaking the silence. The general's uniform was adorned with medals and badges. His eyes were red, his jaw set tight. "I strongly advise an air strike. They've planted IEDs and booby-trapped the property."

"Do we have reinforcements?" John asked.

"It would be irresponsible to send in more men without the engineers and minesweepers to clear the area."

"How long would that take?"

"They'd be coming from Philadelphia. I'd estimate at least four hours."

John shook his head. "That's too long."

The dust cleared. A few men moved now. Bloody bodies were pulled from the vehicles. Some still groaned and wailed, but now a few barked orders.

"What about the security team?" John asked.

"Mr. President, we don't know what they're walking into," General Webb said. "Again I strongly recommend an air strike."

John glared at General Webb. "Do you have any idea what will happen to this country if I order an air strike on US soil to take out arguably the most popular man in America?"

General Webb didn't respond.

"Send in the security team," John said.

"Mr. President," Secretary of Defense Gates said, "I agree with General Webb. An air strike is the prudent course of action at this time. The area is remote. The chances of civilian casualties are near zero, and it's remote enough that the average person will never know about the strike."

"They'll never know?" John said, glaring at Secretary Gates. "There's no secrecy anymore." John turned to General Webb. "Send in the security team."

"We need to evacuate the wounded," General Webb said.

"Evacuate the wounded, then send in the security team and what's left of the QRF."

"Yes, Mr. President." General Webb spoke into the mike, to Colonel Erickson and the command outpost. "Evacuate the wounded, then send in the security team and what's left of the QRF."

"Roger that, sir," Colonel Erickson replied.

Fifteen minutes later, boots marched alongside the wreckage toward George's property. Again there was an explosion. The Situation Room was dead silent, waiting for signs of life. This time nobody cried out in agony.

John pounded the side of his fist on the table and turned to General Webb. John said, "Blow 'em off the fucking map."

126: Julie and the Drone Strike

An unarmed Julie followed Max, drowning in her oversize camo fatigues. They both wore their NVGs. They chose speed over stealth. Their breathing and the crunch of their feet on leaves caused a racket. Julie tried not to think of the consequences of meeting the US Army in these woods.

A massive blast came from George's house that shook the mountain. Max and Julie instinctively fell to the ground and covered their heads. After a moment of silence, their gazes met. Julie's eyes were wide.

"They're already at the rally point," Max said, as if he read her mind. Max stood and helped his mother upright. "Let's get moving. They're waiting on us."

They hiked a safe distance from the north edge of the property, careful to stay far away from the cartridge traps. The outskirts of George's property were dead silent. Max found the concealed entrance to the game trail. They slipped around the brush. Fifty yards farther, they found the downed oaks. Yet no sign of anyone.

"Shit show," Max said.

"We're here," George said.

Julie breathed a sigh of relief. *He's okay.* George slipped through a narrow opening between the trees. He looked like death. His eyes were red-rimmed and dark-circled, his face pale and dirty. He hugged Max, then Julie. He held Julie tight for a moment. The other men exited the hiding place.

"Where's Katie?" Max asked Zach.

Zach was unresponsive, his head hanging.

"She's gone," George said.

Max's shoulders slumped, his bravado vanquished.

Julie began to cry softly.

"We have to go," Gideon said. "They'll come back with reinforcements and maybe more air strikes. We can't be anywhere near here when that happens."

The group, now only eleven strong, moved quickly along the game trail, single file.

127: George and the Sacrifice

The group was just inside the forest canopy, a few hundred yards away from the Baxters' farmhouse. It looked exactly as Mr. Baxter said it would—deserted and pitch black.

"Can you tack this up in the barn?" Max asked Freddie, holding out a folded envelope. "There's a corkboard inside, next to the door."

George shook his head. "No, Max. Any information you give the Baxters puts them and us in danger."

"George is right," Gideon said.

"It's just an envelope," Max said. "There's no letter. I told Daisy that I would leave her an empty envelope to let her know I'm alive."

George looked to Gideon.

"That's fine," Gideon said.

Freddie put the envelope in his pocket.

Freddie, Nelson, and the other two men who had volunteered to be the diversion sprinted from the woods to the barn. A few minutes later, four black SUVs raced from the barn. Three sped down the gravel road without headlights. Freddie backed his vehicle to the forest edge. He hopped out, opened the rear hatch, and tossed out gear and supplies into the woods. Gideon helped for a minute.

"See you on the other side," Freddie said to Gideon as he climbed back into the driver's seat.

Gideon nodded. "See you on the other side."

Freddie sped away.

The remaining individuals collected the packs and dispersed the supplies. Everyone was loaded down with twenty to eighty pounds of gear and supplies, depending on the individual's carrying capacity.

The group was down to seven: George, Julie, Max, Zach, Gideon, and his two remaining men, Xavier and Vince.

They hiked through the forest, slowed and burdened by their packs. Gideon navigated by compass. He was too paranoid to turn on his GPS. George knew the woods better than anyone, so he was behind Gideon, assisting with navigation.

"Driving those trucks—it's a suicide mission, isn't it?" George asked Gideon.

Gideon didn't turn around. "Probably."

128: John and No Escape

President John Bradley and the National Security Council watched the three black SUVs speed down a gravel road, leaving a cloud of dust in their wake.

"Mr. President, we need a decision," General Webb said.

"Frank?" John said.

Secretary of State Frank Whitehead said, "Civilians in central PA don't drive SUVs like that at 2:00 a.m. without headlights. It's them."

John nodded to General Webb. "Attack."

"Target approved," General Webb said into the laptop mike. "Fire when ready."

"Roger that, sir," Colonel Erickson replied from the command outpost.

The White House Situation Room was dead silent as they waited in anticipation of the payload.

"Ten seconds to impact," Colonel Erickson said, breaking the silence. "Eight, seven, six, five, four, three, two, one."

The three black SUVs on the screen disappeared in a cloud of dust. A few members of the National Security Council cheered. The cheering quieted as one SUV emerged from the dust and turned onto the main road.

"Goddamn it," John said.

"Permission to fire on the vehicle," Colonel Erickson said.

"Mr. President, permission to fire on the vehicle?" General Webb asked.

"Permission granted," John said.

"Target approved," General Webb said into the laptop mike. "Fire when ready."

"Roger that, sir," Colonel Erickson replied.

Ten seconds later, the SUV was obliterated.

129: Julie and the Life of a Fugitive

Julie trudged through the forest, following in lockstep with the man in front of her. She didn't bother with the NVGs anymore; the moonlight was enough for a follower. Her legs were rubbery; her lower back ached from the pack—a pack she knew was the lightest of the group. There was strict noise discipline, so they rarely spoke.

Julie was alone with her thoughts. *Are we fugitives now? We're probably on the FBI's most wanted list. Our names and faces will be in post offices across the country. Gideon said they destroyed our home with a drone strike. Even if they didn't, we can't go home ... ever. What about Max? Will he spend the rest of his life in prison? Maybe people will hide us, like a modern underground railroad.*

There was commotion from the front of the group.

"Whoa," someone said. "Are you okay, George?"

Julie rushed forward, passing the men in front of her. George lay on the ground, Gideon, Zach, and Max huddled around him.

Julie dropped to her knees next to George, opposite Gideon. George was pale in the moonlight and dripping with sweat. She put the back of her hand to his forehead. He was listless, his eyes droopy.

"He's burning up. He has a fever," Julie said, glancing at Gideon. "We have to stop."

It began to rain. The group moved into a flat area. Gideon and Xavier carried George. Xavier was a brawny former soldier from Gideon's old SF unit. The group made lean-to shelters with their ponchos, branches, and existing trees. They covered George first while Julie dabbed his head with a cold, moist handkerchief.

Julie spoke to him, even though he was out of it. "We're resting now," she said. "Everything will be fine. You'll get some rest, and you'll feel better in the morning."

George was unresponsive.

The men rotated guard duty throughout the night. The rain continued unabated. Julie watched George, terrified by every hitch of his breathing.

* * *

Shortly before daybreak, the rain stopped, and George's eyes fluttered and opened.

"Where are we?" he asked, his voice gravelly.

Julie smiled wide. "We're still on the trail. You passed out last night."

He nodded.

Julie unscrewed the cap on her canteen. "Have some water."

The men stirred as light filtered through the tree canopy. Julie ate half an MRE and lightened her load by drinking some water. She tried to get George to eat, but he was nauseated. He did drink water. After breakfast, the group moved out. George was able to walk, but he was given a lighter pack.

Julie and Max were toward the rear of the single-file line. George was in front near Gideon to help with navigation again.

"How's he doing?" Max asked, as they hiked.

"His fever broke," Julie said. "He's just weak."

Julie thought about the distance to the hunting camp—twenty-six miles. She thought they must've hiked at least ten the night before, so sixteen more. She used to do four miles around her neighborhood for her workout. She thought she'd be fine, but walking on flat ground in running pants and sneakers was a lot different than walking through mountainous terrain with a pack and boots.

For most of the day, they hiked though the mountains in silence. Julie developed blisters on her feet, and her back ached. She didn't complain. She put one foot in front of the other, calculating her gait and foot placement for the least amount of pain. George was weak, but he also hiked without complaint. It helped that the men took most of his supplies, lightening his load. Late in the afternoon, everyone running on fumes, Julie saw the deserted hunting cabin.

130: George and the Beast Defanged

The hunting cabin had spring-fed water, a wood stove in the kitchen, and two bedrooms with six single beds. The only bathroom was an outhouse, and there was no electricity. George sat at the kitchen table, eating an MRE of hash browns and bacon. Sunlight streamed through the windows of the stone cabin. Gideon and Julie sat with George at the table, drinking coffee. Max was outside setting up the solar panel Gideon had packed to recharge batteries and electronic devices.

"You look better," Julie said, smiling.

"I feel better," George replied.

"I wasn't sure you were gonna make it," Gideon said.

"Neither was I."

Zach burst into the cabin. "I found a signal at the top of the mountain," he said. Everyone turned to Zach as he approached the table. "Adam sent me a text. They released three hundred thousand nonviolent drug offenders from prison to make room for the arrests, but they only arrested a small fraction of what they planned, maybe twenty thousand. People resisted. There've been reports of armed resistance across the country, and a slew of reports of local and even some state police ignoring the arrest warrants from the Feds." Zach took a deep breath and looked at Gideon. "Three of the four SUVs were hit with drone strikes."

Gideon clenched his jaw. "Who made it?"

"Adam doesn't know."

"I'm sorry, Gideon," George said.

Gideon stared at the table, his face twisted in agony.

"It had to be Freddie that made it," George said. "He left a few minutes after the others."

Gideon nodded.

Zach looked at George. "Adam wants you to make a statement of demands for the government."

"How many demands?" George asked.

"Excuse me?"

"How many demands does Adam have for the government?"

"Twenty-five."

"I'm not reading that," George said.

Zach furrowed his brow. "Why not?"

"We only need two things."

"Then we'll record that." Zach removed his phone from his pocket. "Where do you want to record?"

"Not here," George replied. "I don't want them to see the cabin in the video. I'll walk up the mountain with you."

George hiked in the dappled shade of the forest. His quads and calves burned as he moved up an Appalachian Mountain incline. Zach waited upslope. George put his hands on his hips and stopped to rest once he reached Zach. "My legs are still a little weak. You mind if we rest a minute?"

George and Zach both wore forest camo. Zach had a rifle slung across his chest. George had his Glock holstered to his hip.

"I'm sorry about Katie," George said.

"Me too," Zach said, his head bowed.

"She spoke highly of you."

Zach looked up, his eyes wet. "I should've forgiven her."

George took a deep breath. "I should've jumped on that grenade."

Zach turned away and wiped his eyes discreetly. He pivoted back to George. "You ready?"

"Yeah."

They hiked to the peak and caught their breath. Zach retrieved his phone and powered it on. After a brief wait, Zach said, "I have a signal."

George stood in front of an old oak, Zach recording with his phone.

"The US government wanted to arrest three hundred thousand people," George said into the camera, "not because they were hurting others but because these people opposed or were deemed to be a threat to government power. The US government made arrests, but they fell far short of their goal, only arresting twenty thousand people. People everywhere resisted these immoral arrests. This resistance exposed the impotence of the US government. If they don't have the power to arrest us, they have no power. The brutal Chinese Communist Mao Zedong said, 'Political power grows out of the barrel of a gun.' George paused for a moment. "Again, if they can't control us with violence, they have no power."

George was straight-faced, his jaw set tight. "Like so many across the country, my home was attacked and destroyed by the US government. My friend Katie Fitzgerald was killed by Delta Force commandos, along with volunteers Neil and Darren. Three more volunteers—Nelson, Lincoln, and Roland—were killed by drone air strikes. President Bradley authorized drone strikes on American citizens, without due process.

"I won't mention these brave volunteers' last names because I don't know if their families want the notoriety. I will say that these men gave their lives for me and Julie and Max. They weren't forced to protect my family. They didn't do it for pay. They did it because they thought it was the right thing to do. They sacrificed their lives for an idea that they'll never experience—true freedom. I am eternally grateful for their sacrifice.

"Katie and I were in a bunker together." George took a deep breath. "A Delta Force commando threw a grenade into our bunker that landed next to Katie. She told me to get down, and I did. She kicked the grenade into the trench dug specifically for grenades. Unfortunately she didn't have time to move away from the trench before the grenade exploded. Katie was killed by the blast. I walked out of that bunker without a scratch.

"Every day since I think about her. She saved my life. Without her, there wouldn't have been an effective freedom movement. There certainly wouldn't have been a George 2020 campaign. It's very likely the US government would've been far more successful in their mass arrests. She was the great disseminator of this message of freedom, a message that resonated with so many, so much so that untold numbers of you were also willing to fight and die for it." George cleared his throat and looked down for a moment. "I miss her terribly."

George rubbed his eyes with his thumb and index finger. He composed himself and looked into the camera. "We're almost free. The federal government's falling apart under the weight of their own largesse and incompetence. State and local governments are dissolving for the same reasons. With the arrests and brutality we've endured at the hands of the US government, you may have a desire for revenge. You may have a desire to destroy, but those government buildings, equipment, and vehicles belong to us. We paid for them through taxation and inflation.

"We can have our freedom without destroying property. If we truly want freedom, we don't have to beg the government for anything. Thus I have no demands. We don't have to ask for anything. We don't even have to do anything. We simply have to *stop* doing two things.

"First, we will no longer pay taxes of any kind. When we say *freedom*, we must have free trade and the freedom to keep our income.

"Second, we as individuals in a free society will decide for ourselves what to use for money. No longer will we be forced into debt slavery with fiat currencies."

131: John and the Slipping Grip of Power

President John Bradley sat at the head of the oval table with his twenty cabinet members. Each person at the table had a glass of water, a coaster, and an open binder.

"Chapman's body wasn't found at the property or in any of the three SUVs," FBI Director, Michael Hewitt said. "We believe the video was recorded after the assault."

John pinched the bridge of his nose. "This is a total unmitigated disaster."

"Katie Fitzgerald's body *was* found at the property."

John pictured Katie in the Mandarin Oriental, her smooth body wrapped in white sheets, her face young and vibrant. "What's the latest on the arrests?" John asked.

"Arrests have slowed considerably since the resistance." Hewitt cleared his throat. "We've arrested around twenty thousand. At this point we're having diminishing returns. I think it would be prudent to suspend the arrests, until conditions stabilize."

"*Stabilize?*" John glared at Hewitt. "If we can't make arrests, there's nothing to stabilize. We have no power."

Hewitt blanched.

"I agree with Director Hewitt," Secretary of State Frank Whitehead said. "Over 4,500 arresting officers and soldiers have been killed in the line of duty, and many more were wounded. Many departments are ignoring our warrants. If we keep pushing, our impotence becomes more evident."

John scowled at Hewitt. "Suspend the arrests temporarily."

"Yes, Mr. President," Hewitt said.

John flipped the page of the binder in front of him. Everyone else at the table did the same. "From bad to worse," John said, looking at the page. He glowered at Secretary of the Treasury Walter Moody. "This independent assay, is it correct?"

"Yes, Mr. President," Secretary Moody replied.

"According to the World Gold Council, we have over eight thousand tons of gold reserves. This independent assay claims we only have 2,100 tons. How are we supposed to roll out a gold exchange standard without gold?"

"Twenty-one hundred tons is a sufficient amount of gold. Unfortunately the currency will have less purchasing power. The government will have to shrink accordingly. This will ultimately be positive for the economy."

"Do I need to ask the question? Jesus Christ, Moody, what the fuck happened to six thousand tons of gold?"

Moody was unemotional, his face stoic, his mouth perpetually down-turned. He should've been an undertaker. Scratch that. Banking was perfect for him.

"Gold is often loaned to other nations and banks and often owned by multiple parties," Secretary Moody said. "We had massive outflows of gold in the late sixties and early seventies. More recently Germany and Venezuela contributed to the outflows by demanding a return of their gold reserves. Furthermore we've provided the COMEX with gold on many occasions to settle contracts to prevent a default and a run up in price. This strategy of gold-price suppression has been an integral part in maintaining US-dollar hegemony and limiting inflation in the face of generous government budgets. The US dollar as the reserve currency has run its course."

132: Julie and the Fat of the Land

Julie and George hiked through knee-high vegetation alongside the forest edge. The meadow teemed with butterflies and bees, and was dotted with splashes of red and yellow flowers. George carried a sack over his shoulder, Julie a cloth bag.

She stopped to inspect the brambles. "Look at all the raspberries," Julie said. "They're almost ready."

"In a week or two," George said, "we'll have all the raspberries, serviceberries, and mulberries that we can eat."

"It'll be nice to have fresh fruit again. It's been over a month."

"Yeah, the packs of Skittles that come with the MREs don't exactly count as a fruit."

Julie stopped at a patch of wild violets, their tiny purple flowers partially shaded by an old maple. She kneeled and plucked the triangular-shaped leaves, adding them to her cloth bag. George kneeled next to her, doing the same.

"These are getting past their prime," George said. "We'll have to be on the lookout for purslane and oxalis as we get into summer."

Julie turned to George. He wore his forest camos and a full beard. "How much longer do you think we'll be here?" Julie asked.

"At the cabin?" George asked.

"Yes."

"Until it's safe."

"How long can we last up here, living like this?"

George looked at Julie, his face serious as calculus. "Through the summer and fall, but we're not prepared for winter."

"We need to get your medicine. I'm deathly afraid you'll get sick again. We could ask Gideon to help us."

"Gideon and the guys already risked their lives for me. Five of his guys died. I don't want anyone else to die for me."

They stood after a few minutes of picking greens and continued along the forest edge. George checked one of his snap-snare traps. The noose still hung six inches from the ground of a well-traveled game trail and connected to an overhead tree.

They moved to the next trap. This one had a rabbit dangling from a small tree. George grabbed its feet and removed it from the snare. The rabbit jerked. George wrapped his left thumb and index finger around the rabbit's neck. He lifted the rabbit's legs quickly with his right hand and bent the rabbit back, breaking its neck with an audible pop. Julie winced. It was the sixth one that day and at least fifty over the past month, but she was still a bit horrified. He added the rabbit to his sack and slung it over his shoulder.

"You ready to head back?" George asked. "Zach's probably back from the mountaintop."

"I like it out here. It's nice to be alone. No snoring, no body odors, no messy men, and Max has been so sullen."

"I know. He just misses Daisy," George replied. "Imagine how we'd feel if we couldn't see or even contact each other."

They hiked back to the cabin. When Julie and George emerged from the trail, they found Max, pacing on the front porch. As they approached, Max hurried toward them.

"Zach has big news," Max said.

133: George and Rats from a Sinking Ship

George handed his sack of dead rabbits to Max. "Can you start dressing these? I'll give you a hand in a minute," George said.

"I got it," Max replied, taking the sacks. "You guys need to talk to Zach."

George and Julie stepped into the cabin. Zach and Gideon sat at the kitchen table.

"What's going on?" George asked.

"You ready to get outta here?" Gideon asked with a grin.

George and Julie sat at the table.

"Armed people are marching and taking over government buildings," Zach said.

"What people?" George asked.

"Some Anarchists but mostly people who were on Social Security and government pensions."

"There've been plenty of marches. They rarely make a difference."

"I agree, but the government's not doing anything about it. They can't. They're broke, and this is exposing their powerlessness. Police officers and soldiers are quitting by the thousands. They're going home to take care of their families."

George smiled wide. "They can't stop a bunch of retirees?"

"It gets better," Zach said. "Politicians are fleeing, like rats from a sinking ship."

134: John and Ill-Gotten Gains

John stood with his brother, Will, at the window of his new penthouse apartment. They sipped a single malt scotch. John looked down at the most beautiful city he had ever seen. Basel, Switzerland, was clean, cultured, and overflowing with the ill-gotten gains of the world's central bankers. The city had forty museums, gothic and Romanesque cathedrals, and buildings made from sandstone. He hadn't spotted a single piece of vinyl siding in the city. Despite the stunning buildings, John was focused on one of the many stone bridges across the Rhine River. The bridge was empty of cars and people; the water below, devoid of boats.

"I still can't believe it's come to this," John said. "How did people get so goddamn angry?"

"Every man has his breaking point," Will replied. "It seems they all had it at the same time."

"Chapman saved my life, only to dismantle it piece by piece. My legacy will be the leader who destroyed the most powerful empire the world has ever known." John took a swig of the caramel-colored concoction.

"That may be, but it's not true. This revolution was a long time coming, and the United States won't be the only one. Without taxes and debt-backed banker currencies, real money's already flowing to the United States, not to mention talented people and businesses looking to get in on the ground floor of real freedom. The blueprint's there for every country in the world. You watch. They'll topple like dominoes."

John shook his head. "Not in our lifetime."

"I hope you're right, because being a former president seems to have lost its luster at the moment." Will took a hearty drink.

"It's worse being the current president without a country."

"Have you heard from Linda?" Will asked.

"Not since we left the States." John groaned. "Shit, it's hard enough to get the kids on the phone. Divorce is … tough, especially with kids."

"They still at Linda's parents?"

"As far as I know." John checked his watch and changed the subject. "They're late. Maybe the Swiss won't protect the BIS or the gold."

"Don't worry. There's a reason Hitler was afraid to attack this place. The Swiss have over three thousand charges wired and ready to secure this country from invaders. It's more secure than Fort Knox."

John laughed. "Which, as it turns out, wasn't so secure."

Will chuckled. "That's true."

The beautiful stone bridge exploded in a series of perfectly placed charges meant to render it unusable. When the dust settled, the bridge was on the bottom of the Rhine.

"Happy Fourth of July," Will said, raising his glass.

"Happy Fourth of July," John replied, expressionless as he clinked glasses with his brother.

135: Julie and the End of the Line

Julie stood onstage, the Lincoln Memorial behind her, the largest reflecting pool in DC in front of her. The crowd covered every nook and cranny of the National Mall's 146 acres. She bent over George's wheelchair and kissed him on the cheek.

"I love you," she said in his ear.

His face was ghostlike. He had dark lesions on his skin and an oxygen mask over his mouth. George looked up at her, smiling, his dark eyes sunken but still alive. The clear mask fogged with his breath.

Julie moved from his side. Gideon and Max helped him to his feet and grabbed the oxygen tank from under his chair. George leaned on the men as they helped him to the podium. Gideon set the oxygen tank behind the podium and returned to his post. Max hugged George and made sure he was okay before walking away.

George leaned against the podium, his clothes hanging off him like a loose sail that could catch a wind and take him at any moment. He stared at the crowd—a mass of humanity, four million strong, and dead silent. He pulled the oxygen mask from his mouth, now wrapped around his neck.

George spoke into the microphone attached to the podium. "About six years ago, Katie Fitzgerald talked me into debating on the Internet. Mostly what I talked about was just common sense and truth. George Orwell said, 'In a time of universal deceit, telling the truth is a revolutionary act.'

"I suppose that's true, but I certainly wasn't the only one, and, more important, people were primed for it. People were disillusioned. Most knew something wasn't right, and they were searching for answers and meaning. At first it was a trickle, but, over time, more and more people resonated with the idea of universal morality and the implications when applied to government." George took a couple of breaths from his oxygen mask. "Inherently we all know the golden rule—do to others what you want them to do to you. This simple idea is elegant and perfect in its description of ethical conduct, but we were systematically propagandized to believe that government and government actors didn't have to abide by the same rules of moral conduct, that they were somehow godlike in their judgments and abilities with the donning of a uniform or a power suit. People were waking to the lie; they just needed a spark.

"Almost three years ago, the fuse was lit when the US government attempted to arrest three hundred thousand people for violating arbitrary rules made by politicians. We resisted, and we exposed their impotence. Since that time, we've learned a very important truth—they needed us, not the other way around.

"The last time I was here, I was so afraid. I had stage fright. I was worried I might be shot. I suppose I was right to be worried as I was shot at this very spot where I stand now." George took a breath of oxygen from his mask. "I don't expect I'll be shot this time. I might welcome it at this point."

The audience was silent.

"That was a joke. Not a good one I guess."

Nervous laughter came from the crowd.

"I've made my peace with dying. None of us leave this planet alive, and none of us knows exactly how much time we'll have here. Every second is a gift to be cherished." George wheezed and took a few more breaths from his mask. "Human beings aren't meant to live as slaves or dependents. We're meant to live free, purposeful lives doing meaningful work, loving our families and friends, and helping our fellow man.

"I never thought I'd live to see true freedom. I'm filled with joy when I think about the future—the future for our young people and the future for their children. I wish I was coming along for the ride, but I'm afraid this is the end of the line for me."

George removed a handkerchief from his pocket and coughed repeatedly into the cloth. Julie started for the podium, but Max intervened.

"I got it, Mom," Max said.

George placed his oxygen mask over his mouth. Max approached, placing his hand softly on George's back. Max spoke to George for a moment, and George nodded. Max returned to his spot on the stage next to Julie.

"He wants to finish," Max said.

George's breath regulated now, and he removed the oxygen mask once again. He said, "I'll leave you with the words of another dying man by the name of Randy Pausch. His words moved me throughout my life. I hope they do the same for you.

"'If I could only give three words of advice they would be, 'Tell the truth.' If I got three more words they would be, 'All the time.'"

136: Max and the Second Enlightenment

Max stepped into the kitchen, lured by the smell of bacon. Daisy pushed scrambled eggs around a cast iron pan. Max's wife was petite and fair, her brown hair in a loose braided ponytail. He kissed her on the cheek, her skin radiant without makeup.

"Good morning," Daisy said with a smile. "I thought you were gonna sleep in?"

"Too much to do," Max replied, grabbing a piece of bacon and moving to the kitchen table.

Two girls, six and eleven years old, both wearing jeans, sat at the kitchen table. They were the spitting image of their mother, except for the younger one's golden hair.

"Will you walk me to school?" Katie, the younger one, asked her father.

"What time did you come to bed?" Daisy asked Max.

Max turned to his wife, swallowing the bacon. "It was two. I work with a bunch of procrastinators. It seems everyone on the team gets these great ideas at the eleventh hour."

"The most popular cartoon on the streaming network."

"For now," Max said.

Katie tugged at her father's pants. "You didn't answer my question."

Max bent down and kissed Katie on the forehead. "Sorry, sweet pea."

"Will you walk me to school?" she asked, her voice tinged with urgency.

"Of course, honey."

"You have to take me all the way in."

"Come on, Dad," Emma, the older one said. "School's like fifty meters away. She's using you to boost her popularity."

Katie crossed her arms in a huff. "Am not."

Emma looked at her father. "We're studying the Second Enlightenment, and your name's in the book and Grandma's too. Katie told Becky that she was named after Katie Fitzgerald and that she knew Grandpa George when she was a baby. That part was a lie, because Grandpa George died a long time ago—"

"It's not a lie—" Katie interrupted.

"Now Becky doesn't believe that you're our dad, even with Grandma right there." Emma glowered at her sister. "See what happens when you lie?"

"It's not a lie. Daddy and Grandma talk about Grandpa George all the time. It *is* like I know him. He's still my grandpa, even if he's not here." Katie looked up at Max with big blue eyes. "Right, Daddy?"

"Grandpa George would've loved you both very much," Max said, "and you're right, sweet pea. He'll always be your grandpa, but I think you know you never met him."

"You should tell the truth all the time," Emma said. "That's what Grandpa George said in his last speech."

Katie hung her head. "I'm sorry, Daddy."

"Emma, honey, why don't you set the table," Daisy said, as she removed the pan of eggs from the stove.

Emma stood and grabbed plates and silverware from the counter.

Max bent down next to Katie. He raised her chin with his index finger. "Nobody's perfect, honey. You'll feel better if you tell Becky the truth."

"What if she doesn't believe me?"

Max smiled, his blond beard spreading across his face. "Then you'll know how Grandpa George felt before the Second Enlightenment."

Emma set the table, and Max and Daisy served the food and drinks. The young family sat together, enjoying their breakfast.

"I almost forgot," Daisy said, standing from the table. She grabbed her iPad from the counter and returned to her seat. "We have to make a decision on federal, state, and local services."

Max smirked. "We don't *have* to do anything."

"You know what I mean," Daisy said, opening her iPad. She handed it to Max.

Max scanned the screen.

The Federal Service
Washington, DC

Max and Daisy Welch
2300 Elmhurst Road
Lititz, PA 17543

Donation Year: 2036

Choose where you'd like your hard-earned money put to work!
It's a privilege and a duty to support the Federal Service. We
are now accepting gold, silver, platinum, palladium, Bitcoin,
Ethereum, and Litecoin.

Federal Service Donation Departments

Department of Defense
Department of Agriculture
Department of Health and Human Services
Department of Labor
Department of State
Department of Transportation
Department of Veteran Affairs

"I'm surprised anyone gives money to these clowns," Max said.

"Nostalgia?" Daisy asked.

"You don't actually wanna give them any money, do you?"

"Not federal or state. I think the local security guys are doing a good job, and I think we should invest in that wind project."

Max ignored the federal and state donation forms. He and Daisy sent digital silver to invest in the town wind project, as well as the security firm, the fire department, and the shared parks.

After breakfast, Max and Katie walked hand in hand toward the front door. Max stopped in the attached glass house and checked the pH of the fish tanks. The wicking beds were overflowing with produce.

"We're gonna be late, Daddy," Katie said.

"Sorry, you know I get distracted," Max replied.

Katie had her hands on her hips. "That's why I'm telling you."

Outside, the sky was light blue and cloudless. Frogs croaked, and the morning sun reflected off the pond. Bees buzzed in the surrounding wild-flower meadow. A helix-shaped wind turbine spun in the gentle breeze. Next to the earth-sheltered house was a carport covered in solar cells. One small car was plugged in underneath.

Emma wasn't exaggerating; the one-room schoolhouse was literally a stone's throw away. Very few of the old megaschool complexes still operated for education. The roof of this single-story building was also covered in solar cells.

Inside, kids of various elementary ages talked and joked and gesticulated. The room had six round tables that sat groups of five. Julie sat behind her desk, staring at her laptop, her hair gray but her face young-looking for her age. Katie led Max to a front round table. There a group of six- and seven-year-olds stood and talked. Katie marched up to the tallest kid in the group. She was thin with long silky straight hair.

"Dad, this is Becky," Katie said, motioning to the girl.

"Hi, Becky," Max said, holding out his hand.

The girl shook it tentatively.

"My dad's name is Max Welch," Katie said, "just like in the book, because he is the man in the book."

"That's cool," Becky replied.

"And George Chapman was my grandpa, but I never met him because he died before I was born." Katie bit the lower corner of her lip. "I'm sorry I lied."

"I knew it was a lie because of math and stuff. George Chapman died in 2024. You'd have to be at least thirteen to have met him."

Katie looked at the floor.

Becky put her arm around Katie and gave her a hug. "It's okay. You told the truth now. Mrs. Chapman said it's good to say you're sorry if you do something bad."

Max left Katie with her friends and approached Julie's desk.

"Good morning," Max said.

"Oh, hi, honey," Julie said, looking up from her laptop.

"You'll be at dinner tonight, right?"

"I wouldn't miss it."

Max smiled. "Have a good day, Mom."

A small grin tugged at the corners of her mouth. "You too."

Max walked toward the door.

Julie started her lesson. "Everyone, take your seat please."

The children quieted and sat in their chairs.

Max stopped at the door, watching his mother teach. The screen behind her read *What did people learn from the Second Enlightenment?*

"Over the past week we've studied the Second Enlightenment," Julie said. "Does anyone know the answer to the question behind me?"

A stocky boy raised his hand.

"Colby," Julie said.

"That government's stupid," Colby replied.

"Well, a lot of people did begin to think that, but I'm looking for something more specific."

Becky raised her hand.

"Becky," Julie said.

"People learned that you shouldn't make other people do things," Becky said.

"You're on the right track. What do you mean by, 'make other people do things'?"

"Like when my cousins get spanked for being bad. You're not supposed to hit to make people do things."

"That's good, Becky, and you're right. Using violence to influence is a bad idea. What if your parents want you to do something that's good for you, like have you eat your vegetables?"

"They can use, like, facts and stuff to tell us how good vegetables are."

"That's true," Julie said, nodding. "Children being raised without spanking or violence of any kind has certainly increased since the Second Enlightenment, but we also learned something very fundamental, something that keeps us safe from repeating the errors of the past."

Emma raised her hand.

"Emma," Julie said.

"We learned that it doesn't matter if you wear a uniform or have a flag or laws or even a constitution. Right and wrong is the same for every person, every government, and every business. You can't take people away for doing drugs and call it justice. It's still kidnapping. You can't take people's money and call it taxes. It's still stealing. You can't kill people and call it war. It's still murder. I own myself, my work, and my possessions. Nobody can have what I don't choose to give."

For the Reader

Dear Reader,

I'm thrilled that you took precious time out of your life to read my novel. Thank you! I hope you found it entertaining, engaging, and thought-provoking. If so, please consider writing a positive review on Amazon and Goodreads. Five-star reviews have a huge impact on future sales. The review doesn't need to be long and detailed, if you're more of a reader than a writer. As an author and a small businessman, competing against the big publishers, every reader, every review, and every referral is greatly appreciated.

If you're interested in receiving my novel *Against the Grain* for free and/or reading my other titles for free or .99 cents, go to the following link: http://www.PhilWBooks.com. You're probably thinking, *What's the catch?* There is no catch.

If you want to contact me, don't be bashful. I can be found at Phil@PhilWBooks.com. I do my best to respond to all emails.

Sincerely,
Phil M. Williams

Author's Note

I researched and wrote much of this novel during the 2016 presidential race. I was shocked at the division I saw among the American public. Families and friends and Facebook warriors fought over their brand of politics, so certain that, if their candidate was elected, things would be better. People who I've never seen passionate about anything—not their family and certainly not their jobs—were passionate about the D or the R. It was eye-opening.

The Revolutionary War was fought and won with 3 percent of the population at the time. A tiny minority of Americans believe any government to be the antithesis to freedom and a scourge to be ignored out of existence. Many of these Anarchists and Voluntarists have well-reasoned, logical, and ethical arguments against government.

What if this group were to grow to 3 percent and beyond?

Governments around the world are responsible for 250–300 million democide deaths in the past century. These are deaths of a government killing its own people and do not include war-related deaths. In the United States today, we have endless wars, the largest prison population on the planet, debt money created out of thin air, and many layers of government that grow in size each year like tumors. Maybe it's time to stop looking to the government to solve our problems. Maybe it's time to see through the propaganda perpetrated by our schooling, our culture, and our media. Maybe it's time to see the true source of the problem.

Gratitude

I'd like to thank my wife. She's my first reader and always will be. Without her support and unwavering belief in my skill as an author, I'm not sure I would have embarked on this career. I love you, Denise.

I'd also like to thank my editors. My developmental editor, Caroline Smailes, did a fantastic job finding the holes in my plot and suggesting remedies. As always, my line editor, Denise Barker (not to be confused with my wife, Denise Williams), did a fantastic job making sure the manuscript was error-free. I love her comments and feedback.

Thank you to Deborah Bradseth of Tugboat Design for her excellent cover art and formatting. She's the consummate professional. I look forward to many more beautiful covers in the future.

Thank you to my brother, Mark, for his expert advice as a former combat infantryman. Any inaccuracies in the assault on George's residence are mine alone.

Thank you to my sister, Mary, and my friend Elaine for their encouragement to write a dystopian novel. Thank you to my mother-in-law, Joy, for her expert advice on all things medical.

Lastly, thank you to Voluntarists, Anarchists, and all critics of government power who have spoken the truth and inspired me to do the same. Many are listed in the bibliography below. I am indebted and grateful to each and every one of them.

Bibliography

This novel is a work of fiction, but many facts are embedded in the narrative. Many of these ideas are not entirely my own. I've benefited from brilliant people with brilliant books, articles, and podcasts. Below is a list of the sources I used for my research. Three books in particular have had the biggest impact on me: *The Creature from Jekyll Island* by G. Edward Griffin, *Manufacturing Consent* by Noam Chomsky and Edward Herman, and *The Crash Course* by Chris Martenson. I wholeheartedly recommend reading the aforementioned books as well as the sources listed below.

Alexander, Michelle, "Go to Trial: Crash the Justice System," *The New York Times* (March 10, 2012), http://www.nytimes.com/2012/03/11/opinion/sunday/go-to-trial-crash-the-justice-system.html?_r=0

Appelbaum, Binyamin, "2% Inflation Rate Target Is Questioned as Fed Policy Panel Prepares to Meet," *The New York Times* (April 28, 2015), http://www.nytimes.com/2015/04/29/business/economy/2-inflation-rate-target-is-questioned-as-fed-policy-panel-prepares-to-meet.html?_r=0

Ariely, Dan, Predictably Irrational: The Hidden Forces That Shape Our Decisions (New York, NY: Harper Collins Publishers, 2010)

Boniello, Kathianne, "City Says Cops Had No Duty to Protect Subway Hero Who Subdued Killer," *New York Post* (January 27, 2013), http://nypost.com/2013/01/27/city-says-cops-had-no-duty-to-protect-subway-hero-who-subdued-killer/

"Bretton Woods System," *Wikipedia* (2016), https://en.wikipedia.org/wiki/Bretton_Woods_system

Butler, John, The Golden Revolution: How to Prepare for the Coming Global Gold Standard (Hoboken, New Jersey: John Wiley and Sons, Inc., 2012)

Butler, General Smedley D., *War Is a Racket* (Aristeus Books, 2014)

Cali, Jeanine, "Frequent Reference Question: How Many Federal Laws Are There?" Library of Congress (March 12, 2013), https://blogs.loc.gov/law/2013/03/frequent-reference-question-how-many-federal-laws-are-there/

"CalPERS Retirees Outnumber Active Workers Soon," *Calpensions* (November 2014), https://calpensions.com/2014/11/24/calpers-retirees-outnumber-active-workers-soon/

Carr, David, "Blurred Line between Espionage and Truth," *The New York Times* (February 26, 2012), http://www.nytimes.com/2012/02/27/business/media/white-house-uses-espionage-act-to-pursue-leak-cases-media-equation.html?_r=0

"Casualties of the Iraq War," *Wikipedia* (2016), https://en.wikipedia.org/wiki/Casualties_of_the_Iraq_War

"Celtic Anarchism," *Anarchopedia* (October 2014)

Chantrill, Christopher, *USGovernmentspending.com* (September 2016), http://www.usgovernmentspending.com/federal_spending_chart

"Common Arguments against a Stateless Society," *Thrive* (2016), http://www.thrivemovement.com/common-arguments-against-stateless-society

Crovitz, L. Gordon, "You Commit Three Felonies a Day," *The Wall Street Journal* (September 27, 2009), http://www.wsj.com/articles/SB10001424052 748704471504574438900830760842

Cuellar, Danilo. "Monopolies in a Stateless Society," *The Conscious Resistance* (December 20, 2014), http://theconsciousresistance.com/2014/12/monopolies-in-a-stateless-society/

"Dispute Resolution Organization," *Wikipedia* (2016), https://en.wikipedia.org/wiki/Dispute_resolution_organization

"Edward Snowden," *Wikipedia* (2016), https://en.wikipedia.org/wiki/Edward_Snowden

"Export Land Model," *Wikipedia* (2017), https://en.wikipedia.org/wiki/Export_Land_Model

Fang, Lee, "Congress Tells Court That Congress Can't Be Investigated for Insider Trading," *The Intercept* (May 7, 2015), https://theintercept.com/2015/05/07/congress-argues-cant-investigated-insider-trading/

"Federal Revenue: Where Does the Money Come From?" *National Priorities Project* (2015), https://www.nationalpriorities.org/budget-basics/federal-budget-101/revenues/

Fields, Gary, and John R. Emshwiller, "As Arrest Records Rise, Americans Find Consequences Can Last a Lifetime," *The Wall Street Journal* (August 18, 2014), http://www.wsj.com/articles/as-arrest-records-rise-americans-find-consequences-can-last-a-lifetime-1408415402

Flatow, Nicole, "The United States Has the Largest Prison Population in the World—And It's Growing," *Think Progress* (September 2014), https://thinkprogress.org/the-united-states-has-the-largest-prison-population-in-the-world-and-its-growing-d4a35bc9652f/

"George Carlin's 'The American Dream,' The Best 3 Minutes of His Career," YouTube, https://www.youtube.com/watch?v=rsL6mKxtOlQ

Ginn, Vance, "You Think the Deficit Is Bad? Federal Unfunded Liabilities Exceed $127 Trillion," *Forbes* (January 17, 2014), http://www.forbes.com/sites/realspin/2014/01/17/you-think-the-deficit-is-bad-federal-unfunded-liabilities-exceed-127-trillion/#6219cfd410d3

Greenburg, Jon, "CNN's Tapper: Obama Has Used Espionage Act More Than All Previous Administrations," *Politifact* (January 10, 2014), http://www.politifact.com/punditfact/statements/2014/jan/10/jake-tapper/cnns-tapper-obama-has-used-espionage-act-more-all-/

Griffin, G. Edward, *The Creature from Jekyll Island* (Westlake Village, California: American Media, 2010)

Haynes, Chris, "Has Anarchy Existed Before?" *The Rule of Freedom* (June 11, 2012), https://theruleoffreedom.wordpress.com/2012/06/11/has-anarchy-existed-before/

Herman, Edward S., and Noam Chomsky, *Manufacturing Consent* (New York: Pantheon Books, 2002)

"How the Antiterrorism Bill Permits Indefinite Detention of Immigrants," *ACLU* (October 2001), https://www.aclu.org/how-anti-terrorism-bill-permits-indefinite-detention-immigrants

"Indefinite Detention without Trial," *Wikipedia* (2016), https://en.wikipedia.org/wiki/Indefinite_detention_without_trial

Islam, Faisal, "Iraq Nets Handsome Profit by Dumping Dollar for Euro," *The Guardian* (February 15, 2003), https://www.theguardian.com/business/2003/feb/16/iraq.theeuro

"Lawrence Kohlberg's Stages of Moral Development," *Wikipedia* (2016), https://en.wikipedia.org/wiki/Lawrence_Kohlberg%27s_stages_of_moral_development

Leeson, Peter T., "Better Off Stateless: Somalia Before and After Government Collapse," *Journal of Comparative Economics* (February 3, 2006), https://ssrn.com/abstract=879798

Lutz, Ashley, "These 6 Corporations Control 90% of the Media in America," *Business Insider* (June 14, 2012), http://www.businessinsider.com/these-6-corporations-control-90-of-the-media-in-america-2012-6

MacAskill, Ewen, "Fivefold Increase in Terrorism Fatalities since 9/11, Says Report," *The Guardian* (November 17, 2014), https://www.theguardian.com/uk-news/2014/nov/18/fivefold-increase-terrorism-fatalities-global-index

Martenson, Chris, PhD, *The Crash Course* (Hoboken, New Jersey: John Wiley & Sons, Inc., 2011)

Masnick, Mike, "New Snowden Doc Reveals How GCHQ/NSA Use the Internet to 'Manipulate, Deceive and Destroy Reputations,'" *Tech Dirt* (February 25, 2014), https://www.techdirt.com/articles/20140224/17054826340/new-snowden-doc-reveals-how-gchqnsa-use-internet-to-manipulate-deceive-destroy-reputations.shtml

McElroy, Damien, "Colonel Gaddafi Died after Being Stabbed with Bayonet, Says Report," *The Telegraph* (October 17, 2012), http://www.telegraph.co.uk/news/worldnews/africaandindianocean/libya/9613394/Colonel-Gaddafi-died-after-being-stabbed-with-bayonet-says-report.html

McLeod, Saul, "Kohlberg," *Simply Psychology* (2013), http://www.simplypsychology.org/kohlberg.html

McLeod, Saul, "The Milgram Experiment," *Simply Psychology* (2007), http://www.simplypsychology.org/milgram.html

Miles, Kathleen, "Just How Much the War on Drugs Impacts Our Over-crowded Prisons, In One Chart," *The Huffington Post* (March 10, 2014), http://www.huffingtonpost.com/2014/03/10/war-on-drugs-prisons-info-graphic_n_4914884.html

"Milgram Experiment," *Wikipedia* (2016), https://en.wikipedia.org/wiki/Milgram_experiment

Mollison, Bill, PERMACULTURE: *A Designer's Manual* (Australia: Tagari Publications, 1988), ix.

Molyneux, Stefan, "The Social Contract: Defined and Destroyed in under 5 Mins," YouTube, *Freedomain Radio* (May, 2008), https://www.youtube.com/watch?v=jNj0VhK19QU

"More Men Are Raped in the US than Women, Figures on Prison Assaults Reveal," *Daily Mail* (October 3, 2013), http://www.daily-mail.co.uk/news/article-2449454/More-men-raped-US-women-in-cluding-prison-sexual-abuse.html

Newman, Alex, "Gadhafi's Gold-Money Plan Would Have Devastated Dollar," *The New American* (November 11, 2011), http://www.thenewamer-ican.com/economy/markets/item/4630-gadhafi-s-gold-money-plan-would-have-devastated-dollar

Norris, Floyd, "No Surprise, Fed Was Biggest Buyer of Treasuries in 2013," *The New York Times* (February 21, 2014), http://www.nytimes.com/2014/02/22/business/economy/no-surprise-fed-was-biggest-buyer-of-treasuries-in-2013.html?_r=0

Palmer, Steve, "Ending Prohibition: Yet Another Nullification Success Story," *Tenth Amendment Center* (December 2013), http://tenthamend-mentcenter.com/2013/12/05/ending-prohibition-yet-another-nullificati on-success-story/

Pausch, Randy and Jeffrey Zaslow, *The Last Lecture* (London: Hodder & Stoughton, 2008)

Pratkanis, Anthony, and Elliot Aronson, *Age of Propaganda: The Everyday Use and Abuse of Persuasion* (New York: Henry Holt and Company, LLC, 2001)

Prins, Nomi, All the Presidents' Bankers: The Hidden Alliances that Drive American Power (New York, New York: Nation Books, 2014)

Prison Writers, (2016), http://prisonwriters.com/

Reilly, Steve, "Tens of Thousands of Rape Kits Go Untested across USA," *USA TODAY* (July 2015), http://www.usatoday.com/story/news/2015/07/16/untested-rape-kits-evidence-across-usa/29902199/

Reynolds, Glenn Harlan, "You Are Probably Breaking the Law Right Now," *USA Today* (March 29, 2015), http://www.usatoday.com/story/opinion/2015/03/29/crime-law-criminal-unfair-column/70630978/

Robinson, Jerry, "The Rise of the Petrodollar System: Dollars for Oil," Part Two of Four-Part Article, *Financial Sense* (February 23, 2012), http://www.financialsense.com/contributors/jerry-robinson/the-rise-of-the-petrodollar-system-dollars-for-oil

Rose, Larken, *The Most Dangerous Superstition* (Larken Rose, 2012)

Rothbard, Murray, *Anatomy of the State* (Ludwig von Mises Institute, 2009)

Rummel, R. J., "20th Century Democide," The University of Hawaii, http://www.hawaii.edu/powerkills/20TH.HTM

"Sanctions against Iran," *Wikipedia* (2016), https://en.wikipedia.org/wiki/Sanctions_against_Iran

Sanders, Laura, "Smartphones May Be Changing the Way We Think," *Science News* (March 17, 2017), https://www.sciencenews.org/article/smartphones-may-be-changing-way-we-think

SilverShieldGrp, "Greenspan States, Cannot Guarantee Purchasing Power," Senate Banking Committee 2005, YouTube (May 23, 2011), https://www.youtube.com/watch?v=gqUzQjXNliU

Spirko, Jack, *The Survival Podcast* (2011), http://www.thesurvivalpodcast.com/

"Standard Oil," *Wikipedia* (2016), https://en.wikipedia.org/wiki/Standard_Oil

"The Art of Not Being Governed," *Wikipedia* (2016), https://en.wikipedia.org/wiki/The_Art_of_Not_Being_Governed

"Warren v. District of Columbia," *Wikipedia* (2016), https://en.wikipedia.org/wiki/Warren_v._District_of_Columbia

Williams, Phil M., *The Propaganda Project* (Phil W. Books, 2016)

Wong, Andrea, "The Untold Story behind Saudi Arabia's 41-Year US Debt Secret," *Bloomberg* (May 30, 2016), http://www.bloomberg.com/news/features/2016-05-30/the-untold-story-behind-saudi-arabia-s-41-year-u-s-debt-secret

Verma, Nidhi, "Iran Wants Euro Payment for New and Outstanding Oil Sales," *Reuters* (February 5, 2016), http://www.reuters.com/article/us-oil-iran-exclusive-idUSKCN0VE21S

"You're 55 Times More Likely to Be Killed by a Police Officer than a Terrorist," *Washington's Blog* (March 4, 2015), http://www.washingtonsblog.com/2015/03/youre-55-times-likely-killed-police-officer-terrorist.html

"Zomia (geography)," *Wikipedia* (2016), https://en.wikipedia.org/wiki/Zomia_(geography)

www.ingramcontent.com/pod-product-compliance
Lightning Source LLC
Chambersburg PA
CBHW030739030726
47497CB00001B/55